THE SOUTHERN VOICE

There are stories in this anthology from all classes, from the impoverished elite of Susan Petigru King to the impoverished working class of Erskine Caldwell. There are stories about the questioning vision of children by Truman Capote, Zora Neale Hurston, Constance Fenimore Woolson, and Ernest J. Gaines. And there are stories about characters as old as Peter Taylor's pilgrims.

The literary heritage of the American South is as complex and as often distorted as the geographic area it represents, a region identified with a special creativity and anguish, a mythology equally rooted in memory and dreams. This collection of short stories creates a picture of the South as a place of many residents with diverse voices. A place in which the people we read about are ones in whom we can—no matter what our accent, color, gender, culture, social status, or political ideology—recognize ourselves.

Dorothy Abbott is the editor of a four-volume Mississippi writers' series and former assistant director of the literature program at the National Endowment for the Arts. **Susan Koppelman** has edited many anthologies, including *May Your Days Be Merry & Bright: Christmas Stories by Women.*

THE
SIGNET CLASSIC BOOK OF
SOUTHERN
SHORT STORIES

Edited and with an Introduction by
Dorothy Abbott
and Susan Koppelman

SIGNET CLASSICS

SIGNET CLASSICS
Published by New American Library, a division of
Penguin Group (USA) Inc., 375 Hudson Street,
New York, New York 10014, USA
Penguin Group (Canada), 90 Eglinton Avenue East, Suite 700, Toronto,
Ontario M4P 2Y3, Canada (a division of Pearson Penguin Canada Inc.)
Penguin Books Ltd., 80 Strand, London WC2R 0RL, England
Penguin Ireland, 25 St. Stephen's Green, Dublin 2,
Ireland (a division of Penguin Books Ltd.)
Penguin Group (Australia), 250 Camberwell Road, Camberwell, Victoria 3124,
Australia (a division of Pearson Australia Group Pty. Ltd.)
Penguin Books India Pvt. Ltd., 11 Community Centre, Panchsheel Park,
New Delhi - 110 017, India
Penguin Group (NZ), 67 Apollo Drive, Rosedale, North Shore 0632,
New Zealand (a division of Pearson New Zealand Ltd.)
Penguin Books (South Africa) (Pty.) Ltd., 24 Sturdee Avenue,
Rosebank, Johannesburg 2196, South Africa

Penguin Books Ltd., Registered Offices:
80 Strand, London WC2R 0RL, England

Published by Signet Classics, an imprint of New American Library,
a division of Penguin Group (USA) Inc.

First Signet Classics Printing (Second Revised Edition), January 1999
20   19   18

Copyright © Dorothy Abbott, 1991
All rights reserved

 REGISTered TRADEMARK — MARCA REGISTRADA

Printed in the United States of America

CONTENTS

Acknowledgments

"Confessions of a Murderer" by William Gilmore Simms first appeared in *Southern Literary Gazette* (November 1, 1829). Reprinted from *Centennial Simms, Stories and Tales* (1974) edited by John Caldwell Guilds by permission of University of South Carolina Press.

"The Dance" by Augustus Baldwin Longstreet first appeared in *Southern Reader* (October 30, 1833). Reprinted from *Georgia Scenes, Characters, Incidents etc., in the First Half Century of the Republic* (1835).

"A Tale of the Ragged Mountains" by Edgar Allan Poe first appeared in *Godey's Lady's Book* (April 1844).

"A Marriage of Persuasion" by Susan Petigru King (Bowen) first appeared under the pen name Anne Marion Green in *Russell's Magazine* (1857). Reprinted from *Crimes Which the Law Does Not Reach* (1859).

"Felipa" by Constance Fenimore Woolson first appeared in *Lippincott's Magazine* (June 1876). Reprinted from *Rodman the Keeper: Southern Sketches* (1880). Published by D. Appleton & Co.

"Jean-ah Poquelin" by George Washington Cable first appeared in *Scribner's Monthly* (May 1875). Reprinted from *Old Creole Days* (1879). Published by Scribners.

"The Sheriff's Children" by Charles W. Chesnutt first appeared in *Independent* (November 7, 1889). Reprinted from *The Wife of His Youth and Other Stories of the Color Line* (1899). Published by Houghton Mifflin.

"La Belle Zoraide" by Kate Chopin first appeared in *Vogue* (January 4, 1894) under the title "La Belle Zoraide: A Tragedy of the Old Regime." Reprinted from *Bayou Folk* (1894). Published by Houghton Mifflin.

"Tony's Wife" by Alice Dunbar-Nelson first appeared in *The Goodness of St. Rocque and Other Stories* (1899). Published by Dodd, Mead & Co.

"The Heart of It" by Sarah Barnwell Elliott (written in the late 1890s) first appeared in *Some Data and Other Stories of Southern Life* (1981) edited by Clara Childs Mackenzie. (c) 1981 by Seaforth Publications. Reprinted by permission of Clara C. Mackenzie and Seaforth Publications.

"Dare's Gift" by Ellen Glasgow first appeared as a two-part story in *Harper's Magazine* (February and March 1917). (c) 1923 by Doubleday and Company; (c) renewed 1951 by First Merchants National Bank of Richmond. Reprinted from *The Shadowy Third and Other Stories* by permission of Harcourt Brace Jovanovich, Inc.

"Drenched in Light" by Zora Neale Hurston first appeared in *Opportunity: A Journal of Negro Life* (December 1924). (c) 1924 by Zora Neale Hurston. Reprinted by permission of the National Urban League.

"Dry September" by William Faulkner first appeared in *Scribner's Magazine* (February 5, 1930). (c) 1930 and renewed 1958 by William Faulkner. Reprinted from *Collected Stories of William Faulkner* by permission of Random House, Inc.

"Kneel to the Rising Sun" by Erskine Caldwell first appeared in *Scribner's Magazine* (February 1935). (c) 1935 by Charles Scribner's Sons; (c) renewed 1963 by Erskine Caldwell. Reprinted by permission of McIntosh and Otis, Inc.

"The Last Day in the Field" by Caroline Gordon first appeared in *Scribner's Magazine* (March 1935). (c) 1935 and renewed 1981 by Caroline Gordon. Reprinted from *The Collected Stories of Caroline Gordon* by permission of Farrar, Straus and Giroux, Inc.

"When the Light Gets Green" by Robert Penn Warren. (c) 1936 and renewed 1964 by Robert Penn Warren. Reprinted from *The Circus in the Attic and Other Stories* by permission of Harcourt Brace Jovanovich, Inc.

"Big Boy Leaves Home" by Richard Wright first appeared in *The New Caravan* (eds. Alfred Kreymborg et al., Norton, 1936). (c) 1936 by Richard Wright; (c) renewed 1964 by Ellen Wright. Reprinted from *Uncle Tom's Children* (1938) by permission of Harper & Row, Publishers, Inc.

"The Pelican's Shadow" by Marjorie Kinnan Rawlings first

appeared in *The New Yorker* (January 6, 1940). (c) 1940 by Marjorie Kinnan Rawlings; (c) renewed 1968 by Norton Baskin. Reprinted by permission of Brandt & Brandt Literary Agents, Inc.

"A Tree • A Rock • A Cloud" by Carson McCullers first appeared in *Harper's Bazaar* (November 1942). (c) 1942 by Carson McCullers; (c) renewed 1979 by Floria V. Lasky. Reprinted from *The Ballad of the Sad Cafe and Other Works* by permission of Houghton Mifflin Company.

"Health Card" by Frank Yerby first appeared in *Harper's* (May 1944). (c) 1944 and renewed 1972 by Frank Yerby. Reprinted by permission of William Morris Agency, Inc. on behalf of the author.

"The Angel in the Alcove" by Tennessee Williams first appeared in *One Arm* (1948). (c) 1948 by Tennessee Williams. Reprinted from *Collected Stories* by permission of New Directions Publishing Corporation.

"No Place for You, My Love" by Eudora Welty first appeared in *The New Yorker* (September 20, 1952). (c) 1952 by Eudora Welty; renewed (c) 1980 by Eudora Welty. Reprinted from *The Collected Stories of Eudora Welty* by permission of Russell and Volkening, Inc.

"The New Order" by Nancy Hale first appeared in *The New Yorker* (November 27, 1954). (c) 1954 and renewed 1982 by Nancy Hale. Reprinted by permission of Harold Ober Associates Incorporated.

"A Christmas Memory" by Truman Capote first appeared in *Mademoiselle* (December 1956). (c) 1956 by Truman Capote. Reprinted from *Selected Writings of Truman Capote* by permission of Random House, Inc.

"Northerners Can Be So Smug" by Alice Childress. (c) 1956 and renewed 1984 by Alice Childress. Reprinted from *Like One of the Family* by permission of Flora Roberts, Inc.

"First Dark" by Elizabeth Spencer first appeared in *The New Yorker* (June 20, 1959). (c) 1959 by Elizabeth Spencer. Reprinted from *The Stories of Elizabeth Spencer* by permission of Doubleday, a division of Bantam, Doubleday, Dell Publishing Group, Inc.

"On the Lake" by Ellen Douglas first appeared in *The New*

Yorker (August 26, 1961); (c) 1961 by Houghton Mifflin Company; (c) renewed 1985 by Ellen Douglas. Reprinted from *Black Cloud, White Cloud* (1964) by permission of the author.

"The Sky Is Gray" by Ernest J. Gaines first appeared in *Negro Digest* (August 1963). (c) 1963 by Ernest J. Gaines. Reprinted from *Bloodline* by permission of Doubleday, a division of Bantam, Doubleday, Dell Publishing Group, Inc.

"Two Pilgrims" by Peter Taylor first appeared in *The New Yorker* (September 7, 1963). (c) 1969 by Peter Taylor. Reprinted from *The Collected Stories of Peter Taylor* by permission of Farrar, Straus and Giroux, Inc.

"Revelation" by Flannery O'Connor first appeared in *Everything that Rises Must Converge* (1964). (c) 1964, 1965 by the Estate of Mary Flannery O'Connor. Reprinted by permission of Farrar, Straus and Giroux, Inc.

"Neighbors" by Diane Oliver first appeared in *Sewanee Review* (Spring, 1966). (c) 1966 by the University of the South. Reprinted by permission of the editor.

"Talk to the Music" by Arna Bontemps first appeared in *Cimarron Review* (July 1971). (c) 1971 by Board of Regents, Oklahoma State University. Reprinted by permission of Harold Ober Associates Incorporated and the Board of Regents for Oklahoma State University.

"The Ugliest Pilgrim" by Doris Betts first appeared in *Beasts of the Southern Wild and Other Stories* (1973) published by Harper and Row. (c) 1973 by Doris Betts. Reprinted by permission of Russell and Volkening, Inc., as agents for the author.

"Everyday Use" by Alice Walker first appeared in *Harper's* (April 1, 1973). (c) 1973 by Alice Walker. Reprinted from *In Love & Trouble: Stories of Black Women* by permission of Harcourt Brace Jovanovich, Inc.

INTRODUCTION

The literary heritage of the American South is as complex, and as often distorted, as the lives and the land it represents. Contained in these pages are almost a century and a half of the passion of human life as portrayed by Southerners—female and male, black and white, rural and urban, rich and poor, those isolated and those embraced. These short stories present a tradition identified with a special creativity and anguish; one which arose from a mythology equally rooted in memory and dreams. What is created is a picture in which the people we read about—no matter what our accent, gender, ethnicity, culture, economic class, social status, or political ideology—are ones in whom we can recognize ourselves.

The South has often been defined as a region through anthologies of works by its writers. It is our hope that this collection will provide a new definition—a more democratic sense of the South by presenting a stronger voice for white women and African Americans. In collecting these stories, we are excited to see the new shape of southern literature that has emerged when the riches of scholarship in African American literature and women's studies are joined to the white patriarchal tradition.

Never before has there been a collection of southern short stories that has made so evident the long and continuous tradition of short story writing among African American citizens of the southern United States. Charles Chesnutt's "The Sheriff's Children" published in 1889 probes some of the consequences of the racial and sexual exploitation of enslaved women. Diane Oliver's "Neighbors" confronts the crisis of integration and the burden it places on children. Alice Childress writes of the southern struggle against injustice by both black and white Southerners in "Northerners Can Be So Smug." And Alice Walker's 1973 story "Everyday Use," a moving tale of love and family pride, takes us to the close of this anthology.

Southern women writers have accepted the challenge of subject matter growing out of the history of their region.

Sarah Barnwell Elliott's "The Heart of It" and Kate Chopin's "The Belle Zoraide" both explore variations on the theme of Chesnutt's "The Sheriff's Children." But Chopin takes this theme of sexual exploitation of black women a step farther—this time white women are as implicated as white men. In "The Pelican's Shadow," Marjorie Kinnan Rawlings depicts the struggle with gender role expectations that still concern us today. And Ellen Glasgow's "Dare's Gift," a powerful and densely layered story, reminiscent of Charlotte Perkins Gilman's *The Yellow Wallpaper*, portrays a marriage in which the partners understand reality so differently that the moral courage of one is seen as madness by the other. In "Tony's Wife" Alice Dunbar-Nelson explores a pattern of spouse abuse in words familiar to anyone with an awareness of present-day shelters for battered women.

These are but a few of the stories included in this anthology that span the years 1829 to 1973. Our collection begins with "Confessions of a Murderer," first published in 1829, a period particularly important in the growth of a southern regional consciousness, and closes with "Everyday Use," first read in 1973, the same month the last United States ground forces were leaving Vietnam and coming home.

During and after each of the United States' foreign wars, except the one in Vietnam, an upsurge of nationalism was expressed in all aspects of life, including literary studies. After World War I, for instance, public school curriculums were designed to teach citizenship duties and rights, and teachers in all disciplines were encouraged to incorporate lessons of patriotism into their teaching.

And with each resurgence of nationalism, there has been a concomitant resurgence of interest in regionalism and a rediscovery of the beauty and value of the American scene as a subject for literature.

Among the many reasons suggested to explain why the interest in regionalism has always accompanied the passion of nationalism is the suggestion that human beings aren't emotionally "large" enough to identify with geographical areas as vast as the United States. They need something smaller to attach themselves to, something that feels more like "home," something more familiar, like neighborhood. And the biggest "neighborhood" people can feel comfortable with is their region.

A region is usually defined by topographical features: mountain ranges, bodies of water, or abrupt changes in terrain; shared characteristics within those boundaries such as agricultural productivity, prevailing weather conditions, and populations who share ethnic, religious, linguistic, and regional histories; by shared hatred or estrangement from "others"—outsiders or perceived enemies—that is, by xenophobia.

The sharecropping that renders Lonnie Newsome and Clem Henry so vulnerable to Arch Gunnard in Erskine Caldwell's "Kneel to the Rising Sun" is a regionally based agriculture. In Nancy Hale's "The New Order" the black nurse and the white woman cross the borderland of race and give each other comfort based on their connected history.

The perceived boundaries of any region shift as each intellectual discipline orders criteria to fit its needs. In this sense, one value of the concept of region its elasticity— the many different ways a region can be defined. This elasticity is best demonstrated by the regional "maps" produced by linguists, geographers, political and social historians, agronomists, ethnographers, economists, geologists, ecologists, and marketing and transportation planners. These regional maps do not overlap when they are overlaid.

Our literary map of the South, for this anthology, includes the Old Dominion (Virginia); the Blue Grass (Kentucky and Tennessee); the Old South (North and South Carolina); the Lower South (Georgia, Alabama, and Mississippi to the Mississippi delta); the Swamp Region (southern Georgia, Alabama, and the greater part of Florida); and the Creole Country (lower Louisiana). We have based our study on Robert L. Ramsay and his twenty-five "literary states" published in *Short Stories of America* (1921).

Further, the criteria defining a region changes over time. Augustus Baldwin Longstreet's 1833 story, "The Dance," reminds us that the earlier we look at United States history, the closer "the west" or "the frontier" is to "the east" or the Atlantic Ocean. This story of the American frontier, an early example of local color writing, is rich in details of daily life and the idioms of local speech. But are we reading "southern literature" or "frontier literature"? Or is this story both?

The conditions and effects of Charlottesville's Indian Summer in Poe's story, "A Tale of the Ragged Mountains," provide us with another perspective on regional literature. Human moods, experiences, diurnal habits, are tied to the weather characteristic of geographical area. Another natural influence, botany, also serves to move the story along, for it is the palm tree, the sign of a different region, that signals to Bedloe his changed circumstances.

The regions of the nineteenth century were less difficult to isolate than are those of the present, where forces as subtle as the uniform highway signs—white letters, green background—loom out of the darkness to remind us that "here" could be anywhere. We careen along one vast interstate highway system, and off-ramps lead into a myriad of cities that are becoming more and more alike—at least along the main-traveled roads. Such standardizations erase the distinction of place—as do the neon strings of franchise hamburger, taco, ice cream, chicken, pizza, fish, and quasi-ethnic restaurants; the muffler, transmission, tire, and quick-serve auto shops; and the real estate companies selling the same house across the continental United States.

In a time where interstate gas stations have cut off one of the first and most frequent ways travelers entered the world of different regions, literature still remains an opening to discover the beauty of the American landscape. As poet Wendell Berry writes, "our voices arrive from the landscape."

Literature is the embodiment of the "sacred stories" of a people—those cherished stories defining the central issues and questions of a people, the stories that record the history of their search for meaning, identity, and justice.

When we sift through the short stories written by southern writers, we are shifting through a literary repository, the secular texts, of the sacred dimensions of a people (and their ancestors), a place, and a history. Just as the canons of sacred texts have been the foci of spiritual struggle, so, too, have the secular canons of literature been the foci of struggle over the decades. Whose stories are important enough, representative enough, universal enough to rate being included in the canon? And not only whose stories, but which kinds of telling ought a people to preserve and call their own?

For many years now, the study of regional literature has been seen as a quaint or marginal study rather than a necessary pursuit. But as our society returns to our various roots, we have come to understand that all literature is, in some sense, regional or parochial or provincial literature. Once again regional literature is not only being self-consciously (in the best sense) created, but critically acclaimed and rigorously collected as regional literature rather than being transformed or translated into universal literature. We understand better that there is no universal except in the particular.

There are stories in this anthology from all classes, from the impoverished elite of Susan Petigru King's "A Marriage of Persuasion" to the dirt poor of Erskine Caldwell's "Kneel to the Rising Sun." There are visions of children by Truman Capote, Zora Neale Hurston, Constance Fenimore Woolson, and Ernest J. Gaines. There are stories about the quests of young adults searching for self by Arna Bontemps, Doris Betts, and Alice Walker. There are stories about characters as old as Peter Taylor's pilgrims.

In these stories, there are the issues that concern all writers, all readers, the whole world over—issues of economic survival, of familial responsibility and love, conflicts between generations, races, sexes; the difficulty of negotiating a safe and satisfying life, the conflicts between internal prompting and external expectations, between private desire and public demands. Writers whose roots are in the South struggle as vigorously with these issues as have any of the writers and philosophers in the world.

That their focus and the clarity of their vision gives us a better understanding of their region and how it shapes the people who live there makes these stories even more deserving of our attention, gratitude, and admiration.

William Gilmore Simms (April 17, 1806–June 11, 1870) was born in Charleston, South Carolina. He was a prolific writer who published fiction, poetry, drama, criticism, history, biography, and journalism with predominantly southern themes. Today few of his works are in print.

Simms was the second of three children and the only one to survive infancy. His mother died in childbirth in 1808 and his father moved to the Southwest and left him to grow up with his maternal grandmother, who was an outstanding storyteller. She sent him to school at age six and at age ten he entered the College of Charleston where he developed his lasting interest in language. Two years later Simms became an apprentice in a Charleston pharmacist's shop. When his apprenticeship ended six years later he entered the office of a friend to study law. His love of literature continued to thrive and *Monody, on the Death of Gen. Charles Cotesworth Pinckney*, his first published book, appeared in 1825. It was during this period that he left Charleston to journey to his father's plantation near what is now Hattiesburg, Mississippi. There, he gathered stories and experiences by traveling with his father into Indian and backwoods territory. In 1828 in addition to his legal work and writing, Simms began publishing and editing the *Southern Literary Gazette*, but because of financial strain it was discontinued after two issues. In the November 1829 issue his short fiction, "Confessions of a Murderer," was printed. Later Simms expanded this story into the novel *Martin Faber*.

With publication of *Martin Faber* (1833) and *Guy Rivers* (1834), his first border romance, Simms achieved the literary success he desired. Other major works—*The Yemassee* (1835), *The Partisan* (1835), and *Mellichampe* (1836)—followed.

During the 1850s, Simms published four Revolutionary War romances—*Katharine Walton* (1851), *The Sword and the Distaff* (1852, later retitled *Woodcraft*), *The Forayers* (1855), and *Eutaw* (1856). Also in the 1850s the important fifteen-volume Redfield edition of his work (1853-1859) was published. *The Cassique of Kiawah* (1859), which Simms

1

thought to be his best romance, ended his three decades of literary achievement.

CONFESSIONS OF A MURDERER

by William Gilmore Simms

I was born in an obscure country village in D——; the place had not more than ten or twelve families, and that of my parents was one of the most intelligent and respectable. The village was one of that class which is never known to vary its position; it neither increased nor diminished, and my father was one of the principal, if not the only principal man in it. Would he had been less so. Had he thought more of his own and the business of his own family and less of those around, I should not this day recount the history of my own disgrace. But my father was the great man, the lion of the village, and I became no less so of my mama's fireside. I was a spoiled boy even before I could read—so early are the principles of the human mind subject to misdirection. I was perverse, unruly and puerile, and my father mended the matter very considerably by damning at me on all warrantable occasions. To him and to my mother I charge my crime and its punishment, and while they are wondering how so bad a scion should spring from so good a stock, they have been weaving the rope about my neck. I shall render amends to the laws of the land; they are accountable to God, and to his mercies I leave them.

I was a truant from school and exulted in it without punishment. I was brutal while a mere boy to all around me; was a boor in decent society; was insolent to my parents; rude and boisterous at table; savage and ferocious among my associates and received no punishment. Sometimes when

I exceeded even the bounds of toleration, tacitly joined to my conduct by my father, I received some such rebuke as—'now my dear how can you do so,' or, 'I will be vexed with you, my son, if you do not behave.'

What was all this to an overgrown boy, nursed in full ideas of his own importance, licentious in his habits, and admitted to all and any irregularities, for which my father furnished an ample model. I bade defiance to threats, and scorned reproaches. I laughed at the soothings of my mother and took her gifts and favors, furnished in order to persuade me to do better, as things of course which she was obliged to give me. I was brought up a brute, and fulfilled to the letter the seeming objects of my education. Their lessons fitted me to be what I have been, and have reduced me to the miserable situation in which I now am. But let that rest.

I was sent to school, but learnt nothing, or what I learnt was entirely obliterated and counteracted by the nature of my education at home. I cared little to learn; my tutor dared not coerce me; he was a poor miserable hireling from the east, who cringed to all for his bread and who considered my father's influence as a matter which would not allow him to restrain or chastise his favorite son. Whatever I did, therefore, went by with impunity. However extravagant, violent or insolent my amusements, I was unpunished. Grown bold and confident, I even ventured to assume the burdens of my companions, announce myself as the offender and get them off free of punishment, while I escaped myself. One day, however, a circumstance occurred which could not pass so easily. It was under the master's own eye, and I was brought up to receive the award which his sense of justice or his lenity might think proper to bestow. He did not even flog me, he spoke to me like a father; as my father never spoke to me; his words were those of kindness, of friendship. I laughed in his face. He was indignant, as well he might be, and gave me a smart blow with his open hand on my face. I looked round upon my companions in order to ascertain if I should be supported, but they were kept in more subjection than myself and dreaded him accordingly. I submitted, though my heart rankled and my spirit burned within me for revenge. I had it—many years afterwards I had it. A deep and dreadful revenge. For the time, however, I contented myself with one more congenial with the little spirit of a bad and brutal boy. He kept me in, as a punishment, after the boys generally had been dismissed. He left me in the schoolroom and retired to his dinner. While in that room shut up, what were my emotions! The spirit of a demon was working in me, and the passion of my heart nearly exhausted my body; I threw myself on the floor and wept; hot, scalding tears. I rose—I strode for a long time to and fro; a sudden thought seized me; a mean and paltry revenge filled my bosom, as I stopt before a couple of large, new and beautiful globes that had just come to my teacher at a vast expense. I now perceived my revenge. Though small in proportion, to what it appeared to me that my wrongs required, I well knew that the injury of his globes would be almost the most severe revenge I could take upon their owner. A jug of ink lay beside them. I opened it carefully and poured its contents upon the beautifully varnished lines of the heavens and the earth. They were ruined, irrevocably ruined. These are trifles you will say, but you are mistaken. To people advanced in years the life of a boy is made up of trifles; but these incidents are developed with the growth of the child to maturity. The same feeling which prompted to the act just related, would prompt an incendiary to the firing of his enemy's dwelling; the same feeling grown mature with my years, prompted me to the commission of a murder—the crime which to-morrow I shall partially expiate upon the gallows.

Weakly could I describe his rage upon discovering what I had done. I was in the school-room, where he had left me, when he returned. For some time he did not perceive them, but walking up and down he spoke to me for a long time in a manner, which, had I not been acted on by something of the spirit of the arch-enemy of man, must have had the effect of compelling me to acknowledge and atone by the only mode in my power for my errors and misconduct. In vain—I was callous alike to reason and kindness. Suddenly, the globes caught his eye—he stopt short; he approached them; passed his hand over his face and actually shed tears. But human passion triumphed; he turned shortly upon me and smote me with his fist upon the face. The blow was a severe one and felled me to the earth. In the first movement of anger, he took me by the arm and with his school strap inflicted upon me a severe but richly deserved flogging. But I thought not so then. I did not for a moment consider the vast robbery I had made from that poor man's small stock of happiness and enjoyment. My feelings were all concentrated in my self—all my own and according with the manner of my education. The revenge of my boyhood did not rest here. A solemn convocation of the chief men of the village, at the head of which stood my father, highly incensed at the indignity, determined upon the offence. The man lost his school and another more indulgent and tractable took his place. What became of the unfortunate man thus turned out of employment by the babble of a boy, for some time I knew not. My revenge contemplated him reduced to necessity, and exulted at the picture which its own desires had presented. He was not the only sufferer. A wife and two infant children—girls—claimed his care. They departed from the village and took a road farther into the country. I did not care to follow them.

Years glided on, and brought something like an improvement to my physical appearance at least. I became manly, and rather graceful and active. My features underwent a considerable change for the better, and perhaps, my manners were less objectionable. My heart, however, remained the same. There was a spell upon it; it seemed seared and while it blighted the fortunes and the feelings of others, partook somewhat of the blight itself. My time, as before, was consumed in idleness. Such amusements as tended to the encouragement of this disposition were always an object of concern with me. Angling, hunting, and frolicking made the day and night of my existence; an existence that I now perceive has been all night. Talk not of the darkness of Greenland; the moral night is the worst of all darkness; the heart and the affections are there, prisoners in a dungeon of space and vacuity.

One morning, with my gun, I had wandered for some time through a part of the country into which I had never before penetrated. The game was plentiful and any thing but shy. I was easily seduced therefore into a long, but encouraging pursuit. I had gone some fourteen or fifteen miles from our village on the opposite river. My way led through a close and umbrageous forest. A grove of dwarf or scrub oaks, woven about with thick and sheltering vines gave a delightful air of quietness to the scene, which while I felt pleased with, my natural inquietude of disposition would not permit me to enjoy. Wheeling to return, I perceived for the first time a clear and sheltered creek, that stole in among the shrubbery and again made its way into the light at a considerable distance beyond. I followed its bendings. It was a sweet place and the hum of the wind among the tree tops alone broke the solemn and mysterious repose of silence. A small arbor arose upon a bank that jutted into the creek so far, that but for a small and narrow neck which united it to the main, might almost be considered an island. I approached it from the point where it was most sheltered, and saw not and was also unseen, by a tall and beautiful girl that reclined on a small hillock beyond it. We both started with surprise at the same moment. I cannot say that our emotions were those of love, but the surprise was productive of pleasure, to me at least, and I feel too much to her. I apologized for my intrusion, and how we grew familiar I cannot now say. My heart has been an Etna and preyed upon its own vitals. Suffice it—we parted, with a hope, though neither of us expressed it, to meet again. We did meet, and every successive day found me with my gun and on the same journey; I killed no birds, however, as before.

That girl was the most artless, the most innocent of all God's creatures! Strange that she should be condemned to a union with the worst and wildest!—need I say, that I, whose touch has contaminated all whose ill fortunes doomed them to any connection with me, blighted and blasted that innocence and changed the smile into the tear and the hope into the fear of that fond and confiding woman. We were both comparatively children; but I—I had lived many; many years of dissipation and crime. I had concentered a long life of wickedness into a few brief years and its concentrated venom fell upon her. But our commerce while it continued was productive of but few sorrows. She gave every thing up to her affection for me: she taught me to love, she loved me, as the young and morning flower has been seen to entwine itself about the deadly and poisonous nightshade.

I had grown to man's estate, my father was returning to a state of second childhood and his principal employment, at this time, was that of looking out a fitting and proper match for his son. Wealth, entered largely into the essentials required of the lady, and his labors were not entirely unavailing. He made a selection. His choice was concurred in by all parties, save myself, and I had, as yet, heard nothing of the matter. But that was no objection. It proved none. I had long been reduced to many straits for ready money. My pursuits rendered much of this necessary; for though my time was greatly given to my intercourse with Emily (such was her name) yet I had not so entirely divested myself of old employments and associates, as to do without this necessary. I saw no difficulty, at the same time, in marrying the heiress, and enjoying as before the society of the poor sweet girl I had dishonored. My resolution was taken, and a few days saw me in preparation for the bridal. For two days I went not to my place of rendesvous. I was too busily employed. On the third a smart but pensive faced boy, arrested me at the door of the mansion house of the lady to whom I was engaged. I recognized her with surprise and apprehension. I took her aside. Emily, said I, what brings you here. Can you ask, she replied; could I fail to see you for two whole days, nor fear every thing. Alas! you know not, I see, how long two days are to me. Where have you been, what has detained you, were you sick. I have been sick, Emily, I replied unhesitatingly, but am not now. Tomorrow you will see me without fail. But where are you going now she continued. Is this the house you live in—'tis very handsome. But Walter, you will come, dear Walter? I will Emily, go now, and expect me. We parted. How like a child, a sweet confiding child, she spoke to me. Yet at the very moment that the accents of her voice were most tender and touching I had begun to hate her. She was in my way. I kept my appointment however. She was in waiting, and seemingly in very bad spirits. Had she heard any thing? She had. In a few words she gave me to understand that the rumour of my intended marriage had met her ear, and she now enquired of me if it was so. I denied it.

'Walter,' she exclaimed earnestly, 'I believe you, I cannot think for a moment you would wrong me so. But Walter, a something tells me that I shall not live very long, and I would be your wife before the time comes, when my sin will stand embodied before me. You have promised me frequently; say that you will marry me this week, I don't care what time, dear Walter, only let it be this week.'

Her eyes filled as she spoke and her heart palpitated violently as I pressed it against my own. It was the prayer of an apprehensive and almost subdued spirit. Disappointment, for I had long deceived her with promises, had worn and harassed her to a skeleton. But I had no notion of complying. I was inflexible; I was brutally stern, I repulsed and when in the tenderest and most endearing accents she repeated her request, I quickly and pettishly replied that it was impossible.

'It is all true then, as they have said,' she exclaimed passionately. 'Oh, God, now do I feel my infirmity. But think not,' she continued as her face assumed all the majesty and loveliness of inspiration, 'think not thus to injure me unpunished, unpursued. I will go to the village, I will see this lady for whose love mine and my spirit must be sacrificed. She shall know whether it be compatible with her honor or the dignity of the female character, to unite herself with one who has so grievously injured one of her own sex,' and she burst into a passion of tears.

I was alarmed—I had never seen her exhibit so much firmness of purpose on any occasion before. How could I expect it, there had been no occasion whatever for such an exhibition 'till now. I seized her hand. She withdrew it quickly and indignantly. 'Emily,' I exclaimed, while I again took hold of and retained it firmly. She struggled, her strength was opposed to mine and in the heat of the struggle I forgot that victory in such a case would be the greatest shame. I hurled her to the ground, she looked up to me imploringly, apparently strove to speak, but in vain, and she turned her face despairingly upon the still dewy grass and sobbed as if the strings of her heart kept breaking with every motion of her lips. I know not what demon possessed me at that moment. There seemed to be a more than customary silence around me. I knelt beside her, and the fury was in me. My eyes wandered wildly around the forest. I uttered no word, but my left hand grasped her throat, she partly turned her head and exclaimed, while the tones came rattling forth, 'Walter, spare me, do Walter; I am too young, too bad to perish in my sins, dear Walter, I will not reproach you, I will not accuse you, I——O——God!' and she was dead—dead under my hands. I breathed not, I moved not for a minute. My eyes were in the air, on the water, in the woods, but I dared not turn them to the still imploring glance of that fixed and terrified look.

Need I say more, than that I am now about to suffer for that crime? Need I say that Emily Stephenson was the eldest daughter of the poor man, who had been driven from his occupation by the boy, whose manhood had now proved so fatal to him. She was his eldest, most beloved, and tenderly nursed child. I have seen him once since; he spoke not to me; but when he looked upon me, he passed his hands over his eyes as if they had been seared and scathed by a bar of blistering fire. He rushed from my presence but now, and I am alone.

*　　*　　*　　*

I look once more from the window of my dungeon; what a crowd are in waiting. There are parents in that crowd; Alas! is there one whose son's education has been like mine? let him beware!

Augustus Baldwin Longstreet (September 22, 1790–July 9, 1870) was born in Augusta, Georgia. His father was an inventor and business person. Although he wrote many books and pamphlets, he is best known for his collection of stories, *Georgia Scenes, Characters, Incidents, in the First Half Century of the Republic* (1835). These humorous sketches, first printed in the Midgeville *Southern Recorder* and in the Augusta *State Rights Sentinel,* have been called the first significant contribution to southwestern humor. Longstreet said these stories were "fanciful combinations of real incidents and characters." A graduate of Yale University in 1813, Longstreet studied law in Litchfield, Connecticut, before returning to Georgia to be admitted to the bar. In addition to practicing law, Longstreet served as a state legislator, a superior court judge, a newspaper editor and proprietor, a Methodist minister, and president of four colleges—Emory College (1839–1848), Centenary College (1849), University of Mississippi (1849–1856), University of South Carolina (1858–1861). After the Civil War he retired to Mississippi.

Edgar Allan Poe was one of the first to recognize Longstreet's contribution to literature when he praised the anonymous author (the 1835 edition was attributed to a "Native Georgian") for his "penetrating understanding of *character* in general, and of Southern character in particular." In his "Preface" Longstreet states that the sketches "consist of nothing more than fanciful *combinations* of *real* incidents and characters."

THE DANCE

by Augustus Baldwin Longstreet

Some years ago I was called by business to one of the frontier counties, then but recently settled. It became necessary for me, while there, to enlist the services of Thomas Gibson, Esq., one of the magistrates of the county, who resided about a mile and a half from my lodgings; and to this circumstance was I indebted for my introduction to him. I had made the intended disposition of my business, and was on the eve of my departure for the city of my residence, when I was induced to remain a day longer by an invitation from the squire to attend a dance at his house on the following day. Having learned from my landlord that I would probably "be expected at the frolic" about the hour of 10 in the forenoon, and being desirous of seeing all that passed upon the occasion, I went over about an hour before the time.

The squire's dwelling consisted of but one room, which answered the threefold purpose of dining-room, bedroom, and kitchen. The house was constructed of logs, and the floor was of *puncheons*; a term which, in Georgia, means split logs, with their faces a little smoothed with the axe or hatchet. To gratify his daughters, Polly and Silvy, the old gentleman and his lady had consented to *camp out* for a day, and to surrender the habitation to the girls and their young friends.

When I reached there I found all things in readiness for the promised amusement. The girls, as the old gentleman informed me, had compelled the family to breakfast under the trees, for they had completely stripped the house of its furniture before the sun rose. They were already attired for the dance, in neat but plain habiliments of their own manufacture. "What!" says some weakly, sickly, delicate, useless, affected, "charming creature" of the city, "dressed for a ball at 9 in the morning!" Even so, my delectable Miss Octavia Matilda Juliana Claudia Ipecacuanha: and what have you to say against it? If people must dance is it not much more rational to employ the hour allotted to exercise in that amusement, than the hours sacred to repose and meditation? And which is entitled to the most credit; the young lady who rises with the dawn, and puts herself and whole house in order for a ball four hours before it begins, or the one who requires a fortnight to get herself dressed for it?

The squire and I employed the interval in conversation about the first settlement of the country, in the course of which I picked up some useful and much interesting information. We were at length interrupted, however, by the sound of a violin, which proceeded from a thick wood at my left. The performer soon after made his appearance, and proved to be no other than Billy Porter, a negro fellow of much harmless wit and humour, who was well known throughout the state. Poor Billy! "his harp is now hung upon the willow;" and I would not blush to offer a tear to his memory, for his name is associated with some of the happiest scenes of my life, and he sleeps with many a dear friend, who used to join me in provoking his wit and in laughing at his eccentricities; but I am leading my reader to the grave instead of the dance, which I promised. If, however, his memory reaches twelve years back, he will excuse this short tribute of respect to BILLY PORTER.

Billy, to give his own account of himself, "had been taking a turn with the brethren (the Bar); and, hearing the ladies wanted to see *pretty Billy*, had come to give them a benefit." The squire had not seen him before; and it is no disrespect to his understanding or politeness to say, that he found it impossible to give me his attention for half an hour after Billy arrived. I had nothing to do, therefore, while the young people were assembling, but to improve my knowledge of Billy's character, to the squire's amusement. I had been thus engaged about thirty minutes, when I saw several fine, bouncing, ruddy-cheeked girls descending a hill about the eighth of a mile off. They, too, were attired in manufactures of their own hands. The refinements of the present day in female dress had not even reached our republican *cities* at this time; and, of course, the *country girls* were wholly ignorant of them. They carried no more cloth upon their arms or straw upon their heads than was necessary to cover them. They used no artificial means of speading their frock tails to an interesting extent from their ankles. They had no boards laced to their breasts, nor any corsets laced to their sides; consequently, they looked, for all the world, like human beings, and could be distinctly recognised as such at the distance of two hundred paces. Their movements were as free and active as nature would permit them to be. Let me not be understood as interposing the least objection to any lady in this land of liberty dressing just as she pleases. If she choose to lay her neck and shoulders bare, what right have I to look at them? much less to find fault with them. If she choose to put three yards of muslin in a frock sleeve, what right have I to ask why a little strip of it was not put in the body? If she like the pattern of a hoisted umbrella for a frock, and the shape of a cheese-cask for her body, what is all that to me? But to return.

The girls were met by Polly and Silvy Gibson at some distance from the house, who welcomed them—"with a kiss, of course"—oh, no; but with something much less equivocal: a hearty shake of the hand and smiling countenances, which had some meaning.

[*Note.*—The custom of kissing, as practised in these days by the *amiables*, is borrowed from the French, and by them from Judas.]

The young ladies had generally collected before any of the young men appeared. It was not long, however, before a large number of both sexes were assembled, and they adjourned to the *ballroom*.

But for the snapping of a fiddle-string, the young people would have been engaged in the amusement of the day in less than three minutes from the time they entered the house. Here were no formal introductions to be given, no drawing for places or partners, no parade of managers, no ceremonies. It was perfectly understood that all were invited *to dance*, and that none were invited who were unworthy to be danced with; consequently, no gentleman hesitated to ask any lady present to dance with him, and no lady refused to dance with a gentleman merely because she had not been made acquainted with him.

In a short time the string was repaired, and off went the party to a good old republican six reel. I had been thrown among *fashionables* so long that I had almost forgotten my native dance. But it revived rapidly as they wheeled through its mazes, and with it returned many long-forgotten, pleasing recollections. Not only did the reel return to me, but the very persons who used to figure in it with me, in the heyday of youth.

Here was my old sweetheart, Polly Jackson, identically personified in Polly Gibson; and here was Jim Johnson's, in Silvy; and Bill Martin's, in Nancy Ware. Polly Gibson had my old flames's very steps as well as her looks. "Ah!" said I, "squire, this puts me in mind of old times. I have not seen a six reel for five-and-twenty years. It recalls to my mind many a happy hour, and many a jovial friend who used to enliven it with me. Your Polly looks so much like my old sweetheart, Polly Jackson, that, were I young again, I certainly should fall in love with her."

"That was the name of her mother," said the squire.

"Where did you marry her?" inquired I.

"In Wilkes," said he; "she was the daughter of old Nathan Jackson, of that county."

"It isn't possible!" returned I. "Then it is the very girl of whom I am speaking. Where is she?"

"She's out," said the squire, "preparing dinner for the young people; but she'll be in towards the close of the day. But come along, and I'll make you acquainted with her at once, if you'll promise not to run away with her, for I tell you what it is, she's the likeliest *gal* in all these parts yet."

"Well," said I, "I'll promise not to run away with her, but you must not let her know who I am. I wish to make myself known to her; and, for fear of the worst, you shall witness the introduction. But don't get jealous, squire, if she seems a little too glad to see me; for, I assure you, we had a strong notion of each other when we were young."

"No danger," replied the squire; "she hadn't seen *me* then, or she never could have loved such a hard favoured man as you are."

In the mean time the dance went on, and I employed myself in selecting from the party the best examples of the dancers of my day and Mrs. Gibson's for her entertainment. In this I had not the least difficulty; for the dancers before me and those of my day were in all respects identical.

Jim Johnson kept up the double shuffle from the beginning to the end of the reel: and here was Jim over again in

Sammy Tant. Bill Martin always set to his partner with the same step; and a very curious step it was. He brought his right foot close behind his left, and with it performed precisely the motion of the thumb in cracking that insect which Burns has immortalized; then moved his right back, threw his weight upon it, brought his left behind it, and *cracked* with that as before; and so on alternately. Just so did Bill Kemp, to a nail. Bob Simons danced for all the world like a "Suple Jack" (or, as we commonly call it, a "*Suple* Sawney"), when the string is pulled with varied force, at intervals of seconds: and so did *Jake* Slack. Davy Moore went like a suit of clothes upon a clothing line on a windy day: and here was his antitype in Ned Clark. Rhoda Noble swam through the reel like a cork on wavy waters; always giving two or three pretty little perchbite *diddles* as she rose from a coupee: Nancy Ware was her very self. Becky Lewis made a business of dancing; she disposed of her part as quick as possible, stopped dead short as soon as she got through, and looked as sober as a judge all the time; even so did Chloe Dawson. I used to tell Polly Jackson, that Becky's countenance, when she closed a dance, always seemed to say, "Now, if you want any more dancing, you may do it yourself."

The dance grew merrier as it progressed; the young people became more easy in each other's company, and often enlivened the scene with most humorous remarks. Occasionally some sharp cuts passed between the boys, such as would have produced half a dozen duels at a city ball; but here they were taken as they were meant, in good humour. Jim Johnson being a little tardy in meeting his partner at a turn of the reel, "I *ax* pardon, Miss Chloe," said he, "Jake Slack went to make a crosshop just now, and tied his legs in a hard knot, and I stop'd to help him untie them." A little after, Jake hung his toe in a crack of the floor, and nearly fell; "Ding my buttons," said he, "if I didn't know I should stumble over Jim Johnson's foot at last; Jim, draw your foot up to your own end of the reel." (Jim was at the other end of the reel, and had, in truth, a prodigious foot.)

Towards the middle of the day, many of the neighbouring farmers dropped in, and joined the squire and myself in talking of old times. At length dinner was announced. It consisted of plain *fare*, but there was a profusion of it. Rough planks, supported by stakes driven in the ground, served for a table; at which the old and young of both sexes seated themselves at the same time. I soon recognised Mrs. Gibson from all the matrons present. Thirty years had wrought great changes in her appearance, but they had left some of her features entirely unimpaired. Her eye beamed with all its youthful fire; and, to my astonishment, her mouth was still beautified with a full set of teeth, unblemished by time. The rose on her cheek had rather freshened than faded, and her smile was the very same that first subdued my heart; but her fine form was wholly lost, and, with it, all the grace of her movements. Pleasing but melancholy reflections occupied my mind as I gazed on her dispensing her cheerful hospitalities. I thought of the sad history of many of her companions and mine, who used to carry light hearts through the merry dance. I compared my after life with the cloudless days of my attachment to Polly. Then I was light hearted, gay, contented, and happy. I aspired to nothing but a good name, a good wife, and an easy competence. The first and last were mine already; and Polly had given me too many little tokens of her favour to leave a doubt now that the second was at my command. But I was foolishly told that my talents were of too high an order to be employed in the drudgeries of a farm, and I more foolishly believed it. I forsook the pleasures which I had tried and proved, and went in pursuit of those imaginary joys which seemed to encircle the seat of Fame. From that moment to the present, my life had been little else than one unbroken scene of disaster, disappointment, vexation, and toil. And now, when I was too old to enjoy the pleasures which I had discarded, I found that my aim was absolutely hopeless; and that my pursuits had only served to unfit me for the humbler walks of life, and to exclude me from the higher. The gloom of these reflections was, however, lightened in a measure by the promises of the coming hour, when I was to live over again with Mrs. Gibson some of the happiest moments of my life.

After a hasty repast the young people returned to their amusement, followed by myself, with several of the elders of the company. An hour had scarcely elapsed before Mrs. Gibson entered, accompanied by a goodly number of matrons of her own age. This accession to the company produced its usual effects. It raised the tone of conversation a full octave, and gave it a triple time movement; added new life to the wit and limbs of the young folks, and set the old men to cracking jokes.

At length the time arrived for me to surprise and delight Mrs. Gibson. The young people insisted upon the old folks taking a reel; and this was just what I had been waiting for; for, after many plans for making the discovery, I had finally concluded upon that which I thought would make *her* joy general among the company: and that was, to announce myself, just before leading her to the dance, in a voice audible to most of the assembly. I therefore readily assented to the proposition of the young folks, as did two others of my age, and we made to the ladies for our partners. I, of course, offered my hand to Mrs. Gibson.

"Come," said I, "Mrs. Gibson, let us see if we can't out-dance these young people."

"Dear me, sir," said she, "I haven't danced a step these twenty years."

"Neither have I; but I've resolved to try once more, if you will join me, just for old time's sake."

"I really cannot think of dancing," said she.

"Well," continued I (raising my voice to a pretty high pitch, on purpose to be heard, while my countenance kindled with exultation at the astonishment and delight which I was about to produce), "you surely will dance with an old friend and sweetheart, who used to dance with you when a girl!"

At this disclosure her features assumed a vast variety of expressions; but none of them responded precisely to my expectation: indeed, some of them were of such an equivocal and alarming character, that I deemed it advisable not to prolong her suspense. I therefore proceeded:

"Have you forgot your old sweetheart, Abram Baldwin?"

"What!" said she, looking more astonished and confused than ever. "Abram Baldwin! Abram Baldwin! I don't think I ever heard the name before."

"Do you remember Jim Johnson?" said I.

"Oh, yes," said she, "mighty well," her countenance brightening with a smile.

"And Bill Martin?"

"Yes, perfectly well; why, *who* are you?"

Here we were interrupted by one of the gentlemen, who had led his partner to the floor, with, "Come, stranger, we're getting mighty tired o' standing. It won't do for old

people that's going to dance to take up much time in standing; they'll lose all their *spryness*. Don't stand begging Polly
Gibson, she never dances; but take my Sal there, next to
her; she'll run a reel with you, to old Nick's house and back
agin."

No alternative was left me, and therefore I offered my
hand to Mrs. Sally—I didn't know who.

"Well," thought I, as I moved to my place, "the squire is
pretty secure from jealousy; but Polly will soon remember
me when she sees my steps in the reel. I will dance precisely
as I used to in my youth, if it tire me to death." There was
one step that was almost exclusively my own, for few of the
dancers of my day could perform it at all, and none with the
grace and ease that I did. "She'll remember Abram Baldwin," thought I, "as soon as she sees the *double cross-
hop*." It was performed by rising and crossing the legs twice
or thrice before lighting, and I used to carry it to the third
cross with considerable ease. It was a step solely adapted to
setting or balancing, as all will perceive; but I thought the
occasion would justify a little perversion of it, and therefore
resolved to lead off with it, that Polly might be at once
relieved from suspense. Just, however, as I reached my
place, Mrs. Gibson's youngest son, a boy about eight years
old, ran in and cried out, "Mammy, old Boler's jump'd
upon the planks, and dragg'd off a great hunk o' meat as big
as your head, and broke a dish and two plates all to darn
smashes!" Away went Mrs. Gibson, and off went the music.
Still I hoped that matters would be adjusted in time for
Polly to return and see the double cross-hop; and I felt the
mortification which my delay in getting a partner had occasioned somewhat solaced by the reflection that it had thrown
me at the foot of the reel.

The first and second couples had nearly completed their
performances, and Polly had not returned. I began to grow
uneasy, and to interpose as many delays as I could without
attracting notice.

The six reel is closed by the foot couple balancing at the
head of the set, then in the middle, then at the foot, again in
the middle, meeting at the head, and leading down.

My partner and I had commenced balancing at the head,
and Polly had not returned. I balanced until my partner
forced me on. I now deemed it advisable to give myself up
wholly to the double cross-hop; so that, if Polly should

return in time to see any step, it should be this, though I was already nearly exhausted. Accordingly, I made the attempt to introduce it in the turns of the reel; but the first experiment convinced me of three things at once; 1st. That I could not have used the step in this way in my best days; 2nd. That my strength would not more than support it in its proper place for the remainder of the reel; and, 3rd. If I tried it again in this way, I should knock my brains out against the puncheons; for my partner, who seemed determined to confirm her husband's report of her, evinced no disposition to wait upon experiments; but, fetching me a jerk while I was up and my legs crossed, had wellnigh sent me head foremost to Old Nick's house, sure enough.

We met in the middle, my back to the door, and from the silence that prevailed in the yard, I flattered myself that Polly might be even now catching the first glimpse of the favourite step, when I heard her voice at some distance from the house: "Get you gone! G-e-e-e-t you gone! G-e-e-e-e-t you gone!" Matters out doors were now clearly explained. There had been a struggle to get the meat from Boler; Boler had triumphed, and retreated to the woods with his booty, and Mrs. Gibson was heaping indignities upon him in the last resort.

The three "*Get-you-gones*" met me precisely at the three closing balances; and the last brought my moral energies to a perfect level with my physical.

Mrs. Gibson returned, however, in a few minutes after, in a good humour; for she possessed a lovely disposition, which even marriage could not spoil. As soon as I could collect breath enough for regular conversation (for, to speak in my native dialect, I was "*mortal tired*"), I took a seat by her, resolved not to quit the house without making myself known to her, if possible.

"How much," said I, "your Polly looks and dances like you used to, at her age."

"I've told my old man so a hundred times," said she. "Why, who upon earth are you!"

"Did you ever see two persons dance more alike than Jim Johnson and Sammy Tant?"

"Never. Why, who can you be!"

"You remember Becky Lewis?"

"Yes!"

"Well, look at Chloe Dawson, and you'll see her over again."

"Well, law me! Now I know I must have seen you somewhere; but, to save my life, I can't tell where. Where did your father live?"

"He died when I was small."

"And where did you use to see me?"

"At your father's, and old Mr. Dawson's, and at Mrs. Barnes's, and at Squire Noble's, and many other places."

"Well, goodness me! it's mighty strange I can't call you to mind."

I now began to get petulant, and thought it best to leave her.

The dance wound up with the old merry jig, and the company dispersed.

The next day I set out for my residence. I had been at home rather more than two months, when I received the following letter from Squire Gibson:

"DEAR SIR: I send you the money collected on the notes you left with me. Since you left here, Polly has been thinking about old times, and she says, to save her life, she can't recollect you."

Edgar Allan Poe (January 19, 1809–October 7, 1849) was born in Boston, Massachusetts. After his father mysteriously disappeared in 1810 and his mother died in December 1811, Poe became the ward of Frances and John Allan who lived in Richmond, Virginia. They placed great value on education and could afford special academy training for Poe. In 1826 he entered the University of Virginia. It was during this time that many of the poems in his first published book were written. His story of metempsychosis, "A Tale of the Ragged Mountains," (1844), reflects the influence of his years there; the Ragged Mountains were observable from his college room. Although a brilliant student, enormous gambling debts and arguments over money with John Allan caused him to leave the University in December 1826 and enter the army under the name Edgar A. Perry. Between his military duties Poe had time to write poems and other short pieces. He was later to use Sullivan's Island as the setting for "The Gold Bug." His first volume of poems, *Tamerlaine and Other Poems By a Bostonian*, was published in 1827 and a second volume, *Al Aaraaf, Tamerlane, and Minor Poems*, appeared in 1829 shortly after he was honorably discharged from the army. Poe was enrolled in West Point as a cadet on July 1, 1830 but was shortly after expelled for failing to obey regulations. *Poems by Edgar A. Poe, Second Edition* was published in 1831.

For the next four years Poe lived in Baltimore and supported himself with odd jobs and the occasional sale of a story. The Philadelphia *Saturday Courier* published five of Poe's stories in 1832. The *Southern Literary Messenger* hired him in 1835 and he at last had secured a literary profession. In 1836 he married his thirteen year old cousin, Virginia, and returned to Baltimore to write for the *Messenger* which he helped develop into a nationally acclaimed magazine. Poe was fired (or resigned) early in 1837 and moved to New York where life was financially difficult but he was able to publish his novel *The Narrative of Arthur Gordon Pym* (1838). After publication Poe moved his family to Philadel-

21

phia where he lived for the next five years. His first short story collection (1839), *Tales of the Grotesque and Arabesque*, and his poem "The Raven" printed in the New York *Evening Mirror* (January 29, 1845) brought him public attention. *Tales by Edgar A. Poe*, a second collection of short stories, and *The Raven and Other Poems*, his fourth collection of poetry, were both published in 1845. When his wife died in January 1847 Poe went into a period of depression and his own health became worse. He died in a Baltimore hospital after being found unconscious on a street in Baltimore.

Poe is credited with defining the short story as a distinct literary form and some say with inventing the detective story.

A TALE OF THE RAGGED MOUNTAINS

by Edgar Allan Poe

During the fall of the year 1827, while residing near Charlottesville, Virginia, I casually made the acquaintance of Mr. Augustus Bedloe. This young gentleman was remarkable in every respect, and excited in me a profound interest and curiosity. I found it impossible to comprehend him either in his moral or his physical relations. Of his family I could obtain no satisfactory account. Whence he came, I never ascertained. Even about his age—although I call him a young gentleman—there was something which perplexed me in no little degree. He certainly *seemed* young—and he made a point of speaking about his youth—yet there were moments when I should have had little trouble in imagining him a hundred years of age. But in no regard was he more peculiar than in his personal appearance. He was singularly tall and thin. He stoopéd much. His limbs were exceedingly long and emaciated. His forehead was broad and low. His complexion was absolutely bloodless. His mouth was large and flexible, and his teeth were more wildly un-even, although sound, than I had ever before seen teeth in a human head. The expression of his smile, however, was by no means unpleasing, as might be supposed; but it had no variation whatever. It was one of profound melancholy—of a phaseless and unceasing gloom. His eyes were abnormally large, and round like those of a cat. The pupils, too, upon any accession or diminution of light, underwent contraction or dilation, just such as is observed in the feline tribe. In moments of excitement the orbs grew bright to a degree almost inconceivable; seeming to emit luminous rays, not of a reflected but of an intrinsic lustre, as does a candle or the sun; yet their ordinary condition was so totally vapid, filmy, and dull, as to convey the idea of the eyes of a long-interred corpse.

These peculiarities of person appeared to cause him much annoyance, and he was continually alluding to them in a sort of half explanatory, half apologetic strain, which, when I first heard it, impressed me very painfully. I soon, however, grew accustomed to it, and my uneasiness wore off. It seemed to be his design rather to insinuate than directly to assert that, physically, he had not always been what he was—that a long series of neuralgic attacks had reduced him from a condition of more than usual personal beauty, to that which I saw. For many years past he had been attended by a physician, named Templeton—an old gentleman, perhaps seventy years of age—whom he had first encountered at Saratoga, and from whose attention, while there, he either received, or fancied that he received, great benefit. The result was that Bedloe, who was wealthy, had made an arrangement with Dr. Templeton, by which the latter, in consideration of a liberal annual allowance, had consented to devote his time and medical experience exclusively to the care of the invalid.

Doctor Templeton had been a traveller in his younger days, and at Paris had become a convert, in great measure, to the doctrine of Mesmer. It was altogether by means of magnetic remedies that he had succeeded in alleviating the

acute pains of his patient; and this success had very naturally inspired the latter with a certain degree of confidence
in the opinions from which the remedies had been educed.
The Doctor, however, like all enthusiasts, had struggled
hard to make a thorough convert of his pupil, and finally so
far gained his point as to induce the sufferer to submit to
numerous experiments. By a frequent repetition of these, a
result had arisen, which of late days has become so common
as to attract little or no attention, but which, at the period
of which I write, had very rarely been known in America. I
mean to say, that between Doctor Templeton and Bedloe
there had grown up, little by little, a very distinct and
strongly marked *rapport*, or magnetic relation. I am not
prepared to assert, however, that this *rapport* extended
beyond the limits of the simple sleep-producing power; but
this power itself had attained great intensity. At the first
attempt to induce the magnetic somnolency, the mesmerist
entirely failed. In the fifth or sixth he succeeded very partially, and after long-continued effort. Only at the twelfth
was the triumph complete. After this the will of the patient
succumbed rapidly to that of the physician, so that, when I
first became acquainted with the two, sleep was brought
about almost instantaneously by the mere volition of the
operator, even when the invalid was unaware of his presence. It is only now, in the year 1845, when similar miracles
are witnessed daily by thousands, that I dare venture to
record this apparent impossibility as a matter of serious fact.

The temperature of Bedloe was, in the highest degree
sensitive, excitable, enthusiastic. His imagination was singularly vigorous and creative; and no doubt it derived addi-
tional force from the habitual use of morphine, which he
swallowed in great quantity, and without which he would
have found it impossible to exist. It was his practice to take
a very large does of it immediately after breakfast each
morning,—or, rather, immediately after a cup of strong
coffee, for he ate nothing in the forenoon, —and then set
forth alone, or attended only by a dog, upon a long ramble
among the chain of wild and dreary hills that lie westward
and southward of Charlottesville, and are there dignified by
the title of the Ragged Mountains.

Upon a dim, warm, misty day, toward the close of November, and during the strange *interregnum* of the seasons
which in America is termed the Indian summer, Mr. Bedloe

departed as usual for the hills. The day passed, and still he did not return.

About eight o'clock at night, having become seriously alarmed at his protracted absence, we were about setting out in search of him, when he unexpectedly made his appearance, in health no worse than usual, and in rather more than ordinary spirits. The account which he gave of his expedition, and of the events which had detained him, was a singular one indeed.

"You will remember," said he, "that it was about nine in the morning when I left Charlottesville. I bent my steps immediately to the mountains, and, about ten, entered a gorge which was entirely new to me. I followed the windings of this pass with much interest. The scenery which presented itself on all sides, although scarcely entitled to be called grand, had about it an indescribable and to me a delicious aspect of dreary desolation. The solitude seemed absolutely virgin. I could not help believing that the green sods and the gray rocks upon which I trod had been trodden never before by the foot of a human being. So entirely secluded, and in fact inaccessible, except through a series of accidents, is the entrance of the ravine, that it is by no means impossible that I was indeed the first adventurer—the very first and sole adventurer who had ever penetrated its recesses.

"The thick and peculiar mist, or smoke, which distinguishes the Indian summer, and which now hung heavily over all objects, served, no doubt, to deepen the vague impressions which these objects created. So dense was this pleasant fog that I could at no time see more than a dozen yards of the path before me. This path was excessively sinuous, and as the sun could not be seen, I soon lost all idea of the direction in which I journeyed. In the meantime the morphine had its customary effect—that of enduing all the external world with an intensity of interest. In the quivering of a leaf—in the hue of a blade of grass—in the shape of a trefoil—in the humming of a bee—in the gleaming of a dew-drop—in the breathing of the wind—in the faint odors that came from the forest— there came a whole universe of suggestion—a gay and motley train of rhapsodical and immethodical thought.

"Busied in this, I walked on for several hours, during which the mist deepened around me to so great an extent that at length I was reduced to an absolute groping of the way. And now an indescribable uneasiness possessed me—a species of nervous hesitation and tremor. I feared to tread, lest I should be precipitated into some abyss. I remembered, too, strange stories told about these Ragged Hills, and of the uncouth and fierce races of men who tenanted their groves and caverns. A thousand vague fancies oppressed and disconcerted me—fancies the more distressing because vague. Very suddenly my attention was arrested by the loud beating of a drum.

"My amazement was, of course, extreme. A drum in these hills was a thing unknown. I could not have been more surprised at the sound of the trump of the Archangel. But a new and still more astounding source of interest and perplexity arose. There came a wild rattling or jingling sound, as if of a bunch of large keys, and upon the instant a dusky-visaged and half-naked man rushed past me with a shriek. He came so close to my person that I felt his hot breath upon my face. He bore in one hand an instrument composed of an assemblage of steel rings, and shook them vigorously as he ran. Scarcely had he disappeared in the mist, before, panting after him, with open mouth and glaring eyes, there darted a huge beast. I could not be mistaken in its character. It was a hyena.

"The sight of this monster rather relieved than heightened my terrors—for I now made sure that I dreamed, and endeavored to arouse myself to waking consciousness. I stepped boldly and briskly forward. I rubbed my eyes. I called aloud. I pinched my limbs. A small spring of water presented itself to my view, and here, stooping, I bathed my hands and my head and neck. This seemed to dissipate the equivocal sensations which had hitherto annoyed me. I arose, as I thought, a new man, and proceeded steadily and complacently on my unknown way.

"At length, quite overcome by exertion, and by a certain oppressive closeness of the atmosphere, I seated myself beneath a tree. Presently there came a feeble gleam of sunshine, and the shadow of the leaves of the tree fell faintly but definitely upon the grass. At this shadow I gazed wonderingly for many minutes. Its character stupefied me with astonishment. I looked upward. The tree was a palm.

"I now arose hurriedly, and in a state of fearful agitation—for the fancy that I dreamed would serve me no longer. I saw—I felt that I had perfect command of my senses—and these senses now brought to my soul a world of novel and singular sensation. The heat became all at once intolerable. A strange odor loaded the breeze. A low, continuous murmur, like that arising from a full, but gently flowing river, came to my ears, intermingled with the peculiar hum of multitudinous human voices.

"While I listened in an extremity of astonishment which I need not attempt to describe, a strong and brief gust of wind bore off the incumbent fog as if by the wand of an enchanter.

"I found myself at the foot of a high mountain, and looking down into a vast plain, through which wound a majestic river. On the margin of this river stood an Eastern-looking city, such as we read of in the Arabian Tales, but of a character even more singular than any there described. From my position, which was far above the level of the town, I could perceive its every nook and corner, as if delineated on a map. The streets seemed innumerable, and crossed each other irregularly in all directions, but were rather long winding alleys than streets, and absolutely swarmed with inhabitants. The houses were wildly picturesque. On every hand was a wilderness of balconies, of verandas, of minarets, of shrines, and fantastically carved oriels. Bazaars abounded; and there were displayed rich wares in infinite variety and profusion—silks, muslins, the most dazzling cutlery, the most magnificent jewels and gems. Besides these things, were seen, on all sides, banners and palanquins, litters with stately dames close-veiled, elephants gorgeously caparisoned, idols grotesquely hewn, drums, banners, and gongs, spears, silver and gilded maces. And amid the crowd, and the clamor, and the general intricacy and confusion—amid the million of black and yellow men, turbaned and robed, and of flowing beard, there roamed a countless multitude of holy filleted bulls, while vast legions of the filthy but sacred ape clambered, chattering and shrieking, about the cornices of the mosques, or clung to the minarets and oriels. From the swarming streets to the banks of the river, there descended innumerable flights of steps leading to bathing places, while the river itself seemed to force a passage with difficulty through the vast fleets of deeply burdened ships that far and wide encountered its surface. Beyond the limits of the city arose, in frequent majestic groups, the palm and the cocoa, with other gigantic and weird trees of vast age; and here and there might be

seen a field of rice, the thatched hut of a peasant, a tank, a
stray temple, a gypsy camp, or a solitary graceful maiden
taking her way, with a pitcher upon her head, to the banks
of the magnificent river.

"You will say now, of course, that I dreamed; but not so.
What I saw—what I heard—what I felt—what I thought—
had about it nothing of the unmistakable idiosyncrasy of the
dream. All was rigorously self-consistent. At first, doubting
that I was really awake, I entered into a series of tests,
which soon convinced me that I really was. Now, when one
dreams, and, in the dream, suspects that he dreams, the
suspicion *never fails to confirm itself*, and the sleeper is
almost immediately aroused. Thus Novalis errs not in saying
that 'we are near waking when we dream that we dream.'
Had the vision occurred to me as I described it, without my
suspecting it as a dream, then a dream it might absolutely
have been, but, occurring as it did, and suspected and tested
as it was, I am forced to class it among other phenomena."

"In this I am not sure that you are wrong," observed Dr.
Templeton, "but proceed. You arose and descended into
the city."

"I arose," continued Bedloe, regarding the Doctor with
an air of profound astonishment, "I arose, as you say, and
descended into the city. On my way I fell in with an immense populace, crowding through every avenue, all in the
same direction, and exhibiting in every action the wildest
excitement. Very suddenly, and by some inconceivable impulse, I became intensely imbued with personal interest in
what was going on. I seemed to feel that I had an important
part to play, without exactly understanding what it was.
Against the crowd which environed me, however, I experienced a deep sentiment of animosity. I shrank from amid
them, and, swiftly, by a circuitous path, reached and entered the city. Here all was the wildest tumult and conten-
tion. A small party of men, clad in garments half Indian,
half European, and officered by gentlemen in a uniform
partly British, were engaged, at great odds, with the swarming rabble of the alleys. I joined the weaker party, arming
myself with the weapons of a fallen officer, and fighting I
knew not whom with the nervous ferocity of despair. We
were soon overpowered by numbers, and driven to seek
refuge in a species of kiosk. Here we barricaded ourselves,
and, for the present, were secure. From a loop-hole near

the summit of the kiosk, I perceived a vast crowd, in furious agitation, surrounding and assaulting a gay palace that overhung the river. Presently, from an upper window of this palace, there descended an effeminate-looking person, by means of a string made of the turbans of his attendants. A boat was at hand, in which he escaped to the opposite bank of the river.

"And now a new object took possession of my soul. I spoke a few hurried but energetic words to my companions, and, having succeeded in gaining over a few of them to my purpose, made a frantic sally from the kiosk. We rushed amid the crowd that surrounded it. They retreated, at first, before us. They rallied, fought madly, and retreated again. In the meantime we were borne far from the kiosk, and became bewildered and entangled among the narrow streets of tall, overhanging houses, into the recesses of which the sun had never been able to shine. The rabble pressed impetuously upon us, harassing us with their spears, and overwhelming us with flights of arrows. These latter were very remarkable, and resembled in some respects the writhing creese of the Malay. They were made to imitate the body of a creeping serpent, and were long and black, with a poisoned barb. One of them struck me upon the right temple. I reeled and fell. An instantaneous and dreadful sickness seized me. I struggled—I gasped—I died."

"You will hardly persist *now*," said I, smiling, "that the whole of your adventure was not a dream. You are not prepared to maintain that you are dead?"

When I said these words, I of course expected some lively sally from Bedloe in reply; but, to my astonishment, he hesitated, trembled, became fearfully pallid, and remained silent. I looked toward Templeton. He sat erect and rigid in his chair—his teeth chattered, and his eyes were starting from their sockets. "Proceed!" he at length said hoarsely to Bedloe.

"For many minutes," continued the latter, "my sole sentiment—my sole feeling—was that of darkness and nonentity, with the consciousness of death. At length there seemed to pass a violent and sudden shock through my soul, as if of electricity. With it came the sense of elasticity and of light. This latter I felt—not saw. In an instant I seemed to rise from the ground. But I had no bodily, no visible, audible, or palpable presence. The crowd had departed.

The tumult had ceased. The city was in comparative repose. Beneath me lay my corpse, with the arrow in my temple, the whole head greatly swollen and disfigured. But all these things I felt—not saw. I took interest in nothing. Even the corpse seemed a matter in which I had no concern. Volition I had none, but appeared to be impelled into motion, and flitted buoyantly out of the city, retracing the circuitous path by which I had entered it. When I had attained that point of the ravine in the mountains at which I had encountered the hyena, I again experienced a shock as of a galvanic battery; the sense of weight, of volition, of substance, returned. I became my original self, and bent my steps eagerly homeward—but the past had not lost the vividness of the real—and not now, even for an instant, can I compel my understanding to regard it as a dream."

"Nor was it," said Templeton, with an air of deep solemnity, "yet it would be difficult to say how otherwise it should be termed. Let us suppose only, that the soul of the man of to-day is upon the verge of some stupendous psychical discoveries. Let us content ourselves with this supposition. For the rest I have some explanation to make. Here is a water-color drawing, which I should have shown you before, but which an unaccountable sentiment of horror has hitherto prevented me from showing."

We looked at the picture which he presented. I saw nothing in it of an extraordinary character; but its effect upon Bedloe was prodigious. He nearly fainted as he gazed. And yet it was but a miniature portrait—a miraculously accurate one, to be sure—of his own very remarkable features. At least this was my thought as I regarded it.

"You will perceive," said Templeton, "the date of this picture—it is here, scarcely visible, in this corner—1780. In this year was the portrait taken. It is the likeness of a dead friend—a Mr. Oldeb—to whom I became much attached at Calcutta, during the administration of Warren Hastings. I was then only twenty years old. When I first saw you, Mr. Bedloe, at Saratoga, it was the miraculous similarity which existed between yourself and the painting which induced me to accost you, to seek your friendship, and to bring about those arrangements which resulted in my becoming your constant companion. In accomplishing this point, I was urged partly, and perhaps principally, by a regretful memory of the deceased, but also, in part by an uneasy, and not altogether horrorless curiosity respecting yourself.

"In your detail of the vision which presented itself to you amid the hills, you have described, with the minutest accuracy, the Indian city of Benares, upon the Holy River. The riots, the combat, the massacre, were the actual events of the insurrection of Cheyte Sing, which took place in 1780, when Hastings was put in imminent peril of his life. The man escaping by the string of turbans was Cheyte Sing himself. The party in the kiosk were sepoys and British officers, headed by Hastings. Of this party I was one, and did all I could to prevent the rash and fatal sally of the officer who fell, in the crowded alleys, by the poisoned arrow of a Bengalee. That officer was my dearest friend. It was Oldeb. You will perceive by these manuscripts," (here the speaker produced a notebook in which several pages appeared to have been freshly written) "that at the very period in which you fancied these things amid the hills, I was engaged in detailing them upon paper here at home."

In about a week after this conversation, the following paragraphs appeared in a Charlottesville paper:

"We have the painful duty of announcing the death of MR. AUGUSTUS BEDLO, a gentleman whose amiable manners and many virtues have long endeared him to the citizens of Charlottesville.

"Mr. B., for some years past, has been subject to neuralgia, which has often threatened to terminate fatally; but this can be regarded only as the mediate cause of his decease. The proximate cause was one of especial singularity. In an excursion to the Ragged Mountains, a few days since, a slight cold and fever were contracted, attended with great determination of blood to the head. To relieve this, Dr. Templeton resorted to topical bleeding. Leeches were applied to the temples. In a fearfully brief period the patient died, when it appeared that, in the jar containing the leeches, had been introduced, by accident, one of the venomous vermicular sangsues which are now and then found in the neighboring ponds. This creature fastened itself upon a small artery in the right temple. Its close resemblance to the medicinal leech caused the mistake to be overlooked until too late.

"N. B.—The poisonous sangsue of Charlottesville may always be distinguished from the medicinal leech by its blackness, and especially by its writhing or vermicular motions, which very nearly resemble those of a snake."

I was speaking with the editor of the paper in question, upon the topic of this remarkable accident, when it occurred to me to ask how it happened that the name of the deceased had been given as Bedlo.

"I presume," said I, "you have authority for this spelling, but I have always supposed the name to be written with an *e* at the end."

"Authority?—no," he replied. "It is a mere typographical error. The name is Bedlo with an *e*, all the world over, and I never knew it to be spelt otherwise in my life."

"Then," said I mutteringly, as I turned upon my heel, "then indeed has it come to pass that one truth is stranger than any fiction—for Bedlo, without the *e*, what is it but Oldeb conversed! And this man tells me it is a typographical error."

Susan Petigru King (Bowen) (October 23, 1824–December 11, 1875) was born and lived most of her life in Charleston, South Carolina. Once described as "the most distinguished woman novelist of ante-bellum South Carolina," this early realist and colleague of William Gilmore Simms, Henry Timrod, and Paul Hamilton Hayne published *Busy Moments of an Idle Woman* (1854), *Lily* (1855), *Sylvia's World* and *Crimes Which the Law Does Not Reach* (1859), and *Gerald Gray's Wife* (1864). Personal and family scandal contributed to her exclusion from literary history. Her second husband, Christopher Columbus Bowen, who represented South Carolina in Congress from 1868 to 1871 and thereafter served as Sheriff for Charleston County, a position of considerable power, stood trial for bigamy after their marriage. One historian reports that he was acquitted; another that he was convicted and served time in prison. Historians of the Reconstruction period treat Christopher Columbus Bowen as a dishonest and murderous villain.

"A Marriage of Persuasion," from *Crimes Which the Law Does Not Reach*, was first published under the pen name Anne Marion Green in 1857 in *Russell's Magazine*, the preeminent literary monthly in antebellum Charleston, one of the chief cultural centers of the South.

A MARRIAGE OF PERSUASION

by Susan Petigru King

A nd so you refused him?"
　　"Yes, mamma."
"Without one word of hope?"
"Not one."

"Harshly? rudely?"

"I trust not. Finally and positively, I certainly did."

"Anna! I can't forgive you."

"My dear mamma, what have I done?"

"What have you done? Refused an excellent man; one whom any mother would be proud to see as her daughter's husband. Sent from the house the best friend I have—deprived us of our mainstay and support—insulted him—and—destroyed the great hope of my life!" The tears streamed from Mrs. Mansfield's eyes. She drew away her hand from her daughter's clasp, and tried to leave the room. Anna detained her.

"Dearest mother! you cannot be more grieved than I am. Mr. Gordon is a very worthy man—he has been a kind friend to us in adversity—he is, I believe, truly sincere in his love for me, and I regret very deeply that it should have brought us to this pass. I have not wounded him further than I could help, I assure you. He will return to visit us in his usual way, after a while; indeed, I hope to see so little change in our intercourse, that I would have spared you the annoyance of knowing this, had he not expressly desired that I should tell you."

"Ah, he is a forgiving and generous creature; a true Christian. Such a man as that to be so treated!"

Anna was silent.

"Anna," resumed her mother, with sudden energy, after a moment's pause, "do you love any one else? have you formed some absurd attachment which interferes with Mr. Gordon's undeniable claim to your affections?"

Miss Mansfield's noble and expressive face was calmly lifted to her mother's heated and excited gaze.

"No, mamma," she simply answered.

"Then, *why* can't you marry Mr. Gordon, and make me happy?"

"Because," and Anna's voice was firm, decided and honest. "Because I do not love him, and to marry him would make me very unhappy."

"Selfish as ever!" ejaculated Mrs. Mansfield. "Will you tell me what you dislike in him?" she pursued.

"I did not say I disliked Mr. Gordon, mamma."

"What you don't like, then? Why you don't love him?"

Anna smiled faintly. "Dear mamma! is there not a great difference between liking and being in love?"

"You are trifling with me most disrespectfully. Is it not

enough that I should suffer this disappointment at your hands, and can you not spare me this beating about the bush? I wish a plain answer to a plain question. Is there anything about Mr. Gordon especially disagreeable to you? If so, what is it?"

"Nothing especially disagreeable, as a friend—as a man whom one sees three or four times a week; but as a husband, several things."

"May I, as only your mother—of course a very insignificant creature to wish or have your confidence—ask these several things?"

"In the first place, then, his appearance is not attractive to me."

"Gracious heaven!" cried Mrs. Mansfield, starting up; "do I live to hear my daughter express such a sentiment! His appearance! Do you not know that to think of such an objection is—the—the—very reverse of modest? Where have you got such ideas? To a truly virtuous woman, what are a man's looks? I might expect such an objection from a girl of low mind and vicious ideas, but not from Anna Mansfield. So this is your reason for not marrying an excellent, kind"——

"Not my only one, mamma," Anna interrupted gently; "it is one of them, but not the greatest. I named it first because it is, I think, very important; and I cannot see the impropriety which strikes you." A slight blush rose to her cheek, as she continued, "I should not like to engage myself to pass my life with a man whose attentions would be repulsive to me, if he had the right to take my hand—or—excuse me, mamma, I don't like to say any more on this point;" and then as the color deepened, she added in a lower voice, "You saw Frederick yesterday put his arm around Maria's waist, as he lifted her from the saddle; and, not caring for the presence of you, his aunt, and us, his cousins, he—a bridegroom of three months—he kissed her pretty blooming cheek, and drew her close to him. She blushed, and said, 'don't, Fred,' but evidently was not displeased. Now, could I endure?—Oh, mamma, pray don't talk about it. It makes me ill. I have named one of the smallest, and at the same time one of the greatest objections. Why dwell upon a difference of opinion, in many essential cases—a total want of congeniality—sympathy—taste, when this trivial reason (provided he possessed the others) is in itself so strong? Dear mamma, don't be angry—

don't be disappointed. You would not wish to make me truly miserable? Perhaps in a year or two, Sally may be Mr. Gordon's choice; and Sally may take him as her beau ideal. Why do you want to get rid of me so soon?"

"Ah, my dear," said Mrs. Mansfield, "you know how poor we are now. Here I am with you four girls, and an income not much larger than in your dear father's time I spent upon my own dress. Is it wonderful that I long to see you settled? Heaven knows that I am not one of those mercenary mothers who would give their children to any man with money. No, indeed. I would not be so wicked. But when a gentleman like Norman Gordon—an honorable, trustworthy, generous creature—wishes to become my son, do you wonder that I should desire it too? I knew his father before him—I knew his mother—all good people; it is good blood, my child—the best dependence in the world. You are nearly twenty years old, and there are three younger than you; how can I help being anxious? And I who know what 'love-matches' are—how many a girl goes to her ruin by that foolish idea; marrying some boy in haste, and repenting at leisure—children—no money—bills to pay—oh! my dear Anna, where is the love then?"

"Mamma, am I making or thinking of making any such match?"

"But you may do it. I want to save you from this. I have a horror of these romantic 'love-matches.' "

"Did you not love my father, mamma?" Anna asked, in a low voice.

"Of course I did. All women should love their husbands. All proper, well-regulated women do love their husbands."

"And yet you wish me to marry without love!"

"Love comes after marriage—every woman with good principles loves her husband. She makes the best of her bargain. Life is a lottery, and if you draw a prize or a blank, you must accept it as it is and be satisfied. Then, when a woman has sworn, in the face of God and man, 'to love, honor and obey' her husband, how can she reconcile herself to not doing it?"

"But, if she should not? if she finds it impossible? Oh, think of that, mamma. Think of vowing solemnly in the face of heaven—and breaking one's oath! Swearing to love, where you feel indifference—promising to honor, where you see little to respect—and vowing to obey, where your reason tells you there is no judgment to make obedience possible! Taking upon your shoulders, *for life*, a burden you cannot bear, and which it is a crime to struggle under, or to cast aside!"

"You know nothing about it, Anna," Mrs. Mansfield said impatiently; "it is not proper for a young girl to think and speak in this wild way. Your mother is here to guide and direct you. No good ever comes of a child arguing and setting herself up in this manner, to teach those older and wiser than herself. The Bible says, 'Honor thy father and thy mother'—it don't say,'dispute with them.' I tell you what I heard from *my* mother, and what every right-minded person knows. 'Make a good choice in life; marry, and love will come afterward.' Love comes with the—never mind. I will not say any more now. I hope sincerely you have been careful of poor Norman's feelings. But you are not apt to do that. You have lacerated mine enough, Heaven knows."

"Oh, mamma! when—how?"

"In this business. When it would be so easy for you to make us all happy, and you prefer your own notions, and willfully act up to them."

A flush of transient anger and indignation swept gustily over Miss Mansfield's face; but she conquered the emotion, and playfully taking a volume from a book-stand near, said, with perfect good humor, and meaningly, "May I read 'Clarissa Harlowe,' mamma?"

"No, put it down, Anna, and don't bother me with any further nonsense."

The daughter obediently withdrew, glad to escape so painful and so disagreeable an interview.

But although this was the first, it was by no means the last of such conversations. Every day the subject was renewed, but gradually Mrs. Mansfield changed her tactics. She no longer scolded or insisted; her reproaches were silent looks of misery—pathetic appeals to heaven "to grant her patience under her afflictions." She was very affectionate to her daughter—heartrendingly so. Anna was called upon constantly to notice what a tender parent she was distressing. Each necessary privation in their reduced household (the father's honorable failure and death had brought them from affluence to comparative poverty,) was prologued and epilogued by sighs and suggestions. "If only Anna could" —and then a sudden pause and deep respiration.

"My own dear child," Mrs. Mansfield would sometimes say; "how I wish you had a new dress. That brown silk is very shabby; but we cannot, with our limited means, buy another, and yet I saw Jane Berryman sneering at it, with her flounced skirts spreading a mile behind her."

"Indeed, mamma, I don't care for Jane Berryman's sneers. It is very good of you to be anxious about it, but *I* think the old brown very becoming."

The next day a rich plaid silk, glossy and fresh, lay upon Anna's bed. "I could not stand it, my dear," said Mrs. Mansfield. "I must do without a new cloak this winter. A mother would rather starve with cold than see her daughter less handsomely dressed than she ought to be. Nothing is a sacrifice to *me*, for *you*, Anna."

In vain poor Anna protested and tried to return the silk, and exchange it for the very necessary cloak, whose purchase was now impossible. Mrs. Mansfield positively forbade her, and the thin black shawl which covered the widow's last year's bombazine was worn with a prolonged shiver, whenever Anna was near enough to hear and see.

Mr. Gordon soon returned to pay his usual visits—to offer his usual attentions—to make his usual presents, at stated times, of things which could permissibly be tendered. The visits Mrs. Mansfield received with great delight—the attentions were allowed; but the first basket of winter produce which arrived from Mr. Gordon's farm, she requested decidedly should be the last.

Clara, the youngest girl, a child of seven, cried lustily because her mamma said "These will be the last potatoes we shall ever eat." From the solemnity of the tone, the little thing fancied that potatoes—a very important item in her daily consumption—were tabooed forever. She desisted when she found that it was only the potatoes from the Gordon farm that fell under the restriction.

Day by day, week after week, this persecution continued. It was the unceasing drop of water that "stayed not itself" for a single instant. In despair, Anna went to consult an aunt, whose opinion she highly valued—whose principles were undoubted—an exemplary wife and mother, and a kind friend always to her niece. Anna recited her woes. "What must I do to escape this torment, my dear Aunt Mary? I feel and know my duty to mamma, I trust; but this life is wearing me out."

Aunt Mary smiled.

"And you don't like Mr. Gordon, dear?"

"I now detest him."

"Oh, for shame! How can you say so? Indeed, my child, I cannot but agree with your mother. This is an excellent match; and it seems to me that if you have no positive objection against his character and standing, you ought to reconsider Mr. Gordon's proposal."

"But, don't you understand that I don't in the least care for the man, except as an ordinary acquaintance. He is well enough as he is; but, do you too advocate a marriage made on such a foundation?"

"Anna! a love-match makes no marriage of love."

"*Voilà une chanson dont je connais l'air!*" said Anna, smiling bitterly in her turn. "You will all force me to marry this man, actually to get rid of him."

"Well, you could not do a better thing, I think?"

Anna returned home disconsolately; returned to the same wearying, petty, incessant, pin pricks, unencouraged by a single word. With all her affection for her mother, she could not but see her weakness in most cases; but on her aunt's judgment she relied, and what had been the result of the interview?—a decided approval of Mrs. Mansfield's wishes.

Let those who blame Anna Mansfield for her next step, pray to be kept from the same pit-fall. This is a mere sketch; but an outline to which all who choose may fill up the hints given. Those who believe that *they* would have been steadfast to the end, will have my admiration, if, when their day of trial comes, they hold firmly to the right; but—as we look around, have we not cause to think that there are many Mrs. Mansfields, and, alas! many Annas?

There came an evening, at length, when on Miss Mansfield's finger shone a great diamond, which dazzled tiny Clara's eyes and made her uncognizant of the tears in her sister's, as she asked wonderingly, "Where did you get such a beau-ti-ful ring?"

Mrs. Mansfield triumphantly said, "That is a secret, Clara."

"No secret for you, my little darling," Anna answered very low and gravely. "Mr. Gordon gave it to me as a pledge that I am to marry him."

"Do you love him, Annie?" Clara said, swallowing her surprise, with great, open, childish eyes.

"Don't ask foolish questions, Clara," her mother cried

angrily. But the tears now rolled down the elder sister's white cheek, and she held the little girl close to her bosom, as she whispered, "you shall come and live with me, my own, and when you marry, I will not need, if God helps me, to ask *you* that question."

The day came—hurried on—and Anna Mansfield was Mrs. Norman Gordon. She was the owner of houses and lands—gold and silver—a perjured conscience and a bleeding heart. Very fine possessions were they, truly, and very proud Mrs. Mansfield was and is, of the hand she had in this righteous barter.

I see Mrs. Gordon frequently; she is very pale and cold, and kind. She has no children—Clara does live with her. Mr. Gordon is not happy, evidently; he has nothing to complain of in his wife. She is scrupulously polite to him, but there is not an atom of sympathy between them. He is prejudiced, uncultivated; and now that he has her, is terribly afraid of being ruled by her. It is a joyless household, and a very rich one. I watch Mrs. Mansfield's greedy gaze lighten broader and broader as the blaze of plate—the measured footfall of a train of servants—the luxurious profusion of their constant service, are spread out before her. She treads the "velvet pile" of carpets with a happy step, and adores her daughter's noble brow, when she sees shimmering upon it—reflecting a thousand lights—the mass of brilliants that binds, in its costly clasp, the struggling thoughts of what was once Anna Mansfield.

So we leave them. What of the end of all this? Is this grand automaton really dead, or does a heart, young and still untouched, lurk—strong, free and dangerous—in that quiet, unmoved and stately figure?

George Washington Cable (October 12, 1844–January 31, 1925) was born in New Orleans, Louisiana. Cable is regarded by many scholars as one of the first progressive writers of the New South.

When his father died in 1859, Cable dropped out of school to work in a customhouse to help support his mother and sisters. At the age of nineteen he enlisted in the Confederate cavalry and was wounded twice in battle. After the surrender, Cable returned to New Orleans penniless and worked as a clerk for a cotton merchant, a rodman with a surveying company, an accountant, and a reporter for the *New Orleans Picayune*. His first story, " 'Sieur George," published in the October 1873 issue of *Scribner's Monthly*, was a great success and more stories followed. His first published book, *Old Creole Days* (1879) was a collection of these stories.

In addition to the praise Cable continues to receive for his short stories, he is respected for his courageous essays on civil rights, such as *The Silent South* (1885; expanded, 1889) and *The Negro Question* (1890), and for his other writings about New Orleans—*The Grandissimes* (1880) and *Madame Delphine* (1881). In these writings Cable was sometimes the lone voice insisting that the country had a responsibility to protect its newly freed citizens. He wrote that mutual education of the races was critical, and that the New South's claim that the freedman's fate was best left in the care of his former master was a trick. Not until the revival of conscience in the 1940s and 1950s did Cable's writing find a sympathetic audience.

In 1884 Cable spent twenty-two weeks on a reading tour with Mark Twain. They were billed as "The Twins of Genius" and traveled to eighty-five cities. After the tour ended Cable moved his family to Northampton, Massachusetts, and named his house Tarryawhile. There, in 1886, Cable founded the Home Culture clubs, racially integrated reading groups. The clubs published a journal first called *Letter* (1892) and later named *Symposium* (1896). He died while wintering in St. Petersburg, Florida, at work on a manuscript.

JEAN-AH POQUELIN

by *George Washington Cable*

In the first decade of the present century, when the newly established American Government was the most hateful thing in Louisiana—when the Creoles were still kicking at such vile innovations as the trial by jury, American dances, antismuggling laws, and the printing of the governor's proclamation in English—when the Anglo-American flood that was presently to burst in a crevasse of immigration upon the delta had thus far been felt only as slippery seepage which made the Creole tremble for his footing—there stood, a short distance above what is now Canal Street, and considerably back from the line of villas which fringed the riverbank on Tchoupitoulas Road, an old colonial plantation house half in ruin.

It stood aloof from civilization, the tracts that had once been its indigo fields given over to their first noxious wildness, and grown up into one of the horridest marshes within a circuit of fifty miles.

The house was of heavy cypress, lifted up on pillars, grim, solid, and spiritless, its massive build a strong reminder of days still earlier, when every man had been his own peace officer and the insurrection of the blacks a daily contingency. Its dark, weather-beaten roof and sides were hoisted up above the jungly plain in a distracted way, like a gigantic ammunition wagon stuck in the mud and abandoned by some retreating army. Around it was a dense growth of low water willows, with half a hundred sorts of thorny or fetid bushes, savage strangers alike to the "language of flowers" and to the botanist's Greek. They were hung with countless strands of discolored and prickly smilax, and the impassable mud below bristled with *chevaux de frise* of the dwarf palmetto. Two lone forest trees, dead cypresses, stood in the center of the marsh, dotted with roosting vultures. The shallow strips of water were hid by myriads of aquatic plants, under whose coarse and spiritless flowers, could one have seen it, was a harbor of reptiles, great and small, to make one shudder to the end of his days.

The house was on a slightly raised spot, the levee of a draining canal. The waters of this canal did not run; they crawled, and were full of big, ravening fish and alligators that held it against all comers.

Such was the home of old Jean Marie Poquelin, once an opulent indigo planter, standing high in the esteem of his small, proud circle of exclusively male acquaintances in the old city; now a hermit, alike shunned by and shunning all who had ever known him. "The last of his line," said the gossips. His father lies under the floor of the St. Louis Cathedral, with the wife of his youth on one side, and the wife of his old age on the other. Old Jean visits the spot daily. His half brother—alas! there was a mystery; no one knew what had become of the gentle, young half-brother, more than thirty years his junior, whom once he seemed so fondly to love, but who, seven years ago, had disappeared suddenly, once for all, and left no clue of his fate.

They had seemed to live so happily in each other's love. No father, mother, wife to either, no kindred upon earth. The elder a bold, frank, impetuous, chivalric adventurer; the younger a gentle, studious, book-loving recluse; they lived upon the ancestral estate like mated birds, one always on the wing, the other always in the nest.

There was no trait in Jean Marie Poquelin, said the old gossips, for which he was so well known among his few friends as his apparent fondness for his "little brother." "Jacques said this," and "Jacques said that"; he "would leave this or that, or any thing to Jacques," for Jacques was a scholar, and "Jacques was good," or "wise," or "just," or "farsighted," as the nature of the case required; and "he should ask Jacques as soon as he got home," since Jacques was never elsewhere to be seen.

It was between the roving character of the one brother, and the bookishness of the other, that the estate fell into decay. Jean Marie, generous gentleman, gambled the slaves away one by one, until none was left, man or woman, but one old African mute.

The indigo fields and vats of Louisiana had been generally abandoned as unremunerative. Certain enterprising men had substituted the culture of sugar; but while the recluse was too apathetic to take so active a course, the other saw larger, and, at that time, equally respectable profits, first in smuggling, and later in the African slave trade. What harm could he see in it? The whole people said it was vitally necessary, and to minister to a vital public necessity—good enough, certainly, and so he laid up many a doubloon, that made him none the worse in the public regard.

One day old Jean Marie was about to start upon a voyage that was to be longer, much longer, than any that he had yet made. Jacques had begged him hard for many days not to go, but he laughed him off, and finally said, kissing him:

"*Adieu, 'tit frère.*"

"No," said Jacques, "I shall go with you."

They left the old hulk of a house in the sole care of the African mute, and went away to the Guinea coast together.

Two years after, old Poquelin came home without his vessel. He must have arrived at his house by night. No one saw him come. No one saw "his little brother"; rumor whispered that he, too, had returned, but he had never been seen again.

A dark suspicion fell upon the old slave trader. No matter that the few kept the many reminded of the tenderness that had ever marked his bearing to the missing man. The many shook their heads. "You know he has a quick and fearful temper"; and "why does he cover his loss with mystery?"

"Grief would out with the truth."

"But," said the charitable few, "look in his face; see that expression of true humanity." The many did look in his face, and, as he looked in theirs, he read the silent question: "Where is thy brother Abel?" The few were silenced, his former friends died off, and the name of Jean Marie Poquelin became a symbol of witchery, devilish crime, and hideous nursery fictions.

The man and his house were alike shunned. The snipe and duck hunters forsook the marsh, and the woodcutters abandoned the canal. Sometimes the hardier boys who ventured out there snake-shooting heard a low thumping of oarlocks on the canal. They would look at each other for a moment half in consternation, half in glee, then rush from their sport in wanton haste to assail with their gibes the unoffending, withered old man who, in rusty attire, sat in the stern of a skiff, rowed homeward by his white-headed African mute.

"O Jean-ah Poquelin! O Jean-ah! Jean-ah Poquelin!"

It was not necessary to utter more than that. No hint of wickedness, deformity, or any physical or moral demerit; merely the name and tone of mockery: "Oh, Jean-ah Poquelin!" and while they tumbled one over another in their needless haste to fly, he would rise carefully from his seat, while the aged mute, with downcast face, went on rowing, and, rolling up his brown fist and extending it toward the urchins, would pour forth such an unholy broadside of French imprecation and invective as would all but craze them with delight.

Among both blacks and whites the house was the object of a thousand superstitions. Every midnight, they affirmed, the *feu follet* came out of the marsh and ran in and out of the rooms, flashing from window to window. The story of some lads, whose word in ordinary statements was worthless, was generally credited, that the night they camped in the woods, rather than pass the place after dark, they saw, about sunset, every window blood-red, and on each of the four chimneys an owl sitting, which turned his head three times around, and moaned and laughed with a human voice. There was a bottomless well, everybody professed to know, beneath the sill of the big front door under the rotten veranda; whoever set his foot upon that threshold disappeared forever in the depth below.

What wonder the marsh grew as wild as Africa! Take all the Faubourg Ste. Marie, and half the ancient city, you would not find one graceless daredevil reckless enough to pass within a hundred yards of the house after nightfall.

The alien races pouring into old New Orleans began to find the few streets named for the Bourbon princes too strait for them. The wheel of fortune, beginning to whirl, threw them off beyond the ancient corporation lines, and sowed civilization and even trade upon the lands of the Graviers and Girods. Fields became roads, roads streets. Everywhere the leveler was peering through his glass, rodsmen were whacking their way through willow brakes and rose hedges, and the sweating Irishmen tossed the blue clay up with their long-handled shovels.

"Ha! that is all very well," quoth the Jean-Baptistes, feeling the reproach of an enterprise that asked neither cooperation nor advice of them, "but wait till they come yonder to Jean Poquelin's marsh; ha! ha! ha!" The supposed predicament so delighted them that they put on a mock terror and whirled about in an assumed stampede, then caught their clasped hands between their knees in excess of mirth, and laughed till the tears ran; for whether the streetmakers mired in the marsh, or contrived to cut through old "Jeanah's" property, either event would be joyful. Meantime a line of tiny rods, with bits of white paper in their split tops, gradually extended its way straight through the haunted ground and across the canal diagonally.

"We shall fill that ditch," said the men in mudboots, and brushed close along the chained and padlocked gate of the haunted mansion. Ah, Jean-ah Poquelin, those were not Creole boys, to be stampeded with a little hard swearing.

He went to the Governor. That official scanned the odd figure with no slight interest. Jean Poquelin was of short, broad frame, with a bronzed leonine face. His brow was ample and deeply furrowed. His eye, large and black, was bold and open like that of a war horse, and his jaws shut together with the firmness of iron. He was dressed in a suit of Attakapas cottonade, and his shirt unbuttoned and thrown back from the throat and bosom, sailorwise, showed a herculean breast, hard and grizzled. There was no fierceness or defiance in his look, no harsh ungentleness, no symptom of his unlawful life or violent temper; but rather a peaceful and peaceable fearlessness. Across the whole face, not marked in one or another feature, but as it were laid softly upon the countenance like an almost imperceptible veil, was the imprint of some great grief. A careless eye might easily overlook it, but, once seen, there it hung—faint, but unmistakable.

The Governor bowed.

"*Parlez-vous français?*" asked the figure.

"I would rather talk English, if you can do so," said the Governor.

"My name, Jean Poquelin."

"How can I serve you, Mr. Poquelin?"

"My 'ouse is yond'; *dans le marais là-bas.*"

The Governor bowed.

"Dat *marais* billong to me."

"Yes, sir."

"To me; Jean Poquelin; I hown 'im meself."

"Well, sir?"

"He don't billong to you; I get him from me father."

"That is perfectly true, Mr. Poquelin, as far as I am aware."

"You want to make strit pass yond'?"

"I do not know, sir; it is quite probable; but the city will indemnify you for any loss you may suffer—you will get paid, you understand."

"Strit can't pass dare."

"You will have to see the municipal authorities about that, Mr. Poquelin."

A bitter smile came upon the old man's face.

"*Pardon, Monsieur*, you is not *le Gouverneur*?"

"Yes."

"*Mais*, yes. You har *le Gouverneur*—yes. Veh-well. I come to you. I tell you, strit can't pass at me 'ouse."

"But you will have to see—"

"I come to you. You is *le Gouverneur*. I know not the new laws. I ham a Fr-r-rench-a-man! Fr-rench-a-man have something *aller au contraire*—he come at his *Gouverneur*. I come at you. If me not had been bought from me king like *bossals* in the hold time, ze king gof—France would-a-show *Monsieur le Gouverneur* to take care his men to make strit in right places. *Mais*, I know; we billong to *Monsieur le Président*. I want you do somesin for me, eh?"

"What is it?" asked the patient Governor.

"I want you tell *Monsieur le Président*, strit—can't—pass—at—me—'ouse."

"Have a chair, Mr. Poquelin"; but the old man did not stir. The Governor took a quill and wrote a line to a city official, introducing Mr. Poquelin, and asking for him every possible courtesy. He handed it to him, instructing him where to present it.

"Mr. Poquelin," he said, with a conciliatory smile, "tell me, is it your house that our Creole citizens tell such odd stories about?"

The old man glared sternly upon the speaker, and with immovable features, said:

"You don't see me trade some Guinea nigga'?"

"Oh, no."

"You don't see me make some smugglin'?"

"No, sir; not at all."

"But, I am Jean Marie Poquelin. I mine me hown bizniss. Dat all right? Adieu."

He put his hat on and withdrew. By and by he stood, letter in hand, before the person to whom it was addressed. This person employed an interpreter.

"He says," said the interpreter to the officer, "he come to make you the fair warning how you muz not make the street pas' at his 'ouse."

The officer remarked that "such impudence was refreshing"; but the experienced interpreter translated freely.

"He says: 'Why you don't want?' " said the interpreter.

The old slave trader answered at some length.

"He says," said the interpreter, again turning to the officer, "the morass is a too unhealth' for peopl' to live."

"But we expect to drain his old marsh; it's not going to be a marsh."

"*Il dit*"—the interpreter explained in French.

The old man answered tersely.

"He says the canal is a private," said the interpreter.

"Oh! *that* old ditch; that's to be filled up. Tell the old man we're going to fix him up nicely."

Translation being duly made, the man in power was amused to see a thundercloud gathering on the old man's face.

"Tell him," he added, "by the time we finish, there'll not be a ghost left in his shanty."

The interpreter began to translate, but—

"*J' comprends, j' comprends*," said the old man, with an impatient gesture, and burst forth, pouring curses upon the United States, the President, the Territory of Orleans, Congress, the Governor and all his subordinates, striding out of the apartment as he cursed, while the object of his maledictions roared with merriment and rammed the floor with his foot.

"Why, it will make his old place worth ten dollars to one," said the official to the interpreter.

" 'Tis not for de worse of de property," said the interpreter.

"I should guess not," said the other, whittling his chair—"seems to me as if some of these old Creoles would liever live in a crawfish hole than to have a neighbor."

"You know what make old Jean Poquelin make like that? I will tell you. You know—"

The interpreter was rolling a cigarette, and paused to light his tinder; then, as the smoke poured in a thick double stream from his nostrils, he said, in a solemn whisper:

"He is a witch."

"Ho,ho,ho!" laughed the other.

"You don't believe it? What you want to bet?" cried the interpreter, jerking himself half up and thrusting out one arm while he bared it of its coat sleeve with the hand of the other. "What you want to bet?"

"How do you know?" asked the official.

"Dass what I goin' to tell you. You know, one evening I was shooting some *grosbec*. I killed three; but I had trouble to find them, it was becoming so dark. When I have them I start' to come home; then I got to pas' at Jean Poquelin's house."

"Ho,ho,ho!" laughed the other, throwing his leg over the arm of his chair.

"Wait," said the interpreter. "I come along slow, not making some noises; still, still—"

"And scared," said the smiling one.

"*Mais*, wait. I get all pas' the 'ouse. 'Ah!' I say; 'all right!' Then I see two thing' before! Hah! I get as cold and humide, and shake like a leaf. You think it was nothing? There I see, so plain as can be (though it was making nearly dark), I see Jean—Marie—Po-que-lin walkin' right in front, and right there beside of him was something like a man—but not a man—white like paint!—I dropp' on the grass from scared—they pass'; so sure as I live 'twas the ghos' of Jacques Poquelin, his brother!"

"Pooh!" said the listener.

"I'll put my han' in the fire," said the interpreter.

"But did you never think," asked the other, "that that might be Jack Poquelin, as you call him, alive and well, and for some cause hid away by his brother?"

"But there har' no cause!" said the other, and the entrance of third parties changed the subject.

Some months passed and the street was opened. A canal was first dug through the marsh, the small one which passed so close to Jean Poquelin's house was filled, and the street, or rather a sunny road, just touched a corner of the old mansion's dooryard. The morass ran dry. Its venomous denizens slipped away through the bulrushes; the cattle roaming freely upon its hardened surface trampled the superabundant undergrowth. The bellowing frogs croaked to westward. Lilies and the flower-de-luce sprang up in the place of reeds; smilax and poison oak gave way to the purple-plumed ironweed and pink spiderwort; the bindweeds ran everywhere blooming as they ran, and on one of the dead cypresses a giant creeper hung its green burden of foliage and lifted its scarlet trumpets. Sparrows and redbirds flitted through the bushes, and dewberries grew ripe beneath. Over all these came a sweet, dry smell of salubrity which the place had not known since the sediments of the Mississippi first lifted it from the sea.

But its owner did not build. Over the willow brakes, and down the vista of the open street, bright new houses, some singly, some by ranks, were prying in upon the old man's privacy. They even settled down toward his southern side. First a woodcutter's hut or two, then a market gardener's shanty, then a painted cottage, and all at once the *faubourg* had flanked and half surrounded him and his dried-up marsh.

Ah! then the common people began to hate him. "The old tyrant!" "You don't mean an old *tyrant*?" "Well, then, why don't he build when the public need demands it? What does he live in that unneighborly way for?" "The old pirate!" "The old kidnaper!" How easily even the most ultra Louisianians put on the imported virtues of the North when they could be brought to bear against the hermit. "There he goes, with the boys after him! Ah! ha! ha! Jean-ah Poquelin! Ah! Jean-ah! Aha! aha! Jean-ah Marie! Jean-ah Poquelin! The old villain!" How merrily the swarming *Américains* echo the spirit of persecution! "The old fraud," they say— "pretends to live in a haunted house, does he? We'll tar and feather him someday. Guess we can fix him."

He cannot be rowed home along the old canal now; he walks. He has broken sadly of late, and the street urchins are ever at his heels. It is like the days when they cried: "Go up, thou baldhead," and the old man now and then turns and delivers ineffectual curses.

To the Creoles—to the incoming lower class of superstitious Germans, Irish, Sicilians, and others—he became an omen and embodiment of public and private ill fortune. Upon him all the vagaries of their superstitions gathered and grew. If a house caught fire, it was imputed to his machinations. Did a woman go off in a fit, he had bewitched her. Did a child stray off for an hour, the mother shivered with the apprehension that Jean Poquelin had offered him to strange gods. The house was the subject of every bad boy's invention who loved to contrive ghostly lies. "As long as that house stands we shall have bad luck. Do you not see our peas and beans dying, our cabbages and lettuce going to seed and our gardens turning to dust, while every day you can see it raining in the woods? The rain will never pass old Poquelin's house. He keeps a fetish. He has conjured the whole Faubourg Ste. Marie. And why, the old wretch? Simply because our playful and innocent children call after him as he passes."

A "Building and Improvement Company," which had not yet got its charter, "but was going to," and which had not, indeed, any tangible capital yet, but "was going to have some," joined the "Jean-ah Poquelin" war. The haunted property would be such a capital site for a market house! They sent a deputation to the old mansion to ask its occupant to sell. The deputation never got beyond the chained gate and a very barren interview with the African mute. The President of the Board was then empowered (for he had studied French in Pennsylvania and was considered qualified) to call and persuade M. Poquelin to subscribe to the company's stock; but—

"Fact is, gentlemen," he said at the next meeting, "it would take us at least twelve months to make Mr. Pokaleen understand the rather original features of our system, and he wouldn't subscribe when we'd done; besides, the only way to see him is to stop him on the street."

There was a great laugh from the Board; they couldn't help it. "Better meet a bear robbed of her whelps," said one.

"You're mistaken as to that," said the President. "I did meet him, and stopped him, and found him quite polite. But I could get no satisfaction from him; the fellow wouldn't talk in French, and when I spoke in English he hoisted his old shoulders up, and gave the same answer to everything I said."

"And that was—?" asked one or two, impatient of the pause.

"That it 'don't worse w'ile?' "

One of the Board said: "Mr.President, this market-house project, as I take it, is not altogether a selfish one; the community is to be benefited by it. We may feel that we are working in the public interest [the Board smiled knowingly], if we employ all possible means to oust this old nuisance from among us. You may know that at the time the street was cut through, this old Poquelann did all he could to prevent it. It was owing to a certain connection which I had with that affair that I heard a ghost story [smiles, followed by a sudden dignified check]—ghost story, which, of course, I am not going to relate; but I *may* say that my profound conviction, arising from a prolonged study of that story, is, that this old villain, John Poquelann, has his brother locked up in that old house. Now, if this is so, and we can fix it on him, I merely *suggest* that we can make the matter highly useful. I don't know," he added, beginning to sit down, "but that it is an action we owe to the community—ahem!"

"How do you propose to handle the subject?" asked the President.

"I was thinking," said the speaker, "that, as a Board of Directors, it would be unadvisable for us to authorize any action involving trespass; but if you, for instance, Mr. President, should, as it were, for mere curiosity, *request* someone, as, for instance, our excellent Secretary, simply as a personal favor, to look into the matter— this is merely a suggestion."

The Secretary smiled sufficiently to be understood that, while he certainly did not consider such preposterous service a part of his duties as secretary, he might, notwithstanding, accede to the President's request; and the Board adjourned.

Little White, as the Secretary was called, was a mild, kindhearted little man, who, nevertheless, had no fear of anything, unless it was the fear of being unkind.

"I tell you frankly," he privately said to the President, "I go into this purely for reasons of my own."

The next day, a little after nightfall, one might have descried this little man slipping along the rear fence of the Poquelin place, preparatory to vaulting over into the rank, grass-grown yard, and bearing himself altogether more after the manner of a collector of rare chickens than according to the usage of secretaries.

The picture presented to his eye was not calculated to enliven his mind. The old mansion stood out against the western sky, black and silent. One long, lurid pencil stroke along a sky of slate was all that was left of daylight. No sign of life was apparent; no light at any window, unless it might have been on the side of the house hidden from view. No owls were on the chimneys, no dogs were in the yard.

He entered the place, and ventured up behind a small cabin which stood apart from the house. Through one of its many crannies he easily detected the African mute crouched before a flickering pine knot, his head on his knees, fast asleep.

He concluded to enter the mansion, and, with that view, stood and scanned it. The broad rear steps of the veranda would not serve him; he might meet someone midway. He was measuring, with his eye, the proportions of one of the pillars which supported it, and estimating the practicability of climbing it, when he heard a footstep. Someone dragged a chair out toward the railing, then seemed to change his mind and began to pace the veranda, his footfalls resounding on the dry boards with singular loudness. Little White drew a step backward, got the figure between himself and the sky, and at once recognized the short, broad-shouldered form of old Jean Poquelin.

He sat down upon a billet of wood, and, to escape the stings of a whining cloud of mosquitoes, shrouded his face and neck in his handkerchief, leaving his eyes uncovered.

He had sat there but a moment when he noticed a strange, sickening odor, faint, as if coming from a distance, but loathsome and horrid.

Whence could it come? Not from the cabin; not from the marsh, for it was as dry as powder. It was not in the air; it seemed to come from the ground.

Rising up, he noticed, for the first time, a few steps before him a narrow footpath leading toward the house. He glanced down it—ha! right there was someone coming —ghostly white!

Quick as thought, and as noiselessly, he lay down at full length against the cabin. It was bold strategy, and yet, there was no denying it, Little White felt that he was frightened. "It is not a ghost," he said to himself. "I *know* it cannot be a ghost"; but the perspiration burst out at every pore, and the air seemed to thicken with heat. "It is a living man," he said in his thoughts. "I hear his footstep, and I hear old Poquelin's footsteps, too, separately, over on the veranda. I am not discovered; the thing has passed; there is that odor again; what a smell of death! Is it coming back? Yes. It stops at the door of the cabin. Is it peering in at the sleeping mute? It moves away. It is in the path again. Now it is gone." He shuddered. "Now, if I dare venture, the mystery is solved." He rose cautiously, close against the cabin, and peered along the path.

The figure of a man, a presence if not a body—but whether

clad in some white stuff or naked, the darkness would not allow him to determine—had turned, and now, with a seeming painful gait, moved slowly from him. "Great Heaven! can it be that the dead do walk?" He withdrew again the hands which had gone to his eyes. The dreadful object passed between two pillars and under the house. He listened. There was a faint sound as of feet upon a staircase; then all was still except the measured tread of Jean Poquelin walking on the veranda, and the heavy respirations of the mute slumbering in the cabin.

The little Secretary was about to retreat; but as he looked once more toward the haunted house a dim light appeared in the crack of a closed window, and presently old Jean Poquelin came, dragging his chair, and sat down close against the shining cranny. He spoke in a low, tender tone in the French tongue, making some inquiry. An answer came from within. Was it the voice of a human? So unnatural was it—so hollow, so discordant, so unearthly—that the stealthy listener shuddered again from head to foot; and when something stirred in some bushes nearby—though it may have been nothing more than a rat—and came scuttling through the grass, the little Secretary actually turned and fled. As he left the enclosure he moved with bolder leisure through the bushes; yet now and then he spoke aloud: "Oh, oh! I see, I understand!" and shut his eyes in his hands.

How strange that henceforth Little White was the champion of Jean Poquelin! In season and out of season—wherever a word was uttered against him—the Secretary, with a quiet, aggressive force that instantly arrested gossip, demanded upon what authority the statement or conjecture was made; but as he did not condescend to explain his own remarkable attitude, it was not long before the disrelish and suspicion which had followed Jean Poquelin so many years fell also upon him.

It was only the next evening but one after his adventure that he made himself a source of sullen amazement to one hundred and fifty boys, by ordering them to desist from their wanton hallooing. Old Jean Poquelin, standing and shaking his cane, rolling out his long-drawn maledictions, paused and stared, then gave the Secretary a courteous bow and started on. The boys, save one, from pure astonishment, ceased; but a ruffianly little Irish lad, more daring than any had yet been, threw a big hurtling clod that struck old Poquelin between the shoulders and burst like a shell. The enraged old man wheeled with uplifted staff to give chase to the scampering vagabond; and—he may have tripped, or he may not, but he fell full length. Little White hastened to help him up, but he waved him off with a fierce imprecation and, staggering to his feet, resumed his way homeward. His lips were reddened with blood.

Little White was on his way to the meeting of the Board. He would have given all he dared spend to have stayed away, for he felt both too fierce and too tremulous to brook the criticisms that were likely to be made.

"I can't help it, gentlemen; I can't help you to make a case against the old man, and I'm not going to."

"We did not expect this disappointment, Mr. White."

"I can't help that, sir. No, sir; you had better not appoint any more investigations. Somebody'll investigate himself into trouble. No, sir; it isn't a threat, it is only my advice, but I warn you that whoever takes the task in hand will rue it to his dying day—which may be hastened, too."

The President expressed himself surprised.

"I don't care a rush," answered Little White, wildly and foolishly. "I don't care a rush if you are, sir. No, my nerves are not disordered; my head's as clear as a bell. No, I'm *not* excited."

A Director remarked that the Secretary looked as though he had waked from a nightmare.

"Well, sir, if you want to know the fact, I have; and if you choose to cultivate old Poquelin's society you can have one, too."

"White," called a facetious member, but White did not notice. "White," he called again.

"What?" demanded White, with a scowl.

"Did you see the ghost?"

"Yes, sir; I did," cried White, hitting the table, and handing the President a paper which brought the Board to other business.

The story got among the gossips that somebody (they were afraid to say little White) had been to the Poquelin mansion by night and beheld something appalling. The rumor was but a shadow of the truth, magnified and distorted as is the manner of shadows. He had seen skeletons walking, and had barely escaped the clutches of one by making the sign of the cross.

Some madcap boys with an appetite for the horrible plucked up courage to venture through the dried marsh by the cattle path, and come before the house at a spectral hour when the air was full of bats. Something which they but half saw—half a sight was enough—sent them tearing back through the willow brakes and acacia bushes to their homes, where they fairly dropped down, and cried:

"Was it white?" "No—yes—nearly so—we can't tell—but we saw it." And one could hardly doubt, to look at their ashen faces, that they had, whatever it was.

"If that old rascal lived in the country we come from," said certain *Américains*, "he'd have been tarred and feathered before now, wouldn't he, Sanders?"

"Well, now he just would."

"And we'd have rid him on a rail, wouldn't we?"

"That's what I allow."

"Tell you what you *could* do." They were talking to some rollicking Creoles who had assumed an absolute necessity for doing *something*. "What is it you call this thing where an old man marries a young girl, and you come out with horns and—"

"*Charivari?*" asked the Creoles.

"Yes, that's it. Why don't you shivaree him?" Felicitous suggestion.

Little White, with his wife beside him, was sitting on their doorsteps on the sidewalk, as Creole custom had taught them, looking toward the sunset. They had moved into the lately opened street. The view was not attractive on the score of beauty. The houses were small and scattered, and across the flat commons, in spite of the lofty tangle of weeds and bushes, and in spite of the thickets of acacia, they needs must see the dismal old Poquelin mansion, tilted awry and shutting out the declining sun. The moon, white and slender, was hanging the tip of its horn over one of the chimneys.

"And you say," said the Secretary, "the old black man has been going by here alone? Patty, suppose old Poquelin should be concocting some mischief; he don't lack provocation; the way that clod hit him the other day was enough to have killed him. Why, Patty, he dropped as quick as *that!* No wonder you haven't seen him. I wonder if they haven't heard something about him up at the drugstore. Suppose I go and see."

"Do," said his wife.

She sat alone for half an hour, watching that sudden going out of the day peculiar to the latitude.

"That moon is ghost enough for one house," she said, as her husband returned. "It has gone right down the chimney."

"Patty," said little White, "the drug clerk says the boys are going to shivaree old Poquelin tonight. I'm going to try to stop it."

"Why, White," said his wife, "you'd better not. You'll get hurt."

"No, I'll not."

"Yes, you will."

"I'm going to sit out here until they come along. They're compelled to pass right by here."

"Why, White, it may be midnight before they start; you're not going to sit out here till then."

"Yes, I am."

"Well, you're very foolish," said Mrs. White in an undertone, looking anxious, and tapping one of the steps with her foot.

They sat a very long time talking over little family matters.

"What's that?" at last said Mrs. White.

"That's the nine-o'clock gun," said White, and they relapsed into a long-sustained, drowsy silence.

"Patty, you'd better go in and go to bed," said he at last.

"I'm not sleepy."

"Well, you're very foolish," quietly remarked little White, and again silence fell upon them.

"Patty, suppose I walk out to the old house and see if I can find out anything."

"Suppose," said she, "you don't do any such—listen!"

Down the street arose a great hubbub. Dogs and boys were howling and barking; men were laughing, shouting, groaning, and blowing horns, whooping, and clanking cowbells, whinnying, and howling, and rattling pots and pans.

"They are coming this way," said little White. "You had better go into the house, Patty."

"So had you."

"No. I'm going to see if I can't stop them."

"Why, White!"

"I'll be back in a minute," said White, and went toward the noise.

In a few moments the little Secretary met the mob. The pen hesitates on the word, for there is a respectable difference, measurable only on the scale of the half century, between a mob and a *charivari*. Little White lifted his ineffectual voice. He faced the head of the disorderly column, and cast himself about as if he were made of wood and moved by the jerk of a string. He rushed to one who seemed, from the size and clatter of his tin pan, to be a leader. *"Stop these fellows, Bienvenu, stop them just a minute, till I tell them something."* Bienvenu turned and brandished his instruments of discord in an imploring way to the crowd. They slackened their pace, two or three hushed their horns and joined the prayer of little White and Bienvenu for silence. The throng halted. The hush was delicious.

"Bienvenu," said little White, "don't shivaree old Poquelin tonight; he's—"

"My fwang," said the swaying Bienvenu, "who tail you I goin' to chahivahi somebody, eh? You sink bickause I make a little playfool wiz zis tin pan zat I am *dhonk?*"

"Oh, no, Bienvenu, old fellow, you're all right. I was afraid you might not know that old Poquelin was sick, you know, but you're not going there, are you?"

"My fwang, I vay soy to tail you zat you ah dhonk as de dev'. I am *shem* of you. I ham ze servan' of *ze publique*. Zese *citoyens* goin' to wickwest Jean Poquelin to give to the Ursuline' two hondred fifty dolla'—"

"Hé quoi!" cried a listener. *"Cinq cent piastres, oui!"*

"Oui!" said Bienvenu, "and if he wiffuse we make him some lit' *musique*; ta-ra-ta!" He hoisted a merry hand and foot, then frowning, added: "Old Poquelin got no bizniz dhink s'much w'isky."

"But, gentlemen," said little White, around whom a circle had gathered, "the old man is very sick."

"My faith!" cried a tiny Creole, "we did not make him to be sick. W'en we have say we going make *le charivari*, do you want that we hall tell a lie? My faith! 'sfools!"

"But you can shivaree somebody else," said desperate little White.

"Oui!" cried Bienvenu, *"et chahivahi* Jean-ah Poquelin tomo'w!"

"Let us go to Madame Schneider!" cried two or three, and amid huzzas and confused cries, among which was heard a stentorian Celtic call for drinks, the crowd again began to move.

"Cent piastres pour l'hôpital de charité!"

"Hurrah!"

"One hongred dolla' for Charity Hospital!"

"Hurrah!"

"Whang!" went a tin pan, the crowd yelled, and Pandemonium gaped again. They were off at a right angle.

Nodding, Mrs. White looked at the mantel clock.

"Well, if it isn't away after midnight."

The hideous noise downstreet was passing beyond earshot. She raised a sash and listened. For a moment there was silence. Someone came to the door.

"Is that you, White?"

"Yes. They've gone down to shivaree the old Dutch-woman who married her stepdaughter's sweetheart. They say she has got to pay a hundred dollars to the hospital before they stop."

The couple retired, and Mrs. White slumbered. She was awakened by her husband snapping the lid of his watch.

"What time?" she asked.

"Half past three, Patty, I haven't slept a wink. Those fellows are out yet. Don't you hear them?"

"Why, White, they're coming this way!"

"I know they are," said White, sliding out of bed and drawing on his clothes, "and they're coming fast. You'd better go away from that window, Patty! My! what a clatter!"

"Here they are," said Mrs. White, but her husband was gone. Two or three hundred men and boys passed the place at a rapid walk straight down the broad, new street, toward the hated house of ghosts. The din was terrific. She saw Little White at the head of the rabble brandishing his arms and trying in vain to make himself heard; but they only shook their heads, laughing and hooting the louder, and so passed, bearing him on before them.

Swiftly they pass out from among the houses, away from the dim oil lamps of the street, out into the broad starlit commons, and enter the willowy jungles of the haunted ground. Some hearts fail and their owners lag behind and turn back, suddenly remembering how near morning it is. But the most part push on, tearing the air with their clamor.

Down ahead of them in the long, thicket-darkened way there is—singularly enough—a faint, dancing light. It must be very near the old house; it is. It has stopped now. It is a lantern, and is under a well-known sapling which has grown up on the wayside since the canal was filled. Now it swings mysteriously to and fro. A goodly number of the more ghost-fearing give up the sport; but a full hundred move forward at a run, doubling their devilish howling and banging.

Yes; it is a lantern, and there are two persons under the tree. The crowd draws near—drops into a walk; one of the two is the old African mute; he lifts the lantern up so that it shines on the other; the crowd recoils; there is a hush of all clangor, and all at once, with a cry of mingled fright and horror from every throat, the whole throng rushes back, dropping everything, sweeping past little White and hurrying on, never stopping until the jungle is left behind, and then to find that not one in ten has seen the cause of the stampede, and not one of the tenth is certain what it was.

There is one huge fellow among them who looks capable of any villainy. He finds something to mount on, and, in the Creole *patois*, calls a general halt. Bienvenu sinks down, and, vainly trying to recline gracefully, resigns the leadership. The herd gather around the speaker; he assures them that they have been outraged. Their right peaceably to traverse the public streets has been trampled upon. Shall such encroachments be endured? It is now daybreak. Let them go now by the open light of day and force a free passage of the public highway!

A scattering consent was the response, and the crowd, thinned now and drowsy, straggled quietly down toward the old house. Some drifted ahead, others sauntered behind, but everyone, as he again neared the tree, came to a standstill. Little White sat upon a bank of turf on the opposite side of the way looking very stern and sad. To each newcomer he put the same question:

"Did you come here to go to old Poquelin's?"

"Yes."

"He's dead." And if the shocked hearer started away he would say: "Don't go away."

"Why not?"

"I want you to go to the funeral presently."

If some Louisianian, too loyal to dear France or Spain to understand English, looked bewildered, someone would interpret for him; and presently they went. Little White led the van, the crowd trooping after him down the middle of the way. The gate, that had never been seen before unchained, was open. Stern little White stopped a short distance from it; the rabble stopped behind him. Something was moving out from under the veranda. The many whisperers stretched upward to see. The African mute came very slowly toward the gate, leading by a cord in the nose a small brown bull, which was harnessed to a rude cart. On the flat body of the cart, under a black cloth, were seen the outlines of a long box.

"Hats off, gentlemen," said little White, as the box came in view, and the crowd silently uncovered.

"Gentlemen," said little White, "here come the last remains of Jean Marie Poquelin, a better man, I'm afraid, with all his sins—yes, a better—a kinder man to his blood—a man of more self-forgetful goodness—than all of you put together will ever dare to be."

There was a profound hush as the vehicle came creaking through the gate; but when it turned away from them toward the forest, those in front started suddenly. There was a backward rush, then all stood still again staring one way; for there, behind the bier, with eyes cast down and labored step, walked the living remains—all that was left—of little Jacques Poquelin, the long-hidden brother—a leper, as white as snow.

Dumb with horror, the cringing crowd gazed upon the walking death. They watched, in silent awe, the slow *cortège* creep down the long, straight road and lessen on the view, until by and by it stopped where a wild, unfrequented path branched off into the undergrowth toward the rear of the ancient city.

"They are going to the *Terre aux Lépreux*," said one in the crowd. The rest watched them in silence.

The little bull was set free; the mute, with the strength of an ape, lifted the long box to his shoulder. For a moment more the mute and the leper stood in sight, while the former adjusted his heavy burden; then, without one backward glance upon the unkind human world, turning their faces toward the ridge in the depths of the swamp known as the Leper's Land, they stepped into the jungle, disappeared, and were never seen again.

Constance Fenimore Woolson (March 5, 1840–January 24, 1894) was born in New Hampshire and educated in Cleveland, Ohio,. and in New York. She was one of the first American writers to use local color in her novels. In her thirties she moved to Florida because she was attracted by the richness of its history. Many of Woolson's sketches and poems were about an unspoiled Florida, and are considered by many scholars to be her finest work. Woolson described the swamps and pine barrens of a Florida that was settled earlier than Virginia and New England. Her writing dominated American fiction in the 1880s, and she gave northern readers what was probably the first true picture of the post-Civil War South.

East Angels, Woolson's only novel of her five set in Florida, was popular with her readers and sold over 10,000 copies. It is set in a small village and the central characters are wealthy Northerners who come south and end up saving the mistress of East Angels, a nearby plantation, and her daughter from poverty. "Felipa" first appeared in *Lippincott's Magazine* in June 1876 and was reprinted in Woolson's collected stories, *Rodman the Keeper: Southern Sketches* (1880). The title story takes place near the Andersonville prison.

FELIPA

by Constance Fenimore Woolson

Glooms of the live-oaks, beautiful-braided and woven
With intricate shades of the vines that, myriad cloven,
Clamber the forks of the multiform boughs.
                 . . . . Green colonnades
Of the dim sweet woods, of the dear dark woods,

Of the heavenly woods and glades,
That run to the radiant marginal sand-beach within
      The wide sea-marshes of Glynn.

              . . . . Free
By a world of marsh that borders a world of sea.
Sinuous southward and sinuous northward of the shim-
   mering band
Of the sand-beach fastens the fringe of the marsh to
   the folds of the land.

Inward and outward to northward and southward
   the beach-lines linger and curl
As a silver-wrought garment that clings to and follows
   the firm, sweet limbs of a girl.
A league and a league of marsh-grass, waist-high,
   broad n the blade,
Green, and all of a height, and unflecked with a light
   or a shade.
                       SIDNEY LANIER

Christine and I found her there. She was a small, dark-skinned, yellow-eyed child, the offspring of the ocean and the heats, tawny, lithe and wild, shy yet fearless—not unlike one of the little brown deer that bounded through the open reaches of the pine-barren behind the house. She did not come to us—we came to her; we loomed into her life like genii from another world, and she was partly afraid and partly proud of us. For were we not her guests? proud thought! and, better still, were we not women? "I have only seen three women in all my life," said Felipa, inspecting us gravely, "and I like women. I am a woman too, although these clothes of the son of Pedro make me appear as a boy; I wear them on account of the boat and the hauling in of the fish. The son of Pedro being dead at a convenient age, and his clothes fitting me, what would you have? It was a chance not to be despised. But when I am grown I shall wear robes long and beautiful like the señora's." The little creature was dressed in a boy's suit of dark-blue linen, much the worse for wear, and torn.

"If you are a girl, why do you not mend your clothes?" I said.

"Do you mend, señora?"

"Certainly: all women sew and mend."

"The other lady?"

Christine laughed as she lay at ease upon the brown carpet of pine-needles, warm and aromatic after the tropic day's sunshine. "The child has divined me already, Catherine," she said.

Christine was a tall, lissome maid, with an unusually long stretch of arm, long sloping shoulders, and a long fair throat; her straight hair fell to her knees when unbound, and its clear flaxen hue had not one shade of gold, as her clear gray eyes had not one shade of blue. Her small, straight, rose-leaf lips parted over small, dazzlingly white teeth, and the outline of her face in profile reminded you of an etching in its distinctness, although it was by no means perfect according to the rules of art. Still, what a comfort it was, after the blurred outlines and smudged profiles many of us possess—seen to best advantage, I think, in church on Sundays, crowned with flower-decked bonnets, listening calmly serene to favorite ministers, unconscious of noses! When Christine had finished her laugh—and she never hurried anything—she stretched out her arm carelessly and patted Felipa's curly head. The child caught the descending hand and kissed the long white fingers.

It was a wild place where we were, yet not new or crude—the coast of Florida, that old-new land, with its deserted plantations, its skies of Paradise, and its broad wastes open to the changeless sunshine. The old house stood on the edge of the dry land, where the pine-barren ended and the salt-marsh began; in front curved the tide-water river that seemed ever trying to come up close to the barren and make its acquaintance, but could not quite succeed, since it must always turn and flee at a fixed hour, like Cinderella at the ball, leaving not a silver slipper behind, but purple drift-wood and bright seaweeds, brought in from the Gulf Stream outside. A planked platform ran out into the marsh from the edge of the barren, and at its end the boats were moored; for, although at high tide the river was at our feet, at low tide it was far away out in the green waste somewhere, and if we wanted it we must go and seek it. We did not want it, however; we let it glide up to us twice a day with its fresh salt odors and flotsam of the ocean, and the rest of the time we wandered over the barrens or lay under the trees looking up into the wonderful blue above, listening to the winds as they rushed across from sea to sea. I was an artist, poor and painstaking. Christine was my kind friend. She had brought me South because my cough was troublesome, and here because Edward Bowne recommended the place. He and three fellow sportsmen were down at the Madre Lagoon, farther south; I thought it probable we should see him, without his three fellow sportsmen, before very long.

"Who were the three women you have seen, Felipa?" said Christine.

"The grandmother, an Indian woman of the Seminoles who comes sometimes with baskets, and the wife of Miguel of the island. But they are all old, and their skins are curled: I like better the silver skin of the señora."

Poor little Felipa lived on the edge of the great salt-marsh alone with her grandparents, for her mother was dead. The yellow old couple were slow-witted Minorcans, part pagan, part Catholic, and wholly ignorant; their minds rarely rose above the level of their orange-trees and their fish-nets. Felipa's father was a Spanish sailor, and, as he had died only the year before, the child's Spanish was fairly correct, and we could converse with her readily, although we were slow to comprehend the patois of the old people, which seemed to borrow as much from the Italian tongue and the Greek as from its mother Spanish. "I know a great deal," Felipa remarked confidently, "for my father taught me. He had sailed on the ocean out of sight of land, and he knew many things. These he taught to me. Do the gracious ladies think there is anything else to know?"

One of the gracious ladies thought not, decidedly. In answer to my remonstrance, expressed in English, she said, "Teach a child like that, and you ruin her."

"Ruin her?"

"Ruin her happiness—the same thing."

Felipa had a dog, a second self—a great gaunt yellow creature of unknown breed, with crooked legs, big feet, and the name Drollo. What Drollo meant, or whether it was an abbreviation, we never knew; but there was a certain satisfaction in it, for the dog was droll: the fact that the Minorcan title, whatever it was, meant nothing of that sort, made it all the better. We never saw Felipa without Drollo. "They look a good deal alike," observed Christine—"the same coloring."

"For shame!" I said.

But it was true. The child's bronzed yellow skin and soft

eyes were not unlike the dog's, but her head was crowned with a mass of short black curls, while Drollo had only his two great flapping ears and his low smooth head. Give him an inch or two more of skull, and what a creature a dog would be! For love and faithfulness even now what man can match him? But, although ugly, Felipa was a picturesque little object always, whether attired in boy's clothes or in her own forlorn bodice and skirt. Olive-hued and meager-faced, lithe and thin, she flew over the pine-barrens like a creature of air, laughing to feel her short curls toss and her thin childish arms buoyed up on the breeze as she ran, with Drollo barking behind. For she loved the winds, and always knew when they were coming—whether down from the north, in from the ocean, or across from the Gulf of Mexico: she watched for them, sitting in the doorway, where she could feel their first breath, and she taught us the signs of the clouds. She was a queer little thing: we used to find her sometimes dancing alone out on the barren in a circle she had marked out with pine-cones, and once she confided to us that she talked to the trees. "They hear," she said in a whisper; "you should see how knowing they look, and how their leaves listen."

Once we came upon her most secret lair in a dense thicket of thorn-myrtle and wild smilax—a little bower she had made, where was hidden a horrible-looking image formed of the rough pieces of saw-palmetto grubbed up by old Bartolo from his garden. She must have dragged these fragments thither one by one, and with infinite pains bound them together with her rude withes of strong marsh-grass, until at last she had formed a rough trunk with crooked arms and a sort of a head, the red hairy surface of the palmetto looking not unlike the skin of some beast, and making the creature all the more grotesque. This fetich was kept crowned with flowers, and after this we often saw the child stealing away with Drollo to carry to it portions of her meals or a new-found treasure—a sea-shell, a broken saucer, or a fragment of ribbon. The food always mysteriously disappeared, and my suspicion is that Drollo used to go back secretly in the night and devour it, asking no questions and telling no lies: it fitted in nicely, however, Drollo merely performing the ancient part of the priests of Jupiter, men who have been much admired. "What a little pagan she is!" I said.

"Oh, no, it is only her doll," replied Christine.

I tried several times to paint Felipa during these first weeks, but those eyes of hers always evaded me. They were, as I have said before, yellow—that is, they were brown with yellow lights—and they stared at you with the most inflexible openness. The child had the full-curved, half-open mouth of the tropics, and a low Greek forehead. "Why isn't she pretty?" I said.

"She is hideous," replied Christine; "look at her elbows."

Now Felipa's arms *were* unpleasant: they were brown and lean, scratched and stained, and they terminated in a pair of determined little paws that could hold on like grim Death. I shall never forget coming upon a tableau one day out on the barren—a little Florida cow and Felipa, she holding on by the horns, and the beast with its small fore feet stubbornly set in the sand; girl pulling one way, cow the other; both silent and determined. It was a hard contest, but the girl won.

"And if you pass over her elbows, there are her feet," continued Christine languidly. For she was a sybaritic lover of the fine linens of life, that friend of mine—a pre-Raphaelite lady with clinging draperies and a mediæval clasp on her belt. Her whole being rebelled against ugliness, and the mere sight of a sharp-nosed, light-eyed woman on a cold day made her uncomfortable.

"Have we not feet too?" I replied sharply.

But I knew what she meant. Bare feet are not pleasant to the eye nowadays, whatever they may have been in the days of the ancient Greeks; and Felipa's little brown insteps were half the time torn or bruised by the thorns of the chaparral. Besides, there was always the disagreeable idea that she might step upon something cold and squirming when she prowled through the thickets knee-deep in the matted grasses. Snakes abounded, although we never saw them; but Felipa went up to their very doors, as it were, and rang the bell defiantly.

One day old Grandfather Bartolo took the child with him down to the coast: she was always wild to go to the beach, where she could gather shells and sea-beans, and chase the little ocean-birds that ran along close to the waves with that swift gliding motion of theirs, and where she could listen to the roar of the breakers. We were several miles up the salt-marsh, and to go down to the ocean was quite a voyage to Felipa. She bade us good-by joyously; then ran back to hug Christine a second time, then to the boat again; then back.

"I thought you wanted to go, child?" I said, a little impatiently; for I was reading aloud, and these small irruptions were disturbing.

"Yes," said Felipa, "I want to go; and still— Perhaps if the gracious señora would kiss me again—"

Christine only patted her cheek and told her to run away: she obeyed, but there was a wistful look in her eyes, and, even after the boat had started, her face, watching us from the stern, haunted me.

"Now that the little monkey has gone, I may be able at last to catch and fix a likeness of her," I said; "in this case a recollection is better than the changing quicksilver reality."

"You take it as a study of ugliness?"

"Do not be hard upon the child, Christine."

"Hard? Why, she adores me," said my friend, going off to her hammock under the tree.

Several days passed, and the boat returned not. I accomplished a fine amount of work, and Christine a fine amount of swinging in the hammock and dreaming. At length one afternoon I gave my final touch, and carried my sketch over to the pre-Raphaelite lady for criticism. "What do you see?" I said.

"I see a wild-looking child with yellow eyes, a mat of curly black hair, a lank little bodice, her two thin brown arms embracing a gaunt old dog with crooked legs, big feet, and turned-in toes."

"Is that all?"

"All."

"You do not see latent beauty, courage, and a possible great gulf of love in that poor wild little face?"

"Nothing of the kind," replied Christine decidedly. "I see an ugly little girl; that is all."

The next day the boat returned, and brought back five persons, the old grandfather, Felipa, Drollo, Miguel of the island, and—Edward Bowne.

"Already?" I said.

"Tired of the Madre, Kitty; thought I would come up here and see you for a while. I knew you must be pining for me."

"Certainly," I replied; "do you not see how I have wasted away?"

He drew my arm through his and raced me down the plank-walk toward the shore, where I arrived laughing and out of breath.

"Where is Christine?" he asked.

I came back into the traces at once. "Over there in the hammock. You wish to go to the house first, I suppose?"

"Of course not."

"But she did not come to meet you, Edward, although she knew you had landed."

"Of course not, also."

"I do not understand you two."

"And of course not, a third time," said Edward, looking down at me with a smile. "What do peaceful little artists know about war?"

"Is it war?"

"Something very like it, Kitty. What is that you are carrying?"

"Oh! my new sketch. What do you think of it?"

"Good, very good. Some little girl about here, I suppose?"

"Why, it is Felipa!"

"And who is Felipa? Seems to me I have seen that old dog, though."

"Of course you have; he was in the boat with you, and so was Felipa; but she was dressed in boy's clothes, and that gives her a different look."

"Oh! that boy? I remember him. His name is Philip. He is a funny little fellow," said Edward calmly.

"Her name is Felipa, and she is not a boy or a funny little fellow at all," I replied.

"Isn't she? I thought she was both," replied Ned carelessly; and then he went off toward the hammock. I turned away, after noting Christine's cool greeting, and went back to the boat.

Felipa came bounding to meet me. "What is his name?" she demanded.

"Bowne."

"Buon—Buona; I can not say it."

"Bowne, child—Edward Bowne."

"Oh! Eduardo; I know that. Eduardo—Eduardo—a name of honey."

She flew off singing the name, followed by Drollo carrying his mistress's palmetto basket in his big patient mouth; but when I passed the house a few moments afterward she

was singing, or rather talking volubly of, another name—
"Miguel," and "the wife of Miguel," who were apparently
important personages on the canvas of her life. As it happened, I never really saw that wife of Miguel, who seemingly had no name of her own; but I imagined her. She lived
on a sand-bar in the ocean not far from the mouth of our
salt-marsh; she drove pelicans like ducks with a long switch,
and she had a tame eagle; she had an old horse also, who
dragged the driftwood across the sand on a sledge, and this
old horse seemed like a giant horse always, outlined as he
was against the flat bar and the sky. She went out at dawn,
and she went out at sunset, but during the middle of the
burning day she sat at home and polished sea-beans, for
which she obtained untold sums; she was very tall, she was
very yellow, and she had but one eye. These items, one by
one, had been dropped by Felipa at various times, and it
was with curiosity that I gazed upon the original Miguel, the
possessor of this remarkable spouse. He was a grave-eyed,
yellow man, who said little and thought less, applying *cui
bono*? to mental much as the city man applies it to bodily
exertion, and therefore achieving, I think, a finer degree of
inanition. The tame eagle, the pelicans, were nothing to
him; and, when I saw his lethargic, gentle countenance, my
own curiosity about them seemed to die away in haze, as
though I had breathed in an invisible opiate. He came, he
went, and that was all; exit Miguel.

Felipa was constantly with us now. She and Drollo followed the three of us wherever we went—followed the two
also whenever I staid behind to sketch, as I often staid, for
in those days I was trying to catch the secret of the salt-
marsh; a hopeless effort—I know it now. "Stay with me,
Felipa," I said; for it was natural to suppose that the lovers
might like to be alone. (I call them lovers for want of a
better name, but they were more like haters; however, in
such cases it is nearly the same thing.) And then Christine,
hearing this, would immediately call "Felipa!" and the child
would dart after them, happy as a bird. She wore her boy's
suit now all the time, because the señora had said she
"looked well in it." What the señora really said was, that in
boy's clothes she looked less like a grasshopper. But this
had been translated as above by Edward Bowne when Felipa
suddenly descended upon him one day and demanded to be
instantly told what the gracious lady was saying about her;

for she seemed to know by intuition when we spoke of her, although we talked in English and mentioned no names. When told, her small face beamed, and she kissed Christine's hand joyfully and bounded away. Christine took out her handkerchief and wiped the spot.

"Christine," I said, "do you remember the fate of the proud girl who walked upon bread?"

"You think that I may starve for kisses some time?" said my friend, going on with the wiping.

"Not while I am alive," called out Edward from behind. His style of courtship *was* of the sledge-hammer sort sometimes. But he did not get much for it on that day; only lofty tolerance, which seemed to amuse him greatly.

Edward played with Felipa very much as if she was a rubber toy or a little trapeze performer. He held her out at arm's length in mid-air, he poised her on his shoulder, he tossed her up into the low myrtle-trees, and dangled her by her little belt over the claret-colored pools on the barren; but he could not frighten her; she only laughed and grew wilder and wilder, like a squirrel. "She has muscles and nerves of steel," he said admiringly.

"Do put her down; she is too excitable for such games." I said in French, for Felipa seemed to divine our English now. "See the color she has."

For there was a trail of dark red over the child's thin oval cheeks which made her look unlike herself. As she caught our eyes fixed upon her, she suddenly stopped her climbing and came and sat at Christine's feet. "Some day I shall wear robes like the señora's," she said, passing her hand over the soft fabric; "and I think," she added after some slow consideration, "that my face will be like the señora's too."

Edward burst out laughing. The little creature stopped abruptly and scanned his face.

"Do not tease her," I said.

Quick as a flash she veered around upon me. "He does not tease me," she said angrily in Spanish; "and, besides, what if he does? I like it." She looked at me with gleaming eyes and stamped her foot.

"What a little tempest!" said Christine.

Then Edward, man-like, began to explain. "You could not look much like this lady, Felipa," he said, "because you are so dark, you know."

"Am I dark?"

"Very dark; but many people are dark, of course; and for my part I always liked dark eyes," said this mendacious person.

"Do you like my eyes?" asked Felipa anxiously.

"Indeed I do: they are like the eyes of a dear little calf I once owned when I was a boy."

The child was satisfied, and went back to her place beside Christine. "Yes, I shall wear robes like this," she said dreamily, drawing the flowing drapery over her knees clad in the little linen trousers, and scanning the effect; "they would trail behind me—so." Her bare feet peeped out below the hem, and again we all laughed, the little brown toes looked so comical coming out from the silk and the snowy embroideries. She came down to reality again, looked at us, looked at herself, and for the first time seemed to comprehend the difference. Then suddenly she threw herself down on the ground like a little animal, and buried her head in her arms. She would not speak, she would not look up: she only relaxed one arm a little to take in Drollo, and then lay motionless. Drollo looked at us out of one eye solemnly from his uncomfortable position, as much as to say: "No use; leave her to me." So after a while we went away and left them there.

That evening I heard a low knock at my door. "Come in," I said, and Felipa entered. I hardly knew her. She was dressed in a flowered muslin gown which had probably belonged to her mother, and she wore her grandmother's stockings and large baggy slippers; on her mat of curly hair was perched a high-crowned, stiff white cap adorned with a ribbon streamer; and her lank little neck, coming out of the big gown, was decked with a chain of large sea-beans, like exaggerated lockets. She carried a Cuban fan in her hand which was as large as a parasol, and Drollo, walking behind, fairly clanked with the chain of large sea-shells which she had wound around him from head to tail. The droll tableau and the supreme pride on Felipa's countenance overcame me, and I laughed aloud. A sudden cloud of rage and disappointment came over the poor child's face: she threw her cap on the floor and stamped on it; she tore off her necklace and writhed herself out of her big flowered gown, and, running to Drollo, nearly strangled him in her fierce efforts to drag off his shell chains. Then, a half-dressed, wild little phantom, she seized me by the skirts and dragged me toward the looking-glass. "You are not pretty either," she cried. "Look at yourself! look at yourself!"

"I did not mean to laugh at you, Felipa," I said gently; "I would not laugh at any one; and it is true I am not pretty, as you say. I can never be pretty, child; but, if you will try to be more gentle, I could teach you how to dress yourself so that no one would laugh at you again. I could make you a little bright-barred skirt and a scarlet bodice: you could help, and that would teach you to sew. But a little girl who wants all this done for her must be quiet and good."

"I am good," said Felipa; "as good as everything."

The tears still stood in her eyes, but her anger was forgotten: she improvised a sort of dance around my room, followed by Drollo dragging his twisted chain, stepping on it with his big feet, and finally winding himself up into a knot around the chair-legs.

"Couldn't we make Drollo something too? dear old Drollo!" said Felipa, going to him and squeezing him in an enthusiastic embrace. I used to wonder how his poor ribs stood it: Felipa used him as a safety-valve for her impetuous feelings.

She kissed me good night, and then asked for "the other lady."

"Go to bed, child," I said; "I will give her your good night."

"But I want to kiss her too," said Felipa.

She lingered at the door and would not go; she played with the latch, and made me nervous with its clicking; at last I ordered her out. But on opening my door half an hour afterward there she was sitting on the floor outside in the darkness, she and Drollo, patiently waiting. Annoyed, but unable to reprove her, I wrapped the child in my shawl and carried her out into the moonlight, where Christine and Edward were strolling to and fro under the pines. "She will not go to bed, Christine, without kissing you," I explained.

"Funny little monkey!" said my friend, passively allowing the embrace.

"Me too," said Edward, bending down. Then I carried my bundle back satisfied.

The next day Felipa and I in secret began our labors: hers consisted in worrying me out of my life and spoiling material—mine in keeping my temper and trying to sew. The result, however, was satisfactory, never mind how we got there. I led Christine out one afternoon: Edward followed. "Do you like tableaux?" I said. "There is one I have arranged for you."

Felipa sat on the edge of the low, square-curbed Spanish well, and Drollo stood behind her, his great yellow body and solemn head serving as a background. She wore a brown petticoat barred with bright colors, and a little scarlet bodice fitting her slender waist closely; a chemisette of soft cream-color with loose sleeves covered her neck and arms, and set off the dark hues of her cheeks and eyes; and around her curly hair a red scarf was twisted, its fringed edges forming a drapery at the back of the head, which, more than anything else, seemed to bring out the latent character of her face. Brown moccasins, red stockings, and a quantity of bright beads completed her costume.

"By Jove!" cried Edward, "the little thing is almost pretty."

Felipa understood this, and a great light came into her face: forgetting her pose, she bounded forward to Christine's side. "I am pretty, then?" she said with exultation; "I *am* pretty, then, after all? For now you yourself have said it—have said it."

"No, Felipa," I interposed, "the gentleman said it." For the child had a curious habit of confounding the two identities which puzzled me then as now. But this afternoon, this happy afternoon, she was content, for she was allowed to sit at Christine's feet and look up into her fair face unmolested. I was forgotten, as usual.

"It is always so," I said to myself. But cynicism, as Mr. Aldrich says, is a small brass field-piece that eventually bursts and kills the artilleryman. I knew this, having been blown up myself more than once; so I went back to my painting and forgot the world. Our world down there on the edge of the salt-marsh, however, was a small one: when two persons went out of it there was a vacuum.

One morning Felipa came sadly to my side. "They have gone away," she said.

"Yes, child."

"Down to the beach to spend all the day."

"Yes, I know it."

"And without me!"

This was the climax. I looked up. Her eyes were dry, but there was a hollow look of disappointment in her face that made her seem old; it was as though for an instant you caught what her old-woman face would be half a century on.

"Why did they not take me?" she said. "I am pretty now: she herself said it."

"They can not always take you, Felipa," I replied, giving up the point as to who had said it.

"Why not? I am pretty now: she herself said it," persisted the child. "In these clothes, you know: she herself said it. The clothes of the son of Pedro you will never see more: they are burned."

"Burned?"

"Yes, burned," replied Felipa composedly. "I carried them out on the barren and burned them. Drollo singed his paw. They burned quite nicely. But they are gone, and I am pretty now, and yet they did not take me! What shall I do?"

"Take these colors and make me a picture," I suggested. Generally, this was a prized privilege, but to-day it did not attract; she turned away, and a few moments after I saw her going down to the end of the plank-walk, where she stood gazing wistfully toward the ocean. There she staid all day, going into camp with Drollo, and refusing to come to dinner in spite of old Dominga's calls and beckonings. At last the patient old grandmother went down herself to the end of the long walk where they were, with some bread and venison on a plate. Felipa ate but little, but Drollo, after waiting politely until she had finished, devoured everything that was left in his calmly hungry way, and then sat back on his haunches with one paw on the plate, as though for the sake of memory. Drollo's hunger was of the chronic kind; it seemed impossible either to assuage it or to fill him. There was a gaunt leanness about him which I am satisfied no amount of food could ever fatten. I think he knew it too, and that accounted for his resignation. At length, just before sunset, the boat returned, floating up the marsh with the tide, old Bartolo steering and managing the brown sails. Felipa sprang up joyfully; I thought she would spring into the boat in her eagerness. What did she receive for her long vigil? A short word or two; that was all. Christine and Edward had quarreled.

How do lovers quarrel ordinarily? But I should not ask that, for these were no ordinary lovers: they were extraordinary.

"You should not submit to her caprices so readily," I said the next day while strolling on the barren with Edward. (He was not so much cast down, however, as he might have been.)

"I adore the very ground her foot touches, Kitty."

"I know it. But how will it end?"

"I will tell you: some of these days I shall win her, and then—she will adore me."

Here Felipa came running after us, and Edward immediately challenged her to a race: a game of romps began. If Christine had been looking from her window she might have thought he was not especially disconsolate over her absence; but she was not looking. She was never looking out of anything or for anybody. She was always serenely content where she was. Edward and Felipa strayed off among the pine-trees, and gradually I lost sight of them. But as I sat sketching an hour afterward Edward came into view, carrying the child in his arms. I hurried to meet them.

"I shall never forgive myself," he said; "the little thing has fallen and injured her foot badly, I fear."

"I do not care at all," said Felipa; "I like to have it hurt. It is *my* foot, isn't it?"

These remarks she threw at me defiantly, as though I had laid claim to the member in question. I could not help laughing.

"The other lady will not laugh," said the child proudly. And in truth Christine, most unexpectedly, took up the *rôle* of nurse. She carried Felipa to her own room—for we each had a little cell opening out of the main apartment—and as white-robed Charity she shone with new radiance, "Shone" is the proper word; for through the open door of the dim cell, with the dark little face of Felipa on her shoulder, her white robe and skin seemed fairly to shine, as white lilies shine on a dark night. The old grandmother left the child in our care and watched our proceedings wistfully, very much as a dog watches the human hands that extract the thorn from the swollen foot of her puppy. She was grateful and asked no questions; in fact, thought was not one of her mental processes. She did not think much; she felt. As for Felipa, the child lived in rapture during those days in spite of her suffering. She scarcely slept at all—she was too happy: I heard her voice rippling on through the night, and Christine's low replies. She adored her beautiful nurse.

The fourth day came: Edward Bowne walked into the

cell. "Go out and breathe the fresh air for an hour or two," he said in the tone more of a command than a request.

"The child will never consent," replied Christine sweetly.

"Oh, yes, she will; I will stay with her," said the young man, lifting the feverish little head on his arm and passing his hand softly over the bright eyes.

"Felipa, do you not want me?" said Christine, bending down.

"He stays; it is all the same," murmured the child.

"So it is.—Go, Christine," said Edward with a little smile of triumph.

Without a word Christine left the cell. But she did not go to walk; she came to my room, and, throwing herself on my bed, fell in a moment into a deep sleep, the reaction after her three nights of wakefulness. When she awoke it was long after dark, and I had relieved Edward in his watch.

"You will have to give it up," he said as our lily came forth at last with sleep-flushed cheeks and starry eyes shielded from the light. "The spell is broken; we have all been taking care of Felipa, and she likes one as well as the other."

Which was not true, in my case at least, since Felipa had openly derided my small strength when I lifted her, and beat off the sponge with which I attempted to bathe her hot face, "They" used no sponges, she said, only their nice cool hands; and she wished "they" would come and take care of her again. But Christine had resigned *in toto*. If Felipa did not prefer her to all others, then Felipa should not have her; she was not a common nurse. And indeed she was not. Her fair face, ideal grace, cooing voice, and the strength of her long arms and flexible hands, were like magic to the sick, and—distraction to the well; the well in this case being Edward Bowne looking in at the door.

"You love them very much, do you not, Felipa?" I said one day when the child was sitting up for the first time in a cushioned chair.

"Ah, yes; it is so strong when they carry me," she replied. But it was Edward who carried her.

"He is very strong," I said.

"Yes; and their long soft hair, with the smell of roses in it too," said Felipa dreamily. But the hair was Christine's.

"I shall love them for ever, and they will love me for ever," continued the child. "Drollo too." She patted the dog's head as she spoke, and then concluded to kiss him on his little inch of forehead; next she offered him all her medicines and lotions in turn, and he smelled at them grimly. "He likes to know what I am taking," she explained.

I went on: "You love them, Felipa, and they are fond of you. They will always remember you, no doubt."

"Remember!" cried Felipa, starting up from her cushions like a Jack-in-the-box. "They are not going away? Never! never!"

"But of course they must go some time, for—"

But Felipa was gone. Before I could divine her intent she had flung herself out of her chair down on the floor, and was crawling on her hands and knees toward the outer room. I ran after her, but she reached the door before me, and, dragging her bandaged foot behind her, drew herself toward Christine. "You are *not* going away! You are not! you are not!" she sobbed, clinging to her skirts.

Christine was reading tranquilly; Edward stood at the outer door mending his fishing-tackle. The coolness between them remained, unwarmed by so much as a breath. "Run away, child; you disturb me," said Christine, turning over a leaf. She did not even look at the pathetic little bundle at her feet. Pathetic little bundles must be taught some time what ingratitude deserves.

"How can she run, lame as she is?" said Edward from the doorway.

"You are not going away, are you? Tell me you are not," sobbed Felipa in a passion of tears, beating on the floor with one hand, and with the other clinging to Christine.

"I am not going," said Edward. "Do not sob so, you poor little thing!"

She crawled to him, and he took her up in his arms and soothed her into stillness again; then he carried her out on the barren for a breath of fresh air.

"It is a most extraordinary thing how that child confounds you two," I said. "It is a case of color-blindness, as it were—supposing you two were colors."

"Which we are not," replied Christine carelessly. "Do not stray off into mysticism, Catherine."

"It is not mysticism; it is a study of character—"

"Where there is no character," replied my friend.

I gave it up, but I said to myself: "Fate, in the next world make me one of those long, lithe, light-haired women, will you? I want to see how it feels."

Felipa's foot was well again, and spring had come. Soon we must leave our lodge on the edge of the pine-barren, our outlook over the salt-marsh, with the river sweeping up twice a day, bringing in the briny odors of the ocean; soon we should see no more the eagles far above us or hear the night-cry of the great owls, and we must go without the little fairy flowers of the barren, so small that a hundred of them scarcely made a tangible bouquet, yet what beauty! what sweetness! In my portfolio were sketches and studies of the salt-marsh, and in my heart were hopes. Somebody says somewhere:"Hope is more than a blessing; it is a duty and a virtue." But I fail to appreciate preserved hope—hope put up in cans and served out in seasons of depression. I like it fresh from the tree. And so when I hope it *is* hope, and not that well-dried, monotonous cheerfulness which makes one long to throw the persistent smilers out of the window. Felipa danced no more on the barrens; her illness had toned her down; she seemed content to sit at our feet while we talked, looking up dreamily into our faces, but no longer eagerly endeavoring to comprehend. We were there; that was enough.

"She is growing like a reed," I said; "her illness has left her weak."

"-Minded," suggested Christine.

At this moment Felipa stroked the lady's white hand tenderly and laid her brown cheek against it.

"Do you not feel reproached?" I said.

"Why? Must we give our love to whoever loves us? A fine parcel of paupers we should all be, wasting our inheritance in pitiful small change! Shall I give a thousand beggars a half hour's happiness, or shall I make one soul rich his whole life long?"

"The latter," remarked Edward, who had come up unobserved.

They gazed at each other unflinchingly. They had come to open battle during those last days, and I knew that the end was near. Their words had been cold as ice, cutting as steel, and I said to myself, "At any moment." There would be a deadly struggle, and then Christine would yield. Even I comprehended something of what that yielding would be.

"Why do they hate each other so?" Felipa said to me sadly.

"Do they hate each other?"

"Yes, for I feel it here," she answered, touching her breast with a dramatic little gesture.

"Nonsense! Go and play with your doll, child." For I had made her a respectable, orderly doll to take the place of the ungainly fetich out on the barren.

Felipa gave me a look and walked away. A moment afterward she brought the doll out of the house before my very eyes, and, going down to the end of the dock, deliberately threw it into the water; the tide was flowing out, and away went my toy-woman out of sight, out to sea.

"Well!" I said to myself. "What next?"

I had not told Felipa we were going; I thought it best to let it take her by surprise. I had various small articles of finery ready as farewell gifts, which should act as sponges to absorb her tears. But Fate took the whole matter out of my hands. This is how it happened: One evening in the jasmine arbor, in the fragrant darkness of the warm spring night, the end came; Christine was won. She glided in like a wraith, and I, divining at once what had happened, followed her into her little room, where I found her lying on her bed, her hands clasped on her breast, her eyes open and veiled in soft shadows, her white robe drenched with dew. I kissed her fondly—I never could help loving her then or now—and next I went out to find Edward. He had been kind to me all my poor gray life; should I not go to him now? He was still in the arbor, and I sat down by his side quietly; I knew that the words would come in time. They came; what a flood! English was not enough for him. He poured forth his love in the rich-voweled Spanish tongue also; it has sounded doubly sweet to me ever since.

> "Have you felt the wool of the beaver?
>   Or swan's down ever?
> Or have smelt the bud o' the brier?
>   Or the nard in the fire?
> Or ha' tasted the bag o' the bee?
> Oh so white, oh so soft, oh so sweet is she!"

said the young lover; and I, listening there in the dark fragrant night, with the dew heavy upon me, felt glad that the old simple-hearted love was not entirely gone from our tired metallic world.

It was late when we returned to the house. After reaching

my room I found that I had left my cloak in the arbor. It was a strong fabric; the dew could not hurt it, but it could hurt my sketching materials and various trifles in the wide inside pockets—*objets de luxe* to me, souvenirs of happy times, little artistic properties that I hang on the walls of my poor studio when in the city. I went softly out into the darkness again and sought the arbor; groping on the ground I found, not the cloak, but—Felipa! She was crouched under the foliage, face downward; she would not move or answer.

"What is the matter, child?" I said, but she would not speak. I tried to draw her from her lair, but she tangled herself stubbornly still farther among the thorny vines, and I could not move her. I touched her neck; it was cold. Frightened, I ran back to the house for a candle.

"Go away," she said in a low hoarse voice when I flashed the light over her. "I know all, and I am going to die. I have eaten the poison things in your box, and just now a snake came on my neck and I let him. He has bitten me, and I am glad. Go away; I am going to die."

I looked around; there was my color-case rifled and empty, and the other articles were scattered on the ground. "Good Heavens, child!" I cried, "what have you eaten?"

"Enough," replied Felipa gloomily. "I knew they were poisons; you told me so. And I let the snake stay."

By this time the household, aroused by my hurried exit with the candle, came toward the arbor. The moment Edward appeared Felipa rolled herself up like a hedgehog again and refused to speak. But the old grandmother knelt down and drew the little crouching figure into her arms with gentle tenderness, smoothing its hair and murmuring loving words in her soft dialect.

"What is it?" said Edward; but even then his eyes were devouring Christine, who stood in the dark vine-wreathed doorway like a picture in a frame. I explained.

Christine smiled. "Jealousy," she said in a low voice. "I am not surprised."

But at the first sound of her voice Felipa had started up, and, wrenching herself free from old Dominga's arms, threw herself at Christine's feet. "Look at *me* so," she cried—"*me* too; do not look at him. He has forgotten poor Felipa; he does not love her any more. But *you* do not forget, señora; *you* love me—*you* love me. Say you do, or I shall die!"

We were all shocked by the pallor and the wild, hungry look of her uplifted face. Edward bent down and tried to lift her in his arms; but when she saw him a sudden fierceness came into her eyes; they shot out yellow light and seemed to narrow to a point of flame. Before we knew it she had turned, seized something, and plunged it into his encircling arm. It was my little Venetian dagger.

We sprang forward; our dresses were spotted with the fast-flowing blood; but Edward did not relax his hold on the writhing, wild little body he held until it lay exhausted in his arms. "I am glad I did it," said the child, looking up into his face with her inflexible eyes. "Put me down—put me down, I say, by the gracious señora, that I may die with the trailing of her white robe over me." And the old grandmother with trembling hands received her and laid her down mutely at Christine's feet.

Ah, well! Felipa did not die. The poisons racked but did not kill her, and the snake must have spared the little thin brown neck so despairingly offered to him. We went away; there was nothing for us to do but to go away as quickly as possible and leave her to her kind. To the silent old grandfather I said: "It will pass; she is but a child."

"She is nearly twelve, señora. Her mother was married at thirteen."

"But she loved them both alike, Bartolo. It is nothing; she does not know."

"You are right, lady; she does not know," replied the old man slowly; "but *I* know. It was two loves, and the stronger thrust the knife."

Charles Waddell Chesnutt (June 20, 1858–November 15, 1932) was born in Cleveland, Ohio, to parents who left their family home in Fayetteville, North Carolina in 1856 to escape slavery. In 1866, when Chesnutt was eight, his family returned to Fayetteville where he grew up and attended grade school, his only formal education. For nine years Chesnutt taught school and served as a school principal in North Carolina. In 1883 he decided to leave the South to escape the oppressive limits it placed on his career and education. He lived in New York where he worked as a journalist and taught himself to take shorthand at 200 words per minute. Shortly after, he moved his family to Cleveland and enjoyed a successful career as a court reporter. He also "read law" in the office of a Cleveland attorney and was admitted to the Ohio bar. Chesnutt lived the rest of his life in Cleveland and remained active in a number of political and cultural organizations.

In August 1887 the *Atlantic Monthly* published his short story "The Goophered Grapevine" but concealed the fact that they were printing the writing of an African American. His first novel, *The House Behind the Cedars*, was rejected in early draft by the publisher because, they said, it was a "controversial novel of the color line." In 1899 his two collections of short stories, *The Conjure Woman* and *The Wife of His Youth, and Other Stories of the Color Line* were published. In that same year his biography *Frederick Douglass* appeared. These volumes met with such success that his publisher decided to publish *The House Behind the Cedars*, the story of two blacks that pass for white in the postwar South. Chesnutt's second novel, *The Marrow of Tradition*, based on the 1898 race riots in Wilmington, North Carolina, followed in 1901. His third and final novel, *The Colonel's Dream*, was published in 1905.

THE SHERIFF'S CHILDREN

by *Charles W. Chesnutt*

Branson County, North Carolina, is in a sequestered district of one of the staidest and most conservative States of the Union. Society in Branson County is almost primitive in its simplicity. Most of the white people own the farms they till, and even before the war there were no very wealthy families to force their neighbors, by comparison, into the category of "poor whites."

To Branson County, as to most rural communities in the South, the war is the one historical event that overshadows all others. It is the era from which all local chronicles are dated,—births, deaths, marriages, storms, freshets. No description of the life of any Southern community would be perfect that failed to emphasize the all pervading influence of the great conflict.

Yet the fierce tide of war that had rushed through the cities and along the great highways of the country had comparatively speaking but slightly disturbed the sluggish current of life in this region, remote from railroads and navigable streams. To the north in Virginia, to the west in Tennessee, and all along the seaboard the war had raged; but the thunder of its cannon had not disturbed the echoes of Branson County, where the loudest sounds heard were the crack of some hunter's rifle, the baying of some deep-mouthed hound, or the yodel of some tuneful negro on his way through the pine forest. To the east, Sherman's army had passed on its march to the sea; but no straggling band of "bummers" had penetrated the confines of Branson County. The war, it is true, had robbed the county of the flower of its young manhood; but the burden of taxation, the doubt and uncertainty of the conflict, and the sting of ultimate defeat, had been borne by the people with an apathy that robbed misfortune of half its sharpness.

The nearest approach to town life afforded by Branson County is found in the little village of Troy, the county seat, a hamlet with a population of four or five hundred.

Ten years make little difference in the appearance of these remote Southern towns. If a railroad is built through one of them, it infuses some enterprise; the social corpse is galvanized by the fresh blood of civilization that pulses along the farthest ramifications of our great system of commercial highways. At the period of which I write, no railroad had come to Troy. If a traveler, accustomed to the bustling life of cities, could have ridden through Troy on a summer day, he might easily have fancied himself in a deserted village. Around him he would have seen weather-beaten houses, innocent of paint, the shingled roofs in many instances covered with a rich growth of moss. Here and there he would have met a razor-backed hog lazily rooting his way along the principal thoroughfare; and more than once he would probably have had to disturb the slumbers of some yellow dog, dozing away the hours in the ardent sunshine, and reluctantly yielding up his place in the middle of the dusty road.

On Saturdays the village presented a somewhat livelier appearance, and the shade trees around the court house square and along Front Street served as hitching-posts for a goodly number of horses and mules and stunted oxen, belonging to the farmer-folk who had come in to trade at the two or three local stores.

A murder was a rare event in Branson County. Every well-informed citizen could tell the number of homicides committed in the county for fifty years back, and whether the slayer, in any given instance, had escaped, either by flight or acquittal, or had suffered the penalty of the law. So, when it became known in Troy early one Friday morning in summer, about ten years after the war, that old Captain Walker, who had served in Mexico under Scott, and had left an arm on the field of Gettysburg, had been foully murdered during the night, there was intense excitement in the village. Business was practically suspended, and the citizens gathered in little groups to discuss the murder,

and speculate upon the identity of the murderer. It tran-
spired from testimony at the coroner's inquest, held during
the morning, that a strange mulatto had been seen going in
the direction of Captain Walker's house the night before,
and had been met going away from Troy early Friday morning, by a farmer on his way to town. Other circumstances
seemed to connect the stranger with the crime. The sheriff
organized a posse to search for him, and early in the evening, when most of the citizens of Troy were at supper, the
suspected man was brought in and lodged in the county jail.

By the following morning the news of the capture had
spread to the farthest limits of the county. A much larger
number of people than usual came to town that Saturday,
—bearded men in straw hats and blue homespun shirts, and
butternut trousers of great amplitude of material and vague-
ness of outline; women in homespun frocks and slat-bonnets,
with faces as expressionless as the dreary sandhills which
gave them a meagre sustenance.

The murder was almost the sole topic of conversation. A
steady stream of curious observers visited the house of mourning, and gazed upon the rugged face of the old veteran, now
stiff and cold in death; and more than one eye dropped a
tear at the remembrance of the cheery smile, and the joke—
sometimes superannuated, generally feeble, but always good-
natured—with which the captain had been wont to greet his
acquaintances. There was a growing sentiment of anger
among these stern men, toward the murderer who had thus
cut down their friend, and a strong feeling that ordinary
justice was too slight a punishment for such a crime.

Toward noon there was an informal gathering of citizens
in Dan Tyson's store.

"I hear it 'lowed that Square Kyahtah's too sick ter hol'
co'te this evenin'," said one, "an' that the purlim'nary hearin'
'll haf ter go over 'tel nex' week."

A look of disappointment went round the crowd.

"Hit 's the durndes', meanes' murder ever committed in
this caounty," said another, with moody emphasis.

"I s'pose the nigger 'lowed the Cap'n had some green-
backs," observed a third speaker.

"The Cap'n," said another, with an air of superior information, "has left two bairls of Confedrit money, which he
'spected 'ud be good some day er nuther."

This statement gave rise to a discussion of the speculative

value of Confederate money; but in a little while the conversation returned to the murder.

"Hangin' air too good fer the murderer," said one; "he oughter be burnt, stidier bein' hung."

There was an impressive pause at this point, during which a jug of moonlight whiskey went the round of the crowd.

"Well," said a round-shouldered farmer, who, in spite of his peaceable expression and faded gray eye, was known to have been one of the most daring followers of a rebel guerrilla chieftain, "what air yer gwine ter do about it? Ef you fellers air gwine ter set down an' let a wuthless nigger kill the bes' white man in Branson, an' not say nuthin' ner do nuthin', I'll move outen the caounty."

This speech gave tone and direction to the rest of the conversation. Whether the fear of losing the round-shouldered farmer operated to bring about the result or not is immaterial to this narrative; but, at all events, the crowd decided to lynch the negro. They agreed that this was the least that could be done to avenge the death of their murdered friend, and that it was a becoming way in which to honor his memory. They had some vague notions of the majesty of the law and the rights of the citizen, but in the passion of the moment these sunk into oblivion; a white man had been killed by a negro.

"The Cap'n was an ole sodger," said one of his friends solemnly. "He'll sleep better when he knows that a co'te-martial has be'n hilt an' jestice done."

By agreement the lynchers were to meet at Tyson's store at five o'clock in the afternoon, and proceed thence to the jail, which was situated down the Lumberton Dirt Road (as the old turnpike antedating the plank-road was called), about half a mile south of the court-house. When the preliminaries of the lynching had been arranged, and a committee appointed to manage the affair, the crowd dispersed, some to go to their dinners, and some to secure recruits for the lynching party.

It was twenty minutes to five o'clock, when an excited negro, panting and perspiring, rushed up to the back door of Sheriff Campbell's dwelling, which stood at a little distance from the jail and somewhat farther than the latter building from the courthouse. A turbaned colored woman came to the door in response to the negro's knock.

"Hoddy, Sis' Nance."

"Hoddy, Brer Sam."

"Is de shurff in," inquired the negro.

"Yas, Brer Sam, he's eatin' his dinner," was the answer.

"Will yer ax 'im ter step ter de do' a minute, Sis' Nance?"

The woman went into the dining-room, and a moment later the sheriff came to the door. He was a tall, muscular man, of a ruddier complexion than is usual among Southerners. A pair of keen, deep-set gray eyes looked out from under bushy eyebrows, and about his mouth was a masterful expression, which a full beard, once sandy in color, but now profusely sprinkled with gray, could not entirely conceal. The day was hot; the sheriff had discarded his coat and vest, and had his white shirt open at the throat.

"What do you want, Sam?" he inquired of the negro, who stood hat in hand, wiping the moisture from his face with a ragged shirt-sleeve.

"Shurff, dey gwine ter hang de pris'ner w'at's lock' up in de jail. Dey're comin' dis a-way now. I wuz layin' down on a sack er corn down at de sto', behine a pile er flour-bairls, w'en I hearn Doc' Cain en Kunnel Wright talkin' erbout it. I slip' outen de back do', en run here as fas' as I could. I hearn you say down ter de sto' once't dat you would n't let nobody take a pris'ner 'way fum you widout walkin' over yo' dead body, en I thought I'd let you know 'fo' dey come, so yer could pertec' de pris'ner."

The sheriff listened calmly, but his face grew firmer, and a determined gleam lit up his gray eyes. His frame grew more erect, and he unconsciously assumed the attitude of a soldier who momentarily expects to meet the enemy face to face.

"Much obliged, Sam," he answered. "I'll protect the prisoner. Who's coming?"

"I dunno who-all *is* comin'," replied the negro. "Dere's Mistah McSwayne, en Doc' Cain, en Maje' McDonal', en Kunnel Wright, en a heap er yuthers. I wuz so skeered I done furgot mo' d'n half un em. I spec' dey mus' be mos' here by dis time, so I'll git outen de way, fer I don' want nobody fer ter think I wuz mix' up in dis business." The negro glanced nervously down the road toward the town, and made a movement as if to go away.

"Won't you have some dinner first?" asked the sheriff.

The negro looked longingly in at the open door, and sniffed the appetizing odor of boiled pork and collards.

"I ain't got no time fer ter tarry, Shurff," he said, "but Sis' Nance mought gin me sump'n I could kyar in my han' en eat on de way."

A moment later Nancy brought him a huge sandwich of split corn-pone, with a thick slice of fat bacon inserted between the halves, and a couple of baked yams. The negro hastily replaced his ragged hat on his head, dropped the yams in the pocket of his capacious trousers, and, taking the sandwich in his hand, hurried across the road and disappeared in the woods beyond.

The sheriff reëntered the house, and put on his coat and hat. He then took down a double-barreled shotgun and loaded it with buckshot. Filling the chambers of a revolver with fresh cartridges, he slipped it into the pocket of the sack-coat which he wore.

A comely young woman in a calico dress watched these proceedings with anxious surprise.

"Where are you going, father?" she asked. She had not heard the conversation with the negro.

"I am goin' over to the jail," responded the sheriff. "There's a mob comin' this way to lynch the nigger we've got locked up. But they won't do it," he added, with emphasis.

"Oh, father! don't go!" pleaded the girl, clinging to his arm; "they'll shoot you if you don't give him up."

"You never mind me, Polly," said her father reassuringly, as he gently unclasped her hands from his arm. "I'll take care of myself and the prisoner, too. There ain't a man in Branson County that would shoot me. Besides, I have faced fire too often to be scared away from my duty. You keep close in the house," he continued, "and if any one disturbs you just use the old horse-pistol in the top bureau drawer. It's a little old-fashioned, but it did good work a few years ago."

The young girl shuddered at this sanguinary allusion, but made no further objection to her father's departure.

The sheriff of Branson was a man far above the average of the community in wealth, education, and social position. His had been one of the few families in the county that before the war had owned large estates and numerous slaves. He had graduated at the State University at Chapel Hill, and had kept up some acquaintance with current literature and advanced thought. He had traveled some in his youth, and was looked up to in the county as an authority on all subjects connected with the outer world. At first an ardent supporter of the Union, he had opposed the secession movement in his native State as long as opposition availed to stem the tide of public opinion. Yielding at last to the force of circumstances, he had entered the Confederate service rather late in the war, and served with distinction through several campaigns, rising in time to the rank of colonel. After the war he had taken the oath of allegiance, and had been chosen by the people as the most available candidate for the office of sheriff, to which he had been elected without opposition. He had filled the office for several terms, and was universally popular with his constituents.

Colonel or Sheriff Campbell, as he was indifferently called, as the military or civil title happened to be most important in the opinion of the person addressing him, had a high sense of the responsibility attaching to his office. He had sworn to do his duty faithfully, and he knew what his duty was, as sheriff, perhaps more clearly than he had apprehended it in other passages of his life. It was, therefore, with no uncertainty in regard to his course that he prepared his weapons and went over to the jail. He had no fears for Polly's safety.

The sheriff had just locked the heavy front door of the jail behind him when a half dozen horsemen, followed by a crowd of men on foot, came round a bend in the road and drew near the jail. They halted in front of the picket fence that surrounded the building, while several of the committee of arrangements rode on a few rods farther to the sheriff's house. One of them dismounted and rapped on the door with his riding-whip.

"Is the sheriff at home?" he inquired.

"No, he has just gone out," replied Polly, who had come to the door.

"We want the jail keys," he continued.

"They are not here," said Polly. "The sheriff has them himself." Then she added, with assumed indifference, "He is at the jail now."

The man turned away, and Polly went into the front room, from which she peered anxiously between the slats of the green blinds of a window that looked toward the jail. Meanwhile the messenger returned to his companions and announced his discovery. It looked as though the sheriff had learned of their design and was preparing to resist it.

One of them stepped forward and rapped on the jail door.

"Well, what is it?" said the sheriff, from within.

"We want to talk to you, Sheriff," replied the spokesman. There was a little wicket in the door; this the sheriff opened, and answered through it.

"All right, boys, talk away. You are all strangers to me, and I don't know what business you can have." The sheriff did not think it necessary to recognize anybody in particular on such an occasion; the question of identity sometimes comes up in the investigation of these extra-judicial executions.

"We're a committee of citizens and we want to get into the jail."

"What for? It ain't much trouble to get into jail. Most people want to keep out."

The mob was in no humor to appreciate a joke, and the sheriff's witticism fell dead upon an unresponsive audience.

"We want to have a talk with the nigger that killed Cap'n Walker."

"You can talk to that nigger in the courthouse, when he's brought out for trial. Court will be in session here next week. I know what you fellows want, but you can't get my prisoner to-day. Do you want to take the bread out of a poor man's mouth? I get seventy-five cents a day for keeping this prisoner, and he's the only one in jail. I can't have my family suffer just to please you fellows."

One or two young men in the crowd laughed at the idea of Sheriff Campbell's suffering for want of seventy-five cents a day; but they were frowned into silence by those who stood near them.

"Ef yer don't let us in," cried a voice, "we'll bu's' the do' open."

"Bust away," answered the sheriff, raising his voice so that all could hear. "But I give you fair warning. The first man that tries it will be filled with buckshot. I'm sheriff of this county; I know my duty, and I mean to do it."

"What's the use of kicking, Sheriff?" argued one of the leaders of the mob. "The nigger is sure to hang anyhow; he richly deserves it; and we've got to do something to teach the niggers their places, or white people won't be able to live in the county."

"There's no use talking, boys," responded the sheriff. "I'm a white man outside, but in this jail I'm sheriff; and if this nigger's to be hung in this county, I propose to do the hanging. So you fellows might as well right-about-face, and march back to Troy. You've had a pleasant trip, and the exercise will be good for you. You know *me*. I've got powder and ball, and I've faced fire before now, with nothing between me and the enemy, and I don't mean to surrender this jail while I'm able to shoot." Having thus announced his determination, the sheriff closed and fastened the wicket, and looked around for the best position from which to defend the building.

The crowd drew off a little, and the leaders conversed together in low tones.

The Branson County jail was a small, two-story brick building, strongly constructed, with no attempt at architectural ornamentation. Each story was divided into two large cells by a passage running from front to rear. A grated iron door gave entrance from the passage to each of the four cells. The jail seldom had many prisoners in it, and the lower windows had been boarded up. When the sheriff had closed the wicket, he ascended the steep wooden stairs to the upper floor. There was no window at the front of the upper passage, and the most available position from which to watch the movements of the crowd below was the front window of the cell occupied by the solitary prisoner.

The sheriff unlocked the door and entered the cell. The prisoner was crouched in a corner, his yellow face, blanched with terror, looking ghastly in the semi-darkness of the room. A cold perspiration had gathered on his forehead, and his teeth were chattering with affright.

"For God's sake, Sheriff," he murmured hoarsely, "don't let 'em lynch me; I did n't kill the old man."

The sheriff glanced at the cowering wretch with a look of mingled contempt and loathing.

"Get up," he said sharply. "You will probably be hung sooner or later, but it shall not be to-day, if I can help it. I'll unlock your fetters, and if I can't hold the jail, you'll have to make the best fight you can. If I'm shot, I'll consider my responsibility at an end."

There were iron fetters on the prisoner's ankles, and handcuffs on his wrists. These the sheriff unlocked, and they fell clanking to the floor.

"Keep back from the window," said the sheriff. "They might shoot if they saw you."

The sheriff drew toward the window a pine bench which formed a part of the scanty furniture of the cell, and laid his revolver upon it. Then he took his gun in hand, and took his stand at the side of the window where he could with least exposure of himself watch the movements of the crowd below.

The lynchers had not anticipated any determined resistance. Of course they had looked for a formal protest, and perhaps a sufficient show of opposition to excuse the sheriff in the eye of any stickler for legal formalities. They had not however come prepared to fight a battle, and no one of them seemed willing to lead an attack upon the jail. The leaders of the party conferred together with a good deal of animated gesticulation, which was visible to the sheriff from his outlook, though the distance was too great for him to hear what was said. At length one of them broke away from the group, and rode back to the main body of the lynchers, who were restlessly awaiting orders.

"Well, boys," said the messenger, "we'll have to let it go for the present. The sheriff says he'll shoot, and he's got the drop on us this time. There ain't any of us that want to follow Cap'n Walker jest yet. Besides, the sheriff is a good fellow, and we don't want to hurt 'im. But," he added, as if to reassure the crowd, which began to show signs of disappointment, "the nigger might as well say his prayers, for he ain't got long to live."

There was a murmur of dissent from the mob, and several voices insisted that an attack be made on the jail. But pacific counsels finally prevailed, and the mob sullenly withdrew.

The sheriff stood at the window until they had disappeared around the bend in the road. He did not relax his watchfulness when the last one was out of sight. Their withdrawal might be a mere feint, to be followed by a further attempt. So closely, indeed, was his attention drawn to the outside, that he neither saw nor heard the prisoner creep stealthily across the floor, reach out his hand and secure the revolver which lay on the bench behind the sheriff, and creep as noiselessly back to his place in the corner of the room.

A moment after the last of the lynching party had disappeared there was a shot fired from the woods across the road; a bullet whistled by the window and buried itself in the wooden casing a few inches from where the sheriff was standing. Quick as thought, with the instinct born of a semi-guerrilla army experience, he raised his gun and fired twice at the point from which a faint puff of smoke showed the hostile bullet to have been sent. He stood a moment watching, and then rested his gun against the window, and reached behind him mechanically for the other weapon. It was not on the bench. As the sheriff realized this fact, he turned his head and looked into the muzzle of the revolver.

"Stay where you are, Sheriff," said the prisoner, his eyes glistening, his face almost ruddy with excitement.

The sheriff mentally cursed his own carelessness for allowing him to be caught in such a predicament. He had not expected anything of the kind. He had relied on the negro's cowardice and subordination in the presence of an armed white man as a matter of course. The sheriff was a brave man, but realized that the prisoner had him at an immense disadvantage. The two men stood thus for a moment, fighting a harmless duel with their eyes.

"Well, what do you mean to do?" asked the sheriff with apparent calmness.

"To get away, of course," said the prisoner, in a tone which caused the sheriff to look at him more closely, and with an involuntary feeling of apprehension; if the man was not mad, he was in a state of mind akin to madness, and quite as dangerous. The sheriff felt that he must speak the prisoner fair, and watch for a chance to turn the tables on him. The keen-eyed, desperate man before him was a different being altogether from the groveling wretch who had begged so piteously for life a few minutes before.

At length the sheriff spoke:—

"Is this your gratitude to me for saving your life at the risk of my own? If I had not done so, you would now be swinging from the limb of some neighboring tree."

"True," said the prisoner, "you saved my life, but for how long? When you came in, you said Court would sit next week. When the crowd went away they said I had not long to live. It is merely a choice of two ropes."

"While there's life there's hope," replied the sheriff. He uttered this commonplace mechanically, while his brain was busy in trying to think out some way of escape. "If you are innocent you can prove it."

The mulatto kept his eye upon the sheriff. "I didn't kill

the old man," he replied; "but I shall never be able to clear myself. I was at his house at nine o'clock. I stole from it the coat that was on my back when I was taken. I would be convicted, even with a fair trial, unless the real murderer were discovered beforehand."

The sheriff knew this only too well. While he was thinking what argument next to use, the prisoner continued:—

"Throw me the keys—no, unlock the door."

The sheriff stood a moment irresolute. The mulatto's eye glittered ominously. The sheriff crossed the room and unlocked the door leading into the passage.

"Now go down and unlock the outside door."

The heart of the sheriff leaped within him. Perhaps he might make a dash for liberty, and gain the outside. He descended the narrow stairs, the prisoner keeping close behind him.

The sheriff inserted the huge iron key into the lock. The rusty bolt yielded slowly. It still remained for him to pull the door open.

"Stop!" thundered the mulatto, who seemed to divine the sheriff's purpose. "Move a muscle, and I'll blow your brains out."

The sheriff obeyed; he realized that his chance had not yet come.

"Now keep on that side of the passage, and go back upstairs."

Keeping the sheriff under cover of the revolver, the mulatto followed him up the stairs. The sheriff expected the prisoner to lock him into the cell and make his own escape. He had about come to the conclusion that the best thing he could do under the circumstances was to submit quietly, and take his chances of recapturing the prisoner after the alarm had been given. The sheriff had faced death more than once upon the battlefield. A few minutes before, well armed, and with a brick wall between him and them he had dared a hundred men to fight; but he felt instinctively that the desperate man confronting him was not to be trifled with, and he was too prudent a man to risk his life against such heavy odds. He had Polly to look after, and there was a limit beyond which devotion to duty would be quixotic and even foolish.

"I want to get away," said the prisoner, "and I don't want to be captured; for if I am I know I will be hung on the spot.

I am afraid," he added somewhat reflectively, "that in order to save myself I shall have to kill you."

"Good God!" exclaimed the sheriff in involuntary terror; "you would not kill the man to whom you owe your own life."

"You speak more truly than you know," replied the mulatto. "I indeed owe my life to you."

The sheriff started. He was capable of surprise, even in that moment of extreme peril. "Who are you?" he asked in amazement.

"Tom, Cicely's son," returned the other. He had closed the door and stood talking to the sheriff through the grated opening. "Don't you remember Cicely—Cicely whom you sold, with her child, to the speculator on his way to Alabama?"

The sheriff did remember. He had been sorry for it many a time since. It had been the old story of debts, mortgages, and bad crops. He had quarreled with the mother. The price offered for her and her child had been unusually large, and he had yielded to the combination of anger and pecuniary stress.

"Good God!" he gasped, "you would not murder your own father?"

"My father?" replied the mulatto. "It were well enough for me to claim the relationship, but it comes with poor grace from you to ask anything by reason of it. What father's duty have you ever performed for me? Did you give me your name, or even your protection? Other white men gave their colored sons freedom and money, and sent them to the free States. *You* sold *me* to the rice swamps."

"I at least gave you the life you cling to," murmured the sheriff.

"Life?" said the prisoner, with a sarcastic laugh. "What kind of a life? You gave me your own blood, your own features,—no man need look at us together twice to see that,—and you gave me a black mother. Poor wretch! She died under the lash, because she had enough womanhood to call her soul her own. You gave me a white man's spirit, and you made me a slave, and crushed it out."

"But you are free now," said the sheriff. He had not doubted, could not doubt, the mulatto's word. He knew whose passions coursed beneath that swarthy skin and burned in the black eyes opposite his own. He saw in this mulatto what he himself might have become had not the safeguards of parental restraint and public opinion been thrown around him.

"Free to do what?" replied the mulatto. "Free in name, but despised and scorned and set aside by the people to whose race I belong far more than to my mother's."

"There are schools," said the sheriff. "You have been to school." He had noticed that the mulatto spoke more eloquently and used better language than most Branson County people.

"I have been to school, and dreamed when I went that it would work some marvelous change in my condition. But what did I learn? I learned to feel that no degree of learning or wisdom will change the color of my skin and that I shall always wear what in my own country is a badge of degradation. When I think about it seriously I do not care particularly for such a life. It is the animal in me, not the man, that flees the gallows. I owe you nothing," he went on, "and expect nothing of you; and it would be no more than justice if I should avenge upon you my mother's wrongs and my own. But still I hate to shoot you; I have never yet taken human life—for I did *not* kill the old captain. Will you promise to give no alarm and make no attempt to capture me until morning, if I do not shoot?"

So absorbed were the two men in their colloquy and their own tumultuous thoughts that neither of them had heard the door below move upon its hinges. Neither of them had heard a light step come stealthily up the stairs, nor seen a slender form creep along the darkening passage toward the mulatto.

The sheriff hesitated. The struggle between his love of life and his sense of duty was a terrific one. It may seem strange that a man who could sell his own child into slavery should hesitate at such a moment, when his life was trembling in the balance. But the baleful influence of human slavery poisoned the very fountains of life and created new standards of right. The sheriff was conscientious; his conscience had merely been warped by his environment. Let no one ask what his answer would have been; he was spared the necessity of a decision.

"Stop," said the mulatto, "you need not promise. I could not trust you if you did. It is your life for mine; there is but one safe way for me; you must die."

He raised his arm to fire, when there was a flash—a report from the passage behind him. His arm fell heavily at his side, and the pistol dropped at his feet.

The sheriff recovered first from his surprise, and throwing open the door secured the fallen weapon. Then seizing the prisoner he thrust him into the cell and locked the door upon him; after which he turned to Polly, who leaned half-fainting against the wall, her hands clasped over her heart.

"Oh, father, I was just in time!" she cried hysterically, and, wildly sobbing, threw herself into her father's arms.

"I watched until they all went away," she said. "I heard the shot from the woods and I saw you shoot. Then when you did not come out I feared something had happened, that perhaps you had been wounded. I got out the other pistol and ran over here. When I found the door open, I knew something was wrong and when I heard voices I crept upstairs, and reached the top just in time to hear him say he would kill you. Oh, it was a narrow escape!"

When she had grown somewhat calmer, the sheriff left her standing there and went back into the cell. The prisoner's arm was bleeding from a flesh wound. His bravado had given place to a stony apathy. There was no sign in his face of fear or disappointment or feeling of any kind. The sheriff sent Polly to the house for cloth, and bound up the prisoner's wound with a rude skill acquired during his army life.

"I'll have a doctor come and dress the wound in the morning," he said to the prisoner. "It will do very well until then, if you will keep quiet. If the doctor asks you how the wound was caused, you can say that you were struck by the bullet fired from the woods. It would do you no good to have it known that you were shot while attempting to escape."

The prisoner uttered no word of thanks or apology, but sat in sullen silence. When the wounded arm had been bandaged, Polly and her father returned to the house.

The sheriff was in an unusually thoughtful mood that evening. He put salt in his coffee at supper, and poured vinegar over his pancakes. To many of Polly's questions he returned random answers. When he had gone to bed he lay awake for several hours.

In the silent watches of the night, when he was alone with God, there came into his mind a flood of unaccustomed thoughts. An hour or two before, standing face to face with death, he had experienced a sensation similar to that which drowning men are said to feel—a kind of clarifying of the moral faculty, in which the veil of the flesh, with its obscuring passions and prejudices, is pushed aside for a moment, and all the acts of one's life stand out, in the clear light of truth, in their correct proportions and relations,—a state of mind in which one sees himself as God may be supposed to see him. In the reaction following his rescue, this feeling had given place for a time to far different emotions. But now, in the silence of midnight, something of this clearness of spirit returned to the sheriff. He saw that he had owed some duty to this son of his,—that neither law nor custom could destroy a responsibility inherent in the nature of mankind. He could not thus, in the eyes of God at least, shake off the consequences of his sin. Had he never sinned, this wayward spirit would never have come back from the vanished past to haunt him. As these thoughts came, his anger against the mulatto died away, and in its place there sprang up a great pity. The hand of parental authority might have restrained the passions he had seen burning in the prisoner's eyes when the desperate man spoke the words which had seemed to doom his father to death. The sheriff felt that he might have saved this fiery spirit from the slough of slavery; that he might have sent him to the free North, and given him there, or in some other land, an opportunity to turn to usefulness and honorable pursuits the talents that had run to crime, perhaps to madness; he might, still less, have given this son of his the poor simulacrum of liberty which men of his caste could possess in a slave-holding community; or least of all, but still something, he might have kept the boy on the plantation, where the burdens of slavery would have fallen lightly upon him.

The sheriff recalled his own youth. He had inherited an honored name to keep untarnished; he had had a future to make; the picture of a fair young bride had beckoned him on to happiness. The poor wretch now stretched upon a pallet of straw between the brick walls of the jail had had none of these things,—no name, no father, no mother—in the true meaning of motherhood,—and until the past few years no possible future, and then one vague and shadowy in its outline, and dependent for form and substance upon the slow solution of a problem in which there were many unknown quantities.

From what he might have done to what he might yet do

was an easy transition for the awakened conscience of the sheriff. It occurred to him, purely as a hypothesis, that he might permit his prisoner to escape; but his oath of office, his duty as sheriff, stood in the way of such a course, and the sheriff dismissed the idea from his mind. He could, however, investigate the circumstances of the murder, and move Heaven and earth to discover the real criminal, for he no longer doubted the prisoner's innocence; he could employ counsel for the accused, and perhaps influence public opinion in his favor. An acquittal once secured, some plan could be devised by which the sheriff might in some degree atone for his crime against this son of his—against society—against God.

When the sheriff had reached this conclusion he fell into an unquiet slumber, from which he awoke late the next morning.

He went over to the jail before breakfast and found the prisoner lying on his pallet, his face turned to the wall; he did not move when the sheriff rattled the door.

"Good-morning," said the latter, in a tone intended to waken the prisoner.

There was no response. The sheriff looked more keenly at the recumbent figure; there was an unnatural rigidity about its attitude.

He hastily unlocked the door and, entering the cell, bent over the prostrate form. There was no sound of breathing; he turned the body over—it was cold and stiff. The prisoner had torn the bandage from his wound and bled to death during the night. He had evidently been dead several hours.

Kate Chopin (February 8, 1851–August 22, 1904) was born in St. Louis, Missouri, to socially prominent parents. Her mother was of French-Creole descent and her father was an Irish immigrant. When she was growing up her great-grandmother, Mme. Victoria Verdon Charleville, lived in the O'Flaherty home and told Chopin tales of the earliest settlers of the Louisiana Territory and taught her French. At age nineteen, Kate O'Flaherty moved to New Orleans and married Oscar Chopin, a Creole. Later she moved with her husband to his family home in Cloutierville, Natchitoches Parish, near the Red River. A year after her husband's death (1883) from swamp fever, Chopin returned with her six children to St. Louis to live with her mother. In 1887, she wrote a poem, "If it might be" which was published January 10, 1888 in *America*, a progressive Chicago magazine. Her first published novel, *At Fault* (1890), and her published collections of short fiction, *Bayou Folk* (1894) and *A Night in Acadie* (1897), are set along the Cane River of Natchitoches Parish and reflect the culture, language, and customs of the Creole and "Canadians of that area." *The Awakening* (1899), a subject of scandal and censure during her lifetime, is now considered her masterpiece. According to Chopin's notes *The Awakening* earned $145 between 1899 and 1901. In the 1970s the rediscovery of *The Awakening* brought Chopin's works to international attention.

LA BELLE ZORAÏDE

by Kate Chopin

The summer night was hot and still; not a ripple of air swept over the *marais*. Yonder, across Bayou St. John, lights twinkled here and there in the darkness, and in the dark sky above a few stars were blinking. A lugger that had come out of the lake was moving with slow, lazy motion down the bayou. A man in the boat was singing a song.

The notes of the song came faintly to the ears of old Manna-Loulou, herself as black as the night, who had gone out upon the gallery to open the shutters wide.

Something in the refrain reminded the woman of an old, half-forgotten Creole romance, and she began to sing it low to herself while she threw the shutters open:—

> "Lisett' to kité la plaine,
>   Mo perdi bonhair à moué;
>   Ziés à moué semblé fontaine,
>   Dépi mo pa miré toué."

And then this old song, a lover's lament for the loss of his mistress, floating into her memory, brought with it the story she would tell to Madame, who lay in her sumptuous mahogany bed, waiting to be fanned and put to sleep to the sound of one of Manna-Loulou's stories. The old negress had already bathed her mistress's pretty white feet and kissed them lovingly, one, then the other. She had brushed her mistress's beautiful hair, that was as soft and shining as satin, and was the color of Madame's wedding-ring. Now, when she reëntered the room, she moved softly toward the bed, and seating herself there began gently to fan Madame Delisle.

Manna-Loulou was not always ready with her story, for Madame would hear none but those which were true. But to-night the story was all there in Manna-Loulou's head— the story of la belle Zoraïde—and she told it to her mistress in the soft Creole patois, whose music and charm no English words can convey.

"La belle Zoraïde had eyes that were so dusky, so beautiful, that any man who gazed too long into their depths was sure to lose his head, and even his heart sometimes. Her soft, smooth skin was the color of *café-au-lait*. As for her elegant manners, her *svelte* and graceful figure, they were the envy of half the ladies who visited her mistress, Madame Delarivière.

"No wonder Zoraïde was as charming and as dainty as the finest lady of la rue Royale: from a toddling thing she had been brought up at her mistress's side; her fingers had never done rougher work than sewing a fine muslin seam; and she even had her own little black servant to wait upon her.

Madame, who was her godmother as well as her mistress, would often say to her:—

" 'Remember, Zoraïde, when you are ready to marry, it must be in a way to do honor to your bringing up. It will be at the Cathedral. Your wedding gown, your *corbeille*, all will be of the best; I shall see to that myself. You know, M'sieur Ambroise is ready whenever you say the word; and his master is willing to do as much for him as I shall do for you. It is a union that will please me in every way.'

"M'sieur Ambroise was then the body servant of Doctor Langlé. La belle Zoraïde detested the little mulatto, with his shining whiskers like a white man's, and his small eyes, that were cruel and false as a snake's. She would cast down her own mischievous eyes, and say:—

" 'Ah, nénaine, I am so happy, so contented here at your side just as I am. I don't want to marry now; next year, perhaps, or the next.' And Madame would smile indulgently and remind Zoraïde that a woman's charms are not everlasting.

"But the truth of the matter was, Zoraïde had seen le beau Mézor dance the Bamboula in Congo Square. That was a sight to hold one rooted to the ground. Mézor was as straight as a cypress-tree and as proud looking as a king. His body, bare to the waist, was like a column of ebony and it glistened like oil.

"Poor Zoraïde's heart grew sick in her bosom with love for le beau Mézor from the moment she saw the fierce gleam of his eye, lighted by the inspiring strains of the Bamboula, and beheld the stately movements of his splendid body swaying and quivering through the figures of the dance.

"But when she knew him later, and he came near her to speak with her, all the fierceness was gone out of his eyes, and she saw only kindness in them and heard only gentleness in his voice; for love had taken possession of him also, and Zoraïde was more distracted than ever. When Mézor was not dancing Bamboula in Congo Square, he was hoeing sugar-cane, barefooted and half-naked, in his master's field outside of the city. Doctor Langlé age was his master as well as M'sieur Ambroise's.

"One day, when Zoraïde kneeled before her mistress, drawing on Madame's silken stockings, that were of the finest, she said:

" 'Nénaine, you have spoken to me often of marrying. Now, at last, I have chosen a husband, but it is not M'sieur Ambroise; it is le beau Mézor that I want and no other.' And Zoraïde hid her face in her hands when she had said that, for she guessed, rightly enough, that her mistress would be very angry. And, indeed, Madame Delarivière was at first speechless with rage. When she finally spoke it was only to gasp out, exasperated:—

" 'That negro! that negro! Bon Dieu Seigneur, but this is too much!'

" 'Am I white, nénaine?' pleaded Zoraïde.

" 'You white! *Malheureuse!* You deserve to have the lash laid upon you like any other slave; you have proven yourself no better than the worst.'

" 'I am not white,' persisted Zoraïde, respectfully and gently. 'Doctor Langlé gives me his slave to marry, but he would not give me his son. Then, since I am not white, let me have from out of my own race the one whom my heart has chosen.'

"However, you may well believe that Madame would not hear to that. Zoraïde was forbidden to speak to Mézor, and Mézor was cautioned against seeing Zoraïde again. But you know how the negroes are, Ma'zélle Titite," added Manna-Loulou, smiling a little sadly. "There is no mistress, no master, no king nor priest who can hinder them from loving when they will. And these two found ways and means.

"When months had passed by, Zoraïde, who had grown unlike herself,—sober and preoccupied,—said again to her mistress:—

" 'Nénaine, you would not let me have Mézor for my husband; but I have disobeyed you, I have sinned. Kill me if you wish, Nénaine: forgive me if you will; but when I heard le beau Mézor say to me, "Zoraïde, mo l'aime toi," I could have died, but I could not have helped loving him.'

"This time Madame Delarivière was so actually pained, so wounded at hearing Zoraïde's confession, that there was no place left in her heart for anger. She could utter only confused reproaches. But she was a woman of action rather than of words, and she acted promptly. Her first step was to induce Doctor Langlé to sell Mézor. Doctor Langlé, who was a widower, had long wanted to marry Madame Delarivière, and he would willingly have walked on all fours at noon through the Place d'Armes if she wanted him to. Naturally he lost no time in disposing of le beau Mézor, who was sold away into Georgia, or the Carolinas, or one of those distant countries far away, where he would no longer hear his Creole tongue spoken, nor dance Calinda, nor hold la belle Zoraïde in his arms.

"The poor thing was heartbroken when Mézor was sent away from her, but she took comfort and hope in the thought of her baby that she would soon be able to clasp to her breast.

"La belle Zoraïde's sorrows had now begun in earnest. Not only sorrows but sufferings, and with the anguish of maternity came the shadow of death. But there is no agony that a mother will not forget when she holds her first-born to her heart, and presses her lips upon the baby flesh that is her own, yet far more precious than her own.

"So, instinctively, when Zoraïde came out of the awful shadow she gazed questioningly about her and felt with her trembling hands upon either side of her. 'Où li, mo piti a moin? (Where is my little one?)' she asked imploringly. Madame who was there and the nurse who was there both told her in turn, 'To piti à toi, li mouri' ('Your little one is dead'), which was a wicked falsehood that must have caused the angels in heaven to weep. For the baby was living and well and strong. It had at once been removed from its mother's side, to be sent away to Madame's plantation, far up the coast. Zoraïde could only moan in reply, 'Li, mouri, li mouri,' and she turned her face to the wall.

"Madame had hoped, in thus depriving Zoraïde of her child, to have her young waiting-maid again at her side free, happy, and beautiful as of old. But there was a more powerful will than Madame's at work—the will of the good God, who had already designed that Zoraïde should grieve with a sorrow that was never more to be lifted in this world. La belle Zoraïde was no more. In her stead was a sad-eyed woman who mourned night and day for her baby. 'Li mouri, li mouri,' she would sigh over and over again to those about her, and to herself when others grew weary of her complaint.

"Yet, in spite of all, M'sieur Ambroise was still in the notion to marry her. A sad wife or a merry one was all the same to him so long as that wife was Zoraïde. And she seemed to consent, or rather submit, to the approaching marriage as though nothing mattered any longer in this world.

"One day a black servant entered a little noisily the room in which Zoraïde sat sewing. With a look of strange and vacuous happiness upon her face, Zoraïde arose hastily. 'Hush, hush,' she whispered, lifting a warning finger, 'my little one is asleep; you must not awaken her.'

"Upon the bed was a senseless bundle of rags shaped like an infant in swaddling clothes. Over this dummy the woman had drawn the mosquito bar, and she was sitting contentedly beside it. In short, from that day Zoraïde was demented. Night nor day did she lose sight of the doll that lay in her bed or in her arms.

"And now was Madame stung with sorrow and remorse at seeing this terrible affliction that had befallen her dear Zoraïde. Consulting with Doctor Langlé, they decided to bring back to the mother the real baby of flesh and blood that was now toddling about, and kicking its heels in the dust yonder upon the plantation.

"It was Madame herself who led the pretty, tiny little "griffe" girl to her mother. Zoraïde was sitting upon a stone bench in the courtyard, listening to the soft splashing of the fountain, and watching the fitful shadows of the palm leaves upon the broad, white flagging.

" 'Here,' said Madame, approaching, 'here, my poor dear Zoraïde, is your own little child. Keep her; she is yours. No one will ever take her from you again.'

"Zoraïde looked with sullen suspicion upon her mistress and the child before her. Reaching out a hand she thrust the little one mistrustfully away from her. With the other hand she clasped the rag bundle fiercely to her breast; for she suspected a plot to deprive her of it.

"Nor could she ever be induced to let her own child approach her; and finally the little one was sent back to the plantation, where she was never to know the love of mother or father.

"And now this is the end of Zoraïde's story. She was never known again as la belle Zoraïde, but ever after as Zoraïde la folle, whom no one ever wanted to marry— not even M'sieur Ambroise. She lived to be an old woman, whom some people pitied and others laughed at—always clasping her bundle of rags—her 'piti.'

"Are you asleep, Ma'zélle Titite?"

"No, I am not asleep; I was thinking. Ah, the poor little one, Man Loulou, the poor little one! better had she died!"

But this is the way Madame Delisle and Manna-Loulou really talked to each other:—

"Vou pré droumi, Ma'zélle Titite?"

"Non, pa pré droumi; mo yapré zongler. Ah, la pauv' piti, Man Loulou. La pauv' piti! Mieux li mouri!"

Alice Dunbar-Nelson (July 19,1875–September 18, 1935) was born Alice Ruth Moore in New Orleans and educated at Straight College (now Dillard University). Her first book, *Violets and Other Tales* (1895), was published under her birth name, Alice Ruth Moore. It is a collection of sketches, essays, stories, and poems. Following her marriage to Paul Laurence Dunbar in 1898, she published her second book, *The Goodness of St. Rocque and Other Stories* (1899) under the name Alice Dunbar. It was the first collection of short stories to be published by a black woman.

After her divorce from Dunbar, she taught and administered at Howard High School in Wilmington, Delaware, from 1902 to 1920. She edited and published *Masterpieces of Negro Eloquence: The Best Speeches Delivered by the Negro from the Days of Slavery to the Present Time* (1914). In 1916 she married journalist Robert J. Nelson and together they edited and published the *Wilmington Advocate*, a progressive newspaper, from 1920 to 1922. *The Dunbar Speaker and Entertainer*, a collection of poems, speeches, and stories selected from the writing of both Dunbar-Nelson and Paul Laurence Dunbar, was published in 1920.

In the last years of her life in addition to being a writer and educator Dunbar-Nelson was a suffragist, parole and probation officer, politician, lecturer, and civic worker. In 1984 *Give Us Each Day: The Diary of Alice Dunbar-Nelson* was edited by Gloria T. Hull. The diary, covering 1921 and 1926–1931, was the second book-length diary by an African-American woman to be published.

TONY'S WIFE

by Alice Dunbar-Nelson

"Gimme fi' cents worth o'candy, please." It was the little Jew girl who spoke, and Tony's wife roused herself from her knitting to rise and count out the multi-hued candy which should go in exchange for the dingy nickel grasped in warm, damp fingers. Three long sticks, carefully wrapped in crispest brown paper, and a half dozen or more of pink candy fish for lagniappe, and the little Jew girl sped away in blissful contentment. Tony's wife resumed her knitting with a stifled sigh until the next customer should come.

A low growl caused her to look up apprehensively. Tony himself stood beetle-browned and huge in the small doorway.

"Get up from there," he muttered, "and open two dozen oysters right away; the Eliots want 'em." His English was unaccented. It was long since he had seen Italy.

She moved meekly behind the counter, and began work on the thick shells. Tony stretched his long neck up the street.

"Mr. Tony, mama wants some charcoal." The very small voice at his feet must have pleased him, for his black brows relaxed into a smile, and he poked the little one's chin with a hard, dirty finger, as he emptied the ridiculously small bucket of charcoal into the child's bucket, and gave a banana for lagniappe.

The crackling of shells went on behind, and a stifled sob arose as a bit of sharp edge cut into the thin, worn fingers that clasped the knife.

"Hurry up there, will you?" growled the black brows; "the Eliots are sending for the oysters."

She deftly strained and counted them, and, after wiping

her fingers, resumed her seat, and took up the endless crochet work, with her usual stifled sigh.

Tony and his wife had always been in this same little queer old shop on Prytania Street, at least to the memory of the oldest inhabitant in the neighbourhood. When or how they came, or how they stayed, no one knew; it was enough that they were there, like a sort of ancestral fixture to the street. The neighbourhood was fine enough to look down upon these two tumble-down shops at the corner, kept by Tony and Mrs. Murphy, the grocer. It was a semi-fashionable locality, far up-town, away from the old-time French quarter. It was the sort of neighbourhood where millionaires live before their fortunes are made and fashionable, high-priced private schools flourish, where the small cottages are occupied by aspiring school-teachers and choir-singers. Such was this locality, and you must admit that it was indeed a condescension to tolerate Tony and Mrs. Murphy.

He was a great, black-bearded, hoarse-voiced, six-foot specimen of Italian humanity, who looked in his little shop and on the prosaic pavement of Prytania Street somewhat as Hercules might seem in a modern drawing-room. You instinctively thought of wild mountain-passes, and the gleaming dirks of bandit contadini in looking at him. What his last name was, no one knew. Someone had maintained once that he had been christened Antonio Malatesta, but that was unauthentic, and as little to be believed as that other wild theory that her name was Mary.

She was meek, pale, little, ugly, and German. Altogether part of his arms and legs would have very decently made another larger than she. Her hair was pale and drawn in sleek, thin tightness away from a pinched, pitiful face, whose dull cold eyes hurt you, because you knew they were trying to mirror sorrow, and could not because of their expressionless quality. No matter what the weather or what her other toilet, she always wore a thin little shawl of dingy brick-dust hue about her shoulders. No matter what the occasion or what the day, she always carried her knitting with her, and seldom ceased the incessant twist, twist of the shining steel among the white cotton meshes. She might put down the needles and lace into the spool-box long enough to open oysters, or wrap up fruit and candy, or count out wood and coal into infinitesimal portions, or do her housework; but the knitting was snatched with avidity at the first spare moment, and the worn, white, blue-marked fingers, half enclosed in kid-glove stalls for protection, would writhe and twist in and out again. Little girls just learning to crochet borrowed their patterns from Tony's wife, and it was considered quite a mark of advancement to have her inspect a bit of lace done by eager, chubby fingers. The ladies in larger houses, whose husbands would be millionaires some day, bought her lace, and gave it to their servants for Christmas presents.

As for Tony, when she was slow in opening his oysters or in cooking his red beans and spaghetti, he roared at her, and prefixed picturesque adjectives to her lace, which made her hide it under her apron with a fearsome look in her dull eyes.

He hated her in a lusty, roaring fashion, as a healthy beefy boy hates a sick cat and torments it to madness. When she displeased him, he beat her, and knocked her frail form on the floor. The children could tell when this had happened. Her eyes would be red, and there would be blue marks on her face and neck. "Poor Mrs. Tony," they would say, and nestle close to her. Tony did not roar at her for petting them, perhaps, because they spent money on the multi-hued candy in glass jars on the shelves.

Her mother appeared upon the scene once, and stayed a short time; but Tony got drunk one day and beat her because she ate too much, and she disappeared soon after. Whence she came and where she departed, no one could tell, not even Mrs. Murphy, the Pauline Pry and Gazette of the block.

Tony had gout, and suffered for many days in roaring helplessness, the while his foot, bound and swathed in many folds of red flannel, lay on the chair before him. In proportion as his gout increased and he bawled from pure physical discomfort, she became light-hearted, and moved about the shop with real, brisk cheeriness. He could not hit her then without such pain that after one or two trials he gave up in disgust.

So the dull years had passed, and life had gone on pretty much the same for Tony and the German wife and the shop. The children came on Sunday evenings to buy the stick candy, and on week-days for coal and wood. The servants came to buy oysters for the larger houses, and to gossip over the counter about their employers. The little dry woman knitted, and the big man moved lazily in and out in his red flannel shirt, exchanged politics with the tailor next door through the window, or lounged into Mrs. Murphy's bar and drank fiercely. Some of the children grew up and moved away, and other little girls came to buy candy and eat pink lagniappe fishes, and the shop still thrived.

One day Tony was ill, more than the mummied foot of gout, or the wheeze of asthma; he must keep his bed and send for the doctor.

She clutched his arm when he came, and pulled him into the tiny room.

"Is it——is it anything much, doctor?" she gasped.

Æsculapius shook his head as wisely as the occasion would permit. She followed him out of the room into the shop.

"Do you——will he get well, doctor?"

Æsculapius buttoned up his frock coat, smoothed his shining hat, cleared his throat, then replied oracularly,

"Madam, he is completely burned out inside. Empty as a shell, madam, empty as a shell. He cannot live, for he has nothing to live on."

As the cobblestones rattled under the doctor's equipage rolling leisurely up Prytania Street, Tony's wife sat in her chair and laughed,—laughed with a hearty joyousness that lifted the film from the dull eyes and disclosed a sparkle beneath.

The drear days went by, and Tony lay like a veritable Samson shorn of his strength, for his voice was sunken to a hoarse, sibilant whisper, and his black eyes gazed fiercely from the shock of hair and beard about a white face. Life went on pretty much as before in the shop; the children paused to ask how Mr. Tony was, and even hushed the jingles on their bell hoops as they passed the door. Red-headed Jimmie, Mrs. Murphy's nephew, did the hard jobs, such as splitting wood and lifting coal from the bin; and in the intervals between tending the fallen giant and waiting on the customers, Tony's wife sat in her accustomed chair, knitting fiercely, with an inscrutable smile about her purple compressed mouth.

Then John came, introducing himself, serpent-wise, into the Eden of her bosom.

John was Tony's brother, huge and bluff too, but fair and blond, with the beauty of Northern Italy. With the same lack of race pride which Tony had displayed in selecting his

German spouse, John had taken unto himself Betty, a daughter of Erin, aggressive, powerful, and cross-eyed. He turned up now, having heard of this illness, and assumed an air of remarkable authority at once.

A hunted look stole into the dull eyes, and after John had departed with blustering directions as to Tony's welfare, she crept to his bedside timidly.

"Tony," she said,—"Tony, you are very sick."

An inarticulate growl was the only response.

"Tony, you ought to see the priest; you mustn't go any longer without taking the sacrament."

The growl deepened into words.

"Don't want any priest; you're always after some snivelling old woman's fuss. You and Mrs. Murphy go on with your church; it won't make *you* any better."

She shivered under this parting shot, and crept back into the shop. Still the priest came the next day.

She followed him in to the bedside and knelt timidly.

"Tony," she whispered, "here's Father Leblanc."

Tony was too languid to curse out loud; he only expressed his hate in a toss of the black beard and shaggy mane.

"Tony," she said nervously, "won't you do it now? It won't take long, and it will be better for you when you go——Oh, Tony, don't——don't laugh. Please, Tony, here's the priest."

But the Titan roared aloud: "No; get out. Think I'm a-going to give you a chance to grab my money now? Let me die and go to hell in peace."

Father Leblanc knelt meekly and prayed, and the woman's weak pleadings continued,——

"Tony, I've been true and good and faithful to you. Don't die and leave me no better than before. Tony, I do want to be a good woman once, a real-for-true married woman. Tony, here's the priest; say yes." And she wrung her ringless hands.

"You want my money," said Tony, slowly, "and you sha'n't have it, not a cent; John shall have it."

Father Leblanc shrank away like a fading spectre. He came next day and next day, only to see re-enacted the same piteous scene,—the woman pleading to be made a wife ere death hushed Tony's blasphemies, the man chuckling in pain-racked glee at the prospect of her bereaved misery. Not all the prayers of Father Leblanc nor the wailings of Mrs. Murphy could alter the determination of the will beneath the shock of hair; he gloated in his physical weakness at the tenacious grasp on his mentality.

"Tony," she wailed on the last day, her voice rising to a shriek in its eagerness, "tell them I'm your wife; it'll be the same. Only say it, Tony, before you die!"

He raised his head, and turned stiff eyes and gibbering mouth on her; then, with one chill finger pointing at John, fell back dully and heavily.

They buried him with many honours by the Society of Italia's Sons. John took possession of the shop when they returned home, and found the money hidden in the chimney corner.

As for Tony's wife, since she was not his wife after all, they sent her forth in the world penniless, her worn fingers clutching her bundle of clothes in nervous agitation, as though they regretted the time lost from knitting.

Sarah Barnwell Elliott (November 29, 1848–August 30, 1928) was born in Montpelier, Georgia, and lived in Savannah until December, 1864, when she left on the last train to depart Savannah before the town was seized by Sherman's troops. For the next six years she was without a permanent home. In 1871 she moved to Sewanee, Tennessee, to the newly opened University of the South, which her father had helped establish. Except for a year at John Hopkins University in 1886, Elliott's education was completed at home. At the age of twelve she had begun to write stories and once settled in Sewanee she resumed her writing. *The Felmeres*, her first novel, was published in 1879, followed by a series of sketches and short travel pieces. It was on a trip to Europe in 1886 that she met the writer Constance Fenimore Woolson who encouraged her to write from the remembrances of her childhood. This counsel, combined with the new techniques of Realism, resulted in a style of writing that did not glamorize the South's past.

Aside from six years in New York City (1896–1902) the remainder of Elliott's life was spent in Sewanee, Tennessee. From 1887 onward her writing was in demand. She published six more novels, a biography of Sam Houston, more than thirty short stories, a play, essays, reviews, and poems. In New York she began activities for the suffrage movement and women's rights. Returning to Tennessee she assumed a position of leadership and addressed the legislature, lectured nationally, and lobbied on behalf of the Nineteenth Amendment. It should be noted that Tennessee was the only southern state to ratify the amendment.

During her lifetime Elliott published one collection of short stories, *An Incident and Other Happenings* (1899). Because of Elliott's realistic writing about the South many of her stories were not published during her lifetime. "The Heart of It" is one such story. In 1981 twenty-two stories, five for the first time, were published in *Some Data and Other Stories of Southern Life.*

THE HEART OF IT

by Sarah Barnwell Elliott

It was a dark night and raining, and the level, sandy road could be distinguished only because of the greater dark of the wilderness on either side. A broad, white road it was, that led by swamp, and river, and pine barren, and now was greatly under water, not only because of rain, but because of a spring freshet that had swelled the great river that was an arm of the sea. Along this road a large blur was moving, with creakings and splashings; gradually emerging as a cart with a canvas cover and one horse, going at a leisurely gait. It was heavy traveling and slow, and reaching a little upward incline, the horse stopped.

"Mos' dead, is you Job?" said the man sitting just under the cover; "an' yo' travelin' ain't half done."

"Are we there?" a woman's voice asked from the recesses of the cart.

"In jest about five yards of it."

"You mean . . ."

"The railroad track; my horse is restin' a min'it; it ain't rainin' now, if you're sure goin' to git out."

"Yes, thank you, I must get this next train that passes."

"Well, if you git out here, you've got fo' miles to walk down the track; but I kin drive you three miles fu'ther on to Mr. Percy Lasston's place an' you might hire a horse there an' drive down to the nex' station."

"No, thank you, I'll get out here and walk."

"Fo' miles on the crossties."

"Yes."

"An' you ain't skeered?"

"No."

"Well, I'm right sorry, but I can't drive down the crossties."

"No, and I thank you for bringing me so far. You mentioned a name just now."

"Mr. Percy Lasston."

"Do you know the people about here?"

"No, I don't. I'm only a peddler sellin' to the niggers; but I knows the names of the planters. I've stopped tradin' round here though, its too po'. I never stops to sell nothin' this side o' Jonesborough, an' that's nigh to thirty miles fu'ther on; an' frum there I goes on to Greensborough. This is Friday night, an' I muss git to Jonesborough by Sat'day night, for then the man's gits paid off an' comes to town, an' that's my chance."

"Do you expect to travel all night?"

"I do; an' I hate to leave a white woman in the road 'leven o'clock of a rainy night; I certainly do."

"It doesn't matter. No, you need not bother to help me out. Good-bye."

"Good-bye, an' good luck to you, Lady; you're travelin' back to yo' own people, you say? They ought to be mightly proud you'd take sicher journey, an' I hopes you gits there safe; good-bye. You ain't skeered?"

"No, good-bye," and the woman stood still in the mist and the darkness, watching the wagon toil up the incline to the railway.

Not long, then the wagon became a blur, then the sounds faded. Still she stood there poised attentive as if one more "Git up" of the kindly voice; one more grind of wheel, or splash of hoof might reach her; waited in the silence where, gradually, there intruded a soft sound as of whispering rain, or sweeping wings; a sound that as she listened seemed to grow on her awakening senses into a tremulous terror! She caught the stem of a young tree; what was coming? People with panting dogs? A train with glaring lights that would reveal her?

The river! Only the old river; brimful, rushing, swirling, deep and strong; the river that went by home! The young tree swayed a little for she sobbed against it. Dogs, people, would they search for her? Would they bring the dogs? To the pond, to the swamp, to the river? The dogs could not tell, no, at the junction of the three ways the wagon had come. How kind the man had been, a stranger, and white, how fortunate.

Fortunate? The pond, the swamp, the river would have

been better. Search for her? Never! As that morning—was it only that morning—? In the awful light that had searched her heart, her life; that had seemed to scorch her physical eyeballs as she had read the letter thrust under her door, so now, she went over slowly, but with the bitterness of death, all the things of her life that had hurt her. From her orphaned babyhood there had been a lack of love, a lack that Alan partly filled, and yet, she had never told him of the lack because he was her Aunt Alicia's only child. But Percy—the leaves of the young tree shivered as in a sudden gust of wind.

That was all past, and now—now it was only a few steps to the railway; here it was; now, four miles on the crossties to the station. The night train passed at two o'clock. The man had said it was eleven now; yes, she had time. Once at the station, she would look up a schedule and decide where she would go. Fifteen dollars she would spend on traveling; this would leave her ten dollars for expenses until she found work. Meanwhile, she would slip off her frock skirt and fold it under her coat where, for the sake of dryness, her thick veil now was. Just before she reached the station, she would put them on. The thick veil would hide her face. Besides, the man at the station would be too sleepy to observe much.

Tired—tired, too tired! The river was just beyond that bank? They'd find her body beaten up against one of the rice dams; or swept aside, entangled in brush and logs; and they would realize. But it did not matter what they realized. They had done what they thought was their duty by her. Better, less cruel, it seemed, to have drowned her as they did the worthless puppies, far better.

Yes, she had told Percy. Percy was her third cousin; lived on his own plantation, and was the head of the family. How he laughed at that; land-poor, tax-ridden, poverty-stricken. And talk of 'The Head of the Family'! But she had been so proud of it; it was fine, she declared, and it was. She—she was still a Lasston! She must go on; must think of something else.

Yes, Percy was older than Alan, and Alan older than she, and on the fateful day when she had been driven to the conclusion that her aunt did not love her—a day in February when the fires were still necessary—those great fires, how sweet they smelled—her despair had demanded outlet and she had told Percy; had poured out all the longings of her life, all the pain of loneliness that had been with her day and night, had told it all clinging to his arm. And he?

The rushing river was nearer now! The friendly river that would lodge her somewhere near the old place. And, yes, she had not hauled her boat up! She stopped a moment, they might think she'd gone out in the boat. Why had she not thought of that? Out on that wild, sweeping tide in her little boat; out with the wind and the rain beating in her face! And she could have fought for her life then; have had the battle that would have dulled her fear of death, and with all her fighting, not have saved her life.

Again she sobbed a little, a tearless sob with a catch in it, and plodded on in the darkness. She knew she would never have entered the boat. She had courage only to endure; endure life a little longer, a little longer until her vision cleared. Had she not endured—endured herself—her life, since—since when? How long was it? The morning before this night, the morning which she could only remember in fragments as she moved along the dark railway track.

She had been about to do something that morning. What was it? She was on her way out the door of the big old house which had always been home to her and Aunt Alicia—taking breakfast to old George. It was old George who had kept the place running after Aunt Alicia was left a widow, until Alan had become old enough to begin to look after things. All this had been her knowledge for all her life. Old George, good old George, the special care of the family—all who were left, her Aunt Alicia, Alan and—not herself now—no. And old Mawm Sue, George's daughter, she was good too, was cook and general servant at the big house, and his great-grand daughter, little Juno, black little Juno, down at the cabin to wait on the old man. All her life they had been about her, and it was this morning she had gone down carrying George's breakfast in a basket, and with it a pitcher of hot coffee. This morning!

She must not hasten; she could not run away, not escape; this thing, no, it would be with her forever—forever. And it was too dark to run; she would fall, would injure herself, perhaps be unable to get even to the river! She must walk quietly, steadily.

The woolly little dog, dirty, but with a ribbon about its neck, had rushed out at her, had stopped her, not its small bark, but the surprise of such an anomaly. Instantly, old

George had stood in the door, blocking the entrance. She could hear his—"Mawnin, Li'l Missy Hagar, mawnin' ma'm," and his call—"Juno, come teck dese t'ings! Come quick, gal!" And Juno had dodged under his arm that to steady him, was against the door frame, and had taken the basket and pitcher.

"But the dog," she had insisted. If she had not; if she had gone away, her curiosity unsatisfied, would it all have happened?

He said, "Lou's dawg, Li'l Missy Hagar; Lou come las' night." Then behind the old man, lolling in a rocking chair, she saw a figure in white. Old George had been careful to block the door, but she, she had moved forward. Her own fault. The old man had made way for her, but the figure in white had not moved from the rocking chair. Instead, she had said, "How do you do, Miss Lasston?"

Her face burned now, remembering. She had paused and had stood looking down on the girl who as a child had been a runner of messages up at the big house; a clever, light-footed little creature whom her Aunt Alicia had sent to a mission school in the city. The little thing had cried, had begged not to go, and all her own child sympathy had gone out to the black child. And that had been ten years ago; Lou must be twenty now.

Yes, even now her face burned as she remembered the interview; but then, she had said quietly, "How are you, Lou," How careful the girl's pronunciation had been, how emphasized the "Grandpar-par", how slowly and carelessly she had rocked, old George's great-granddaughter, Lou, yes, all these things she must remember, and the old man leaning on his stick with his old wrinkled face so full of pain. But he was not well, he said, and Lou explained, "I told him all my plans, Miss Lasston, not wise at night; but I wished him to share my joy. I am engaged to be married, Miss Lasston, to a gentleman at the school, one of the teachers." Then old George's sharp interpolation; "A yaller nigger, Miss Hagar!"

"And Grandpar-par," Lou had gone on smoothly; "and Aunt Susan, and Juno must come to live with me. My family must not be servants any longer." But Old George would have none of it. His dim eyes flashed.

"No, ma'm, Miss Hagar!" he had cried quite loud, striking his stick on the floor; "no, ma'm en ef Missis'll lemme stay, I ent gwine; no, ma'm; en Sue ent gwine, en Juno ent gwine nurrer, no, ma'm! En we is berry mad, Miss Hagar; en we ent to say been want you fuh see Lou, no, ma'm!" They had been wise, these old people; but she had pushed in.

Then Lou had talked of the unholy slavery to which her race had been subjected. And she had turned on the Negro girl. "Slavery raised your race," she had said sharply; "you came to this country, savages!" She seemed to hear her own voice now as she announced that; it was true; and once more she sobbed a little as she plodded on in the darkness. Then Lou's retort—"You mean that we are an inferior race," she cried; "made lower than the whites!" And old George's—"Cose, gal!" and he raised his stick as if to strike the girl. Quickly she had saved Lou from the stick, and pushing on, ever pushing on, she had asked, "What do you think, Lou?"

"That we are a little backward," had come glibly, then her voice sharpening; "it is a great tragedy; an awful tragedy! Yes, and you don't care! But there is an outlet, yes, an outlet to this terrible tragedy, yes, we cross over to you whites!" How the words seemed to echo about her out here in the darkness, and the cry, "We cross over and you don't know it, ah ha!"

It had been as a physical blow and she had caught her breath while all the teachings of her life as to the awfulness of amalgamation; the hopelessness of the hybrid; the horrors of the "Return to Race" had swept over her. Her aunt had taught her all this—how carefully it had been done—it had sickened her at the time, and the assertion of the Negro girl was as a sword trust!

"Impossible!" she had faltered, and at last had turned toward the open door, while through the horrid confusion old George had cried, "En who wants ter be er yaller-white nigger! Ole Mawsa always drown dem half-breed puppy." And she, weakly, "You could never be pure white, Lou, never!"

"But if nobody knows the black blood is in us?"

"Somebody always knows!" She had been taught that too.

"But I know better!" Lou had cried; "wait! Last night I found that my own family had crossed over! That I have white cousins; as white as you! Wait!" and she had run out of the room. Then old George had wailed, the tears running down his face. "Oh, Miss Hagar, Miss Hagar! Please ma'm scuze Lou? Please ma'm? Dee school is done meck she foolish, ma'm? She ent hab no manners, ma'm; en dat letter what she is gittin', Miss Hagar, she done git out she Mah trunk w'at is lef' yer w'en she Mah daid, yes, ma'm; en I ent know say she Mah is keep dat letter, no, ma'm, I ent know it. Dat letter hot my feelin's w'en I fust git it, Miss Hagar, en it hots my feelin's now, ma'm; hots my feelin's des dee same dis berry min'it. Oh, Lawd!"

It was almost a cry as Lou had rushed in. "Read that!" she ordered. Race instinct, race experience, all had then risen up within her, all were with her now as she remembered, even now! And would she ever forget the grime and dirt of the letter, the worn age of it! Written in the thirties, and to old George from his aunt, telling him that after she had gone North, her Negro husband had left her to return South, and that then she had married a 'very white man', so she had expressed it; a German carpenter; that George's first cousin, her daughter by this German, had also married a white man and had gone west, where she was considered a white woman, and her name was 'Mrs. Henry Smithers'. That her advice to George was to run away from slavery and to do as she had done, so as to give his children a better place in life; and the letter was signed "Lualamba Siegers." And during the reading old George had sat with covered eyes, but Lou's eyes had watched her as she read. She had paused a second before looking up, then all that she could find to say was, "What a curious name."

"Her African name!" Lou cried.

Then at last she had stepped out of the open door which she had better never have entered, and in a maze of confusion had returned to the house, to her sewing with her aunt in the study. And for once she had felt that she must talk, must say all that was in her to say as to what she had been through, and her aunt had listened, quiet, unanswering, until she reached the letter, then, without one sign of interest she had said, "I have read the letter." And then had explained the story, how Lualamba and her brother, old George's father, had been bought by the Lasstons out of pity for their condition, as they seemed of a better tribe. "There was a great difference in the tribes," her aunt had added. How strange that seemed. Superior tribe. Lualamba had married a Negro! How foolish to shut her eyes. Of course a Negro, and on the Howard plantation. Then

Lualamba had been sold to the Howards, that was the custom, so that she would not be separated from her husband. Then old Mr. Howard dying, Mrs. Howard, having no children, and being a Northern woman, had sold to Mr. Howard's nephew, everything except Lualamba and her husband; she had taken them with her to the North. "When the letter came," her aunt had finished, "old George could not read it, and brought it to my mother. At her death I found it, read it to see what I should do with it. I returned it to George. He would not let me read it to him this second time; said it was a wicked, sinful letter."

And she had cried—"It is, Aunt Alicia, it is!" "Yes," her aunt had answered in a toneless voice. "And what good does it do them to 'Cross Over,' " she had pushed on. "It is forever in the blood; they are always Negro, always, forever!" "Forever," her aunt had agreed. "I'd kill myself," she had cried! There had been a second's pause, and then, "Perhaps," was all the answer, but in the voice there had been a strange tone and her aunt had added, "But the Negroes would not feel it as you do; they have not been trained—" and she had interrupted sharply—"They have not my blood! My blood that goes back and back!"

"Nor your prejudices," came the quiet reply.

"Race instinct!" her aunt had cried. "Prejudices," was repeated.

"The world calls it prejudice; and the Negro does not mind," her aunt had gone on; "and ambitious, they do not tell their secret, and many, many people do not know the marks," then she had added slowly—"all the marks."

"Do you know them?" and now she had leaned forward, and—"tell me?" she had whispered, had slipped from off her low chair to her knees close beside her aunt. Then like a physical blow came a low, fierce "No!" and a quick movement away from her as if she were a repulsive thing—"the subject is abhorrent to me! Hush!"

She felt the hot tears in her eyes, tears for the poor girl who was herself, kneeling there. She had got up slowly, had tried to go on with her sewing. Her heart had seemed wrung, somehow; she longed that her aunt should talk to her of this dreadful question; should say something, something pitiful for the poor Negroes. Never until that moment had she thought of them as having any feeling on the subject of being black. That they were black and were servants, had seemed to her a foregone conclusion. But that they had this hopeless desire—wicked, horrible desire, she had called it—to be white, to mingle their blood with the blood of the white race, was too appalling, it seemed almost to suffocate her! Poor things, poor things! They could not escape their fate; they were blacks just as birds were birds. "Cross Over!" Unendurable! Better raise themselves as a black race, as a black nation, so she had thought; had wondered why some leader did not rise to tell them this; to preach a hegira; to take them quickly back to their own country, such a rich country, before the white nations took it all; rouse their self-respect, their ambition as blacks! "Poor things, poor things!" and in her absorption she had said this last aloud, and started, looking up, "I meant the Negroes, Aunt Alicia," she had explained; "the poor things who long to be white and cannot. I wonder if they know about the 'Return to Race'," Then she had caught sight of the clock. "Already eleven," she said.

She stopped in her walk. Twelve hours ago! Twelve years— twelve centuries! All time had swept over her, had blighted her! What remained? She must not think, no, just walk. Her life lay all before her in which to think; now she must walk, step from crosstie to crosstie until she reached the station.

Twelve hours ago when her aunt had said, "You cannot go to walk, the dogs are out with Alan." Then she had got her hat and a small pistol that Percy had given her; she did not know it was an expensive one; "Just down the Avenue," she had explained.

"How could Percy afford it?" was demanded; and—"Is he in the habit of giving you things?" And the look! One moment it held her, then, "You may go." And she had gone.

That look burned and seared her still! Down the avenue she had sped, under the live oaks, that draped in the long gray moss did what was possible to keep out the brilliant sunlight. On either side, beyond the avenue, had stretched the level pine woods, and wherever there was a hillock or any support for a vine, there grew the yellow jessamine, filling the air with an ineffable sweetness. She could see it all, this dear home of all her life, could smell the jessamine; out here in the darkness as she walked, the picture seemed to shine about her, and yonder, at the end; there, by the big gate—Percy!

She had a right to dream—to remember? How fair and tall he was, how blue his eyes with ever a laugh in them. How strong the clasp of his hand, how rich his voice.

"And what are you running from?" he had demanded. But she had not told.

The haste had given her a color, it made her beautiful, he said, quite gave him "indigestion of the heart!" And she was so "Fizzy, always driving the cork out; not at all a Lasston; a changeling, with red-black eyes." His "Blossom" for whose love he was "hungry and thirsty."

And she—"I give you all! My life, my soul!"

"Hagar!" was all he said; her name that she hated, that she had not understood; why—why name her Hagar?

Then, "We must tell Aunt Alicia," she had declared; "She murdered me with a look!"

"And so you ran—of course we'll tell; I've always wanted to tell, but you, little coward, would not. But now I've sold the pine lands, and we can be married at once."

For a little moment she had looked within the gates of Paradise, at least she had done that; then again fear had cowed her. "But that look!" she had whispered; "that look about the pistol; I felt burned up! Now that you love me perhaps she will love me." And to his assertions she had answered, "Never, and yet she adored my father; he was 'The Head of the Family' and if I had been a boy—"

She paused a moment. If she had been a boy? It was a new line of thought and she followed it as she tramped; if she had been a boy. She must think that out in the days to come.

Then Percy had untied his horse and had gone with her to the house. "It's unlucky touching perfect happiness," he said.

Then she—"I am not happy."

Once more he called her "little coward" as they walked together. From the garden gate where he tied his horse, she could see her aunt standing at the study window that was a door, and upstairs, in the sunshine by an open window, her cousin Sabina Lasston, sewing. How her fair hair glittered in the sunshine; and all the connection had wanted Percy to marry Sabina. A choking came in her throat. He would, in time.

He had laughed at her when they reached the gate. "I'll kiss you here where they can see," he said; "such an easy way to tell them. Why so terrified? You really are a coward." He had held her hand as they went around the big tea olive bush, how sweet it smelled! Then her aunt had called them in at the study window. How gay and debonair he had been about it all.

"Cousin Alicia wants us to go in there," he whispered; "trap us as it were; don't worry, I'll protect you. Here goes! Hullo, 'Bina!", and he waved his hand to the upstairs window. "Good morning, Cousin Alicia, how are you? Shall we come in there? I love this dear old study. Too cool? Let me close that window; the wind has still a little nip in it, only we've been walking."

Then—"You went to meet him, Hagar?"

"We are engaged, Cousin Alicia," he had struck in; "third cousins, no harm, and I've come to ask you to the wedding. Why—why, are you not well!"

"Yes, yes, I—I think so; I had, I have had, no suspicion of this; Hagar—"

Then for once she had been brave. "My fault," she had cried; "my fault, I would not let him tell you."

The the order—"Leave the room." And she had gone despite Percy's order to stay, despite his clasp of her arm.

That was the end. She was glad she had got to the end; had it all clear of confusion in her mind even though she could not remember how she had got up the stairs.

Lying face downwards on her bed was the next clear thing she could remember; then to the window; and he had not turned his head, had gone slowly away from the house, as if suddenly crippled. In silence she had endured this, endured, yes.

She had eaten the food put down outside her door for the sake of the strength to endure. She had not died, no, she had endured the horrors of the letter thrust under her door, the hideous anticlimax of its ending: "I have said that you have a nervous headache and must not be disturbed"! All this she had endured; but not yet had she dared. She had not dared even to think, not dared to realize, not dared to feel—to die! Not yet. Recalling and arranging memories, scenes, that was all. "Afraid?" the man had asked. Yesterday, this walk would have been a terrifying impossibility. Now? Well, now, if anything further happened to her, perhaps, perhaps she would have the courage for the river; no, she was not afraid of this.

The day was still as death; a fine rain was falling noiselessly; the bright jessamine of the day before now were hanging heavy with moisture, the long moss showed a pale, dim green because of the wetness. Near one of the windows stood Mrs. Jarnigan, still and gray as the day. She seemed to be watching, listening. She walked from window to window, then out to the front door, standing for a moment to look down the avenue. Something sent a shiver through her, perhaps the rain, or the wind that now and then came in little gusts, and she went in again.

She was cold, colder than the rain or the wind could have made her. For twenty-four hours she had not rested, had not slept; had again and again gone over the scenes of the day before. How radiant Percy had looked; had come to ask her to his wedding—wedding with Hagar!

Great God! Blind! How blind she had been, how foolish; had she not eyes to see that the girl was beautiful? How his fair, level brows had drawn together when Hagar at her order had left the room, closing the door, how his blue eyes had flashed! What avail that she had pleaded to him, "Before God, I had no thought of this! I have kept the girl so secluded." How he had stared.

"What!" he had whispered it. Then her own voice answering, low, intense, that seemed to still the universe.

"It killed my brother," she had said; "it crucified me!" Then dimly, through the closed windows she had heard a mockingbird singing.

"Think," she had gone on, and she had come closer, peering into his face; "think had there ever before been a brunette Lasston?" A white line had settled about Percy's lips.

"Sit down, sit down," she had ordered; "it is a long story;" but he would not. Then with her hand on his shoulder, she had told him the story.

"My brother, so young, that when he finished his part in the war went to college, and there met his wife, older than he, but very beautiful. We opposed this stranger; he was infatuated. He brought her here a bride. Just before the child was born, an old German came on a visit, a scientific man. He stayed here for two days. The German said to me, "You do not mind the Negro blood, then?"

In telling the terrible story to Percy she had given the German's very words that for years had been burned into her heart, her memory.

"She has one mark of Negro blood," the German had

said, "that may fade in her child; but she lacks, she has not the mark of the pure white. The hair, the modeling of the nose—one drop of Negro blood eliminated that delicate modelling."

The words seemed even now actually to sound in her ears; she shivered and went to the fire. How cold she was. She put on a fresh log, made it blaze cheerfully, then stood there warming herself. Why could she not forget; would she be always seeing Percy's face gone so gray, so drawn? And beyond that seeing again, as she had seemed to see the day before, the face of her young brother, dead all these years? He had overheard the German telling her! He had come in at the door—the door there behind Percy—and his fair young face had gone gray and drawn just as Percy's had; and yesterday he had come and stood behind Percy—she had had a vision of him and of his dead wife standing there!

And the wife had known that she had black blood; after the German left them, the whole story had been told. She had known that the Lasstons had owned her ancestors, but not that in old George and old Sue she had black cousins left there. That had been a terrible shock to her; unknowing, they had bowed down before her as their master's wife—before Hagar as their master's daughter! They had been as an awful nightmare to the young wife and she had died when her child was born. Hagar, the father had named the child; Hagar, " 'An alien,' he said; 'an outcast'."

The story told, Percy had turned his dead eyes, his ashen face to her; "Thank you," he had said. "Thank you—may I go this way?" and had put his hand on the window latch. How loud the mockingbird had sounded as the window opened, singing its heart out! Still singing as when he and Hagar had come inside. The sun was still shining. Then he had crossed the broad piazza to the steps, down to the garden path, round the olive bushes to where his horse stood at the gate. He did not once turn, not once look back.

She drew a sobbing breath; how still the house was. Not a footstep, not a voice, no sound anywhere, just the wind outside, the drip of the rain from the roof. She started away from the cheerful fire so suddenly that she overturned a small screen; the sound seemed to echo, to come, to go. Hastily she went from the window to the door and back again; up and down; out to the piazza. And old George had hobbled up to the kitchen this morning, hearing the awful news that his young mistress was missing, and she was waiting there in the kitchen now for some word. His kinswoman. He had a right to know it all? Never!

She wrung her hands together; she must stop thinking. Would this terrible waiting never end—would no one ever come! Once more she went from window to door and back again; up and down the piazza. At last she bent her head, stopped, went quickly to the door. Yes, there, she could see her son now, and coming alone!

A horseman dismounted at the gate and tied his horse, slowly he came as if neither rain nor shelter meant anything to him. She met him at the step.

"No sign," he said, going into the study; "We've dragged the pond, have searched the swamp out to the river; the freshet makes the river impossible; but the dogs did not go to the river—"

"Where?" It was a whisper.

"They lost scent in the middle of the public road, and I found this." In his extended palm there lay a gray button.

Her whole being seemed to relax. "Her gray frock," she said; "that tells nothing; she had that on yesterday, too."

"You say that so quietly, mother," laying his hands on her two shoulders. "Mother," swaying her slightly; "why did you let her live here as our equal?"

"A girl, I could not cast her off; poverty-stricken, I had no money to place her elsewhere; I could not bring myself to explain, the disgrace would have killed me! The disgrace, the horror of it, killed my brother. But, where's Sabina?"

"She and the Doctor have ridden again to the river; she will not give up the search."

"She does not know our secret; and Percy?"

"Percy? Good God!"

"What?"

"Says, God has been merciful!"

"He has; and Hagar has been well trained."

"Mother!" Staring into Mrs. Jarnigan's eyes; "your niece, your—"

"Hush!"

"Your only brother's only child; trained by you; beautiful, gentle! Mother, did you not love her?"

"Love her? God! My life has been torture! When she touched me my blood turned backward in my veins! Eating at my table; sitting near you; treating you as a brother! The unspeakable misery! Her black hair, coarse, curly! Could you not see, boy? And I, I cut myself off from my people; I could not take her into their homes any more than I would take a disease there. Lonely, wretched, I've lived here with that calamity, turning over and over in my mind what to do for her—with her. A boy, I would have sent away, but a girl? A little black-eyed, black-haired baby, she killed her father. He died within the year. 'My blood!' he cried; 'My race!"

"And now, mother, she has vanished; that is noble, mother."

"She has Lasston blood in her; she has been well trained."

"She might not have lived up to it."

"She may not yet."

"She may not be alive, mother."

"In all my training of her I looked forward to this day, and now, in the first trial, she has done the right thing."

"I say, she may not be alive."

"She is afraid; she would not kill herself. She loves the soft things; she was not direct; was hard to train. I taught her daily the 'Noblesse Oblige' of the Lasstons; it became her creed; it is guiding her now; pray God it will continue. Her father named her 'Hagar Black'; if I should go out into the world to hunt for her, I should hunt for Hagar Black. Thank God, Percy needed no arguments! Your attitude, Alan, shames me."

"Suppose Sabina find trace of her?"

"I should send Percy to lose it."

"Oh, mother!"

"What would you have? Bring her back as our equal? Place her in old George's cabin? You have no answer. There is no answer. To lose herself to us; to make her own place in life, that is the only thing. Pray God she may remain true to her training and not marry a white man—"

"How dare you, mother!"

"Not marry at all; her children might—"

"Here is Sabina."

"We have ridden miles and miles, cousin, down the river. It is over the banks; the current is terrific!"

"Thank you, dear Sabina, you must be wet."

"No, the clouds are breaking."

"And Doctor Bruce?"

"He left me at the gate, cousin," she paused, "cousin, he has no hope."

"Yes, Sabina."

"She must have gone out early this morning in her boat; old George said she often did—she did not mind weather."

"Perhaps."

"And, cousin, if you do not mind, will you let Alan ride home with me now? And bring the buggy back for you? Won't you come too? A little change, cousin?"

"Oh, Sabina, yes! Thank you dear."

"And Alan, too?"

"Thank you, dear," her voice faltering a little; "thank you."

"Poor cousin," putting her arm about the elder woman; "Mama will be so glad to see you; the first time in all my life that you have come to us; you'd never bring Hagar, too many, you said; but now?"

"Yes, now I can come; I shall be ready when Alan returns."

"You've led such a hermit life; you seemed to need no one but dear Hagar; but now you must come out to us."

"I shall be glad; but none of you must be pitiful, sorrowful; it would kill me! Good-bye, dear Sabina; I shall be ready; yes, close the door."

She stood quite still until the door was fast, then she went to the window. "In her boat on the river; that story will do; and old George suggested it." She raised her arms above her head. "Free!" she said, looking up, while a great light broke over her face; "once more, once more myself—free among my own kind, once more!" Her voice broke and the sobs came, deep, heart-rending, almost cries, that shook her from head to foot. Down on her knees she prayed, "God have mercy! If I have failed, have mercy!"

And out in the olive bushes a bird was singing—singing.

Ellen Glasgow (April 22, 1873–November 21, 1945) was born in Richmond, Virginia, the eighth of ten children. Glasgow described her childhood as "painfully lonely but occasionally blissful." Glasgow had no formal education, yet through self-determination, she developed an energetic, intelligent mind.

Glasgow steered her writing toward a creative vision of "a series of sketches dealing with life in Virginia." In constructing this vision she rejected the Victorian definition of femininity which dominated the social attitude of her day. *In A Certain Measure: An Interpretation of Prose Fiction* (1943) Glasgow said what the South needed was "blood and irony." In writing this she felt it needed *blood* "because southern culture had strained too far away from its roots in the earth; it had grown thin and pale; it was satisfied to exist on borrowed ideas, to copy instead of create. And *irony* is an indispensable ingredient of the critical vision; it is the safest antidote to sentimental decay."

Glasgow authored twenty novels, a collection of poems, one volume of short stories, and a book of literary criticism. She was also a popular writer; five of her books appeared on the best-seller list. Some of her best known novels are *Barren Ground* (1925), *The Romantic Comedians* (1926), *They Stooped to Folly* (1929), *The Sheltered Life* (1932), and *Vein of Iron* (1935). In 1942 she received the Pulitzer Prize for *In This Our Life*, her last published novel. It was made into a film with Olivia de Havilland and Bette Davis. Her autobiography, *The Woman Within*, was published posthumously in 1954.

DARE'S GIFT

by Ellen Glasgow

A year has passed, and I am beginning to ask myself if the thing actually happened? The whole episode, seen in clear perspective, is obviously incredible. There are, of course, no haunted houses in this age of science; there are merely hallucinations, neurotic symptoms, and optical illusions. Any one of these practical diagnoses would, no doubt, cover the impossible occurrence, from my first view of that dusky sunset on James River to the erratic behaviour of Mildred during the spring we spent in Virginia. There is—I admit it readily!—a perfectly rational explanation of every mystery. Yet, while I assure myself that the supernatural has been banished, in the evil company of devils, black plagues, and witches, from this sanitary century, a vision of Dare's Gift, amid its clustering cedars under the shadowy arch of the sunset, rises before me, and my feeble scepticism surrenders to that invincible spirit of darkness. For once in my life—the ordinary life of a corporation lawyer in Washington—the impossible really happened.

It was the year after Mildred's first nervous breakdown, and Drayton, the great specialist in whose care she had been for some months, advised me to take her away from Washington until she recovered her health. As a busy man I couldn't spend the whole week out of town; but if we could find a place near enough—somewhere in Virginia! we both exclaimed, I remember—it would be easy for me to run down once a fortnight. The thought was with me when Harrison asked me to join him for a week's hunting on James River; and it was still in my mind, though less distinctly, on the evening when I stumbled alone, and for the first time, on Dare's Gift.

I had hunted all day—a divine day in October—and at sunset, with a bag full of partridges, I was returning for the night to Chericoke, where Harrison kept his bachelor's house. The sunset had been wonderful; and I had paused for a moment with my back to the bronze sweep of the land, when I had a swift impression that the memories of the old river gathered around me. It was at this instant—I recall even the trivial detail that my foot caught in a brier as I wheeled quickly about—that I looked past the sunken wharf on my right, and saw the garden of Dare's Gift falling gently from its almost obliterated terraces to the scalloped edge of the river. Following the steep road, which ran in curves through a stretch of pines and across an abandoned pasture or two, I came at last to an iron gate and a grassy walk leading, between walls of box, to the open lawn planted in elms. With that first glimpse the Old World charm of the scene held me captive. From the warm red of its brick walls to the pure Colonial lines of its doorway, and its curving wings mantled in roses and ivy, the house stood there, splendid and solitary. The rows of darkened windows sucked in without giving back the last flare of daylight; the heavy cedars crowding thick up the short avenue did not stir as the wind blew from the river; and above the carved pineapple on the roof, a lonely bat was wheeling high against the red disc of the sun. While I had climbed the rough road, and passed more slowly between the marvelous walls of the box, I had told myself that the place must be Mildred's and mine at any cost. On the upper terrace, before several crude modern additions to the wings, my enthusiasm gradually ebbed, though I still asked myself incredulously, "Why have I never heard of it? To whom does it belong? Has it a name as well known in Virginia as Shirley or Brandon?" The house was of great age, I knew, and yet from obvious signs I discovered that it was not too old to be lived in. Nowhere could I detect a hint of decay or dilapidation. The sound of cattle bells floated up from a pasture somewhere in the distance. Through the long grass on the lawn little twisted paths, like sheep tracks, wound back and forth under the fine old elms, from which a rain of bronze leaves fell slowly and ceaselessly in the wind. Nearer at hand, on the upper terrace, a few roses were blooming; and when I passed between two marble urns on the right of the house, my feet crushed a garden of "simples" such as our grandmothers used to grow.

As I stepped on the porch I heard a child's voice on the lawn, and a moment afterwards a small boy, driving a cow, appeared under the two cedars at the end of the avenue. At sight of me he flicked the cow with the hickory switch he held, and bawled, "Ma! thar's a stranger out here, an' I don't know what he wants."

At his call the front door opened, and a woman in a calico dress, with a sunbonnet pushed back from her forehead, came out on the porch.

"Hush yo' fuss, Eddy!" she remarked authoritatively. "He don't want nothin'." Then, turning to me, she added civilly, "Good evenin', suh. You must be the gentleman who is visitin' over at Chericoke?"

"Yes, I am staying with Mr. Harrison. You know him, of course?"

"Oh, Lordy, yes. Everybody aroun' here knows Mr. Harrison. His folks have been here goin' on mighty near forever. I don't know what me and my children would come to if it wa'n't for him. He is gettin' me my divorce now. It's been three years and mo' sence Tom deserted me."

"Divorce?" I had not expected to find this innovation on James River.

"Of course it ain't the sort of thing anybody would want to come to. But if a woman in the State ought to have one easy, I reckon it's me. Tom went off with another woman— and she my own sister—from this very house—"

"From this house—and, by the way, what is the name of it?"

"Name of what? This place? Why, it's Dare's Gift. Didn't you know it? Yes, suh, it happened right here in this very house, and that, too, when we hadn't been livin' over here mo' than three months. After Mr. Duncan got tired and went away he left us as caretakers, Tom and me, and I asked Tilly to come and stay with us and help me look after the children. It came like a lightning stroke to me, for Tom and Tilly had known each other all their lives, and he'd never taken any particular notice of her till they moved over here and began to tend the cows together. She wa'n't much for beauty, either. I was always the handsome one of the family—though you mightn't think it now, to look at me— and Tom was the sort that never could abide red hair—"

"And you've lived at Dare's Gift ever since?" I was more interested in the house than in the tenant.

"I didn't have nowhere else to go, and the house has got to have a caretaker till it is sold. It ain't likely that anybody will want to rent an out-of-the-way place like this—though now that automobiles have come to stay that don't make so much difference."

"Does it still belong to the Dares?"

"Naw, suh; they had to sell it at auction right after the war on account of mortgages and debts—old Colonel Dare died the very year Lee surrendered, and Miss Lucy she went off somewhere to strange parts. Sence their day it has belonged to so many different folks that you can't keep account of it. Right now it's owned by a Mr. Duncan, who lives out in California. I don't know that he'll ever come back here—he couldn't get on with the neighbours—and he is trying to sell it. No wonder, too, a great big place like this, and he ain't even a Virginian—"

"I wonder if he would let it for a season?" It was then, while I stood there in the brooding dusk of the doorway, that the idea of the spring at Dare's Gift first occurred to me.

"If you want it, you can have it for 'most nothing, I reckon. Would you like to step inside and go over the rooms?"

That evening at supper I asked Harrison about Dare's Gift, and gleaned the salient facts of its history.

"Strange to say, the place, charming as it is, has never been well known in Virginia. There's historical luck, you know, as well as other kinds, and the Dares—after that first Sir Roderick, who came over in time to take a stirring part in Bacon's Rebellion, and, tradition says, to betray his leader—have never distinguished themselves in the records of the State. The place itself, by the way, is about a fifth of the original plantation of three thousand acres, which was given—though I imagine there was more in that than appears in history—by some Indian chief of forgotten name to this notorious Sir Roderick. The old chap—Sir Roderick, I mean—seems to have been something of a fascinator in his day. Even Governor Berkeley, who hanged half the colony, relented, I believe, in the case of Sir Roderick, and that unusual clemency gave rise, I suppose, to the legend of the betrayal. But, however that may be, Sir Roderick had more miraculous escapes than John Smith himself, and died at last in his bed at the age of eighty from overeating cherry-pie."

"And now the place has passed away from the family?"

"Oh, long ago—though not so long, after all, when one comes to think of it. When the old Colonel died the year after the war, it was discovered that he had mortgaged the farm up to the last acre. At that time real estate on James River wasn't regarded as a particularly profitable investment, and under the hammer Dare's Gift went for a song."

"Was the Colonel the last of his name?"

"He left a daughter—a belle, too, in her youth, my mother says—but she died—at least I think she did—only a few months after her father."

Coffee was served on the veranda, and while I smoked my cigar and sipped my brandy—Harrison had an excellent wine-cellar—I watched the full moon shining like a yellow lantern through the diaphanous mist on the river. Downshore, in the sparkling reach of the water, an immense cloud hung low over the horizon, and between the cloud and the river a band of silver light quivered faintly, as if it would go out in an instant.

"It is over there, isn't it?"—I pointed to the silver light—"Dare's Gift, I mean."

"Yes, it's somewhere over yonder—five miles away by the river, and nearly seven by the road."

"It is the dream of a house, Harrison, and there isn't too much history attached to it—nothing that would make a modern beggar ashamed to live in it."

"By Jove! so you are thinking of buying it?" Harrison was beaming. "It is downright ridiculous, I declare, the attraction that place has for strangers. I never knew a Virginian who wanted it; but you are the third Yankee of my acquaintance—and I don't know many—who has fallen in love with it. I searched the title and drew up the deed for John Duncan exactly six years ago—though I'd better not boast of that transaction, I reckon."

"He still owns it, doesn't he?"

"He still owns it, and it looks as if he would continue to own it unless you can be persuaded to buy it. It is hard to find purchasers for these old places, especially when the roads are uncertain and they happen to be situated on the James River. We live too rapidly in these days to want to depend on a river, even on a placid old fellow like the James."

"Duncan never really lived here, did he?"

"At first he did. He began on quite a royal scale; but, somehow, from the very start things appeared to go wrong with him. At the outset he prejudiced the neighbours against him—I never knew exactly why—by putting on airs, I imagine, and boasting about his money. There is something in the Virginia blood that resents boasting about money. However that may be, he hadn't been here six months before he was at odds with every living thing in the county, white, black, and spotted—for even the dogs snarled at him. Then his secretary—a chap he had picked up starving in London, and had trusted absolutely for years—made off with a lot of cash and securities, and that seemed the last straw in poor Duncan's ill luck. I believe he didn't mind the loss half so much—he refused to prosecute the fellow—as he minded the betrayal of confidence. He told me, I remember, before he went away, that it had spoiled Dare's Gift for him. He said he had a feeling that the place had come too high; it had cost him his belief in human nature."

"Then I imagine he'd be disposed to consider an offer?"

"Oh, there isn't a doubt of it. But, if I were you, I shouldn't be too hasty. Why not rent the place for the spring months? It's beautiful here in the spring, and Duncan has left furniture enough to make the house fairly comfortable."

"Well, I'll ask Mildred. Of course Mildred must have the final word in the matter."

"As if Mildred's final word would be anything but a repetition of yours!" Harrison laughed slyly—for the perfect harmony in which we lived had been for ten years a pleasant jest among our friends. Harrison had once classified wives as belonging to two distinct groups—the group of those who talked and knew nothing about their husbands' affairs, and the group of those who knew everything and kept silent. Mildred, he had added politely, had chosen to belong to the latter division.

The next day I went back to Washington, and Mildred's first words to me in the station were,

"Why, Harold, you look as if you had bagged all the game in Virginia!"

"I look as if I had found just the place for you!"

When I told her about my discovery, her charming face

sparkled with interest. Never once, not even during her illness, had she failed to share a single one of my enthusiasms; never once, in all the years of our marriage, had there been so much as a shadow between us. To understand the story of Dare's Gift, it is necessary to realize at the beginning all that Mildred meant and means in my life.

Well, to hasten my slow narrative, the negotiations dragged through most of the winter. At first, Harrison wrote me, Duncan couldn't be found, and a little later that he was found, but that he was opposed, from some inscrutable motive, to the plan of renting Dare's Gift. He wanted to sell it outright, and he'd be hanged if he'd do anything less than get the place clean off his hands. "As sure as I let it" —Harrison sent me his letter—"there is going to be trouble, and somebody will come down on me for damages. The damned place has cost me already twice as much as I paid for it."

In the end, however—Harrison has a persuasive way— the arrangements were concluded. "Of course," Duncan wrote after a long silence, "Dare's Gift may be as healthy as heaven. I may quite as easily have contracted this confounded rheumatism, which makes life a burden, either in Italy or from too many cocktails. I've no reason whatever for my dislike for the place; none, that is, except the incivility of my neighbours—where, by the way, did you Virginians manufacture your reputation for manners?—and my unfortunate episode with Paul Grymes. That, as you remark, might, no doubt, have occurred anywhere else, and if a man is going to steal he could have found all the opportunities he wanted in New York or London. But the fact remains that one can't help harbouring associations, pleasant or unpleasant, with the house in which one has lived, and from start to finish my associations with Dare's Gift are frankly unpleasant. If, after all, however, your friend wants the place, and can afford to pay for his whims—let him have it! I hope to Heaven he'll be ready to buy it when his lease has run out. Since he wants it for a hobby, I suppose one place is as good as another; and I can assure him that by the time he has owned it for a few years—especially if he undertakes to improve the motor road up to Richmond—he will regard a taste for Chinese porcelain as an inexpensive diversion." Then, as if impelled by a twist of ironic humour, he added, "He will find the shooting good anyhow."

By early spring Dare's Gift was turned over to us— Mildred was satisfied, if Duncan wasn't—and on a showery day in April, when drifting clouds cast faint gauzy shadows over the river, our boat touched at the old wharf, where carpenters were working, and rested a minute before steaming on to Chericoke Landing five miles away. The spring was early that year—or perhaps the spring is always early on James River. I remember the song of birds in the trees; the veil of bright green over the distant forests; the broad reach of the river scalloped with silver; the dappled sunlight on the steep road which climbed from the wharf to the iron gates; the roving fragrance from lilacs on the lower terrace; and, surmounting all, the two giant cedars which rose like black crags against the changeable blue of the sky—I remember these things as distinctly as if I had seen them this morning.

We entered the wall of box through a living door, and strolled up the grassy walk from the lawn to the terraced garden. Within the garden the air was perfumed with a thousand scents—with lilacs, with young box, with flags and violets and lilies, with aromatic odours from the garden of "simples," and with the sharp sweetness of sheep-mint from the mown grass on the lawn.

"This spring is fine, isn't it?" As I turned to Mildred with the question, I saw for the first time that she looked pale and tired—or was it merely the green light from the box wall that fell over her features? "The trip has been too much for you. Next time we'll come by motor."

"Oh, no, I had a sudden feeling of faintness. It will pass in a minute. What an adorable place, Harold!"

She was smiling again with her usual brightness, and as we passed from the box wall to the clear sunshine on the terrace her face quickly resumed its natural colour. To this day—for Mildred has been strangely reticent about Dare's Gift—I do not know whether her pallor was due to the shade in which we walked or whether, at the instant when I turned to her, she was visited by some intuitive warning against the house we were approaching. Even after a year the events of Dare's Gift are not things I can talk over with Mildred; and, for my part, the occurrence remains, like the house in its grove of cedars, wrapped in an impenetrable mystery. I don't in the least pretend to know how or why the thing happened. I only know that it did happen—that it happened, word for word as I record it. Mildred's share in it will, I think, never become clear to me. What she felt, what she imagined, what she believed, I have never asked her. Whether the doctor's explanation is history or fiction, I do not attempt to decide. He is an old man, and old men, since Biblical times, have seen visions. There were places in his story where it seemed to me that he got historical data a little mixed—or it may be that his memory failed him. Yet, in spite of his liking for romance and his French education, he is without constructive imagination —at least he says that he is without it—and the secret of Dare's Gift, if it is not fact, could have sprung only from the ultimate chaos of imagination.

But I think of these things a year afterwards, and on that April morning the house stood there in the sunlight, presiding over its grassy terraces with an air of gracious and intimate hospitality. From the symbolic pineapple on its sloping roof to the twittering sparrows that flew in and out of its ivied wings, it reaffirmed that first flawless impression. Flaws, of course, there were in the fact, yet the recollection of it to-day—the garnered impression of age, of formal beauty, of clustering memories—is one of exquisite harmony. We found later, as Mildred pointed out, architectural absurdities—wanton excrescences in the modern additions, which had been designed apparently with the purpose of providing space at the least possible cost of material and labour. The rooms, when we passed through the fine old doorway, appeared cramped and poorly lighted; broken pieces of the queer mullioned window, where the tracery was of wood, not stone, had been badly repaired, and much of the original detail work of the mantels and cornices had been blurred by recent disfigurements. But these discoveries came afterwards. The first view of the place worked like a magic spell—like an intoxicating perfume—on our senses.

"It is just as if we had stepped into another world," said Mildred, looking up at the row of windows, from which the ivy had been carefully clipped. "I feel as if I had ceased to be myself since I left Washington." Then she turned to meet Harrison, who had ridden over to welcome us.

We spent a charming fortnight together at Dare's Gift— Mildred happy as a child in her garden, and I satisfied to lie in the shadow of the box wall and watch her bloom back to health. At the end of the fortnight I was summoned to an urgent conference in Washington. Some philanthropic busybody, employed to nose out corruption, had scented legal game in the affairs of the Atlantic & Eastern Railroad, and I had been retained as special counsel by that corporation. The fight would be long, I knew—I had already thought of it as one of my great cases—and the evidence was giving me no little anxiety. "It is my last big battle," I told Mildred, as I kissed her good-by on the steps. "If I win, Dare's Gift shall be your share of the spoils; if I lose—well, I'll be like any other general who has met a better man in the field."

"Don't hurry back, and don't worry about me. I am quite happy here."

"I shan't worry, but all the same I don't like leaving you. Remember, if you need advice or help about anything, Harrison is always at hand."

"Yes, I'll remember."

With this assurance I left her standing in the sunshine, with the windows of the house staring vacantly down on her.

When I try now to recall the next month, I can bring back merely a turmoil of legal wrangles. I contrived in the midst of it all to spend two Sundays with Mildred, but I remember nothing of them except the blessed wave of rest that swept over me as I lay on the grass under the elms. On my second visit I saw that she was looking badly, though when I commented on her pallor and the darkened circles under her eyes, she laughed and put my anxious questions aside.

"Oh, I've lost sleep, that's all," she answered, vaguely, with a swift glance at the house. "Did you ever think how many sounds there are in the country that keep one awake?"

As the day went on I noticed, too, that she had grown restless, and once or twice while I was going over my case with her—I always talked over my cases with Mildred because it helped to clarify my opinions—she returned with irritation to some obscure legal point I had passed over. The flutter of her movements—so unlike my calm Mildred—disturbed me more than I confessed to her, and I made up my mind before night that I would consult Drayton when I went back to Washington. Though she had always been sensitive and impressionable, I had never seen her until that second Sunday in a condition of feverish excitability.

In the morning she was so much better that by the time I reached Washington I forgot my determination to call on her physician. My work was heavy that week—the case was developing into a direct attack upon the management of the road—and in seeking evidence to rebut the charges of illegal rebates to the American Steel Company, I stumbled by accident upon a mass of damaging records. It was a clear case of somebody having blundered—or the records would not have been left for me to discover—and with disturbed thoughts I went down for my third visit to Dare's Gift. It was in my mind to draw out of the case, if an honourable way could be found, and I could barely wait until dinner was over before I unburdened my conscience to Mildred.

"The question has come to one of personal honesty." I remember that I was emphatic. "I've nosed out something real enough this time. There is material for a dozen investigations in Dowling's transactions alone."

The exposure of the Atlantic & Eastern Railroad is public property by this time, and I needn't resurrect the dry bones of that deplorable scandal. I lost the case, as everyone knows; but all that concerns me in it to-day is the talk I had with Mildred on the darkening terrace at Dare's Gift. It was a reckless talk, when one comes to think of it. I said, I know, a great deal that I ought to have kept to myself; but, after all, she is my wife; I had learned in ten years that I could trust her discretion, and there was more than a river between us and the Atlantic & Eastern Railroad.

Well, the sum of it is that I talked foolishly, and went to bed feeling justified in my folly. Afterwards I recalled that Mildred had been very quiet, though whenever I paused she questioned me closely, with a flash of irritation as if she were impatient of my slowness or my lack of lucidity. At the end she flared out for a moment into the excitement I had noticed the week before; but at the time I was so engrossed in my own affairs that this scarcely struck me as unnatural. Not until the blow fell did I recall the hectic flush in her face and the quivering sound of her voice, as if she were trying not to break down and weep.

It was long before either of us got to sleep that night, and Mildred moaned a little under her breath as she sank into unconsciousness. She was not well, I knew, and I resolved again that I would see Drayton as soon as I reached Washington. Then, just before falling asleep, I became acutely aware of all the noises of the country which Mildred said had kept her awake—of the chirping of the crickets in the fireplace, of the fluttering of swallows in the chimney, of the sawing of innumerable insects in the night outside, of the croaking of frogs in the marshes, of the distant solitary hooting of an owl, of the whispering sound of wind in the leaves, of the stealthy movement of a myriad creeping lives in the ivy. Through the open window the moonlight fell in a milk-white flood, and in the darkness the old house seemed to speak with a thousand voices. As I dropped off I had a confused sensation—less a perception than an apprehension—that all these voices were urging me to something—somewhere—

The next day I was busy with a mass of evidence—dull stuff, I remember. Harrison rode over for luncheon, and not until late afternoon, when I strolled out, with my hands full of papers, for a cup of tea on the terrace, did I have a chance to see Mildred alone. Then I noticed that she was breathing quickly, as if from a hurried walk.

"Did you go to meet the boat, Mildred?"

"No, I've been nowhere—nowhere. I've been on the lawn all day," she answered sharply—so sharply that I looked at her in surprise.

In the ten years that I had lived with her I had never before seen her irritated without cause—Mildred's disposition, I had once said, was as flawless as her profile—and I had for the first time in my life that baffled sensation which comes to men whose perfectly normal wives reveal flashes of abnormal psychology. Mildred wasn't Mildred, that was the upshot of my conclusions; and, hang it all! I didn't know any more than Adam what was the matter with her. There were lines around her eyes, and her sweet mouth had taken an edge of bitterness.

"Aren't you well, dear?" I asked.

"Oh, I'm perfectly well," she replied, in a shaking voice, "only I wish you would leave me alone!" And then she burst into tears.

While I was trying to comfort her the servant came with the tea things, and she kept him about some trivial orders until the big touring-car of one of our neighbours rushed up the drive and halted under the terrace.

In the morning Harrison motored up to Richmond with me, and on the way he spoke gravely of Mildred.

"Your wife isn't looking well, Beckwith. I shouldn't won-der if she were a bit seedy—and if I were you I'd get a doctor to look at her. There is a good man down at Chericoke Landing—old Pelham Lakeby. I don't care if he did get his training in France half a century ago; he knows more than your half-baked modern scientists."

"I'll speak to Drayton this very day," I answered, ignoring his suggestion of the physician. "You have seen more of Mildred this last month than I have. How long have you noticed that she isn't herself?"

"A couple of weeks. She is usually so jolly, you know." Harrison had played with Mildred in his childhood. "Yes, I shouldn't lose any time over the doctor. Though, of course, it may be only the spring," he added, reassuringly.

"I'll drop by Drayton's office on my way uptown," I replied, more alarmed by Harrison's manner than I had been by Mildred's condition.

But Drayton was not in his office, and his assistant told me that the great specialist would not return to town until the end of the week. It was impossible for me to discuss Mildred with the earnest young man who discoursed so eloquently of the experiments in the Neurological Institute, and I left without mentioning her, after making an appointment for Saturday morning. Even if the consultation delayed my return to Dare's Gift until the afternoon, I was determined to see Drayton, and, if possible, take him back with me. Mildred's last nervous breakdown had been too serious for me to neglect this warning.

I was still worrying over that case—wondering if I could find a way to draw out of it—when the catastrophe overtook me. It was on Saturday morning, I remember, and after a reassuring talk with Drayton, who had promised to run down to Dare's Gift for the coming week-end, I was hurrying to catch the noon train for Richmond. As I passed through the station, one of the *Observer*'s sensational "war extras" caught my eye, and I stopped for an instant to buy the paper before I hastened through the gate to the train. Not until we had started, and I had gone back to the dining-car, did I unfold the pink sheets and spread them out on the table before me. Then, while the waiter hung over me for the order, I felt the headlines on the front page slowly burn themselves into my brain—for, instead of the news of the great French drive I was expecting, there flashed back at me, in large type, the name of the opposing counsel in the case against the Atlantic & Eastern. The *Observer's* "extra" battened not on the war this time, but on the gross scandal of the railroad; and the front page of the paper was devoted to a personal interview with Herbert Tremaine, the great Tremaine, that philanthropic busybody who had first scented corruption. It was all there, every ugly detail— every secret proof of the illegal transactions on which I had stumbled. It was all there, phrase for phrase, as I alone could have told it—as I alone, in my folly, had told it to Mildred. The Atlantic & Eastern had been betrayed, not privately, not secretly, but in large type in the public print of a sensational newspaper. And not only the road! I also had been betrayed—betrayed so wantonly, so irrationally, that it was like an incident out of melodrama. It was conceivable that the simple facts might have leaked out through other channels, but the phrases, the very words of Tremaine's interview, were mine.

The train had started; I couldn't have turned back even if I had wanted to do so. I was bound to go on, and some intuition told me that the mystery lay at the end of my journey. Mildred had talked indiscreetly to someone, but to whom? Not to Harrison, surely! Harrison, I knew, I could count on, and yet whom had she seen except Harrison? After my first shock the absurdity of the thing made me laugh aloud. It was all as ridiculous, I realized, as it was disastrous! It might so easily not have happened. If only I hadn't stumbled on those accursed records! If only I had kept my mouth shut about them! If only Mildred had not talked unwisely to someone! But I wonder if there was ever a tragedy so inevitable that the victim, in looking back, could not see a hundred ways, great or small, of avoiding or preventing it?—a hundred trivial incidents which, falling differently, might have transformed the event into pure comedy?

The journey was unmitigated torment. In Richmond the car did not meet me, and I wasted half an hour in looking for a motor to take me to Dare's Gift. When at last I got off, the road was rougher than ever, plowed into heavy furrows after the recent rains, and filled with mudholes from which it seemed we should never emerge. By the time we puffed exhaustedly up the rocky road from the river's edge, and ran into the avenue, I had worked myself into a state of nervous apprehension bordering on panic. I don't know what I expected, but I think I shouldn't have been surprised if Dare's Gift had lain in ruins before me. Had I found the house levelled to ashes by a divine visitation, I believe I should have accepted the occurrence as within the bounds of natural phenomena.

But everything—even the young peacocks on the lawn—was just as I had left it. The sun, setting in a golden ball over the pineapple on the roof, appeared as unchangeable, while it hung there in the glittering sky, as if it were made of metal. From the somber dusk of the wings, where the ivy lay like a black shadow, the clear front of the house, with its formal doorway and its mullioned windows, shone with an intense brightness, the last beams of sunshine lingering there before they faded into the profound gloom of the cedars. The same scents of roses and sage and mown grass and sheep-mint hung about me; the same sounds—the croaking of frogs and the sawing of katydids—floated up from the low grounds; the very books I had been reading lay on one of the tables on the terrace, and the front door still stood ajar as if it had not closed since I passed through it.

I dashed up the steps, and in the hall Mildred's maid met me. "Mrs. Beckwith was so bad that we sent for the doctor—the one Mr. Harrison recommended. I don't know what it is, sir, but she doesn't seem like herself. She talks as if she were quite out of her head."

"What does the doctor say?"

"He didn't tell me. Mr. Harrison saw him. He—the doctor, I mean—has sent a nurse, and he is coming again in the morning. But she isn't herself, Mr. Beckwith. She says she doesn't want you to come to her——"

"Mildred!" I had already sprung past the woman, calling the beloved name aloud as I ran up the stairs.

In her chamber, standing very straight, with hard eyes, Mildred met me. "I had to do it, Harold," she said coldly—so coldly that my outstretched arms fell to my sides. "I had to tell all I knew."

"You mean you told Tremaine—you wrote to him—you, Mildred?"

"I wrote to him—I had to write. I couldn't keep it back any longer. No, don't touch me. You must not touch me. I had to do it. I would do it again."

Then it was, while she stood there, straight and hard, and rejoiced because she had betrayed me—then it was that I knew that Mildred's mind was unhinged.

"I had to do it. I would do it again," she repeated, pushing me from her.

II

All night I sat by Mildred's bedside, and in the morning, without having slept, I went downstairs to meet Harrison and the doctor.

"You must get her away, Beckwith," began Harrison with a curious, suppressed excitement. "Dr. Lakeby says she will be all right again as soon as she gets back to Washington."

"But I brought her away from Washington because Drayton said it was not good for her."

"I know, I know." His tone was sharp, "But it's different now. Dr. Lakeby wants you to take her back as soon as you can."

The old doctor was silent while Harrison spoke, and it was only after I had agreed to take Mildred away to-morrow that he murmured something about "bromide and chloral," and vanished up the staircase. He impressed me then as a very old man—old not so much in years as in experience, as if, living there in that flat and remote country, he had exhausted all human desires. A leg was missing, I saw, and Harrison explained that the doctor had been dangerously wounded in the battle of Seven Pines, and had been obliged after that to leave the army and take up again the practice of medicine.

"You had better get some rest," Harrison said, as he parted from me. "It is all right about Mildred, and nothing else matters. The doctor will see you in the afternoon, when you have had some sleep, and have a talk with you. He can explain things better than I can."

Some hours later, after a profound slumber, which lasted well into the afternoon, I waited for the doctor by the tea-table, which had been laid out on the upper terrace. It was a perfect afternoon—a serene and cloudless afternoon in early summer. All the brightness of the day gathered on the white porch and the red walls, while the clustering shadows slipped slowly over the box garden to the lawn and the river.

I was sitting there, with a book I had not even attempted to read, when the doctor joined me; and while I rose to shake hands with him I received again the impression of weariness, of pathos and disappointment, which his face had given me in the morning. He was like sun-dried fruit, I thought, fruit that has ripened and dried under the open sky, not withered in tissue paper.

Declining my offer of tea, he sat down in one of the wicker chairs, selecting, I noticed, the least comfortable among them, and filled his pipe from a worn leather pouch.

"She will sleep all night," he said; "I am giving her bromide every three hours, and to-morrow you will be able to take her away. In a week she will be herself again. These nervous natures yield quickest to the influence, but they recover quickest also. In a little while this illness, as you choose to call it, will have left no mark upon her. She may even have forgotten it. I have known this to happen."

"You have known this to happen?" I edged my chair nearer.

"They all succumb to it—the neurotic temperament soonest, the phlegmatic one later—but they all succumb to it in the end. The spirit of the place is too strong for them. They surrender to the thought of the house—to the psychic force of its memories——"

"There are memories, then? Things have happened here?"

"All old houses have memories, I suppose. Did you ever stop to wonder about the thoughts that must have gathered within walls like these?—to wonder about the impressions that must have lodged in the bricks, in the crevices, in the timber and the masonry? Have you ever stopped to think that these multiplied impressions might create a current of thought—a mental atmosphere—an inscrutable power of suggestion?"

"Even when one is ignorant? When one does not know the story?"

"She may have heard scraps of it from the servants—who knows? One can never tell how traditions are kept alive. Many things have been whispered about Dare's Gift; some of these whispers may have reached her. Even without her knowledge she may have absorbed the suggestion; and some day, with that suggestion in her mind, she may have gazed too long at the sunshine on these marble urns before she turned back into the haunted rooms where she lived. After all, we know so little, so pitifully little about these things. We have only touched, we physicians, the outer edges of psychology. The rest lies in darkness——"

I jerked him up sharply. "The house, then, is haunted?"

For a moment he hesitated. "The house is saturated with a thought. It is haunted by treachery."

"You mean something happened here?"

"I mean——" He bent forward, groping for the right word, while his gaze sought the river, where a golden web of mist hung midway between sky and water. "I am an old man, and I have lived long enough to see every act merely as the husk of an idea. The act dies; it decays like the body, but the idea is immortal. The thing that happened at Dare's Gift was over fifty years ago, but the thought of it still lives—still utters its profound and terrible message. The house is a shell, and if one listens long enough one can hear in its heart the low murmur of the past—of that past which is but a single wave of the great sea of human experience——"

"But the story?" I was becoming impatient of his theories. After all, if Mildred was the victim of some phantasmal hypnosis, I was anxious to meet the ghost who had hypnotized her. Even Drayton, I reflected, keen as he was about the fact of mental suggestion, would never have regarded seriously the suggestion of a phantom. And the house looked so peaceful—so hospitable in the afternoon light.

"The story? Oh, I am coming to that—but of late the story has meant so little to me beside the idea. I like to stop by the way. I am getting old, and an amble suits me better than too brisk a trot—particularly in this weather——"

Yes, he was getting old. I lit a fresh cigarette and waited impatiently. After all, this ghost that he rambled about was real enough to destroy me, and my nerves were quivering like harp-strings.

"Well, I came into the story—I was in the very thick of it, by accident, if there is such a thing as accident in this world of incomprehensible laws. The Incomprehensible! That has always seemed to me the supreme fact of life, the one truth overshadowing all others—the truth that we know nothing. We nibble at the edges of the mystery, and the great Reality— the Incomprehensible—is still untouched, undiscovered. It unfolds hour by hour, day by day, creating, enslaving, killing us, while we painfully gnaw off—what? A crumb or two, a grain from that vastness which envelops us, which remains impenetrable——"

Again he broke off, and again I jerked him back from his reverie.

"As I have said, I was placed, by an act of Providence, or of chance, in the very heart of the tragedy. I was with Lucy Dare on the day, the unforgettable day, when she made her choice—her heroic or devilish choice, according to the way one has been educated. In Europe a thousand years ago such an act committed for the sake of religion would have made her a saint; in New England, a few centuries past, it would have entitled her to a respectable position in history— the little history of New England. But Lucy Dare was a Virginian, and in Virginia—except in the brief, exalted Virginia of the Confederacy—the personal loyalties have always been esteemed beyond the impersonal. I cannot imagine us as a people canonizing a woman who sacrificed the human ties for the superhuman—even for the divine. I cannot imagine it, I repeat; and so Lucy Dare—though she rose to greatness in that one instant of sacrifice—has not even a name among us to-day. I doubt if you can find a child in the State who has ever heard of her—or a grown man, outside of this neighbourhood, who could give you a single fact of her history. She is as completely forgotten as Sir Roderick, who betrayed Bacon—she is forgotten . because the thing she did, though it might have made a Greek tragedy, was alien to the temperament of the people among whom she lived. Her tremendous sacrifice failed to arrest the imagination of her time. After all, the sublime cannot touch us unless it is akin to our ideal; and though Lucy Dare was sublime, according to the moral code of the Romans, she was a stranger to the racial soul of the South. Her memory died because it was the bloom of an hour—because there was nothing in the soil of her age for it to thrive on. She missed her time; she is one of the mute inglorious heroines of history; and yet, born in another century, she might have stood side by side with Antigone——" For an instant he paused. "But she has always seemed to me diabolical," he added.

"What she did, then, was so terrible that it has haunted the house ever since?" I asked again, for, wrapped in memories, he had lost the thread of his story.

"What she did was so terrible that the house has never forgotten. The thought in Lucy Dare's mind during those hours while she made her choice has left an ineffaceable impression on the things that surrounded her. She created in the horror of that hour an unseen environment more real, because more spiritual, than the material fact of the house. You won't believe this, of course—if people believed in the unseen as in the seen, would life be what it is?"

The afternoon light slept on the river; the birds were mute in the elm-trees; from the garden of herbs at the end of the terrace an aromatic fragrance rose like invisible incense.

"To understand it all, you must remember that the South was dominated, was possessed by an idea—the idea of the Confederacy. It was an exalted idea—supremely vivid, supremely romantic—but, after all, it was only an idea. It existed nowhere within the bounds of the actual unless the souls of its devoted people may be regarded as actual. But it is the dream, not the actuality, that commands the noblest devotion, the completest self-sacrifice. It is the dream, the ideal, that has ruled mankind from the beginning.

"I saw a great deal of the Dares that year. It was a lonely life I led after I lost my leg at Seven Pines, and dropped out of the army, and, as you may imagine, a country doctor's practice in wartimes was far from lucrative. Our one comfort was that we were all poor, that we were all starving together; and the Dares—there were only two of them, father and daughter—were as poor as the rest of us. They had given their last coin to the government—had poured their last bushel of meal into the sacks of the army. I can imagine the superb gesture with which Lucy Dare flung her dearest heirloom—her one remaining brooch or pin—into the bare coffers of the Confederacy. She was a small woman, pretty rather than beautiful—not the least heroic in build— yet I wager that she was heroic enough on that occasion. She was a strange soul, though I never so much as suspected her strangeness while I knew her—while she moved among us with her small oval face, her gentle blue eyes, her smoothly banded hair, which shone like satin in the sunlight. Beauty she must have had in a way, though I confess a natural preference for queenly women; I dare say I should have preferred Octavia to Cleopatra, who, they tell me, was small and slight. But Lucy Dare wasn't the sort to blind your eyes when you first looked at her. Her charm was like a fragrance rather than a colour—a subtle fragrance that steals into the senses and is the last thing a man ever forgets. I knew half a dozen men who would have died for her—and yet she gave them nothing, nothing, barely a smile. She appeared cold—she who was destined to flame to life in an act. I can see her distinctly as she looked then, in that last year—grave, still, with the curious, unearthly loveliness that comes to pretty women who are underfed—who are slowly starving for bread and meat, for bodily nourishment. She had the look of one dedicated—as ethereal as a saint, and yet I never saw it at the time; I only remember it now, after fifty years, when I think of her. Starvation, when it is slow, not quick—when it means, not acute hunger, but merely lack of the right food, of the blood-making, nerve-building elements—starvation like this often plays strange pranks with one. The visions of the saints, the glories of martyrdom, come to the underfed, the anemic. Can you recall one of the saints—the genuine sort—whose regular diet was roast beef and ale?

"Well, I have said that Lucy Dare was a strange soul, and she was, though to this day I don't know how much of her strangeness was the result of improper nourishment, of too little blood to the brain. Be that as it may, she seems to me when I look back on her to have been one of those women whose characters are shaped entirely by external events— who are the playthings of circumstance. There are many such women. They move among us in obscurity—reserved, passive, commonplace—and we never suspect the spark of fire in their natures until it flares up at the touch of the unexpected. In ordinary circumstances Lucy Dare would have been ordinary, submissive, feminine, domestic; she adored children. That she possessed a stronger will than the average Southern girl, brought up in the conventional manner, none of us—least of all I, myself—ever imagined. She was, of course, intoxicated, obsessed, with the idea of the Confederacy; but, then, so were all of us. There wasn't anything unusual or abnormal in that exalted illusion. It was the common property of our generation. . . .

"Like most non-combatants, the Dares were extremists, and I, who had got rid of a little of my bad blood when I lost my leg, used to regret sometimes that the Colonel—I never knew where he got his title—was too old to do a share of the actual fighting. There is nothing that takes the fever out of one so quickly as a fight; and in the army I had never met a hint of this concentrated, vitriolic bitterness towards the enemy. Why, I've seen the Colonel, sitting here on this terrace, and crippled to the knees with gout, grow purple in the face if I spoke so much as a good word for the climate of the North. For him, and for the girl, too, the Lord had drawn a divine circle round the Confederacy. Everything inside of that circle was perfection; everything outside of it was evil. Well, that was fifty years ago, and his hate is all dust now; yet I can sit here, where he used to brood on this terrace, sipping his blackberry wine—I can sit here and remember it all as if it were yesterday. The place has changed so little, except for Duncan's grotesque additions to the wings, that one can scarcely believe all these years have passed over it. Many an afternoon just like this I've sat here, while the Colonel nodded and Lucy knitted for the soldiers, and watched these same shadows creep down the terrace and that mist of light—it looks just as it used to— hang there over the James. Even the smell from those herbs hasn't changed. Lucy used to keep her little garden at the end of the terrace, for she was fond of making essences and beauty lotions. I used to give her all the prescriptions I could find in old books I read—and I've heard people say that she owed her wonderful white skin to the concoctions she brewed from shrubs and herbs. I couldn't convince them that lack of meat, not lotions, was responsible for the pallor— pallor was all the fashion then—that they admired and envied."

He stopped a minute, just long enough to refill his pipe, while I glanced with fresh interest at the garden of herbs.

"It was a March day when it happened," he went on presently; "cloudless, mild, with the taste and smell of spring in the air. I had been at Dare's Gift almost every day for a year. We had suffered together, hoped, feared, and wept together, hungered and sacrificed together. We had felt together the divine, invincible sway of an idea.

"Stop for a minute and picture to yourself what it is to be of a war and yet not in it; to live in imagination until the mind becomes inflamed with the vision; to have no outlet for the passion that consumes one except the outlet of thought. Add to this the fact that we really knew nothing. We were as far away from the truth, stranded here on our river, as if we had been anchored in a canal on Mars. Two men—one crippled, one too old to fight—and a girl—and the three living for a country which in a few weeks would be nothing—would be nowhere—not on any map of the world. . . .

"When I look back now it seems to me incredible that at that time any persons in the Confederacy should have been ignorant of its want of resources. Yet remember we lived apart, remote, unvisited, out of touch with realities, thinking the one thought. We believed in the ultimate triumph of the South with that indomitable belief which is rooted not in reason, but in emotion. To believe had become an act of religion; to doubt was rank infidelity. So we sat there in our little world, the world of unrealities, bounded by the river and the garden, and talked from noon till sunset about our illusion—not daring to look a single naked fact in the face—talking of plenty when there were no crops in the ground and no flour in the storeroom, prophesying victory while the Confederacy was in her death struggle. Folly! All folly, and yet I am sure even now that we were sincere, that we believed the nonsense we were uttering. We believed, I have said, because to doubt would have been far too horrible. Hemmed in by the river and the garden, there wasn't anything left for us to do—since we couldn't fight—but believe. Someone has said, or ought to have said, that faith is the last refuge of the inefficient. The twin devils of famine and despair were at work in the country, and we sat there—we three, on this damned terrace—and prophesied about the second president of the Confederacy. We agreed, I remember, that Lee would be the next president. And all the time, a few miles away, the demoralization of defeat was abroad, was around us, was in the air. . . .

"It was a March afternoon when Lucy sent for me, and while I walked up the drive—there was not a horse left among us, and I made all my rounds on foot—I noticed that patches of spring flowers were blooming in the long grass on the lawn. The air was as soft as May, and in the woods at the back of the house buds of maple-trees ran like a flame. There were, I remember, leaves—dead leaves, last year's leaves—everywhere, as if, in the demoralization of panic, the place had been forgotten, had been untouched since autumn. I remember rotting leaves that gave like moss underfoot; dried leaves that stirred and murmured as one walked over them; black leaves, brown leaves, wine-coloured leaves, and the still glossy leaves of the evergreens. But they were everywhere—in the road, over the grass on the lawn, beside the steps, piled in wind-drifts against the walls of the house.

"On the terrace, wrapped in shawls, the old Colonel was

sitting; and he called out excitedly, 'Are you bringing news of a victory?' Victory! when the whole country had been scraped with a fine-tooth comb for provisions.

" 'No, I bring no news except that Mrs. Morson has just heard of the death of her youngest son in Petersburg. Gangrene, they say. The truth is the men are so ill-nourished that the smallest scratch turns to gangrene——'

" 'Well, it won't be for long—not for long. Let Lee and Johnston get together and things will go our way with a rush. A victory or two, and the enemy will be asking for terms of peace before the summer is over.'

"A lock of his silver-white hair had fallen over his forehead, and pushing it back with his clawlike hand, he peered up at me with his little nearsighted eyes, which were of a peculiar burning blackness, like the eyes of some small enraged animal. I can see him now as vividly as if I had left him only an hour ago, and yet it is fifty years since then— fifty years filled with memories and with forgetfulness. Behind him the warm red of the bricks glowed as the sunshine fell, sprinkled with shadows, through the elm boughs. Even the soft wind was too much for him, for he shivered occasionally in his blanket shawls, and coughed the dry, hacking cough which had troubled him for a year. He was a shell of a man—a shell vitalized and animated by an immense, and indestructible illusion. While he sat there, sipping his blackberry wine, with his little fiery dark eyes searching the river in hope of something that would end his interminable expectancy, there was about him a fitful sombre gleam of romance. For him the external world, the actual truth of things, had vanished—all of it, that is, except the shawl that wrapped him and the glass of blackberry wine he sipped. He had died already to the material fact, but he lived intensely, vividly, profoundly, in the idea. It was the idea that nourished him, that gave him his one hold on reality.

" 'It was Lucy who sent for you,' said the old man presently. 'She has been on the upper veranda all day overlooking something—the sunning of winter clothes, I think. She wants to see you about one of the servants—a sick child, Nancy's child, in the quarters.'

" 'Then I'll find her,' I answered readily, for I had, I confess, a mild curiosity to find out why Lucy had sent for me.

"She was alone on the upper veranda, and I noticed that she closed her Bible and laid it aside as I stepped through the long window that opened from the end of the hall. Her face, usually so pale, glowed now with a wan illumination, like ivory before the flame of a lamp. In this illumination her eyes, beneath delicately pencilled eyebrows, looked unnaturally large and brilliant, and so deeply, so angelically blue that they made me think of the Biblical heaven of my childhood. Her beauty, which had never struck me sharply before, pierced through me. But it was her fate—her misfortune perhaps—to appear commonplace, to pass unrecognized, until the fire shot from her soul.

" 'No, I want to see you about myself, not about one of the servants.'

"At my first question she had risen and held out her hand—a white, thin hand, small and frail as a child's.

" 'You are not well, then?' I had known from the first that her starved look meant something.

" 'It isn't that; I am quite well.' She paused a moment, and then looked at me with a clear shining gaze. 'I have had a letter,' she said.

" 'A letter?' I have realized since how dull I must have seemed to her in that moment of excitement, of exaltation.

" 'You didn't know. I forgot that you didn't know that I was once engaged—long ago—before the beginning of the war. I cared a great deal—we both cared a great deal, but he was not one of us; he was on the other side—and when the war came, of course there was no question. We broke it off; we had to break it off. How could it have been possible to do otherwise?'

" 'How, indeed!' I murmured; and I had a vision of the old man downstairs on the terrace, of the intrepid and absurd old man.

" 'My first duty is to my country,' she went on after a minute, and the words might have been spoken by her father. 'There has been no thought of anything else in my mind since the beginning of the war. Even if peace comes I can never feel the same again—I can never forget that he has been a part of all we have suffered—of the thing that has made us suffer. I could never forget—I can never forgive.'

"Her words sound strange now, you think, after fifty years; but on that day, in this house surrounded by dead leaves, inhabited by an inextinguishable ideal—in this country, where the spirit had fed on the body until the impoverished brain reacted to transcendent visions—in this place, at that time, they were natural enough. Scarcely a woman of the South but would have uttered them from her soul. In every age one ideal enthralls the imagination of mankind; it is in the air; it subjugates the will; it enchants the emotions. Well, in the South fifty years ago this ideal was patriotism; and the passion of patriotism, which bloomed like some red flower, the flower of carnage, over the land, had grown in Lucy Dare's soul into an exotic blossom.

"Yet even to-day, after fifty years, I cannot get over the impression she made upon me of a woman who was, in the essence of her nature, thin and colourless. I may have been wrong. Perhaps I never knew her. It is not easy to judge people, especially women, who wear a mask by instinct. What I thought lack of character, of personality, may have been merely reticence; but again and again there comes back to me the thought that she never said or did a thing—except the one terrible thing—that one could remember. There was nothing remarkable that one could point to about her. I cannot recall either her smile or her voice, though both were sweet, no doubt, as the smile and the voice of a Southern woman would be. Until that morning on the upper veranda I had not noticed that her eyes were wonderful. She was like a shadow, a phantom, that attains in one supreme instant, by one immortal gesture, union with reality. Even I remember her only by that one lurid flash.

" 'And you say you have had a letter?'

" 'It was brought by one of the old servants—Jacob, the one who used to wait on him when he stayed here. He was a prisoner. A few days ago he escaped. He asked me to see him—and I told him to come. He wishes to see me once again before he goes North—for ever——' She spoke in gasps in a dry voice. Never once did she mention his name. Long afterwards I remembered that I had never heard his name spoken. Even to-day I do not know it. He also was a shadow, a phantom—a part of the encompassing unreality.

" 'And he will come here?'

For a moment she hesitated; then she spoke quite simply, knowing that she could trust me.

" 'He is here. He is in the chamber beyond.' She pointed

to one of the long windows that gave on the veranda. The blue chamber at the front.

I remember that I made a step towards the window when her voice arrested me. 'Don't go in. He is resting. He is very tired and hungry.'

" 'You didn't send for me, then, to see him?'

" 'I sent for you to be with father. I knew you would help me—that you would keep him from suspecting. He must not know, of course. He must be kept quiet.'

" 'I will stay with him,' I answered, and then, 'Is that all you wish to say to me?'

" 'That is all. It is only for a day or two. He will go on in a little while, and I can never see him again. I do not wish to see him again.'

"I turned away, across the veranda, entered the hall, walked the length of it, and descended the staircase. The sun was going down in a ball—just as it will begin to go down in a few minutes—and as I descended the stairs I saw it through the mullioned window over the door— huge and red and round above the black cloud of the cedars.

"The old man was still on the terrace. I wondered vaguely why the servants had not brought him indoors; and then, as I stepped over the threshold, I saw that a company of soldiers—Confederates—had crossed the lawn and were already gathering about the house. The commanding officer—I was shaking hands with him presently—was a Dare, a distant cousin of the Colonel's, one of those excitable, nervous, and slightly theatrical natures who become utterly demoralized under the spell of any violent emotion. He had been wounded at least a dozen times, and his lean, sallow, still handsome features had the greenish look which I had learned to associate with chronic malaria.

"When I look back now I can see it all as a part of the general disorganization—of the fever, the malnutrition, the complete demoralization of panic. I know now that each man of us was facing in his soul defeat and despair; and that we—each one of us—had gone mad with the thought of it. In a little while, after the certainty of failure had come to us, we met it quietly—we braced our souls for the issue; but in those last weeks defeat had all the horror, all the insane terror of a nightmare, and all the vividness. The thought was like a delusion from which we fled, and which no flight could put farther away from us.

"Have you ever lived, I wonder, from day to day in that ever-present and unchanging sense of unreality, as if the moment before you were but an imaginary experience which must dissolve and evaporate before the touch of an actual event? Well, that was the sensation I had felt for days, weeks, months, and it swept over me again while I stood there, shaking hands with the Colonel's cousin, on the terrace. The soldiers, in their ragged uniforms, appeared as visionary as the world in which we had been living. I think now that they were as ignorant as we were of the things that had happened—that were happening day by day to the army. The truth is that it was impossible for a single one of us to believe that our heroic army could be beaten even by unseen powers—even by hunger and death.

" 'And you say he was a prisoner?' It was the old man's quavering voice, and it sounded avid for news, for certainty.

" 'Caught in disguise. Then he slipped through our fingers.' The cousin's tone was querulous, as if he were irritated by loss of sleep or of food. 'Nobody knows how it happened. Nobody ever knows. But he has found out things that will ruin us. He has plans. He has learned things that mean the fall of Richmond if he escapes.'

"Since then I have wondered how much they sincerely believed—how much was simply the hallucination of fever, of desperation? Were they trying to bully themselves by violence into hoping? Or had they honestly convinced themselves that victory was still possible? If one only repeats a phrase often and emphatically enough one comes in time to believe it; and they had talked so long of that coming triumph, of the established Confederacy, that it had ceased to be, for them at least, merely a phrase. It wasn't the first occasion in life when I had seen words bullied—yes, literally bullied into beliefs.

"Well, looking back now after fifty years, you see, of course, the weakness of it all, the futility. At that instant, when all was lost, how could any plans, any plotting have ruined us? It seems irrational enough now—a dream, a shadow, that belief—and yet not one of us but would have given our lives for it. In order to understand you must remember that we were, one and all, victims of an idea—of a divine frenzy.

" 'And we are lost—the Confederacy is lost, you say, if he escapes?'

"It was Lucy's voice; and turning quickly, I saw that she was standing in the doorway. She must have followed me closely. It was possible that she had overheard every word of the conversation.

" 'If Lucy knows anything, she will tell you. There is no need to search the house,' quavered the old man, 'she is my daughter.'

" 'Of course we wouldn't search the house—not Dare's Gift,' said the cousin. He was excited, famished, malarial, but he was a gentleman, every inch of him.

"He talked on rapidly, giving details of the capture, the escape, the pursuit. It was all rather confused. I think he must have frightfully exaggerated the incident. Nothing could have been more unreal than it sounded. And he was just out of a hospital—was suffering still, I could see, from malaria. While he drank his blackberry wine—the best the house had to offer—I remember wishing that I had a good dose of quinine and whiskey to give him.

"The narrative lasted a long time; I think he was glad of a rest and of the blackberry wine and biscuits. Lucy had gone to fetch food for the soldiers; but after she had brought it she sat down in her accustomed chair by the old man's side and bent her head over her knitting. She was a wonderful knitter. During all the years of the war I seldom saw her without her ball of yarn and her needles—the long wooden kind that the women used at that time. Even after the dusk fell in the evenings the click of her needles sounded in the darkness.

" 'And if he escapes it will mean the capture of Richmond?' she asked once again when the story was finished. There was no hint of excitement in her manner. Her voice was perfectly toneless. To this day I have no idea what she felt—what she was thinking.

" 'If he gets away it is the ruin of us—but he won't get away. We'll find him before morning.'

"Rising from his chair, he turned to shake hands with the old man before descending the steps. 'We've got to go on now. I shouldn't have stopped if we hadn't been half starved. You've done us a world of good, Cousin Lucy. I reckon you'd give your last crust to the soldiers?'

" 'She'd give more than that,' quavered the old man. 'You'd give more than that, wouldn't you, Lucy?'

" 'Yes, I'd give more than that,' repeated the girl quietly, so quietly that it came as a shock to me—like a throb of actual pain in the midst of a nightmare—when she rose to her feet and added, without a movement, without a gesture, 'You must not go, Cousin George. He is upstairs in the blue chamber at the front of the house.'

"For an instant surprise held me speechless, transfixed, incredulous; and in that instant I saw a face—a white face of horror and disbelief—look down on us from one of the side-windows of the blue chamber. Then, in a rush it seemed to me the soldiers were everywhere, swarming over the terrace, into the hall, surrounding the house. I had never imagined that a small body of men in uniforms, even ragged uniforms, could so possess and obscure one's surroundings. The three of us waited there—Lucy had sat down again and taken up her knitting—for what seemed hours, or an eternity. We were still waiting—though, for once, I noticed, the needles did not click in her fingers—when a single shot, followed by a volley, rang out from the rear of the house, from the veranda that looked down on the grove of oaks and the kitchen.

"Rising, I left them—the old man and the girl—and passed from the terrace down the little walk which led to the back. As I reached the lower veranda one of the soldiers ran into me.

"'I was coming after you,' he said, and I observed that his excitement had left him. 'We brought him down while he was trying to jump from the veranda. He is there now on the grass.'

"The man on the grass was quite dead, shot through the heart; and while I bent over to wipe the blood from his lips, I saw him for the first time distinctly. A young face, hardly more than a boy—twenty-five at the most. Handsome, too, in a poetic and dreamy way; just the face, I thought, that a woman might have fallen in love with. He had dark hair, I remember, though his features have long ago faded from my memory. What will never fade, what I shall never forget, is the look he wore—the look he was still wearing when we laid him in the old graveyard next day—a look of mingled surprise, disbelief, terror, and indignation.

"I had done all that I could, which was nothing, and rising to my feet, I saw for the first time that Lucy had joined me. She was standing perfectly motionless. Her knitting was still in her hands, but the light had gone from her face, and she

looked old—old and gray—beside the glowing youth of her
lover. For a moment her eyes held me while she spoke as
quietly as she had spoken to the soldiers on the terrace.

" 'I had to do it,' she said. 'I would do it again.' "

Suddenly, like the cessation of running water, or of wind
in the treetops, the doctor's voice ceased. For a long pause
we stared in silence at the sunset; then, without looking at
me, he added slowly:

"Three weeks later Lee surrendered and the Confederacy
was over."

The sun had slipped, as if by magic, behind the tops of
the cedars, and dusk fell quickly, like a heavy shadow, over
the terrace. In the dimness a piercing sweetness floated up
from the garden of herbs, and it seemed to me that in a
minute the twilight was saturated with fragrance. Then I
heard the cry of a solitary whippoorwill in the graveyard,
and it sounded so near that I started.

"So she died of the futility, and her unhappy ghost haunts
the house?"

"No, she is not dead. It is not her ghost; it is the memory
of her act that has haunted the house. Lucy Dare is still
living. I saw her a few months ago."

"You saw her? You spoke to her after all these years?"

He had refilled his pipe, and the smell of it gave me a
comfortable assurance that I was living here, now, in the
present. A moment ago I had shivered as if the hand of the
past, reaching from the open door at my back, had touched
my shoulder.

"I was in Richmond. My friend Beverly, an old classmate,
had asked me up for a week-end, and on Saturday afternoon, before motoring into the country for supper, we started
out to make a few calls which had been left over from the
morning. For a doctor, a busy doctor, he had always seemed
to me to possess unlimited leisure, so I was not surprised
when a single visit sometimes stretched over twenty-five
minutes. We had stopped several times, and I confess that I
was getting a little impatient when he remarked abruptly
while he turned his car into a shady street.

" 'There is only one more. If you don't mind, I'd like you
to see her. She is a friend of yours, I believe.'

"Before us, as the car stopped, I saw a red-brick house,

very large, with green shutters, and over the wide door, which stood open, a sign reading 'St. Luke's Church Home.' Several old ladies sat, half asleep, on the long veranda; a clergyman, with a prayer book in his hand, was just leaving; a few pots of red geraniums stood on little green-wicker stands; and from the hall, through which floated the smell of freshly baked bread, there came the music of a victrola— sacred music, I remember. Not one of these details escaped me. It was as if every trivial impression was stamped indelibly in my memory by the shock of the next instant.

"In the centre of the large, smoothly shaven lawn an old woman was sitting on a wooden bench under an ailantus-tree which was in blossom. As we approached her, I saw that her figure was shapeless, and that her eyes, of a faded blue, had the vacant and listless expression of the old who have ceased to think, who have ceased even to wonder or regret. So unlike was she to anything I had ever imagined Lucy Dare could become, that not until my friend called her name and she glanced up from the muffler she was knitting— the omnipresent dun-coloured muffler for the war relief associations—not until then did I recognize her.

" 'I have brought an old friend to see you, Miss Lucy.'

"She looked up, smiled slightly, and after greeting me pleasantly, relapsed into silence. I remembered that the Lucy Dare I had known was never much of a talker.

"Dropping on the bench at her side, my friend began asking her about her sciatica, and, to my surprise, she became almost animated. Yes, the pain in her hip was better—far better than it had been for weeks. The new medicine had done her a great deal of good; but her fingers were getting rheumatic. She found trouble holding her needles. She couldn't knit as fast as she used to.

"Unfolding the end of the muffler, she held it out to us. 'I have managed to do twenty of these since Christmas. I've promised fifty to the War Relief Association by autumn, and if my fingers don't get stiff I can easily do them.'

"The sunshine falling through the ailantus-tree powdered with dusty gold her shapeless, relaxed figure and the dun-coloured wool of the muffler. While she talked her fingers flew with the click of the needles—older fingers than they had been at Dare's Gift, heavier, stiffer, a little knotted in the joints. As I watched her the old familiar sense of strangeness, of encompassing and hostile mystery, stole over me.

"When we rose to go she looked up, and, without pausing for an instant in her knitting, said, gravely, 'It gives me something to do, this work for the Allies. It helps to pass the time, and in an Old Ladies' Home one has so much time on one's hands.'

"Then, as we parted from her, she dropped her eyes again to her needles. Looking back at the gate, I saw that she still sat there in the faint sunshine—knitting—knitting——"

"And you think she has forgotten?"

He hesitated, as if gathering his thoughts, "I was with her when she came back from the shock—from the illness that followed—and she had forgotten. Yes, she has forgotten, but the house has remembered."

Pushing back his chair, he rose unsteadily on his crutch, and stood staring across the twilight which was spangled with fireflies. While I waited I heard again the loud cry of the whippoorwill.

"Well, what could one expect?" he asked, presently. "She had drained the whole of experience in an instant, and there was left to her only the empty and withered husks of the hours. She had felt too much ever to feel again. After all," he added slowly, "it is the high moments that make a life, and the flat ones that fill the years."

Zora Neale Hurston (January 7, 1891–January 28, 1960) grew up in Eatonville, Florida. Eatonville was founded by ex-slaves and their families in August of 1887 and is recognized as the oldest incorporated black town in the United States. The town was rich in black folk culture and became, as the poet June Jordan writes, "a supportive, nourishing environment" for Hurston. As Hurston wrote in *Mules and Men*, "I hurried back to Eatonville because I knew that the town was full of material and that I could get it without hurt, harm or danger."

Hurston was a bold and outspoken woman who was one of the first women to wear trousers in public. She collected folklore, wrote novels, plays, and short stories, and staged dramatic readings. She completed high school at Morgan Academy (now Morgan State University) and studied at Howard University. With the aid of a scholarship Hurston studied along with Margaret Mead under the respected Franz Boas at Barnard College where she graduated in 1928. She became a well-known figure among the intellectuals of the Harlem Renaissance. After devoting five years to field research in Florida, Alabama, Louisiana, and the Bahamas she published her classic *Mules and Men* (1935).

Hurston published four novels—*Jonah's Gourd Vine* (1934), *Their Eyes Were Watching God* (1937), *Moses, Man of the Mountain* (1939), and *Seraph on the Sewanee* (1948). *Dust Tracks on a Road*, her autobiography, was published in 1948. Between the 1920s and 1950s she was one of America's most prolific black women writers. Hurston believed in the "beauty of black expression and traditions and in the psychological wholeness of black."

At the time of her death, with all her books out-of-print, Hurston lived in a welfare home in Florida. She was never to make a living from her writing. A collection of her writings, *I Love Myself When I Am Laughing and Then Again When I Am Looking Mean and Impressive* edited by Alice Walker, was published in 1979. Over the past decade much of Hurston's writing has been reprinted. She left a legacy that will not be forgotten.

DRENCHED IN LIGHT

by Zora Neale Hurston

"You Isie Watts! Git 'own offen dat gate post an' rake up dis yahd!"

The small brown girl perched upon the gate post looked yearningly up the gleaming shell road that lead to Orlando. After awhile, she shrugged her thin shoulders. This only seemed to heap still more kindling on Grandma Potts' already burning ire.

"Lawd a-mussy!" she screamed, enraged—"Heah Joel, gimme dat wash stick. Ah'll show dat limb of Satan she cain't shake herself at *me*. If she ain't down by the time Ah gets dere, Ah'll break huh down in de lines."

"Aw Gran'ma, Ah see Mist' George and Jim Robinson comin' and Ah wanted to wave at 'em," the child said impatiently.

"You jes' wave dat rake at dis heah yahd, madame, else Ah'll take you down a button hole lower. Youse too'oomanish jumpin' up in everybody's face dat pass."

This struck the child sorely for nothing pleased her so much as to sit atop of the gate post and hail the passing vehicles on their way South to Orlando, or North to Sanford. That white shell road was her great attraction. She raced up and down the stretch of it that lay before her gate like a round-eyed puppy hailing gleefully all travelers. Everybody in the country, white and colored, knew little Isis Watts, Isis the Joyful. The Robinson brothers, white cattlemen, were particularly fond of her and always extended a stirrup for her to climb up behind one of them for a short ride, or let her try to crack the long bull whips and *yee whoo* at the cows.

Grandma Potts went inside and Isis literally waved the

rake at the 'chaws' of ribbon cane that lay so bountifully about the yard in company with the knots and peelings, with a thick sprinkling of peanut hulls.

The herd of cattle in their envelope of gray dust came alongside and Isis dashed out to the nearest stirrup and was lifted up.

"Hello theah Snidlits, I was wonderin' wheah you was," said Jim Robinson as she snuggled down behind him in the saddle. They were almost out of the danger zone when Grandma emerged. "You Isie," she bawled.

The child slid down on the opposite side of the house and executed a flank movement through the corn patch that brought her into the yard from behind the privy.

"You li'l hasion you! Wheah you been?"

"Out in de back yahd," Isis lied and did a cart wheel and a few fancy steps on her way to the front again.

"If you doan git in dat yahd, Ah make a mommuk of you!" Isis observed that Grandma was cutting a fancy assortment of switches from peach, guana and cherry trees.

She finished the yard by raking everything under the edge of the porch and began a romp with the dogs, those lean, floppy-eared hounds that all country folks keep. But Grandma vetoed this also.

"Isie, you set on dat porch! Uh great big 'leben yeah ole gal racin' an' rompin' lak dat—set 'own!"

Isis flung herself upon the steps.

"Git up offa dem steps, you aggravatin' limb, 'fore Ah git dem hick'ries tuh you, an' set yo' seff on a cheah."

Isis arose, and then sat down as violently as possible in the chair. She slid down, and down, until she all but sat on her own shoulder blades.

"Now look atcher," Grandma screamed, "Put yo' knees together, an' git up offen yo' backbone! Lawd, you know dis hellion is gwine make me stomp huh insides out."

Isis sat bold upright as if she wore a ramrod down her back and began to whistle. Now there are certain things that Grandma Potts felt no one of this female persuasion should do—one was to sit with the knees separated, 'settin' brazen' she called it; another was whistling, another playing with boys. Finally, a lady must never cross her legs.

Grandma jumped up from her seat to get the switches.

"So youse whistlin' in mah face, huh!" She glared till her eyes were beady and Isis bolted for safety. But the noon hour brought John Watts the widowed father, and this excused the child from sitting for criticism.

Being the only girl in the family, of course she must wash the dishes, which she did in intervals between frolics with the dogs. She even gave Jake, the puppy, a swim in the dishpan by holding him suspended above the water that reeked of 'pot likker'—just high enough so that his feet would be immersed. The deluded puppy swam and swam without ever crossing the pan, much to his annoyance. Hearing Grandma she hurriedly dropped him on the floor, which he tracked-up with feet wet with dishwater.

Grandma took her patching and settled down in the front room to sew. She did this every afternoon, and invariably slept in the big red rocker with her head lolled back over the back, the sewing falling from her hand.

Isis had crawled under the center table with its red plush cover with little round balls for fringe. She was lying on her back imagining herself various personages. She wore trailing robes, golden slippers with blue bottoms. She rode white horses with flaring pink nostrils to the horizon, for she still believed that to be land's end. She was picturing herself gazing over the edge of the world into the abyss when the spool of cotton fell from Grandma's lap and rolled away under the whatnot. Isis drew back from her contemplation of the nothingness at the horizon and glanced up at the sleeping woman. Her head had fallen far back. She breathed with a regular 'mark' intake and 'poosah' exhaust. But Isis was a visual-minded child. She heard the snores only subconsciously but she saw the straggling beard of Grandma's chin, trembling a little with every 'mark' and 'poosah'. They were long gray hairs curled every here and there against the dark brown skin. Isis was moved with pity for her mother's mother.

"Poah Gran-ma needs a shave," she murmured, and set about it. Just then Joel, next older than Isis, entered with a can of bait.

"Come on Isie, les' we all go fishin'. The Perch is bitin' fine in Blue Sink."

"Sh-sh—" cautioned his sister, "Ah got to shave Gran'ma."

"Who say so?" Joel asked, surprised.

"Nobody doan hafta tell me. Look at her chin. No ladies don't weah whiskers if they kin help it. But Gran-ma gittin ole an' she doan know how to shave lak *me*."

The conference adjourned to the back porch lest Grandma wake.

"Aw, Isie, you doan know nothin' 'bout shavin' a-tall—but a *man* lak *me*—"

"Ah do so know."

"You don't not. Ah'm goin' shave her mahseff."

"Naw, you won't neither, Smarty. Ah saw her first an' thought it all up first," Isis declared, and ran to the calico-covered box on the wall above the wash basin and seized her father's razor. Joel was quick and seized the mug and brush.

"Now!" Isis cried defiantly, "Ah got the razor."

"Goody, goody, goody, pussy cat, Ah got th' brush an' you can't shave 'thout lather—see! Ah know mo' than you," Joel retorted.

"Aw, who don't know dat?" Isis pretended to scorn. But seeing her progress blocked from lack of lather she compromised.

"Ah know! Les' we all shave her. You lather an' Ah shave."

This was agreeable to Joel. He made mountains of lather and anointed his own chin, and the chin of Isis and the dogs, splashed the wall and at last was persuaded to lather Grandma's chin. Not that he was loath but he wanted his new plaything to last as long as possible.

Isis stood on one side of the chair with the razor clutched cleaver fashion. The niceties of razor-handling had passed over her head. The thing with her was to *hold* the razor—sufficient in itself.

Joel splashed on the lather in great gobs and Grandma awoke.

For one bewildered moment she stared at the grinning boy with the brush and mug but sensing another presence, she turned to behold the business face of Isis and the razor-clutching hand. Her jaw dropped and Grandma, forgetting years and rheumatism, bolted from the chair and fled the house, screaming.

"She's gone to tell papa, Isie. You didn't have no business wid his razor and he's gonna lick yo' hide," Joel cried, running to replace mug and brush.

"You too, chuckle-head, you too," retorted Isis. "You was playin' wid his brush and put it all over the dogs—Ah seen you put in on Ned an' Beulah." Isis shaved and replaced it in the box. Joel took his bait and pole and hurried to Blue Sink. Isis crawled under the house to brood over the whipping she knew would come. She had meant well.

But sounding brass and tinkling cymbal drew her forth. The local lodge of the Grand United Order of Odd Fellows, led by a braying, thudding band, was marching in full regalia down the road. She had forgotten the barbecue and log-rolling to be held today for the benefit of the new hall.

Music to Isis meant motion. In a minute razor and whipping forgotten, she was doing a fair imitation of a Spanish dancer she had seen in a medicine show some time before. Isis' feet were gifted—she could dance most anything she saw.

Up, up, went her spirits, her small feet doing all sorts of intricate things and her body in rhythm, hand curving above her head. But the music was growing faint. Grandma was nowhere in sight. Isis stole out of the gate, running and dancing after the band.

Not far down the road, Isis stopped. She realized she couldn't dance at the carnival. Her dress was torn and dirty. She picked a long-stemmed daisy, and placed it behind her ear, but her dress remained torn and dirty just the same. Then Isis had an idea. Her thoughts returned to the battered, round-topped trunk back in the bedroom. She raced back to the house; then, happier, she raced down the white dusty road to the picnic grove, gorgeously clad. People laughed good-naturedly at her, the band played and Isis danced because she couldn't help it. A crowd of children gathered admiringly about her as she wheeled lightly about, hand on hip, flower between her teeth with the red and white fringe of the tablecloth—Grandma's new red tablecloth that she wore in lieu of a Spanish shawl—trailing in the dust. It was too ample for her meager form, but she wore it like a gypsy. Her brown feet twinkled in and out of the fringe. Some grown people joined the children about her. The Grand Exalted Ruler rose to speak; the band was hushed, but Isis danced on, the crowd clapping their hands for her. No one listened to the Exalted one, for little by little the multitude had surrounded the small brown dancer.

An automobile drove up to the Crown and halted. Two white men and a lady got out and pushed into the crowd, suppressing mirth discretely behind gloved hands. Isis looked up and waved them a magnificent hail and went on dancing until—

Grandma had returned to the house, and missed Isis. She straightaway sought her at the festivities, expecting to find her in her soiled dress, shoeless, standing at the far edge of the crowd. What she saw now drove her frantic. Here was her granddaughter dancing before a gaping crowd in her brand new red tablecloth, and reeking of lemon extract. Isis had added the final touch to her costume. Of course she must also have perfume.

When Isis saw her Grandma, she bolted. She heard her Grandma cry—"Mah Gawd, mah brand new tablecloth Ah just bought f'um O'landah!"—as Isis fled through the crowd and on into the woods.

Isis followed the little creek until she came to the ford in a rutty wagon road that led to Apopka and laid down on the cool grass at the roadside. The April sun was quite warm.

Misery, misery and woe settled down upon her. The child wept. She knew another whipping was in store.

"Oh, Ah wish Ah could die, then Gran'ma an' papa would be sorry they beat me so much. Ah b'leeve Ah'll run away and never go home no mo'. Ah'm goin' drown mahseff in th' creek!"

Isis got up and waded into the water. She routed out a tiny 'gator and a huge bullfrog. She splashed and sang. Soon she was enjoying herself immensely. The purr of a motor struck her ear and she saw a large, powerful car jolting along the rutty road toward her. It stopped at the water's edge.

"Well, I declare, it's our little gypsy," exclaimed the man at the wheel. "What are you doing here, now?"

"Ah'm killin' mahseff," Isis declared dramatically, "Cause Gran'ma beats me too much."

There was a hearty burst of laughter from the machine.

"You'll last some time the way you are going about it. Is this the way to Maitland? We want to go to the Park Hotel."

Isis saw no longer any reason to die. She came up out of the water, holding up the dripping fringe of the tablecloth.

"Naw, indeedy. You go to Maitlan' by the shell road—it goes by mah house—an'turn off at Lake Sebelia to the clay road that takes you right to the do'."

"Well," went on the driver, smiling furtively, "Could you quit dying long enough to go with us?"

"Yessuh," she said thoughtfully, "Ah wanta go wid you."

The door of the car swung open. She was invited to a seat beside the driver. She had often dreamed of riding in one of these heavenly chariots but never thought she would, actually.

"Jump in then, Madame Tragedy, and show us. We lost ourselves after we left your barbecue."

During the drive Isis explained to the kind lady who smelt faintly of violets and to the indifferent men that she was really a princess. She told them about her trips to the horizon, about the trailing gowns, the gold shoes with blue bottoms—she insisted on the blue bottoms—the white charger, the time when she was Hercules and had slain numerous dragons and sundry giants. At last the car approached her gate over which stood the umbrella chinaberry tree. The car was abreast of the gate and had all but passed when Grandma spied her glorious tablecloth lying back against the upholstery of the Packard.

"You Isie-e!" she bawled, "You li'l wretch you! Come heah *dis instant.*"

"That's me," the child confessed, mortified, to the lady on the rear seat.

"Oh Sewell, stop the car. This is where the child lives. I hate to give her up though."

"Do you wanta keep me?" Isis brightened.

"Oh, I wish I could. Wait, I'll try to save you a whipping this time."

She dismounted with the gaudy lemon-flavored culprit and advanced to the gate where Grandma stood glowering, switches in hand.

"You're gointuh ketchit f'um yo' haid to yo' heels m'lady. Jes' come in heah."

"Why, good afternoon," she accosted the furious grandparent. "You're not going to whip this poor little thing, are you?" the lady asked in conciliatory tones.

"Yes, Ma'am. She's de wustest li'l limb dat ever drawed bref. Jes' look at mah new tablecloth, dat ain't never been washed. She done traipsed all over de woods, uh dancin' an' uh prancin' in it. She done took a razor to me t'day an' Lawd knows whut mo'."

Isis clung to the stranger's hand fearfully.

"Ah wuzn't gointer hurt Gran'ma, miss—Ah wuz just

gointer shave her whiskers fuh huh 'cause she's old an' can't.''

The white hand closed tightly over the little brown one that was quite soiled. She could understand a voluntary act of love even though it miscarried.

"Now, Mrs. er-er-I didn't get the name—how much did your tablecloth cost?"

"One whole big silvah dollar down at O'landah—ain't had it a week yit."

"Now here's five dollars to get another one. I want her to go to the hotel and dance for me. I could stand a little light today—"

"Oh, yessum, yessum," Grandma cut in, "Everything's alright, sho' she kin go, yessum."

Feeling that Grandma had been somewhat squelched did not detract from Isis' spirit at all. She pranced over to the waiting motor-car and this time seated herself on the rear seat between the sweet-smiling lady and the rather aloof man in gray.

"Ah'm gointer stay wid you all," she said with a great deal of warmth, and snuggled up to her benefactress. "Want me tuh sing a song fuh you?"

"There, Helen, you've been adopted," said the man with a short, harsh laugh.

"Oh, I hope so, Harry." She put her arm about the red-draped figure at her side and drew it close until she felt the warm puffs of the child's breath against her side. She looked hungrily ahead of her and spoke into space rather than to anyone in the car. "I would like just a little of her sunshine to soak into my soul. I would like that alot."

William Faulkner (September 25, 1897–July 6, 1962) was born in New Albany, Mississippi. When he was five years old his family moved to Oxford, Mississippi, where he lived most of his life except for brief periods spent in Hollywood and Charlottesville, Virginia. Faulkner's education was sporadic. Dropping out of high school in his senior year, he attended the University of Mississippi as a special student for only one year (1919–20). He was a voracious reader and, through his friend and earliest critic, Phil Stone, was introduced to modern writers, including the French Symbolist poets. Their influence, along with the influence of Thomas Hardy and William Butler Yeats, can be seen in Faulkner's first book, a collection of poetry, *The Marble Faun*.

Influenced by Sherwood Anderson, Faulkner wrote his first novel, *Soldier's Pay*, which appeared in 1926. Its publication began an extraordinarily prolific career. The next decade produced eight novels, including many of the finest he would write: *The Sound and the Fury* (1929), *As I Lay Dying* (1930), *Light in August* (1932), and *Absalom, Absalom!* (1936). However, his creative output was not matched by financial returns, so, in 1932, Faulkner went to Hollywood as a screen writer, a position he kept, under financial duress, until 1948, when the commercial success of *Intruder in the Dust* and its subsequent sale to the movies enabled him to return to Mississippi. With the exception of tours for the State Department and time spent as a writer-in-residence at the University of Virginia, he remained in Oxford the rest of his life. Faulkner won numerous awards for his fiction, including the 1949 Nobel Prize and two Pulitzer Prizes, one for *A Fable* (1954) and another for *The Reivers* (1962). His accomplished short fiction appears in *Collected Stories* (1950) and *Uncollected Stories* (1979). Faulkner, who admitted that he had learned to write "from other writers," advised hopeful poets and novelists to "read all you can."

DRY SEPTEMBER

by William Faulkner

Through the bloody September twilight, aftermath of sixty-two rainless days, it had gone like a fire in dry grass—the rumor, the story, whatever it was. Something about Miss Minnie Cooper and a Negro. Attacked, insulted, frightened: none of them, gathered in the barber shop on that Saturday evening where the ceiling fan stirred, without freshening it, the vitiated air, sending back upon them, in recurrent surges of stale pomade and lotion, their own stale breath and odors, knew exactly what had happened.

"Except it wasn't Will Mayes," a barber said. He was a man of middle age; a thin, sand-colored man with a mild face, who was shaving a client. "I know Will Mayes. He's a good nigger. And I know Miss Minnie Cooper, too."

"What do you know about her?" a second barber said.

"Who is she?" the client said. "A young girl?"

"No," the barber said. "She's about forty, I reckon. She aint married. That's why I dont believe—"

"Believe, hell!" a hulking youth in a sweat-stained silk shirt said. "Wont you take a white woman's word before a nigger's?"

"I dont believe Will Mayes did it," the barber said. "I know Will Mayes."

"Maybe you know who did it, then. Maybe you already got him out of town, you damn niggerlover."

"I dont believe anybody did anything. I dont believe anything happened. I leave it to you fellows if them ladies that get old without getting married dont have notions that a man cant—"

"Then you are a hell of a white man," the client said. He moved under the cloth. The youth had sprung to his feet.

"You dont?" he said. "Do you accuse a white woman of lying?"

The barber held the razor poised above the half-risen client. He did not look around.

"It's this durn weather," another said. "It's enough to make a man do anything. Even to her."

Nobody laughed. The barber said in his mild, stubborn tone: "I aint accusing nobody of nothing. I just know and you fellows know how a woman that never—"

"You damn niggerlover!" the youth said.

"Shut up, Butch," another said. "We'll get the facts in plenty of time to act."

"Who is? Who's getting them?" the youth said. "Facts, hell! I—"

"You're a fine white man," the client said. "Aint you?" In his frothy beard he looked like a desert rat in the moving pictures. "You tell them, Jack," he said to the youth. "If there aint any white men in this town, you can count on me, even if I aint only a drummer and a stranger."

"That's right, boys," the barber said. "Find out the truth first. I know Will Mayes."

"Well, by God!" the youth shouted. "To think that a white man in this town—"

"Shut up, Butch," the second speaker said. "We got plenty of time."

The client sat up. He looked at the speaker. "Do you claim that anything excuses a nigger attacking a white woman? Do you mean to tell me you are a white man and you'll stand for it? You better go back North where you came from. The South dont want your kind here."

"North what?" the second said. "I was born and raised in this town."

"Well, by God!" the youth said. He looked about with a strained, baffled gaze, as if he was trying to remember what it was he wanted to say or to do. He drew his sleeve across his sweating face. "Damn if I'm going to let a white woman—"

"You tell them, Jack," the drummer said. "By God, if they—"

The screen door crashed open. A man stood in the floor, his feet apart and his heavy-set body poised easily. His white shirt was open at the throat; he wore a felt hat. His hot, bold glance swept the group. His name was McLendon. He had commanded troops at the front in France and had been decorated for valor.

"Well," he said, "are you going to sit there and let a black son rape a white woman on the streets of Jefferson?"

Butch sprang up again. The silk of his shirt clung flat to his heavy shoulders. At each armpit was a dark halfmoon. "That's what I been telling them! That's what I—"

"Did it really happen?" a third said. "This aint the first man scare she ever had, like Hawkshaw says. Wasn't there something about a man on the kitchen roof, watching her undress, about a year ago?"

"What?" the client said. "What's that?" The barber had been slowly forcing him back into the chair; he arrested himself reclining, his head lifted, the barber still pressing him down.

McLendon whirled on the third speaker. "Happen? What the hell difference does it make? Are you going to let the black sons get away with it until one really does it?"

"That's what I'm telling them!" Butch shouted. He cursed, long and steady, pointless.

"Here, here," a fourth said. "Not so loud. Dont talk so loud."

"Sure," McLendon said; "no talking necessary at all. I've done my talking. Who's with me?" He poised on the balls of his feet, roving his gaze.

The barber held the drummer's face down, the razor poised. "Find out the facts first, boys. I know Willy Mayes. It wasn't him. Let's get the sheriff and do this thing right."

McLendon whirled upon him his furious, rigid face. The barber did not look away. They looked like men of different races. The other barbers had ceased also above their prone clients. "You mean to tell me," McLendon said, "that you'd take a nigger's word before a white woman's? Why, you damn niggerloving—"

The third speaker rose and grasped McLendon's arm; he too had been a soldier. "Now, now. Let's figure this thing out. Who knows anything about what really happened?"

"Figure out hell!" McLendon jerked his arm free. "All that're with me get up from there. The ones that aint—" He roved his gaze, draggin his sleeve across his face.

Three men rose. The drummer sat in the chair sat up. "Here," he said, jerking at the cloth about his neck; "get this rag off me. I'm with him. I dont live here, but by God, if our mothers and wives and sisters—" He smeared the cloth over his face and flung it to the floor. McLendon stood in the floor and cursed the others. Another rose and moved toward him. The remainder sat uncomfortable, not looking at one another, then one by one they rose and joined him.

The barber picked the cloth from the floor. He began to fold it neatly. "Boys, dont do that. Will Mayes never done it. I know."

"Come on," McLendon said. He whirled. From his hip pocket protruded the butt of a heavy automatic pistol. They went out. The screen door crashed behind them reverberant in the dead air.

The barber wiped the razor carefully and swiftly, and put it away, and ran to the rear, and took his hat from the wall. "I'll be back as soon as I can," he said to the other barbers. "I cant let—" He went out, running. The two other barbers followed him to the door and caught in to the rebound, leaning out and looking up the street after him. The air was flat and dead. It had a metallic taste at the base of the tongue.

"What can he do?" the first said. The second one was saying "Jees Christ, Jees Christ" under his breath. "I'd just as lief be Will Mayes as Hawk, if he gets McLendon riled."

"Jees Christ, Jees Christ," the second whispered.

"You reckon he really done it to her?" the first said.

II

She was thirty-eight or thirty-nine. She lived in a small frame house with her invalid mother and a thin, sallow, unflagging aunt, where each morning between ten and eleven she would appear on the porch in a lace-trimmed boudoir cap, to sit swinging in the porch swing until noon. After dinner she lay down for a while, until the afternoon began to cool. Then, in one of the three or four new voile dresses which she had each summer, she would go downtown to spend the afternoon in the stores with the other ladies, where they would handle the goods and haggle over the prices in cold, immediate voices, without any intention of buying.

She was of comfortable people—not the best in Jefferson, but good people enough—and she was still on the slender side of ordinary looking, with a bright, faintly haggard manner and dress. When she was young she had had a slender, nervous body and a sort of hard vivacity which had enabled her for a time to ride upon the crest of the town's social life as exemplified by the huge school party and church social period of her contemporaries while still children enough to be unclassconscious.

She was the last to realize that she was losing ground; that those among whom she had been a little brighter and louder flame than any other were beginning to learn the pleasure of snobbery—male—and retaliation—female. That was when her face began to wear that bright, haggard look. She still carried it to parties on shadowy porticoes and summer lawns, like a mask or a flag, with that bafflement of furious repudiation of truth in her eyes. One evening at a party she heard a boy and two girls, all schoolmates, talking. She never accepted another invitation.

She watched the girls with whom she had grown up as they married and got homes and children, but no man ever called on her steadily until the children of the other girls had been calling her "aunty" for several years, the while their mothers told them in bright voices about how popular Aunt Minnie had been as a girl. Then the town began to see her driving on Sunday afternoons with the cashier in the bank. He was a widower of about forty—a high-colored man, smelling always faintly of the barber shop or of whisky. He owned the first automobile in town, a red runabout; Minnie had the first motoring bonnet and veil the town ever saw. Then the town began to say: "Poor Minnie." "But she is old enough to take care of herself," others said. That was when she began to ask her old schoolmates that their children call her "cousin" instead of "aunty."

It was twelve years now since she had been relegated into adultery by public opinion, and eight years since the cashier had gone to a Memphis bank, returning one day each Christmas, which he spent at an annual bachelors' party at a hunting club on the river. From behind their curtains the neighbors would see the party pass, and during the over-the-way Christmas day visiting they would tell her about him, about how well he looked, and how they heard that he was prospering in the city, watching with bright, secret eyes her haggard, bright face. Usually by that hour there would be the scent of whisky on her breath. It was supplied her by a youth, a clerk at the soda fountain: "Sure; I buy it for the old gal. I reckon she's entitled to a little fun."

Her mother kept to her room altogether now; the gaunt aunt ran the house. Against that background Minnie's bright dresses, her idle and empty days, had a quality of furious unreality. She went out in the evenings only with women now, neighbors, to the moving pictures. Each afternoon she dressed in one of the new dresses and went downtown alone, where her young "cousins" were already strolling in the late afternoons with their delicate, silken heads and thin, awkward arms and conscious hips, clinging to one another or shrieking and giggling with paired boys in the soda fountain when she passed and went on along the serried store fronts, in the doors of which the sitting and lounging men did not even follow her with their eyes any more.

III

The barber went swiftly up the street where the sparse lights, insect-swirled, glared in rigid and violent suspension in the lifeless air. The day had died in a pall of dust; above the darkened square, shrouded by the spent dust, the sky was as clear as the inside of a brass bell. Below the east was a rumor of the twice-waxed moon.

When he overtook them McLendon and three others were getting into a car parked in an alley. McLendon stooped his thick head, peering out beneath the top. "Changed your mind, did you?" he said. "Damn good thing; by God, tomorrow when this town hears about how you talked tonight—"

"Now, now," the other ex-soldier said. "Hawkshaw's all right. Come on, Hawk; jump in."

"Will Mayes never done it, boys," the barber said. "If anybody done it. Why, you all know well as I do there aint any town where they got better niggers than us. And you know how a lady will kind of think things about men when there aint any reason to, and Miss Minnie anyway—"

"Sure, sure," the soldier said. "We're just going to talk to him a little; that's all."

"Talk hell!" Butch said. "When we're through with the—"

"Shut up, for God's sake!" the soldier said. "Do you want everybody in town—"

"Tell them, by God!" McLendon said. "Tell every one of the sons that'll let a white woman—"

"Let's go; let's go: here's the other car." The second car slid squealing out of a cloud of dust at the alley mouth. McLendon started his car and took the lead. Dust lay like fog in the street. The street lights hung nimbused as in water. They drove on out of town.

A rutted lane turned at right angles. Dust hung above it too, and above all the land. The dark bulk of the ice plant, where the Negro Mayes was night watchman, rose against the sky. "Better stop here, hadn't we?" the soldier said. McLendon did not reply. He hurled the car up and slammed to a stop, the headlights glaring on the blank wall.

"Listen here, boys," the barber said; "if he's here, dont that prove he never done it? Dont it? If it was him, he would run. Dont you see he would?" The second car came up and stopped. McLendon got down; Butch spring down beside him. "Listen, boys," the barber said.

"Cut the lights off!" McLendon said. The breathless dark rushed down. There was no sound in it save their lungs as they sought air in the parched dust in which for two months they had lived; then the diminishing crunch of McLendon's and Butch's feet, and a moment later McLendon's voice:

"Will! . . . Will!"

Below the east the wan hemorrhage of the moon increased. It heaved above the ridge, silvering the air, the dust, so that they seemed to breathe, live, in a bowl of molten lead. There was no sound of nightbird nor insect, no sound save their breathing and a faint ticking of contracting metal about the cars. Where their bodies touched one another they seemed to sweat dryly, for no more moisture came. "Christ!" a voice said; "let's get out of here."

But they didn't move until vague noises began to grow out of the darkness ahead; then they got out and waited tensely in the breathless dark. There was another sound: a blow, a hissing expulsion of breath and McLendon cursing in undertone. They stood a moment longer, then they ran forward. They ran in a stumbling clump, as though they were fleeing something. "Kill him, kill the son," a voice whispered. McLendon flung them back.

"Not here," he said. "Get him into the car." "Kill him, kill the black son!" the voice murmured. They dragged the Negro to the car. The barber had waited beside the car. He could feel himself sweating and he knew he was going to be sick at the stomach.

"What is it, captains?" the Negro said. "I aint done nothing. 'Fore God, Mr John." Someone produced handcuffs. They worked busily about the Negro as though he were a post, quiet, intent, getting in one another's way. He submitted to the handcuffs, looking swiftly and constantly from dim face to dim face. "Who's here, captains?" he said, leaning to peer into the faces until they could feel his breath and smell his sweaty reek. He spoke a name or two. "What you all say I done, Mr John?"

McLendon jerked the car door open. "Get in!" he said.

The Negro did not move. "What you all going to do with me, Mr John? I aint done nothing. White folks, captains, I aint done nothing: I swear 'fore God." He called another name.

"Get in!" McLendon said. He struck the Negro. The others expelled their breath in a dry hissing and struck him with random blows and he whirled and cursed them, and swept his manacled hands across their faces and slashed the barber upon the mouth, and the barber struck him also. "Get him in there," McLendon said. They pushed at him. He ceased struggling and got in and sat quietly as the others took their places. He sat between the barber and the soldier, drawing his limbs in so as not to touch them, his eyes going swiftly and constantly from face to face. Butch clung to the running board. The car moved on. The barber nursed his mouth with his handkerchief.

"What's the matter, Hawk?" the soldier said.

"Nothing," the barber said. They regained the highroad and turned away from town. The second car dropped back out of the dust. They went on, gaining speed; the final fringe of houses dropped behind.

"Goddamn, he stinks!" the soldier said.

"We'll fix that," the drummer in front beside McLendon said. On the running board Butch cursed into the hot rush of air. The barber leaned suddenly forward and touched McLendon's arm.

"Let me out, John," he said.

"Jump out, niggerlover," McLendon said without turning his head. He drove swiftly. Behind them the sourceless lights of the second car glared in the dust. Presently McLendon turned into a narrow road. It was rutted with disuse. It led back to an abandoned brick kiln—a series of reddish mounds and weed- and vine-choked vats without bottom. It had been used for pasture once, until one day the owner missed one of his mules. Although he prodded carefully in the vats with a long pole, he could not even find the bottom of them.

"John," the barber said.

"Jump out, then," McLendon said, hurling the car along the ruts. Beside the barber the Negro spoke:

"Mr Henry."

The barber sat forward. The narrow tunnel of the road rushed up and past. Their motion was like an extinct furnace blast: cooler, but utterly dead. The car bounded from rut to rut.

"Mr Henry," the Negro said.

The barber began to tug furiously at the door. "Look out, there!" the soldier said, but the barber had already kicked the door open and swung onto the running board. The soldier leaned across the Negro and grasped at him, but he had already jumped. The car went on without checking speed.

The impetus hurled him crashing through dust-sheathed weeds, into the ditch. Dust puffed about him, and in a thin, vicious crackling of sapless stems he lay choking and retching until the second car passed and died away. Then he rose and limped on until he reached the highroad and turned toward town, brushing at his clothes with his hands. The moon was higher, riding high and clear of the dust at last, and after a while the town began to glare beneath the dust. He went on, limping. Presently he heard cars and the glow of them grew in the dust behind him and he left the road and crouched again in the weeds until they passed. McLendon's car came last now. There were four people in it and Butch was not on the running board.

They went on; the dust swallowed them; the glare and the sound died away. The dust of them hung for a while, but soon the eternal dust absorbed it again. The barber climbed back onto the road and limped on toward town.

IV

As she dressed for supper on that Saturday evening, her own flesh felt like fever. Her hands trembled among the hooks and eyes, and her eyes had a feverish look, and her hair swirled crisp and crackling under the comb. While she was still dressing the friends called for her and sat while she donned her sheerest underthings and stockings and a new voile dress. "Do you feel strong enough to go out?" they said, their eyes bright too, with a dark glitter. "When you have had time to get over the shock, you must tell us what happened. What he said and did; everything."

In the leafed darkness, as they walked toward the square, she began to breathe deeply, something like a swimmer preparing to dive, until she ceased trembling, the four of them walking slowly because of the terrible heat and out of solicitude for her. But as they neared the square she began to tremble again, walking with her head up, her hands clenched at her sides, their voices about her murmurous, also with that feverish, glittering quality of their eyes.

They entered the square, she in the center of the group, fragile in her fresh dress. She was trembling worse. She walked slower and slower, as children eat ice cream, her head up and her eyes bright in the haggard banner of her face, passing the hotel and the coatless drummers in chairs along the curb looking around at her: "That's the one: see? The one in pink in the middle." "Is that her? What did they do with the nigger? Did they—?" "Sure. He's all right." "All right, is he?" "Sure. He went on a little trip." Then the drug store, where even the young men lounging in the doorway tipped their hats and followed with their eyes the motion of her hips and legs when she passed.

They went on, passing the lifted hats of the gentlemen, the suddenly ceased voices, deferent, protective. "Do you see?" the friends said. Their voices sounded like long, hovering sighs of hissing exultation. "There's not a Negro on the square. Not one."

They reached the picture show. It was like a miniature fairyland with its lighted lobby and colored lithographs of life caught in its terrible and beautiful mutations. Her lips began to tingle. In the dark, when the picture began, it would be all right; she could hold back the laughing so it would not waste away so fast and so soon. So she hurried on before the turning faces, the undertones of low astonishment, and they took their accustomed places where she could see the aisle against the silver glare and the young men and girls coming in two and two against it.

The lights flicked away; the screen glowed silver, and

soon life began to unfold, beautiful and passionate and sad, while still the young men and girls entered, scented and sibilant in the half dark, their paired backs in silhouette delicate and sleek, their slim, quick bodies awkward, divinely young, while beyond them the silver dream accumulated, inevitably on and on. She began to laugh. In trying to suppress it, it made more noise than ever; heads began to turn. Still laughing, her friends raised her and led her out, and she stood at the curb, laughing on a high, sustained note, until the taxi came up and they helped her in.

They removed the pink voile and the sheer underthings and the stockings, and put her to bed, and cracked ice for her temples, and sent for the doctor. He was hard to locate, so they ministered to her with hushed ejaculations, renewing the ice and fanning her. While the ice was fresh and cold she stopped laughing and lay still for a time, moaning only a little. But soon the laughing welled again and her voice rose screaming.

"Shhhhhhhhhhh! Shhhhhhhhhhhhhhh!" they said, freshening the icepack, smoothing her hair, examining it for gray; "poor girl!" Then to one another: "Do you suppose anything really happened?" their eyes darkly aglitter, secret and passionate. "Shhhhhhhhhh! Poor girl! Poor Minnie!"

V

It was midnight when McLendon drove up to his neat new house. It was trim and fresh as a birdcage and almost as small, with its clean, green-and-white paint. He locked the car and mounted the porch and entered. His wife rose from a chair beside the reading lamp. McLendon stopped in the floor and stared at her until she looked down.

"Look at that clock," he said, lifting his arm, pointing. She stood before him, her face lowered, a magazine in her hands. Her face was pale, strained, and weary-looking. "Haven't I told you about sitting up like this, waiting to see when I come in?"

"John," she said. She laid the magazine down. Poised on the balls of his feet, he glared at her with his hot eyes, his sweating face.

"Didn't I tell you?" He went toward her. She looked up then. He caught her shoulder. She stood passive, looking at him.

"Don't, John. I couldn't sleep . . . The heat; something. Please, John. You're hurting me."

"Didn't I tell you?" He released her and half struck, half flung her across the chair, and she lay there and watched him quietly as he left the room.

He went on through the house, ripping off his shirt, and on the dark, screened porch at the rear he stood and mopped his head and shoulders with the shirt and flung it away. He took the pistol from his hip and laid it on the table beside the bed, and sat on the bed and removed his shoes, and rose and slipped his trousers off. He was sweating again already, and he stopped and hunted furiously for the shirt. At last he found it and wiped his body again, and, with his body pressed against the dusty screen, he stood panting. There was no movement, no sound, not even an insect. The dark world seemed to lie stricken beneath the cold moon and the lidless stars.

Erskine Caldwell (December 17, 1903–April 11, 1987) was born in Coweta County, Georgia. Because his father was Associated Reformed Presbyterian minister and trouble-shooting arbiter for his denomination, Caldwell moved a great deal. His mother, a former teacher of Latin and English, taught him at home until he was thirteen. Caldwell began to write short stories after a brief formal education which included college in Georgia, Virginia, and Pennsylvania. He lived in Maine for several years and many other parts of the country, including Arizona, California, and Florida.

His first published writing was "The Georgia Cracker" in 1926. His early writing was noticed by the editor Maxwell Perkins who published some of Caldwell's stories in *Scribner's* and published *American Earth* (1931) and *Tobacco Road* (1932),two of his early novels about southern life. Subsequently Viking Press issued *God's Little Acre* (1933), *Journeyman* (1935), and his first two short-story collections—*We Are the Living* (1933) and *Kneel to the Rising Sun* (1935).

Caldwell had a variety of occupations. He worked on the Atlanta *Journal*, wrote for Hollywood, worked as a foreign correspondent, covered the Spanish Civil War, and lectured at the New School for Social Research in New York City.

Caldwell and photographer Margaret Bourke-White married in 1939. Before divorcing in 1942 they collaborated on three books—*You Have Seen Their Faces* (1937), *North of the Danube* (1939), and *Say! Is This the U.S.A.?* (1941).

In addition to twenty-five novels, twelve works of nonfiction, picture-texts with Bourke-White, and two children's books, Caldwell published 128 short stories. In a 1958 interview with *Atlantic Monthly* Caldwell told literary scholar Carvel Collins: "I don't think there is anything to compare with the short story. I think it's the best form of writing there is."

Caldwell spent the last years of his life in Florida writing his autobiography, *With All My Might*. It was published first in France in 1986 and in the United States by Peachtree Press a month before his death from cancer.

KNEEL TO THE RISING SUN

by Erskine Caldwell

A shiver went through Lonnie. He drew his hand away from his sharp chin, remembering what Clem had said. It made him feel now as if he were committing a crime by standing in Arch Gunnard's presence and allowing his face to be seen.

He and Clem had been walking up the road together that afternoon on their way to the filling station when he told Clem how much he needed rations. Clem stopped a moment to kick a rock out of the road, and said that if you worked for Arch Gunnard long enough, your face would be sharp enough to split the boards for your own coffin.

As Lonnie turned away to sit down on an empty box beside the gasoline pump, he could not help wishing that he could be as unafraid of Arch Gunnard as Clem was. Even if Clem was a Negro, he never hesitated to ask for rations when he needed something to eat; and when he and his family did not get enough, Clem came right out and told Arch so. Arch stood for that, but he swore that he was going to run Clem out of the country the first chance he got.

Lonnie knew without turning around that Clem was standing at the corner of the filling station with two or three other Negroes and looking at him, but for some reason he was unable to meet Clem's eyes.

Arch Gunnard was sitting in the sun, honing his jackknife blade on his boot top. He glanced once or twice at Lonnie's hound, Nancy, who was lying in the middle of the road waiting for Lonnie to go home.

"That your dog, Lonnie?"

Jumping with fear, Lonnie's hand went to his chin to hide the lean face that would accuse Arch of short-rationing.

Arch snapped his fingers and the hound stood up, wagging her tail. She waited to be called.

"Mr. Arch, I—"

Arch called the dog. She began crawling towards them on her belly, wagging her tail a little faster each time Arch's fingers snapped. When she was several feet away, she turned over on her back and lay on the ground with her four paws in the air.

Dudley Smith and Jim Weaver, who were lounging around the filling station, laughed. They had been leaning against the side of the building, but they straightened up to see what Arch was up to.

Arch spat some more tobacco juice on his boot top and whetted the jackknife blade some more.

"What kind of a hound dog is that, anyway, Lonnie?" Arch said. "Looks like to me it might be a ketch hound."

Lonnie could feel Clem Henry's eyes boring into the back of his head. He wondered what Clem would do if it had been his dog Arch Gunnard was snapping his fingers at and calling like that.

"His tail's way too long for a coon hound or a bird dog, ain't it, Arch?" somebody behind Lonnie said, laughing out loud.

Everybody laughed then, including Arch. They looked at Lonnie, waiting to hear what he was going to say to Arch.

"Is he a ketch hound, Lonnie?" Arch said, snapping his finger again.

"Mr. Arch, I—"

"Don't be ashamed of him, Lonnie, if he don't show signs of turning out to be a bird dog or a foxhound. Everybody needs a hound around the house that can go out and catch pigs and rabbits when you are in a hurry for them. A ketch hound is a mighty respectable animal. I've known the time when I was mighty proud to own one."

Everybody laughed.

Arch Gunnard was getting ready to grab Nancy by the tail. Lonnie sat up, twisting his neck until he caught a glimpse of Clem Henry at the other corner of the filling station. Clem was staring at him with unmistakable meaning, with the same look in his eyes he had had that afternoon when he said that nobody who worked for Arch

Gunnard ought to stand for short-rationing. Lonnie lowered his eyes. He could not figure out how a Negro could be braver than he was. There were a lot of times like that when he would have given anything he had to be able to jump into Clem's shoes and change places with him.

"The trouble with this hound of yours, Lonnie, is that he's too heavy on his feet. Don't you reckon it would be a pretty slick little trick to lighten the load some, being as how he's a ketch hound to begin with?"

Lonnie remembered then what Clem Henry had said he would do if Arch Gunnard ever tried to cut off his dog's tail. Lonnie knew, and Clem knew, and everybody else knew, that that would give Arch the chance he was waiting for. All Arch asked, he had said, was for Clem Henry to overstep his place just one little half inch, or to talk back to him with just one little short word, and he would do the rest. Everybody knew what Arch meant by that, especially if Clem did not turn and run. And Clem had not been known to run from anybody, after fifteen years in the country.

Arch reached down and grabbed Nancy's tail while Lonnie was wondering about Clem. Nancy acted as if she thought Arch were playing some kind of game with her. She turned her head around until she could reach Arch's hand to lick it. He cracked her on the bridge of the nose with the end of the jackknife.

"He's a mighty playful dog, Lonnie," Arch said, catching up a shorter grip on the tail, "but his wagpole is way too long for a dog his size, especially when he wants to be a ketch hound."

Lonnie swallowed hard.

"Mr. Arch, she's a mighty fine rabbit tracker. I—"

"Shucks, Lonnie," Arch said, whetting the knife blade on the dog's tail, "I ain't ever seen a hound in all my life that needed a tail that long to hunt rabbits with. It's way too long for just a common, ordinary, everyday ketch hound."

Lonnie looked up hopefully at Dudley Smith and the others. None of them offered any help. It was useless for him to try to stop Arch, because Arch Gunnard would let nothing stand in his way when once he had set his head on what he wished to do. Lonnie knew that if he should let himself show any anger or resentment, Arch would drive him off the farm before sundown that night. Clem Henry was the only person there who would help him, but Clem . . .

The white men and the Negroes at both corners of the filling station waited to see what Lonnie was going to do about it. All of them hoped he would put up a fight for his hound. If anyone ever had the nerve to stop Arch Gunnard from cutting off a dog's tail, it might put an end to it. It was plain, though, that Lonnie, who was one of Arch's share-croppers, was afraid to speak up. Clem Henry might; Clem was the only one who might try to stop Arch, even if it meant trouble. And all of them knew that Arch would insist on running Clem out of the country, or filling him full of lead.

"I reckon it's all right with you, ain't it, Lonnie?" Arch said. "I don't seem to hear no objections."

Clem Henry stepped forward several paces, and stopped.

Arch laughed, watching Lonnie's face, and jerked Nancy to her feet. The hound cried out in pain and surprise, but Arch made her be quiet by kicking her in the belly.

Lonnie winced. He could hardly bear to see anybody kick his dog like that.

"Mr. Arch, I. . . ."

A contraction in his throat almost choked him for several moments, and he had to open his mouth wide and fight for breath. The other white men around him were silent. Nobody liked to see a dog kicked in the belly like that.

Lonnie could see the other end of the filling station from the corner of his eye. He saw a couple of Negroes go up behind Clem and grasp his overalls. Clem spat on the ground, between outspread feet, but he did not try to break away from them.

"Being as how I don't hear no objections, I reckon it's all right to go ahead and cut it off," Arch said, spitting.

Lonnie's head went forward and all he could see of Nancy was her hind feet. He had come to ask for a slab of sowbelly and some molasses, or something. Now he did not know if he could ever bring himself to ask for rations, no matter how much hungrier they became at home.

"I always make it a habit of asking a man first," Arch said. "I wouldn't want to go ahead and cut off a tail if a man had any objections. That wouldn't be right. No, sir, it just wouldn't be fair and square."

Arch caught a shorter grip on the hound's tail and placed the knife blade on it two or three inches from the rump. It looked to those who were watching as if his mouth were watering, because tobacco juice began to trickle down the corners of his lips. He brought up the back of his hand and wiped his mouth.

A noisy automobile came plowing down the road through the deep red dust. Everyone looked up as it passed in order to see who was in it.

Lonnie glanced at it, but he could not keep his eyes raised. His head fell downward once more until he could feel his sharp chin cutting into his chest. He wondered then if Arch had noticed how lean his face was.

"I keep two or three ketch hounds around my place," Arch said, honing the blade on the tail of the dog as if it were a razor strop until his actions brought smiles to the faces of the men grouped around him, "but I never could see the sense of a ketch hound having a long tail. It only gets in their way when I send them out to catch a pig or a rabbit for my supper."

Pulling with his left hand and pushing with his right, Arch Gunnard docked the hound's tail as quickly and as easily as if he were cutting a willow switch in the pasture to drive the cows home with. The dog sprang forward with the release of her tail until she was far beyond Arch's reach, and began howling so loud she could be heard half a mile away. Nancy stopped once and looked back at Arch, and then she sprang to the middle of the road and began leaping and twisting in circles. All that time she was yelping and biting at the bleeding stub of her tail.

Arch leaned backward and twirled the severed tail in one hand while he wiped the jackknife blade on his boot sole. He watched Lonnie's dog chasing herself around in circles in the red dust.

Nobody had anything to say then. Lonnie tried not to watch his dog's agony, and he forced himself to keep from looking at Clem Henry. Then, with his eyes shut, he wondered why he had remained on Arch Gunnard's plantation all those past years, sharecropping for a mere living on short rations, and becoming leaner and leaner all the time. He knew then how true it was what Clem had said about Arch's sharecroppers' faces becoming sharp enough to hew their own coffins. His hands went to his chin before he knew what he was doing. His hand dropped when he had felt the bones of jaw and the exposed tendons of his cheeks.

As hungry as he was, he knew that even if Arch did give

him some rations then, there would not be nearly enough for them to eat for the following week. Hatty, his wife, was already broken down from hunger and work in the fields, and his father, Mark Newsome, stone-deaf for the past twenty years, was always asking him why there was never enough food in the house for them to have a solid meal. Lonnie's head fell forward a little more, and he could feel his eyes becoming damp.

The pressure of his sharp chin against his chest made him so uncomfortable that he had to raise his head at last in order to ease the pain of it.

The first thing he saw when he looked up was Arch Gunnard twirling Nancy's tail in his left hand. Arch Gunnard had a trunk full of dogs' tails at home. He had been cutting off tails ever since anyone could remember, and during all those years he had accumulated a collection of which he was so proud that he kept the trunk locked and the key tied around his neck on a string. On Sunday afternoons when the preacher came to visit, or when a crowd was there to loll on the front porch and swap stories, Arch showed them off, naming each tail from memory just as well as if he had had a tag on it.

Clem Henry had left the filling station and was walking alone down the road towards the plantation. Clem Henry's house was in a cluster of Negro cabins below Arch's big house, and he had to pass Lonnie's house to get there. Lonnie was on the verge of getting up and leaving when he saw Arch looking at him. He did not know whether Arch was looking at his lean face, or whether he was watching to see if he were going to get up and go down the road with Clem.

The thought of leaving reminded him of his reason for being there. He had to have some rations before suppertime that night, no matter how short they were.

"Mr. Arch, I. . . ."

Arch stared at him for a moment, appearing as if he had turned to listen to some strange sound unheard of before that moment.

Lonnie bit his lips, wondering if Arch was going to say anything about how lean and hungry he looked. But Arch was thinking about something else. He slapped his hand on his leg and laughed out loud.

"I sometimes wish niggers had tails," Arch said, coiling

Nancy's tail into a ball and putting it into his pocket. "I'd a heap rather cut off nigger tails than dog tails. There'd be more to cut, for one thing."

Dudley Smith and somebody else behind them laughed for a brief moment. The laughter died out almost as suddenly as it had risen.

The Negroes who had heard Arch shuffled their feet in the dust and moved backwards. It was only a few minutes until not one was left at the filling station. They went up the road behind the red wooden building until they were out of sight.

Arch got up and stretched. The sun was getting low, and it was no longer comfortable in the October air. "Well, I reckon I'll be getting on home to get me some supper," he said.

He walked slowly to the middle of the road and stopped to look at Nancy retreating along the ditch.

"Nobody going my way?" he asked. "What's wrong with you, Lonnie? Going home to supper, ain't you?"

"Mr. Arch, I. . . ."

Lonnie found himself jumping to his feet. His first thought was to ask for the sowbelly and molasses, and maybe some corn meal; but when he opened his mouth, the words refused to come out. He took several steps forward and shook his head. He did not know what Arch might say or do if he said "No."

"Hatty'll be looking for you," Arch said, turning his back and walking off.

He reached into his hip pocket and took out Nancy's tail. He began twirling it as he walked down the road towards the big house in the distance.

Dudley Smith went inside the filling station, and the others walked away.

After Arch had gone several hundred yards, Lonnie sat down heavily on the box beside the gas pump from which he had got up when Arch spoke to him. He sat down heavily, his shoulders drooping, his arms falling between his outspread legs.

Lonnie did not know how long his eyes had been closed, but when he opened them, he saw Nancy lying between his feet, licking the docked tail. While he watched her, he felt the sharp point of his chin cutting into his chest again.

Presently the door behind him was slammed shut, and a minute later he could hear Dudley Smith walking away from the filling station on his way home.

II

Lonnie had been sleeping fitfully for several hours when he suddenly found himself wide awake. Hatty shook him again. He raised himself on his elbow and tried to see into the darkness of the room. Without knowing what time it was, he was able to determine that it was still nearly two hours until sunrise.

"Lonnie," Hatty said again, trembling in the cold night air, "Lonnie, your pa ain't in the house."

Lonnie sat upright in bed.

"How do you know he ain't?" he said.

"I've been lying here wide awake ever since I got in bed, and I heard him when he went out. He's been gone all that time."

"Maybe he just stepped out for a while," Lonnie said, turning and trying to see through the bedroom window.

"I know what I'm saying, Lonnie," Hatty insisted. "Your pa's been gone a heap too long."

Both of them sat without a sound for several minutes while they listened for Mark Newsome.

Lonnie got up and lit a lamp. He shivered while he was putting on his shirt, overalls, and shoes. He tied his shoe-laces in hard knots because he couldn't see in the faint light. Outside the window it was almost pitch-dark, and Lonnie could feel the damp October air blowing against his face.

"I'll go help look," Hatty said, throwing the covers off and starting to get up.

Lonnie went to the bed and drew the covers back over her and pushed her back into place.

"You try to get some sleep, Hatty," he said; "you can't stay awake the whole night. I'll go bring Pa back."

He left Hatty, blowing out the lamp, and stumbled through the dark hall, feeling his way to the front porch by touching the wall with his hands. When he got to the porch, he could still barely see any distance ahead, but his eyes were becoming more accustomed to the darkness. He waited a minute, listening.

Feeling his way down the steps into the yard, he walked

around the corner of the house and stopped to listen again before calling his father.

"Oh, Pa!" he said loudly. "Oh, Pa!"

He stopped under the bedroom window when he realized what he had been doing.

"Now that's a fool thing for me to be out here doing," he said, scolding himself. "Pa couldn't hear it thunder."

He heard a rustling of the bed.

"He's been gone long enough to get clear to the crossroads, or more," Hatty said, calling through the window.

"Now you lay down and try to get a little sleep, Hatty," Lonnie told her. "I'll bring him back in no time."

He could hear Nancy scratching fleas under the house, but he knew she was in no condition to help look for Mark. It would be several days before she recovered from the shock of losing her tail.

"He's been gone a long time," Hatty said, unable to keep still.

"That don't make no difference," Lonnie said. "I'll find him sooner or later. Now you go on to sleep like I told you, Hatty."

Lonnie walked towards the barn, listening for some sound. Over at the big house he could hear the hogs grunting and squealing, and he wished they would be quiet so he could hear other sounds. Arch Gunnard's dogs were howling occasionally, but they were not making any more noise than they usually did at night, and he was accustomed to their howling.

Lonnie went to the barn, looking inside and out. After walking around the barn, he went into the field as far as the cotton shed. He knew it was useless, but he could not keep from calling his father time after time.

"Oh, Pa!" he said, trying to penetrate the darkness.

He went farther into the field.

"Now, what in the world could have become of Pa?" he said, stopping and wondering where to look next.

After he had gone back to the front yard, he began to feel uneasy for the first time. Mark had not acted any more strangely during the past week than he ordinarily did, but Lonnie knew he was upset over the way Arch Gunnard was giving out short rations. Mark had even said that, at the rate they were being fed, all of them would starve to death inside another three months.

Lonnie left the yard and went down the road towards the

Negro cabins. When he got to Clem's house, he turned in and walked up the path to the door. He knocked several times and waited. There was no answer, and he rapped louder.

"Who's that?" he heard Clem say from bed.

"It's me," Lonnie said. "I've got to see you a minute, Clem. I'm out in the front yard."

He sat down and waited for Clem to dress and come outside. While he waited, he strained his ears to catch any sound that might be in the air. Over the fields towards the big house he could hear the fattening hogs grunt and squeal.

Clem came out and shut the door. He stood on the doorsill a moment speaking to his wife in bed, telling her he would be back and not to worry.

"Who's that?" Clem said, coming down into the yard.

Lonnie got up and met Clem halfway.

"What's the trouble?" Clem asked then, buttoning up his overall jumper.

"Pa's not in his bed," Lonnie said, "and Hatty says he's been gone from the house most all night. I went out in the field, and all around the barn, but I couldn't find a trace of him anywhere."

Clem then finished buttoning his jumper and began rolling a cigarette. He walked slowly down the path to the road. It was still dark, and it would be at least an hour before dawn made it any lighter.

"Maybe he was too hungry to stay in bed any longer," Clem said. "When I saw him yesterday, he said he was so shrunk up and weak he didn't know if he could last much longer. He looked like his skin and bones couldn't shrivel much more."

"I asked Arch last night after suppertime for some rations—just a little piece of sowbelly and some molasses. He said he'd get around to letting me have some the first thing this morning."

"Why don't you tell him to give you full rations or none?" Clem said. "If you knew you wasn't going to get none at all, you could move away and find a better man to sharecrop for, couldn't you?"

"I've been loyal to Arch Gunnard for a long time now," Lonnie said. "I'd hate to haul off and leave him like that."

Clem looked at Lonnie, but he did not say anything more just then. They turned up the road towards the driveway that led up to the big house. The fattening hogs were still grunting and squealing in the pen, and one of Arch's hounds came down a cotton row beside the driveway to smell their shoes.

"Them fattening hogs always get enough to eat," Clem said. "There's not a one of them that don't weigh seven hundred pounds right now, and they're getting bigger every day. Besides taking all that's thrown to them, they make a lot of meals off the chickens that get in there to peck around."

Lonnie listened to the grunting of the hogs as they walked up the driveway towards the big house.

"Reckon we'd better get Arch up to help look for Pa?" Lonnie said. "I'd hate to wake him up, but I'm scared Pa might stray off into the swamp and get lost for good. He couldn't hear it thunder, even. I never could find him back there in all that tangle if he got into it."

Clem said something under his breath and went on towards the barn and hog pen. He reached the pen before Lonnie got there.

"You'd better come here quick," Clem said, turning around to see where Lonnie was.

Lonnie ran to the hog pen. He stopped and climbed halfway up the wooden-and-wire sides of the fence. At first he could see nothing, but gradually he was able to see the moving mass of black fattening hogs on the other side of the pen. They were biting and snarling at each other like a pack of hungry hounds turned loose on a dead rabbit.

Lonnie scrambled to the top of the fence, but Clem caught him and pulled him back.

"Don't go in that hog pen that way," he said. "Them hogs will tear you to pieces, they're that wild. They're fighting over something."

Both of them ran around the corner of the pen and got to the side where the hogs were. Down under their feet on the ground Lonnie caught a glimpse of a dark mass splotched with white. He was able to see it for a moment only, because one of the hogs trampled over it.

Clem opened and closed his mouth several times before he was able to say anything at all. He clutched at Lonnie's arm, shaking him.

"That looks like it might be your pa," he said. "I swear before goodness, Lonnie, it does look like it."

Lonnie still could not believe it. He climbed to the top of the fence and began kicking his feet at the hogs, trying to drive them away. They paid no attention to him.

While Lonnie was perched there, Clem had gone to the wagon shed, and he ran back with two singletrees he had somehow managed to find there in the dark. He handed one to Lonnie, poking it at him until Lonnie's attention was drawn from the hogs long enough to take it.

Clem leaped over the fence and began swinging the singletree at the hogs. Lonnie slid down beside him, yelling at them. One hog turned on Lonnie and snapped at him, and Clem struck it over the back of the neck with enough force to drive it off momentarily.

By then Lonnie was able to realize what had happened. He ran to the mass of hogs, kicking them with his heavy stiff shoes and striking them on their heads with the iron-tipped singletree. Once he felt a stinging sensation, and looked down to see one of the hogs biting the calf of his leg. He had just enough time to hit the hog and drive it away before his leg was torn. He knew most of his overall leg had been ripped away, because he could feel the night air on his bare wet calf.

Clem had gone ahead and had driven the hogs back. There was no other way to do anything. They were in a snarling circle around them, and both of them had to keep the singletrees swinging back and forth all the time to keep the hogs off. Finally Lonnie reached down and got a grip on Mark's leg. With Clem helping, Lonnie carried his father to the fence and lifted him over to the other side.

They were too much out of breath for a while to say anything, or to do anything else. The snarling, fattening hogs were at the fence, biting the wood and wire, and making more noise than ever.

While Lonnie was searching in his pockets for a match, Clem struck one. He held the flame close to Mark Newsome's head.

They both stared unbelievingly, and then Clem blew out the match. There was nothing said as they stared at each other in the darkness.

Clem walked several steps away, and turned and came back beside Lonnie.

"It's him, though," Clem said, sitting down on the ground. "It's him, all right."

"I reckon so," Lonnie said. He could think of nothing else to say then.

They sat on the ground, one on each side of Mark, looking at the body. There had been no sign of life in the body beside them since they had first touched it. The face, throat, and stomach had been completely devoured.

"You'd better go wake up Arch Gunnard," Clem said after a while.

"What for?" Lonnie said. "He can't help none now. It's too late for help."

"Makes no difference," Clem insisted. "You'd better go wake him up and let him see what there is to see. If you wait till morning, he might take it into his head to say the hogs didn't do it. Right now is the time to get him up so he can see what his hogs did."

Clem turned around and looked at the big house. The dark outline against the dark sky made him hesitate.

"A man who short-rations tenants ought to have to sit and look at that till it's buried."

Lonnie looked at Clem fearfully. He knew Clem was right, but he was scared to hear a Negro say anything like that about a white man.

"You oughtn't talk like that about Arch," Lonnie said. "He's in bed asleep. He didn't have a thing to do with it. He didn't have no more to do with it than I did."

Clem laughed a little, and threw the singletree on the ground between his feet. After letting it lie there a little while, he picked it up and began beating the ground with it.

Lonnie got to his feet slowly. He had never seen Clem act like that before, and he did not know what to think about it. He left without saying anything and walked stiffly to the house in the darkness to wake up Arch Gunnard.

III

Arch was hard to wake up. And even after he was awake, he was in no hurry to get up. Lonnie was standing outside the bedroom window, and Arch was lying in bed six or eight feet away. Lonnie could hear him toss and grumble.

"Who told you to come and wake me up in the middle of the night?" Arch said.

"Well, Clem Henry's out here, and he said maybe you'd like to know about it."

Arch tossed around on the bed, flailing the pillow with his fists.

"You tell Clem Henry I said that one of these days he's going to find himself turned inside out, like a coat sleeve."

Lonnie waited doggedly. He knew Clem was right in insisting that Arch ought to wake up and come out there to see what had happened. Lonnie was afraid to go back to the barnyard and tell Clem that Arch was not coming. He did not know, but he had a feeling that Clem might go into the bedroom and drag Arch out of bed. He did not like to think of anything like that taking place.

"Are you still out there, Lonnie?" Arch shouted.

"I'm right here, Mr. Arch. I—"

"If I wasn't so sleepy, I'd come out there and take a stick and—I don't know what I wouldn't do!"

Lonnie met Arch at the back step. On the way out to the hog pen Arch did not speak to him. Arch walked heavily ahead, not even waiting to see if Lonnie was coming. The lantern that Arch was carrying cast long flat beams of yellow light over the ground; and when they got to where Clem was waiting beside Mark's body, the Negro's face shone in the night like a highly polished plowshare.

"What was Mark doing in my hog pen at night, anyway?" Arch said, shouting at them both.

Neither Clem nor Lonnie replied. Arch glared at them for not answering. But no matter how many times he looked at them, his eyes returned each time to stare at the torn body of Mark Newsome on the ground at his feet.

"There's nothing to be done now," Arch said finally. "We'll just have to wait till daylight and send for the undertaker." He walked a few steps away. "Looks like you could have waited till morning in the first place. There wasn't no sense in getting me up."

He turned his back and looked sideways at Clem. Clem stood up and looked him straight in the eyes.

"What do you want, Clem Henry?" he said. "Who told you to be coming around my house in the middle of the night? I don't want niggers coming here except when I send for them."

"I couldn't stand to see anybody eaten up by the hogs, and not do anything about it," Clem said.

"You mind your own business," Arch told him. "And when you talk to me, take off your hat, or you'll be sorry for it. It wouldn't take much to make me do you up the way you belong."

Lonnie backed away. There was a feeling of uneasiness around them. That was how trouble between Clem and Arch always began. He had seen it start that way dozens of times before. As long as Clem turned and went away, nothing happened, but sometimes he stayed right where he was and talked up to Arch just as if he had been a white man, too.

Lonnie hoped it would not happen this time. Arch was already mad enough about being waked up in the middle of the night, and Lonnie knew there was no limit to what Arch would do when he got good and mad at a Negro. Nobody had ever seen him kill a Negro, but he had said he had, and he told people that he was not scared to do it again.

"I reckon you know how he came to get eaten up by the hogs like that," Clem said, looking straight at Arch.

Arch whirled around.

"Are you talking to me. . . ?"

"I asked you that," Clem stated.

"God damn you, yellow-blooded . . ." Arch yelled.

He swung the lantern at Clem's head. Clem dodged, but the bottom of it hit his shoulder, and it was smashed to pieces. The oil splattered on the ground, igniting in the air from the flaming wick. Clem was lucky not to have it splash on his face and overalls.

"Now, look here . . ." Clem said.

"You yellow-blooded nigger," Arch said, rushing at him. "I'll teach you to talk back to me. You've got too big for your place for the last time. I've been taking too much from you, but I ain't doing it no more."

"Mr. Arch, I . . ." Lonnie said, stepping forward partly between them. No one heard him.

Arch stood back and watched the kerosene flicker out on the ground.

"You know good and well why he got eaten up by the fattening hogs," Clem said, standing his ground. "He was so hungry he had to get up out of bed in the middle of the night and come up here in the dark trying to find something to eat. Maybe he was trying to find the smokehouse. It makes no difference, either way. He's been on short rations like everybody else working on your place, and he was so old he didn't know where else to look for food except in your smokehouse. You know good and well that's how he got lost up here in the dark and fell in the hog pen."

The kerosene had died out completely. In the last faint flare, Arch had reached down and grabbed up the singletree that had been lying on the ground where Lonnie had dropped it.

Arch raised the singletree over his head and struck with all his might at Clem. Clem dodged, but Arch drew back again quickly and landed a blow on his arm just above the elbow before Clem could dodge it. Clem's arm dropped to his side, dangling lifelessly.

"You God-damn yellow-blooded nigger!" Arch shouted. "Now's your time, you black bastard! I've been waiting for the chance to teach you your lesson. And this's going to be one you won't never forget."

Clem felt the ground with his feet until he had located the other singletree. He stooped down and got it. Raising it, he did not try to hit Arch, but held it in front of him so he could ward off Arch's blows at his head. He continued to stand his ground, not giving Arch an inch.

"Drop that singletree," Arch said.

"I won't stand here and let you beat me like that," Clem protested.

"By God, that's all I want to hear," Arch said, his mouth curling. "Nigger, your time has come, by God!"

He swung once more at Clem, but Clem turned and ran towards the barn. Arch went after him a few steps and stopped. He threw aside the singletree and turned and ran back to the house.

Lonnie went to the fence and tried to think what was best for him to do. He knew he could not take sides with a Negro, in the open, even if Clem had helped him, and especially after Clem had talked to Arch in the way he wished he could himself. He was a white man, and to save his life he could not stand to think of turning against Arch, no matter what happened.

Presently a light burst through one of the windows of the house, and he heard Arch shouting at his wife to wake her up.

When he saw Arch's wife go to the telephone, Lonnie realized what was going to happen. She was calling up the neighbors and Arch's friends. They would not mind getting up in the night when they found out what was going to take place.

Out behind the barn he could hear Clem calling him. Leaving the yard, Lonnie felt his way out there in the dark.

"What's the trouble, Clem?" he said.

"I reckon my time has come," Clem said . "Arch Gunnard talks that way when he's good and mad. He talked just like he did that time he carried Jim Moffin off to the swamp— and Jim never came back."

"Arch wouldn't do anything like that to you, Clem," Lonnie said excitedly, but he knew better.

Clem said nothing.

"Maybe you'd better strike out for the swamps till he changes his mind and cools off some," Lonnie said. "You might be right, Clem."

Lonnie could feel Clem's eyes burning into him.

"Wouldn't be no sense in that, if you'd help me," Clem said. "Wouldn't you stand by me?"

Lonnie trembled as the meaning of Clem's suggestion became clear to him. His back was to the side of the barn, and he leaned against it while sheets of black and white passed before his eyes.

"Wouldn't you stand by me?" Clem asked again.

"I don't know what Arch would say to that," Lonnie told him haltingly.

Clem walked away several paces. He stood with his back to Lonnie while he looked across the field towards the quarter where his home was.

"I could go in that little patch of woods out there and stay till they get tired of looking for me," Clem said, turning around to see Lonnie.

"You'd better go somewhere," Lonnie said uneasily. "I know Arch Gunnard. He's hard to handle when he makes up his mind to do something he wants to do. I couldn't stop him an inch. Maybe you'd better get clear out of the country, Clem."

"I couldn't do that, and leave my family down there across the field," Clem said.

"He's going to get you if you don't."

"If you'd only sort of help me out a little, he wouldn't. I would only have to go and hide out in that little patch of woods over there a while. Looks like you could do that for me, being as how I helped you find your pa when he was in the hog pen."

Lonnie nodded, listening for sounds from the big house. He continued to nod at Clem while Clem was waiting to be assured.

"If you're going to stand up for me," Clem said, "I can just go over there in the woods and wait till they get it off their minds. You won't be telling them where I'm at, and you could say I struck out for the swamp. They wouldn't ever find me without bloodhounds."

"That's right," Lonnie said, listening for sounds of Arch's coming out of the house. He did not wish to be found back there behind the barn where Arch could accuse him of talking to Clem.

The moment Lonnie replied, Clem turned and ran off into the night. Lonnie went after him a few steps, as if he had suddenly changed his mind about helping him, but Clem was lost in the darkness by then.

Lonnie waited for a few minutes, listening to Clem crashing through the underbrush in the patch of woods a quarter of a mile away. When he could hear Clem no longer, he went around the barn to meet Arch.

Arch came out of the house carrying his double-barreled shotgun and the lantern he had picked up in the house. His pockets were bulging with shells.

"Where is that damn nigger, Lonnie?" Arch asked him. "Where'd he go to?"

Lonnie opened his mouth, but no words came out.

"You know which way he went, don't you?"

Lonnie again tried to say something, but there were no sounds. He jumped when he found himself nodding his head to Arch.

"Mr. Arch, I—"

"That's all right, then," Arch said. "That's all I need to know now. Dudley Smith and Tom Hawkins and Frank and Dave Howard and the rest will be here in a minute, and you can stay right here so you can show us where he's hiding out."

Frantically Lonnie tried to say something. Then he reached for Arch's sleeve to stop him, but Arch had gone.

Arch ran around the house to the front yard. Soon a car came racing down the road, its headlights lighting up the whole place, hog pen and all. Lonnie knew it was probably

Dudley Smith, because his was the first house in that direction, only half a mile away. While he was turning into the driveway, several other automobiles came into sight, both up the road and down it.

Lonnie trembled. He was afraid Arch was going to tell him to point out where Clem had gone to hide. Then he knew Arch would tell him. He had promised Clem he would not do that. But try as he might, he could not make himself believe that Arch Gunnard would do anything more than whip Clem.

Clem had not done anything that called for lynching. He had not raped a white woman, he had not shot at a white man; he had only talked back to Arch, with his hat on. But Arch was mad enough to do anything; he was mad enough at Clem not to stop at anything short of lynching.

The whole crowd of men was swarming around him before he realized it. And there was Arch clutching his arm and shouting into his face.

"Mr. Arch, I—"

Lonnie recognized every man in the feeble dawn. They were excited, and they looked like men on the last lap of an all-night fox-hunting party. Their shotguns and pistols were held at their waist, ready for the kill.

"What's the matter with you, Lonnie?" Arch said, shouting into his ear. "Wake up and say where Clem Henry went to hide out. We're ready to go get him."

Lonnie remembered looking up and seeing Frank Howard dropping yellow twelve-gauge shells into the breech of his gun. Frank bent forward so he could hear Lonnie tell Arch where Clem was hiding.

"You ain't going to kill Clem this time, are you, Mr. Arch?" Lonnie asked.

"Kill him?" Dudley Smith repeated. "What do you reckon I've been waiting all this time for if it wasn't for a chance to get Clem. That nigger has had it coming to him ever since he came to this county. He's a bad nigger, and it's coming to him."

"It wasn't exactly Clem's fault," Lonnie said. "If Pa hadn't come up here and fell in the hog pen, Clem wouldn't have had a thing to do with it. He was helping me, that's all."

"Shut up, Lonnie," somebody shouted at him. "You're so excited you don't know what you're saying. You're taking up for a nigger when you talk like that."

People were crowding around him so tightly he felt as if he were being squeezed to death. He had to get some air, get his breath, get out of the crowd.

"That's right," Lonnie said.

He heard himself speak, but he did not know what he was saying.

"But Clem helped me find Pa when he got lost looking around for something to eat."

"Shut up, Lonnie," somebody said again. "You damn fool, shut up!"

Arch grabbed his shoulder and shook him until his teeth rattled. Then Lonnie realized what he had been saying.

"Now, look here, Lonnie," Arch shouted. "You must be out of your head, because you know good and well you wouldn't talk like a nigger-lover in your right mind."

"That's right," Lonnie said, trembling all over. "I sure wouldn't want to talk like that."

He could still feel the grip on his shoulder where Arch's strong fingers had hurt him.

"Did Clem go to the swamp, Lonnie?" Dudley Smith said. "Is that right, Lonnie?"

Lonnie tried to shake his head; he tried to nod his head. Then Arch's fingers squeezed his thin neck. Lonnie looked at the men wild-eyed.

"Where's Clem hiding, Lonnie?" Arch demanded, squeezing.

Lonnie went three or four steps towards the barn. When he stopped, the men behind him pushed forward again. He found himself being rushed behind the barn and beyond it.

"All right, Lonnie," Arch said. "Now which way?"

Lonnie pointed towards the patch of woods where the creek was. The swamp was in the other direction.

"He said he was going to hide out in that little patch of woods along the creek over there, Mr. Arch," Lonnie said. "I reckon he's over there now."

Lonnie felt himself being swept forward, and he stumbled over the rough ground trying to keep from being knocked down and trampled upon. Nobody was talking, and everyone seemed to be walking on tiptoes. The gray light of early dawn was increasing enough both to hide them and to show the way ahead.

Just before they reached the fringe of the woods, the men separated, and Lonnie found himself a part of the circle that was closing in on Clem.

Lonnie was alone, and there was nobody to stop him, but he was unable to move forward or backward. It began to be clear to him what he had done.

Clem was probably up a tree somewhere in the woods ahead, but by that time he had been surrounded on all sides. If he should attempt to break and run, he would be shot down like a rabbit.

Lonnie sat down on a log and tried to think what to do. The sun would be up in a few more minutes, and as soon as it came up, the men would close in on the creek and Clem. He would have no chance at all among all those shotguns and pistols.

Once or twice he saw the flare of a match through the underbrush where some of the men were lying in wait. A whiff of cigarette smoke struck his nostrils, and he found himself wondering if Clem could smell it wherever he was in the woods.

There was still no sound anywhere around him, and he knew that Arch Gunnard and the rest of the men were waiting for the sun, which would in a few minutes come up behind him in the east.

It was light enough by that time to see plainly the rough ground and the tangled underbrush and the curling bark on the pine trees.

The men had already begun to creep forward, guns raised as if stalking a deer. The woods were not large, and the circle of men would be able to cover it in a few minutes at the rate they were going forward. There was still a chance that Clem had slipped through the circle before dawn broke, but Lonnie felt that he was still there. He began to feel then that Clem was there because he himself had placed him there for the men to find easily.

Lonnie found himself moving forward, drawn into the narrowing circle. Presently he could see the men all around him in dim outline. Their eyes were searching the heavy green pine tops as they went forward from tree to tree.

"Oh, Pa!" he said in a hoarse whisper. "Oh, Pa!"

He went forward a few steps, looking into the bushes and up into the treetops. When he saw the other men again, he realized that it was not Mark Newsome being sought. He did not know what had made him forget like that.

The creeping forward began to work into the movement of Lonnie's body. He found himself springing forward on his toes, and his body was leaning in that direction. It was like creeping up on a rabbit when you did not have a gun to hunt with.

He forgot again what he was doing there. The springing motion in his legs seemed to be growing stronger with each step. He bent forward so far he could almost touch the ground with his fingertips. He could not stop now. He was keeping up with the circle of men.

The fifteen men were drawing closer and closer together. The dawn had broken enough to show the time on the face of a watch. The sun was beginning to color the sky above.

Lonnie was far in advance of anyone else by then. He could not hold himself back. The strength in his legs was more than he could hold in check.

He had for so long been unable to buy shells for his gun that he had forgotten how much he liked to hunt.

The sound of the men's steady creeping had become a rhythm in his ears.

"Here's the bastard!" somebody shouted, and there was a concerted crashing through the dry underbrush. Lonnie dashed forward, reaching the tree almost as quickly as anyone else.

He could see everybody with guns raised, and far into the sky above the sharply outlined face of Clem Henry gleamed in the rising sun. His body was hugging the slender top of the pine.

Lonnie did not know who was the first to fire, but the rest of the men did not hesitate. There was a deafening roar as the shotguns and revolvers flared and smoked around the trunk of the tree.

He closed his eyes; he was afraid to look again at the face above. The firing continued without break. Clem hugged the tree with all his might, and then, with the faraway sound of splintering wood, the top of the tree and Clem came crashing through the lower limbs to the ground. The body, sprawling and torn, landed on the ground with a thud that stopped Lonnie's heart for a moment.

He turned, clutching for the support of a tree, as the firing began once more. The crumpled body was tossed time after time, like a sackful of kittens being killed with an automatic shotgun, as charges of lead were fired into it from all sides. A cloud of dust rose from the ground and drifted overhead with the choking odor of burned powder.

Lonnie did not remember how long the shooting lasted.

He found himself running from tree to tree, clutching at the rough pine bark, stumbling wildly towards the cleared ground. The sky had turned from gray to red when he emerged in the open, and as he ran, falling over the hard clods in the plowed field, he tried to keep his eyes on the house ahead.

Once he fell and found it almost impossible to rise again to his feet. He struggled to his knees, facing the round red sun. The warmth gave him the strength to rise to his feet, and he muttered unintelligibly to himself. He tried to say things he had never thought to say before.

When he got home, Hatty was waiting for him in the yard. She had heard the shots in the woods, and she had seen him stumbling over the hard clods in the field, and she had seen him kneeling there looking straight into the face of the sun. Hatty was trembling as she ran to Lonnie to find out what the matter was.

Once in his own yard, Lonnie turned and looked for a second over his shoulder. He saw the men climbing over the fence at Arch Gunnard's. Arch's wife was standing on the back porch, and she was speaking to them.

"Where's your pa, Lonnie?" Hatty said. "And what in the world was all that shooting in the woods for?" Lonnie stumbled forward until he had reached the front porch. He fell upon the steps.

"Lonnie, Lonnie!" Hatty was saying. "Wake up and tell me what in the world is the matter. I've never seen the like of all that's going on."

"Nothing," Lonnie said. "Nothing."

"Well, if there's nothing the matter, can't you go up to the big house and ask for a little piece of streak-of-lean? We ain't got a thing to cook for breakfast. Your pa's going to be hungrier than ever after being up walking around all night."

Caroline Gordon (October 6, 1895–April 11, 1981) was born at Merry Mont Farm in Todd County, Kentucky, on the Tennessee-Kentucky border. She did not attend a formal school until she was fourteen, because her father, a teacher at a classical school for boys, thought it necessary only to learn mathematics, Latin, and Greek to be educated. She attended Bethany College in West Virginia where she graduated in 1916. Gordon then taught high school for three years and worked as a journalist for the Chattanooga *News* for four years. Through Robert Penn Warren, who also grew up in Todd County, she met Allen Tate, whom she married in 1924. They divorced in 1959.

From 1924 to 1928 Gordon and Tate lived in New York. In 1928 they went to France for two years when Tate received a Guggenheim Fellowship. During this period Gordon published her first short story, "Summer Dust," in *Gyroscope*. In 1930 Gordon returned to Tennessee with her husband and daughter and they lived in Benfolly, near Clarksville, for the next eight years. It was there that Gordon published many short stories and four of her nine novels. In 1931 Maxwell Perkins accepted *Penhally*, her first novel, for publication by Scribner's. In *Penhally* Gordon wrote about several generations of a family living on a Kentucky plantation.

Over the next four decades Gordon worked as a writer in residence at many colleges and universities, developing her career as a critic and teacher. Two of her lasting achievements are *The House of Fiction: An Anthology of the Short Story* (1950; revised edition, 1960) which she edited with Allen Tate and *How to Read a Novel* (1957), a book which expresses a great many of her ideas about writing and pays tribute to Flaubert, James, and Joyce. Gordon spent the last years of her life teaching at the University of Dallas, a small Catholic college in Irving, Texas. In 1978 she retired to live with her daughter in San Cristobal de las Casas in Chiapas, Mexico. *The Collected Stories of Caroline Gordon* with an introduction by Robert Penn Warren was published the year of her death.

Close Connections: Caroline Gordon and the Southern Renaissance, a biography by Ann Waldron, was published in 1987.

THE LAST DAY IN THE FIELD

by Caroline Gordon

That was the fall when the leaves stayed green so long. We had a drought in August and the ponds everywhere were dry and the watercourses shrunken. Then in September heavy rains came. Things greened up. It looked like winter was never coming.

"You aren't going to hunt this year, Aleck?" Molly said. "Remember how you stayed awake nights last fall with that pain in your leg."

In October light frosts came. In the afternoons when I sat on the back porch going over my fishing tackle I marked their progress on the elderberry bushes that were left standing against the stable fence. The lower, spreading branches had turned yellow and were already sinking to the ground but the leaves in the top clusters still stood up stiff and straight.

"Ah-ha, it'll get you yet!" I said, thinking how frost creeps higher and higher out of the ground each night of fall.

The dogs next door felt it and would thrust their noses through the wire fence scenting the wind from the north. When I walked in the back yard they would bound twice their height and whine, for meat scraps Molly said, but it was because they smelled blood on my old hunting coat.

They were almost matched liver-and-white pointers. The big dog had a beautiful, square muzzle and was deep-chested and rangy. The bitch, Judy, had a smaller head and not so good a muzzle but she was springy-loined too and had one of the merriest tails I've ever watched.

When Joe Thomas, the boy that owned them, came home from the hardware store he would change his clothes and then come down the back way and we would stand there watching the dogs and wondering how they would work. They had just been with a trainer up in Kentucky for three months. Joe said they were keen as mustard. He was going to take them out the first good Saturday and he wanted me to come along.

"I can't make it," I said. "My leg's worse this fall than it was last."

The fifteenth of November was clear and so warm that we sat out on the porch till nine o'clock. It was still warm when we went to bed toward eleven. The change must have come in the middle of the night. I woke once, hearing the clock strike two, and felt the air cold on my face and thought before I went back to sleep that the weather had broken at last. When I woke again toward dawn the cold air slapped my face hard. I came wide awake, turned over in bed, and looked out of the window. The sun was just coming up behind a wall of purple clouds streaked with amber. As I watched, it burned through and the light everywhere got bright.

There was a scaly bark hickory tree growing on the east side of the house. You could see its upper branches from the bedroom window. The leaves had turned yellow a week ago. But yesterday evening when I walked out there in the yard they had still been flat, with green streaks showing in them. Now they were curled up tight and a lot of leaves had fallen to the ground.

I got out of bed quietly so as not to wake Molly, dressed, and went down the back way over to the Thomas house. There was no one stirring but I knew which room Joe's was. The window was open and I could hear him snoring. I went up and stuck my head in.

"Hey," I said, "killing frost!"

He opened his eyes and looked at me and then his eyes

went shut. I reached my arm through the window and shook him. "Get up," I said. "We got to start right away."

He was awake now and out on the floor stretching. I told him to dress and be over at the house as quick as he could. I'd have breakfast ready for us both.

Aunt Martha had a way of leaving fire in the kitchen stove at night. There were red embers there now. I poked the ashes out and piled kindling on top of them. When the flame came up I put some heavier wood on, filled the coffeepot, and put some grease on in a skillet. By the time Joe got there I had coffee ready and had stirred up some hoecakes to go with our fried eggs. Joe had brought a thermos bottle. We put the rest of the coffee in it and I found a ham in the pantry and made some sandwiches.

While I was fixing the lunch Joe went down to the lot to hitch up. He was just driving the buggy out of the stable when I came down the back steps. The dogs knew what was up, all right. They were whining and surging against the fence and Bob, the big dog, thrust his paw through and into the pocket of my hunting coat as I passed. While Joe was snapping on the leashes I got a few handfuls of straw from the rack and put it in the foot of the buggy. It was twelve miles where we were going; the dogs would need to ride warm coming back.

Joe said he would drive. We got in the buggy and started out, up Seventh Street, on over to College, and out through Scufftown. When we got into the nigger section we could see what a killing frost it had been. A light shimmer over all the ground still and the weeds around all the cabins dark and matted the way they are when the frost hits them hard and twists them.

We drove on over the Red River bridge and out into the open country. At Jim Gill's place the cows had come up and were standing there waiting to be milked but nobody was stirring yet from the house. I looked back from the top of the hill and saw that the frost mists still hung heavy in the bottom and thought it was a good sign. A day like this when the earth is warmer than the air currents is good for the hunter. Scent particles are borne on the warm air; and birds will forage far on such a day.

It took us over an hour to get from Gloversville to Spring Creek. Joe wanted to get out as soon as we hit the big bottom there but I held him down and we drove on through and up Rollow's hill to the top of the ridge. We got out there, unhitched Old Dick and turned him into one of Rob Fayerlee's pastures—I thought how surprised Rob would be when he looked out and saw him grazing there—put our guns together, and started out, with the dogs still on leash.

It was rough, broken ground, scrub oak with a few gum trees and lots of buckberry bushes. One place a patch of corn ran clear up to the top of the ridge. As we passed along between the rows, I could see the frost glistening on the north side of every stalk. I knew it was going to be a good day.

I walked over to the brow of the hill. From there you could see off over the whole valley—I've hunted over every foot of it in my time—tobacco land, mostly. One or two patches of cowpeas there on the side of the ridge. I thought we might start there and then I knew that wouldn't do. Quail will linger on the roost a cold day and feed in shelter during the morning. It is only in the afternoon that they will work out well into the open.

The dogs' whining made me turn around. Joe had bent down and was about to slip the leashes. "Hey, boy," I said, "wait a minute."

I turned around and looked down the other side of the hill. It looked better that way. The corn land of the bottoms ran high up onto the ridge in several places there and where the corn stopped there were big patches of ironweed and buckberry. I stooped and knocked my pipe out on a stump.

"Let's go that way," I said.

Joe was looking at my old buckhorn whistle that I had slung around my neck. "I forgot to bring mine," he said.

"All right," I said, "I'll handle 'em."

He unfastened their collars and cast off. They broke away, racing for the first hundred yards and barking, then suddenly swerved. The big dog took off to the right along the hillside. The bitch, Judy, skirted a belt of corn along the upper bottomlands. I kept my eye on the big dog. A dog that has bird sense knows cover when he sees it. This big Bob was an independent hunter. I could see him moving fast through the scrub oaks, working his way down toward a patch of ironweed. He caught the first scent traces just on the edge of the weed patch and froze. Judy, meanwhile, had been following the line of the cornfield. A hundred yards away she caught sight of Bob's point and backed him.

We went up and flushed the birds. They got up in two bunches. I heard Joe's shot while I was in the act of raising my gun and I saw his bird fall not thirty paces from where I stood. I had covered a middle bird of the larger bunch—that's the one led by the boss cock—the way I usually do. He fell, whirling head over heels, driven a little forward by the impact. A well-centered shot. I could tell by the way the feathers fluffed as he tumbled.

The dogs were off through the grass. They had retrieved both birds. Joe stuck his in his pocket. He laughed. "I thought there for a minute you were going to let him get away."

I looked at him but I didn't say anything. It's a wonderful thing to be twenty years old.

The majority of the singles had flown straight ahead to settle in the rank grass that jutted out from the bottomland. Judy got down to work at once but the big dog broke off to the left, wanting to get footloose to find another covey. I thought of how Gyges, the best dog I ever had—the best dog any man ever had—used always to want to do the same thing, and I laughed.

"Naw, you won't," I said. "Come back here, you scoundrel, and hunt these singles."

He stopped on the edge of a briar patch, looked at me, and heeled up promptly. I clucked him out again. He gave me another look. I thought we were beginning to understand each other better. We got some nice points among those singles and I found him reasonably steady to both wing and shot, needing only a little control.

We followed that valley along the creek bed through two or three more cornfields without finding another covey. Joe was disappointed but I wasn't worrying yet; you always make your bag in the afternoon.

It was twelve o'clock by this time. We turned up the ravine toward Buck Springs. They had cleared out some of the big trees on the sides of the ravine but the spring itself was just the same: the tall sycamore tree and the water pouring in a thin stream over the slick rocks. I unwrapped the sandwiches and the pieces of cake and laid them on a stump. Joe had got the thermos bottle out of his pocket. Something had gone wrong with it and the coffee was stone cold. We were about to drink it that way when Joe saw a good tin can flung down beside the spring. He made a trash fire and we put the coffee in the can and heated it to boiling.

Joe finished his last sandwich and reached for the cake. "Good ham," he said.

"It's John Ferguson's," I said. I was watching the dogs. They were tired, all right. Judy had scooped out a soft place between the roots of a sycamore but the big dog, Bob, lay there with his forepaws stretched out before him, never taking his eyes off our faces. I looked at him and thought how different he was from his mate and like some dogs I had known—and men, too—who lived only for hunting and could never get enough no matter how long the day was. There was something about his head and his markings that reminded me of another dog I used to hunt with a long time ago and I asked the boy who had trained him. He said the old fellow he bought the dogs from had been killed last spring, over in Trigg: Charley Morrison.

Charley Morrison. I remembered how he died. Out hunting by himself and the gun had gone off, accidentally, they said. Charley had called the dog to him, got blood all over him, and sent him home. The dog went, all right, but when they got there Charley was dead. Two years ago that was and now I was hunting the last dogs he'd ever trained. . . .

Joe lifted the thermos bottle. "Another cup?"

I held my cup out and he filled it. The coffee was still good and hot. I lit my pipe and ran my eye over the country in front of us. I always enjoy figuring out which way they'll go. This afternoon with the hot coffee in me and the ache gone from my leg I felt like I could do it. It's not as hard as it looks. A well-organized covey has a range, like chickens. I knew what they'd be doing this time of day: in a thicket, dusting—sometimes they'll get up in grapevine swings. Then after they've fed and rested they'll start out again, working always toward the open.

Joe was stamping out his cigarette. "Let's go."

The dogs were already out of sight but I could see the sedge grass ahead moving and I knew they'd be making for the same thing that took my eye: a spearhead of thicket that ran far out into this open field. We came up over a little rise. There they were. Bob on a point and Judy, the staunch little devil, backing him, not fifty feet from the thicket. I saw it was going to be tough shooting. No way to tell whether the birds were between the dog and the thicket or in the thicket itself. Then I saw that the cover was more open along the side of the thicket and I thought that that was the way they'd go if they were in the thicket. But Joe had already broken away to the left. He got too far to the side. The birds flushed to the right and left him standing, flat-footed, without a shot.

He looked sort of foolish and grinned.

I thought I wouldn't say anything and then found myself speaking:

"Trouble with you, you try to outthink the dog."

There was nothing to do about it now, though, and the chances were that the singles had pitched through the trees below. We went down there. It was hard hunting. The woods were open, the ground heavily carpeted everywhere with leaves. Dead leaves make a tremendous rustle when the dogs surge through them; it takes a good nose to cut scent keenly in such dry, noisy cover. I kept my eye on Bob. He never faltered, getting over the ground in big, springy strides but combing every inch of it. We came to an open place in the woods. Nothing but big hickory trees and bramble thickets overhung with trailing vines. Bob passed the first thicket and came to a beautiful point. We went up. He stood perfectly steady but the bird flushed out fifteen or twenty steps ahead of him. I saw it swing to the right, gaining altitude very quickly, and it came to me how it would be.

I called to Joe: "Don't shoot yet."

He nodded and raised his gun, following the bird with the barrel. It was directly over the treetops when I gave the word and he shot, scoring a clean kill.

He laughed excitedly as he stuck the bird in his pocket. "*Man!* I didn't know you could take that much time!"

We went on through the open woods. I was thinking about a day I'd had years ago, in the woods at Grassdale, with my uncle James Morris and his son Julian. Uncle James had given Julian and me hell for missing just such a shot. I can see him now, standing up against a big pine tree, his face red from liquor and his gray hair ruffling in the wind: "*Let him alone. Let him alone!* And establish your lead as he climbs!*"

Joe was still talking about the shot he'd made. "Lord, I wish I could get another one like that."

"You won't," I said. "We're getting out of the woods now."

We struck a path that led through the woods. My leg was stiff from the hip down and every time I brought it over the pain would start in my knee, zing, and travel up and settle in the small of my back. I walked with my head down, watching the light catch on the ridges of Joe's brown corduroy trousers and then shift and catch again as he moved forward. Sometimes he would get on ahead and then there would be nothing but the black tree trunks coming up out of the dead leaves that were all over the ground.

Joe was talking about that wild land up on the Cumberland. We could get up there some Saturday on an early train. Have a good day. Might even spend the night. When I didn't answer he turned around. "Man, you're sweating!"

I pulled my handkerchief out and wiped my face. "Hot work," I said.

He had stopped and was looking about him. "Used to be a spring somewhere around here."

He had found the path and was off. I sat down on a stump and mopped my face some more. The sun was halfway down through the trees, the whole west woods ablaze with light. I sat there and thought that in another hour it would be good dark and I wished that the day could go on and not end so soon and yet I didn't see how I could make it much farther with my leg the way it was.

Joe was coming up the path with his folding cup full of water. I hadn't thought I was thirsty but the cold water tasted good. We sat there awhile and smoked. It was Joe said we ought to be starting back, that we must be a good piece from the rig by this time.

We set out, working north through the edge of the woods. It was rough going and I was thinking that it would be all I could do to make it back to the rig when we climbed a fence and came out at one end of a long field. It sloped down to a wooded ravine, broken ground badly gullied and covered with sedge everywhere except where sumac thickets had sprung up—as birdy a place as ever I saw. I looked it over and I knew I'd have to hunt it, leg or no leg, but it would be close work, for me and the dogs too.

I blew them in a bit and we stood there watching them cut up the cover. The sun was down now; there was just enough light left to see the dogs work. The big dog circled the far wall of the basin and came upwind just off the drain, then stiffened to a point. We walked down to it. The birds had obviously run a bit, into the scraggly sumac stalks that bordered the ditch. My mind was so much on the dogs that I forgot Joe. He took one step too many and the fullest-blown bevy of the day roared up through the tangle. It had to be fast work. I raised my gun and scored with the only barrel I had time to peg. Joe shouted: I knew he had got one too.

We stood awhile trying to figure out which way the singles had gone. But they had fanned out too quick for us and after beating around the thicket for fifteen minutes or so we gave up and went on.

We came to the rim of the swale, eased over it, crossed the dry creek bed that was drifted thick with leaves, and started up the other side. I had blown in the dogs, thinking there was no use for them to run their heads off now we'd started home, but they didn't come. I walked a little way, then I looked back and saw Bob's white shoulders through a tangle of cinnamon vines.

Joe had turned around too. "Look a yonder! They've pinned a single out of that last covey."

"Your shot," I told him.

He shook his head. "No, you take it."

I went back and flushed the bird. It went skimming along the buckberry bushes that covered that side of the swale. In the fading light I could hardly make it out and I shot too quick. It swerved over the thicket and I let go with the second barrel. It staggered, then zoomed up. Up, up, up, over the rim of the hill and above the tallest hickories. I saw it there for a second, its wings black against the gold light, before, wings still spread, it came whirling down, like an autumn leaf, like the leaves that were everywhere about us, all over the ground.

Robert Penn Warren (April 24, 1905–September 15, 1989) was born in Guthrie, Kentucky, a small town near the Tennessee-Kentucky border. At Vanderbilt University he developed a passion for literature during an English course with John Crowe Ransom. While at Vanderbilt, Warren became friends with Allen Tate and became part of the Nashville Fugitives, so named for their literary publication *Fugitive* magazine (1922–1925). In 1930 he contributed to the Fugitives publication, *I'll Take My Stand: The South and the Agrarian Tradition*, a landmark book in Southern literature that rejected industrialism and advocated a return to agriculture as the economic base of the South.

After graduating summa cum laude from Vanderbilt in 1925, Warren went to graduate school at the University of California at Berkeley, Yale University, and on a Rhodes Scholarship to Oxford University in England. Warren taught at Southwestern Presbyterian College (now Rhodes College) in Memphis (1930–1931), Vanderbilt (1931–1943), and Louisiana State University (1934–1942) where he met Cleanth Brooks and Charles W. Pipkin. Together the three founded the *Southern Review* and Warren and Brooks edited the classic *Understanding Poetry: An Anthology for College Students* (1938), which promoted their theories of New Criticism. In 1942 Warren left L.S.U. to take the position of professor at the University of Minnesota. There he completed *Selected Poems, 1923–1943* (1944) and two novels, *All the King's Men* (1946) and *World Enough and Time* (1950), as well as many important essays. In the early fifties Warren accepted a professorship at Yale University and married his second wife, the poet Eleanor Clark. His long poem *Brother to Dragons* (1953) is seen as a benchmark in his publishing career, separating him from the formal verse of his previous books.

Warren is the only writer to have received the Pulitzer Prize for both fiction and poetry in 1946 for *All the King's Men* and in 1957 for *Promises: Poems 1954–1956*. In addition, he received the National Book Award, two Guggenheim awards, a MacArthur Foundation Fellowship, the Bollinger Prize for poetry, the National Medal for Literature, and a third Pulitzer Prize for *Now and Then* (1978). In 1986 Warren was named the nation's first Poet Laureate.

WHEN THE LIGHT GETS GREEN

by Robert Penn Warren

My grandfather had a long white beard and sat under the cedar tree. The beard, as a matter of fact, was not very long and not white, only gray, but when I was a child and was away from him at school during the winter, I would think of him, not seeing him in my mind's eye, and say: He has a long white beard. Therefore, it was a shock to me, on the first morning back home, to watch him lean over the dresser toward the wavy green mirror, which in his always shadowy room reflected things like deep water riffled by a little wind, and clip his gray beard to a point. It is gray and pointed, I would say then, remembering what I had thought before.

He turned his face to the green wavy glass, first one side and then the other in quarter profile, and lifted the long shears, which trembled a little, to cut the beard. His face being turned like that, with his good nose and pointed gray beard, he looked like General Robert E. Lee, without any white horse to ride. My grandfather had been a soldier, too, but now he wore blue-jean pants and when he leaned over like that toward the mirror, I couldn't help but notice how small his hips and backsides were. Only they weren't just small, they were shrunken. I noticed how the blue jeans hung loose from his suspenders and loose off his legs and down around his shoes. And in the morning when I noticed all this about his legs and backsides, I felt a tight feeling in my stomach like when you walk behind a woman and see the high heel of her shoe is worn and twisted and jerks her ankle every time she takes a step.

Always before my grandfather had finished clipping his beard, my Uncle Kirby came to the door and beat on it for breakfast. "I'll be down in just a minute, thank you, sir," my grandfather said. My uncle called him Mr. Barden. "Mr. Barden, breakfast is ready." It was because my Uncle Kirby was not my real uncle, having married my Aunt Lucy, who lived with my grandfather. Then my grandfather put on a black vest and put his gold watch and chain in the vest and picked up his cob pipe from the dresser top, and he and I went down to breakfast, after Uncle Kirby was already downstairs.

When he came into the dining room, Aunt Lucy was sitting at the foot of the table with the iron coffee pot on a plate beside her. She said, "Good morning, Papa."

"Good morning, Lucy," he said, and sat down at the head of the table, taking one more big puff off his pipe before laying it beside his plate.

"You've brought that old pipe down to breakfast again," my aunt said, while she poured the bright-looking coffee into the cups.

"Don't it stink," he always said.

My uncle never talked at breakfast, but when my grandfather said that, my uncle always opened his lips to grin like a dog panting, and showed his hooked teeth. His teeth were yellow because he chewed tobacco, which my grandfather didn't do, although his beard was yellow around the mouth from smoking. Aunt Lucy didn't like my uncle to chew, that was the whole trouble. So she rode my grandfather for bringing his pipe down, all in fun at first before she got serious about it. But he always brought it down just the same, and said to her, "Don't it stink."

After we ate, my uncle got up and said, "I got to get going," and went out through the kitchen where the cook was knocking and sloshing around. If it had rained right and was a good tobacco-setting season, my grandfather went off with me down to the stable to get his mare, for he had to see the setting. We saddled up the mare and went across the lot, where limestone bunched out of the ground and cedar trees and blue grass grew out of the split rock. A branch of cold water with minnows in it went through the lot between rocks and under the cedar trees; it was where I used to play before I got big enough to go to the river with the niggers to swim.

My grandfather rode across the lot and over the rise back of the house. He sat up pretty straight for an old man, holding the bridle in his left hand, and in his right hand a long hickory tobacco stick whittled down to make a walking cane. I walked behind him and watched the big straw hat he wore waggle a little above his narrow neck, or how he held the stick in the middle, firm and straight up like something carried in a parade, or how smooth and slow the muscles in the mare's flanks worked as she put each hoof down in the ground, going up hill. Sassafras bushes and blackberry bushes grew thick along the lane over the rise. In summer, tufts of hay would catch and hang on the dry bushes and showed that the hay wagons had been that way; but when we went that way in setting time, just after breakfast, the blackberry blooms were hardly gone, only a few rusty patches of white left, and the sassafras leaves showed still wet with dew or maybe the rain.

From the rise we could look back on the house. The shingles were black with damp, and the whitewash grayish, except in spots where the sun already struck it and it was drying. The tops of the cedar trees, too, were below us, very dark green and quiet. When we crossed the rise, there were the fields going down toward the river, all checked off and ready for setting, very even, only for the gullies where brush was piled to stop the washing. The fields were reddish from the wet, not yet steaming. Across them, the green woods and the sycamores showing white far off told where the river was.

The hands were standing at the edge of the field under the trees when we got there. The little niggers were filling their baskets with the wet plants to drop, and I got me a basket and filled it. My Uncle Kirby gave me fifty cents for dropping plants, but he didn't give the little niggers that much, I remember. The hands and women stood around waiting a minute, watching Uncle Kirby, who always fumed around, waving his dibble, his blue shirt already sticking to his arms with sweat. "Get the lead out," he said. The little niggers filled faster, grinning with their teeth at him. "God-damn, get the lead out!" My grandfather sat on his mare under the trees, still holding the walking cane, and said, "Why don't you start 'em, sir?"

Then, all of a sudden, they all moved out into the field, scattering out down the rows, the droppers first, and after a minute the setters, who lurched along, never straightening up, down the rows toward the river. I walked down my row, separating out the plants and dropping them at the hills, while it got hotter and the ground steamed. The sun broke out now and then, making my shadow on the ground, then the cloud would come again, and I could see its shadow drifting at me on the red field.

My grandfather rode very slow along the edge of the field to watch the setting, or stayed still under the trees. After a while, maybe about ten o'clock, he would leave and go home. I could see him riding the mare up the rise and then go over the rise; or if I was working the other way toward the river, when I turned round at the end, the lane would be empty and nothing on top the rise, with the cloudy, blue-gray sky low behind it.

The tobacco was all he cared about, now we didn't have any horses that were any real good. He had some silver cups, only one real silver one though, that his horses won at fairs, but all that was before I was born. The real silver one, the one he kept on his dresser and kept string and old minnie balls and pins and things in, had *1859* on it because his horse won it then before the War, when he was a young man. Uncle Kirby said horses were foolishness, and Grandfather said, yes, he reckoned horses were foolishness, all right. So what he cared about now was the tobacco. One time he was a tobacco-buyer for three years, but after he bought a lot of tobacco and had it in his sheds, the sheds burned up on him. He didn't have enough insurance to do any good and he was a ruined man. After that all his children, he had all girls and his money was gone, said about him, "Papa's just visionary, he tried to be a tobacco-buyer but he's too visionary and not practical." But he always said, "All tobacco-buyers are sons-of-bitches, and three years is enough of a man's life for him to be a son-of-a-bitch, I reckon." Now he was old, the corn could get the rust or the hay get rained on for all he cared, it was Uncle Kirby's worry, but all summer, off and on, he had to go down to the tobacco field to watch them sucker or plow or worm, and sometimes he pulled a few suckers himself. And when a cloud would blow up black in summer, he got nervous as a cat, not knowing whether it was the rain they needed or maybe a hail storm coming that would cut the tobacco up bad.

Mornings he didn't go down to the field, he went out under the cedar tree where his chair was. Most of the time he took a book with him along with his pipe, for he was an inveterate reader. His being an inveterate reader was one of the things made his children say he was visionary. He read a lot until his eyes went bad the summer before he had his stroke, then after that, I read to him some, but not as much as I ought. He used to read out loud some from Macaulay's *History of England* or Gibbon's *Decline and Fall*, about Flodden Field or about how the Janizaries took Constantinople amid great slaughter and how the Turk surveyed the carnage and quoted from the Persian poet about the lizard keeping the courts of the mighty. My grandfather knew some poetry, too, and he said it to himself when he didn't have anything else to do. I lay on my back on the ground, feeling the grass cool and tickly on the back of my neck, and looked upside down into the cedar tree where the limbs were tangled and black-green like big hairy fern fronds with the sky blue all around, while he said some poetry. Like the "Isles of Greece, the Isles of Greece, where burning Sappho loved and sung." Or like "Roll on, thou deep and dark blue ocean, roll."

But he never read poetry, he just said what he already knew. He only read history and *Napoleon and His Marshals*, having been a soldier and fought in the War himself. He rode off and joined the cavalry, but he never told me whether he took the horse that won the real silver cup or not. He was with Forrest before Forrest was a general. He said Forrest was a great general, and if they had done what Forrest wanted and cleaned the country ahead of the Yankees, like the Russians beat Napoleon, they'd whipped the Yankees sure. He told me about Fort Donelson, how they fought in the winter woods, and how they got away with Forrest at night, splashing through the cold water. And how the dead men looked in the river bottoms in winter, and I lay on my back on the grass, looking up in the thick cedar limbs, and thought how it was to be dead.

After Shiloh was fought and they pushed the Yankees down in the river, my grandfather was a captain, for he raised a cavalry company of his own out of West Tennessee. He was a captain, but he never got promoted after the War; when I was a little boy everybody still called him Captain Barden, though they called lots of other people in our section Colonel and Major. One time I said to him: "Grandpa, did you ever kill any Yankees?" He said: "God-a-Mighty, how do I know?" So, being little, I thought he was just a captain because he never killed anybody and I was ashamed. He talked about how they took Fort Pillow, and the drunk niggers under the bluff. And one time he said niggers couldn't stand a charge or stand the cold steel, so I thought maybe he killed some of them. But then I thought, Niggers don't count, maybe.

He only talked much in the morning. Almost every afternoon right after dinner, he went to sleep in his chair, with his hands curled up in his lap, one of them holding the pipe that still sent up a little smoke in the shadow, and his head propped back on the tree trunk. His mouth hung open, and under the hairs of his mustache, all yellow with nicotine, you could see his black teeth and his lips that were wet and pink like a baby's. Usually I remember him that way, asleep.

I remember him that way, or else trampling up and down the front porch, nervous as a cat, while a cloud blew up and the trees began to rustle. He tapped his walking cane on the boards and whistled through his teeth with his breath and kept looking off at the sky where the cloud and sometimes the lightning was. Then of a sudden it came, and if it was rain he used to go up to his room and lie down; but if it came hail on the tobacco, he stayed on the front porch, not trampling any more, and watched the hail rattle off the roof and bounce soft on the grass. "God-a-Mighty," he always said, "bigger'n minnie balls," even when it wasn't so big.

In 1914, just before the war began, it was a hot summer with the tobacco mighty good but needing rain. And when the dry spell broke and a cloud blew up, my grandfather came out on the front porch, watching it like that. It was mighty still, with lightning way off, so far you couldn't hardly hear the thunder. Then the leaves began to ruffle like they do when the light gets green, and my grandfather said to me, "Son, it's gonna hail." And he stood still. Down in the pasture, that far off, you could see the cattle bunching up and the white horse charging across the pasture, looking bright, for the sun was shining bright before the cloud struck it all at once. "It's gonna hail," my grandfather said. It was dark, with jagged lightning and the thunder high and steady. And there the hail was.

He just turned around and went in the house. I watched the hail bouncing, then I heard a noise and my aunt yelled. I ran back in the dining room where the noise was, and my grandfather was lying on the floor with the old silver pitcher he dropped and a broken glass. We tried to drag him, but he was too heavy; then my Uncle Kirby came up wet from the stable and we carried my grandfather upstairs and put him on his bed. My aunt tried to call the doctor even if the lightning might hit the telephone. I stayed back in the dining room and picked up the broken glass and the pitcher and wiped up the floor with a rag. After a while Dr. Blake came from town; then he went away.

When Dr. Blake was gone, I went upstairs to see my grandfather. I shut the door and went in his room, which was almost dark, like always, and quiet because the hail didn't beat on the roof any more. He was lying on his back in the featherbed, with a sheet pulled up over him, lying there in the dark. He had his hands curled loose on his stomach, like when he went to sleep in his chair holding the pipe. I sat on a split-bottom chair by the bed and looked at him: he had his eyes shut and his mouth hung loose, but you couldn't hear his breathing. Then I quit looking at him and looked round the room, my eyes getting used to the shadow. I could see his pants on the floor, and the silver cup on the dresser by the mirror, which was green and wavy like water.

When he said something, I almost jumped out of my skin, hearing his voice like that. He said, "Son, I'm gonna die." I tried to say something, but I couldn't. And he waited, then he said, "I'm on borrowed time, it's time to die." I said, "No!" so sudden and loud I jumped. He waited a long time and said, "It's time to die. Nobody loves me." I tried to say, "Grandpa, I love you." And then I did say it all right, feeling like it hadn't been me said it, and knowing all of a sudden it was a lie, because I didn't feel anything. He just lay there; and I went downstairs.

It was sunshiny in the yard, the clouds gone, but the grass was wet. I walked down toward the gate, rubbing my bare feet over the slick cold grass. A hen was in the yard and she kept trying to peck up a piece of hail, like a fool chicken will do after it hails; but every time she pecked, it bounced away from her over the green grass. I leaned against the gate, noticing the ground on one side the posts, close up, was still dry and dusty. I wondered if the tobacco was cut up bad, because Uncle Kirby had gone to see. And while I looked through the gate down across the pasture where everything in the sun was green and shiny with wet and the cattle grazed, I thought about my grandfather, not feeling anything. But I said out loud anyway, "Grandpa, I love you."

My grandfather lived four more years. The year after his stroke they sold the farm and moved away, so I didn't stay with them any more. My grandfather died in 1918, just before the news came that my Uncle Kirby was killed in France, and my aunt had to go to work in a store. I got the letter about my grandfather, who died of flu, but I thought about four years back, and it didn't matter much.

Richard Wright (September 4, 1908–November 28, 1960) was born in Adams County, Mississippi, "too far back in the woods to hear the train whistle," to a country schoolteacher mother and an illiterate sharecropper father. Because of his mother's illness and his father's eventual abandonment, his childhood was one of poverty, frequent moves from relative to relative, and interrupted schooling. His first published story, "The Voodoo of Hell's Half Acre," was printed in September 1924 in the *Southern Register*, the local black newspaper in Jackson, Mississippi. In 1925 he graduated from Jackson's Smith-Robertson Public School. It was the last year he spent in school.

In 1927 Wright moved to Chicago, where he would remain for ten years. In 1932 he joined the American Communist Party, believing that he had finally found a group interested in the plight of the American black. He had begun writing poetry and short stories earlier, and now, on behalf of the Party, his work began to appear in such publications as *New Masses, Left Front,* and *Partisan Review.*

In 1937 Wright moved to New York, where he was Harlem editor of the *Daily Worker.* His first book, *Uncle Tom's Children,* was published in 1938. This was followed by his two most famous works. *Native Son,* published in 1940, is the tragic tale of a Mississippi-born black in Chicago. Its success was phenomenal, and assured Wright a place in American literature. In 1945 *Black Boy,* an autobiographical work based on his traumatic childhood in Mississippi, was released.

By 1944 Wright had left the Communist Party and in 1946, unreconciled to the continuing racism in the United States, he and his family moved to Paris, France. There he was to remain until his death. Among Wright's nonfiction works of this time are *Black Power* (1954) and *Pagan Spain* (1957).

Wright's fiction includes *The Outsider* (1953) and *Savage Holiday* (1954). In addition, three works were published posthumously—*Eight Men* (1961), *Lawd Today* (1963) and *American Hunger* (1977).

BIG BOY LEAVES HOME

by Richard Wright

Is it true what they say about Dixie?
Does the sun really shine all the time?
Do sweet magnolias blossom at everybody's door?
Do folks keep eating 'possum, till they can't eat no more?
Is it true what they say about Swanee?
Is a dream by that stream so sublime?
Do they laugh, do they love, like they say in ev'ry song? . . .
If it's true, that's where I belong.

                                                           Popular Song

I

Yo mama don wear no drawers . . .
    Clearly, the voice rose out of the woods, and died away.
Like an echo another voice caught it up:
    Ah seena when she pulled em off . . .
    Another, shrill, cracking, adolescent:
    N she washed 'em in alcohol . . .
    Then a quartet of voices, blending in harmony, floated
high above the tree tops:
    N she hung 'em out in the hall . . .
    Laughing easily, four black boys came out of the woods
into cleared pasture. They walked lollingly in bare feet,
beating tangled vines and bushes with long sticks.
    "Ah wished Ah knowed some mo lines t tha song."
    "Me too."
    "Yeah, when yuh gits t where she hangs em out in the
hall yuh has t stop."
    "Shucks, what goes wid *hall*?"
    "*Call.*"

"Fall."

"Wall."

"Quall."

They threw themselves on the grass, laughing.

"Big Boy?"

"Huh?"

"Yuh know one thing?"

"Whut?"

"Yuh sho is crazy!"

"Crazy?"

"Yeah. yuh crazys a bed-bug!"

"Crazy bout whut?"

"Man, whoever hearda *quall*?"

"Yuh said yuh wanted something to go wid *hall*, didn't yuh?"

"Yeah, but whuts a *quall*?"

"Nigger, a *qualls* a *quall*."

They laughed easily, catching and pulling long green blades of grass with their toes.

"Waal, ef a *qualls* a *quall*, whut IS a *quall*?"

"Oh, Ah know."

"Whut?"

"Tha ol song goes something like this:

> *Yo mama don wear no drawers,*
> *Ah seena when she pulled em off.*
> *N she washed em in alcohol,*
> *N she hung em out in the hall,*
> *N then she put em back on her QUALL!*

They laughed again. Their shoulders went flat to the earth, their knees propped up, and their faces square to the sun.

"Big Boy, yuhs CRAZY!"

"Don ax me nothin else."

"Nigger, yuhs CRAZY!"

They fell silent, smiling, drooping the lids of their eyes softly against the sunlight.

"Man, don the groun feel warm?"

"Jus lika bed."

"Jeeesus, Ah could stay here ferever."

"Me too."

"Ah kin feel tha ol sun goin all thu me."

"Feels like mah bones is warm."

In the distance a train whistled mournfully.
"There goes number fo!"
"Hittin on all six!"
"Highballin it down the line!"
"Boun fer up Noth, Lawd, boun fer up Noth!"
They began to chant, pounding bare heels in the grass.

> *Dis train boun fo Glory*
> *Dis train, Oh Hallelujah*
> *Dis train boun fo Glory*
> *Dis train, Oh Hallelujah*
> *Dis train boun fo Glory*
> *Ef yuh ride no need fer fret er worry*
> *Dis train, Oh Hallelujah*
> *Dis train. . . .*
>
> *Dis train don carry no gambler*
> *Dis train, Oh Hallelujah*
> *Dis train don carry no gambler*
> *Dis train, Oh Hallelujah*
> *Dis train don carry no gambler*
> *No fo day creeper er midnight rambler*
> *Dis train, Oh Hallelujah*
> *Dis train . . .*

When the song ended they burst out laughing, thinking of a
train bound for Glory.
"Gee, thas a good ol song!"
"Huuuuummmmmmmmman . . ."
"Whut?"
"Gee whiiiiiiz . . ."
"Whut?"
"Somebody don let win! Das whut!"
Buck, Bobo and Lester jumped up. Big Boy stayed on the
ground, feigning sleep.
"Jeeesus, tha sho stinks!"
"Big Boy!"
Big Boy feigned to snore.
"Big Boy!"
Big Boy stirred as though in sleep.
"Big Boy!"
"Hunh?"
"Yuh rotten inside!"

"Rotten?"

"Lawd, cant yuh smell it?"

"Smell whut?"

"Nigger, yuh mus gotta bad col!"

"Smell whut?"

"NIGGER, YUH BROKE WIN!"

Big Boy laughed and fell back on the grass, closing his eyes.

"The hen whut cackles is the hen whut laid the egg."

"We ain no hens."

"Yuh cackled, didnt yuh?"

The three moved off with noses turned up.

"C mon!"

"Where yuh-all goin?"

"T the creek fer a swim."

"Yeah, les swim."

"Naw buddy naw!" said Big Boy, slapping the air with a scornful palm.

"Aw, c mon! Don be a heel!"

"N git *lynched?* Hell naw!"

"He ain gonna see us."

"How yuh know?"

"Cause he ain."

"Yuh-all go on. Ahma stay right here," said Big Boy.

"Hell, let im stay! C mon, les go," said Buck.

The three walked off, swishing at grass and bushes with sticks. Big Boy looked lazily at their backs.

"Hey!"

Walking on, they glanced over their shoulders.

"Hey, niggers!"

"C mon!"

Big Boy grunted, pick up his stick, pulled to his feet and stumbled off.

"Wait!"

"C mon!"

He ran, caught up with them, leaped upon their backs, bearing them to the ground.

"Quit, Big Boy!"

"Gawddam, nigger!"

"Git t hell offa me!"

Big Boy sprawled in the grass beside them, laughing and pounding his heels in the ground.

"Nigger, whut yuh think we is, hosses?"

"How come yuh awways hoppin on us?"

"Lissen, wes gonna double-team on yuh one of these days n beat yo ol ass good."

Big Boy smiled.

"Sho nough?"

"Yeah, don yuh like it?"

"We gonna beat yuh sos yuh cant walk!"

"N dare yuh t do nothing erbout it!"

Big Boy bared his teeth.

"C mon! Try it now!"

The three circle around him.

"Say, Buck, yuh grab his feets!"

"N yuh git his head, Lester!"

"N Bobo, yuh git berhin n grab his arms!"

Keeping more than arm's length, they circled round and round Big Boy.

"C mon!" said Big Boy, feinting at one and then the other.

Round and round they circled, but could not seem to get any closer. Big Boy stopped and braced his hands on his hips.

"Is all three of yuh-all scareda me?"

"Les git im some other time," said Bobo, grinning.

"Yeah, we kin ketch yuh when yuh ain thinkin," said Lester.

"We kin trick yuh," said Buck.

They laughed and walked together.

Big Boy belched.

"Ahm hongry," he said.

"Me too."

"Ah wished Ah hada big hot pota belly-busters!"

"Cooked wid some good ol salty ribs . . ."

"N some good ol egg cornbread . . ."

"N some buttermilk . . ."

"N some hot peach cobbler swimmin in juice . . ."

"Nigger, hush!"

They began to chant, emphasizing the rhythm by cutting at grass with sticks.

> *Bye n bye*
> *Ah wanna piece of pie*
> *Pies too sweet*
> *Ah wanna piece of meat*
> *Meats too red*

"Waal, wes here now," said Big Boy. "Ef he ketched us even like this thered be trouble, so we just as waal go on in . . ."

"Ahm wid the nex one!"

"Ahl go ef anybody else goes!"

Big Boy looked carefully in all directions. Seeing nobody, he began jerking off his overalls.

"LAS ONE INS A OL DEAD DOG!"

"THAS YO MA!"

"THAS YO PA!"

"THAS BOTH YO MA N YO PA!"

They jerked off their clothes and threw them in a pile under a tree. Thirty seconds later they stood, black and naked, on the edge of the hole under a sloping embankment. Gingerly Big Boy touched the water with his foot.

"Man, this waters col," he said.

"Ahm gonna put mah cloes back on," said Bobo, withdrawing his foot.

Big Boy grabbed him about the waist.

"Like hell yuh is!"

"Git outta the way, nigger!" Bobo yelled.

"Throw im in!" said Lester.

"Duck im!"

Bobo crouched, spread his legs, and braced himself against Big Boy's body. Locked in each other's arms, they tussled on the edge of the hole, neither able to throw the other.

"C mon, les me n yuh push em in."

Laughing, Lester and Buck gave the two locked bodies a running push. Big Boy and Bobo splashed, sending up silver spray in the sunlight. When Big Boy's head came up he yelled:

"Yuh bastard!"

"That wuz yo ma yuh pushed!" said Bobo, shaking his head to clear the water from his eyes.

They did a surface dive, came up and struck out across the creek. The muddy water foamed. They swam back, waded into shallow water, breathing heavily and blinking eyes.

"C mon in!"

"Man, the waters fine!"

Lester and Buck hesitated.

"Les wet em," Big Boy whispered to Bobo.

Before Lester and Buck could back away, they were dripping wet from handsful of scooped water.

"Hey, quit!"

"Gawddam, nigger! Tha waters col!"

"C mon in!" called Big Boy.

"We jus as waal go on in now," said Buck.

> *Ah wanna piece of bread*
> *Breads too brown*
> *Ah wanna go t town*
> *Towns too far*
> *Ah wanna ketch a car*
> *Cars too fas*
> *Ah fall n break mah ass*
> *Ahll understan it better bye n bye . . .*

They climbed over a barbed-wire fence and entered a stretch of thick woods. Big Boy was whistling softly, his eyes half-closed.

"LES GIT IM!"

Buck, Lester, and Bobo whirled, grabbed Big Boy about the neck, arms, and legs, bearing him to the ground. He grunted and kicked wildly as he went back into weeds.

"Hol him tight!"

"Git his arms! Git his arms!"

"Set on his legs so he cant kick!"

Big Boy puffed heavily, trying to get loose.

"WE GOT YUH NOW, GAWDDAMMIT, WE GOT YUH NOW!"

"Thas a Gawddam lie!" said Big Boy. He kicked, twisted, and clutched for a hold on one and then the other.

"Say, yuh-all hep me hol his arms!" said Bobo.

"Aw, we got this basterd now!" said Lester.

"Thas a Gawddam lie!" said Big Boy again.

"Say, yuh-all hep me hol his arms!" called Bobo.

Big Boy managed to encircle the neck of Bobo with his left arm. He tightened his elbow scissors-like and hissed through his teeth:

"Yuh got me, ain yuh?"

"Hol im."

"Les, beat this bastard's ass!"

"Say, hep me hol his *arms!* Hes got aholda mah *neck!*" cried Bobo.

Big Boy squeezed Bobo's neck and twisted his head to the ground.

"Yuh got me, ain yuh?"

"Quit, Big Boy, yuh chokin me; yuh hurtin mah neck!" cried Bobo.

"Turn me loose!" said Big Boy.

"Ah ain got yuh! Its the others whut got yuh!" pleaded Bobo.

"Tell them others t git t hell offa me or Ahma break yo neck," said Big Boy.

"Ssssay, yyyuh-all gggit ooooffa Bbig Boy. Hhhes got me," gurgled Bobo.

"Cant yuh hol im?"

"Nnaw, hhes ggot mmah nneck . . ."

Big Boy squeezed tighter.

"N Ahma break it too less yuh tell em t git t hell offa me!"

"Ttturn mmmeee lllloose," panted Bobo, tears gushing.

"Cant yuh hol im, Bobo?" asked Buck.

"Nnaw, yuh-all tturn im lloose; hhhes got mah nnneck. . ."

"Grab his neck, Bobo . . ."

"Ah cant; yugurgur . . ."

To save Bobo, Lester and Buck got up and ran to a safe distance. Big Boy released Bobo, who staggered to his feet, slobbering and trying to stretch a crick out of his neck.

"Shucks, nigger, yuh almos broke mah neck," whimpered Bobo.

"Ahm gonna break yo ass nex time," said Big Boy.

"Ef Bobo coulda hel yuh we woulda had yuh," yelled Lester.

"Ah waznt gonna let im do that," said Big Boy.

They walked together again, swishing sticks.

"Yuh see," began Big Boy, "when a ganga guys jump on yuh, all yuh gotta do is just put the heat on one of them n make im tell the others to let up, see?"

"Gee, thas a good idee!"

"Yeah, thas a good idee!"

"But yuh almos broke mah neck, man," said Bobo.

"Ahma smart nigger," said Big Boy, thrusting out his chest.

II

They came to the swimming hole.

"Ah ain goin in," said Bobo.

"Done got scared?" asked Big Boy.

"Naw, Ah ain scared. . . ."

"How come yuh ain going in?"

"Yuh know ol man Harvey don erllow no niggers to swim in his hole."

"N jus las year he took a shot at Bob fer swimmin in here," said Lester.

"Shucks, ol man Harvey ain studyin bout us niggers," said Big Boy.

"Hes at home thinkin about his jelly-roll," said Buck.

They laughed.

"Buck, yo mins lowern a snakes belly," said Lester.

"Ol man Harvey too doggone ol t think erbout jelly-roll," said Big Boy.

"Hes dried up: all the saps done lef im," said Bobo.

"C mon, les go!" said Big Boy.

Bobo pointed.

"See tha sign over yonder?"

"Yeah."

"Whut it say?"

"NO TRESPASSIN," read Lester.

"Know whut tha mean?"

"Mean ain no dogs n niggers erllowed," said Buck.

"Look n see ef anybodys comin."

Kneeling, they squinted among the trees.

"Ain nobody."

"C mon, les go."

They waded in slowly, pausing each few steps to catch their breath. A desperate water battle began. Closing eyes and backing away, they shunted water into one another's faces with the flat palms of hands.

"Hey, cut it out!"

"Yeah, Ahm bout drownin!"

They came together in water up to their navels, blowing and blinking. Big Boy ducked, upsetting Bobo.

"Look out, nigger!"

"Don holler so loud!"

"Yeah, they kin hear yo ol big mouth a mile erway."

"This waters too col fer me."

"Thas cause it rained yistiddy."

They swam across and back again.

"Ah wish we hada bigger place to swim in."

"The white folks got plenty swimmin pools n we ain got none."

"Ah useta swim in the ol Missipi when we lived in Vicksburg."

Big Boy put his head under the water and blew his breath. A sound came like that of a hippopotamus.

"C mon, les be hippos."

Each went to a corner of the creek and put his mouth just below the surface and blew like a hippopotamus. Tiring, they came and sat under the embankment.

"Look like Ah gotta chill."

"Me too."

"Les stay here n dry off."

"Jeeesus, Ahm col!"

They kept still in the sun, suppressing shivers. After some of the water had dried off their bodies they began to talk through clattering teeth.

"Whut would yuh do ef ol man Harveyd come erlong right now?"

"Run like hell."

"Man, Ahd run so fas hed thinka black streaka lightnin shot pass im."

"But spose he hada gun?"

"Aw, nigger, shut up!"

They were silent. They ran their hands over wet, trembling legs, brushing water away. Then their eyes watched the sun sparkling on the restless creek.

Far away a train whistled.

"There goes number seven!"

"Headin fer up Noth!"

"Blazin it down the line!"

"Lawd, Ahm going Noth some day."

"Me too, man."

"They say colored folks up Noth is got ekual rights."

They grew pensive. A black winged butterfly hovered at the water's edge. A bee droned. From somewhere came the sweet scent of honeysuckles. Dimly they could hear sparrows twittering in the woods. They rolled from side to side, letting sunshine dry their skins and warm their blood. They plucked blades of grass and chewed them.

"Oh!"

They looked up, their lips parting.

"Oh!"

A white woman, poised on the edge of the opposite

embankment, stood directly in front of them, her hat in her hand and her hair lit by the sun.

"Its a woman!" whispered Big Boy in an underbreath. "A *white* woman!"

They stared, their hands instinctively covering their groins. Then they scrambled to their feet. The white woman backed slowly out of sight. They stood for a moment looking at one another.

"Les git outta here!" Big Boy whispered.

"Wait till she goes erway."

"Les run, theyll ketch us here naked like this!"

"Mabbe theres a man wid her."

"C mon, les git our cloes," said Big Boy.

They waited a moment longer, listening.

"Whut t hell! Ahma git mah cloes," said Big Boy.

Grabbing at short tufts of grass, he climbed the embankment.

"Don run out there now!"

"C mon back, fool!"

Bobo hesitated. He looked at Big Boy, and then at Buck and Lester.

"Ahm goin wid Big Boy n git mah cloes," he said.

"Don run out there naked like tha, fool!" said Buck. "Yuh don know whos out there!"

Big Boy was climbing over the edge of the embankment.

"C mon," he whispered.

Bobo climbed after. Twenty-five feet away the woman stood. She had one hand over her mouth. Hanging by fingers, Buck and Lester peeped over the edge.

"C mon back; that womans scared," said Lester.

Big Boy stopped, puzzled. He looked at the woman. He looked at the bundle of clothes. Then he looked at Buck and Lester.

"C mon, les git our cloes!"

He made a step.

"Jim!" the woman screamed.

Big Boy stopped and looked around. His hands hung loosely at his sides. The woman, her eyes wide, her hand over her mouth, backed away to the tree where their clothes lay in a heap.

"Big Boy, come back n wait till shes gone!"

Bobo ran to Big Boy's side.

"Les go home! Theyll ketch us here," he urged.

Big Boy's throat felt tight.

"Lady, we wanna git our cloes," he said.

Buck and Lester climbed the embankment and stood indecisively. Big Boy ran toward the tree.

"Jim!" the woman screamed. "Jim! Jim!"

Black and naked, Big Boy stopped three feet from her.

"We wanna git our cloes," he said again, his words coming mechanically.

He made a motion.

"You go away! You go away! I tell you, you go away!"

Big Boy stopped again, afraid. Bobo ran and snatched the clothes. Buck and Lester tied to grab theirs out of his hands.

"You go away! You go away! You go away!" the woman screamed.

"Les go!" said Bobo, running toward the woods.

CRACK!

Lester grunted, stiffened, and pitched forward. His forehead struck a toe of the woman's shoes.

Bobo stopped, clutching the clothes. Buck whirled. Big Boy stared at Lester, his lips moving.

"Hes gotta gun; hes gotta gun!" yelled Buck, running wildly.

CRACK!

Buck stopped at the edge of the embankment, his head jerked backward, his body arched stiffly to one side; he toppled headlong, sending up a shower of bright spray to the sunlight. The creek bubbled.

Big Boy and Bobo backed away, their eyes fastened fearfully on a white man who was running toward them. He had a rifle and wore an army officer's uniform. He ran to the woman's side and grabbed her hand.

"You hurt, Bertha, you hurt?"

She stared at him and did not answer.

The man turned quickly. His face was red. He raised the rifle and pointed it at Bobo. Bobo ran back, holding the clothes in front of his chest.

"Don shoot me, Mistah, don shoot me . . ."

Big Boy lunged for the rifle, grabbing the barrel.

"You black sonofabitch!"

Big Boy clung desperately.

"Let go, you black bastard!"

The barrel pointed skyward.

CRACK!

The white man, taller and heavier, flung Big Boy to the

ground. Bobo dropped the clothes, ran up, and jumped onto the white man's back.

"You black sonsofbitches!"

The white man released the rifle, jerked Bobo to the ground, and began to batter the naked boy with his fists. Then Big Boy swung, striking the man in the mouth with the barrel. His teeth caved in and he fell, dazed. Bobo was on his feet.

"C mon, Big Boy, les go!"

Breathing hard, the white man got up and faced Big Boy. His lips were trembling, his neck and chin wet with blood. He spoke quietly.

"Give me that gun, boy!"

Big Boy leveled the rifle and backed away.

The white man advanced.

"Boy, I say give me that gun!"

Bobo had the clothes in his arms.

"Run, Big Boy, run!"

The man came at Big Boy.

"Ahll kill yuh; Ahll kill yuh!" said Big Boy.

His fingers fumbled for the trigger.

The man stopped, blinked, spat blood. His eyes were bewildered. His face whitened. Suddenly, he lunged for the rifle, his hands outstretched.

CRACK!

He fell forward on his face.

"Jim!"

Big Boy and Bobo turned in surprise to look at the woman.

"Jim!" she screamed again, and fell weakly at the foot of the tree.

Big Boy dropped the rifle, his eyes wide. He looked around. Bobo was crying and clutching the clothes.

"Big Boy, Big Boy . . ."

Big Boy looked at the rifle, started to pick it up, but didn't. He seemed at a loss. He looked at Lester, then at the white man; his eyes followed a thin stream of blood that seeped to the ground.

"Yoh don killed im," mumbled Bobo.

"Les go home!"

Naked, they turned and ran toward the woods. When they reached the barbed-wire fence they stopped.

"Les git our cloes on," said Big Boy.

They slipped quickly into overalls. Bobo held Lester's and Buck's clothes.

"Whut we gonna do wid these?"

Big Boy stared. His hands twitched.

"Leave em."

They climbed the fence and ran through the woods. Vines and leaves switched their faces. Once Bobo tripped and fell.

"C mon!" said Big Boy.

Bobo started crying, blood streaming from his scratches.

"Ahm scared!"

"C mon! Don cry! We wanna git home fo they ketches us!"

Big Boy grabbed his hand and dragged him along.

"C mon!"

III

They stopped when they got to the end of the woods. They could see the open road leading home, home to ma and pa. But they hung back, afraid. The thick shadows cast from the trees were friendly and sheltering. But the wide glare of sun stretching out over the fields was pitiless. They crouched behind an old log.

"We gotta git home," said Big Boy.

"Theys gonna lynch us," said Bobo, half questioningly.

Big Boy did not answer.

"Theys gonna lynch us," said Bobo again.

Big Boy shuddered.

"Hush!" he said. He did not want to think of it. He could not think of it; there was but one thought, and he clung to that one blindly. He had to get home, home to ma and pa.

Their heads jerked up. Their ears had caught the rhythmic jingle of a wagon. They fell to the ground and clung flat to the side of a log. Over the crest of the hill came the top of a hat. A white face. Then shoulders in a blue shirt. A wagon drawn by two horses pulled into full view.

Big Boy and Bobo held their breath, waiting. Their eyes followed the wagon till it was lost in dust around a bend of the road.

"We gotta git home," said Big Boy.

"Ahm scared," said Bobo.

"C mon! Les keep t the fields."

They ran till they came to the cornfields. Then they went slower, for last year's corn stubbles bruised their feet.

They came in sight of a brickyard.

"Wait a minute," gasped Big Boy.

They stopped.

"Ahm goin on t mah home n yuh better go on t yos."

Bobo's eyes grew round.

"Ahm scared!"

"Yuh better go on!"

"Lemme go wid yuh; theyll ketch me . . ."

"Ef yuh kin git home mabbe yo folks kin hep yuh t git erway."

Big Boy started off. Bobo grabbed him.

"Lemme go wid yuh!"

Big Boy shook free.

"Ef yuh stay here theys gonna lynch yuh!" he yelled, running.

After he had gone about twenty-five yards he turned and looked. Bobo was flying through the woods like the wind.

Big Boy slowed when he came to the railroad. He wondered if he ought to go through the streets or down the track. He decided on the tracks. He could dodge a train better than a mob.

He trotted along the ties, looking ahead and back. His cheek itched and he felt it. His hand came away smeared with blood. He wiped it nervously on his overalls.

When he came to his back fence he heaved himself over. He landed among a flock of startled chickens. A bantam rooster tried to spur him. He slipped and fell in front of the kitchen steps, grunting heavily. The ground was slick with greasy dishwater.

Panting, he stumbled through the doorway.

"Lawd, Big Boy, whuts wrong wid yuh?"

His mother stood gaping in the middle of the floor. Big Boy flopped wordlessly onto a stool, almost toppling over. Pots simmered on the stove. The kitchen smelled of food cooking.

"Whuts the matter, Big Boy?"

Mutely, he looked at her. Then he burst into tears. She came and felt the scratches on his face.

"Whut happened t yuh, Big Boy? Somebody been botherin yuh?"

"They after me, Ma! They after me . . ."

"Who!"

"Ah . . . Ah . . . We. . . ."

"Big Boy, whuts wrong wid yuh?"

"He killed Lester n Buck," he muttered simply.

"Killed!"

"Yessum."

"Lester n Buck!"

"Yessum, Ma!"

"How killed?"

"He shot em, Ma!"

"Lawd Gawd in Heaven, have mercy on us all! This is mo trouble, mo trouble," she moaned, wringing her hands.

"N Ah killed im, Ma . . ."

She stared, trying to understand.

"Whut happened, Big Boy?"

"We tried t git our cloes from the tree . . ."

"Whut tree?"

"We wuz swimmin, Ma. N the white woman . . ."

"*White* woman? . . ."

"Yessum. She wuz at the swimmin hole . . ."

"Lawd have mercy! Ah knowed yuh boys wuz gonna keep on til yuh got into somethin like this!"

She ran into the hall.

"Lucy!"

"Mam?"

"C mere!"

"Mam?"

"C mere, Ah say!"

"Wutcha wan, Ma? Ahm sewin."

"Chile, wil yuh c mere like Ah ast yuh?"

Lucy came to the door holding an unfinished apron in her hands. When she saw Big Boy's face she looked wildly at her mother.

"Whuts the matter?"

"Wheres Pa?"

"Hes out front, Ah reckon."

"Git im, quick!"

"Whuts the matter, Ma?"

"Go git yo Pa, Ah say!"

Lucy ran out, the mother sank into a chair, holding a dish rag. Suddenly, she sat up.

"Big Boy, Ah thought yuh wuz at school?"

Big Boy looked at the floor.

"How come yuh didnt go t school?"

"We went t the woods."

She sighed.

"Ah done done all Ah kin fer yuh, Big Boy. Only Gawd kin hep yuh now."

"Ma, don let em git me; don let em git me . . ."

His father came into the doorway. He stared at Big Boy, then at his wife.

"Whuts Big Boy inter now?" he asked sternly.

"Saul, Big Boys done gone n got inter trouble wid the white folks."

The old man's mouth dropped, and he looked from one to the other.

"Saul, we gotta git im erway from here."

"Open yo mouth n talk! Whut yuh been doin?" The old man gripped Big Boy's shoulders and peered at the scratches on his face.

"Me n Lester n Buck n Bobo wuz out on ol man Harveys place swimmin . . ."

"Saul, its a *white* woman!"

Big Boy winced. The old man compressed his lips and stared at his wife. Lucy gaped at her brother as though she had never seen him before.

"Whut happened? Cant yuh-all talk?" the old man thundered with a certain helplessness in his voice.

"We wuz swimmin," Big Boy began, "n then a white woman comes up t the hole. We got up right erway t git our cloes sos we could git erway, n she started screamin. Our cloes wuz right by the tree where she wuz standin, n when we started t git em she jus screamed. We tol her we wanted our cloes . . . Yuh see, Pa, she wuz standin right *by* our cloes; n when we went t git em she jus screamed . . . Bobo got the cloes, n then he shot Lester . . ."

"*Who* shot Lester?"

"The white man."

"Whut white man?"

"Ah dunno, Pa. He wuz a soljer, n he had a rifle."

"A soljer?"

"Yessuh."

"A *soljer?*"

"Yessuh, Pa. A soljer."

The old man frowned.

"N then whut yuh-all do?"

"Waal, Buck said, 'He's gotta gun!' N we started runnin. N then he shot Buck, n he fell in the swimmin hole. We didnt see im no mo . . . He wuz close on us then. He looked at the white woman n then he started t shoot Bobo. Ah grabbed the gun, n we started fightin. Bobo jumped on his back. He started beatin Bobo. Then Ah hit im wid the gun. Then he started at me n Ah shot im. Then we run . . ."

"Who seen?"

"Nobody."

"Wheres Bobo?"

"He went home."

"Anybody run after yuh-all?"

"Nawsuh."

"Yuh see anybody?"

"Nawsuh. Nobody but a white man. But he didnt see us."

"How long fo yuh-all lef the swimmin hole?"

"Little while ergo."

The old man nervously brushed his hand across his eyes and walked to the door. His lips moved, but no words came.

"Saul, whut we gonna do?"

"Lucy," began the old man, "go t Brother Sanders n tell im Ah said c mere; n go t Brother Jenkins n tell im Ah said c mere; n go t Elder Peters n tel im Ah said c mere. N don say nothin t nobody but whut Ah tol yuh. N when yuh git thu come straight back. Now go!"

Lucy dropped her apron across the back of a chair and ran down the steps. The mother bent over, crying and praying. The old man walked slowly over to Big Boy.

"Big Boy?"

Big Boy swallowed.

"Ahm talkin t yuh!"

"Yessuh."

"How come yuh didnt go t school this mawnin?"

"We went t the woods."

"Didnt yo ma send yuh t school?"

"Yessuh."

"How come yuh didnt go?"

"We went t the woods."

"Don yuh know thas wrong?"

"Yessuh."

"How come yuh go?"

Big Boy looked at his fingers, knotted them, and squirmed in his seat.

"AHM TALKIN T YUH!"

His wife straightened up and said reprovingly:

"Saul!"

The old man desisted, yanking nervously at the shoulder straps of his overalls.

"How long wuz the woman there?"

"Not long."

"Wuz she young?"

"Yessuh. Lika gal."

"Did yuh-all say anythin t her?"

"Nawsuh. We jus said we wanted our cloes."

"N whut she say?"

"Nothin, Pa. She jus backed erway t the tree n screamed."

The old man stared, his lips trying to form a question.

"Big Boy, did yuh-all bother her?"

"Nawsuh, Pa. We didnt *touch* her."

"How long fo the white man come up?"

"Right erway."

"Whut he say?"

"Nothin. He jus cussed us."

Abruptly the old man left the kitchen.

"Ma, cant Ah go fo they ketches me?"

"Sauls doin whut he kin."

"Ma, Ma, Ah don wan em t ketch me . . ."

"Sauls doin whut he kin. Nobody but the good Lawd kin hep us now."

The old man came back with a shotgun and leaned it in a corner. Fascinatedly, Big Boy looked at it.

There was a knock at the front door.

"Liza, see whos there."

She went. They were silent, listening. They could hear her talking.

"Whos there?"

"Me."

"Who?"

"Me, Brother Sanders."

"C mon in. Sauls waitin fer yuh."

Sanders paused in the doorway, smiling.

"Yuh sent fer me, Brother Morrison?"

"Brother Sanders, wes in deep trouble here."

Sanders came all the way into the kitchen.

"Yeah?"

"Big Boy done gone n killed a white man."

Sanders stopped short, then came forward, his face thrust out, his mouth open. His lips moved several times before he could speak.

"A *white* man?"

"They gonna kill me; they gonna kill me!" Big Boy cried, running to the old man.

"Saul, cant we git im erway somewhere?"

"Here now, take it easy; take it easy," said Sanders, holding Big Boy's wrists.

"They gonna kill me; they gonna lynch me!"

Big Boy slipped to the floor. They lifted him to a stool. His mother held him closely, pressing his head to her bosom.

"Whut we gonna do?" asked Sanders.

"Ah done sent fer Brother Jenkins n Elder Peters."

Sanders leaned his shoulders against the wall. Then, as the full meaning of it all came to him, he exclaimed:

"Theys gonna git a mob! . . ." His voice broke off and his eyes fell on the shotgun.

Feet came pounding on the steps. They turned toward the door. Lucy ran in crying. Jenkins followed. The old man met him in the middle of the room, taking his hand.

"Wes in bad trouble here. Brother Jenkins. Big Boy's done gone n killed a white man. Yuh-alls gotta hep me . . ."

Jenkins looked hard at Big Boy.

"Elder Peters says hes comin," said Lucy.

"When all this happen?" asked Jenkins.

"Near bout a hour ergo, now," said the old man.

"Whut we gonna do?" asked Jenkins.

"Ah wanna wait till Elder Peters come," said the old man helplessly.

"But we gotta work fas ef we gonna do anythin," said Sanders. "Well git in trouble jus standin here like this."

Big Boy pulled away from his mother.

"Pa, lemme go now! Lemme go now!"

"Be still, Big Boy!"

"Where kin yuh go?"

"Ah could ketch a freight!"

"Thas *sho* death!" said Jenkins. "They'll be watchin em all!"

"Kin yuh-all hep me wid some money?" the old man asked.

They shook their heads.

"Saul, whut kin we do? Big Boy cant stay here."

There was another knock at the door.

The old man backed stealthily to the shotgun.

"Lucy go!"

Lucy looked at him, hesitating.

"Ah better go," said Jenkins.

It was Elder Peters. He came in hurriedly.

"Good evenin, everybody!"

"How yuh, Elder?"

"Good evenin."

"How yuh today?"

Peters looked around the crowded kitchen.

"Whuts the matter?"

"Elder, wes in deep trouble," began the old man. "Big Boy n some mo boys . . ."

". . . Lester n Buck n Bobo . . ."

". . . wuz over on ol man Harveys place swimmin . . ."

"N he don like us niggers *none*," said Peters emphatically. He widened his legs and put his thumbs in the armholes of his vest.

". . . n some white woman . . ."

"Yeah?" said Peters, coming closer.

". . . comes erlong n the boys tries t git their cloes where they done lef em under a tree. Waal, she started screamin n all, see? Reckon she thought the boys wuz after her. Then a white man in a soljers suit shoots two of em . . ."

". . . Lester n Buck . . ."

"Huummm," said Peters. "Tha wuz ol man Harveys son."

"Harveys son?"

"Yuh mean the one tha wuz in the Army?"

"Yuh mean Jim?"

"Yeh," said Peters. "The papers said he wuz here for a vacation from his regiment. N tha woman the boys saw wuz jus erbout his wife . . ."

They stared at Peters. Now that they knew what white person had been killed, their fears became definite.

"N whut else happened?"

"Big Boy shot the man . . ."

"Harveys *son*?"

"He had t, Elder. He wuz gonna shoot im ef he didnt . . ."

"Lawd!" said Peters. He looked around and put his hat back on.

"How long ergo wuz this?"

"Mighty near an hour, now, Ah reckon."

"Do the white folks know yit?"

"Don know, Elder."

"Yuh-all better git this boy outta here right now," said Peters. "Cause ef yuh don theres gonna be a lynchin . . ."

"Where kin Ah go, Elder?" Big Boy ran up to him.

They crowded around Peters. He stood with his legs wide apart, looking up at the ceiling.

"Mabbe we kin hide im in the church till he kin git erway," said Jenkins.

Peters' lips flexed.

"Naw, Brother, thall never do! Theyll git im there sho. N anyhow, ef they ketch im there itll ruin us all. We gotta git the boy outta town . . ."

Sanders went up to the old man.

"Lissen," he said in a whisper. "Mah son, Will, the one whut drives for the Magnolia Express Company, is taking a truck o goods t Chicawgo in the mawnin. If we kin hide Big Boy somewhere till then, we kin put im on the truck . . ."

"Pa, please, lemme go wid Will when he goes in the mawnin," Big Boy begged.

The old man stared at Sanders.

"Yuh reckon thas safe?"

"Its the only thing yuh *kin* do," said Peters.

"But where we gonna hide im till then?"

"Whut time yo boy leavin out in the mawnin?"

"At six."

They were quiet, thinking. The water kettle on the stove sang.

"Pa, Ah knows where Will passes erlong wid the truck out on Bullards Road. Ah kin hide in one of them ol kilns . . ."

"Where?"

"In one of them kilns we built . . ."

"But theyll git yuh there," wailed the mother.

"But there ain no place else fer im t go."

"Theres some holes big ernough fer me t git in n stay till Will comes erlong," said Big Boy. "Please, Pa, lemme go fo they ketches me . . ."

"Let im go!"

"Please, Pa . . ."

The old man breathed heavily.

"Lucy, git his things!"

"Saul, theyll git im out there!" wailed the mother, grabbing Big Boy.

Peters pulled her way.

"Sister Morrison, ef yuh don let im go n git erway from here hes gonna be caught shos theres a Gawd in Heaven!"

Lucy came running with Big Boy's shoes and pulled them on his feet. The old man thrust a battered hat on his head. The mother went to the stove and dumped the skillet of corn pone into her apron. She wrapped it, and unbuttoning Big Boy's overalls, pushed it into his bosom.

"Heres somethin fer yuh t eat; n pray, Big Boy, cause thas all anybody kin do now . . ."

Big Boy pulled to the door, his mother clinging to him.

"Let im go, Sister Morrison!"

"Run fas, Big Boy!"

Big Boy raced across the yard, scattering the chickens. He paused at the fence and hollered back:

"Tell Bobo where Ahm hidin n tell im t c mon!"

IV

He made for the railroad, running straight toward the sunset. He held his left hand tightly over his heart, holding the hot pone of corn bread there. At times he stumbled over the ties, for his shoes were tight and hurt his feet. His throat burned from thirst; he had had no water since noon.

He veered off the track and trotted over the crest of a hill, following Bullard's Road. His feet slipped and slid in the dust. He kept his eyes straight ahead, fearing every clump of shrubbery, every tree. He wished it were night. If he could only get to the kilns without meeting anyone. Suddenly a thought came to him like a blow. He recalled hearing the old folks tell tales of blood-hounds, and fear made him run slower. None of them had thought of that. Spose blood-houns wuz put on his trail? Lawd! Spose a whole pack of em, foamin n howlin tore im t pieces? He went limp and his feet dragged. Yeah, thas whut they wuz gonna send after im, blood-houns! N then thered be no way fer im to dodge! Why hadnt Pa let im take tha shotgun? He stopped. He oughta go back n git tha shotgun. And then when the mob came he would take some with him.

In the distance he heard the approach of a train. It jarred him back to a sharp sense of danger. He ran again, his big shoes sopping up and down in the dust. He was tired and his lungs were bursting from running. He wet his lips, wanting water. As he turned from the road across a plowed field he heard the train roaring at his heels. He ran faster, gripped in terror.

He was nearly there now. He could see the black clay on the sloping hillside. Once inside a kiln he would be safe. For a little while, at least. He thought of the shotgun again. If he only had something; Someone to talk to . . . Thas right! Bobo! Bobod be wid im. Hed almost fergot Bobo. Bobod bringa gun; he knowed he would. N tergether they could kill the whole mob. Then in the mawning theyd git inter Will's truck n go far erway, t Chicawgo . . .

He slowed to a walk, looking back and ahead. A light wind skipped over the grass. A beetle lit on his cheek and he brushed it off. Behind the dark pines hung a red sun. Two bats flapped against that sun. He shivered, for he was growing cold; the sweat on his body was drying.

He stopped at the foot of the hill, trying to choose between two patches of black kilns high above him. He went to the the left, for there lay the ones he, Bobo, Lester, and Buck had dug only last week. He looked around again; the landscape was bare. He climbed the embankment and stood before a row of black pits sinking four and five feet deep into the earth. He went to the largest and peered in. He stiffened when his ears caught the sound of a whir. He ran back a few steps and poised on his toes. Six foot of snake slid out of the pit and went into coil. Big Boy looked around wildly for a stick. He ran down the slope, peering into the grass. He stumbled over a tree limb. He picked it up and tested it by striking it against the ground.

Warily, he crept back up the slope, his stick poised. When about seven feet from the snake he stopped and waved the stick. The coil grew tighter, the whir sounded louder, and a flat head reared to strike. He went to the right, and the flat head followed him, the blue-black tongue darting forth; he went to the left, and the flat head followed him there too.

He stopped, teeth clenched. He had to kill this snake. Jus had t kill im! This wuz the safest pit on the hillside. He waved the stick again, looking at the snake before, thinking of a mob behind. The flat head reared higher. With stick over shoulder, he jumped in, swinging. The stick sang through the air, catching the snake on the side of the head, sweeping him out of coil. There was a brown writhing mass. Then Big Boy was upon him, pounding blows home, one on top of the other. He fought viciously, his eyes red, his teeth bared in a snarl. He beat till the snake lay still; then he stomped it with his heel, grinding its head into the dirt.

He stopped, limp, wet. The corners of his lips were white with spittle. He spat and shuddered.

Cautiously, he went to the hole and peered. He longed for a match. He imagined whole nests of them in there waiting. He put the stick into the hole and waved it around. Stooping, he peered again. It mus be awright. He looked over the hillside, his eyes coming back to the dead snake. Then he got to his knees and backed slowly into the hole.

When inside he felt there must be snakes all about him, ready to strike. It seemed he could see and feel them there, waiting tensely in coil. In the dark he imagined long white fangs ready to sink into his neck, his side, his legs. He wanted to come out, but kept still. Shucks, he told himself, ef there wuz any snakes in here they sho woulda done bit me by now. Some of his fear left, and he relaxed.

With elbows on ground and chin on palms, he settled. The clay was cold to his knees and thighs, but his bosom was kept warm by the hot pone of corn bread. His thirst returned and he longed for a drink. He was hungry, too. But he did not want to eat the corn pone. Naw, not now. Mabbe after erwhile, after Bobo came. Then theyd both eat the corn pone.

The view from his hole was fringed by the long tufts of grass. He could see all the way to Bullard's Road, and even beyond. The wind was blowing, and in the east the first touch of dusk was rising. Every now and then a bird floated past, a spot of wheeling black printed against the sky. Big Boy sighed, shifted his weight, and chewed at a blade of grass. A wasp droned. He heard number nine, far away and mournful.

The train made him remember how they had dug these kilns on long hot summer days, how they had made boilers out of big tin cans, filled them with water, fixed stoppers for steam, cemented them in holes with wet clay, and built fires under them. He recalled how they had danced and yelled when a stopper blew out of a boiler, letting out a big spout of steam and a shrill whistle. There were times when they had the whole hillside blazing and smoking. Yeah, yuh see,

Big Boy wuz Casey Jones n wuz speedin it down the gleamin
rails of the Southern Pacific. Bobo had number two on the
Santa Fe. Buck wuz on the Illinoy Central. Lester the Nickel
Plate. Lawd, how they shelved the wood in! The boiling
water would almost jar the cans loose from the clay. More
and more pine-knots and dry leaves would be piled under
the cans. Flames would grow so tall they would have to
shield their eyes. Sweat would pour off their faces. Then,
suddenly, a peg would shoot high into the air, and
    Pssseeeeezzzzzzzzzzzzzzzzzzzzzzzzz . . .
Big Boy sighed and stretched out his arm, quenching the
flames and scattering the smoke. Why didnt Bobo c mon?
He looked over the fields; there was nothing but dying
sunlight. His mind drifted back to the kilns. He remembered the day when Buck, jealous of his winning, had tried
to smash his kiln. Yeah, that ol sonofabitch! Naw, Lawd!
He didnt go t say tha! Whut wuz he thinkin erbout? Cussin
the dead! Yeah, po ol Buck wuz dead now. N Lester too.
Yeah, it wuz awright fer Buck t smash his kiln. Sho. N he
wished he hadnt socked ol Buck so hard tha day. He wuz
sorry fer Buck now. N he sho wished he hadnt cussed po ol
Bucks ma, neither. Tha wuz sinful! Mabbe Gawd would git
im fer tha? But he didnt go t do it! Po Buck! Po Lester! Hed
never treat anybody like tha ergin, never . . .
Dusk was slowly deepening. Somewhere, he could not tell
exactly where, a cricket took up a fitful song. The air was
growing soft and heavy. He looked over the fields, longing
for Bobo . . .
He shifted his body to ease the cold damp of the ground,
and thought back over the day. Yeah, hed been dam right
erbout not wantin t go swimmin. N ef hed followed his right
min hed neverve gone n got inter all this trouble. At first
hed said naw. But shucks, somehow hed just went on wid
the res. Yeah, he shoulda went on t school tha mawnin, like
Ma told im t do. But, hell, who wouldnt git tireda school?
T hell wid school! Tha wuz the big trouble, awways drivin a
guy t school. He would'nt be in all this trouble now ef it
wuznt for that Gawddam school! Impatiently, he took the
grass out of his mouth and threw it away, demolishing the
little red school house . . .
Yeah, ef they had all kept still n quiet when that ol white
woman showed-up, mabbe shedve went on off. But yuh
never kin tell erbout these white folks. Mabbe she wouldntve

went. Mabbe that white man woulda killed all of em! All *fo* of em! Yeah, yuh never kin tell erbout white folks. Then, ergin, mabbe tha white woman woulda went on off n laffed. Yeah, mabbe tha white man woulda said: *Yuh nigger bastards git t hell outta here! Yuh know Gawddam well yuh don berlong here!* N then they woulda grabbed their cloes n run like all hell . . . He blinked the white man away. Where wuz Bobo? Why didnt he hurry up n c mon?

He jerked another blade and chewed. Yeah, ef pa had only let im have tha shotgun? He could stan off a whole mob wid a shotgun. He looked at the ground as he turned a shotgun over in his hands. Then he leveled it at an advancing white man. *Boooom!* The man curled up. Another came. He reloaded quickly, and let him have what the other had got. He too curled up. Then another came. He got the same medicine. Then the whole mob swirled around him, and he blazed away, getting as many as he could. They closed in; but, by Gawd, he had done his part, hadnt he? N the newspapersd say: NIGGER KILLS DOZEN OF MOB BEFO LYNCHED! Er mabbe theyd say: TRAPPED NIGGER SLAYS TWENTY BEFO KILLED! He smiled a little. Tha wouldnt be so bad, would it? Blinking the newspaper away, he looked over the fields. Where wuz Bobo? Why didnt he hurry up n c mon?

He shifted, trying to get a crick out of his legs. Shucks, he wuz gittin tireda this. N it wuz almos dark now. Yeah, there wuz a little bittie star way over yonder in the eas. Mabbe that white man wuznt dead? Mabbe they wuznt even lookin for im? Mabbe he could go back home now? Naw, better wait erwhile. Thad be bes. But, Lawd, ef he only had some water! He could hardly swallow, his throat was so dry. Gawddam them white folks! Thas all they wuz good fer, t run a nigger down lika rabbit! Yeah, they git yuh in a corner n then they let yuh have it. A thousan of em! He shivered, for the cold of the clay was chilling his bones. Lawd, spose they foun im here in this hole? N wid nobody t hep im? . . . But ain no use in thinkin erbout tha; wait till trouble come fo yuh start fightin it. But ef tha mob came one by one hed wipe em all out. Clean up the whole bunch. He caught one by the neck and choked him long and hard, choked him till his tongue and eyes popped out. Then he jumped upon his chest and stomped him like he had stomped that snake. When he had finished with one, another came.

He choked him too. Choked till he sank slowly to the ground, gasping . . .

"Hoalo!"

Big Boy snatched his fingers from the white man's neck and looked over the fields. He saw nobody. Had someone spied him? He was sure that somebody had hollered. His heart pounded. But, shucks, nobody couldnt see im here in this hole . . . But mabbe theyd seen im when he wuz comin n had laid low n wuz now closin in on im! Praps they wuz signalin fer the others? Yeah, they wuz creepin up on im! Mabbe he oughta git up n run . . . Oh! Mabbe tha wuz Bobo! Yeah, Bobo! He oughta clim out n see ef Bobo wuz lookin fer im . . . He stiffened.

"Hoalo!"

"Hoalo!"

"Wheres yuh?"

"Over here on Bullards Road!"

"C mon over!"

"Awright!"

He heard footsteps. Then voices came again, low and far away this time.

"Seen anybody?"

"Naw. Yuh?"

"Naw."

"Yuh reckon they got erway?"

"Ah dunno. Its hard t tell."

"Gawddam them sonofabitchin niggers!"

"We oughta kill ever black bastard in this country!"

"Waal, Jim got two of em, anyhow."

"But Bertha said there wuz *fo*!"

"Where in hell they hidin?"

"She said one of em wuz named Big Boy, or somethin like tha."

"We went t his shack lookin fer im."

"Yeah?"

"But we didnt fin im."

"These niggers stick together; they don never tell on each other."

"We looked all thu the shack n couldnt fin hide ner hair of im. Then we drove the ol woman n man out n set the shack on fire . . ."

"Jeesus! Ah wished Ah coulda been there!"

"Yuh shoulda heard the ol nigger woman howl . . ."

"Hoalo!"

"C mon over!"

Big Boy eased to the edge and peeped. He saw a white man with a gun slung over his shoulder running down the slope. Wuz they gonna search the hill? Lawd, there wuz no way fer im t git erway now; he wuz caught! He shoulda knowed theyd git im here. N he didnt hava thing, notta thing t fight wid. Yeah, soon as the blood-houns came theyd fin im. Lawd, have mercy! Theyd lynch im right here on the hill . . . Theyd git im n tie im t a stake n burn im erlive! Lawd! Nobody but the good Lawd could hep im now, nobody . . .

He heard more feet running. He nestled deeper. His chest ached. Nobody but the good Lawd could hep now. They wuz crowdin all round im n when they hada big crowd theyd close in on im. Then itd be over . . . The good Lawd would have t hep im, cause nobody could hep im now, nobody . . .

And then he went numb when he remembered Bobo. Spose Bobod come now? Hed be caught sho! Both of em would be caught! They'd make Bobo tell where he wuz! Bobo oughta not try to come now. Somebody oughta tell im . . . But there wuz nobody; there wuz no way . . .

He eased slowly back to the opening. There was a large group of men. More were coming. Many had guns. Some had coils of rope slung over shoulders.

"Ah tell yuh they still here, somewhere . . ."

"But we looked all over!"

"What t hell! Wouldnt do t let em git erway!"

"Naw. Ef they git erway notta woman in this town would be safe."

"Say, whuts tha yuh got?"

"Er pillar."

"Fer whut?"

"Feathers, fool!"

"Chris! Thisll be hot ef we kin ketch them niggers!"

"Ol Anderson said he wuz gonna bringa barrela tar!"

"Ah got some gasoline in mah car ef yuh need it."

Big Boy had no feelings now. He was waiting. He did not wonder if they were coming after him. He just waited. He did not wonder about Bobo. He rested his cheek against the cold clay, waiting.

A dog barked. He stiffened. It barked again. He balled

himself into a knot at the bottom of the hole, waiting. Then he heard the patter of dog feet.

"Look!"

"Whuts he got?"

"Its a snake!"

"Yeah, the dogs foun a snake!"

"Gee, its a big one!"

"Shucks, Ah wish he could fin one of them sonofabitchin niggers!"

The voices sank to low murmurs. Then he heard number twelve, its bell tolling and whistle crying as it slid along the rails. He flattened himself against the clay. Someone was singing:

"We'll hang ever nigger t a sour apple tree . . ."

When the song ended there was hard laughter. From the other side of the hill he heard the dog barking furiously. He listened. There was more than one dog now. There were many and they were barking their throats out.

"Hush. Ah hear them dogs!"

"When theys barking like tha they foun somethin!"

"Here they come over the hill!"

"WE GOT IM! WE GOT IM!"

There came a roar. Tha mus be Bobo; tha mus be Bobo . . . In spite of his fear, Big Boy looked. The road, and half of the hillside across the road, were covered with men. A few were at the top of the hill, stenciled against the sky. He could see dark forms moving up the slopes. They were yelling.

"By Gawd, we got im!"

"C mon!"

"Where is he?"

"Theyre bringin im over the hill!"

"Ah got a rope fer im!"

"Say, somebody go n git the others!"

"Where is he? Cant we see im, Mister?"

"They say Berthas comin, too."

"Jack! Jack! Don leave me! Ah wanna see im!"

"Theyre bringin im over the hill, sweetheart!"

"AH WANNA BE THE FIRS T PUT A ROPE ON THA BLACK BASTARDS NECK!"

"Les start the fire!"

"Heat the tar!"

"Ah got some chains t chain im."

"Bring im over this way!"

"Chris, Ah wished Ah hada drink . . ."

Big Boy saw men moving over the hill. Among them was a long dark spot. Tha mus be Bobo; tha mus be Bobo theys carryin . . . They'll git im here. He oughta git up n run. He clamped his teeth and ran his hand across his forehead, bringing it away wet. He tried to swallow, but could not; his throat was dry.

They had started the song again:

"We'll hang ever nigger t a sour apple tree . . ."

There were women singing now. Their voices made the song round and full. Song waves rolled over the top of pine trees. The sky sagged low, heavy with clouds. Wind was rising. Sometimes cricket cries cut surprisingly across the mob song. A dog had gone to the utmost top of the hill. At each lull of the song his howl floated full into the night.

Big Boy shrank when he saw the first tall flame light the hillside. Would they see im here? Then he remembered you could not see into the dark if you were standing in the light. As flames leaped higher he saw two men rolling a barrel up the slope.

"Say, gimme a han here, will yuh?"

"Awright, heave!"

"C mon! Straight up! Git t the other end!"

"Ah got the feathers here in this pillar!"

"BRING SOME MO WOOD!"

Big Boy could see the barrel surrounded by flames. The mob fell back, forming a dark circle. Theyd fin im here! He had a wild impulse to climb out and fly across the hills. But his legs would not move. He stared hard, trying to find Bobo. His eyes played over a long dark spot near the fire. Fanned by wind, flames leaped higher. He jumped. That dark spot had moved. Lawd, thas Bobo; thas Bobo . . .

He smelt the scent of tar, faint at first, then stronger. The wind brought it full into his face, then blew it away. His eyes burned and he rubbed them with his knuckles. He sneezed.

"LES GIT SOURVINEERS!"

He saw the mob close in around the fire. Their faces were

hard and sharp in the light of the flames. More men and women were coming over the hill. The long dark spot was smudged out.

"Everybody git back!"

"Look! Hes gotta finger!"

"C MON! GIT THE GALS BACK FROM THE FIRE!"

"Hes got one of his ears, see?"

"Whuts the matter!"

"A woman fell out! Fainted, Ah reckon . . ."

The stench of tar permeated the hillside. The sky was black and the wind was blowing hard.

"HURRY UP N BURN THE NIGGER FO IT RAINS!"

Big Boy saw the mob fall back, leaving a small knot of men about the fire. Then, for the first time, he had a full glimpse of Bobo. A black body flashed in the light. Bobo was struggling, twisting; they were binding his arms and legs . . .

When he saw them tilt the barrel he stiffened. A scream quivered. He knew the tar was on Bobo. The mob fell back. He saw a tar-drenched body glistening and turning.

"THE BASTARDS GOT IT!"

There was a sudden quiet. Then he shrank violently as the wind carried, like a flury of snow, a widening spiral of white feathers into the night. The flames leaped tall as the trees. The scream came again. Big Boy trembled and looked. The mob was running down the slopes, leaving the fire clear. The he saw a writhing white mass cradled in yellow flame, and heard screams, one on top of the other, each shriller and shorter than the last. The mob was quiet now, standing still, looking up the slopes at the writhing white mass gradually growing black, growing black in a cradle of yellow flame.

"PO ON MO GAS!"

"Gimme a lif, will yuh!"

Two men were struggling, carrying between them a heavy can. They set it down, tilted it, leaving it so that the gas would trickle down to the hollowed earth around the fire.

Big Boy slid back into the hole, his face buried in clay. He had no feelings now, no fears. He was numb, empty, as though all blood had been drawn from him. Then his muscles flexed taut when he heard a faint patter. A tiny stream of cold water seeped to his knees, making him push back to a drier spot. He looked up; rain was beating in the grass.

"Its rainin!"

"C mon, les git t town!"

". . . don worry, when the fire git thu wid im hell be gone . . ."

"Wait, Charles! Don leave me; its slippery here . . ."

"Ahll take some of yuh ladies back in mah car . . ."

Big Boy heard the dogs barking again, this time closer. Running feet pounded past. Cold water chilled his ankles. He could hear rain-drops steadily hissing.

Now a dog was barking at the mouth of the hole, barking furiously, sensing a presence there. He balled himself into a knot and clung to the bottom, his knees and shins buried in water. The bark came louder. He heard paws scraping and felt the hot scent of dog breath on his face. Green eyes glowed and drew nearer as the barking, muffled by the closeness of the hole, beat upon his eardrums. Backing till his shoulders pressed against the clay, he held his breath. He pushed out his hands, his fingers stiff. The dog yawped louder, advancing, his bark rising sharp and thin. Big Boy rose to his knees, his hands before him. Then he flattened out still more against the bottom, breathing lungsful of hot dog scent, breathing it slowly, hard, but evenly. The dog came closer, bringing hotter dog scent. Big Boy could go back no more. His knees were slipping and slopping in the water. He braced himself, ready. Then, he never exactly knew how—he never knew whether he had lunged or the dog had lunged—they were together, rolling in the water. The green eyes were beneath him, between his legs. Dognails bit into his arms. His knees slipped backward and he landed full on the dog; the dog's breath left in a heavy gasp. Instinctively, he fumbled for the throat as he felt the dog twisting between his knees. The dog snarled, long and low, as though gathering strength. Big Boy's hands traveled swiftly over the dog's back, groping for the throat. He felt dognails again and saw green eyes, but his fingers had found the throat. He choked, feeling his fingers sink; he choked, throwing back his head and stiffening his arms. He felt the dog's body heave, felt dognails digging into his loins. With strength flowing from fear, he closed his fingers, pushing his full weight on the dog's throat. The dog heaved again, and lay still . . . Big Boy heard the sound of his own breathing filling the hole, and heard shouts and footsteps above him going past.

For a long, long time he held the dog, held it long after the last footstep had died out, long after the rain had stopped.

V

Morning found him still on his knees in a puddle of rainwater, staring at the stiff body of a dog. As the air brightened he came to himself slowly. He held still for a long time, as though waking from a dream, as though trying to remember.

The chug of a truck came over the hill. He tried to crawl to the opening. His knees were stiff and a thousand needle-like pains shot from the bottom of his feet to the calves of his legs. Giddiness made his eyes blur. He pulled up and looked. Through brackish light he saw Will's truck standing some twenty-five yards away, the engine running. Will stood on the running board, looking over the slopes of the hill.

Big Boy scuffled out, falling weakly in the wet grass. He tried to call to Will, but his dry throat would make no sound. He tried again.

"Will!"

Will heard, answering:

"Big Boy, c mon!"

He tried to run, and fell. Will came, meeting him in the tall grass.

"C mon," Will said, catching his arm.

They struggled to the truck.

"Hurry up!" said Will, pushing him onto the runningboard.

Will pushed back a square trapdoor which swung above the back of the driver's seat. Big Boy pulled through, landing with a thud on the bottom. On hands and knees he looked around in the semi-darkness.

"Wheres Bobo?"

Big Boy stared.

"Wheres Bobo?"

"They got im."

"When?"

"Las night."

"The mob?"

Big Boy pointed in the direction of a charred sapling on the slope of the opposite hill. Will looked. The trapdoor fell. The engine purred, the gears whined, and the truck lurched forward over the muddy road, sending Big Boy on his side.

For a while he lay as he had fallen, on his side, too weak to move. As he felt the truck swing around a curve he straightened up and rested his back against a stack of wooden boxes. Slowly, he began to make out objects in the darkness. Through two long cracks fell thin blades of daylight. The floor was of smooth steel, and cold to his thighs. Splinters and bits of sawdust danced with the rumble of the truck. Each time they swung around a curve he was pulled over the floor; he grabbed at corners of boxes to steady himself. Once he heard the crow of a rooster. It made him think of home, of ma and pa. He thought he remembered hearing somewhere that the house had burned, but could not remember where . . . It all seemed unreal now.

He was tired. He dozed, swaying with the lurch. Then he jumped awake. The truck was running smoothly, on gravel. Far away he heard two short blasts from the Buckeye Lumber Mill. Unconsciously, the thought sang through his mind: Its six erclock . . .

The trapdoor swung in. Will spoke through a corner of his mouth.

"How yuh comin?"

"Awright."

"How they git Bobo?"

"He wuz comin over the hill."

"What they do?"

"They burnt im . . . Will, Ah wan some water; mah throats like fire . . ."

"Well git some when we pass a fillin station."

Big Boy leaned back and dozed. He jerked awake when the truck stopped. He heard Will git out. He wanted to peep through the trapdoor, but was afraid. For a moment, the wild fear he had known in the hole came back. Spose theyd search n fin im? He quieted when he heard Will's footstep on the runningboard. The trapdoor pushed in. Will's hat came through dripping.

"Take it quick!"

Big Boy grabbed, spilling water into his face. The truck lurched. He drank. Hard cold lumps of brick rolled into his hot stomach. A dull pain made him bend over. His intestines seemed to be drawing into a tight knot. After a bit it eased, and he sat up, breathing softly.

The truck swerved. He blinked his eyes. The blades of daylight had turned brightly golden. The sun had risen.

The truck sped over the asphalt miles, sped northward, jolting him, shaking out of his bosom the crumbs of corn bread, making them dance with the splinters and sawdust in the golden blades of sunshine.

He turned on his side and slept.

Marjorie Kinnan Rawlings (August 8, 1896–December 14, 1953) was born in Washington, D.C. and in 1918 received a degree from the University of Wisconsin. In 1928, after spending a spring vacation tramping through the wilderness area of Florida known as the Ocala scrub, she bought sight-unseen a farmhouse on the shore of Orange Lake in a tiny place called Cross Creek. She felt from the beginning that she had "come home."

In her farmhouse, often on the screened-in front porch, Rawlings composed *South Moon Under* (1933), *Golden Apples* (1935), *The Yearling* (1938), *When the Whippoorwill* (1940), *Cross Creek* (1942), *Cross Creek Cookery* (1942), and *The Sojourner* (1953). *The Yearling*, her Pulitzer Prize winning novel, is Rawlings's best-known book, but it is *Cross Creek* that offers her richest portrayal of Florida. This autobiographical work gives the reader an account of her life and describes vividly the local people, the vegetation, the animals, and the folklore of the region.

When Rawlings died in 1953 she was researching the life of Ellen Glasgow in preparation for a biography.

THE PELICAN'S SHADOW

by Marjorie Kinnan Rawlings

The lemon-colored awning over the terrace swelled in the southeasterly breeze from the ocean. Dr Tifton had chosen lemon so that when the hungry Florida sun had fed on the canvas the color would still be approximately the same.

"Being practical on one's honeymoon," he had said to Elsa, "stabilizes one's future."

At the moment she had thought it would have been nicer to say "our" honeymoon and "our" future, but she had dismissed it as another indication of her gift for critical analysis which her husband considered unfortunate.

"I am the scientist of the family, my mouse," he said often. "Let me do the analyzing. I want you to develop all your latent femininity."

Being called "my mouse" was probably part of the development. It had seemed quite sweet at the beginning, but repetition had made the mouse feel somehow as though the fur were being worn off in patches.

Elsa leaned back in the long beach chair and let the magazine containing her husband's new article drop to the rough coquina paving of the terrace. Howard did express himself with an exquisite precision. The article was a gem, just scientific enough, just humorous, just human enough to give the impression of a choice mind back of it. It was his semiscientific writings that had brought them together.

Fresh from college, she had tumbled, butter side up, into a job as assistant to the feature editor of *Home Life*. Because of her enthusiasm for the Tifton series of articles, she had been allowed to handle the magazine's correspondence with him. He had written her, on her letter of acceptance of "Algae and Their Human Brothers":

MY DEAR MISS WHITTINGTON:

Fancy a woman's editor being appealed to by my algae! Will you have tea with me, so that my eyes, accustomed to the microscope, may feast themselves on a *femme du monde* who recognizes not only that science is important but that in the proper hands it may be made important even to those little fire-lit circles of domesticity for which your publication is the *raison d'être!*

She had had tea with him, and he had proved as distinguished as his articles. He was not handsome. He was, in fact, definitely tubby. His hair was steel-gray and he wore gray tweed suits, so that, for all his squattiness, the effect was smoothly sharp. His age, forty-odd, was a part of his distinction. He had marriage, it appeared, in the back of his mind. He informed her with engaging frankness that his wife must be young and therefore malleable. His charm, his prestige, were irresistible. The "union," as he called it, had followed quickly, and of course she had dropped her meaningless career to give a feminine backing to his endeavors, scientific and literary.

"It is not enough," he said, "to be a scientist. One must also be articulate."

He was immensely articulate. No problem, from the simple ones of a fresh matrimony to the involved matters of his studies and his writings, found him without an expression.

"Howard intellectualizes about everything," she wrote her former editor, May Morrow, from her honeymoon. She felt a vague disloyalty as she wrote it, for it did not convey his terrific humanity.

"A man is a man first," he said, "and *then* a scientist."

His science took care of itself, in his capable hands. It was his manhood that occupied her energies. Not his male potency—which again took care of itself, with no particular concern for her own needs—but all the elaborate mechanism that, to him, made up the substance of a man's life. Hollandaise sauce, for instance. He had a passion for hollandaise, and like his microscopic studies, like his essays, it must be perfect. She looked at her wrist watch. It was his wedding gift. She would have liked something delicate and diamond-studded and feminine, something suitable for "the mouse," but he had chosen a large, plain-faced gold Hamilton of railroad accuracy. It was six o'clock. It was not time for the hollandaise, but it was time to check up on Jones, the manservant and cook. Jones had a trick of boiling the vegetables too early, so that they lay limply under the hollandaise instead of standing up firm and decisive. She stirred in the beach chair and picked up the magazine. It would seem as though she were careless, indifferent to his achievements, if he found it sprawled on the coquina instead of arranged on top of the copies of *Fortune* on the red velvet fire seat.

She gave a start. A shadow passed between the terrace and the ocean. It flapped along on the sand with a reality greater than whatever cast the shadow. She looked out from under the awning. One of those obnoxious pelicans was flapping slowly down the coast. She felt an unreasonable irritation at sight of the thick, hunched shoulders, the out-of-proportion wings, the peculiar contour of the head, lifting at the back to something of a peak. She could not understand why she so disliked the birds. They were hungry; they searched out their food; they moved and mated like every living thing. They were basically drab, like most human beings, but all that was no reason for giving a slight shudder when one passed over the lemon-colored awning and winged its self-satisfied way down the Florida coast line.

She rose from the beach chair, controlling her annoyance. Howard was not sensitive to her moods, for which she was grateful, but she had found that the inexplicable crossness which sometimes seized her made her unduly sensitive to his. As she feared, Jones had started the cauliflower ahead of time. It was only just in the boiling water so she snatched it out and plunged it in ice water.

"Put the cauliflower in the boiling water at exactly six-thirty," she said to Jones.

As Howard so wisely pointed out, most of the trouble with servants lay in not giving exact orders.

"If servants knew as much as you do," he said, "they would not be working for you. Their minds are vague. That is why they are servants."

Whenever she caught herself being vague she had a moment's unhappy feeling that she should probably have been a lady's maid. It would at least have been a preparation for matrimony. Turning now from the cauliflower, she wondered if marriage always laid these necessities for exactness on a woman. Perhaps all men were not concerned with domestic precision. She shook off the thought, with the sense of disloyalty that always stabbed her when she was critical. As Howard said, a household either ran smoothly, with the mechanism hidden, or it clanked and jangled. No one wanted clanking and jangling.

She went to her room to comb her hair and powder her face and freshen her lipstick. Howard liked her careful grooming. He was himself immaculate. His gray hair smoothed back over his scientist's head that lifted to a little peak in the back; his gray suits, even his gray pajamas were incredibly neat, as smooth and trim as feathers.

She heard the car on the shell drive and went to meet him. He had brought the mail from the adjacent city, where he had the use of a laboratory.

"A ghost from the past," he said sententiously and handed her a letter from *Home Life*.

He kissed her with a longer clinging than usual, so that she checked the date in her mind. Two weeks ago—yes, this was his evening to make love to her. Their months of marriage were marked off into two-week periods as definitely as though the / line on the typewriter cut through them. He drew off from her with disapproval if she showed fondness between a / and a /. She went to the living room to read her letter from May Morrow.

DEAR ELSA:

Your beach house sounds altogether too idyllic. What previous incarnated suffering has licenced you to drop into an idyll? And so young in life. Well, maybe I'll get mine next time.

As you can imagine, there have been a hundred people after your job. The Collins girl that I rushed into it temporarily didn't work out at all, and I was beginning to despair when Jane Maxe, from *Woman's Outlook*, gave me a ring and said she was fed up with their politics and would come to us if the job was permanent. I assured her that it was hers until she had to be carried out on her shield. You see, I know your young type. You've burned your bridges and set out to be A Good Wife, and hell will freeze before you quit anything you tackle.

Glad the Distinguished Spouse proves as clever in daily conversation as in print. Have you had time to notice that trick writers have of saying something neat, recognizing it at once as a precious nut to be stored then bringing it out later in the long hard winter of literary composition? You will. Drop me a line. I wonder about things sometimes.

MAY

She wanted to sit down at the portable at once, but Dr Tifton came into the room.

"I'll have my shower later," he said and rolled his round gray eyes with meaning.

His mouth, she noticed, made a long, thin line that gave the impression of a perpetual half-smile. She mixed the martinis and he sipped his with appreciation. He had a smug expectancy that she recognized from her brief dealings with established authors. He was waiting for her favorable comment on his article.

"Your article was grand," she said. "If I were still an editor I'd have grabbed it."

He lifted his eyebrows. "Of course," he said, "editors were grabbing my articles before I knew you." He added complacently, "And after."

"I mean," she said uncomfortably, "that an editor can only judge things by her own acceptance."

"An editor?" He looked sideways at her. His eye seemed to have the ability to focus backward. "And what does a wife think of my article?"

She laughed. "Oh, a wife thinks that anything you do is perfect." She added, "Isn't that what wives are for?"

She regretted the comment immediately, but he was bland.

"I really think I gave the effect I wanted," he said. "Science is of no use to the layman unless it's humanized."

They sipped the martinis.

"I'd like to have you read it aloud," he said, studying his glass casually. "One learns things from another's reading."

She picked up the magazine gratefully. The reading would fill nicely the time between cocktails and dinner.

"It really gives the effect, doesn't it?" he said when she had finished. "I think anyone would get the connection, of which I am always conscious, between the lower forms of life and the human."

"It's a swell job," she said.

Dinner began successfully. The donac broth was strong enough. She had gone out in her bathing suit to gather the tiny clams just before high tide. The broiled pompano was delicately brown and flaky. The cauliflower was all right after all. The hollandaise, unfortunately, was thin. She had so frightened Jones about the heinousness of cooking it too long that he had taken it off the fire before it had quite thickened.

"My dear," Dr Tifton said, laying down his fork, "surely it is not too much to ask of an intelligent woman to teach a servant to make a simple sauce."

She felt a little hysterical. "Maybe I'm not intelligent," she said.

"Of course you are," he said soothingly. "Don't misunderstand me. I am not questioning your intelligence. You just do not realize the importance of being exact with an inferior."

He took a large mouthful of the cauliflower and hollandaise. The flavor was beyond reproach, and he weakened.

"I know," he said, swallowing and scooping generously again, "I know that I am a perfectionist. It's a bit of a bother sometimes, but of course it is the quality that makes me a scientist. A literary—shall I say literate?—no, articulate scientist."

He helped himself to a large pat of curled butter for his roll. The salad, the pineapple mousse, the after-dinner coffee and liqueur went off acceptably. He smacked his lips ever so faintly.

"Excuse me a moment, my mouse," he said. His digestion was rapid and perfect.

Now that he was in the bathroom, it had evidently occurred to him to take his shower and get into his dressing gown. She heard the water running and the satisfied humming he emitted when all was well. She would have time, for he was meticulous with his fortnightly special toilet, to begin a letter to May Morrow. She took the portable typewriter out to a glass-covered table on the terrace. The setting sun reached benignly under the awning. She drew a deep breath. It was a little difficult to begin. May had almost sounded as though she did not put full credence in the idyll. She wanted to write enthusiastically but judiciously, so May would understand that she, Elsa, was indeed a fortunate young woman, wed irrevocably, by her own deliberate, intelligent choice, to a brilliant man—a real man, second only in scientific and literary rating to Dr Beebe.

DEAR MAY:

It was grand to hear from you. I'm thrilled about Jane Maxe. What a scoop! I could almost be jealous of both of you if my lines hadn't fallen into such gloriously pleasant places.

I am, of course, supremely happy—

She leaned back. She was writing gushily. Married women had the damnedest way, she had always noticed, of gushing. Perhaps the true feminine nature was sloppy after all. She deleted "gloriously," crossed out "supremely," and inserted "tremendously." She would have to copy the letter.

A shadow passed between the terrace and the ocean. She looked up. One of those beastly pelicans was flapping down the coast over the sand dunes. He had already fed, or he would be flapping, in that same sure way of finding what he wanted, over the surf. It was ridiculous to be disturbed by him. Yet somewhere she suspected there must be an association of thoughts that had its base in an unrecognized antipathy. Something about the pelican's shadow, darkening her heart and mind with that absurd desperation, must be connected with some profound and secret dread, but she could not seem to put her finger on it.

She looked out from under the lemon-colored awning. The pelican had turned and was flapping back again. She had a good look at him. He was neatly gray, objectionably neat for a creature with such greedy habits. His round head, lifted to a peak, was sunk against his heavy shoulders. His round gray eye looked down below him, a little behind him, with a cold, pleased, superior expression. His long, thin mouth was unbearably smug with the expression of a partial smile.

"Oh, go on about your business!" she shouted at him.

Carson McCullers (February 19, 1917–September 29, 1967) was born Lula Carson Smith in Columbus, Georgia. Her mother, Marguerite Smith, convinced she would be unique, confided to friends that there had been prenatal signs her child would achieve greatness as an artist. In her early years McCullers was devoted to music and the piano. It was only when she developed rheumatic fever at fifteen that she turned to writing as a less strenuous form of artistic expression. She began to write family plays that she described as "thick with incest, lunacy, and murder." At seventeen she left Georgia to work in New York and attend classes at Barnard. She published her first short story, "Wunderkind," in *Story* magazine when she was nineteen. McCullers was forced to return to Georgia after she suffered another attack of rheumatic fever. Her novel *The Heart Is a Lonely Hunter* (1940) established her reputation and many critics consider it her finest work. McCullers followed it with *Reflections in a Golden Eye* (1941), *The Member of the Wedding* (1946), *The Ballad of the Sad Cafe* (1951), and *Clock without Hands* (1961). She died at age fifty after suffering a variety of ailments.

A TREE · A ROCK · A CLOUD

by Carson McCullers

It was raining that morning, and still very dark. When the boy reached the streetcar café he had almost finished his route and he went in for a cup of coffee. The place was an all-night café owned by a bitter and stingy man called Leo. After the raw, empty street the café seemed friendly and bright: along the counter there were a couple of soldiers, three spinners from the cotton mill, and in a corner a man who sat hunched over with his nose and half his face down in a beer mug. The boy wore a helmet such as aviators wear. When he went into the café he unbuckled the chin strap and raised the right flap up over his pink little ear; often as he drank his coffee someone would speak to him in a friendly way. But this morning Leo did not look into his face and none of the men were talking. He paid and was leaving the café when a voice called out to him:

"Son! Hey Son!"

He turned back and the man in the corner was crooking his finger and nodding to him. He had brought his face out of the beer mug and he seemed suddenly very happy. The man was long and pale, with a big nose and faded orange hair.

"Hey Son!"

The boy went toward him. He was an undersized boy of about twelve, with one shoulder drawn higher than the other because of the weight of the paper sack. His face was shallow, freckled, and his eyes were round child eyes.

"Yeah Mister?"

The man laid one hand on the paper boy's shoulders, then

grasped the boy's chin and turned his face slowly from one side to the other. The boy shrank back uneasily.

"Say! What's the big idea?"

The boy's voice was shrill; inside the café it was suddenly very quiet.

The man said slowly: "I love you."

All along the counter the men laughed. The boy, who had scowled and sidled away, did not know what to do. He looked over the counter at Leo, and Leo watched him with a weary, brittle jeer. The boy tried to laugh also. But the man was serious and sad.

"I did not mean to tease you, Son," he said. "Sit down and have a beer with me. There is something I have to explain."

Cautiously, out of the corner of his eye, the paper boy questioned the men along the counter to see what he should do. But they had gone back to their beer or their breakfast and did not notice him. Leo put a cup of coffee on the counter and a little jug of cream.

"He is a minor," Leo said.

The paper boy slid himself up onto the stool. His ear beneath the upturned flap of the helmet was very small and red. The man was nodding at him soberly. "It is important," he said. Then he reached in his hip pocket and brought out something which he held up in the palm of his hand for the boy to see.

"Look very carefully," he said.

The boy stared, but there was nothing to look at very carefully. The man held in his big, grimy palm a photograph. It was the face of a woman, but blurred, so that only the hat and the dress she was wearing stood out clearly.

"See?" the man asked.

The boy nodded and the man placed another picture in his palm. The woman was standing on a beach in a bathing suit. The suit made her stomach very big, and that was the main thing you noticed.

"Got a good look?" He leaned over closer and finally asked: "You ever seen her before?"

The boy sat motionless, staring slantwise at the man. "Not so I know of."

"Very well." The man blew on the photographs and put them back into his pocket. "That was my wife."

"Dead?" the boy asked.

Slowly the man shook his head. He pursed his lips as though about to whistle and answered in a long-drawn way: "Nuuu—" he said. "I will explain."

The beer on the counter before the man was in a large brown mug. He did not pick it up to drink. Instead he bent down and, putting his face over the rim, he rested there for a moment. Then with both hands he tilted the mug and sipped.

"Some night you'll go to sleep with your big nose in a mug and drown," said Leo. "Prominent transient drowns in beer. That would be a cute death."

The paper boy tried to signal to Leo. While the man was not looking he screwed up his face and worked his mouth to question soundlessly: "Drunk?" But Leo only raised his eyebrows and turned away to put some pink strips of bacon on the grill. The man pushed the mug away from him, straightened himself, and folded his loose crooked hands on the counter. His face was sad as he looked at the paper boy. He did not blink, but from time to time the lids closed down with delicate gravity over his pale green eyes. It was nearing dawn and the boy shifted the weight of the paper sack.

"I am talking about love," the man said. "With me it is a science."

The boy half slid down from the stool. But the man raised his forefinger, and there was something about him that held the boy and would not let him go away.

"Twelve years ago I married the woman in the photograph. She was my wife for one year, nine months, three days, and two nights. I loved her. Yes . . ." He tightened his blurred, rambling voice and said again: "I loved her. I thought also that she loved me. I was a railroad engineer. She had all home comforts and luxuries. It never crept into my brain that she was not satisfied. But do you know what happened?"

"Mgneeow!" said Leo.

The man did not take his eyes from the boy's face. "She left me. I came in one night and the house was empty and she was gone. She left me."

"With a fellow?" the boy asked.

Gently the man placed his palm down on the counter. "Why naturally, Son. A woman does not run off like that alone."

The café was quiet, the soft rain black and endless in the

street outside. Leo pressed down the frying bacon with the prongs of his long fork. "So you have been chasing the floozie for eleven years. You frazzled old rascal!"

For the first time the man glanced at Leo. "Please don't be vulgar. Besides, I was not speaking to you." He turned back to the boy and said in a trusting and secretive undertone: "Let's not pay any attention to him. O.K.?"

The paper boy nodded doubtfully.

"It was like this," the man continued. "I am a person who feels many things. All my life one thing after another has impressed me. Moonlight. The leg of a pretty girl. One thing after another. But the point is that when I had enjoyed anything there was a peculiar sensation as though it was laying around loose in me. Nothing seemed to finish itself up or fit in with the other things. Women? I had my portion of them. The same. Afterwards laying around loose in me. I was a man who had never loved."

Very slowly he closed his eyelids, and the gesture was like a curtain drawn at the end of a scene in a play. When he spoke again his voice was excited and the words came fast—the lobes of his large, loose ears seemed to tremble.

"Then I met this woman. I was fifty-one years old and she always said she was thirty. I met her at a filling station and we were married within three days. And do you know what it was like? I just can't tell you. All I had ever felt was gathered together around this woman. Nothing lay around loose in me any more but was finished up by her."

The man stopped suddenly and stroked his long nose. His voice sank down to a steady and reproachful undertone: "I'm not explaining this right. What happened was this. There were these beautiful feelings and loose little pleasures inside me. And this woman was something like an assembly line for my soul. I run these little pieces of myself through her and I come out complete. Now do you follow me?"

"What was her name?" the boy asked.

"Oh," he said. "I called her Dodo. But that is immaterial."

"Did you try to make her come back?"

The man did not seem to hear. "Under the circumstances you can imagine how I felt when she left me."

Leo took the bacon from the grill and folded two strips of it between a bun. He had a gray face, with slitted eyes, and a pinched nose saddled by faint blue shadows. One of the mill workers signaled for more coffee and Leo poured it. He did not give refills on coffee free. The spinner ate breakfast there every morning, but the better Leo knew his customers the stingier he treated them. He nibbled his own bun as though he grudged it to himself.

"And you never got hold of her again?"

The boy did not know what to think of the man, and his child's face was uncertain with mingled curiosity and doubt. He was new on the paper route; it was still strange to him to be out in the town in the black, queer early morning.

"Yes," the man said. "I took a number of steps to get her back. I went around trying to locate her. I went to Tulsa where she had folks. And to Mobile. I went to every town she had ever mentioned to me, and I hunted down every man she had formerly been connected with. Tulsa, Atlanta, Chicago, Cheehaw, Memphis. . . . For the better part of two years I chased around the country trying to lay hold of her."

"But the pair of them had vanished from the face of the earth!" said Leo.

"Don't listen to him," the man said confidentially. "And also just forget those two years. They are not important. What matters is that around the third year a curious thing begun to happen to me."

"What?" the boy asked.

The man leaned down and tilted his mug to take a sip of beer. But as he hovered over the mug his nostrils fluttered slightly; he sniffed the staleness of the beer and did not drink. "Love is a curious thing to begin with. At first I thought only of getting her back. It was a kind of mania. But then as time went on I tried to remember her. But do you know what happened?"

"No," the boy said.

"When I laid myself down on a bed and tried to think about her my mind became a blank. I couldn't see her. I would take out her pictures and look. No good. Nothing doing. A blank. Can you imagine it?"

"Say Mac!" Leo called down the counter. "Can you imagine this bozo's mind a blank!"

Slowly, as though fanning away flies, the man waved his hand. His green eyes were concentrated and fixed on the shallow little face of the paper boy.

"But a sudden piece of glass on a sidewalk. Or a nickel tune in a music box. A shadow on a wall at night. And I would remember. It might happen in a street and I would cry or bang my head against a lamppost. You follow me?"

"A piece of glass . . ." the boy said.

"Anything. I would walk around and I had no power of how and when to remember her. You think you can put up a kind of shield. But remembering don't come to a man face forward—it corners around sideways. I was at the mercy of everything I saw and heard. Suddenly instead of me combing the countryside to find her she begun to chase me around in my very soul. *She* chasing *me*, mind you! And in my soul."

The boy asked finally: "What part of the country were you in then?"

"Ooh," the man groaned. "I was a sick mortal. It was like smallpox. I confess, Son, that I boozed. I fornicated. I committed any sin that suddenly appealed to me. I am loath to confess it but I will do so. When I recall that period it is all curdled in my mind, it was so terrible."

The man leaned his head down and tapped his forehead on the counter. For a few seconds he stayed bowed over in this position, the back of his stringy neck covered with orange furze, his hands with their long warped fingers held palm to palm in an attitude of prayer. Then the man straightened himself; he was smiling and suddenly his face was bright and tremulous and old.

"It was in the fifth year that it happened," he said. "And with it I started my science."

Leo's mouth jerked with a pale, quick grin. "Well none of we boys are getting any younger," he said. Then with sudden anger he balled up a dishcloth he was holding and threw it down hard on the floor. "You draggle-tailed old Romeo!"

"What happened?" the boy asked.

The old man's voice was high and clear: "Peace," he answered.

"Huh?"

"It is hard to explain scientifically, Son," he said. "I guess the logical explanation is that she and I had fleed around from each other for so long that finally we just got tangled up together and lay down and quit. Peace. A queer and beautiful blankness. It was spring in Portland and the rain came every afternoon. All evening I just stayed there on my bed in the dark. And that is how the science come to me."

The windows in the streetcar were pale blue with light.

The two soldiers paid for their beers and opened the door—
one of the soldiers combed his hair and wiped off his muddy
puttees before they went outside. The three mill workers
bent silently over their breakfasts. Leo's clock was ticking
on the wall.

"It is this. And listen carefully. I meditated on love and
reasoned it out. I realized what is wrong with us. Men fall in
love for the first time. And what do they fall in love with?"

The boy's soft mouth was partly open and he did not
answer.

"A woman," the old man said. "Without science, with
nothing to go by, they undertake the most dangerous and
sacred experience in God's earth. They fall in love with a
woman. Is that correct, Son?"

"Yeah," the boy said faintly.

"They start at the wrong end of love. They begin at the
climax. Can you wonder it is so miserable? Do you know
how men should love?"

The old man reached over and grasped the boy by the
collar of his leather jacket. He gave him a gentle little shake
and his green eyes gazed down unblinking and grave.

"Son, do you know how love should be begun?"

The boy sat small and listening and still. Slowly he shook
his head. The old man leaned closer and whispered:

"A tree. A rock. A cloud."

It was still raining outside in the street: a mild, gray,
endless rain. The mill whistle blew for the six o'clock shift
and the three spinners paid and went away. There was no
one in the café but Leo, the old man, and the little paper
boy.

"The weather was like this in Portland," he said. "At the
time my science was begun. I meditated and I started very
cautious. I would pick up something from the street and
take it home with me. I bought a goldfish and I concentrated on the goldfish and I loved it. I graduated from one
thing to another. Day by day I was getting this technique.
On the road from Portland to San Diego—"

"Aw shut up!" screamed Leo suddenly. "Shut up! Shut
up!"

The old man still held the collar of the boy's jacket; he
was trembling and his face was earnest and bright and wild.
"For six years now I have gone around by myself and built
up my science. And now I am a master, Son. I can love

anything. No longer do I have to think about it even. I see a street full of people and a beautiful light comes in me. I watch a bird in the sky. Or I meet a traveler on the road. Everything, Son. And anybody. All stranger and all loved! Do you realize what a science like mine can mean?"

The boy held himself stiffly, his hands curled tight around the counter edge. Finally he asked: "Did you ever really find that lady?"

"What? What say, Son?"

"I mean," the boy asked timidly. "Have you fallen in love with a woman again?"

The old man loosened his grasp on the boy's collar. He turned away and for the first time his green eyes had a vague and scattered look. He lifted the mug from the counter, drank down the yellow beer. His head was shaking slowly from side to side. Then finally he answered: "No, Son. You see that is the last step in my science. I go cautious. And I am not quite ready yet."

"Well!" said Leo. "Well well well!"

The old man stood in the open doorway. "Remember," he said. Framed there in the gray damp light of the early morning he looked shrunken and seedy and frail. But his smile was bright. "Remember I love you," he said with a last nod. And the door closed quietly behind him.

The boy did not speak for a long time. He pulled down the bangs on his forehead and slid his grimy little forefinger around the rim of his empty cup. Then without looking at Leo he finally asked:

"Was he drunk?"

"No," said Leo shortly.

The boy raised his clear voice higher. "Then was he a dope fiend?"

"No."

The boy looked up at Leo, and his flat little face was desperate, his voice urgent and shrill. "Was he crazy? Do you think he was a lunatic?" The paper boy's voice dropped suddenly with doubt. "Leo? Or not?"

But Leo would not answer him. Leo had run a night café for fourteen years, and he held himself to be a critic of craziness. There were the town characters and also the transients who roamed in from the night. He knew the manias of all of them. But he did not want to satisfy the questions of the waiting child. He tightened his pale face and was silent.

So the boy pulled down the right flap of his helmet and as he turned to leave he made the only comment that seemed safe to him, the only remark that could not be laughed down and despised:

"He sure has done a lot of traveling."

Frank Yerby (September 5, 1916) was born in Augusta, Georgia. He completed degrees at Paine College (1937) and Fisk University (1938) and attended graduate school at the University of Chicago and worked on the Federal Writers Project of the WPA. Yerby taught English at Florida A & M College in Tallahassee, Florida (1939–1940) and at Southern University in Baton Rouge, Louisiana (1940–1941). His first major success as a writer was publication of his short story "Health Card" which appeared in *Harper's* magazine. It won the O. Henry Memorial Award for 1944. Between 1944 and 1946 Yerby published several outstanding short stories dealing with the theme of race.

Since 1946 Yerby has concentrated on writing popular romance novels. Some critics have called him the "king" of the costume novel. *The Foxes of Harrow*, his first novel set in the antebellum South, was published in 1946 and sold more than two million copies by the end of the year. For the next twenty-five years, Yerby had more novels on the best-seller list than any other American writer. Some of his most popular novels are *The Vixens* (1947), *The Golden Hawk* (1948), *Pride's Castle* (1949), *Woman Called Fancy* (1951), and *The Saracen Blade* (1952). Three of these books have been made into films.

Since 1959 Yerby has lived in Madrid, Spain.

HEALTH CARD

by Frank Yerby

Johnny stood under one of the street lights on the corner and tried to read the letter. The street lights down in the Bottom were so dim that he couldn't make out half the words, but he didn't need to: he knew them all by heart anyway.

"Sugar," he read, "it took a long time but I done it. I got the money to come to see you. I waited and waited for them to give you a furlough, but it look like they don't mean to. Sugar, I can't wait no longer. I got to see you. I got to. Find a nice place for me to stay—where we can be happy together. You know what I mean. With all my love, Lily."

Johnny folded the letter up and put it back in his pocket. Then he walked swiftly down the street past all the juke joints with the music blaring out and the G.I. brogans pounding. He turned down a side street, scuffing up a cloud of dust as he did so. None of the streets down in Black Bottom was paved, and there were four inches of fine white powder over everything. When it rained the mud would come up over the tops of his army shoes, but it hadn't rained in nearly three months. There were no juke joints on this street, and the Negro shanties were neatly whitewashed. Johnny kept on walking until he came to the end of the street. On the corner stood the little whitewashed Baptist Church, and next to it was the neat, well-kept home of the pastor.

Johnny went up on the porch and hesitated. He thrust his hand in his pocket and the paper crinkled. He took his hand out and knocked on the door.

"Who's that?" a voice called.

"It's me," Johnny answered; "it's a sodjer."

The door opened a crack and a woman peered out. She was middle-aged and fat. Looking down, Johnny could see that her feet were bare.

"Whatcha want, sodjer?"

Johnny took off his cap.

"Please, ma'am, lemme come in. I kin explain it t' yuh better settin' down."

She studied his face for a minute in the darkness.

"Aw right," she said; "you kin come in, son."

Johnny entered the room stiffly and sat down on a cornshuck-bottomed chair.

"It's this way, ma'am," he said. "I got a wife up Nawth. I been tryin' an' tryin' t' git a furlough so I could go t' see huh. But they always put me off. So now she done worked an' saved enuff money t' come an' see me. I wants t' ax you t' rent me a room, ma'am. I doan' know nowheres t' ax."

"This ain't no hotel, son."

"I know it ain't. I cain't take Lily t' no hotel, not lak hotels in this heah town."

"Lily yo wife?"

"Yes'm. She my sho' nuff, honest t' Gawd wife. Married in th' Baptist Church in Deetroit."

The fat woman sat back, and her thick lips widened into a smile.

"She a good girl, ain't she? An' you doan' wanta take her t' one o' these heah ho'houses they calls hotels."

"That's it, ma'am."

"Sho' you kin bring huh heah, son. Be glad t' have huh. Reveren' be glad t' have huh too. What yo' name, son?"

"Johnny. Johnny Green. Ma'am—"

"Yas, son?"

"You understands that I wants t' come heah too?"

The fat woman rocked back in her chair and gurgled with laughter.

"Bless yo' heart, chile, I ain't always been a ole woman! And I ain't always been th' preacher's wife neither!"

"Thank you, ma'am. I gotta go now. Time fur me t' be gettin' back t' camp."

"When you bring Lily?"

"Be Monday night, ma'am. Pays you now if you wants it."

"Monday be aw right. Talk it over with th' Reveren', so

he make it light fur yuh. Know sodjer boys ain't got much money."

"No, ma'am, sho' Lawd ain't. G'night, ma'am."

When he turned back into the main street of the Negro section the doors of the joints were all open and the soldiers were coming out. The girls were clinging onto their arms all the way to the bus stop. Johnny looked at the dresses that stopped halfway between the pelvis and the knee and hugged the backside so that every muscle showed when they walked. He saw the purple lipstick smeared across the wide full lips, and the short hair stiffened with smelly grease so that it covered their heads like a black lacquered cap. They went on down to the bus stop arm in arm, their knotty bare calves bunching with each step as they walked. Johnny thought about Lily. He walked past them very fast without turning his head.

But just as he reached the bus stop he heard the whistles. When he turned around he saw the four M.P.s and the civilian policeman stopping the crowd. He turned around again and walked back until he was standing just behind the white men.

"Aw right," the M.P.s were saying, "you gals git your health cards out."

Some of the girls started digging in their handbags. Johnny could see them dragging out small yellow cardboard squares. But the others just stood there with blank expressions on their faces. The soldiers started muttering, a dark, deep-throated sound. The M.P.s started pushing their way through the crowd, looking at each girl's card as they passed. When they came to a girl who didn't have a card they called out to the civilian policemen:

"Aw right, mister, take A'nt Jemima for a little ride."

Then the city policemen would lead the girl away and put her in the Black Maria.

They kept this up until they had examined every girl except one. She hung back beside her soldier, and the first time the M.P.s didn't see her. When they came back through, one of them caught her by the arm.

"Lemme see your card, Mandy," he said.

The girl looked at him, her little eyes narrowing into slits in her black face.

"Tek yo' hands offen me, white man," she said.

The M.P.s face crimsoned, so that Johnny could see it, even in the darkness.

"Listen, black girl," he said, "I told you to lemme see your card."

"An' I tole you t' tek yo' han' offen me, white man!"

"Gawddammit, you little black bitch, you better do like I tell you!"

Johnny didn't see very clearly what happened after that. There was a sudden explosion of motion, and then the M.P. was trying to jerk his hand back, but he couldn't, for the little old black girl had it between her teeth and was biting it to the bone. He drew his other hand back and slapped her across the face so hard that it sounded like a pistol shot. She went over backwards and her tight skirt split, so that when she got up Johnny could see that she didn't have anything on under it. She came forward like a cat, her nails bared, straight for the M.P.'s eyes. He slapped her down again, but the soldiers surged forward all at once. The M.P.s fell back and drew their guns and one of them blew a whistle.

Johnny, who was behind them, decided it was time for him to get out of there and he did; but not before he saw the squads of white M.P.s hurling around the corner and going to work on the Negroes with their clubs. He reached the bus stop and swung on board. The minute after he had pushed his way to the back behind all the white soldiers he heard the shots. The bus driver put the bus in gear and they roared off toward the camp.

It was after one o'clock when all the soldiers straggled in. Those of them who could still walk. Eight of them came in on the meat wagon, three with gunshot wounds. The colonel declared the town out of bounds for all Negro soldiers for a month.

"Dammit," Johnny said, "I gotta go meet Lily, I gotta. I cain't stay heah. I cain't!"

"Whatcha gonna do," Little Willie asked, "go A.W.O.L.?"

Johnny looked at him, his brow furrowed into a frown.

"Naw," he said, "I'm gonna go see th' colonel!"

"Whut!" Man, you crazy! Colonel kick yo' black ass out fo' you gits yo' mouf open."

"I take a chanct on that."

He walked over to the little half mirror on the wall of the barracks. Carefully he readjusted his cap. He pulled his tie out of his shirt front and drew the knot tighter around his throat. Then he tucked the ends back in at just the right fraction of an inch between the correct pair of buttons. He bent down and dusted his shoes again, although they were already spotless.

"Man," Little Willie said, "you sho' is a fool!"

"Reckon I am," Johnny said; then he went out of the door and down the short wooden steps.

When he got to the road that divided the colored and white sections of the camp his steps faltered. He stood still a minute, drew in a deep breath, and marched very stiffly and erect across the road. The white soldiers gazed at him curiously, but none of them said anything. If a black soldier came over into their section it was because somebody sent him, so they let him alone.

In front of the colonel's headquarters he stopped. He knew what he had to say, but his breath was very short in his throat and he was going to have a hard time saying it.

"Whatcha want, soldier?" the sentry demanded.

"I wants t' see th' colonel."

"Who sent you?"

Johnny drew his breath in sharply.

"I ain't at liberty t' say," he declared, his breath coming out very fast behind the words.

"You ain't at liberty t' say," the sentry mimicked. "Well I'll be damned! If you ain't at liberty t' say, then I ain't at liberty t' let you see the colonel! Git tha hell outa here, nigger, before I pump some lead in you!"

Johnny didn't move.

The sentry started toward him, lifting his rifle butt, but another soldier, a sergeant, came around the corner of the building.

"Hold on there," he called. "What tha hell is th' trouble here?"

"This here nigger says he want t' see tha colonel an' when I ast him who sent him he says he ain't at liberty t' say!"

The sergeant turned to Johnny.

Johnny came to attention and saluted him. You aren't supposed to salute N.C.O.s, but sometimes it helps.

"What you got t' say fur yourself, boy?" the sergeant said, not unkindly. Johnny's breath evened.

"I got uh message fur th' colonel, suh," he said; "I ain't s'posed t' give it t' nobody else but him. I ain't even s'posed t' tell who sont it, suh."

The sergeant peered at him sharply.

"You tellin' tha truth, boy?"

"Yassuh!"

"Aw right. Wait here a minute."

He went into H.Q. After a couple of minutes he came back.

"Aw right, soldier, you kin go on in."

Johnny mounted the steps and went into the colonel's office. The colonel was a lean, white-haired soldier with a face tanned to the color of saddle leather. He was reading a letter through a pair of horn-rimmed glasses which had only one earhook left, so that he had to hold them up to his eyes with one hand. He put them down and looked up. Johnny saw that his eyes were pale blue, so pale that he felt as if he were looking into the eyes of an eagle or some other fierce bird of prey.

"Well?" he said, and Johnny stiffened into a salute. The colonel half smiled.

"At ease, soldier," he said. Then: "The sergeant tells me that you have a very important message for me."

Johnny gulped in the air.

"Beggin' th' sergeant's pardon, suh," he said, "but that ain't so."

"What!"

"Yassuh," Johnny rushed on, "nobody sent me. I come on m' own hook. I had t' talk t' yuh, Colonel, suh! You kin sen' me t' th' guardhouse afterwards, but please, suh, lissen t' me fur jes' a minute!"

The colonel relaxed slowly. Something very like a smile was playing around the corners of his mouth. He looked at his watch.

"All right, soldier," he said. "You've got five minutes."

"Thank yuh, thank yuh, suh!"

"Speak your piece, soldier; you're wasting time!"

"It's about Lily, suh. She my wife. She done worked an' slaved fur nigh onto six months t' git the money t' come an' see me. An' now you give th' order that none of th' cullud boys kin go t' town. Beggin' yo' pahdon, suh, I wasn't in none of that trouble. I ain't neber been in no trouble. You kin ax my cap'n, if you wants to. All I wants is permission to go into town fur one week, an' I'll stay outa town fur two months if yuh wants me to."

The colonel picked up the phone.

"Ring Captain Walters for me," he said. Then: "What's your name, soldier?"

"It's Green, suh. Private Johnny Green."

"Captain Walters? This is Colonel Milton. Do you have anything in your files concerning Private Johnny Green? Oh yes, go ahead. Take all the time you need."

The colonel lit a long black cigar. Johnny waited. The clock on the wall spun its electric arms.

"What's that? Yes. Yes, yes, I see. Thank you, Captain."

He put down the phone and picked up a fountain pen. He wrote swiftly. Finally he straightened up and gave Johnny the slip of paper.

Johnny read it. It said: "Private Johnny Green is given express permission to go into town every evening of the week beginning August seventh and ending August fourteenth. He is further permitted to remain in town overnight every night during said week, so long as he returns to camp for reveille the following morning. By order of the commanding officer, Colonel H. H. Milton."

There was a hard knot at the base of Johnny's throat. He couldn't breathe. But he snapped to attention and saluted smartly.

"Thank yuh, suh," he said at last. Then: "Gawd bless you, suh!"

"Forget it, soldier. I was a young married man once myself. My compliments to Captain Walters."

Johnny saluted again and about-faced, then he marched out of the office and down the stairs. On the way back he saluted everybody—privates, N.C.O.s, and civilian visitors, his white teeth gleaming in a huge smile.

"That's sure one happy darky," one of the white soldiers said.

Johnny stood in the station and watched the train running in. The yellow lights from the windows flickered on and off across his face as the alternating squares of light and darkness flashed past. Then it was slowing and Johnny was running beside it, trying to keep abreast of the Jim Crow coach. He could see her standing up, holding each other, Johnny's arms crushing all the breath out of her, holding her so hard against him that his brass buttons hurt through her thin dress. She opened her mouth to speak but he kissed her, bending her head backward on her neck until her little hat fell off. It lay there on the ground, unnoticed.

"Sugah," she said, "sugah. It was awful."

"I know," he said. "I know."

Then he took her bags and they started walking out of the station toward the Negro section of town.

"I missed yuh so much," Johnny said, "I thought I lose m' mind."

"Me too," she said. Then: "I brought th' marriage license with me like yuh tole me. I doan' wan th' preacher's wife t' think we bad."

"Enybody kin look at yuh an' see yuh uh angel!"

They went very quietly through all the dark streets and the white soldiers turned to look at Johnny and his girl.

Lak a queen, Johnny thought, lak a queen. He looked at the girl beside him, seeing the velvety nightshade skin, the glossy black lacquered curls, the sweet, wide hips and the long, clean legs striding beside him in the darkness. I am black, but comely, O ye daughters of Jerusalem!

They turned into the Bottom where the street lights were dim blobs on the pine poles and the dust rose up in little swirls around their feet. Johnny had his head half turned so that he didn't see the two M.P.s until he had almost bumped into them. He dropped one bag and caught Lily by the arm. Then he drew her aside quickly and the two men went by them without speaking.

They kept on walking, but every two steps Johnny would jerk his head around and look nervously back over his shoulder. The last time he looked the two M.P.s had stopped and were looking back at them. Johnny turned out the elbow of the arm next to Lily so that it hooked into hers a little and began to walk faster, pushing her along with him.

"What's yo' hurry, sugah?" she said. "I be heah a whole week!"

But Johnny was looking over his shoulder at the two M.P.s. They were coming toward them now, walking with long, slow strides, their reddish-white faces set. Johnny started to push Lily along faster, but she shook off his arm and stopped still.

"I do declare, Johnny Green! You th' beatines' man! Whut you walk me so fas' fur?"

Johnny opened his mouth to answer her, but the military police were just behind them now, and the sergeant reached out and laid his hand on her arm.

"C'mon, gal," he said, "lemme see it."

"Let you see whut? Whut he mean, Johnny?"

"Your card," the sergeant growled. "Lemme see your card."

"My card?" Lily said blankly. "Whut kinda card, mister?"

Johnny put the bags down. He was fighting for breath.

"Look heah, Sarge," he said; "this girl my wife!"

"Oh yeah? I said lemme see your card, sister!"

"I ain't got no card, mister. I dunno whut you talkin' about."

"Look, Sarge," the other M.P. said, "th' soldier's got bags. Maybe she's just come t' town."

"These your bags, gal?"

"Yessir."

"Aw right. You got twenty-four hours to git yourself a health card. If you don't have it by then we hafta run you in. Git goin' now."

"Listen," Johnny shouted; "this girl my wife! She ain't no ho'! I tell you she ain't—"

"What you say, nigger—" the M.P. sergeant growled. "Whatcha say?" He started toward Johnny.

Lily swung on Johnny's arm.

"C'mon, Johnny," she said; "they got guns. C'mon, Johnny, please! Please, Johnny!"

Slowly she drew him away.

"Aw, leave 'em be, Sarge," the M.P. corporal said; "maybe she is his wife."

The sergeant spat. The brown tobacco juice splashed in the dirt not an inch from Lily's foot. Then the two of them turned and started away.

Johnny stopped.

"Lemme go, Lily," he said, "lemme go!" He tore her arm loose from his and started back up the street. Lily leaped, her two arms fastening themselves around his neck. He fought silently but she clung to him, doubling her knees so that all her weight was hanging from his neck.

"No, Johnny! Oh Jesus no! You be kilt! Oh, Johnny, listen t' me, sugah! You's all I got!"

He put both hands up to break her grip but she swung her weight sidewise and the two of them went down in the dirt. The M.P.s turned the corner out of sight.

Johnny sat there in the dust staring at her. The dirt had ruined her dress. He sat there a long time looking at her until the hot tears rose up back of his eyelids faster than he could blink them away, so he put his face down in her lap and cried.

"I ain't no man!" he said. "I ain't no man!"

"Hush, sugah," she said. "You's a man aw right. You's my man!"

Gently she drew him to his feet. He picked up the bags and the two of them went down the dark street toward the preacher's house.

Tennessee Williams (March 26, 1911–February 25, 1983) was born Thomas Lanier Williams in Columbus, Mississippi. After living his early years in various Mississippi towns, his family moved to St. Louis. This environment and its effect on the young Williams is described in his play *The Glass Menagerie* and his short story "Portrait of a Girl in Glass." Williams attended the University of Missouri from 1929 to 1931, when he was withdrawn by his father because of his failure to pass ROTC. He then worked for three years (1931–1934) at the International Shoe Company in St. Louis and, as a way of escaping tedium, began to write more and more. Quitting his job, he attended Washington University before receiving a degree from the University of Iowa in 1938.

Williams revised an earlier script called "The Gentleman Caller" into *The Glass Menagerie*. It opened in Chicago on December 26, 1944 and was his first professional success. In 1945 it moved to Broadway. With this impressive start, Williams began his career as one of the world's most popular playwrights. He won two Pulitzer Prizes, one for *A Streetcar Named Desire* and another for *Cat on a Hot Tin Roof*, and four New York Drama Critics Circle Awards for these two plays, as well as for *The Glass Menagerie* and *The Night of the Iguana*. Many of Williams' plays have been made into films.

After he changed his name to "Tennessee," the first work to bear his new name was "The Field of Blue Children," printed in *Story* in September 1939. Williams wrote "The Angel in the Alcove" in October 1943 in Santa Monica. It was published in 1948 in his collection *One Arm*. This short story is a partial basis for his play *Vieux Carré*. Williams divided much of his time between New Orleans, his home in Key West, and the Hotel Elysee on East 54th Street in New York where he died.

THE ANGEL IN THE ALCOVE

by Tennessee Williams

Suspicion is the occupational disease of land-ladies and long association with them has left me with an obscure sense of guilt I will probably never be free of. The initial trauma in this category was inflicted by a land-lady I had in the old French Quarter of New Orleans when I was barely twenty. She was the archetype of the suspicious land-lady. She had a room of her own but preferred to sleep on a rattling cot in the downstairs hall so that none of her tenants could enter or leave the establishment during the night without her grudging permission. When finally I left there I fooled the old woman. I left by way of a balcony and a pair of sheets. I was miles out of town on the Old Spanish Trail to the West before the old woman found out I had gotten past her.

The downstairs hall of this rooming-house on Bourbon Street was totally lightless. You had to grope your way through it with cautious revulsion, trailing your fingers along the damp, cracked plaster until you arrived at the door or the foot of the stairs. You never reached either without the old woman's challenge. Her ghostly figure would spring bolt upright on the rattling iron cot. She would utter one syllable— *Who?* If she were not satisfied with the identification given, or suspected that you were taking your luggage out in a stealthy departure or bringing somebody in for carnal enjoyment, a match would be struck on the floor and held toward you for several moments. In its weirdly flickering light she would squint her eyes at you until her doubts were dismissed. Then she would flop back down in a huddle of sour blankets and if you waited to listen you would hear mutterings vicious and coarse as any that drunks in Quarter barrooms ever gave voice to.

She was a woman of paranoidal suspicion and her suspicion of me was unbounded. Often she came in my room with the morning paper and read aloud some item concerning an act of crime in the Quarter. After the reading she would inspect me closely for any guilty change of countenance, and I would nearly always gratify her suspicion with a deep flush and inability to return her look. I am sure she had chalked up dozens of crimes against me and was only waiting for some more concrete betrayal to call the police, a captain of whom, she had warned me, was her first cousin.

The land-lady was a victim of dead beats, that much should be admitted in her defense. None of her tenants were regular payers. Some of them clung to their rooms for months and months with only promises given of future payment. One of these was a widow named Mrs. Wayne. Mrs. Wayne was the most adroit sponger in the house. She even succeeded in finagling gratuities from the land-lady. Her fortune was in her tongue. She was a wonderful raconteur of horribly morbid or salacious stories. Whenever she smelled food cooking her door would fly open and she would dart forth with a mottled blue and white sauce-pan held to her bosom coquettishly as a lace fan. Undoubtedly she was half starved and the odor of food set her off like a powerful drug, for there was an abnormal brilliance in her chatter. She tapped on the door from which the seductive smell came but entered before there could be any kind of response. Her tongue would be off before she was fairly inside and no amount of rudeness short of forcible ejection from the room would suffice to discourage her. There was something pitifully winning about the old lady. Even her bad-smelling breath became a component of her unwholesome appeal. To me it was the spectacle of so much heroic vitality in so wasted a vessel that warmed my heart toward the widow. I never did any cooking in my attic bedroom. I only met Mrs. Wayne in the land-lady's kitchen on those occasions when I had earned my supper by some small job on the premises. The land-lady herself was not entirely immune to Mrs. Wayne's charm and the stories unmistakably entranced her. As she put things on the stove she would always remark, If the bitch gets a sniff of this cookin' wild horses won't hold'er!

In eight years' time such characters disappear, the earth swallows them up, the walls absorb them like moisture. Undoubtedly old Mrs. Wayne and her battered utensil have made their protesting departure and I am not at all sure that with them the world has not lost the greatest pathological genius since Baudelaire or Poe. Her favorite subject was the deaths of relatives and friends which she had attended with an eye and ear from which no agonizing detail escaped annotation. Her memory served them up in the land-lady's kitchen so graphically that I would find myself sick with horror and yet so fascinated that the risk of losing my appetite for a hard-earned supper would not prevail upon me to shut my ears. The land-lady was equally spell-bound. Gradually her gruff mumblings of disbelief and impatient gestures would give way to such morbid enjoyment that her jaws would slacken and dribble. A faraway mesmerized look would come into her usually pin-sharp eyes. All the while Mrs. Wayne with the sauce-pan held to her bosom would be executing a slow and oblique approach to the great kitchen stove. So powerful was her enchantment that even when she was actually removing the lid from the stew-pot and ladling out some of its contents into her sauce-pan, although the land-lady's look would follow her movements there would not appear to be any recognition. Not until the hapless protagonist of the story had endured his final conclusion—his eyeballs popped from their sockets and ghastly effluvia drenching his bed-clothes—did the charm loosen enough to permit the narrator's listeners any clear knowledge of what went on outside the scene that was painted. By that time Mrs. Wayne had scraped her sauce-pan clean with wolfish relish and made her way so close to the door that if any unpleasantness attended the land-lady's emergence from trance, the widow could be out of ear-shot before it achieved a momentum.

In this old house it was either deathly quiet or else the high plaster walls were ringing like fire-bells with angry voices, with quarrels over the use of the lavatory or accusations of theft or threats of eviction. I had no door to my room which was in the attic, only a ragged curtain that couldn't exclude the barrage of human wretchedness often exploding. The walls of my room were pink and green stippled plaster and there was an alcove window. This alcove window shone faintly in the night. There was a low

bench beneath it. Now and again when the room was otherwise lightless a misty grey figure would appear to be seated
on this bench in the alcove. It was the tender and melancholy figure of an angel or some dim, elderly madonna. The
apparition occurred in the alcove most often on those winter
nights in New Orleans when slow rain is falling from a sky
not clouded heavily enough to altogether separate the town
from the moon. New Orleans and the moon have always
seemed to me to have an understanding between them, an
intimacy of sisters grown old together, no longer needing
more than a speechless look to communicate their feelings
to each other. This lunar atmosphere of the city draws me
back whenever the waves of energy which removed me to
more vital towns have spent themselves and a time of reces-
sion is called for. Each time I have felt some rather profound psychic wound, a loss or a failure, I have returned to
this city. At such periods I would seem to belong there and
no place else in the country.

During this first period in New Orleans none of the small
encouragements in my life as a writer had yet come along
and I had already accepted the terms of anonymity and
failure. I had already learned to make a religion of endur-
ance and a secret of my desperation. The nights were com-
forting. When the naked light-bulb had been turned off and
everything visible gone except the misty alcove set deeply
and narrowly into the wall above Bourbon, I would seem to
slip into another state of being which had no trying associations with the world. For a while the alcove would remain
empty, just a recess that light came faintly into: but after my
thoughts had made some dreamy excursion or other and I
turned again to look in that direction, the transparent figure
would noiselessly have entered and seated herself on the
bench below the window and begun that patient watching
which put me to sleep. The hands of the figure were folded
among the colorless draperies of her lap and her eyes were
fixed up on me with a gentle, unquestioning look which I came
to remember as having belonged to my grandmother during
her sieges of illness when I used to go to her room and sit
by her bed and want to say something or put my hand over
hers but could not do either, knowing that if I did I would
burst into tears that would trouble her more than her illness.

The appearance of this grey figure in the alcove never
preceded the time of falling asleep by more than a few

moments. When I saw her there I thought comfortably, Ah, now, I'm about to slip away, it will all be gone in a moment and won't come back until morning. . . .

On one of those nights a more substantial visitor came to my room. I was jolted out of sleep by a warmth that was not my own, and I awoke to find that someone had entered my room and was crouching over the bed. I jumped up and nearly cried out, but the arms of the visitor passionately restrained me. He whispered his name which was that of a tubercular young artist who slept in the room adjoining. I want to, I want to, he whispered. So I lay back and let him do what he wanted until he was finished. Then without any speech he got up and left my room. For a while afterwards I heard him coughing and muttering to himself through the wall between us. Turbulent feelings were on both sides of that wall. But at last I was drowsy again. I cocked an eye toward the alcove. Yes, she was there. I wondered if she had witnessed the strange goings-on and what her attitude was toward perversions of longing. But nothing gave any sign. The two weightless hands so loosely clasping each other among the colorless draperies of the lap, the cool and believing grey eyes in the faint pearly face, were immobile as statuary. I felt that she had permitted the act to occur and had neither blamed nor approved, and so I went off to sleep.

Not long after the episode in my room the artist was involved in a terrible scene with the land-lady. His disease was entering the final stage, he coughed all the time but managed to go on working. He was a quick-sketch artist at the Court of the Two Parrots which was around the corner on Toulouse. He did not trust anybody or anything. He lived in a world completely hostile to him, unrelentingly hostile, and no other being could enter the walls about him for more than the frantic moments desire drove him to. He would not give in to the mortal fever which licked all the time at his nerves. He invented all sorts of trivial complaints and grudges to hide from himself the knowledge that he was dying. One of these subterfuges to which he resorted was a nightly preoccupation with bed-bugs. He claimed that his mattress was infested with them, and every morning he made an angry report to the land-lady on the number that had bitten him during the night. These numbers grew and grew to appalling figures. The old woman wouldn't believe him. Finally one morning he did get her into the room to take a look at the bed-clothes.

I heard him breathing hoarsely while the old woman shuffled and rattled about the corner his bed was in.

Well, she finally grunted, I ain't found nothin'.

Christ, said the artist, you're blind!

Okay! You show me! What is there on this bed?

Look at that! said the artist.

What?

That spot of blood on the pillow.

Well?

That's where I smashed a bed-bug as big as my thumb-nail!

Ho, ho, ho, said the land-lady. That's where you spit up blood!

There was a pause in which his breathing grew hoarser. His speech when it burst out again was dreadfully altered.

How dare you, God damn you, say that!

Ho, ho, ho! I guess you claim you never spit up no blood?

No, no, never! he shouted.

Ho, ho, ho! You spit up blood all the time. I've seen your spit on the stairs and in the hall and on the floor of this bedroom. You leave a trail of it everywhere that you go, a bloody track like a chicken that runs with its head off. You hawk and you spit and you spread contamination. And that ain't all that you do by a long shot neither!

Now, yelled the artist—What kind of a dirty insinuation is *that*?

Ho, ho, ho! Insinuation of nothin' but what's known facts!

Get out! he shouted.

I'm in my own house and I'll say what I want where I please! I know all about you degenerates in the Quarter. I ain't let rooms ten years in the Quarter for nothin'. A bunch of rotten half breeds and drunks an' degenerates, that's what I've had to cope with. But you're the worst of the bunch, barring none! And it's not just here but at the Two Parrots, too. Your awful condition's become the main topic of talk at the place where you work. You spit all around your easel in the courtyard. It's got to be mopped with a strong disinfectant each night. The management is disgusted. They wish you would fold up your easel and get to hell out. They only don't ask you because you're a pitiful case. Why, one of the waitresses told me some customers left without paying their bill because you was hawking and spitting right next to their table. That's how it is, and the management's fed up with it!

You're making up lies!

It's God's own truth! I got it from the cashier!

I ought to hit you!

Go on!

I ought to knock your ugly old lying face in!

Go on, go on, just try it! I got a nephew that's a captain on the police force! Hit me an you'll land smack in the House of Detention! A rubber hose on your back is what you'll git in there!

I ought to twist those dirty lies out of your neck!

Ho, ho, just try it! Even the effort would kill you!

You'll be punished, he gasped. One of these nights you'll get a knife stuck in you!

By you, I suppose? Ho, ho! You'll die on the street, you'll cough up your lungs in the gutter! You'll go to the morgue. Nobody will claim that skinny cadaver of yours. You'll go in a box and be dumped off a barge in the river. The sooner the better is how I look at it, too. A case like you is a public nuisance and danger. You've got no right to expose healthy people to you. You ought to go into the charity ward at Saint Vincent's. That is the place for a person in dying condition who ain't got the sense to know what is really wrong with him but goes about raising a stink about bugs putting blood on his pillow. Huh! Bugs! You're the bugs that puts blood all over this linen! It's you, not bugs, that makes such, a filthy mess at the Court of Two Parrots it's got to be scoured with lye when you leave ev'ry night! It's you, not bugs, that drives the customers off without paying their checks. The management's not disgusted with bugs, but with you! And if you don't leave of your own sweet accord pretty quick you'll be given y'ur notice. And I'm not keepin' yuh neither. Not after y'ur threats an' the scene that you've made this mawnin'. I want you to gather all of y'ur old junk up, all of y'ur dirty old handkerchiefs an' y'ur bottles, and get 'em all out of here by twelve o'clock noon, or by God, an' by Jesus, anything that's left here is going straight down to the incinerator! I'll gather it up on the end of a ten-foot pole and dump it into the fire, cause nothing you touch is safe for human contact!

He ran from the room. I heard him running downstairs and out of the building. I went to the alcove window and watched him spinning wildly around in the street. He was crazed with fury. A waiter from the Chinese restaurant came out and caught at his arm, a drunk from a bar reasoned with him. He sobbed and lamented and wandered from door to door of the ancient buildings until the drunk had maneuvered him into a bar.

The land-lady and a fat old Negress who worked on the place removed the young man's mattress from his bed and lugged it into the courtyard. They stuffed it into the iron pit of the incinerator and set it afire and stood at respectful distance watching it burn. The land-lady wasn't content with just the burning, she made a long speech at the top of her voice about it.

It's not bein' burned because of no bugs, she shouted. I'm burnin' this mattress because it's contaminated. A T.B. case has been on it, a filthy degenerate and a liar!

She went on and on until the mattress was fully consumed, and after.

Then the old Negress was sent upstairs to remove the young man's belongings. It had begun to rain and despite the land-lady's objections the Negress put all of the things beneath the banana tree in the courtyard and covered them with a discarded sheet of linoleum weighted down with loose bricks.

At sun-down the young man returned to the place. I heard him coughing and gasping in the rainy courtyard as he collected his things from under the fantastic green and yellow umbrella of the banana tree. He seemed to be talking about all the wrongs he had suffered since he had come into the world, but at last the complaints were centered upon the loss of a handsome comb. Oh, my God, he muttered, She's stolen my comb, I had a beautiful comb that I got from my mother, a tortoise-shell comb with a silver and pearl handle on it. That's gone, it's been stolen, the comb that belonged to my mother!

At last it was found, or the young man gave up the search, for his talk died out. A wet silver hush fell over the house on Bourbon as daylight and rain both ended their business there, and in my room the luminous dial of a clock and the misty grey of the alcove were all that remained for me of the visible world.

The episode put an end to my stay at the house. For several nights after that the transparent grey angel failed to appear in the alcove and sleep had to come without any motherly sanction. So I decided to give up my residence there. I felt that the delicate old lady angel had tacitly warned me to leave, and that if I ever was visited by her again, it would be at another time in another place—which still haven't come.

Eudora Welty (April 13, 1909) was born in Jackson, Mississippi. Educated in Jackson's public schools, she began writing and drawing at a young age, publishing poems and sketches in *St. Nicholas* magazine as early as 1920. After attending Mississippi State College for Women for two years (1925–1927), she transferred to the University of Wisconsin, graduating in 1929. In 1930 she attended Columbia University School of Business, but returned to Mississippi in 1931.

Two of her short stories "Death of a Traveling Salesman" and "Magic" were published in *Manuscript* magazine in 1936. Welty's first book, *A Curtain of Green*, appeared in 1941, and was a critical success. Her second volume, *The Robber Bridegroom*, appeared in 1942, and firmly established her reputation as a writer. Since *The Wide Net and Other Stories* (1943), Welty has published *Delta Wedding* (1946), *The Golden Apples* (1949), *The Ponder Heart* (1954), *The Bride of the Innisfallen and Other Stories* (1955), *The Shoe Bird* (1964), *Losing Battles* (1970), *One Time, One Place* (1971), *The Optimist's Daughter* (1972), *The Eye of the Story* (1977), *The Collected Stories of Eudora Welty* (1980), and *One Writer's Beginnings* (1984) among others.

Welty's many honors include the Pulitzer Prize, the American Book Award for fiction, the Gold Medal for the Novel by the National Institute of Arts and Letters, the Howells Medal for Fiction by the American Academy of Arts and Letters, and a Senior Fellowship from the National Endowment for the Arts.

NO PLACE FOR YOU, MY LOVE

by Eudora Welty

They were strangers to each other, both fairly well strangers to the place, now seated side by side at luncheon—a party combined in a free-and-easy way when the friends he and she were with recognized each other across Galatoire's. The time was a Sunday in summer— those hours of afternoon that seem Time Out in New Orleans.

The moment he saw her little blunt, fair face, he thought that here was a woman who was having an affair. It was one of those odd meetings when such an impact is felt that it has to be translated at once into some sort of speculation.

With a married man, most likely, he supposed, slipping quickly into a groove—he was long married—and feeling more conventional, then, in his curiosity as she sat there, leaning her cheek on her hand, looking no further before her than the flowers on the table, and wearing that hat.

He did not like her hat, any more than he liked tropical flowers. It was the wrong hat for her, thought this Eastern businessman who had no interest whatever in women's clothes and no eye for them; he thought the unaccustomed thing crossly.

It must stick out all over me, she thought, so people think they can love me or hate me just by looking at me. How did it leave us—the old, safe, slow way people used to know of learning how one another feels, and the privilege that went with it of shying away if it seemed best? People in love like me, I suppose, give away the short cuts to everybody's secrets.

Something, though, he decided, had been settled about

her predicament—for the time being, anyway; the parties to it were all still alive, no doubt. Nevertheless, her predicament was the only one he felt so sure of here, like the only recognizable shadow in that restaurant, where mirrors and fans were busy agitating the light, as the very local talk drawled across and agitated the peace. The shadow lay between her fingers, between her little square hand and her cheek, like something always best carried about the person. Then suddenly, as she took her hand down, the secret fact was still there—it lighted her. It was a bold and full light, shot up under the brim of that hat, as close to them all as the flowers in the center of the table.

Did he dream of making her disloyal to that hopelessness that he saw very well she'd been cultivating down here? He knew very well that he did not. What they amounted to was two Northerners keeping each other company. She glanced up at the big gold clock on the wall and smiled. He didn't smile back. She had that naïve face that he associated, for no good reason, with the Middle West—because it said "Show me," perhaps. It was a serious, now-watch-out-everybody face, which orphaned her entirely in the company of these Southerners. He guessed her age, as he could not guess theirs: thirty-two. He himself was further along.

Of all human moods, deliberate imperviousness may be the most quickly communicated—it may be the most successful, most fatal signal of all. And two people can indulge in imperviousness as well as in anything else. "You're not very hungry either," he said.

The blades of fan shadows came down over their two heads, as he saw inadvertently in the mirror, with himself smiling at her now like a villain. His remark sounded dominant and rude enough for everybody present to listen back a moment; it even sounded like an answer to a question she might have just asked him. The other women glanced at him. The Southern look—Southern mask—of life-is-a-dream irony, which could turn to pure challenge at the drop of a hat, he could wish well away. He liked naïveté better.

"I find the heat down here depressing," she said, with the heart of Ohio in her voice.

"Well—I'm in somewhat of a temper about it, too," he said.

They looked with grateful dignity at each other.

"I have a car here, just down the street," he said to her as

the luncheon party was rising to leave, all the others wanting to get back to their houses and sleep. "If it's all right
with—Have you ever driven down south of here?"

Out on Bourbon Street, in the bath of July, she asked at
his shoulder, "South of New Orleans? I didn't know there
was any south to *here*. Does it just go on and on?" She
laughed, and adjusted the exasperating hat to her head in a
different way. It was more than frivolous, it was conspicuous, with some sort of glitter or flitter tied in a band around
the straw and hanging down.

"That's what I'm going to show you."

"Oh—you've been there?"

"No!"

His voice rang out over the uneven, narrow sidewalk and
dropped back from the walls. The flaked-off, colored houses
were spotted like the hides of beasts faded and shy, and
were hot as a wall of growth that seemed to breathe flower-
like down onto them as they walked to the car parked there.

"It's just that it couldn't be any worse—we'll see."

"All right, then," she said. "We will."

So, their actions reduced to amiability, they settled into
the car—a faded-red Ford convertible with a rather thread-
bare canvas top, which had been standing in the sun for all
those lunch hours.

"It's rented," he explained. "I asked to have the top put
down, and was told I'd lost my mind."

"It's out of this world. *Degrading* heat," she said and
added, "Doesn't matter."

The stranger in New Orleans always sets out to leave it as
though following the clue in a maze. They were threading
through the narrow and one-way streets, past the pale-violet
bloom of tired squares, the brown steeples and statues, the
balcony with the live and probably famous black monkey
dipping along the railing as over a ballroom floor, past the
grillework and the lattice-work to all the iron swans painted
flesh color on the front steps of bungalows outlying.

Driving, he spread his new map and put his finger down
on it. At the intersection marked Arabi, where their road
led out of the tangle and he took it, a small Negro seated
beneath a black umbrella astride a box chalked "Shou Shine"
lifted his pink-and-black hand and waved them languidly
good-by. She didn't miss it, and waved back.

*   *   *

Below New Orleans there was a raging of insects from both sides of the concrete highway, not quite together, like the playing of separated marching bands. The river and the levee were still on her side, waste and jungle and some occasional settlements on his—poor houses. Families bigger than housefuls thronged the yards. His nodding, driving head would veer from side to side, looking and almost lowering. As time passed and the distance from New Orleans grew, girls ever darker and younger were disposing themselves over the porches and the porch steps, with jet-black hair pulled high, and ragged palm-leaf fans rising and falling like rafts of butterflies. The children running forth were nearly always naked ones.

She watched the road. Crayfish constantly crossed in front of the wheels, looking grim and bonneted, in a great hurry.

"How the Old Woman Got Home," she murmured to herself.

He pointed, as it flew by, at a saucepan full of cut zinnias which stood waiting on the open lid of a mailbox at the roadside, with a little note tied onto the handle.

They rode mostly in silence. The sun bore down. They met fishermen and other men bent on some local pursuits, some in sulphur-colored pants, walking and riding; met wagons, trucks, boats in trucks, autos, boats on top of autos—all coming to meet them, as though something of high moment were doing back where the car came from, and he and she were determined to miss it. There was nearly always a man lying with his shoes off in the bed of any truck otherwise empty—with the raw, red look of a man sleeping in the daytime, being jolted about as he slept. Then there was a sort of dead man's land, where nobody came. He loosened his collar and tie. By rushing through the heat at high speed, they brought themselves the effect of fans turned onto their cheeks. Clearing alternated with jungle and cane-brake like something tried, tried again. Little shell roads led off on both sides; now and then a road of planks led into the yellow-green.

"Like a dance floor in there." She pointed.

He informed her, "In there's your oil, I think."

There were thousands, millions of mosquitoes and gnats—a universe of them, and on the increase.

A family of eight or nine people on foot strung along the road in the same direction the car was going, beating themselves with the wild palmettos. Heels, shoulders, knees, breasts, back of the heads, elbows, hands, were touched in turn—like some game, each playing it with himself.

He struck himself on the forehead, and increased their speed. (His wife would not be at her most charitable if he came bringing malaria home to the family.)

More and more crayfish and other shell creatures littered their path, scuttling or dragging. These little samples, little jokes of creation, persisted and sometimes perished, the more of them the deeper down the road went. Terrapins and turtles came up steadily over the horizons of the ditches.

Back there in the margins were worse—crawling hides you could not penetrate with bullets or quite believe, grins that had come down from the primeval mud.

"Wake up." Her Northern nudge was very timely on his arm. They had veered toward the side of the road. Still driving fast, he spread his map.

Like a misplaced sunrise, the light of the river flowed up; they were mounting the levee on a little shell road.

"Shall we cross here?" he asked politely.

He might have been keeping track over years and miles of how long they could keep that tiny ferry waiting. Now skid-down the levee's flank, they were the last-minute car, the last possible car that could squeeze on. Under the sparse shade of one willow tree, the small, amateurish-looking boat slapped the water, as, expertly, he wedged on board.

"Tell him we put him on hub cap!" shouted one of the numerous olive-skinned, dark-eyed young boys standing dressed up in bright shirts at the railing, hugging each other with delight that that last straw was on board. Another boy drew his affectionate initials in the dust of the door on her side.

She opened the door and stepped out, and, after only a moment's standing at bay, started up a little iron stairway. She appeared above the car, on the tiny bridge beneath the captain's window and the whistle.

From there, while the boat still delayed in what seemed a trance—as if it were too full to attempt the start—she could see the panlike deck below, separated by its rusty rim from the tilting, polished water.

The passengers walking and jostling about there appeared oddly amateurish, too—amateur travelers. They were having such a good time. They all knew each other. Beer was being passed around in cans, bets were being loudly settled and new bets made, about local and special subjects on which they all doted. One red-haired man in a burst of wildness even tried to give away his truckload of shrimp to a man on the other side of the boat—nearly all the trucks were full of shrimp—causing taunts and then protests of "They good! They good!" from the giver. The young boys leaned on each other thinking of what next, rolling their eyes absently.

A radio pricked the air behind her. Looking like a great tomcat just above her head, the captain was digesting the news of a fine stolen automobile.

At last a tremendous explosion burst—the whistle. Everything shuddered in outline from the sound, everybody said something—everybody else.

They started with no perceptible motion, but her hat blew off. It went spiraling to the deck below, where he, thank heaven, sprang out of the car and picked it up. Everybody looked frankly up at her now, holding her hands to her head.

The little willow tree receded as its shade was taken away. The heat was like something falling on her head. She held the hot rail before her. It was like riding a stove. Her shoulders dropping, her hair flying, her skirt buffeted by the sudden strong wind, she stood there, thinking they all must see that with her entire self all she did was wait. Her set hands, with the bag that hung from her wrist and rocked back and forth—all three seemed objects bleaching there, belonging to no one; she could not feel a thing in the skin of her face; perhaps she was crying, and not knowing it. She could look down and see him just below her, his black shadow, her hat, and his black hair. His hair in the wind looked unreasonably long and rippling. Little did he know that from here it had a red undergleam like an animal's. When she looked up and outward, a vortex of light drove through and over the brown waves like a star in the water.

He did after all bring the retrieved hat up the stairs to her. She took it back—useless—and held it to her skirt. What they were saying below was more polite than their searchlight faces.

"Where you think he come from, that man?"

"I bet he come from Lafitte."

"Lafitte? What you bet, eh?"—all crouched in the shade of trucks, squatting and laughing.

Now his shadow fell partly across her; the boat had jolted into some other strand of current. Her shaded arm and shaded hand felt pulled out from the blaze of light and water, and she hoped humbly for more shade for her head. It had seemed so natural to climb up and stand in the sun.

The boys had a surprise—an alligator on board. One of them pulled it by a chain around the deck, between the cars and trucks, like a toy—a hide that could walk. He thought, Well they had to catch one sometime. It's Sunday afternoon. So they have him on board now, riding him across the Mississippi River. . . . The playfulness of it beset everybody on the ferry. The hoarseness of the boat whistle, commenting briefly, seemed part of the general appreciation.

"Who want to rassle him? Who want to, eh?" two boys cried, looking up. A boy with shrimp-colored arms capered from side to side, pretending to have been bitten.

What was there so hilarious about jaws that could bite? And what danger was there once in this repulsiveness—so that the last worldly evidence of some old heroic horror of the dragon had to be paraded in capture before the eyes of country clowns?

He noticed that she looked at the alligator without flinching at all. Her distance was set—the number of feet and inches between herself and it mattered to her.

Perhaps her measuring coolness was to him what his bodily shade was to her, while they stood pat up there riding the river, which felt like the sea and looked like the earth under them—full of the red-brown earth, charged with it. Ahead of the boat it was like an exposed vein of ore. The river seemed to swell in the vast middle with the curve of the earth. The sun rolled under them. As if in memory of the size of things, uprooted trees were drawn across their path, sawing at the air and tumbling one over the other.

When they reached the other side, they felt that they had been racing around an arena in their chariot, among lions. The whistle took and shook the stairs as they went down. The young boys, looking taller, had taken out colored combs and were combing their wet hair back in solemn pompadour above their radiant foreheads. They had been bathing in the river themselves not long before.

The cars and trucks, then the foot passengers and the

alligator, waddling like a child to school, all disembarked and wound up the weed-sprung levee.

Both respectable and merciful, their hides, she thought, forcing herself to dwell on the alligator as she looked back. Deliver us all from the naked in heart. (As she had been told.)

When they regained their paved road, he heard her give a little sigh and saw her turn her straw-colored head to look back once more. Now that she rode with her hat in her lap, her earrings were conspicuous too. A little metal ball set with small pale stones danced beside each square, faintly downy cheek.

Had she felt a wish for someone else to be riding with them? He thought it was more likely that she would wish for her husband if she had one (his wife's voice) than for the lover in whom he believed. Whatever people liked to think, situations (if not scenes) were usually three-way—there was somebody else always. The one who didn't—couldn't—understand the two made the formidable third.

He glanced down at the map flapping on the seat between them, up at his wristwatch, out at the road. Out there was the incredible brightness of four o'clock.

On this side of the river, the road ran beneath the brow of the levee and followed it. Here was a heat that ran deeper and brighter and more intense than all the rest—its nerve. The road grew one with the heat as it was one with the unseen river. Dead snakes stretched across the concrete like markers—inlaid mosaic bands, dry as feathers, which their tires licked at intervals that began to seem clocklike.

No, the heat faced them—it was ahead. They could see it waving at them, shaken in the air above the white of the road, always at a certain distance ahead, shimmering finely as a cloth, with running edges of green and gold, fire and azure.

"It's never anything like this in Syracuse," he said.

"Or in Toledo, either," she replied with dry lips.

They were driving through greater waste down here, through fewer and even more insignificant towns. There was water under everything. Even where a screen of jungle had been left to stand, splashes could be heard from under the trees. In the vast open, sometimes boats moved inch by inch through what appeared endless meadows of rubbery flowers.

Her eyes overcome with brightness and size, she felt a

panic rise, as sudden as nausea. Just how far below questions and answers, concealment and revelation, they were running now—that was still a new question, with a power of its own, waiting. How dear—how costly—could this ride be?

"It looks to me like your road can't go much further," she remarked cheerfully. "Just over there, it's all water."

"Time out," he said, and with that he turned the car into a sudden road of white shells that rushed at them narrowly out of the left.

They bolted over a cattle guard, where some rayed and crested purple flowers burst out of the vines in the ditch, and rolled onto a long, narrow, green, mowed clearing: a churchyard. A paved track ran between two short rows of raised tombs, all neatly white-washed and now brilliant as faces against the vast flushed sky.

The track was the width of the car with a few inches to spare. He passed between the tombs slowly but in the manner of a feat. Names took their places on the walls slowly at a level with the eye, names as near as the eyes of a person stopping in conversation, and as far away in origin, and in all their music and dead longing, as Spain. At intervals were set packed bouquets of zinnias, oleanders, and some kind of purple flowers, all quite fresh, in fruit jars, like nice welcomes on bureaus.

They moved on into an open plot beyond, of violent-green grass, spread before the green-and-white frame church with worked flower beds around it, flowerless poinsettias growing up to the windowsills. Beyond was a house, and left on the doorstep of the house a fresh-caught catfish the size of a baby—a fish wearing whiskers and bleeding. On a clothesline in the yard, a priest's black gown on a hanger hung airing, swaying at man's height, in a vague, trainlike, ladylike sweep along an evening breath that might otherwise have seemed imaginary from the unseen, felt river.

With the motor cut off, with the raging of the insects about them, they sat looking out at the green and white and black and red and pink as they leaned against the sides of the car.

"What is your wife like?" she asked. His right hand came up and spread—iron, wooden, manicured. She lifted her eyes to his face. He looked at her like that hand.

Then he lit a cigarette, and the portrait, and the right-hand testimonial it made, were blown away. She smiled, herself as unaffected as by some stage performance; and he was annoyed in the cemetery. They did not risk going on to her husband—if she had one.

Under the supporting posts of the priest's house, where a boat was, solid ground ended and palmettos and water hyacinths could not wait to begin; suddenly the rays of the sun, from behind the car, reached that lowness and struck the flowers. The priest came out onto the porch in his underwear, stared at the car a moment as if he wondered what time it was, then collected his robe off the line and his fish off the doorstep and returned inside. Vespers was next, for him.

After backing out between the tombs he drove on still south, in the sunset. They caught up with an old man walking in a sprightly way in their direction, all by himself, wearing a clean bright shirt printed with a pair of palm trees fanning green over his chest. It might better be a big colored woman's shirt, but she didn't have it. He flagged the car with gestures like hoops.

"You're coming to the end of the road," the old man told them. He pointed ahead, tipped his hat to the lady, and pointed again. "End of the road." They didn't understand that he meant, "Take me."

They drove on. "If we do go any further, it'll have to be by water—is that it?" he asked her, hesitating at this odd point.

"You know better than I do," she replied politely.

The road had for some time ceased to be paved; it was made of shells. It was leading into a small, sparse settlement like the others a few miles back, but with even more of the camp about it. On the lip of the clearing, directly before a green willow blaze with the sunset gone behind it, the row of houses and shacks faced out on broad, colored, moving water that stretched to reach the horizon and looked like an arm of the sea. The houses on their shaggy posts, patchily built, some with plank runways instead of steps, were flimsy and alike, and not much bigger than the boats tied up at the landing.

"Venice," she heard him announce, and he dropped the crackling map in her lap.

They coasted down the brief remainder. The end of the road—she could not remember ever seeing a road simply end—was a spoon shape, with a tree stump in the bowl to turn around by.

Around it, he stopped the car, and they stepped out, feeling put down in the midst of a sudden vast pause or subduement that was like a yawn. They made their way on foot toward the water, where at an idle-looking landing men in twos and threes stood with their backs to them.

The nearness of darkness, the still uncut trees, bright water partly under a sheet of flowers, shacks, silence, dark shapes of boats tied up, then the first sounds of people just on the other side of thin walls—all this reached them. Mounds of shells like day-old snow, pink-tinted, lay around a central shack with a beer sign on it. An old man up on the porch there sat holding an open newspaper, with a fat white goose sitting opposite him on the floor. Below, in the now shadowless and sunless open, another old man, with a colored pencil bright under his hat brim, was late mending a sail.

When she looked clear around, thinking they had a fire burning somewhere now, out of the heat had risen the full moon. Just beyond the trees, enormous, tangerine-colored, it was going solidly up. Other lights just striking into view, looking farther distant, showed moss shapes hanging, or slipped and broke matchlike on the water that so encroached upon the rim of ground they were standing on.

There was a touch at her arm—his, accidental.

"We're at the jumping-off place," he said.

She laughed, having thought his hand was a bat, while her eyes rushed downward toward a great pale drift of water hyacinths—still partly open, flushed and yet moonlit, level with her feet—through which paths of water for the boats had been hacked. She drew her hands up to her face under the brim of her hat; her own cheeks felt like the hyacinths to her, all her skin still full of too much light and sky, exposed. The harsh vesper bell was ringing.

"I believe there must be something wrong with me, that I came on this excursion to begin with," she said, as if he had already said this and she were merely in hopeful, willing, maddening agreement with him.

He took hold of her arm, and said, "Oh, come on—I see we can get something to drink here, at least."

But there was a beating, muffled sound from over the darkening water. One more boat was coming in, making its way through the tenacious, tough, dark flower traps, by the shaken light of what first appeared to be torches. He and she waited for the boat, as if on each other's patience. As if borne in on a mist of twilight or a breath, a horde of mosquitoes and gnats came singing and striking at them first. The boat bumped, men laughed. Somebody was offering somebody else some shrimp.

Then he might have cocked his dark city head down at her; she did not look up at him, only turned when he did. Now the shell mounds, like the shacks and trees, were solid purple. Lights had appeared in the not-quite-true window squares. A narrow neon sign, the lone sign, had come out in bright blush on the beer shack's roof: "Baba's Place." A light was on on the porch.

The barnlike interior was brightly lit and unpainted, looking not quite finished, with a partition dividing this room from what lay behind. One of the four cardplayers at a table in the middle of the floor was the newspaper reader; the paper was in his pants pocket. Midway along the partition was a bar, in the form of a pass-through to the other room, with a varnished, second-hand fretwork overhang. They crossed the floor and sat, alone there, on wooden stools. An eruption of humorous signs, newspaper cutouts and cartoons, razor-blade cards, and personal messages of significance to the owner or his friends decorated the over-hang, framing where Baba should have been but wasn't.

Through there came a smell of garlic and cloves and red pepper, a blast of hot cloud escaped from a cauldron they could see now on a stove at the back of the other room. A massive back, presumably female, with a twist of gray hair on top, stood with a ladle akimbo. A young man joined her and with his fingers stole something out of the pot and ate it. At Baba's they were boiling shrimp.

When he got ready to wait on them, Baba strolled out to the counter, young, black-headed, and in very good humor.

"Coldest beer you've got. And food—What will you have?"

"Nothing for me, thank you," she said. "I'm not sure I could eat, after all."

"Well, I could," he said, shoving his jaw out. Baba smiled. "I want a good solid ham sandwich."

"I could have asked him for some water," she said, after he had gone.

While they sat waiting, it seemed very quiet. The bubbling of the shrimp, the distant laughing of Baba, and the slap of cards, like the beating of moths on the screens, seemed to come in fits and starts. The steady breathing they heard came from a big rough dog asleep in the corner. But it was bright. Electric lights were strung riotously over the room from a kind of spider web of old wires in the rafters. One of the written messages tacked before them read, "Joe! At the boyy!!" It looked very yellow, older than Baba's Place. Outside, the world was pure dark.

Two little boys, almost alike, almost the same size, and just cleaned up, dived into the room with a double bang of the screen door, and circled around the card game. They ran their hands into the men's pockets.

"Nickel for some pop!"

"Nickel for some pop!"

"Go 'way and let me play, you!"

They circled around and shrieked at the dog, ran under the lid of the counter and raced through the kitchen and back, and hung over the stools at the bar. One child had a live lizard on his shirt, clinging like a breast pin—like lapis lazuli.

Bringing in a strong odor of geranium talcum, some men had come in now—all in bright shirts. They drew near the counter, or stood and watched the game.

When Baba came out bringing the beer and sandwich, "Could I have some water?" she greeted him.

Baba laughed at everybody. She decided the woman back there must be Baba's mother.

Beside her, he was drinking his beer and eating his sandwich—ham, cheese, tomato, pickle, and mustard. Before he finished, one of the men who had come in beckoned from across the room. It was the old man in the palm-tree shirt.

She lifted her head to watch him leave her, and was looked at, from all over the room. As a minute passed, no cards were laid down. In a far-off way, like accepting the light from Arcturus, she accepted it that she was more beautiful or perhaps more fragile than the women they saw every day of their lives. It was just this thought coming into a woman's face, and at this hour, that seemed familiar to them.

Baba was smiling. He had set an opened, frosted brown bottle before her on the counter, and a thick sandwich, and

stood looking at her. Baba made her eat some supper, for
what she was.

"What the old fellow wanted," said he when he came
back at last, "was to have a friend of his apologize. Seems
church is just out. Seems the friend made a remark coming
in just now. His pals told him there was a lady present."

"I see you bought him a beer," she said.

"Well, the old man looked like he wanted *something*."

All at once the juke box interrupted from back in the
corner, with the same old song as anywhere. The half-dozen
slot machines along the wall were suddenly all run to like
Maypoles, and thrown into action—taken over by further
battalions of little boys.

There were three little boys to each slot machine. The
local custom appeared to be that one pulled the lever for the
friend he was holding up to put the nickel in, while the third
covered the pictures with the flat of his hand as they fell into
place, so as to surprise them all if anything happened.

The dog lay sleeping on in front of the raging juke box,
his ribs working fast as a concertina's. At the side of the
room a man with a cap on his white thatch was trying his
best to open a side screen door, but it was stuck fast. It was
he who had come in with the remark considered ribald; now
he was trying to get out the other way. Moths as thick as
ingots were trying to get in. The cardplayers broke into
shouts of derision, then joy, then tired derision among themselves; they might have been here all afternoon—they were
the only ones not cleaned up and shaved. The original pair
of little boys ran in once more, with the hyphenated bang.
They got nickels this time, then were brushed away from the
table like mosquitoes, and they rushed under the counter
and on to the cauldron behind, clinging to Baba's mother
there. The evening was at the threshold.

They were quite unnoticed now. He was eating another
sandwich, and she, having finished part of hers, was fanning
her face with her hat. Baba had lifted the flap of the counter
and come out into the room. Behind his head there was a
sign lettered in orange crayon: "Shrimp Dance Sun.PM."
That was tonight, still to be.

And suddenly she made a move to slide down from her
stool, maybe wishing to walk out into that nowhere down
the front steps to be cool a moment. But he had hold of her
hand. He got down from his stool, and, patiently, reversing

her hand in his own—just as she had had the look of being about to give up, faint—began moving her, leading her. They were dancing.

"I get to thinking this is what we get—what you and I deserve," she whispered, looking past his shoulder into the room. "And all the time, it's real. It's a real place—away off down here. . . ."

They danced gratefully, formally, to some song carried on in what must be the local patois, while no one paid any attention as long as they were together, and the children poured the family nickels steadily into the slot machines, walloping the handles down with regular crashes and troubling nobody with winning.

She said rapidly, as they began moving together too well, "One of those clippings was an account of a shooting right here. I guess they're proud of it. And that awful knife Baba was carrying . . . I wonder what he called me," she whispered in his ear.

"Who?"

"The one who apologized to you."

If they had ever been going to overstep themselves, it would be now as he held her closer and turned her, when she became aware that he could not help but see the bruise at her temple. It would not be six inches from his eyes. She felt it come out like an evil star. (Let it pay him back, then, for the hand he had stuck in her face when she'd tried once to be sympathetic, when she'd asked about his wife.) They danced on still as the record changed, after standing wordless and motionless, linked together in the middle of the room, for the moment between.

Then, they were like a matched team—like professional, Spanish dancers wearing masks—while the slow piece was playing.

Surely even those immune from the world, for the time being, need the touch of one another, or all is lost. Their arms encircling each other, their bodies circling the odorous, just-nailed-down floor, they were, at last, imperviousness in motion. They had found it, and had almost missed it: they had had to dance. They were what their separate hearts desired that day, for themselves and each other.

They were so good together that once she looked up and half smiled. "For whose benefit did we have to show off?"

Like people in love, they had a superstition about them-

NO PLACE FOR YOU, MY LOVE   323

selves almost as soon as they came out on the floor, and
dared not think the words "happy" or "unhappy," which
might strike them, one or the other, like lightning.

In the thickening heat they danced on while Baba himself
sang with the mosquito-voiced singer in the chorus of "*Moi
pas l'aimez ça*," enumerating the *ça*'s with a hot shrimp
between his fingers. He was counting over the platters the
old woman now set out on the counter, each heaped with
shrimp in their shells boiled to iridescence, like mounds of
honeysuckle flowers.

The goose wandered in from the back room under the lid
of the counter and hitched itself around the floor among the
table legs and people's legs, never seeing that it was neatly
avoided by two dancers—who nevertheless vaguely thought
of this goose as learned, having earlier heard an old man
read to it. The children called it Mimi, and lured it away.
The old thatched man was again drunkenly trying to get out
by the stuck side door; now he gave it a kick, but was
prevailed on to remain. The sleeping dog shuddered and
snored.

It was left up to the dancers to provide nickels for the
juke box; Baba kept a drawerful for every use. They had
grown fond of all the selections by now. This was the music
you heard out of the distance at night—out of the roadside
taverns you fled past, around the late corners in cities half
asleep, drifting up from the carnival over the hill, with one
odd little strain always managing to repeat itself. This seemed
a homey place.

Bathed in sweat, and feeling the false coolness that brings,
they stood finally on the porch in the lapping night air for a
moment before leaving. The first arrivals of the girls were
coming up the steps under the porch light—all flowered
fronts, their black pompadours giving out breathlike feelers
from sheer abundance. Where they'd resprinkled it since
church, the talcum shone like mica on their downy arms.
Smelling solidly of geranium, they filed across the porch
with short steps and fingers joined, just timed to turn their
smiles loose inside the room. He held the door open for
them.

"Ready to go?" he asked her.

Going back, the ride was wordless, quiet except for the
motor and the insects driving themselves against the car.

The windshield was soon blinded. The headlights pulled in two other spinning storms, cones of flying things that, it seemed, might ignite at the last minute. He stopped the car and got out to clean the windshield thoroughly with his brisk, angry motions of driving. Dust lay thick and cratered on the roadside scrub. Under the now ash-white moon, the world traveled through very faint stars—very many slow stars, very high, very low.

It was a strange land, amphibious—and whether water-covered or grown with jungle or robbed entirely of water and trees, as now, it had the same loneliness. He regarded the great sweep—like steppes, like moors, like deserts (all of which were imaginary to him); but more than it was like any likeness, it was South. The vast, thin, wide-thrown, pale, unfocused star-sky, with its veils of lightning adrift, hung over this land as it hung over the open sea. Standing out in the night alone, he was struck as powerfully with recognition of the extremity of this place as if all other bearings had vanished—as if snow had suddenly started to fall.

He climbed back inside and drove. When he moved to slap furiously at his shirtsleeves, she shivered in the hot, licking night wind that their speed was making. Once the car lights picked out two people—a Negro couple, sitting on two facing chairs in the yard outside their lonely cabin—half undressed, each battling for self against the hot night, with long white rags in endless, scarflike motions.

In peopleless open places there were lakes of dust, smudge fires burning at their hearts. Cows stood in untended rings around them, motionless in the heat, in the night—their horns standing up sharp against that glow.

At length, he stopped the car again, and this time he put his arm under her shoulder and kissed her—not knowing ever whether gently or harshly. It was the loss of that distinction that told him this was now. Then their faces touched unkissing, unmoving, dark, for a length of time. The heat came inside the car and wrapped them still, and the mosquitoes had begun to coat their arms and even their eyelids.

Later, crossing a large open distance, he saw at the same time two fires. He had the feeling that they had been riding for a long time across a face—great, wide, and upturned. In its eyes and open mouth were those fires they had had glimpses of, where the cattle had drawn together: a face, a head, far down here in the South—south of South, below it. A whole giant body sprawled downward then, on and on, always, constant as a constellation or an angel. Flaming and perhaps falling, he thought.

She appeared to be sound asleep, lying back flat as a child, with her hat in her lap. He drove on with her profile beside his, behind his, for he bent forward to drive faster. The earrings she wore twinkled with their rushing motion in an almost regular beat. They might have spoken like tongues. He looked straight before him and drove on, at a speed that, for the rented, overheated, not at all new Ford car, was demoniac.

It seemed often now that a barnlike shape flashed by, roof and all outlined in lonely neon—a movie house at a crossroads. The long white flat road itself, since they had followed it to the end and turned around to come back, seemed able, this far up, to pull them home.

A thing is incredible, if ever, only after it is told—returned to the world it came out of. For their different reasons, he thought, neither of them would tell this (unless something was dragged out of them): that, strangers, they had ridden down into a strange land together and were getting safely back—by a slight margin, perhaps, but margin enough. Over the levee wall now, like an aurora borealis, the sky of New Orleans, across the river, was flickering gently. This time they crossed by bridge, high above everything, merging into a long light-stream of cars turned cityward.

For a time afterward he was lost in the streets, turning almost at random with the noisy traffic until he found his bearings. When he stopped the car at the next sign and leaned forward frowning to make it out, she sat up straight on her side. It was Arabi. He turned the car right around.

"We're all right now," he muttered, allowing himself a cigarette.

Something that must have been with them all along suddenly, then, was not. In a moment, tall as panic, it rose, cried like a human, and dropped back.

"I never got my water," she said.

She gave him the name of her hotel, he drove her there, and he said good night on the sidewalk. They shook hands.

"Forgive . . ." For, just in time, he saw she expected it of him.

And that was just what she did, forgive him. Indeed, had she waked in time from a deep sleep, she would have told him her story. She disappeared through the revolving door, with a gesture of smoothing her hair, and he thought a figure in the lobby strolled to meet her. He got back in the car and sat there.

He was not leaving for Syracuse until early in the morning. At length, he recalled the reason; his wife had recommended that he stay where he was this extra day so that she could entertain some old, unmarried college friends without him underfoot.

As he started up the car, he recognized in the smell of exhausted, body-warm air in the streets, in which the flow of drink was an inextricable part, the signal that the New Orleans evening was just beginning. In Dickie Grogan's, as he passed, the well-known Josefina at her organ was charging up and down with "*Clair de Lune*," As he drove the little Ford safely to its garage, he remembered for the first time in years when he was young and brash, a student in New York, and the shriek and horror and unholy smother of the subway had its original meaning for him as the lilt and expectation of love.

Nancy Hale (May 6, 1908–September 24, 1988) was born in Boston. Her mother, Lillian Westcott Hale, was the most successful and respected portrait painter of her time in Boston. Her father, Philip Hale, taught at the Boston Museum of Fine Arts, where Hale received her early training as a painter. Hale's other literary relatives include her grandfather Edward Everett Hale, who is remembered for his famous story "The Man Without a Country," and her great aunt Harriet Beecher Stowe, the author of *Uncle Tom's Cabin*.

Nancy Hale published her first short story in the Boston *Herald* when she was eleven. After an early career in editing at *Vogue* and *Vanity Fair*, she became the first woman reporter on *The New York Times*. In 1942, Hale married and moved to Charlottesville, Virginia where she remained until her death.

Frequently anthologized and distinguished with awards, many of Hale's short stories were first published in *The New Yorker*. Her novels include *Never Any More* (1934), *The Prodigal Woman* (1942), and *Dear Beast* (1959). She also wrote a biography of Mary Cassatt, memoirs—*A New England Girlhood* (1958) and *The Life in the Studio* (1969), and *The Realities of Fiction: A Book About Writing* (1962).

THE NEW ORDER

by Nancy Hale

"I BELIEVE in change," Mrs. Shackelford declared the instant the thermometer was out of her mouth. Her operation had been two days before. "To remain young in spirit, we must move with the times. My poor mother set herself against all change . . ." she continued in her silvery voice.

Miss Wickes, one of the colored nurses who had just been introduced into the Southern University Hospital, stood reading the thermometer beside the sunny window; her elbow was at the exactly correct angle. She went then, on noiseless feet, in her white nylon uniform, and put the thermometer back into its tube of alcohol on the washstand. She opened the notebook she had brought into the room with her and recorded Mrs. Shackelford's temperature and pulse. She was severely handsome; dark; hair strained back into a neat bun, features aquiline and regular. She filled a metal basin with warm water and began methodically to give Mrs. Shackelford her bath in bed.

"I welcome the changes that have taken place in this place since I was a patient here fifteen years ago," Mrs. Shackelford went on as her shoulders were being washed. "So much more *sensible*. After all, we must all face reality, mustn't we, Miss Wickes?"

"It is the recommendable attitude," Miss Wickes said as she washed Mrs. Shackelford's still pretty hands, on which the rings had been put back.

"For example, the operation itself," Mrs. Shackelford persisted. "Such an informal procedure today. I mean, they gave me the anesthetic right there, under that great blazing lamp. Why not? In the old days, they gave it to you in another room, so that you wouldn't see all the—Oh, I said to Dr. Calhoun when he came in in his robe and mask, 'This is very informal, Doctor.' I said it gaily, I tried to let him *see* how I felt—they were strapping my arms down to the sides just then, and strapping my legs down. My, they're sore where they were strapped."

The nurse said, "Tsk, tsk, tsk." It reminded Mrs. Shackelford of somebody, she could not quite place whom.

"Did you ever—know Mrs. Harmon, on Bledsoe Avenue, Miss Wickes?" she asked.

"I don't think I ever made her acquaintance," the nurse said, and began on Mrs. Shackelford's legs, working down toward the slender ankles and the delicate feet.

"Well, some people, I know, would think it an indignity to be strapped down like an animal while you are still conscious, but I say, Why not? I'm an intelligent being, I can understand the necessity for it. I must tell you about the orderly—Joe, his name is—who wheeled me to the operating room on the stretcher the other morning. Do you know Joe?"

"I am acquainted with the man," Miss Wickes said, and this phrase, too, struck Mrs. Shackelford as puzzlingly familiar.

"Yes. Well, as we were trundling along through all those long corridors—how like a rabbit warren this old hospital is—somebody, I couldn't see who, some friend of Joe's, called out 'How y'all doin'?' And Joe calls back, 'Still cuttin'.' "

She looked sharply up at Miss Wickes's calm, decorous face, but there was not so much as a twitch in it.

"Some patients might have thought that pretty crude," the patient went on. "*I* thought it was just funny. 'Still cuttin'.' " She waited for a moment. "Then the food they serve you here these days. It's *sensible*. Nourishing, and sufficient. With things as they are, why should they give you steak and chops? In the old days," she said suddenly, "when I was here before, in this wing you could always order steak or chops specially broiled for you if you didn't like what was on the menu. But they don't even bring you the menu to choose from now."

"Tsk, tsk, tsk," Miss Wickes said.

Mrs. Shackelford looked at her for a moment.

"But I *believe* in change," she insisted. "It's the breath of life to me, you might say. The word 'change' is written on my banner. Take that interne, or whoever he was, that they sent to me the night before I was operated on."

"Dr. Fawkes?" Miss Wickes said.

"I guess so. My word, Miss Wickes, *you* know what the name Fawkes means around here. White trash straight out of the mountains with the smell of corn mash still clinging to his heels. But I didn't mind. I was diverted. I'd sat here alone, all that long evening, waiting. Of course, I did imagine Dr. Calhoun would come to see me; in the old days— But why should he? I know he's a *very* busy man. Why shouldn't he send his assistant or whoever this little man was? I waited and waited—it's so silly the way one feels apprehensive before an operation even when one has the greatest confidence in one's surgeon. Anyway, who should walk in but this Fawkes. Now, it's *interesting* that I should come face to face with a Fawkes. I thought it was *amusing*."

Miss Wickes turned the patient over and began to rub her back with alcohol.

"But it's different," Mrs. Shackelford said, lying with her head turned so that her petal-soft, faintly wrinkled cheek lay on the pillow. "You know it's different. I feel as if it's mostly that everybody is so much *busier* nowadays. Doctors, nurses—In the old days there always seemed to be so much time. How I remember sitting here—in one of the rooms in this wing like this—sitting up in bed, and my doctor and a whole flock of internes sitting around laughing. There seemed to be so much time for everybody in the hospital then. And the nurses. When I began to get better, they used to come in and watch how I did my hair up, just gaping. But mostly I remember those doctors, the way they all used to drop in. We'd sit, and talk, and laugh . . ."

"I can see how it would have been extremely enjoyable," Miss Wickes said. She began to make the bed with Mrs. Shackelford in it, using the clean linen she had brought in earlier.

"It was," Mrs. Shackelford said. "It was like a party. I remember when I left here I was going straight to two weeks at the Hot. Well, things have changed, and I, for one, am a hundred percent for it. How would the world's work ever get done if all everybody did was sit around and talk and laugh—and in a hospital, too? Things are done better now, there's no question about it."

"It is well to adjust oneself gracefully to the inevitable," Miss Wickes said.

"Miss Wickes, didn't you ever know Mrs. Starling—Mrs. Hugh Starling, the one who lives way out on Dairy Road?"

Miss Wickes hesitated.

"At one time I was employed by Mrs. Starling," she said, finally. "In a domestic capacity."

"I just love Mrs. Starling, don't you?" the patient said.

"She is a very fine woman," Miss Wickes said.

The door of the hospital room opened abruptly, and Miss Bruce, who was in charge of the corridor, burst in. She was young; dazzlingly blond; with a look of a cross child carrying responsibility.

"Why aren't you up?" she demanded, viewing the patient with disfavor. "Miss Wickes, you know Dr. Calhoun said the patient was to sit up this morning for a little bit. What are you doing making her bed with her in it?"

Miss Wickes said nothing.

"I haven't got time to do *everything*!" Miss Bruce cried impatiently. "Am I supposed to check up on everything you do? Come on, get her up."

She moved a step, so that she could see her lovely face in the hospital bureau mirror, adjusted her cap, looked comprehensively over the room with her blue, expressionless eyes, and whirled out again with the whisper of starch.

For a moment Mrs. Shackelford and Miss Wickes looked bleakly at each other.

"I thought you seemed a trifle fatigued this morning, or I would have—" Miss Wickes began.

"Come on, get me up," Mrs. Shackelford said, echoing Miss Bruce. "This is the new way, I know."

Miss Wickes helped her raise herself in the bed and turn sidewise, and slipped her satin scuffs over those pretty, slender feet. Then, slowly, holding on to Miss Wickes, Mrs. Shackelford slid off the bed and staggered the couple of steps to the big chair by the window.

"There!" She let out a deep breath. "It's the new way, and it's the best way, I'm sure."

Miss Wickes took the folded blanket off the end of the bed and put it over Mrs. Shackelford's knees. She stood back and looked at her.

"Are you entirely comfortable?" she asked.

"Oh, I'm all right," Mrs. Shackelford said. "Perfectly all right. You don't need to worry about me. Just come back after the proper length of time and help me get back to bed, that's all."

"In that case—" Miss Wickes said, and started slowly to leave the room. But just as she was going out the door, Mrs. Shackelford called to her.

"Miss Wickes!"—sharply, pleadingly.

The nurse hurried back to the little figure silhouetted against the window.

"Oh, it's nothing," Mrs. Shackelford said. "Just—for a moment I felt so dizzy, that's all. So—queer. I suppose it's to be expected, the first time up—Just—Miss Wickes, hold my hand for a moment, will you?"

The nurse took the patient's pretty, beringed hand.

"It's just—" the patient went on. Suddenly she began to cry. "It's not true, what I said," she sobbed. "About everything being changed—it's me that's changed, it's me. That's why the doctors don't come around and talk any more; that's why the nurses don't stand and stare. It's me! I'm not pretty any more. I'm not amusing. I'm old. I'm ugly," she wept.

The nurse all at once bent over her and put her arms full around the shaking shoulders.

"No," she said. "Don't say like that. You and your pretty ways—"

"Oh, Miss Wickes—"

"Mattie," the nurse said.

"Oh, Mattie, don't let them see me crying like this—I don't want anyone to see me—to know. You're the only one who understands—"

The nurse pressed her face against the fading golden hair and hugged the little figure and began to murmur, softly, in a kind of loving language that was deeply familiar to both of them.

"Ain't nobody goin' to know," she said. "Ain't nobody in the world here but just plain old me."

Truman Capote (September 30, 1924–August 24, 1984) was born Truman Streckfus Persons in New Orleans. After the divorce of his parents, he spent most of his childhood with relatives in Monroeville, Alabama. One of his friends there was Harper Lee who wrote the classic *To Kill a Mockingbird*. After his mother's remarriage he joined her in New York and took the last name of his stepfather. Capote began work at an early age as an office boy with the *New Yorker*, the magazine that later published much of his creative writing. After moving to New Orleans Capote began his public writing career with the short story "Miriam," published in *Mademoiselle* in 1945. It was honored with the O. Henry Memorial Prize. Although Capote received much praise for his early novels and collections of short stories, it was with the publication of *In Cold Blood* that he became tremendously successful. Originally published serially in the *New Yorker* in 1965, and later published as a book in 1966, *In Cold Blood* is the account of the brutal murder of a Kansas farm family in 1959 by two young killers. In it Capote combined journalistic accuracy and literary imagination to create what he called a "nonfiction novel." It was followed by an equally successful motion picture and one more book, *Music for Chameleons* (1980).

In his later years Capote lived in New York and continued his celebrity life by appearing as a frequent guest on national television talk shows. When he died in California in 1984 his much publicized novel "Answered Prayers" had not been published. Whether he ever finished it remains a mystery.

Capote remembered early years in the South lovingly in his short story "A Christmas Memory," first published in 1956 and later adapted for radio and film.

A CHRISTMAS MEMORY

by *Truman Capote*

Imagine a morning in late November. A coming of winter morning more than twenty years ago. Consider the kitchen of a spreading old house in a country town. A great black stove is its main feature; but there is also a big round table and a fireplace with two rocking chairs placed in front of it. Just today the fireplace commenced its seasonal roar.

A woman with shorn white hair is standing at the kitchen window. She is wearing tennis shoes and a shapeless gray sweater over a summery calico dress. She is small and sprightly, like a bantam hen; but, due to a long youthful illness, her shoulders are pitifully hunched. Her face is remarkable—not unlike Lincoln's, craggy like that, and tinted by sun and wind; but it is delicate too, finely boned, and her eyes are sherry-colored and timid. "Oh my," she exclaims, her breath smoking the windowpane, "it's fruitcake weather!"

The person to whom she is speaking is myself. I am seven; she is sixty-something. We are cousins, very distant ones, and we have lived together—well, as long as I can remember. Other people inhabit the house, relatives; and though they have power over us, and frequently make us cry, we are not, on the whole, too much aware of them. We are each other's best friend. She calls me Buddy, in memory of a boy who was formerly her best friend. The other Buddy died in the 1880's, when she was still a child. She is still a child.

"I knew it before I got out of bed," she says, turning away from the window with a purposeful excitement in her eyes. "The courthouse bell sounded so cold and clear. And there were no birds singing; they've gone to warmer country, yes indeed. Oh, Buddy, stop stuffing biscuit and fetch our buggy. Help me find my hat. We've thirty cakes to bake."

It's always the same: a morning arrives in November, and my friend, as though officially inaugurating the Christmas time of year that exhilarates her imagination and fuels the blaze of her heart, announces: "It's fruitcake weather! Fetch our buggy. Help me find my hat."

The hat is found, a straw cartwheel corsaged with velvet roses out-of-doors has faded: it once belonged to a more fashionable relative. Together, we guide our buggy, a dilapidated baby carriage, out to the garden and into a grove of pecan trees. The buggy is mine; that is, it was bought for me when I was born. It is made of wicker, rather unraveled, and the wheels wobble like a drunkard's legs. But it is a faithful object; spring-times, we take it to the woods and fill it with flowers, herbs, wild fern for our porch pots; in the summer, we pile it with picnic paraphernalia and sugar-cane fishing poles and roll it down to the edge of a creek; it has its winter uses, too: as a truck for hauling firewood from the yard to the kitchen, as a warm bed for Queenie, our tough little orange and white rat terrier, who has survived distemper and two rattlesnake bites. Queenie is trotting beside it now.

Three hours later we are back in the kitchen hulling a heaping buggy-load of windfall pecans. Our backs hurt from gathering them: how hard they were to find (the main crop having been shaken off the trees and sold by the orchard's owners, who are not us) among the concealing leaves, the frosted, deceiving grass. Caaarackle! A cheery crunch, scraps of miniature thunder sound as the shells collapse and the golden mound of sweet oily ivory meat mounts in the milk-glass bowl. Queenie begs to taste, and now and again my friend sneaks her a mite, though insisting we deprive ourselves. "We mustn't, Buddy. If we start, we won't stop. And there's scarcely enough as there is. For thirty cakes." The kitchen is growing dark. Dusk turns the window into a mirror: our reflections mingle with the rising moon as we work by the fireside in the firelight. At last, when the moon is quite high, we toss the final hull into the fire and with joined sighs, watch it catch flame. The buggy is empty, the bowl is brimful.

We eat our supper (cold biscuits, bacon, blackberry jam) and discuss tomorrow. Tomorrow the kind of work I like best begins: buying. Cherries and citron, ginger and vanilla and canned Hawaiian pineapple, rinds and raisins and walnuts and whiskey and oh, so much flour, butter, so many eggs, spices, flavorings: why, we'll need a pony to pull the buggy home.

But before these purchases can be made, there is the question of money. Neither of us has any. Except for skinflint sums persons in the house occasionally provide (a dime is considered very big money); or what we earn ourselves from various activities: holding rummage sales, selling buckets of hand-picked blackberries, jars of homemade jam and apple jelly and peach preserves, rounding up flowers for funerals and weddings. Once we won seventy-ninth prize, five dollars, in a national football contest. Not that we know a fool thing about football. It's just that we enter any contest we hear about: at the moment our hopes are centered on the fifty-thousand-dollar Grand Prize being offered to name a new brand of coffee (we suggested "A.M."; and, after some hesitation, for my friend thought it perhaps sacrilegious, the slogan "A.M.! Amen!"). To tell the truth, our only *really* profitable enterprise was the Fun and Freak museum we conducted in a back-yard woodshed two summers ago. The Fun was a stereopticon with slide views of Washington and New York lent us by a relative who had been to those places (she was furious when she discovered why we'd borrowed it); the Freak was a three-legged biddy chicken hatched by one of our own hens. Everybody hereabouts wanted to see that biddy: we charged grownups a nickel, kids two cents. And took in a good twenty dollars before the museum shut down due to the decease of the main attraction.

But one way and another we do each year accumulate Christmas savings, a Fruitcake Fund. These moneys we keep hidden in an ancient bead purse under a loose board under the floor under a chamber pot under my friend's bed. The purse is seldom removed from this safe location except to make a deposit, or, as happens every Saturday, a withdrawal; for on Saturdays I am allowed ten cents to go to the picture show. My friend has never been to a picture show, nor does she intend to: "I'd rather hear you tell the story, Buddy. That way I can imagine it more. Besides, a person my age shouldn't squander their eyes. When the Lord comes, let me see him clear." In addition to never having seen a movie, she has never: eaten in a restaurant, traveled more than five miles from home, received or sent a telegram, read anything except funny papers and the Bible, worn cosmetics, cursed, wished someone harm, told a lie on purpose, let a hungry dog go hungry. Here are a few things she has done, does do: killed with a hoe the biggest rattlesnake ever seen in this county (sixteen rattles), dip snuff (secretly), tame hummingbirds (just try it) till they balance on her finger, tell ghost stories (we both believe in ghosts) so tingling they chill you in July, talk to herself, take walks in the rain, grow the prettiest japonicas in town, know the recipe for every sort of old-time Indian cure, including a magical wart-remover.

Now, with supper finished, we retire to the room in a faraway part of the house where my friend sleeps in a scrap-quilt-covered iron bed painted rose pink, her favorite color. Silently, wallowing in the pleasures of conspiracy, we take the bead purse from its secret place and spill its contents on the scrap quilt. Dollar bills, tightly rolled and green as May buds. Somber fifty-cent pieces, heavy enough to weight a dead man's eyes. Lovely dimes, the liveliest coin, the one that really jingles. Nickels and quarters, worn smooth as creek pebbles. But mostly a hateful heap of bitter-odored pennies. Last summer others in the house contracted to pay us a penny for every twenty-five flies we killed. Oh, the carnage of August: the flies that flew to heaven! Yet it was not work in which we took pride. And, as we sit counting pennies, it is as though we were back tabulating dead flies. Neither of us has a head for figures; we count slowly, lose track, start again. According to her calculations, we have $12.73. According to mine, exactly $13. "I do hope you're wrong, Buddy. We can't mess around with thirteen. The cakes will fall. Or put somebody in the cemetery. Why, I wouldn't dream of getting out of bed on the thirteenth." This is true: she always spends thirteenths in bed. So, to be on the safe side, we subtract a penny and toss it out the window.

Of the ingredients that go into our fruitcakes, whiskey is the most expensive, as well as the hardest to obtain: State laws forbid its sale. But everybody knows you can buy a bottle from Mr. Haha Jones. And the next day, having completed our more prosaic shopping, we set out for Mr. Haha's business address, a "sinful" (to quote public opinion) fish-fry and dancing café down by the river. We've been there before, and on the same errand; but in previous years our dealings have been with Haha's wife, an iodine-dark Indian woman with brassy peroxided hair and a dead-tired disposition. Actually, we've never laid eyes on her husband, though we've heard that he's an Indian too. A giant with razor scars across his cheeks. They call him Haha because he's so gloomy, a man who never laughs. As we approach his café (a large log cabin festooned inside and out with chains of garish-gay naked light bulbs and standing by the river's muddy edge under the shade of river trees where moss drifts through the branches like gray mist) our steps slow down. Even Queenie stops prancing and sticks close by. People have been murdered in Haha's café. Cut to pieces. Hit on the head. There's a case coming up in court next month. Naturally these goings-on happen at night when the colored lights cast crazy patterns and the victrola wails. In the daytime Haha's is shabby and deserted. I knock at the door, Queenie barks, my friend calls: "Mrs. Haha, ma'am? Anyone to home?"

Footsteps. The door opens. Our hearts overturn. It's Mr. Haha Jones himself! And he *is* a giant; he *does* have scars; he *doesn't* smile. No, he glowers at us through Satan-tilted eyes and demands to know: "What you want with Haha?"

For a moment we are too paralyzed to tell. Presently my friend half-finds her voice, a whispery voice at best: "If you please, Mr. Haha, we'd like a quart of your finest whiskey."

His eyes tilt more. Would you believe it? Haha is smiling! Laughing, too. "Which one of you is a drinkin' man?"

"It's for making fruitcakes, Mr. Haha. Cooking."

This sobers him. He frowns. "That's no way to waste good whiskey." Nevertheless, he retreats into the shadowed café and seconds later appears carrying a bottle of daisy yellow unlabeled liquor. He demonstrates its sparkle in the sunlight and says: "Two dollars."

We pay him with nickels and dimes and pennies. Suddenly, jangling the coins in his hands like a fistful of dice, his face softens. "Tell you what," he proposes, pouring the money back into our bead purse, "just send me one of them fruitcakes instead."

"Well," my friend remarks on our way home, "there's a lovely man. We'll put an extra cup of raisins in *his* cake."

The black stove, stoked with coal and firewood, glows

like a lighted pumpkin. Eggbeaters whirl, spoons spin round
in bowls of butter and sugar, vanilla sweetens the air, ginger
spices it; melting, nose-tingling odors saturate the kitchen,
suffuse the house, drift out to the world on puffs of chimney
smoke. In four days our work is done. Thirty-one cakes,
dampened with whiskey, bask on window sills and shelves.

Who are they for?

Friends. Not necessarily neighbor friends: indeed, the
larger share are intended for persons we've met maybe
once, perhaps not at all. People who've struck our fancy.
Like President Roosevelt. Like the Reverend and Mrs. J.C.
Lucey, Baptist missionaries to Borneo who lectured here
last winter. Or the little knife grinder who comes through
town twice a year. Or Abner Packer, the driver of the six
o'clock bus from Mobile, who exchanges waves with us
every day as he passes in a dust-cloud whoosh. Or the young
Wistons, a California couple whose car one afternoon broke
down outside the house and who spent a pleasant hour
chatting with us on the porch (young Mr. Wiston snapped
our picture, the only one we've ever had taken). Is it because my friend is shy with everyone *except* strangers that
these strangers, or merest acquaintances, seem to us our
truest friends? I think yes. Also, the scrapbooks we keep of
thank-you's on White House stationery, time-to-time com-
munications from California and Borneo, the knife grinder's
penny post cards, make us feel connected to eventual worlds
beyond the kitchen with its view of a sky that stops.

Now a nude December fig branch grates against the window. The kitchen is empty, the cakes are gone; yesterday
we carted the last of them to the post office, where the cost
of stamps turned our purse inside out. We're broke. That
rather depresses me, but my friend insists on celebrating—
with two inches of whiskey left in Haha's bottle. Queenie
has a spoonful in a bowl of coffee (she likes her coffee
chicory-flavored and strong). The rest we divide between a
pair of jelly glasses. We're both quite awed at the prospect
of drinking straight whiskey; the taste of it brings screwed-up
expressions and sour shudders. But by and by we begin to
sing, the two of us singing different songs simultaneously. I
don't know the words to mine, just: *Come on along, come
on along, to the dark-town strutters' ball*. But I can dance:
that's what I mean to be, a tap dancer in the movies. My
dancing shadow rollicks on the walls; our voices rock the

chinaware; we giggle: as if unseen hands were tickling us. Queenie rolls on her back, her paws plow the air, something like a grin stretches her black lips. Inside myself, I feel warm and sparky as those crumbling logs, carefree as the wind in the chimney. My friend waltzes round the stove, the hem of her poor calico skirt pinched between her fingers as though it were a party dress: *Show me the way to go home*, she sings, her tennis shoes squeaking on the floor. *Show me the way to go home*.

Enter: two relatives. Very angry. Potent with eyes that scold, tongues that scald. Listen to what they have to say, the words tumbling together into a wrathful tune: "A child of seven! whiskey on his breath! are you out of your mind? feeding a child of seven! must be loony! road to ruination! remember Cousin Kate? Uncle Charlie? Uncle Charlie's brother-in-law? shame! scandal! humiliation! kneel, pray, beg the Lord!"

Queenie sneaks under the stove. My friend gazes at her shoes, her chin quivers, she lifts her skirt and blows her nose and runs to her room. Long after the town has gone to sleep and the house is silent except for the chimings of clocks and the sputter of fading fires, she is weeping into a pillow already as wet as a widow's handkerchief.

"Don't cry," I say, sitting at the bottom of her bed and shivering despite my flannel nightgown that smells of last winter's cough syrup, "don't cry," I beg, teasing her toes, tickling her feet, "you're too old for that."

"It's because," she hiccups, "I *am* too old. Old and funny."

"Not funny. Fun. More fun than anybody. Listen. If you don't stop crying you'll be so tired tomorrow we can't go cut a tree."

She straightens up. Queenie jumps on the bed (where Queenie is not allowed) to lick her cheeks. "I know where we'll find real pretty trees, Buddy. And holly, too. With berries big as your eyes. It's way off in the woods. Farther than we've ever been. Papa used to bring us Christmas trees from there: carry them on his shoulder. That's fifty years ago. Well, now: I can't wait for morning."

Morning. Frozen rime lusters the grass; the sun, round as an orange and orange as hot-weather moons, balances on the horizon, burnishes the silvered winter woods. A wild turkey calls. A renegade hog grunts in the undergrowth. Soon, by the edge of knee-deep, rapid-running water, we have to abandon the buggy. Queenie wades the stream first, paddles across barking complaints at the swiftness of the current, the pneumonia-making coldness of it. We follow, holding our shoes and equipment (a hatchet, a burlap sack) above our heads. A mile more: of chastising thorns, burs and briers that catch at our clothes; of rusty pine needles brilliant with gaudy fungus and molted feathers. Here, there, a flash, a flutter, an ecstasy of shrillings remind us that not all the birds have flown south. Always, the path unwinds through lemony sun pools and pitch vine tunnels. Another creek to cross: a disturbed armada of speckled trout froths the water round us, and frogs the size of plates practice belly flops; beaver workmen are building a dam. On the farther shore, Queenie shakes herself and trembles. My friend shivers, too: not with cold but enthusiasm. One of her hat's ragged roses sheds a petal as she lifts her head and inhales the pine-heavy air. "We're almost there; can you smell it, Buddy?" she says, as though we were approaching an ocean.

And, indeed, it is a kind of ocean. Scented acres of holiday trees, prickly-leafed holly. Red berries shiny as Chinese bells: black crows swoop upon them screaming. Having stuffed our burlap sacks with enough greenery and crimson to garland a dozen windows, we set about choosing a tree. "It should be," muses my friend, "twice as tall as a boy. So a boy can't steal the star." The one we pick is twice as tall as me. A brave handsome brute that survives thirty hatchet strokes before it keels with a creaking rending cry. Lugging it like a kill, we commence the long trek out. Every few yards we abandon the struggle, sit down and pant. But we have the strength of triumphant huntsmen; that and the tree's virile, icy perfume revive us, goad us on. Many compliments accompany our sunset return along the red clay road to town; but my friend is sly and noncommittal when passers-by praise the treasure perched in our buggy: what a fine tree and where did it come from? "Yonderways," she murmurs vaguely. Once a car stops and the rich mill owner's lazy wife leans out and whines: "Giveya two-bits cash for that ol tree." Ordinarily my friend is afraid of saying no; but on this occasion she promptly shakes her head: "We wouldn't take a dollar." The mill owner's wife persists. "A dollar, my foot! Fifty cents. That's my last offer. Goodness, woman, you can get another one." In answer, my friend gently reflects: "I doubt it. There's never two of anything."

Home: Queenie slumps by the fire and sleeps till tomorrow, snoring loud as a human.

A trunk in the attic contains: a shoebox of ermine tails (off the opera cape of a curious lady who once rented a room in the house), coils of frazzled tinsel gone gold with age, one silver star, a brief rope of dilapidated, undoubtedly dangerous candy-like light bulbs. Excellent decorations, as far as they go, which isn't far enough: my friend wants our tree to blaze "like a Baptist window," droop with weighty snows of ornament. But we can't afford the made-in-Japan splendors at the five-and-dime. So we do what we've always done: sit for days at the kitchen table with scissors and crayons and stacks of colored paper. I make sketches and my friend cuts them out: lots of cats, fish too (because they're easy to draw), some apples, some watermelons, a few winged angels devised from saved-up sheets of Hershey-bar tin foil. We use safety pins to attach these creations to the tree; as a final touch, we sprinkle the branches with shredded cotton (picked in August for this purpose). My friend, surveying the effect, clasps her hands together. "Now honest, Buddy. Doesn't it look good enough to eat?" Queenie tries to eat an angel.

After weaving and ribboning holly wreaths for all the front windows, out next project is the fashioning of family gifts. Tie-dye scarves for the ladies, for the men a home-brewed lemon and licorice and aspirin syrup to be taken "at the first Symptoms of a Cold and after Hunting." But when it comes time for making each other's gift, my friend and I separate to work secretly. I would like to buy her a pearl-handled knife, a radio, a whole pound of chocolate-covered cherries (we tasted some once, and she always swears: "I could live on them, Buddy, Lord yes I could—and that's not taking His name in vain"). Instead, I am building her a kite. She would like to give me a bicycle (she's said so on several million occasions: "If only I could, Buddy. It's bad enough in life to do without something *you* want; but confound it, what gets my goat is not being able to give somebody something you want *them* to have. Only one of these days I will, Buddy. Locate you a bike. Don't ask how. Steal it, maybe"). Instead, I'm fairly certain that she is building me a kite—the same as last year, and the year before: the year before that we exchanged slingshots. All of which is fine by me. For we are champion kite-fliers who study the wind like sailors; my friend, more accomplished than I, can get a kite aloft when there isn't enough breeze to carry clouds.

Christmas Eve afternoon we scrape together a nickel and go to the butcher's to buy Queenie's traditional gift, a good gnawable beef bone. The bone, wrapped in funny paper, is placed high in the tree near the silver star. Queenie knows it's there. She squats at the foot of the tree staring up in a trance of greed: when bedtime arrives she refuses to budge. Her excitement is equaled by my own. I kick the covers and turn my pillow as though it were a scorching summer's night. Somewhere a rooster crows: falsely, for the sun is still on the other side of the world.

"Buddy, are you awake?" It is my friend, calling from her room, which is next to mine; and an instant later she is sitting on my bed holding a candle. "Well, I can't sleep a hoot," she declares. "My mind's jumping like a jack rabbit. Buddy, do you think Mrs. Roosevelt will serve our cake at dinner?" We huddle in the bed, and she squeezes my hand I-love-you. "Seems like your hand used to be so much smaller. I guess I hate to see you grow up. When you're grown up, will we still be friends?" I say always. "But I feel so bad, Buddy. I wanted so bad to give you a bike. I tried to sell my cameo Papa gave me. Buddy—" she hesitates, as though embarrassed—"I made you another kite." Then I confess that I made her one, too; and we laugh. The candle burns too short to hold. Out it goes, exposing the starlight, the stars spinning at the window like a visible caroling that slowly, slowly daybreak silences. Possibly we doze; but the beginnings of dawn splash us like cold water: we're up, wide-eyed and wandering while we wait for others to waken. Quite deliberately my friend drops a kettle on the kitchen floor. I tap-dance in front of closed doors. One by one the household emerges, looking as though they'd like to kill us both; but it's Christmas, so they can't. First, a gorgeous breakfast: just everything you can imagine—from flapjacks and fried squirrel to hominy grits and honey-in-the-comb. Which puts everyone in a good humor except my friend and I. Frankly, we're so impatient to get at the presents we can't eat a mouthful.

Well, I'm disappointed. Who wouldn't be? With socks, a

Sunday school shirt, some handkerchiefs, a hand-me-down sweater and a year's subscription to a religious magazine for children. *The Little Shepherd*. It makes me boil. It really does.

My friend has a better haul. A sack of Satsumas, that's her best present. She is proudest, however, of a white wool shawl knitted by her married sister. But she *says* her favorite gift is the kite I built her. And it *is* very beautiful; though not as beautiful as the one she made me, which is blue and scattered with gold and green Good Conduct stars; moreover, my name is painted on it, "Buddy."

"Buddy, the wind is blowing."

The wind is blowing, and nothing will do till we've run to a pasture below the house where Queenie has scooted to bury her bone (and where, a winter hence, Queenie will be buried, too.) There, plunging through the healthy waist-high grass, we unreel our kites, feel them twitching at the string like sky fish as they swim into the wind. Satisfied, sun-warmed, we sprawl in the grass and peel Satsumas and watch our kites cavort. Soon I forget the socks and hand-me-down sweater. I'm as happy as if we'd already won the fifty-thousand-dollar Grand Prize in that coffee-naming contest.

"My, how foolish I am!" my friend cries, suddenly alert, like a woman remembering too late she has biscuits in the oven. "You know what I've always thought?" she asks in a tone of discovery, and not smiling at me but a point beyond. "I've always thought a body would have to be sick and dying before they saw the Lord. And I imagined that when He came it would be like looking at the Baptist window: pretty as colored glass with the sun pouring through, such a shine you don't know it's getting dark. And it's been a comfort: to think of that shine taking away all the spooky feeling. But I'll wager it never happens. I'll wager at the very end a body realizes the Lord has already shown Himself. That things as they are"—her hand circles in a gesture that gathers clouds and kites and grass and Queenie pawing earth over her bone—"just what they've always seen, was seeing Him. As for me, I could leave the world with today in my eyes."

This is our last Christmas together.

Life separates us. Those who Know Best decide that I belong in a military school. And so follows a miserable succession of bugle-blowing prisons, grim reveille-ridden summer camps. I have a new home too. But it doesn't count. Home is where my friend is, and there I never go.

And there she remains, puttering around the kitchen. Alone with Queenie. Then alone. ("Buddy dear," she writes in her wild hard-to-read script, "yesterday Jim Macy's horse kicked Queenie bad. Be thankful she didn't feel much. I wrapped her in a Fine Linen sheet and rode her in the buggy down to Simpson's pasture where she can be with all her Bones . . ."). For a few Novembers she continues to bake her fruitcakes single-handed; not as many, but some: and, of course, she always sends me "the best of the batch." Also, in every letter she encloses a dime wadded in toilet paper: "See a picture show and write me the story." But gradually in her letters she tends to confuse me with her other friend, the Buddy who died in the 1880's; more and more thirteenths are not the only days she stays in bed: a morning arrives in November, a leafless birdless coming of winter morning, when she cannot rouse herself to exclaim: "Oh my, it's fruitcake weather!"

And when that happens, I know it. A message saying so merely confirms a piece of news some secret vein had already received, severing from me an irreplaceable part of myself, letting it loose like a kite on a broken string. That is why, walking across a school campus on this particular December morning, I keep searching the sky. As if I expected to see, rather like hearts, a lost pair of kites hurrying toward heaven.

Alice Childress (October 12, 1920) was born in Charleston, South Carolina. At the age of five she was taken to New York and grew up in Harlem. She writes, "I never planned to become a writer. I had started a 'career' as an actress with the American Negro Theatre, went to Broadway with *Anna Lucasta*, was nominated for a Tony award. Radio and television work followed, but racism, a double blacklisting system, and a feeling at being somewhat alone in my ideas caused me to know I could more freely express myself as a writer."

In 1956 Childress published *Like One of the Family . . . Conversations from a Domestic Life*, short fiction which Childress first wrote for *Freedom*, a newspaper edited by Paul Robinson in the 1950s, and continued publishing with the *Baltimore Afro-American* in a column titled "Here's Mildred." Mildred is based on Childress's Aunt Lorraine, who worked as a domestic for many years and who unfailingly "refused to exchange dignity for pay."

In the sixties Childress concentrated on writing plays. *Wedding Band: A Love/Hate Story in Black and White*, dealing with the love affair of a black woman and a white man and set in South Carolina in 1918, was performed at the University of Michigan in December 1966 with a cast headed by Ruby Dee. In 1969, Childress completed *String*, an adaptation of Guy de Maupassant's story "A Piece of String." It was followed by *Wine in the Wilderness: A Comedy-Drama* (1969) and *Mojo: A Black Love Story* (1970). *A Hero Ain't Nothin' but a Sandwich* (1973), her first adolescent novel, received many awards and prizes. It was made into a film, for which Childress wrote the screenplay. *When the Rattlesnake Sounds* (1975) and *Let's Hear It for the Queen* (1976), two plays for children, followed. *A Short Walk* (1979), Childress's first adult novel, traced the life of her main character Cora from her birth in South Carolina to her death in New York.

NORTHERNERS CAN
BE SO SMUG

by Alice Childress

Girl, I tried to hold my peace, I tried to let things go by the board, I did my best to remember all the things you told me, but before the night was over, I just had to speak my mind! . . . Yes, it was a nice meetin' as meetin's go. Of course you know I don't consider a meetin' to be the last word as far as a good time is concerned. I go to them 'cause sometimes folks got to meet in order to straighten out things, and I feel that it's my beholden duty to be right there meetin' along with everybody else.

Marge, the church was crowded, and it would have done your heart good if you could of been there to see that fine turnout! . . . It's a good thing that you had a toothache 'cause I wouldn't of taken nothin' else for a excuse! . . . No, I don't mean that I'm glad your tooth is achin', and you know it! . . . Why do you always twist and turn every word I say. . . . I don't mean *every* word, I only mean *some* words! . . . Are you feelin' better now? . . . Well, that's good. Do you want me to tell you 'bout the meetin'? . . . All right, I'll begin at the beginnin'.

Honey, they raised some money this evenin'! This civil rights business has got folks so tore up 'til they're really ready to dig down in their pocketbooks and put some money where their mouth is! The whole idea of givin' the money is simply this: they're gonna send it down South to help out people who are catchin' a hard time 'cause they want to vote and ride the buses and things like that. . . . Yes, they had several speakers there and they spoke right well.

The minister introduced one white man who got up and

started his speech by sayin', "The South today is in a state . . ." and then he went on to tell us all about the state of things. After he finished a colored man got up and started his speech by sayin' "The South has *always* been in a state . . ." Then he went on to further tell us 'bout the state of things. Two or three more people spoke a little bit, and I'm here to tell you that they gave the South a *hard* way to go! Oh, it was the South this and the South that and by the time they got through, I don't think there was another bad word to say 'bout the South 'cause they had said 'em all!

When the question and answer time came, everybody started in on the South all over again and took it from slavery and traveled each day and year right back on up to nineteen hundred and fifty-six. I learned a lot, but it seemed to me that we was forgettin' that this land also has a North, East and West to it! Since I didn't think we should be so forgetful I got up to say my say.

When it came my turn, I said, "We have heard a great deal about the South tonight and rightly so, but I'm wonderin' if we got room to just low-rate the South in such a sweepin' manner. . . ." Marge, before I could go on with what I had to say, there was a little disturbance in the back of the auditorium, and one squeaky-voiced little man jumped up and said, "Yes, that's right, *before* we get on the South, let's take care of the North!"

. . . Now, he wasn't doin' a thing but tryin' to mislead the people, so I kept standin' and got him out of my way! "Never mind that *before* business," I says, "but let's take care of the North *while* we're gettin' on the South! To hear us talk, anybody would think the North was some kind of promiseland come true. All is not sweetness and light just 'cause we're on the North side of the Mason and Dixon line!

"But the main thing I want us to remember is that there's lots of *good* people down South!" Marge, they started to mumble then, and I could see that I wasn't gettin' too much agreement on the last thing that I had said. "Yes," I says, "*good* people. When we talk about slave days let's bear in mind that there was plenty of white folks who helped the slaves to escape, Southern folks. No, they didn't get the honor and the glory like the Abolitionists in the North 'cause they had to work quiet and secret and it was worth their lives if they got caught. I heard about them Southern ship captains who took slaves out of the South and hid them 'til they got to freeland, I heard about Southerners who bought slaves in order to bring them to the North and set them free, I heard of Southern homes where the poor 'run-away' found rest and food and hope. Believe me, when I say that it took nerve and courage to fight slavery right there in the teeth of it, so to speak! It wouldn't be right for us to forget those things 'cause even though there was more help comin' from the North, it was harder to get help in the South and for that reason it was worth its weight in gold!"

One woman sittin' behind me, whispered, "We don't want to make them Southerners sound like no angels now." And I said, "We got to give credit where credit is due at the same time that we're puttin' the blame to the South! Are we goin' to forget the judge in Carolina that spoke up for us, are we goin' to forget how he had to leave his home for sayin' what was on his mind? . . . Are we gonna forget the man in Kentucky who sold a colored family a home and got put in jail for it? Are we goin' to forget those youngsters in Alabama who signed a paper sayin' that they didn't want to have nothin' to do with mobs and that they were for the right of a colored student to go to their college? Are we gonna forget the folks who *refuse* to join up with klans and such? Are we gonna forget them Southerners who made trips to people's homes to warn them that bad white folks was comin' over to molest them? Oh, yes, there's been a lot of good Southerners who took a stand for the right even when the goin' was lonely-like and frightenin', when they got chased from their homes, when 'friends' wouldn't talk to them, when they got ugly telephone calls and letters. Oh, my, but it ain't easy to do right in the midst of all that killin', burnin' and mobbin' that's goin' on!"

One of the speakers interrupted me and said, "They ought to be doin' a whole lot more. After all, it's *their* laws that's makin' all the trouble!" "You are so right," I says, "and we oughta encourage 'em! We got to start showin' that we know how some of the folks are scared and pep-talk 'em a little bit! When we hear that there's a mob made up of hundreds of folks, we got to realize that the other thousands upon thousands was *not* out there with 'em and got to ask 'em how come they can't show some gumption and start doin' and speakin' against the mobs instead of sittin' home washin' their hands of it like Pontius Pilate. For too long they have been allowed to think that we don't expect any *good* to come from them, that we just fold our hands and say, "Oh, well, they're Southerners, so what can you expect?' We got to start sayin' to 'em, 'Speak up so's we can hear you, if everybody ain't for oppressin', then let those that's against it stand up and be counted! We got to include 'em in the *stand!* We got to write some of their churches and clubs and things and ask 'em, 'Where are you and what are you goin' to do?' When we get their answers, we'll have it down in black and white for the whole world to see! And I bet we'll rack up a few more friends down that way!"

The lady behind me says to me, "Honey, they should speak if they feel right! Looks like we'd be goin' out of our way to be askin' 'em about it."

"Yes," I says, "we would, but it's goin' to take some out-of-the-way things to change them Southern laws! After all, we sure hear plenty from the folks who don't want the law to change and from the Northerners who're willin' to go part-way with the civil rights but hang back some when it comes to *livin'* the thing right down the line!"

Marge, I got solid agreement on that 'cause folks know that even though our laws are much better than down home, we still got to put up such a to-do to get what the law promises. Didn't they try to keep the man out of the housin' project out in Chicago, didn't *they* have mobs gatherin'? How 'bout folks tarrin' the colored woman's home out in *Long Island?* Mobs and meanness can happen in any part of the land but them *laws* in the South just make it easier for it to go on!

Sure, I told them all those things and they had to listen to me, too, 'cause while we're settlin' the trouble down South, we got to remember that we want *all our rights, everywhere* and this is no time for Northerners to get so smug. . . . You're right, girl! All the colored folk that's standin' up and talkin' out in Mississippi, Alabama, Kentucky, Carolina and all over the South, ain't they *Southerners*, too! Yes, indeed, we got to send the message East, West, *North*, and *South*. . . . It's high time that the land should be free, from one corner to the other!

Elizabeth Spencer (July 19, 1921) was born in Carrollton, Mississippi, to a family that had lived in Carroll County since the 1830s. In 1942 she received a B.A. in English from Belhaven College in Jackson, Mississippi. Upon graduation, she attended Vanderbilt University where she received an M.A. degree. Spencer later taught at Northwest Mississippi Junior College (Senatobia), at Belmont College (Nashville, Tennessee), and at University of Mississippi (Oxford). While teaching at the University of Mississippi in 1948 she published her first novel, *Fire in the Morning*. Since 1953 she has worked full time as a writer and teacher and her publications include eight novels and more than forty short stories.

In addition to *Fire in the Morning*, Spencer's books include *This Crooked Way* (1952), *The Voice at the Back Door* (1956), *The Light in the Piazza* (1960), *Knights and Dragons* (1965), *No Place for an Angel* (1967), *Ship Island and Other Stories* (1968), *The Snare* (1972), *The Stories of Elizabeth Spencer*(1981), *Marilee* (1981), *The Salt Line* (1984), and *Jack of Diamond* (1988). Her short stories—which have appeared regularly for four decades in such magazines *The New Yorker, Atlantic, Southern Review,* and *McCall's*—have received many awards including *O Henry Prize Stories* and *The Pushcart Prize: Best of the Small Presses*.

Since the late 1950s Spencer's fiction has increasingly reflected the international settings she has come to know from living in Italy and Canada. Yet, Spencer continues to be inspired by the South. She writes: "Mississippi gave me a wonderful crosscurrent to writing—when I was growing up the old had been set in its ways since the Civil War, but the new was making itself felt. Writers respond especially to this sort of tension. Then, too, there was such a wide variety of individuals, so many wildly different characters, everyone with his or her own story, all to be met with daily. The challenge was not where to find material but how best to use it in a modern fiction which would engage intelligence and feeling. All my early books came out of Mississippi and many still do; memory keeps so many things, and rather than lose them, it may even make them richer."

Spencer lived for many years in Montreal, but now lives in Chapel Hill, where she teaches at the University of North Carolina.

FIRST DARK

by *Elizabeth Spencer*

When Tom Beavers started coming back to Richton, Mississippi, on weekends, after the war was over, everybody in town was surprised and pleased. They had never noticed him much before he paid them this compliment; now they could not say enough nice things. There was not much left in Richton for him to call family—just his aunt who had raised him, Miss Rita Beavers, old as God, ugly as sin, deaf as a post. So he must be fond of the town, they reasoned; certainly it was a pretty old place. Far too many young men had left it and never come back at all.

He would drive in every Friday night from Jackson, where he worked. All weekend, his Ford, dusty of flank, like a hard-ridden horse, would sit parked down the hill near Miss Rita's old wire front gate, which sagged from the top hinge and had worn a span in the ground. On Saturday morning, he would head for the drugstore, then the post office; then he would be observed walking here and there around the streets under the shade trees. It was as though he were looking for something.

He wore steel taps on his heels, and in the still the click of them on the sidewalks would sound across the big front lawns and all the way up to the porches of the houses, where two ladies might be sitting behind a row of ferns. They would identify him to one another, murmuring in their fine little voices, and say it was just too bad there was nothing here for young people. It was just a shame they didn't have one or two more old houses, here, for a Pilgrimage—look how Natchez had waked up.

One Saturday morning in early October, Tom Beavers sat at the counter in the drugstore and reminded Totsie Poteet, the drugstore clerk, of a ghost story. Did he remember the strange old man who used to appear to people who were coming into Richton along the Jackson road at twilight— what they called "first dark"?

"Sure I remember," said Totsie. "Old Cud'n Jimmy Wiltshire used to tell us about him every time we went 'possum hunting. I could see him plain as I can see you, the way he used to tell it. Tall, with a top hat on, yeah, and waiting in the weeds alongside the road ditch, so'n you couldn't tell if he wasn't taller than any mortal man could be, because you couldn't tell if he was standing down in the ditch or not. It would look like he just grew up out of the weeds. Then he'd signal to you."

"Them that stopped never saw anybody," said Tom Beavers, stirring his coffee. "There were lots of folks besides Mr. Jimmy that saw him."

"There was, let me see . . ." Totsie enumerated others— some men, some women, some known to drink, others who never touched a drop. There was no way to explain it. "There was that story the road gang told. Do you remember, or were you off at school? It was while they were straightening the road out to the highway—taking the curves out and building a new bridge. Anyway, they said that one night at quitting time, along in the winter and just about dark, this old guy signaled to some of 'em. They said they went over and he asked them to move a bulldozer they had left across the road, because he had a wagon back behind on a little dirt road, with a sick nigger girl in it. Had to get to the doctor and this was the only way. They claimed they knew didn't nobody live back there on that little old road, but niggers can come from anywhere. So they moved the bulldozer and cleared back a whole lot of other stuff, and waited and waited. Not only didn't no wagon ever come, but the man that had stopped them, he was gone, too. They was right shook up over it. You never heard that one?"

"No, I never did." Tom Beavers said this with his eyes looking up over his coffee cup, as though he sat behind a hand of cards. His lashes and brows were heavier than was ordinary, and worked as a veil might, to keep you away from knowing exactly what he was thinking.

"They said he was tall and had a hat on." The screen door flapped to announce a customer, but Totsie kept on talking. "But whether he was a white man or a real light-colored nigger they couldn't say. Some said one and some said another. I figured they'd been pulling on the jug a little earlier than usual. You know why? I never heard of *our* ghost *saying* nothing. Did you, Tom?"

He moved away on the last words, the way a clerk will, talking back over his shoulder and ahead of him to his new customer at the same time, as though he had two voices and two heads. "And what'll it be today, Miss Frances?"

The young woman standing at the counter had a prescription already out of her bag. She stood with it poised between her fingers, but her attention was drawn toward Tom Beavers, his coffee cup, and the conversation she had interrupted. She was a girl whom no ordinary description would fit. One would have to know first of all who she was: Frances Harvey. After that, it was all right for her to be a little odd-looking, with her reddish hair that curled back from her brow, her light eyes, and her high, pale temples. This is not the material for being pretty, but in Frances Harvey it was what could sometimes be beauty. Her family home was laden with history that nobody but the Harveys could remember. It would have been on a Pilgrimage if Richton had had one. Frances still lived in it, looking after an invalid mother.

"What were you-all talking about?" she wanted to know.

"About that ghost they used to tell about," said Totsie, holding out his hand for the prescription. "The one people used to see just outside of town, on the Jackson road."

"But why?" she demanded. "Why were you talking about him?"

"Tom, here—" the clerk began, but Tom Beavers interrupted him.

"I was asking because I was curious," he said. He had been studying her from the corner of his eye. Her face was beginning to show the wear of her mother's long illness, but that couldn't be called change. Changing was something she didn't seem to have done, her own style being the only one natural to her.

"I was asking," he went on, "because I saw him." He

turned away from her somewhat too direct gaze and said to Totsie Poteet, whose mouth had fallen open, "It was where the new road runs close to the old road, and as far as I could tell he was right on the part of the old road where people always used to see him."

"But when?" Frances Harvey demanded.

"Last night," he told her. "Just around first dark. Driving home."

A wealth of quick feeling came up in her face. "So did I! Driving home from Jackson! I saw him, too!"

For some people, a liking for the same phonograph record or for Mayan archaeology is enough of an excuse to get together. Possibly, seeing the same ghost was no more than that. Anyway, a week later, on Saturday at first dark, Frances Harvey and Tom Beavers were sitting together in a car parked just off the highway, near the spot where they agreed the ghost had appeared. The season was that long, peculiar one between summer and fall, and there were so many crickets and tree frogs going full tilt in their periphery that their voices could hardly be distinguished from the background noises, though they both would have heard a single footfall in the grass. An edge of autumn was in the air at night, and Frances had put on a tweed jacket at the last minute, so the smell of moth balls was in the car, brisk and most unghostlike.

But Tom Beavers was not going to forget the value of the ghost, whether it put in an appearance or not. His questions led Frances into reminiscence.

"No, I never saw him before the other night," she admitted. "The Negroes used to talk in the kitchen, and Regina and I—you know my sister Regina—would sit there listening, scared to go and scared to stay. Then finally going to bed upstairs was no relief, either, because sometimes Aunt Henrietta was visiting us, and *she'd* seen it. Or if she wasn't visiting us, the front room next to us, where she stayed, would be empty, which was worse. There was no way to lock ourselves in, and besides, what was there to lock out? We'd lie all night like two sticks in bed, and shiver. Papa finally had to take a hand. He called us in and sat us down and said that the whole thing was easy to explain—it was all automobiles. What their headlights did with the dust and shadows out on the Jackson road. 'Oh, but Sammie and

Jerry!' we said, with great big eyes, sitting side by side on the sofa, with our tennis shoes flat on the floor.''

"Who were Sammie and Jerry?" asked Tom Beavers.

"Sammie was our cook. Jerry was her son, or husband, or something. Anyway, they certainly didn't have cars. Papa called them in. They were standing side by side by the bookcase, and Regina and I were on the sofa—four pairs of big eyes, and Papa pointing his finger. Papa said, 'Now, you made up these stories about ghosts, didn't you?' 'Yes, sir,' said Sammie. 'We made them up.' 'Yes, sir,' said Jerry. 'We sho did.' 'Well, then, you can just stop it,' Papa said. 'See how peaked these children look?' Sammie and Jerry were terribly polite to us for a week, and we got in the car and rode up and down the Jackson road at first dark to see if the headlights really did it. But we never saw anything. We didn't tell Papa, but headlights had nothing whatever to do with it.''

"You had your own *car* then?" He couldn't believe it.

"Oh, no!" She was emphatic. "We were too young for that. Too young to drive, really, but we did anyway.''

She leaned over to let him give her cigarette a light, and saw his hand tremble. Was he afraid of the ghost or of her? She would have to stay away from talking family.

Frances remembered Tommy Beavers from her childhood —a small boy going home from school down a muddy side road alone, walking right down the middle of the road. His old aunt's house was at the bottom of a hill. It was damp there, and the yard was always muddy, with big fat chicken tracks all over it, like Egyptian writing. How did Frances know? She could not remember going there, ever. Miss Rita Beavers was said to order cold ham, mustard, bread, and condensed milk from the grocery store. "I doubt if that child ever has anything hot," Frances's mother had said once. He was always neatly dressed in the same knee pants, high socks, and checked shirt, and sat several rows ahead of Frances in study hall, right in the middle of his seat. He was three grades behind her; in those days, that much younger seemed very young indeed. What had happened to his parents? There was some story, but it was not terribly interesting, and, his people being of no importance, she had forgotten.

"I think it's past time for our ghost," she said. "He's never out so late at night.''

"He gets hungry, like me," said Tom Beavers. "Are you hungry, Frances?"

They agreed on a highway restaurant where an orchestra played on weekends. Everyone went there now.

From the moment they drew up on the graveled entrance, cheerful lights and a blare of music chased the spooks from their heads. Tom Beavers ordered well and danced well, as it turned out. Wasn't there something she had heard about his being "smart"? By "smart," Southerners mean intellectual, and they say it in an almost condescending way, smart being what you are when you can't be anything else, but it is better, at least, than being nothing. Frances Harvey had been away enough not to look at things from a completely Southern point of view, and she was encouraged to discover that she and Tom had other things in common besides a ghost, though all stemming, perhaps, from the imagination it took to see one.

They agreed about books and favorite movies and longing to see more plays. She sighed that life in Richton was so confining, but he assured her that Jackson could be just as bad; *it* was getting to be like any Middle Western city, he said, while Richton at least had a sense of the past. This was the main reason, he went on, gaining confidence in the jumble of commonplace noises—dishes, music, and a couple of drinkers chattering behind them—that he had started coming back to Richton so often. He wanted to keep a connection with the past. He lived in a modern apartment, worked in a soundproof office—he could be in any city. But Richton was where he had been born and raised, and nothing could be more old-fashioned. Too many people seemed to have their lives cut in two. He was earnest in desiring that this should not happen to him.

"You'd better be careful," Frances said lightly. Her mood did not incline her to profound conversation. "There's more than one ghost in Richton: You may turn into one yourself, like the rest of us."

"It's the last thing I'd think of you," he was quick to assure her.

Had Tommy Beavers really said such a thing, in such a natural, charming way? Was Frances Harvey really so pleased? Not only was she pleased but, feeling warmly alive amid the music and small lights, she agreed with him. She could not have agreed with him more.

* * *

"I hear that Thomas Beavers has gotten to be a very attractive man," Frances Harvey's mother said unexpectedly one afternoon.

Frances had been reading aloud—Jane Austen this time. Theirs was one house where the leather-bound sets were actually read. In Jane Austen, men and women seesawed back and forth for two or three hundred pages until they struck a point of balance; then they got married. She had just put aside the book, at the end of a chapter, and risen to lower the shade against the slant of afternoon sun. "Or so Cud'n Jennie and Mrs. Giles Antley and Miss Fannie Stapleton have been coming and telling you," she said.

"People talk, of course, but the consensus is favorable," Mrs. Harvey said. "Wonders never cease; his mother ran away with a brush salesman. But nobody can make out what he's up to, coming back to Richton."

"Does he have to be 'up to' anything?" Frances asked.

"Men are always up to something," said the old lady at once. She added, more slowly, "In Thomas's case, maybe it isn't anything it oughtn't to be. They say he reads a lot. He may just have taken up with some sort of idea."

Frances stole a long glance at her mother's face on the pillow. Age and illness had reduced the image of Mrs. Harvey to a kind of caricature, centered on a mouth that Frances could not help comparing to that of a fish. There was a tension around its rim, as though it were outlined in bone, and the underlip even stuck out a little. The mouth ate, it took medicine, it asked for things, it gasped when breath was short, it commented. But when it commented, it ceased to be just a mouth and became part of Mrs. Harvey, that witty tyrant with the infallible memory for the right detail, who was at her terrible best about men.

"And what could he be thinking of?" she was wont to inquire when some man had acted foolishly. No one could ever defend accurately the man in question, and the only conclusion was Mrs. Harvey's; namely, that he wasn't thinking, if, indeed, he could. Although she had never been a belle, never a flirt, her popularity with men was always formidable. She would be observed talking marathons with one in a corner, and could you ever be sure, when they both burst into laughter, that they had not just exchanged the most shocking stories? "Of course, *he*—" she would begin later, back with the family, and the masculinity that had just been encouraged to strut and preen a little was quickly shown up as idiotic. Perhaps Mrs. Harvey hoped by this method to train her daughters away from a lot of sentimental nonsense that was their birthright as pretty Southern girls in a house with a lawn that moonlight fell on and that was often lit also by Japanese lanterns hung for parties. "Oh, he's not like that, Mama!" the little girls would cry. They were already alert for heroes who would ride up and cart them off. "Well, then, you watch," she would say. Sure enough, if you watched, she would be right.

Mrs. Harvey's younger daughter, Regina, was a credit to her mother's long campaign; she married well. The old lady, however, never tired of pointing out behind her son-in-law's back that his fondness for money was ill-concealed, that he had the longest feet she'd ever seen, and that he sometimes made grammatical errors.

Her elder daughter, Frances, on a trip to Europe, fell in love, alas! The gentlemen was of French extraction but Swiss citizenship, and Frances did not marry him, because he was already married—that much filtered back to Richton. In response to a cable, she had returned home one hot July in time to witness her father's wasted face and last weeks of life. That same September, the war began. When peace came, Richton wanted to know if Frances Harvey would go back to Europe. Certain subtly complicated European matters, little understood in Richton, seemed to be obstructing Romance; one of them was probably named Money. Meanwhile, Frances's mother took to bed, in what was generally known to be her last illness.

So no one crossed the ocean, but eventually Tom Beavers came up to Mrs. Harvey's room one afternoon, to tea.

Though almost all her other faculties were seriously impaired, in ear and tongue Mrs. Harvey was as sound as a young beagle, and she could still weave a more interesting conversation than most people who go about every day and look at the world. She was of the old school of Southern lady talkers; she vexed you with no ideas, she tried to protect you from even a moment of silence. In the old days, when a bright company filled the downstairs rooms, she could keep the ball rolling amongst a crowd. Everyone—all the men especially—got their word in, but the flow of things came back to her. If one of those twenty-minutes-to-or-after silences fell—and even with her they did occur—people would turn and look at her daughter Frances. "And what do you think?" some kind-eyed gentleman would ask. Frances did not credit that she had the sort of face people would turn to, and so did not know how to take advantage of it. What did she think? Well, to answer that honestly took a moment of reflection—a fatal moment, it always turned out. Her mother would be up instructing the maid, offering someone an ashtray or another goody, or remarking outright, "Frances is so timid. She never says a word."

Tom Beavers stayed not only past teatime that day but for a drink as well. Mrs. Harvey was induced to take a glass of sherry, and now her bed became her enormous throne. Her keenest suffering as an invalid was occasioned by the absence of men. "What is a house without a man in it?" she would often cry. From her eagerness to be charming to Frances's guest that afternoon, it seemed that she would have married Tom Beavers herself if he had asked her. The amber liquid set in her small four-sided glass glowed like a jewel, and her diamond flashed; she had put on her best ring for the company. What a pity no longer to show her ankle, that delicious bone, so remarkably slender for so ample a frame.

Since the time had flown so, they all agreed enthusiastically that Tom should wait downstairs while Frances got ready to go out to dinner with him. He was hardly past the stair landing before the old lady was seized by such a fit of coughing that she could hardly speak. "It's been—it's been too much—too *much* for me!" she gasped out.

But after Frances had found the proper sedative for her, she was calmed, and insisted on having her say.

"Thomas Beavers has a good job with an insurance company in Jackson," she informed her daughter, as though Frances were incapable of finding out anything for herself. "He makes a good appearance. He is the kind of man" —she paused—"who would value a wife of good family." She stopped, panting for breath. It was this complimenting a man behind his back that was too much for her—as much out of character, and hence as much of a strain, as if she had got out of bed and tried to tap-dance.

"Heavens, Mama," Frances said, and almost giggled.

At this, the old lady, thinking the girl had made light of her suitor, half screamed at her, "Don't be so critical,

Frances! You can't be so critical of men!" and fell into an even more terrible spasm of coughing. Frances had to lift her from the pillow and hold her straight until the fit passed and her breath returned. Then Mrs. Harvey's old, dry, crooked, ineradicably feminine hand was laid on her daughter's arm, and when she spoke again she shook the arm to emphasize her words.

"When your father knew he didn't have long to live," she whispered, "we discussed whether to send for you or not. You know you were his favorite, Frances. 'Suppose our girl is happy over there,' he said. 'I wouldn't want to bring her back on my account.' I said you had to have the right to choose whether to come back or not. You'd never forgive us, I said, if you didn't have the right to choose."

Frances could visualize this very conversation taking place between her parents; she could see them, decorous and serious, talking over the fact of his approaching death as though it were a piece of property for agreeable disposition in the family. She could never remember him without thinking, with a smile, how he used to come home on Sunday from church (he being the only one of them who went) and how, immediately after hanging his hat and cane in the hall, he would say, "Let all things proceed in orderly progression to their final confusion. How long before dinner?" No, she had had to come home. Some humor had always existed between them—her father and her—and humor, of all things, cannot be betrayed.

"I meant to go back," said Frances now. "But there was the war. At first I kept waiting for it to be over. I still wake up at night sometimes thinking, I wonder how much longer before the war will be over. And then—" She stopped short. For the fact was that her lover had been married to somebody else, and her mother was the very person capable of pointing that out to her. Even in the old lady's present silence she heard the unspoken thought, and got up nervously from the bed, loosing herself from the hand on her arm, smoothing her reddish hair where it was inclined to straggle. "And then he wrote me that he had gone back to his wife. Her family and his had always been close, and the war brought them back together. This was in Switzerland— naturally, he couldn't stay on in Paris during the war. There were the children, too—all of them were Catholic. Oh, I do understand how it happened."

Mrs. Harvey turned her head impatiently on the pillow. She dabbed at her moist upper lip with a crumpled linen handkerchief; her diamond flashed once in motion. "War, religion, wife, children—yes. But men do what they want to."

Could anyone make Frances as angry as her mother could? "Believe what you like then! You always know so much better than I do. *You* would have managed things somehow. Oh, you would have had your way!"

"Frances," said Mrs. Harvey, "I'm an old woman." The hand holding the handkerchief fell wearily, and her eyelids dropped shut. "If you should want to marry Thomas Beavers and bring him here, I will accept it. There will be no distinctions. Next, I suppose, we will be having his old deaf aunt for tea. I hope she has a hearing aid. I haven't got the strength to holler at her."

"I don't think any of these plans are necessary, Mama."

The eyelids slowly lifted. "None?"

"None."

Mrs. Harvey's breathing was as audible as a voice. She spoke, at last, without scorn, honestly. "I cannot bear the thought of leaving you alone. You, nor the house, nor your place in it—alone. I foresaw Tom Beavers here! What has he got that's better than you and this place? I knew he would come!"

Terrible as her mother's meanness was, it was not half so terrible as her love. Answering nothing, explaining nothing, Frances stood without giving in. She trembled, and tears ran down her cheeks. The two women looked at each other helplessly across the darkening room.

In the car, later that night, Tom Beavers asked, "Is your mother trying to get rid of me?" They had passed an unsatisfactory evening, and he was not going away without knowing why.

"No, it's just the other way around," said Frances, in her candid way. "She wants you so much she'd like to eat you up. She wants you in the house. Couldn't you tell?"

"She once chased me out of the yard," he recalled.

"Not really!"

They turned into Harvey Street (that was actually the name of it), and when he had drawn the car up before the dark front steps, he related the incident. He told her that

Mrs. Harvey had been standing just there in the yard, talking to some visitor who was leaving by inches, the way ladies used to—ten minutes' more talk for every forward step. He, a boy not more than nine, had been crossing a corner of the lawn where a faint path had already been worn; he had had nothing to do with wearing the path and had taken it quite innocently and openly. "You, boy!" Mrs. Harvey's fan was an enormous painted thing. She had furled it with a clack so loud he could still hear it. "You don't cut through my yard again! Now, you stop where you are and you go all the way back around by the walk, and don't you ever do that again." He went back and all the way around. She was fanning comfortably as he passed. "Old Miss Rita Beavers' nephew," he heard her say, and though he did not speak of it now to Frances, Mrs. Harvey's rich tone had been as stuffed with wickedness as a fruitcake with goodies. In it you could have found so many things: that, of course, he didn't know any better, that he was poor, that she knew his first name but would not deign to mention it, that she meant him to understand all this and more. Her fan was probably still somewhere in the house, he reflected. If he ever opened the wrong door, it might fall from above and brain him. It seemed impossible that nowadays he could even have the chance to open the wrong door in the Harvey house. With its graceful rooms and big lawn, its camellias and magnolia trees, the house had been one of the enchanted castles of his childhood, and Frances and Regina Harvey had been two princesses running about the lawn one Saturday morning drying their hair with big white towels and not noticing when he passed.

There was a strong wind that evening. On the way home, Frances and Tom had noticed how the night was streaming, but whether with mist or dust or the smoke from some far-off fire in the dry winter woods they could not tell. As they stood on the sidewalk, the clouds raced over them, and moonlight now and again came through. A limb rubbed against a high cornice. Inside the screened area of the porch, the swing jangled in its iron chains. Frances's coat blew about her, and her hair blew. She felt herself to be no different from anything there that the wind was blowing on, her happiness of no relevance in the dark torrent of nature.

"I can't leave her, Tom. But I can't ask you to live with her, either. Of all the horrible ideas! She'd make demands, take all my time, laugh at you behind your back—she has to run everything. You'd hate me in a week."

He did not try to pretty up the picture, because he had a feeling that it was all too accurate. Now, obviously, was the time she should go on to say there was no good his waiting around through the years for her. But hearts are not noted for practicality, and Frances stood with her hair blowing, her hands stuck in her coat pockets, and did not go on to say anything. Tom pulled her close to him—in, as it were, out of the wind.

"I'll be coming by next weekend, just like I've been doing. And the next one, too," he said. "We'll just leave it that way, if it's O.K. with you."

"Oh yes, it is, Tom!" Never so satisfied to be weak, she kissed him and ran inside.

He stood watching on the walk until her light flashed on. Well, he had got what he was looking for; a connection with the past, he had said. It was right upstairs, a splendid old mass of dictatorial female flesh, thinking about him. Well, they could go on, he and Frances, sitting on either side of a sickbed, drinking tea and sipping sherry with streaks of gray broadening on their brows, while the familiar seasons came and went. So he thought. Like Frances, he believed that the old lady had a stranglehold on life.

Suddenly, in March, Mrs. Harvey died.

A heavy spring funeral, with lots of roses and other scented flowers in the house, is the worst kind of all. There is something so recklessly fecund about a south Mississippi spring that death becomes just another word in the dictionary, along with swarms of others, and even so pure and white a thing as a gardenia has too heavy a scent and may suggest decay. Mrs. Harvey, amid such odors, sank to rest with a determined pomp, surrounded by admiring eyes.

While Tom Beavers did not "sit with the family" at this time, he was often observed with the Harveys, and there was whispered speculation among those who were at the church and the cemetery that the Harvey house might soon come into new hands, "after a decent interval." No one would undertake to judge for a Harvey how long an interval was decent.

Frances suffered from insomnia in the weeks that followed, and at night she wandered about the spring-swollen

air of the old house, smelling now spring and now death.
"Let all things proceed in orderly progression to their final
confusion." She had always thought that the final confusion
referred to death, but now she began to think that it could
happen any time; that final confusion, having found the
door ajar, could come into a house and show no inclination
to leave. The worrisome thing, the thing it all came back to,
was her mother's clothes. They were numerous, expensive,
and famous, and Mrs. Harvey had never discarded any of
them. If you opened a closet door, hatboxes as big as crates
towered above your head. The shiny black trim of a great
shawl stuck out of a wardrobe door just below the lock.
Beneath the lid of a cedar chest, the bright eyes of a tippet
were ready to twinkle at you. And the jewels! Frances's
sister had restrained her from burying them all on their
mother, and had even gone off with a wad of them tangled
up like fishing tackle in an envelope, on the ground of
promises made now and again in the course of the years.

("Regina," said Frances, "what else were you two talking
about besides jewelry?" "I don't remember," said Regina,
getting mad.

"Frances makes me so mad," said Regina to her husband
as they were driving home. "I guess I can love Mama and
jewelry, too. Mama certainly loved *us* and jewelry, too.")

One afternoon, Frances went out to the cemetery to take
two wreaths sent by somebody who had "just heard." She
drove out along the winding cemetery road, stopping the car
a good distance before she reached the gate, in order to
walk through the woods. The dogwood was beautiful that
year. She saw a field where a house used to stand but had
burned down; its cedar trees remained, and two bushes of
bridal wreath marked where the front gate had swung. She
stopped to admire the clusters of white bloom massing up
through the young, feathery leaf and stronger now than the
leaf itself. In the woods, the redbud was a smoke along
shadowy ridges, and the dogwood drifted in layers, like
snow suspended to give you all the time you needed to
wonder at it. But why, she wondered, do they call it bridal
wreath? It's not a wreath but a little bouquet. Wreaths are
for funerals, anyway. As if to prove it, she looked down at
the two she held, one in each hand. She walked on, and
such complete desolation came over her that it was more of

a wonder than anything in the woods—more, even, than death.

As she returned to the car from the two parallel graves, she met a thin, elderly, very light-skinned Negro man in the road. He inquired if she would mind moving her car so that he could pass. He said that there was a sick colored girl in his wagon, whom he was driving in to the doctor. He pointed out politely that she had left her car right in the middle of the road. "Oh, I'm terribly sorry," said Frances, and hurried off toward the car.

That night, reading late in bed, she thought, I could have given her a ride into town. No wonder they talk about us up North. A mile into town in a wagon! She might have been having a baby. She became conscience-stricken about it—foolishly so, she realized, but if you start worrying about something in a house like the one Frances Harvey lived in, in the dead of night, alone, you will go on worrying about it until dawn. She was out of sleeping pills.

She remembered having bought a fresh box of sedatives for her mother the day before she died. She got up and went into her mother's closed room, where the bed had been dismantled for airing, its wooden parts propped along the walls. On the closet shelf she found the shoe box into which she had packed away the familiar articles of the bedside table. Inside she found the small enameled-cardboard box, with the date and prescription inked on the cover in Totsie Poteet's somewhat prissy handwriting, but the box was empty. She was surprised, for she realized that her mother could have used only one or two of the pills. Frances was so determined to get some sleep that she searched the entire little store of things in the shoe box quite heartlessly, but there were no pills. She returned to her room and tried to read, but could not, and so smoked instead and stared out at the dawn-blackening sky. The house sighed. She could not take her mind off the Negro girl. If she died . . . When it was light, she dressed and got into the car.

In town, the postman was unlocking the post office to sort the early mail. "I declare," he said to the rural mail carrier who arrived a few minutes later, "Miss Frances Harvey is driving herself crazy. Going back out yonder to the cemetery, and it not seven o'clock in the morning."

"Aw," said the rural deliveryman skeptically, looking at the empty road.

"That's right. I was here and seen her. You wait there, you'll see her come back. She'll drive herself nuts. Them old maids like that, left in them old houses—crazy and sweet, or crazy and mean, or just plain crazy. They just ain't locked up like them that's down in the asylum. That's the only difference."

"Miss Frances Harvey ain't no more than thirty-two, -three years old."

"Then she's just got more time to get crazier in. You'll see."

That day was Friday, and Tom Beavers, back from Jackson, came up Frances Harvey's sidewalk, as usual, at exactly a quarter past seven in the evening. Frances was not "going out" yet, and Regina had telephoned her long distance to say that "in all probability" she should not be receiving gentlemen "in." "What would Mama say?" Regina asked. Frances said she didn't know, which was not true, and went right on cooking dinners for Tom every weekend.

In the dining room that night, she sat across one corner of the long table from Tom. The useless length of polished cherry stretched away from them into the shadows as sadly as a road. Her plate pushed back, her chin resting on one palm, Frances stirred her coffee and said, "I don't know what on earth to do with all of Mama's clothes. I can't give them away, I can't sell them, I can't burn them, and the attic is full already. What can I do?"

"You look better tonight," said Tom.

"I slept," said Frances. "I slept and slept. From early this morning until just 'while ago. I never slept so well."

Then she told him about the Negro near the cemetery the previous afternoon, and how she had driven back out there as soon as dawn came, and found him again. He had been walking across the open field near the remains of the house that had burned down. There was no path to him from her, and she had hurried across ground uneven from old plowing and covered with the kind of small, tender grass it takes a very skillful mule to crop. "Wait!" she had cried. "Please wait!" The Negro had stopped and waited for her to reach him. "Your daughter?" she asked, out of breath.

"Daughter?" he repeated.

"The colored girl that was in the wagon yesterday. She was sick, you said, so I wondered. I could have taken her to town in the car, but I just didn't think. I wanted to know, how is she? Is she very sick?"

He had removed his old felt nigger hat as she approached him. "She a whole lot better, Miss Frances. She going to be all right now." Then he smiled at her. He did not say thank you, or anything more. Frances turned and walked back to the road and the car. And exactly as though the recovery of the Negro girl in the wagon had been her own recovery, she felt the return of a quiet breath and a steady pulse, and sensed the blessed stirring of a morning breeze. Up in her room, she had barely time to draw an old quilt over her before she fell asleep.

"When I woke, I knew about Mama," she said now to Tom. By the deepened intensity of her voice and eyes, it was plain that this was the important part. "It isn't right to say I *knew*," she went on, "because I had known all the time—ever since last night. I just realized it, that's all. I realized she had killed herself. It had to be that."

He listened soberly through the story about the box of sedatives. "But why?" he asked her. "It maybe looks that way, but what would be her reason for doing it?"

"Well, you see—" Frances said, and stopped.

Tom Beavers talked quietly on. "She didn't suffer. With what she had, she could have lived five, ten, who knows how many years. She was well cared for. Not hard up, I wouldn't say. Why?"

The pressure of his questioning could be insistent, and her trust in him, even if he was nobody but old Miss Rita Beavers' nephew, was well-nigh complete. "Because of you and me," she said, finally. "I'm certain of it, Tom. She didn't want to stand in our way. She never knew how to express love, you see." Frances controlled herself with an effort.

He did not reply, but sat industriously balancing a match folder on the tines of an unused serving fork. Anyone who has passed a lonely childhood in the company of an old deaf aunt is not inclined to doubt things hastily, and Tom Beavers would not have said he disbelieved anything Frances had told him. In fact, it seemed only too real to him. Almost before his eyes, that imperial, practical old hand went fumbling for the pills in the dark. But there had been much more to it than just love, he reflected. Bitterness, too, and pride, and control. And humor, perhaps, and the memory of a frightened little boy chased out of the yard by a twitch of her fan. Being invited to tea was one thing; suicide was quite another. Times had certainly changed, he thought.

But, of course, he could not say that he believed it, either. There was only Frances to go by. The match folder came to balance and rested on the tines. He glanced up at her, and a chill walked up his spine, for she was too serene. Cheek on palm, a lock of reddish hair fallen forward, she was staring at nothing with the absorbed silence of a child, or of a sweet, silver-haired old lady engaged in memory. Soon he might find that more and more of her was vanishing beneath this placid surface.

He himself did not know what he had seen that Friday evening so many months ago—what the figure had been that stood forward from the roadside at the tilt of the curve and urgently waved an arm to him. By the time he had braked and backed, the man had disappeared. Maybe it had been somebody drunk (for Richton had plenty of those to offer), walking it off in the cool of the woods at first dark. No such doubts had occurred to Frances. And what if he told her now the story Totsie had related of the road gang and the sick Negro girl in the wagon? Another labyrinth would open before her; she would never get out.

In Richton, the door to the past was always wide open, and what came in through it and went out of it had made people "different." But it scarcely ever happens, even in Richton, that one is able to see the precise moment when fact becomes faith, when life turns into legend, and people start to bend their finest loyalties to make themselves bemused custodians of the grave. Tom Beavers saw that moment now, in the profile of this dreaming girl, and he knew there was no time to lose.

He dropped the match folder into his coat pocket. "I think we should be leaving, Frances."

"Oh well, I don't know about going out yet," she said. "People criticize you so. Regina even had the nerve to telephone. Word had got all the way to her that you came here to have supper with me and we were alone in the house. When I tell the maid I want biscuits made up for two people, she looks like 'What would yo' mama say?' "

"I mean," he said, "I think it's time we left for good."

"And never came back?" It was exactly like Frances to balk at going to a movie but seriously consider an elopement.

"Well, never is a long time. I like to see about Aunt Rita every once in a great while. She can't remember from one time to the next whether it's two days or two years since I last came."

She glanced about the walls and at the furniture, the pictures, and the silver. "But I thought you would want to live here, Tom. It never occurred to me. I know it never occurred to Mama . . . This house . . . It can't be just left."

"It's a fine old house," he agreed. "But what would you do with all your mother's clothes?"

Her freckled hand remained beside the porcelain cup for what seemed a long time. He waited and made no move toward her; he felt her uncertainty keenly, but he believed that some people should not be startled out of a spell.

"It's just as you said," he went on, finally. "You can't give them away, you can't sell them, you can't burn them, and you can't put them in the attic, because the attic is full already. So what are you going to do?"

Between them, the single candle flame achieved a silent altitude. Then, politely, as on any other night, though shaking back her hair in a decided way, she said, "Just let me get my coat, Tom."

She locked the door when they left, and put the key under the mat—a last obsequy to the house. Their hearts were bounding ahead faster than they could walk down the sidewalk or drive off in the car, and, mindful, perhaps, of what happened to people who did, they did not look back.

Had they done so, they would have seen that the Harvey house was more beautiful than ever. All unconscious of its rejection by so mere a person as Tom Beavers, it seemed, instead, to have got rid of what did not suit it, to be free, at last, to enter with abandon the land of mourning and shadows and memory.

Ellen Douglas (July 12, 1921) is the pen name of Josephine Ayres Haxton. Born in Natchez, Mississippi she graduated from the University of Mississippi in 1942. Her first novel, *A Family's Affairs*, published in 1962 received the Houghton Mifflin-Esquire Fellowship Award. Her short story "On the Lake" was published that same year in the *New Yorker* and won an O. Henry Memorial Prize award. The next year "On the Lake" was published in her collection *Black Cloud, White Cloud* as part of that book's novella, "Hold On." These two books were each in turn selected by the *New York Times* for inclusion among the ten best fiction titles of the year. Her other novels include *Apostles of Light* (1973), *The Rock Cried Out* (1979) and *A Lifetime Burning* (1982). Her most recent novel, *Can't Quit You, Baby* (1988), is, like all her other novels, set in Mississippi. "Place is the repository of history," Douglas says. "Place is the means by which you enter a story. I need the familiarity of my own surroundings to hear the voice."

Douglas lives in Jackson, Mississippi, and teaches creative writing at the University of Mississippi.

ON THE LAKE

by Ellen Douglas

Late summer in Philippi is a deadly time of year. Other parts of the United States are hot, it is true, but not like the lower Mississippi Valley. Here the shimmering heat—the thermometer standing day after day in the high nineties and the nights breathless and oppressive—is compounded, even in a drought, by the saturated air. Thunderheads, piling up miles high in the afternoon sky, dwarf the great jet planes that fly through them. The air is heavy with moisture, but for weeks in July and August there is no rain.

In July, Lake Okatukla begins to fall. The lake, named from a meandering bayou that flows into it on the Arkansas side, bounds the town of Philippi on the west. It was once a horseshoe-shaped bend of the Mississippi, but its northern arm is blocked off from the river now by the Nine-Mile Dike, built years ago when a cut-through was made to straighten the river's course. The southern arm of the lake is still a channel into the Mississippi, through which pass towboats pushing strings of barges loaded with gravel, sand, cotton, scrap iron, soybeans, fertilizer, or oil.

In August, the lake drops steadily lower, and at the foot of the levee mud flats begin to appear around the rusty barges that serve as Philippi's municipal terminal and around the old stern-wheeler moored just above them that has been converted into the Philippi Yacht Club. The surface of the mud, covered with discarded beer cans, broken bottles, and tangles of baling wire, cracks and scales like the skin of some scrofulous river beast, and a deathlike stench pervades the hot, still air. But the lake is deep and broad—more than a mile wide at the bend, close to the town—and fifty feet out from the lowest mud flat the steely surface water hides unplumbed black depths.

Late in August, if rain falls all along the course of the Mississippi, there will be a rise of the lake as the river backs into it. The mud flats are covered again. The trees put on pale spikes of new growth. The sandbars are washed clean. Mud runnels stream from the rain-heavy willow fronds, and the willows lift their heads. The fish begin to bite. For a week or two, from the crest of the rise, when the still water begins to clear, dropping the mud that the river has poured into the lake, until another drop has begun to expose the mud flats, Lake Okatukla is beautiful—a serene, broad wilderness of green trees and bright water, bounded at the horizon by the green range of levee sweeping in a slow curve against the sky. Looking down into the water, one can see through drifting forests of moss the quick flash of frightened bream, the shadowy threat of great saw-toothed gar. In the town, there has been little to do for weeks but wait out the heat. Only a few Negroes have braved the stench of the mud flats for the sake of a slimy catfish or a half-dead bream. After the rise, however, fishermen are out again in their skiffs, casting for bass around the trunks of the big willow trees or fishing with cane poles and minnows for white perch along the fringe willows. Family parties picnic here and there along the shore. The lake is big—twelve miles long, with dozens of curving inlets and white sandy islands. Hundreds of fishermen can spend their days trolling its shores and scarcely disturb one another.

One morning just after the August rise a few years ago, Anna Glover set out with two of her three sons, Ralph and Steve, and one of Ralph's friends, Murray McCrae, for a day on the lake. Her oldest son, who at fifteen considered himself too old for such family expeditions, and her husband, Richard, an architect, for whom summer was the busiest season of the year, had stayed behind. It was early, and the waterfront was deserted when Anna drove over the crest of the levee. She parked the car close to the Yacht Club mooring float, where the Glovers kept their fishing skiff tied up, and began to unload the gear—life jackets for the children, tackle box, bait, poles, gas can, and Skotch cooler full of beer, soft drinks, and sandwiches. She had hardly begun when she thought she heard someone shouting her name. "Miss Anna! Hey, Miss Anna!" She looked around, but, seeing the whole slope of the levee empty and no one on the deck of the Yacht Club except Gaines Williamson, the Negro bartender, she called the children back from the water's edge, toward which they had run as soon as the car stopped, and began to distribute the gear among them to carry down to the float.

Anna heaved the heavy cooler out of the car without much effort and untied the poles from the rack on the side of the car, talking as she worked. At thirty-six, she looked scarcely old enough to have three half-grown sons. Her high, round brow was unlined, her brown eyes were clear, and her strong, boyish figure in shorts and a tailored shirt looked almost like a child's. She wore her long sandy-brown hair drawn into a twist on the back of her head. Ralph and his friend Murray were ten; Steve was seven. Ralph's straight nose, solemn expression, and erect, sway-backed carriage made him look like a small preacher. Steve was gentler, with brown eyes like his mother's, fringed by a breathtaking sweep of dark lashes. They were beautiful children, or so Anna thought, for she regarded them with the most intense, subjective passion. Murray was a slender, dark boy with a closed face and a reserve that to Anna seemed impregnable. They were picking up the gear to move it down to the Yacht Club float when they all heard someone calling, and turned around.

"Ralph! Hey there, boys! Here I am, up here!" the voice cried.

"It's Estella, Mama," Ralph said. "There she is, over by the barges."

"Hi, Estella!" Steve shouted. He and Ralph put down the poles and cooler and ran along the rough, uneven slope of the levee, jumping over the iron rings set in the concrete to hold the mooring lines and over the rusty cables that held the terminal barges against the levee.

"Come on, Murray," Anna said. "Let's go speak to Estella. She's over there fishing off the ramp."

Sitting on the galvanized-iron walkway from the levee to the terminal, her legs dangling over the side of the walkway ten feet above the oily surface of the water, was Estella Moseby, a huge and beautiful Negro woman who had worked for the Glover family since the children were small. She had left them a few months before to have a child and had stayed home afterward, at James', her husband's, insistence, to raise her own family. It was the first time that Anna or the children had seen her since shortly after the child was born. Estella held a long cane pole in one hand and with the other waved toward Anna and the children. Her serene, round face was golden brown, the skin flawless even in the cruel light of the August sun, her black hair pulled severely back to a knot on her neck, her enormous dark eyes and wide mouth smiling with pleasure at the unexpected meeting. As the children approached, she drew her line out of the water and pulled herself up by the cable that served as a side rail for the walkway. The walk creaked under her shifting weight. She was fully five feet ten inches tall—at least seven inches taller than Anna—and loomed above the heads of the little group on the levee like an amiable golden giantess, her feet set wide apart to support the weight that fleshed her big frame. Her gaily flowered house dress, printed with daisies and morning-glories in shades of blue, green, and yellow, took on the very quality of her appearance, as if she were some tropical fertility goddess robed to receive her worshippers.

"Lord, Estella," Anna said. "Come on down. We haven't seen you in ages. How have you been?"

"You see me," Estella said. "Fat as ever." She carefully wrapped her line around her pole, secured the hook in the cork, and came down from her high perch to join the others on the levee. "Baby or no baby, I got to go fishing after such a fine rain," she said.

"We're going on a picnic," Steve said.

"Well, isn't that fine," Estella said. "Where is your brother?"

"Oh, he thinks he's too old to associate with us any more," Anna said. "He *scorns* us. How is the baby?"

The two women looked at each other with the shy pleasure of old friends long separated who have not yet fallen back into the easy ways of their friendship.

"Baby's fine," Estella said. "My cousin Bernice is nursing him. I said to myself this morning, 'I haven't been fishing since I got pregnant with Lee Roy. I *got* to go fishing.' So look at me. Here I am sitting on this ramp since seven this morning and no luck."

Steve threw his arms around her legs. "Estella, why don't you come *work* for us again?" he said. "We don't like *anybody* but you."

"I'm coming, honey," she said. "Let me get these kids up a little bit and I'll be back."

"Estella, why don't you go fishing with us today?" Ralph said. "We're going up to the north end of the lake and fish all day."

"Yes, come on," Anna said. "Come on and keep me company. You can't catch any fish around this old barge, and if you do they taste like fuel oil. I heard the bream are really biting in the upper lake—over on the other side, you know, in the willows."

Estella hesitated, looking out over the calm and shining dark water. "I ain't much on boats," she said. "Boats make me nervous."

"Oh, come on, Estella," Anna said. "You know you want to go."

"Well, it's the truth, I'm not catching any fish sitting here. I got two little no-'count bream on my stringer." Estella paused, and then she said, "*All* y'all going to fish from the boat? I'll crowd you."

"We're going to find a good spot and fish off the bank," Anna said. "We're already too many to fish from the boat."

"Well, it'll be a pleasure," Estella said. "I'll just come along. Let me get my stuff." She went up on the walkway again and gathered up her tackle where it lay—a brown paper sack holding sinkers, floats, hooks, and line, and her pole and a coffee can full of worms and dirt.

"I brought my gig along," Ralph said as they all trudged across the levee toward the Yacht Club. "I'm going to gig one of those great big buffalo or a gar or something."

"Well, if you do, give it to me, honey," Estella said. "James is really crazy about buffalo the way I cook it." Pulling a coin purse out of her pocket, she turned to Anna. "You reckon you might get us some beer in the Yacht Club? A nice can of beer 'long about eleven o'clock would be good."

"I've got two cans in the cooler," Anna said, "but maybe we'd better get a couple more." She took the money and, while Murray and Ralph brought the skiff around from the far side of the Yacht Club, where it was tied up, went into the bar and bought two more cans of beer. Estella and Steve, meanwhile, carried the fishing gear down to the float.

Gaines Williamson, a short, powerfully built man in his forties, followed Anna out of the bar and helped stow their gear in the little boat. The children got in first and then he helped Estella in. "Lord, Miss Estella," he said, "you too big for this boat, and that's a fact." He stood back and looked down at her doubtfully, sweat shining on his face and standing in droplets on his shaven scalp.

"I must say it's none of your business," Estella said.

"We'll be all right, Gaines," Anna said. "The lake's smooth as glass."

The boys held the skiff against the float while Anna got in, and they set out, cruising slowly up the lake until they found a spot that Estella and Anna agreed looked promising. Here, on a long, clean sandbar fringed with willows, they beached the boat. The children stripped off their life jackets, pulled off the jeans they wore over their swimming trunks, and began to wade.

"You children wade here in the open water," Estella

ordered. "Don't go over yonder on the other side of the bar, where the willows are growing. You'll bother the fish."

She and Anna stood looking around. Wilderness was all about them. As far as they could see on either side of the lake, not even a road ran down to the water's edge. While they watched, two white herons dragged themselves awkwardly into the air and flapped away, long legs trailing. The southern side of the sandbar, where they had beached the boat, had no trees growing on it, but the edge of the northern side, which curved in on itself and out again, was covered with willows. Here the land was higher. Beyond a low hummock crowned with cottonwood trees, Anna and Estella discovered a pool, twenty-five yards long and nearly as wide, that had been left behind by the last rise, a few days before. Fringe willows grew all around it, and the fallen trunk of a huge cottonwood lay with its roots exposed on the ground, its whole length stretched out into the still water of the pool.

"Here's the place," Estella said decidedly. "Shade for us, and fringe willows for the fish. And looka there." She pointed to the fallen tree. "If there aren't any fish under *there* . . ." They stood looking down at the pool, pleased with their find.

"I'll go get our things," Estella said. "You sit down and rest yourself, Miss Anna."

"I'll come help you."

The two women unloaded the boat, and Anna carried the cooler up the low hill and left it in the shade of one of the cottonwood trees. Then they gathered the fishing tackle and took it over to a shady spot by the pool. In a few minutes, the children joined them, and Anna passed out poles and bait. The bream were rising to crickets, and she had brought a wire cylinder basket full of them.

"You boys scatter out, now," Anna said. "There's plenty of room for everybody, and if you stay too close together you'll hook each other."

Estella helped Steve bait his hook, then baited her own and dropped it into the water as close as she could get it to the trunk of the fallen tree. Almost as soon as it reached the water, her float began to bob and quiver.

"Here we go," she said in a low voice. "Take it under, now. Take it under." She addressed herself to the business of fishing with such delight and concentration that Anna stopped in the middle of rigging a pole to watch her. Even the children, intent on finding places for themselves, turned back to see Estella catch a fish. She stood over the pool like a priestess at her altar, all expectation and willingness, holding the pole lightly, as if her fingers could read the intentions of the fish vibrating through line and pole. Her bare arms were tense, and she gazed down into the still water. A puff of wind made the leafy shadows waver and tremble on the pool, and the float rocked deceptively. Estella's arms quivered with a jerk begun and suppressed. Her flowery dress flapped around her legs, and her skin shone with sweat and oil where the sunlight struck through the leaves across her forehead and down one cheek.

"Not yet," she muttered. "*Take* it." The float bobbed and went under. "Aaah!" She gave her line a quick, short jerk to set the hook; the line tightened, the long pole bent, and she swung a big bream out onto the sand. The fish flopped off the hook and down the slope toward the water; she dropped the pole and dived at it, half falling. Ralph, who had been watching, was ahead of her, shouting with excitement, grabbing up the fish before it could flop back into the pool, and putting it into Estella's hands, careful to avoid the sharp dorsal fin.

"Look, boys, look!" she cried happily. "Just look at him!" She held out the big bream, as wide and thick as her hand, marked with blue around the gills and orange on its swollen belly. The fish twisted and gasped in her hand while she got the stringer. She slid the metal end of the stringer through one gill and out the mouth, secured the other end to an exposed root of the fallen tree, and dropped the fish into the water, far enough away so that the bream's thrashing would not disturb their fishing spot.

"Quick now, Miss Anna," she said. "Get your line in there. I bet this pool is full of bream. Come on, boys, we're going to catch some fish today."

Anna baited her hook and dropped it in. The children scattered around the pool to their own places. In an hour, the two women had caught a dozen bream and four small catfish, and the boys had caught six or seven more bream. Then for ten minutes no one got a bite, and the boys began to lose interest. A school of minnows flashed into the shallow water at Anna's feet, and she pointed them out to Estella. "Bream are gone," she said. "They've quit feeding, or we wouldn't see any minnows."

* * *

Anna laid down her pole and told the children they could swim. "Come on, Estella," she said. "We can sit in the shade and watch them and have a beer, and then in a little while we can move to another spot."

"You aren't going to let them swim in this old lake, are you, Miss Anna?" Estella said.

"Sure. The bottom's nice and sandy here," Anna said. "Murray, your mama said you've got to keep your life preserver on if you swim." She said to Estella in a low voice, "He's not much of a swimmer. He's the only one I would worry about."

The children splashed and tumbled fearlessly in the water, Ralph and Steve popping up and disappearing, sometimes for so long that Anna, in spite of what she had said, would begin to watch anxiously for their blond heads.

"I must say, I don't see how you stand it," Estella said. "That water scares me."

"Nothing to be scared of," Anna said. "They're both good swimmers, and so am I. I could swim across the lake and back, I bet you, old as I am."

She fished two beers out of the Skotch cooler, opened them, and gave one to Estella. Then she sat down with her back against a cottonwood tree, gave Estella a cigarette, took one herself, and leaned back with a sigh. Estella sat down on a fallen log, and the two women smoked and drank their beer in silence for a few minutes. The breeze ran through the cottonwoods, shaking the leaves against each other. "I love the sound of the wind in a cottonwood tree," Anna said. "Especially at night when you wake up and hear it outside your window. I remember there was one outside the window of my room when I was a little girl, so close to the house I could climb out the window and get into it." The breeze freshened and the leaves pattered against each other. "It sounds cool," Anna said, "even in August."

"It's nice," Estella said. "Like a nice, light rain."

"Well, tell me what you've been doing with yourself," Anna said. "When are you going to move into your new house?"

"James wants to keep renting it out another year," Estella said. "He wants us to get ahead a little bit. And you know, Miss Anna, if I can hang on where I am we'll be in a good shape. We can rent that house until we finish paying for it, and then when we move we can rent the one we're in, and, you know, we own that little one next door, too. With four children now, we got to think of the future. And I must say, with all his old man's ways, James is a good provider. He looks after his own. So I go along with him. But, Lord, I can't stand it much longer. We're falling all over each other in that little tiny place. Kids under my feet all day. No place to keep the baby quiet. And in rainy weather! It's worse than a circus. I've gotten so all I do is yell at the kids. It would be a rest to go back to work."

"I wish you *would* come back to work," Anna said.

"No use talking about it," Estella said. "James says I've got to stay home at least until Lee Roy gets up to school age. And you can see for yourself I'd be paying out half what I made to get somebody to keep mine. But I'll tell you, my nerves are tore up."

"It takes a while to get your strength back after a baby," Anna said.

"Oh, I'm strong enough," Estella said. "It's not that." She pulled a stalk of Johnson grass and began to chew it thoughtfully. "I've had something on my mind," she said, "something I've been meaning to tell you ever since the baby came, and I haven't seen you by yourself—"

Anna interrupted her. "Look at the fish, Estella," she said. "They're really kicking up a fuss."

There was a wild, thrashing commotion in the water by the roots of the cottonwood tree where Estella had tied the stringer.

Estella watched a minute. "Lord, Miss Anna," she said, "something's after those fish. A turtle or something." She got up and started toward the pool as a long, dark, whiplike shape flung itself out of the water, slapped the surface, and disappeared.

"Hey," Anna said, "it's a snake! A snake!"

Estella looked around for a weapon and hastily picked up a short, heavy stick and a rock from the ground. Moving lightly and easily in spite of her weight, she ran down to the edge of the water, calling over her shoulder, "I'll scare him off. I'll chunk him. Don't you worry." She threw the rock into the churning water, but it had no effect. "Go, snake. Leave our fish alone." She stood waving her stick threateningly over the water.

Anna came down to the pool now, and they both saw the

whiplike form again. Fearlessly, Estella whacked at it with her stick.

"Keep back, Estella," Anna said. "He might bite you. Wait a minute and I'll get a longer stick."

"Go, snake!" Estella shouted furiously, confidently. "What's the matter with him? He won't go off. Go, you crazy snake!"

Now the children heard the excitement and came running across the beach and over the low hill where Estella and Anna had been sitting, to see what was happening.

"A snake, a snake!" Steve screamed. "He's after the fish. Come on, y'all! It's a big old snake after the fish."

The two older boys ran up. "Get 'em out of the water, Mama," Ralph said. "He's going to eat 'em."

"I'm scared he might bite me," Anna said. "Keep back. He'll go away in a minute." She struck at the water with the stick she had picked up.

Murray looked the situation over calmly. "Why don't we gig him?" he said to Ralph.

Ralph ran down to the boat and brought back the long, barb-pointed gig. "Move, Estella," he said. "I'm gonna gig him." He struck twice at the snake and missed.

"Estella," Anna said, "I saw his head. He can't go away. He's swallowed one of the fish. He's caught on the stringer." She shuddered with disgust. "What are we going to do?" she said. "Let's throw away the stringer. We'll never get him off."

"All them beautiful fish! No, *Ma'am*," Estella said. "Here, Ralph, he can't bite us if he's swallowed a fish. I'll untie the stringer and get him up on land, and then you gig him."

"I'm going away," Steve said. "I don't want to watch." He crossed the hill and went back to the beach, where he sat down alone and began to dig a hole in the sand.

Ralph, wild with excitement, danced impatiently around Estella while she untied the stringer.

"Be calm, child," she said. She pulled the stringer out of the water and dropped it on the ground. "Now!"

The snake had indeed tried to swallow one of the bream on the stringer. Its jaws were stretched so wide as to look dislocated; its body was distended behind the head with the half-swallowed meal, and the fish's head could still be seen protruding from its mouth. The snake, faintly banded with slaty black on a brown background, was a water moccasin.

"Lord, it's a cottonmouth!" Estella cried as soon as she had the stringer out on land, where she could see the snake.

A thrill of horror and disgust raised the hair on Anna's arms. The thought of the helpless fish on the stringer sensing its enemy's approach, and then of the snake, equally and even more grotesquely helpless, filled her with revulsion. "Throw it away," she commanded. And then the thought of the stringer with its living burden of fish and snake struggling and swimming away into the lake struck her as even worse. "No!" she said. "Go on. Kill the snake, Ralph."

Ralph paid no attention to his mother but stood with the long gig poised, looking up at Estella for instructions.

"Kill him," Estella said. "Now."

He drove the gig into the snake's body behind the head and pinned it to the ground, where it coiled and uncoiled convulsively, wrapping its tail around the gig and then unwrapping it and whipping it across the sand.

Anna mastered her horror as well as she could with a shake of her head. "Now what?" she said calmly.

Estella got a knife from the tackle box, held the dead but still writhing snake down with one big foot behind the gig on its body and the other on its tail, squatted, and deftly cut off the fish's head where it protruded from the gaping, fanged mouth. Then she worked the barbed point of the gig out of the body, picked the snake up on the point, and stood holding it away from her.

Ralph whirled around with excitement and circled Estella twice. "We've killed a snake," he chanted. "We've killed a snake. We've killed a snake."

"Look at it wiggle," Murray said. "It keeps on wiggling even after it's dead."

"Yeah, a snake'll wiggle like that for an hour sometimes, even with its head cut off," Estella said. "Look out, Ralph." She swept the gig forward through the air and threw the snake out into the pool, where it continued its aimless writhing on the surface of the water. She handed Ralph the gig and stood watching the snake for a few minutes, holding her hands away from her sides to keep the blood off her clothes. Then she bent down by the water's edge and washed the blood from her hands. She picked up the stringer, dropped the fish into the water, and tied the stringer to the root of the cottonwood. "There!" she said. "I didn't have no idea of throwing away all them—*those* beautiful fish. James would've skinned me if he ever heard about it."

Steve got up from the sand now and came over to his mother. He looked at the wiggling snake, and then he leaned against his mother without saying anything, put his arms around her, and laid his head against her side.

Anna stroked his hair with one hand and held him against her with the other. "It was a moccasin, honey," she said. "They're poison, you know. You have to kill them."

"I'm hungry," Ralph said. "Is it time to eat?"

Anna shook her head, gave Steve a pat, and released him. "Let me smoke a cigarette first and forget about that old snake. Then we'll eat."

Anna and Estella went back to the shade on the hill and settled themselves once more, each with a fresh can of beer and a cigarette. The children returned to the beach.

"I can do without snakes," Anna said. "Indefinitely."

Estella was still breathing hard. "I don't mind killing no snake," she said happily.

"I never saw anything like that before," Anna said. "A snake getting caught on a stringer, I mean. Did you?"

"Once or twice," Estella said. "And I've had 'em get after my stringer plenty of times."

"I don't see how you could stand to cut the fish's head off," Anna said, and shivered.

"Well, somebody had to."

"Yes, I suppose I would have done it if you hadn't been here." She laughed. "*Maybe*. I was mighty tempted to throw the whole thing away."

"I'm just as glad I wasn't pregnant," Estella said. "I'm glad it didn't happen while I was carrying Lee Roy. I would have been *helpless*."

"You might have had a miscarriage," Anna said. She laughed again, still nervous, wanting to stop talking about the snake but not yet able to, feeling somehow that there was more to be said. "Please don't have any miscarriages on fishing trips with me," she went on. "I can do without that, too."

"Miscarriage!" Estella said. "That's not what I'm talking about. And that reminds me, what I was getting ready to tell you when we saw the snake. You know, I said I had something on my mind?"

"Uh-huh."

"You remember last summer when you weren't home that day, and that kid fell out of the tree in the yard, and all?"

"How could I forget it?" Anna said.

"You remember you spoke to me so heavy about it? Why didn't I stay out in the yard with him until his mama got there, instead of leaving him laying on the ground like that, nobody with him but Ralph, and I told you I couldn't go out there to him—couldn't look at that kid with his leg broke, and all—and you didn't understand why?"

"Yes, I remember," Anna said.

"Well, I wanted to tell you I was *blameless*," Estella said. "I didn't want you to know it at the time, but I was pregnant. I *couldn't* go out there. It might have *marked* my child, don't you see? I might have bore a cripple."

"Oh, Estella! You don't believe that kind of foolishness, do you?" Anna said.

"*Believe* it? I've seen it happen," Estella said. "I know it's true." She was sitting on the fallen log, so that she towered above Anna, who had gone back to her place on the ground, leaning against the tree. Now Estella leaned forward with an expression of intense seriousness on her face. "My aunt looked on a two-headed calf when she was carrying a child," she said, "and her child had six fingers on one hand and seven on the other."

Anna hitched herself up higher, then got up and sat down on the log beside Estella. "But that was an accident," she said. "A coincidence. Looking at the calf didn't have anything to do with it."

Estella shook her head stubbornly. "This world is a mysterious place," she said. "Do you think you can understand everything in it?"

"No," Anna said. "Not everything. But I don't believe in magic."

"All this world is full of mystery," Estella repeated. "You got to have respect for what you don't understand. There are times to be brave and times when you go down helpless in spite of all. Like that snake. You were afraid of that snake."

"I thought he might bite me," Anna said. "And besides, it was so horrible the way he was caught."

But Estella went on as if she hadn't heard. "You see,"

she said, "there are things you overlook. Things, like I was telling you about my aunt, that are *true*. My mother in her day saw more wonders than that. She knew more than one that sickened and died of a spell. And this child with the fingers, I know about him for a fact. I lived with them when I was teaching school. I lived in the house with that kid. So I'm not taking any chances."

"But I thought you had lost your head and got scared because he was hurt," Anna said. "When the little boy broke his leg, I mean. I kept thinking it wasn't like you. That's what really happened, isn't it?"

"No," Estella said. "It was like I told you."

Anna said no more, but sat quiet a long time, lighting another cigarette and smoking calmly, her face expressionless. But her thoughts were in a tumult of exasperation, bafflement, and outrage. She tried unsuccessfully to deny, to block out, the overriding sense of the difference between herself and Estella, borne in on her by this strange conversation so foreign to their quiet, sensible friendship. She had often thought, with pride both in herself and in Estella, what an accomplishment their friendship was, knowing how much delicacy of feeling, how much consideration and understanding they had both brought to it. And now it seemed to her that it was this very friendship, so carefully nurtured for years, that Estella had unwittingly attacked. With a few words, she had put between them all that separated them, all the dark and terrible past. In the tumult of Anna's feelings there rose a queer, long-forgotten memory of a nurse she had once had as a child—the memory of a brown hand thrust out at her, holding a greasy black ball of hair combings. "You see, child, I saves my hair. I ain't never th'owed away a hair of my head."

"Why?" she had asked.

"Bad luck to th'ow away combings. Bad luck to lose any part of yourself in this old world. Fingernail parings, too. I gathers them up and carries them home and burns them. And I sits by the fire and watches until every last little bitty hair is turned plumb to smoke."

"But why?" she had asked again.

"Let your enemy possess one hair of your head and you will be in his power," the nurse had said. She had thrust the hair ball into her apron pocket, and now, in the memory, she seemed to be brushing Anna's hair, and Anna remembered standing restive under her hand, hating, as always, to have her hair brushed.

"Hurry up," she had said. "Hurry up. I got to go."

"All right, honey. I'm through." The nurse had given her head one last lick and then, bending toward her, still holding her arm while she struggled to be off and outdoors again, had thrust a dark, brooding face close to hers, had looked at her for a long, scary moment, and had laughed. "I saves your combings, too, honey. You in my power."

With an effort, Anna drew herself up short. She put out her cigarette, threw her beer can into the lake, and stood up. "I reckon we better fix some lunch," she said. "The children are starving."

By the time they had finished lunch, burned the discarded papers, thrown the bread crusts and crumbs of potato chips to the birds, and put the empty soft-drink bottles back in the cooler, it had begun to look like rain. Anna stood gazing thoughtfully into the sky. "Maybe we ought to start back," she said. "We don't want to get caught in the rain up here."

"We're not going to catch any more fish as long as the wind is blowing," Estella said.

"We want to swim some more," Ralph said.

"You can't go swimming right after lunch," Anna said. "You might get a cramp. And it won't be any fun to get caught in the rain. We'd better call it a day." She picked up one of the poles and began to wind the line around it. "Come on, kids," she said. "Let's load up."

They loaded their gear into the skiff and dropped the stringer full of fish in the bottom. Anna directed Murray and Steve to sit in the bow, facing the stern. Estella got in cautiously and took the middle seat. Anna and Ralph waded in together, pushed the skiff off the sandbar, and then got into the stern.

"You all got your life jackets on?" Anna said, glancing at the boys. "That's right."

Ralph pulled on the recoil-starter rope until he had got the little motor started, and they headed down the lake. The heavily loaded skiff showed no more than eight inches of freeboard, and as they cut through the choppy water, waves sprayed over the bow and sprinkled Murray and Steve. Anna moved the tiller and headed the skiff in closer to the shore. "We'll stay close in going down," she said. "Water's not so rough in here. And then we can cut across the lake right opposite the Yacht Club."

Estella sat still in the middle of the skiff, her back to Anna, a hand on each gunwale, as they moved steadily down the lake, rocking with the wind-rocked waves. "I don't like this old lake when it's windy," Estella said. "I don't like no windy water."

When they reached a point opposite the Yacht Club, where the lake was a little more than a mile wide, Anna headed the skiff into the rougher open water. The wind, however, was still no more than a stiff breeze, and the skiff was a quarter of the way across the lake before Anna began to be worried. Spray from the choppy waves was coming in more and more often over the bow; Murray and Steve were drenched, and an inch of water sloshed in the bottom of the skiff. Estella had not spoken since she had said "I don't like no windy water." She sat perfectly still, gripping the gunwales with both hands, her paper sack of tackle in her lap, her worm can on the seat beside her. Suddenly a gust of wind picked up the paper sack and blew it out of the boat. It struck the water and floated back to Anna, who reached out, picked it up, and dropped it by her own feet. Estella did not move, although the sack brushed against her face as it blew out. She made no attempt to catch it. She's scared, Anna thought. She's so scared she didn't even see it blow away. And Anna was frightened herself. She leaned forward, picked up the worm can from the seat beside Estella, dumped out the worms and dirt, and tapped Estella on the shoulder. "Here," she said. "Why don't you bail some of the water out of the bottom of the boat, so your feet won't get wet?"

Estella did not look around, but reached over her shoulder, took the can, and began to bail, still holding to the gunwale tightly with her left hand.

The wind freshened, the waves began to show white at their tips, the clouds in the south raced across the sky, darker and darker. But still, although they could see sheets of rain far away to the south, the sun shone on them brightly. They were now almost halfway across the lake. Anna looked over her shoulder toward the quieter water they had left behind. Along the shore of the lake, the willow trees tossed in the wind like a forest of green plumes. It's just as far one way as the other, she thought, and anyhow there's nothing to be afraid of. But while she looked back, the boat slipped off course, no longer quartering the waves, and immediately they took a big one over their bow.

"Bail, Estella," Anna said quietly, putting the boat back on course. "Get that water out of the boat." Her mind was filled with one paralyzing thought: She can't swim. My God, Estella can't swim.

Far off down the channel she saw the Gay Rosey Jane moving steadily toward the terminal, pushing a string of barges. She looked at Murray and Steve in the bow of the boat, drenched, hair plastered to their heads. "Just sit still, boys," she said. "There's nothing to worry about. We're almost there."

The wind was a gale now, and the black southern sky rushed toward them as if to engulf them. The boat took another wave over the bow, and then another. Estella bailed mechanically with the coffee can. They were still almost half a mile out from the Yacht Club. The boat's overloaded, and we're going to sink, Anna thought. My God, we're going to sink, and Estella can't swim.

"Estella," she said, "the boat will not sink. It may fill up with water, but it won't sink. Do you understand? It is all filled with cork, like a life preserver. It won't sink, do you hear me?" She repeated herself louder and louder above the wind. Estella sat with her back turned and bailed. She did not move or answer, or even nod her head. She went on bailing frantically, mechanically, dumping pint after pint of water over the side while they continued to ship waves over the bow. Murray and Steve sat in their places and stared at Anna. Ralph sat motionless by her side. No one said a word. I've got to take care of them all, Anna thought. Estella kept on bailing. The boat settled in the water and shipped another wave, wallowing now, hardly moving before the labored push of the motor. Estella gave a yell and started to rise, holding to the gunwales with both hands.

"Sit down, you fool!" Anna shouted. *"Sit down!"*

"We're gonna sink!" Estella yelled. "And I can't swim, Miss Anna! I can't swim!" For the first time, she turned, and stared at Anna with wild, blind eyes. She stood all the way up and clutched the air. "I'm gonna drown!" she yelled.

The boat rocked and settled, the motor drowned out, another wave washed in over the bow, and the boat tipped slowly up on its side. An instant later, they were all in the water and the boat was floating upside down beside them.

The children bobbed up immediately, buoyant in their life jackets. Anna glanced around once to see if they were all there. "Stay close to the boat, boys," she said.

And then Estella heaved out of the water, fighting frantically, eyes vacant, mouth open, the broad expanse of her golden face set in mindless desperation.

Anna got hold of one of the handgrips at the stern of the boat and, with her free hand, grabbed Estella's arm. "You're all right," she said. "Come on, I've got hold of the boat."

She tried to pull the huge bulk of the Negro woman toward her and guide her hand to the grip. Estella did not speak, but lunged forward in the water with a strangled yell and threw herself on Anna, flinging her arms across her shoulders. Anna felt herself sinking and scissors-kicked strongly to keep herself up, but she went down. Chin-deep in the water, she threw back her head and took a breath before Estella pushed her under. She hung on to the grip with all her strength, feeling herself battered against the boat and jerked away from it by Estella's struggle. This can't be happening, she thought. We can't be out here drowning. She felt a frantic hand brush across her face and snatch at her nose and hair. My glasses, she thought as she felt them torn away. I've lost my glasses.

Estella's weight slid away, and she, too, went under. Then both women came up and Anna got hold of Estella's arm again. "Come *on*," she gasped. "The *boat*."

Again Estella threw herself forward, the water streaming from her head and shoulders. This time Anna pulled her close enough to get hold of the grip, but Estella did not try to grasp it. Her hand slid, clawing, along Anna's wrist and arm; again she somehow rose up in the water and came down on Anna, and again the two women went under. This time, Estella's whole thrashing bulk was above Anna; she held with all her strength to the handgrip, but felt herself torn away from it. She came up behind Estella, who was now clawing frantically at the side of the skiff, which sank down on their side and tipped gently toward them as she pulled at it.

Anna ducked down and somehow got her shoulder against Estella's rump. Kicking and heaving with a strength she did not possess, she boosted Estella up and forward so that she fell sprawling across the boat. *"There!"* She came up as the rocking skiff began to submerge under Estella's weight. *"Stay* there!" she gasped. *"Stay* on it. For God's . . ."

But the boat was under a foot of water now, rocking and slipping away under Estella's shifting weight. Clutching and kicking crazily, mouth open in a soundless prolonged scream, eyes staring, she slipped off the other side, turned her face toward Anna, gave a strange, strangled grunt, and sank again. The water churned and foamed where she had been.

Anna swam around the boat toward her. As she swam, she realized that Ralph and Steve were screaming for help. Murray floated in the water with a queer, embarrassed smile on his face, as if he had been caught at something shameful. "I'm not here," he seemed to be saying. "This is all just an embarrassing mistake."

By the time Anna got to Estella, the boat was a couple of yards away—too far, she knew, for her to try to get Estella back to it. Estella broke the surface of te water directly in front of her and immediately flung both arms around her neck. Nothing Anna had ever learned in a lifesaving class seemed to have any bearing on this reasonless two hundred pounds of flesh with which she had to deal. They went down. This time they stayed under so long, deep in the softly yielding black water, that Anna thought she would not make it back up. Her very brain seemed ready to burst out of her ears and nostrils. She scissors-kicked again and again with all her strength—not trying to pull loose from Estella's clinging but now more passive weight—and they came up. Anna's head was thrust up and back, ready for a breath, and the instant she felt the air on her face, she took it, deep and gulping, swallowing some water at the same time, and they went down again. Estella's arms rested heavily—trustingly, it seemed—on her shoulders. She did not hug Anna or try to strangle her but simply kept holding on and pushing her down. This time, again deep in the dark water, when Anna raised her arms for a strong downstroke, she touched a foot. One of the boys was floating above their heads. She grabbed the foot without a thought and pulled with all her strength, scissors-kicking at the same time. She and Estella popped out of the water. Gasping in the life-giving air, Anna found herself staring into Steve's face as he floated beside her, weeping.

My God, I'll drown him if he doesn't get out of the way,

she thought. I'll drown my own child. But she had no time to say even a word to warn him off before they went down again.

The next time up, she heard Ralph's voice, high and shrill and almost in her ear, and realized that he, too, was swimming close by, and was pounding on Estella's shoulder. "Estella, let go, let go!" he was crying. "Estella, you're drowning Mama!" Estella did not hear. She seemed not even to try to raise her head or breathe when their heads broke out of the water.

Once more they went under and came up before Anna thought, I've given out. There's no way to keep her up, and nobody is coming. And then, deep in the lake, the brassy taste of fear on her tongue, the yielding water pounding in her ears: *She's going to drown me. I've got to let her drown, or she will drown me.* She drew her knee up under her chin, planted her foot in the soft belly, still swollen from pregnancy, and shoved as hard as she could, pushing herself up and back and Estella down and away. Estella was not holding her tightly, and it was easy to push her away. The big arms slid off Anna's shoulders, the limp hands making no attempt to clutch or hold.

They had been together, close as lovers in the darkness or as twins in the womb of the lake, and now they were apart. Anna shot up into the air with the force of her shove and took a deep, gasping breath. Treading water, she waited for Estella to come up beside her, but nothing happened. The three children floated in a circle and looked at her. A vision passed through her mind of Estella's body drifting downward, downward through layers of increasing darkness, all her golden strength and flowery beauty mud-and-water-dimmed, still, aimless as a drifting log. I ought to surface-dive and look for her, she thought, and the thought of going down again turned her bowels to water.

Before she had to decide to dive, something nudged lightly against her hand, like an inquiring, curious fish. She grabbed at it and felt the inert mass of Estella's body, drained of struggle, floating below the surface of the water. She got hold of the belt of her dress and pulled. Estella's back broke the surface of the water, mounded and rocking in the dead man's float, and then sank gently down again. Anna held on to the belt. She moved her feet tiredly to keep herself afloat and looked around her. I can't even get face out of the water, she thought. I haven't the strength to lift her head.

The boat was floating ten yards away. The Skotch cooler, bright red-and-black plaid, bobbed gaily in the water nearby. Far, far off she could see the levee. In the boat it had looked so near and the distance across the lake so little that she had said she could easily swim it, but now everything in the world except the boat, the children, and this lifeless body was unthinkably far away. Tiny black figures moved back and forth along the levee, people going about their business without a thought of tragedy. The whole sweep of the lake was empty, with not another boat in sight except the Gay Rosey Jane, still moving up the channel. All that had happened had happened so quickly that the towboat seemed no nearer than it had before the skiff overturned. Murray floated in the water a few yards off, still smiling his embarrassed smile. Steve and Ralph stared at their mother with stricken faces. The sun broke through the shifting blackness of the sky, and at the same time a light rain began to fall, pattering on the choppy surface of the lake and splashing into their faces.

All her senses dulled and muffled by shock and exhaustion, Anna moved her feet and worked her way toward the boat, dragging her burden.

"She's gone," Steve said. "Estella's drowned." Tears and rain streamed down his face.

"What shall we do, Mama?" Ralph said.

Dimly, Anna realized that he had sensed her exhaustion and was trying to rouse her.

"Yell," she said. "All three of you yell. Maybe somebody . . ."

The children screamed for help again and again, their thin, piping voices floating away in the wind. With her last strength, Anna continued to work her way toward the boat, pulling Estella after her. She swam on her back, frog-kicking, and feeling the inert bulk bump against her legs at every stroke. When she reached the boat, she took hold of the handgrip and concentrated on holding on to it.

"What shall we do?" Ralph said again. "They can't hear us."

Overcome with despair, Anna let her head droop toward the water. "No one is coming," she said. "It's too far. They can't hear you." And then, from somewhere, dim thoughts of artificial respiration, of snatching back the dead, came into her mind and she raised her head. Still time. I've got to get her out *now*, she thought. "Yell again," she said.

"I'm going to swim to shore and get help," Ralph said. He looked toward his mother for a decision, but his face clearly showed that he knew he could not expect one. He started swimming away, his blond head bobbing in the rough water. He did not look back.

"I don't know," Anna said. Then she remembered vaguely that in an accident you were supposed to stay with the boat. "She's dead," she said to herself. "My God, she's dead. My fault."

Ralph swam on, the beloved head smaller and smaller on the vast expanse of the lake. The Gay Rosey Jane moved steadily up the channel. They might run him down, Anna thought. They'd never see him. She opened her mouth to call him back.

"Somebody's coming!" Murray shouted. "They see us. Somebody's coming. Ralph!"

Ralph heard him and turned back, and now they saw two boats racing toward them, one from the Yacht Club and one from the far side of the lake, across from the terminal. In the nearer one they saw Gaines Williamson.

Thirty yards away, something happened to Gaines' engine; it raced, ground, and died. Standing in the stern of the rocking boat, he worked frantically over it while they floated and watched. It could not have been more than a minute or two before the other boat pulled up beside them, but every moment that passed, Anna knew, might be the moment of Estella's death. In the stern of the second boat they saw a wiry white man wearing a T shirt and jeans. He cut his engine when he was beside them, and, moving quickly to the side of the boat near Anna, bent over her in great excitement. "Are you all right?" he asked. He grabbed her arm with a hard, calloused hand and shook her as if he had seen that she was about to pass out. "Are you all right?" he asked again, his face close to hers.

Anna stared at him, scarcely understanding what the question meant. The children swam over to the boat, and he helped them in and then turned back to Anna. "Come on," he said, and took hold of her arm again. "You've got to help yourself. Can you make it?"

"Get this one first," she said.

"What?" He stared at her with a queer, concentrated gaze, and she realized that he had not even seen Estella.

She hauled on the belt, and Estella's back broke the surface of the water, rolling, rocking, and bumping against the side of the boat. "I've got somebody else here," she said.

He grunted as if someone had hit him in the stomach. Reaching down, he grabbed the back of Estella's dress, pulled her toward him, got one hand into her hair, raised her face out of the water, and, bracing himself against the gunwale, held her there. Estella's peaceful face turned slowly toward him. Her mouth and eyes were closed, her expression was one of deep repose. The man stared at her and then at Anna. "My God," he said.

"We've got to get her into the boat," Anna said. "If we can get her where we can give her artificial respiration . . ."

"It's Estella," Steve said. "Mama had her all the time." He began to cry again. "Let go of her hair," he said. "You're hurting her."

The three children shifted all at once to the side of the boat where the man was still holding Estella, and he turned on them sternly. "Get back," he said. "Sit *down*. And sit still."

The children scuttled back to their places. "You're hurting her," Steve said again.

"It's all right, son," the man said. "She can't feel a thing." To Anna, in a lower voice, he said, "She's dead."

"I'll push and you pull," Anna said. "Maybe we can get her into the boat."

He shifted his position, bracing himself as well as he could in the rocking boat, rested Estella's head on his own shoulder, and put both arms around her. They heaved and pushed at the limp body, but they could not get her into the boat. The man let her down into the water again, this time holding her under the arms. A hundred yards away, Gaines still struggled with his engine.

"Hurry up!" the man shouted. "Get on over here. We can't lift this woman by ourselves."

"Fishing lines tangled in the screw!" Gaines shouted back. His engine caught and died again.

"We're going to have to tow her in," the man said. "That fellow can't start his boat." He reached behind him and got a life jacket. "We'd better put this on her," he said. They worked Estella's arms into the life jacket and fastened the straps. "I've got a rope here somewhere," he said. "Hold her a minute. Wait." He handed Anna a life jacket. "You put one on, too." While he still held Estella by the hair, Anna struggled into the life jacket, and then took hold of the straps of Estella's. Just then, Gaines got his engine started, raced across the open water, and drew up beside them.

The two boats rocked in the rough water with Anna and Estella between them. Anna, with a hand on the gunwale of each, held them apart while the two men, straining and grunting, hauled Estella's body up out of the water and over the gunwale of Gaines' boat. Gaines heaved her legs in. She flopped, face down, across the seat and lay with one arm hanging over the side, the hand trailing in the water. Anna lifted the arm and put it in the boat. Then the white man pulled Anna into his boat. As he helped her over the side, she heard a smacking blow, and, looking back, saw that Gaines had raised and turned Estella's body and was pounding her in the belly. Water poured out of her mouth and, in reflex, air rushed in.

The boats roared off across the lake toward the Yacht Club. The white man's was much the faster of the two, and he quickly pulled away. As soon as they were within calling distance, he stood up in the boat and began to yell at the little group gathered on the Yacht Club mooring float. "Drowned! She's drowned!" he yelled. "Call an ambulance. Get a resuscitator down here. Hurry!"

They drew up to the float. He threw a rope to one of the Negroes standing there and jumped out. Anna dragged herself to a sitting position and stared stupidly at the crowd of Negroes. Gaines Williamson pulled up behind them in the other boat.

"Give us a hand," the white man said. "Let's get her out of there. My God, she's huge. Somebody lend a hand."

To Anna it seemed that all the rest of the scene on the float took place above and far away from her. She saw legs moving back and forth, heard voices and snatches of conversation, felt herself moved from one place to another, but nothing that happened interrupted her absorption in grief and guilt. For the time, nothing existed for her except the belief that Estella was dead.

Someone took her arm and helped her onto the float

while the children climbed up by themselves. She sat down on the splintery boards, surrounded by legs, and no one paid any attention to her.

"I saw 'em." The voice of a Negro woman in the crowd. "I was setting on the levee and I saw 'em. You heard me. 'My Lord save us, some folks out there drowning,' I said. I was up on the levee and I run down to the Yacht Club . . ."

"Did somebody call an ambulance?" the white man asked.

"I run down here to the Yacht Club, like to killed myself running, and . . ."

"How . . ."

"Gay Rosey Jane swamped them. Never even seen them. Them towboats don't stop for nobody. See, there she goes. Never seen them at all."

"Still got a stitch in my side. My Lord, I like to killed myself running."

"Anybody around here know how to give artificial respiration?"

"I was sitting right yonder on the terminal fishing with her this morning. Would you believe that?"

"God have mercy on us."

"Oh, Lord. Oh, Lord God. Lord God."

"Have mercy on us."

A young Negro in Army khakis walked over to where the white man and Gaines Williamson were trying to get Estella out of the bulky jacket. "We'll cut it off," he said calmly. He pulled a straight razor from his pocket, slit one shoulder of the life jacket, pushed it out of the way, and straddled Estella's body. "I know how," he said. "I learned in the Army." He arranged her body in position—lying flat on her stomach, face turned to the side and arms above her head— and set to work, raising her arms and then her body rhythmically. When he lifted her body in the middle, her face dragged on the splintery planks of the float.

Anna crawled through the crowd to where Estella lay. Squatting down without a word, she put her hands under Estella's face to protect it from the splinters. It passed through her mind that she should do something about the children. Looking around, she saw them standing in a row at one side of the float, staring down at her and Estella—no longer crying, just standing and staring. Somebody ought to get them away from here, she thought vaguely, but the thought left her mind and she forgot them. She swayed, rocked back on her heels, sat down suddenly, and then lay on her stomach, her head against Estella's head, her hands cradling the sleeping face.

Who's going to tell James, she thought. Who's going to tell him she's dead? And then, I. I have to tell him. She began to talk to Estella. "Please, darling," she said. "Please, Estella, breathe." Tears of weakness rolled down her face, and she looked up above the forest of legs at the black faces in a circle around them. "She's got four babies," she said. "*Babies*. Who's going to tell her husband she's dead? Who's going to tell him?" And then, again, "Please, Estella, breathe. Please breathe."

No one answered. The young Negro soldier continued to raise the limp arms and body alternately, his motions deliberate and rhythmical, the sweat pouring off his face and dripping down on his sweat-soaked shirt. His thin face was intent and stern. The storm was over, the clouds to the west had blown away, and the sun had come out and beat down bright and hot, raising steamy air from the rain-soaked float.

A long time passed. The soldier giving Estella artificial respiration looked around at the crowd. "Anybody know how to do this? I'm about to give out." He did not pause or break the rhythm of his motions.

A man stepped out of the crowd. "I can do it," he said. "I know how."

"Come on, then," the soldier said. "Get down here by me and do it with me three times, and then, when I stop, you take over. Don't break it."

"Please, Estella," Anna said. "Please."

"One . . . Two . . ."

She felt someone pulling at her arm and looked up. A policeman was standing over her. "Here, lady," he said. "Get up off that dock. You ain't doing no good."

"But the splinters will get in her face," Anna said. "I'm holding her face off the boards."

"It ain't going to matter if her face is tore up if she's dead," the policeman said. "Get up."

Someone handed her a towel, and she folded it and put it under Estella's face. The policeman dragged her to her feet and took her over to a chair near the edge of the float and sat her down in it. He squatted beside her. "Now, who was in the boat?" he said. "I got to make a report."

Anna made a vague gesture. "We were," she said.

"Who is 'we,' lady?"

"Estella and I and the children."

"Lady, give me the names, please," the policeman said.

"Estella Moseby, the Negro woman. She used to work for me, and we *asked* her, we asked her—" She broke off.

"Come on, who else?"

Anna stared at him, a short, bald man with shining pink scalp, and drum belly buttoned tightly into his uniform. A wave of nausea overcame her, and she saw his head surrounded by the shimmering black spokes of a rimless wheel, a black halo. "I'm going to be sick," she said. Collapsing out of the chair onto the dock, she leaned her head over the edge and vomited into the lake.

He waited until she was through and then helped her back into her chair. "Who else was with you?" he said.

"My two children, Ralph and Steve," she said. "Murray McCrae. I am Mrs. Richard Glover."

"Where is this McCrae fellow? He all right?"

"He's a little *boy*," Anna said. "A child. He's over there somewhere."

"You sure there wasn't nobody else with you?"

"No. That's all," Anna said.

"Now, give me the addresses, please. Where did the nigger live?"

"For God's sake," Anna said. "What difference does it make? Go away and let me alone."

"I got to make my report, lady."

Ralph tugged at Anna's arm. "Mama, hadn't I better call Daddy?" he said.

"Yes," she said. "Yes, I guess you had." Oh, God, she thought, he has to find out. I can't put it off. Everybody has to find out that Estella is dead.

Anna heard a commotion on the levee. The steadily increasing crowd separated, and two white-jacketed men appeared and began to work over Estella. Behind them, a woman with a camera snapped pictures.

"What are they taking *pictures* of her for?" Anna asked.

Then she heard her husband's voice shouting, "Get off the damn raft, God damn it! Get off. You want to sink it? Get back there. You want to drown us all?"

The policeman stood up and went toward the crowd. "What the hell?" Anna heard him say.

"And put that camera up, if you don't want me to throw it in the lake." Anna's husband was in a fury of outrage, and concentrated it for the moment on the woman reporter from the local newspaper, who was snapping pictures of Estella.

"You all right, Anna?" Richard asked her.

The people on the float were scuttling back to the levee, and the reporter had disappeared. Anna, who was still sitting where the policeman had left her, nodded and opened her mouth to speak, but her husband was gone before she could say anything. She felt a wave of self-pity. He didn't even stay to help me, she thought.

Then, a moment or an hour later—she did not know how long—she heard a strange high-pitched shriek from the other end of the float. What's that, she thought. It sounded again—a long, rasping rattle and then a shriek. Does the machine they brought make that queer noise?

"She's breathing," somebody said.

"No," Anna said aloud to nobody, for nobody was listening. "No. She's dead. I couldn't help it. I let her drown. Who's going to tell James?"

The float was cleared now. Besides Estella and Anna, only the two policemen, the two men from the ambulance, and Gaines Williamson were on it. The man who had rescued them was gone. The crowd stood quietly on the levee.

"Where is Richard?" Anna said. "Did he leave?"

No one answered.

The long, rasping rattle and shriek sounded again. Gaines Williamson came over to where Anna was sitting, and bent down to her, smiling kindly. "She's alive, Mrs. Glover," he said. "She's going to be all right."

Anna shook her head.

"Yes, Ma'am. She's moving and breathing, and yelling like crazy. She's going to be all right."

Anna got up shakily. She walked over to where the men were working Estella onto a stretcher.

"What's she doing?" she said. "What's the matter with her?"

Estella was thrashing her arms and legs furiously, mouth open, eyes staring, her face again the mask of mindless terror that Anna had seen in the lake. The rattle and shriek were her breathing and screaming.

"She must think she's still in the water," one of the men said. "Shock. But she's O.K. Look at her kick."

Anna sat down on the float, her knees buckling under her, and someone pulled her out of the way while four men carried the stretcher off the float and up the levee toward the ambulance.

Richard reappeared at the foot of the levee and crossed the walkway to the Yacht Club float. He bent down to help her up. "I'm sorry I had to leave you," he said. "I had to get the children away from here and find someone to take them home."

"My God," Anna said. "She's alive. They said she would be all right."

Later, in the car, she said to her husband, "She kept pushing me down, Richard. I tried to hold her up, I tried to make her take hold of the boat. But she kept pushing me down."

"It's all right now," he said. "Try not to think about it any more."

The next day, when Anna visited Estella in the hospital, she learned that Estella remembered almost nothing of what had happened. She recalled getting into the skiff for the trip home, but everything after that was gone.

"James says you saved my life," she said, in a hoarse whisper, "and I thank you."

Her husband stood at the head of her bed, gray-haired and dignified in his Sunday suit. He nodded. "The day won't come when we'll forget it, Miss Anna," he said. "God be my witness."

Anna shook her head. "I never should have taken you out without a life preserver," she said.

"Ain't she suppose to be a grown woman?" James said. "She suppose to know better herself."

"How do you feel?" Anna asked.

"Lord, not a square inch on my body don't ache," Estella said. She laid her hands on the mound of her body under the sheet. "My stomach!" she said, with a wry laugh. "Somebody must've jumped up and down on it."

"I reckon that's from the artificial respiration," Anna said. "I had never seen anyone do it that way before. They pick you up under the stomach and then put you down and lift your arms. And then, too, I kicked you. And we must have banged you up some getting you into the boat. Lord! The more I think about it, the worse it gets. Because Gaines hit you in the stomach, too, as soon as he got you into the boat. That's what really saved your life. As soon as he got you into the boat, he hit you in the stomach and got rid of a lot of the water in your lungs and let in some air. I believe that breath you took in Gaines' boat kept you alive until we got you to the dock."

"You kicked me?" Estella said.

"We were going down," Anna said, feeling that she must confess to Estella the enormity of what she had done, "and I finally knew I couldn't keep you up. I kicked you in the stomach hard, and got loose from you, and then when you came up I grabbed you and held on, and about that time they saw us and the boats came. You passed out just when I kicked you, or else the kick knocked you out, because you didn't struggle any more. I reckon that was lucky, too."

Estella shook her head. "I can't remember anything about it," she whispered. "Not anything." She pointed out the window toward the smokestack rising from the opposite wing of the hospital. "Seems like last night I got the idea there's a little man up there," she said. "He peeps out from behind that smokestack at me, and I'm afraid of him. He leans on the smokestack, and then he jumps away real quick, like it's hot, and one time he came right over here and stood on the window ledge and looked in at me. Lucky the window was shut. I said 'Boo!' and, you know, he fell off! It didn't hurt him; he came right back. He wants to tell me something, yes, but he can't get in." She closed her eyes.

Anna looked anxiously at James.

"They still giving her something to keep her quiet," he said. "Every so often she gets a notion somebody trying to get in here."

Estella opened her eyes. "I thank you, Miss Anna," she said. "James told me you saved my life." She smiled. "Seems like every once in a while I hear your voice," she said. "Way off. Way, way off. You're saying, 'I'll save you, Estella. Don't be afraid. I'll save you.' That's all I can remember."

Ernest J. Gaines (January 15, 1933) was born in Oscar, Louisiana. As a boy he worked in the plantation fields and spent much of his free time with his aunt, Augustine Jefferson. She encouraged him to read and to write letters for many of the old people who were illiterate. Gaines says, "I came up in a place that was oral; we talked stories." In 1948 he moved to Vallejo, California to live with his mother and stepfather, who encouraged his education. Gaines finished high school and two years of junior college before being drafted into the Army in 1953. He entered San Francisco State College on the G.I. bill in 1955 and graduated in 1957. In 1958 he received a Wallace Stegner Creative Writing Fellowship for graduate study at Stanford University, where he concentrated on writing fiction and worked on a novel he had started writing as a teenager. In 1964 this novel, *Catherine Carmier*, the story of discrimination within the black Creole community, was published. It was followed by *Of Love and Dust* (1967), a novel of the convict-lease system in Louisiana, and *Bloodline* (1968), a collection of five stories. His internationally successful, *The Autobiography of Miss Jane Pittman*, a novel he describes as "folk autobiography," was published in 1971. Two more novels followed —*In My Father's House* (1978) and *A Gathering of Old Men* (1983).

Gaines divides his life and writing between San Francisco and Lafayette, Louisiana where he serves as writer in residence at the University of Southwestern Louisiana.

THE SKY IS GRAY

by *Ernest J. Gaines*

Go'n be coming in a few minutes. Coming 'round that bend down there full speed. And I'm go'n get out my handkercher and I'm go'n wave it down and us go'n get on it and go.

I keep on looking for it, but Mama don't look that way no more. She looking down the road where us jest come from. It's a long old road, and far's you can see you don't see nothing but gravel. You got dry weeds on both sides, and you got trees on both sides, and fences on both sides, too. And you got cows in the pastures and they standing close together. And when us was coming out yer to catch the bus I seen the smoke coming out o' the cow's nose.

I look at my mama and I know what she thinking. I been with Mama so much, jest me and her, I know what she thinking all the time. Right now it's home—Auntie and them. She thinking if they got 'nough wood—if she left 'nough there to keep 'em warm till us get back. She thinking if it go'n rain and if any of 'em go'n have to go out in the rain. She thinking 'bout the hog—if he go'n get out, and if Ty and Val be able to get him back in. She always worry like that when she leave the house. She don't worry too much if she leave me there with the smaller ones 'cause she know I'm go'n look after 'em and look after Auntie and everything else. I'm the oldest and she say I'm the man.

I look at my mama and I love my mama. She wearing that black coat and that black hat and she looking sad. I love my mama and I want to put my arm 'round her and tell her. But I'm not s'pose to do that. She say that's weakness and that's cry-baby stuff, and she don't want no cry-baby 'round her. She don't want you to be scared neither. 'Cause Ty scared

of ghosts and she always whipping him. I'm scared of the
dark, too. But I make 'tend I ain't. I make 'tend I ain't
cause I'm the oldest, and I got to set a good sample for the
rest. I can't ever be scared and I can't ever cry. And that's
the reason I didn't never say nothing 'bout my teef. It been
hurting me and hurting me close to a month now. But I
didn't say it. I didn't say it 'cause I didn't want act like no
cry-baby, and 'cause I know us didn't have 'nough money to
have it pulled. But, Lord, it been hurting me. And look like
it won't start till at night when you trying to get little sleep.
Then soon's you shet your eyes—umm-umm, Lord. Look
like it go right down to your heart string.

"Hurting, hanh?" Ty'd say.

I'd shake my head, but I wouldn't open my mouth for
nothing. You open your mouth and let that wind in, and it
almost kill you.

I'd just lay there and listen to 'em snore. Ty, there, right
'side me, and Auntie and Val over by the fireplace. Val
younger 'an me and Ty, and he sleep with Auntie. Mama
sleep 'round the other side with Louis and Walker.

I'd just lay there and listen to 'em, and listen to that wind
out there, and listen to that fire in the fireplace. Sometime
it'd stop long enough to let me get little rest. Sometime it
just hurt, hurt, hurt. Lord, have mercy.

II

Auntie knowed it was hurting me. I didn't tell nobody but
Ty, 'cause us buddies and he ain't go'n tell nobody. But
some kind o' way Auntie found out. When she asked me, I
told her no, nothing was wrong. But she knowed it all the
time. She told me to mash up a piece o' aspirin and wrap it
in some cotton and jugg it down in that hole. I did it, but it
didn't do no good. It stopped for a little while, and started
right back again. She wanted to tell Mama, but I told her
Uh-uh. 'Cause I knowed it didn't have no money, and it jest
was go'n make her mad again. So she told Monsieur Bayonne, and Monsieur Bayonne came to the house and told
me to kneel down 'side him on the fireplace. He put his
finger in his mouth and made the Sign of the Cross on my
jaw. The tip of Monsieur Bayonne finger is some hard,
'cause he always playing on that guitar. If us sit outside at
night us can always hear Monsieur Bayonne playing on his

guitar. Sometime us leave him out there playing on the guitar.

He made the Sign of the Cross over and over on my jaw, but that didn't do no good. Even when he prayed and told me to pray some, too, that teef still hurt.

"How you feeling?" he say.

"Same," I say.

He kept on praying and making the Sign of the Cross and I kept on praying, too.

"Still hurting?" he say.

"Yes, sir."

Monsieur Bayonne mashed harder and harder on my jaw. He mashed so hard he almost pushed me on Ty. But then he stopped.

"What kind o' prayers you praying, boy?" he say.

"Baptist," I say.

"Well, I'll be—no wonder that teef still killing him. I'm going one way and he going the other. Boy, don't you know any Catholic prayers?"

"Hail Mary," I say.

"Then you better start saying it."

"Yes, sir."

He started mashing again, and I could hear him praying at the same time. And, sure 'nough, afterwhile it stopped.

Me and Ty went outside where Monsieur Bayonne two hounds was, and us started playing with 'em. "Let's go hunting," Ty say. "All right," I say; and us went on back in the pasture. Soon the hounds got on a trail, and me and Ty followed 'em all cross the pasture and then back in the woods, too. And then they cornered this little old rabbit and killed him, and me and Ty made 'em get back, and us picked up the rabbit and started on back home. But it had started hurting me again. It was hurting me plenty now, but I wouldn't tell Monsieur Bayonne. That night I didn't sleep a bit, and first thing in the morning Auntie told me go back and let Monsieur Bayonne pray over me some more. Monsieur Bayonne was in his kitchen making coffee when I got there. Soon's he seen me, he knowed what was wrong.

"All right, kneel down there 'side that stove," he say. "And this time pray Catholic. I don't know nothing 'bout Baptist, and don't want know nothing 'bout him."

III

Last night Mama say: "Tomorrow us going to town."

"It ain't hurting me no more," I say. "I can eat anything on it."

"Tomorrow us going to town," she say.

And after she finished eating, she got up and went to bed. She always go to bed early now. 'Fore Daddy went in the Army, she used to stay up late. All o' us sitting out on the gallery or 'round the fire. But now, look like soon's she finish eating she go to bed.

This morning when I woke up, her and Auntie was standing 'fore the fireplace. She say: " 'Nough to get there and back. Dollar and a half to have it pulled. Twenty-five for me to go, twenty-five for him. Twenty-five for me to come back, twenty-five for him. Fifty cents left. Guess I get a little piece o' salt meat with that."

"Sure can use a piece," Auntie say. "White beans and no salt meat ain't white beans."

"I do the best I can," Mama say.

They was quiet after that, and I made 'tend I was still sleep.

"James, hit the floor," Auntie say.

I still made 'tend I was sleep. I didn't want 'em to know I was listening.

"All right," Auntie say, shaking me by the shoulder. "Come on. Today's the day."

I pushed the cover down to get out, and Ty grabbed it and pulled it back.

"You, too, Ty," Auntie say.

"I ain't getting no teef pulled," Ty say.

"Don't mean it ain't time to get up," Auntie say. "Hit it, Ty."

Ty got up grumbling.

"James, you hurry up and get in your clothes and eat your food," Auntie say. "What time y'all coming back?" she say to Mama.

"That 'leven o'clock bus," Mama say. "Got to get back in that field this evening."

"Get a move on you, James," Auntie say.

I went in the kitchen and washed my face, then I ate my breakfast. I was having bread and syrup. The bread was warm and hard and tasted good. And I tried to make it last a long time.

Ty came back there, grumbling and mad at me.

"Got to get up," he say. "I ain't having no teef pulled. What I got to be getting up for."

Ty poured some syrup in his pan and got a piece of bread. He didn't wash his hands, neither his face, and I could see that white stuff in his eyes.

"You the one getting a teef pulled," he say. "What I got to get up for. I bet you if I was getting a teef pulled, you wouldn't be getting up. Shucks; syrup again. I'm getting tired of this old syrup. Syrup, syrup, syrup. I want me some bacon sometime."

"Go out in the field and work and you can have bacon," Auntie say. She stood in the middle door looking at Ty. "You better be glad you got syrup. Some people ain't got that—hard's time is."

"Shucks," Ty say. "How can I be strong."

"I don't know too much 'bout your strength," Auntie say; "but I know where you go'n be hot, you keep that grumbling up. James, get a move on you; your mama waiting."

I ate my last piece of bread and went in the front room. Mama was standing 'fore the fireplace warming her hands. I put on my coat and my cap, and us left the house.

IV

I look down there again, but it still ain't coming. I almost say, "It ain't coming, yet," but I keep my mouth shet. 'Cause that's something else she don't like. She don't like for you to say something just for nothing. She can see it ain't coming, I can see it ain't coming, so why say it ain't coming. I don't say it, and I turn and look at the river that's back o' us. It so cold the smoke just raising up from the water. I see a bunch of pull-doos not too far out—jest on the other side the lilies. I'm wondering if you can eat pull-doos. I ain't too sure, 'cause I ain't never ate none. But I done ate owls and black birds, and I done ate red birds, too. I didn't want kill the red birds, but she made me kill 'em. They had two of 'em back there. One in my trap, one in Ty trap. Me and Ty was go'n play with 'em and let 'em go. But she made me kill 'em 'cause us needed the food.

"I can't," I say. "I can't."

"Here," she say. "Take it."

"I can't," I say. "I can't. I can't kill him, Mama. Please."

"Here," she say. "Take this fork, James."

"Please, Mama, I can't kill him," I say.

I could tell she was go'n hit me. And I jecked back, but I didn't jeck back soon enough.

"Take it," she say.

I took it and reached in for him, but he kept hopping to the back.

"I can't, Mama," I say. The water just kept running down my face. "I can't."

"Get him out o' there," she say.

I reached in for him and he kept hopping to the back. Then I reached in farther, and he pecked me on the hand.

"I can't Mama," I say.

She slapped me again.

I reached in again, but he kept hopping out my way. Then he hopped to one side, and I reached there. The fork got him on the leg and I heard his leg pop. I pulled my hand out 'cause I had hurt him.

"Give it here," she say, and jecked the fork out my hand.

She reached and got the little bird right in the neck. I heard the fork go in his neck, and I heard it go in the ground. She brought him out and helt him right in front o' me.

"That's one," she say. She shook him off and gived me the fork. "Get the other one."

"I can't, Mama. I do anything. But I can't do that."

She went to the corner o' the fence and broke the biggest switch over there. I knelt 'side the trap crying.

"Get him out o' there," she say.

"I can't, Mama."

She started hitting me cross the back. I went down on the ground crying.

"Get him," she say.

"Octavia," Auntie say.

'Cause she had come out o' the house and she was standing by the tree looking at us.

"Get him out o' there," Mama say.

"Octavia," Auntie say; "explain to him. Explain to him. Jest don't beat him. Explain to him."

But she hit me and hit me and hit me.

I'm still young. I ain't no more'an eight. But I know now. I know why I had to. (They was so little, though. They was so little. I 'member how I picked the feathers off 'em and cleaned 'em and helt 'em over the fire. Then us all ate 'em.

Ain't had but little bitty piece, but us all had little bitty piece, and ever'body jest looked at me, 'cause they was so proud.) S'pose she had to go away? That's why I had to do it. S'pose she had to go away like Daddy went away? Then who was go'n look after us? They had to be somebody left to carry on. I didn't know it then, but I know it now. Auntie and Monsieur Bayonne talked to me and made me see.

V

Time I see it, I get out my handkercher and start waving. It still 'way down there, but I keep waving anyhow. Then it come closer and stop and me and Mama get on. Mama tell me go sit in the back while she pay. I do like she say, and the people look at me. When I pass the little sign that say White and Colored, I start looking for a seat. I jest see one of 'em back there, but I don't take it, 'cause I want my mama to sit down herself. She come in the back and sit down, and I lean on the seat. They got seats in the front, but I know I can't sit there, 'cause I have to sit back o' the sign. Anyhow, I don't want sit there if my mama go'n sit back here.

They got a lady sitting 'side my mama and she look at me and grin little bit. I grin back, but I don't open my mouth, 'cause the wind'll get in and make that teef hurt. The lady take out a pack o' gum and reach me a slice, but I shake my head. She reach Mama a slice, and Mama shake her head. The lady jest can't understand why a little boy'll turn down gum and she reached me a slice again. This time I point to my jaw. The lady understand and grin little bit, and I grin little bit, but I don't open my mouth, though.

They got a girl sitting 'cross from me. She got on a red overcoat, and her hair plaited in one big plait. First, I make 'tend I don't even see her. But then I start looking at her little bit. She make 'tend she don't see me neither, but I catch her looking that way. She got a cold, and ever' now and then she hist that little handkercher to her nose. She ought to blow it, but she don't. Must think she too much a lady or something.

Ever' time she hist that little handkercher, the lady 'side her say something in her yer. She shake her head and lay her hands in her lap again. Then I catch her kind o' looking where I'm at. I grin at her. But think she'll grin back? No.

She turn up her little old nose like I got some snot on my face or something. Well, I show her both o' us can turn us head. I turn mine, too, and look out at the river.

The river is gray. The sky is gray. They have pull-doos on the water. The water is wavey, and the pull-doos go up and down. The bus go 'round a turn, and you got plenty trees hiding the river. Then the bus go 'round another turn, and I can see the river again.

I look to the front where all the white people sitting. Then I look at that little old gal again. I don't look right at her, 'cause I don't want all them people to know I love her. I jest look at her little bit, like I'm looking out that window over there. But she know I'm looking that way, and she kind o' look at me, too. The lady sitting 'side her catch her this time, and she lean over and say something in her yer.

"I don't love him nothing," that little old gal say out loud.

Ever'body back there yer her mouth, and all of 'em look at us and laugh.

"I don't love you, neither," I say. "So you don't have to turn up your nose, Miss."

"You the one looking," she say.

"I wasn't looking at you," I say. "I was looking out that window, there."

"Out that window, my foot," she say. "I seen you. Ever' time I turn 'round you look at me."

"You must o' been looking yourself if you seen me all them times," I say.

'   "Shucks," she say. "I got me all kind o' boyfriends."

"I got girlfriends, too," I say.

"Well, I just don't want you to get your hopes up," she say.

I don't say no more to that little old gal, 'cause I don't want have to bust her in the mouth. I lean on the seat where Mama sitting, and I don't even look that way no more. When us get to Bayonne, she jugg her little old tongue out at me. I make 'tend I'm go'n hit her, and she duck down side her mama. And all the people laugh at us again.

VI

Me and Mama get off and start walking in town. Bayonne is a little bitty town. Baton Rouge is a hundred times bigger 'an Bayonne. I went to Baton Rouge once—me, Ty, Mama, and Daddy. But that was 'way back yonder—'fore he went in the Army. I wonder when us go'n see him again. I wonder when. Look like he ain't ever coming home. . . . Even the pavement all cracked in Bayonne. Got grass shooting right out the sidewalk. Got weeds in the ditch, too; jest like they got home.

It some cold in Bayonne. Look like it colder 'an it is home. The wind blow in my face, and I feel that stuff running down my nose. I sniff. Mama say use that handkercher. I blow my nose and put it back.

Us pass a school and I see them white children playing in the yard. Big old red school, and them children jest running and playing. Then us pass a café, and I see a bunch of 'em in there eating. I wish I was in there 'cause I'm cold. Mama tell me keep my eyes in front where they blonks.

Us pass stores that got dummies, and us pass another café, and then us pass a shoe shop, and that baldhead man in there fixing on a shoe. I look at him and I butt into that white lady, and Mama jeck me in front and tell me stay there.

Us come to the courthouse, and I see the flag waving there. This one yer ain't like the one us got at school. This one yer ain't got but a handful of stars. One at school got a big pile of stars—one for ever' state. Us pass it and us turn and there it is—the dentist office. Me and Mama go in, and they got people sitting ever' where you look. They even got a little boy in there younger 'an me.

Me and Mama sit on that bench, and a white lady come in there and ask me what my name. Mama tell her, and the white lady go back. Then I yer somebody hollering in there. And soon's that little boy hear him hollering he, start hollering, too. His mama pat him and pat him, trying to make him hush up, but he ain't thinking 'bout her.

The man that was hollering in there come out holding his jaw.

"Got it, hanh?" another man say.

The man shake his head.

"Man, I thought they was killing you in there," the other man say. "Hollering like a pig under a gate."

The man don't say nothing. He jest head for the door, and the other man follow him.

"John Lee," the white lady say. "John Lee Williams."

The little boy jugg his head down in his mama lap and

holler more now. His mama tell him go with the nurse, but he ain't thinking 'bout her. His mama tell him again, but he don't even yer. His mama pick him up and take him in there, and even when the white lady shet the door I can still hear him hollering.

"I often wonder why the Lord let a child like that suffer," a lady say to my mama. The lady's sitting right in front o' us on another bench. She got on a white dress and a black sweater. She must be a nurse or something herself, I reckoned.

"Not us to question," a man say.

"Sometimes I don't know if we shouldn't," the lady say.

"I know definitely we shouldn't," the man say. The man look like a preacher. He big and fat and he got on a black suit. He got a gold chain, too.

"Why?" the lady say.

"Why anything?" the preacher say.

"Yes," the lady say. "Why anything?"

"Not us to question," the preacher say.

The lady look at the preacher a little while and look at Mama again.

"And look like it's the poor who do most the suffering," she say. "I don't understand it."

"Best not to even try," the preacher say. "He works in mysterious ways. Wonders to perform."

Right then Little John Lee bust out hollering, and ever'body turn they head.

"He's not a good dentist," the lady say. "Dr. Robillard is much better. But more expensive. That's why most of the colored people come here. The white people go to Dr. Robillard. Y'all from Bayonne?"

"Down the river," my mama say. And that's all she go'n say, 'cause she don't talk much. But the lady keep on looking at her, and so she say: "Near Morgan."

"I see," the lady say.

VII

"That's the trouble with the black people in this country today," somebody else say. This one yer sitting on the same side me and Mama sitting, and he kind o'sitting in front of that preacher. He look like a teacher or somebody that go to college. He got on a suit, and he got a book that he been reading. "We don't question is exactly the trouble," he say. "We should question and question and question. Question everything."

The preacher jest look at him a long time. He done put a toothpick or something in his mouth, and he jest keep turning it and turning it. You can see he don't like that boy with that book.

"Maybe you can explain what you mean," he say.

"I said what I meant," the boy say. "Question everything. Every stripe, every star, every word spoken. Everything."

"It 'pears to me this young lady and I was talking 'bout God, young man," the preacher say.

"Question Him, too," the boy say.

"Wait," the preacher say. "Wait now."

"You heard me right," the boy say. "His existence as well as everything else. Everything."

The preacher jest look cross the room at the boy. You can see he getting madder and madder. But mad or no mad, the boy ain't thinking 'bout him. He look at the preacher jest's the preacher look at him.

"Is this what they coming to?" the preacher say. "Is this what we educating them for?"

"You're not educating me," the boy say. "I wash dishes at night to go to school in the day. So even the words you spoke need questioning."

The preacher jest look at him and shake his head.

"When I come in this room and seen you there with your book, I said to myself, There's an intelligent man. How wrong a person can be."

"Show me one reason to believe in the existence of a God," the boy say.

"My heart tell me," the preacher say.

"My heart tells me," the boy say. "My heart tells me. Sure, my heart tells me. And as long as you listen to what your heart tells you, you will have only what the white man gives you and nothing more. Me, I don't listen to my heart. The purpose of the heart is to pump blood throughout the body, and nothing else."

"Who's your paw, boy?" the preacher say.

"Why?"

"Who is he?"

"He's dead."

"And your mom?"

"She's in Charity Hospital with pneumonia. Half killed herself working for nothing."

"And 'cause he's dead and she sick, you mad at the world?"

"I'm not mad at the world. I'm questioning the world. I'm questioning it with cold logic, sir. What do words like Freedom, Liberty, God, White, Colored mean? I want to know. That's why *you* are sending us to school, to read and to ask questions. And because we ask these questions, you call us mad. No, sir, it is not us who are mad."

"You keep saying 'us'?"

" 'Us' . . . why not? I'm not alone."

The preacher jest shake his head. Then he look at ever'body in the room—ever'body. Some of the people look down at the floor, keep from looking at him. I kind o' look 'way myself, but soon's I know he done turn his head, I look that way again.

"I'm sorry for you," he say.

"Why?" the boy say. "Why not be sorry for yourself? Why are you so much better off than I am? Why aren't you sorry for these other people in here? Why not be sorry for the lady who had to drag her child into the dentist office? Why not be sorry for the lady sitting on that bench over there? Be sorry for them. Not for me. Some way or other I'm going to make it."

"No, I'm sorry for you," the preacher say.

"Of course. Of course," the boy say, shaking his head. "You're sorry for me because I rock that pillar you're leaning on."

"You can't ever rock the pillar I'm leaning on, young man. It's stronger than anything man can ever do."

"You believe in God because a man told you to believe in God. A white man told you to believe in God. And why? To keep you ignorant, so he can keep you under his feet."

"So now, we the ignorant?"

"Yes," the boy say. "Yes." And he open his book again.

The preacher jest look at him there. The boy done forgot all about him. Ever'body else make 'tend they done forgot 'bout the squabble, too.

Then I see that preacher getting up real slow. Preacher a great big old man, and he got to brace hisself to get up. He come 'cross the room where the boy is. He jest stand there looking at him, but the boy don't raise his head.

"Stand up, boy," preacher say.

The boy look up at him, then he shet his book real slow and stand up. Preacher jest draw back and hit him in the face. The boy fall 'gainst the wall, but he straighten hisself up and look right back at that preacher.

"You forgot the other cheek," he say.

The preacher hit him again on the other side. But this time the boy don't fall.

"That hasn't changed a thing," he say.

The preacher jest look at the boy. The preacher breathing real hard like he jest run up a hill. The boy sit down and open his book again.

"I feel sorry for you," the preacher say. "I never felt so sorry for a man before."

The boy make 'tend he don't even hear that preacher. He keep on reading his book. The preacher go back and get his hat off the chair.

"Excuse me," he say to us. "I'll come back some other time. Y'all, please excuse me."

And he look at the boy and go out the room. The boy hist his hand up to his mouth one time, to wipe 'way some blood. All the rest o' the time he keep on reading.

VIII

The lady and her little boy come out the dentist, and the nurse call somebody else in. Then little bit later they come out, and the nurse call another name. But fast's she call somebody in there, somebody else come in the place where we at, and the room stay full.

The people coming in now, all of 'em wearing big coats. One of 'em say something 'bout sleeting, and another one say he hope not. Another one say he think it ain't nothing but rain. 'Cause, he say, rain can get awful cold this time o' year.

All 'cross the room they talking. Some of 'em talking to people right by 'em, some of 'em talking to people clare 'cross the room, some of 'em talking to anybody'll listen. It's a little bitty room, no bigger 'an us kitchen, and I can see ever'body in there. The little old room's full of smoke, 'cause you got two old men smoking pipes. I think I feel my teef thumping me some, and I hold my breath and wait. I wait and wait, but it don't thump me no more. Thank God for that.

I feel like going to sleep, and I lean back 'gainst the wall. But I'm scared to go to sleep: Scared 'cause the nurse might call my name and I won't hear her. And Mama might go to sleep, too, and she be mad if neither us heard the nurse.

I look up at Mama. I love my mama. I love my mama. And when cotton come I'm go'n get her a newer coat. And I ain't go'n get a black one neither. I think I'm go'n get her a red one.

"They got some books over there," I say. "Want read one of 'em?"

Mama look at the books, but she don't answer me.

"You got yourself a little man there," the lady say.

Mama don't say nothing to the lady, but she must 'a' grin a little bit, 'cause I seen the lady grinning back. The lady look at me a little while, like she feeling sorry for me.

"You sure got that preacher out here in a hurry," she say to that other boy.

The boy look up at her and look in his book again. When I grow up I want to be jest like him. I want clothes like that and I want keep a book with me, too.

"You really don't believe in God?" the lady say.

"No," he say.

"But why?" the lady say.

"Because the wind is pink," he say.

"What?" the lady say.

The boy don't answer her no more. He jest read in his book.

"Talking 'bout the wind is pink," that old lady say. She sitting on the same bench with the boy, and she trying to look in his face. The boy make 'tend the old lady ain't even there. He jest keep reading. "Wind is pink," she say again. "Eh, Lord, what children go'n be saying next?"

The lady 'cross from us bust out laughing.

"That's a good one," she say. "The wind is pink. Yes, sir, that's a good one."

"Don't you believe the wind is pink?" the boy say. He keep his head down in the book.

"Course I believe it, Honey," the lady say. "Course I do." She look at us and wink her eye. "And what color is grass, Honey?"

"Grass? Grass is black."

She bust out laughing again. The boy look at her.

"Don't you believe grass is black?" he say.

The lady quit laughing and look at him. Ever'body else look at him now. The place quiet, quiet.

"Grass is green, Honey," the lady say. "It was green yesterday, it's green today, and it's go'n be green tomorrow."

"How do you know it's green?"

"I know because I know."

"You don't know it's green. You believe it's green because someone told you it was green. If someone had told you it was black you'd believe it was black."

"It's green," the lady say. "I know green when I see green."

"Prove it's green."

"Surely, now," the lady say. "Don't tell me it's coming to that?"

"It's coming to just that," the boy say. "Words mean nothing. One means no more than the other."

"That's what it all coming to?" that old lady say. That old lady got on a turban and she got on two sweaters. She got a green sweater under a black sweater. I can see the green sweater 'cause some of the buttons on the other sweater missing.

"Yes, ma'am," the boy say. "Words mean nothing. Action is the only thing. Doing. That's the only thing."

"Other words, you want the Lord to come down here and show Hisself to you?" she say.

"Exactly, ma'am."

"You don't mean that, I'm sure?"

"I do, ma'am."

"Done, Jesus," the old lady say, shaking her head.

"I didn't go 'long with that preacher at first," the other lady say; "but now—I don't know. When a person say the grass is black, he's either a lunatic or something wrong."

"Prove to me that it's green."

"It's green because the people say it's green."

"Those same people say we're citizens of the United States."

"I think I'm a citizen."

"Citizens have certain rights. Name me one right that you have. One right, granted by the Constitution, that you can exercise in Bayonne."

The lady don't answer him. She jest look at him like she don't know what he talking 'bout. I know I don't.

"Things changing," she say.

"Things are changing because some black men have begun to follow their brains instead of their hearts."

"You trying to say these people don't believe in God?"

"I'm sure some of them do. Maybe most of them do. But they don't believe that God is going to touch these white people's hearts and change them tomorrow. Things change through action. By no other way."

Ever'body sit quiet and look at the boy. Nobody say a thing. Then the lady 'cross from me and Mama jest shake her head.

"Let's hope that not all your generation feel the same way you do," she say.

"Think what you please, it doesn't matter," the boy say. "But it will be men who listen to their heads and not their hearts who will see that your children have a better chance than you had."

"Let's hope they ain't all like you, though," the old lady say. "Done forgot the heart absolutely."

"Yes, ma'am, I hope they aren't all like me," the boy say. "Unfortunately I was born too late to believe in your God. Let's hope that the ones who come after will have your faith—if not in your God, then in something else, something definitely that they can lean on. I haven't anything. For me, the wind is pink; the grass is black."

IX

The nurse come in the room where us all sitting and waiting and say the doctor won't take no more patients till one o'clock this evening. My mama jump up off the bench and go up to the white lady.

"Nurse, I have to go back in the field this evening," she say.

"The doctor is treating his last patient now," the nurse say. "One o'clock this evening."

"Can I at least speak to the doctor?" my mama say.

"I'm his nurse," the lady say.

"My little boy sick," my mama say. "Right now his teef almost killing him."

The nurse look at me. She trying to make up her mind if to let me come in. I look at her real pitiful. The teef ain't hurting me a tall, but Mama say it is, so I make 'tend for her sake.

"This evening," the nurse say, and go back in the office.

"Don't feel 'jected, Honey," the lady say to Mama. "I been 'round 'em a long time—they take you when they want to. If you was white, that's something else; but you the wrong shade."

Mama don't say nothing to the lady, and me and her go outside and stand 'gainst the wall. It's cold out there. I can feel that wind going through my coat. Some of the other people come out of the room and go up the street. Me and Mama stand there a little while and start to walking. I don't know where us going. When us come to the other street us jest stand there.

"You don't have to make water, do you?" Mama say.

"No, ma'am," I say.

Us go up the street. Walking real slow. I can tell Mama don't know where she going. When us come to a store us stand there and look at the dummies. I look at a little boy with a brown overcoat. He got on brown shoes, too. I look at my old shoes and look at his'n again. You wait till summer, I say.

Me and Mama walk away. Us come up to another store and us stop and look at them dummies, too. Then us go again. Us pass a café where the white people in there eating. Mama tell me keep my eyes in front where they blonks, but I can't help from seeing them people eat. My stomach start to growling 'cause I'm hungry. When I see people eating, I get hungry; when I see a coat, I get cold.

A man whistle at my mama when us go by a filling station. She make 'tend she don't even see him. I look back and I feel like hitting him in the mouth. If I was bigger, I say. If I was bigger, you see.

Us keep on going. I'm getting colder and colder, but I don't say nothing. I feel that stuff running down my nose and I sniff.

"That rag," she say.

I git it out and wipe my nose. I'm getting cold all over now—my face, my hands, my feet, ever'thing. Us pass another little café, but this'n for white people, too, and us can't go in there neither. So us jest walk. I'm so cold now. I'm 'bout ready to say it. If I knowed where us was going, I wouldn't be so cold, but I don't know where us going. Us go, us go, us go. Us walk clean out o' Bayonne. Then us cross the street and us come back. Same thing I seen when I got off the bus. Same old trees, same old walk, same old weeds, same old cracked pave—same old ever'thing.

I sniff again.

"That rag," she say.

I wipe my nose real fast and jugg that handkercher back in my pocket 'fore my hand get too cold. I raise my head and I can see David hardware store. When us come up to it, us go in. I don't know why, but I'm glad.

It warm in there. It so warm in there you don't want ever leave. I look for the heater, and I see it over by them ba'ls. Three white men standing 'round the heater talking in Creole. One of 'em come to see what Mama want.

"Got any ax handle?" she say.

Me, Mama, and the white man start to the back, but Mama stop me when us come to the heater. Her and the white man go on. I hold my hand over the heater and look at 'em. They go all the way in the back, and I see the white man point to the ax handle 'gainst the wall. Mama take one of 'em and shake it like she trying to figure how much it weigh. Then she rub her hand over it from one end to the other. She turn it over and look at the other side, then she shake it again, and shake her head and put it back. She get another one and she do it jest like she did the first one, then she shake her head. Then she get a brown one and do it that, too. But she don't like this one neither. Then she get another one, but 'fore she shake it or anything, she look at me. Look like she trying to say something to me, but I don't know what it is. All I know is I done got warm now and I'm feeling right smart better. Mama shake this ax handle jest like she done the others, and shake her head and say something to the white man. The white man jest look at his pile of ax handle, and when Mama pass by him to come to the front, the white man jest scratch his head and follow her. She tell me come on, and us go on out and start walking again.

Us walk and walk, and no time at all I'm cold again. Look like I'm colder now 'cause I can still remember how good it was back there. My stomach growl and I suck it in to keep Mama from yering it. She walking right 'side me, and it growl so loud you can yer it a mile. But Mama don't say a word.

X

When us come up to the courthouse, I look at the clock. It got quarter to twelve. Mean us got another hour and a quarter to be out yer in the cold. Us go and stand side a building. Something hit my cap and I look up at the sky. Sleet falling.

I look at Mama standing there. I want stand close 'side her, but she don't like that. She say that's cry-baby stuff. She say you got to stand for yourself, by yourself.

"Let's go back to that office," she say.

Us cross the street. When us get to the dentist I try to open the door, but I can't. Mama push me on the side and she twist the knob. But she can't open it neither. She twist it some more, harder, but she can't open it. She turn 'way from the door. I look at her, but I don't move and I don't say nothing. I done seen her like this before and I'm scared.

"You hungry?" she say. She say it like she mad at me, like I'm the one cause of ever'thing.

"No, ma'am," I say.

"You want eat and walk back, or you rather don't eat and ride?"

"I ain't hungry," I say.

I ain't jest hungry, but I'm cold, too. I'm so hungry and I'm so cold I want cry. And look like I'm getting colder and colder. My feet done got numb. I try to work my toes, but I can't. Look like I'm go'n die. Look like I'm go'n stand right here and freeze to death. I think about home. I think about Val and Auntie and Ty and Louis and Walker. It 'bout twelve o'clock and I know they eating dinner. I can hear Ty making jokes. That's Ty. Always trying to make some kind o' joke. I wish I was right there listening to him. Give anything in the world if I was home 'round the fire.

"Come on," Mama say.

Us start walking again. My feet so numb I can't hardly feel 'em. Us turn the corner and go back up the street. The clock start hitting for twelve.

The sleet's coming down plenty now. They hit the pave and bounce like rice. Oh, Lord; oh, Lord, I pray. Don't let me die. Don't let me die. Don't let me die, Lord.

XI

Now I know where us going. Us going back o' town where the colored people eat. I don't care if I don't eat. I been hungry before. I can stand it. But I can't stand the cold.

I can see us go'n have a long walk. It 'bout a mile down there. But I don't mind. I know when I get there I'm go'n warm myself. I think I can hold out. My hands numb in my pockets and my feet numb, too, but if I keep moving I can hold out. Jest don't stop no more, that's all.

The sky's gray. The sleep keeps falling. Falling like rain now—plenty, plenty. You can hear it hitting the pave. You can see it bouncing. Sometimes it bounce two times 'fore it settle.

Us keep going. Us don't say nothing. Us jest keep going, keep going.

I wonder what Mama thinking. I hope she ain't mad with me. When summer come I'm go'n pick plenty cotton and get her a coat. I'm go'n get her a red one.

I hope they make it summer all the time. I be glad if it was summer all the time—but it ain't. Us got to have winter, too. Lord, I hate the winter. I guess ever'body hate the winter.

I don't sniff this time. I get out my handkercher and wipe my nose. My hand so cold I can hardly hold the handkercher.

I think us getting close, but us ain't there yet. I wonder where ever'body is. Can't see nobody but us. Look like us the only two people moving 'round today. Must be too cold for the rest of the people to move 'round.

I can hear my teefes. I hope they don't knock together too hard and make that bad one hurt. Lord, that's all I need, for that bad one to start off.

I hear a church bell somewhere. But today ain't Sunday. They must be ringing for a funeral or something.

I wonder what they doing at home. They must be eating. Monsieur Bayonne might be there with his guitar. One day Ty played with Monsieur Bayonne guitar and broke one o' the string. Monsieur Bayonne got some mad with Ty. He say Ty ain't go'n never 'mount to nothing. Ty can go jest like him when he ain't there. Ty can make ever'body laugh mocking Monsieur Bayonne.

I used to like to be with Mama and Daddy. Us used to be happy. But they took him in the Army. Now, nobody happy no more. . . . I be glad when he come back.

Monsieur Bayonne say it wasn't fair for 'em to take Daddy and give Mama nothing and give us nothing. Auntie say, Shhh, Etienne. Don't let 'em yer you talk like that. Monsieur Bayonne say, It's God truth. What they giving his children? They have to walk three and a half mile to school hot or cold. That's anything to give for a paw? She's got to work in the field rain or shine jest to make ends meet. That's anything to give for a husband? Auntie say, Shhh Etienne, shhh. Yes, you right, Monsieur Bayonne say. Best don't say it in front of 'em now. But one day they go'n find out. One day. Yes, s'pose so, Auntie say. Then what, Rose Mary? Monsieur Bayonne say. I don't know, Etienne, Auntie say. All us can do is us job, and leave ever'thing else in His hand. . . .

Us getting closer, now. Us getting closer. I can see the railroad tracks.

Us cross the tracks, and now I see the café. Jest to get in there, I say. Jest to get in there. Already I'm starting to feel little better.

XII

Us go in. Ahh, it good. I look for the heater; there 'gainst the wall. One of them little brown ones. I jest stand there and hold my hand over it. I can't open my hands too wide 'cause they almost froze.

Mama standing right 'side me. She done unbuttoned her coat. Smoke rise out the coat, and the coat smell like a wet dog.

I move to the side so Mama can have more room. She open out her hands and rub 'em together. I rub mine together, too, 'cause this keeps 'em from hurting. If you let 'em warm too fast, they hurt you sure. But if you let 'em warm jest little bit at a time, and you keep rubbing 'em, they be all right ever' time.

They got jest two more people in the café. A lady back o' the counter, and a man on this side the counter. They been watching us ever since us come in.

Mama get out the handkercher and count the money. Both o' us know how much money she got there. Three dollars. No, she ain't got three dollars. 'Cause she had to pay us way up here. She ain't got but two dollars and a half left. Dollar and a half to get my teef pulled, and fifty cents for us to go back on, and fifty cents worse o' salt meat.

She stir the money 'round with her finger. Most o' the money is change 'cause I can hear it rubbing together. She stir it and stir it. Then she look at the door. It still sleeting. I can yer it hitting 'gainst the wall like rice.

"I ain't hungry, Mama," I say.

"Got to pay 'em something for they heat," she say.

She take a quarter out the handkercher and tie the handkercher up again. She look over her shoulder at the people, but she still don't move. I hope she don't spend the money. I don't want her spend it on me. I'm hungry, I'm almost starving I'm so hungry, but I don't want her spending the money on me.

She flip the quarter over like she thinking. She must be thinking 'bout us walking back home. Lord, I sure don't want walk home. If I thought it done any good to say something, I say it. But my mama make up her own mind.

She turn way from the heater right fast, like she better hurry up and do it 'fore she change her mind. I turn to look at her go to the counter. The man and the lady look at her, too. She tell the lady something and the lady walk away. The man keep on looking at her. Her back turn to the man, and Mama don't even know he standing there.

The lady put some cakes and a glass o' milk on the counter. Then she pour up a cup o' coffee and set it side the other stuff. Mama pay her for the things and come back where I'm at. She tell me sit down at that table 'gainst the wall.

The milk and the cakes for me. The coffee for my mama. I eat slow, and I look at her. She looking outside at the sleet. She looking real sad. I say to myself, I'm go'n make all this up one day. You see, one day, I'm go'n make all this up. I want to say it now. I want to tell how I feel right now. But Mama don't like for us to talk like that.

"I can't eat all this," I say.

"They got just three little cakes there. And I'm so hungry right now, the Lord know I can eat a hundred times three. But I want her to have one.

She don't even look my way. She know I'm hungry. She know I want it. I let it stay there a while, then I get it and eat it. I eat jest on my front teefes, 'cause if it tech that back teef I know what'll happen. Thank God it ain't hurt me a tall today.

After I finish eating I see the man go to the juke box. He drop a nickel in it, then he jest stand there looking at the record. Mama tell me keep my eyes in front where they blonks. I turn my head like she say, but then I yer the man coming towards us.

"Dance, Pretty?" he say.

Mama get up to dance with him. But 'fore you know it, she done grabbed the little man and done throwed him 'side the wall. He hit the wall so hard he stop the juke box from playing.

"Some pimp," the lady back o' the counter say. "Some pimp."

The little man jump off the floor and start towards my mama. 'Fore you know it, Mama done sprung open her knife and she waiting for him.

"Come on," she say. "Come on. I'll cut you from you neighbo to your throat. Come on."

I go up to the little man to hit him, but Mama make me come and stand 'side her. The little man look at me and Mama and go back to the counter.

"Some pimp," the lady back o' the counter say. "Some pimp." She start laughing and pointing at the little man. "Yes, sir, you a pimp, all right. Yes sir."

XIII

"Fasten that coat. Let's go," Mama say.

"You don't have to leave," the lady say.

Mama don't answer the lady, and us right out in the cold again. I'm warm right now—my hands, my yers, my feet— but I know this ain't go'n last too long. It done sleet so much now you got ice ever'where.

Us cross the railroad tracks, and soon's us do, I get cold. That wind go through this little old coat like it ain't nothing. I got a shirt and a sweater under it, but that wind don't pay 'em no mind. I look up and I can see us got a long way to go. I wonder if us go'n make it 'fore I get too cold.

Us cross over to walk on the sidewalk. They got jest one sidewalk back here. It's over there.

After us go jest a little piece, I smell bread cooking. I look, then I see a baker shop. When us get closer, I can smell it more better. I shet my eyes and make 'tend I'm eating. But I keep 'em shet too long and I butt up 'gainst a telephone post. Mama grab me, and see if I'm hurt. I ain't bleeding or nothing and she turn me loose.

I can feel I'm getting colder and colder, and I look up to see how far us still got to go. Uptown is 'way up yonder. A half mile, I reckoned. I try to think of something. They say think and you won't get cold. I think of that poem, *Annabel Lee*. I ain't been to school in so long—this bad weather—I reckoned they done passed *Annabel Lee*. But passed it or not, I'm sure Miss Walker go'n make me recite it when I get there. That woman don't never forget nothing. I ain't never seen nobody like that.

I'm still getting cold. *Annabel Lee* or no *Annabel Lee*, I'm still getting cold. But I can see us getting closer. Us getting there gradually.

Soon's us turn the corner, I see a little old white lady up in front o' us. She the only lady on the street. She all in black and she got a long black rag over her head.

"Stop," she say.

Me and Mama stop and look at her. She must be crazy to be out in all this sleet. Ain't got but a few other people out there, and all of 'em men.

"Yall done ate?" she say.

"Jest finished," Mama say.

"Yall must be cold then?" she say.

"Us headed for the dentist," Mama say. "Us'll warm up when us get there."

"What dentist?" the old lady say. "Mr. Bassett?"

"Yes, ma'am," Mama say.

"Come on in," the old lady say. "I'll telephone him and tell him yall coming."

Me and Mama follow the old lady in the store. It's a little bitty store, and it don't have much in there. The old lady take off her head piece and fold it up.

"Helena?" somebody call from the back.

"Yes, Alnest?" the old lady say.

"Did you see them?"

"They're here. Standing beside me."

"Good. Now you can stay inside."

The old lady look at Mama. Mama waiting to hear what she brought us in here for. I'm waiting for that, too.

"I saw yall each time you went by," she say. "I came out to catch you, but you were gone."

"Us went back 'o town," Mama say.

"Did you eat?"

"Yes, ma'am."

The old lady look at Mama a long time, like she thinking Mama might be jest saying that. Mama look right back at her. The old lady look at me to see what I got to say. I don't say nothing. I sure ain't going 'gainst my mama.

"There's food in the kitchen," she say to Mama. "I've been keeping it warm."

Mama turn right around and start for the door.

"Just a minute," the old lady say. Mama stop. "The boy'll have to work for it. It isn't free."

"Us don't take no handout," Mama say.

"I'm not handing out anything," the old lady say. "I need my garbage moved to the front. Ernest has a bad cold and can't go out there."

"James'll move it for you," Mama say.

"Not unless you eat," the old lady say. "I'm old, but I have my pride, too, you know."

Mama can see she ain't go'n beat this old lady down, so she jest shake her head.

"All right," the old lady say. "Come into the kitchen."

She lead the way with that rag in her hand. The kitchen is a little bitty thing, too. The table and the stove jest about fill it up. They got a little room to the side. Somebody in there laying cross the bed. Must be the person she was talking with: Alnest or Ernest—I forget what she call him.

"Sit down," the old lady say to Mama. "Not you," she say to me. "You have to move the cans."

"Helena?" somebody say in the other room.

"Yes, Alnest?" the old lady say.

"Are you going out there again?"

"I must show the boy where the garbage is," the old lady say.

"Keep that shawl over your head," the old man say.

"You don't have to remind me. Come boy," the old lady say.

Us go out in the yard. Little old back yard ain't no bigger 'an the store or the kitchen. But it can sleet here jest like it can sleet in any big back yard. And 'fore you know it I'm trembling.

"There," the old lady say, pointing to the cans. I pick up one of the cans. The can so light I put it back down to look inside o' it.

"Here," the old lady say. "Leave that cap alone."

I look at her in the door. She got that black rag wrapped

'round her shoulders, and she pointing one of her fingers at me.

"Pick it up and carry it to the front," she say. I go by her with the can. I'm sure the thing's empty. She could 'a' carried the thing by herself, I'm sure. "Set it on the sidewalk by the door and come back for the other one," she say.

I go and come back, Mama look at me when I pass her. I get the other can and take it to the front. It don't feel no heavier 'an the other one. I tell myself to look inside and see just what I been hauling. First, I look up and down the street. Nobody coming. Then I look over my shoulder. Little old lady done slipped there jest's quiet 's mouse, watching me. Look like she knowed I was go'n try that.

"Ehh, Lord," she say. "Children, children. Come in here, boy, and go wash your hands."

I follow her into the kitchen, and she point, and I go to the bathroom. When I come out, the old lady done dished up the food. Rice, gravy, meat, and she even got some lettuce and tomato in a saucer. She even got a glass o' milk and a piece o' cake there, too. It look so good. I almost start eating 'fore I say my blessing.

"Helena?" the old man say.

"Yes Alnest?" she say.

"Are they eating?"

"Yes," she say.

"Good," he say. "Now you'll stay inside."

The old lady go in there where he is and I can hear 'em talking. I look at Mama. She eating slow like she thinking. I wonder what's the matter now. I reckoned she think 'bout home.

The old lady come back in the kitchen.

"I talked to Dr. Bassett's nurse," she say. "Dr. Bassett will take you as soon as you get there."

"Thank you, ma'am," Mama say.

"Perfectly all right," the old lady say. "Which one is it?"

Mama nod towards me. The old lady look at me real sad. I look sad, too.

"You're not afraid, are you?" she say.

"No'm," I say.

"That's a good boy," the old lady say. "Nothing to be afraid of."

When me and Mama get through eating, us thank the old lady again.

"Helena, are they leaving?" the old man say.

"Yes, Alnest."

"Tell them I say good-by."

"They can hear you, Alnest."

"Good-by both mother and son," the old man say. "And may God be with you."

Me and Mama tell the old man good-by, and us follow the old lady in the front. Mama open the door to go out, but she stop and come back in the store.

"You sell salt meat?" she say.

"Yes."

"Give me two bits worse."

"That isn't very much salt meat," the old lady say.

"That'll all I have," Mama say.

The old lady go back o' the counter and cut a big piece off the chunk. Then she wrap it and put it in a paper bag.

"Two bits," she say.

"That look like awful lot of meat for a quarter," Mama say

"Two bits," the old lady say. "I've been selling salt meat behind this counter twenty-five years. I think I know what I'm doing."

"You got a scale there," Mama say.

"What?" the old lady say.

"Weigh it," Mama say.

"What?" the old lady say. "Are you telling me how to run my business?"

"Thanks very much for the food," Mama say.

"Just a minute," the old lady say.

"James," Mama say to me. I move towards the door.

"Just one minute, I said," the old lady say.

Me and Mama stop again and look at her. The old lady take the meat out the bag and unwrap it and cut 'bout half o' it off. Then she wrap it up again and jugg it back in the bag and give it to Mama. Mama lay the quarter on the counter.

"Your kindness will never be forgotten," she say. "James," she say to me.

Us go out, and the old lady come to the door to look at us. After us go a little piece I look back, and she still there watching us.

The sleet's coming down heavy, heavy now, and I turn up my collar to keep my neck warm. My mama tell me turn it right back down.

"You not a bum," she say. "You a man."

Peter Taylor (January 8, 1917) was born in Trenton, Tennessee, and grew up in Nashville, St. Louis, and Memphis. Both his grandfathers were lawyers and politicians, as was his father. Taylor credits his mother with much of his story-telling ability. He dedicated his *Collected Stories* to his mother, "who was the best teller of tales I know and from whose lips I first heard many of the stories in this book."

In 1936 Taylor enrolled in Southwestern at Memphis (now Rhodes College) where he took Allen Tate's English course. When Tate left Southwestern, Taylor transferred to Vanderbilt University where he studied with John Crowe Ransom. At Vanderbilt he formed a friendship with Randall Jarrell. When Ransom left to teach at Kenyon College in 1937, Taylor dropped out of college and sold real estate for a year before transferring to Kenyon to continue his studies with Ransom. Before he graduated from Kenyon in 1940, he published two short stories, "The Party" and "The Lady Is Civilized," in *River*, a literary magazine in Oxford, Mississippi. Taylor studied briefly with Robert Penn Warren and Cleanth Brooks at Louisiana State University before enlisting in the United States Army to participate in World War II. He was discharged in 1945 after serving in the Tidworth Camp, in England.

He is the author of six books of short stories—*A Long Forth and Other Stories (1948), Happy Families Are All Alike: A Collection of Stories* (1959), *Miss Lenora When Last Seen and Fifteen Other Stories* (1963), *The Collected Stories of Peter Taylor* (1969), *In the Miro District and Other Stories* (1977), *The Old Forest and Other Stories* (1985)—two novels—*A Woman of Means* (1950) and *A Summons to Memphis* (1986), and four books of plays.

TWO PILGRIMS

by Peter Taylor

We were on our way from Memphis to a small town in northern Alabama, where my uncle, who was a cotton broker, had a lawsuit that he hoped could be settled out of court. Mr. Lowder, my uncle's old friend and lawyer, was traveling with him. I had just turned seventeen, and I had been engaged to come along in the capacity of chauffeur. I sat alone in the front seat of the car. The two men didn't discuss the lawsuit along the way, as I would have expected them to do. I don't know to this day exactly what was involved, or even whether or not Mr. Lowder managed to settle the matter on that trip. From the time we left the outskirts of Memphis, the two men talked instead about how good the bird hunting used to be there in our section of the country. During the two hours while we were riding through the big cotton counties of West Tennessee, they talked of almost nothing but bird dogs and field trials, interrupting themselves only when we passed through some little town or settlement to speak of the fine people they knew who had once lived there. We went through Collierville, La Grange, Grand Junction, Saulsbury. At La Grange, my uncle pointed out a house with a neoclassic portico and said he had once had a breakfast there that lasted three hours. At Saulsbury, Mr. Lowder commented that it somehow did his soul good to see the name spelled that way. Though it was November, not all the trees had lost their leaves yet. There was even some color still—dull pinks and yellows mixed with reddish browns—and under a bright, limitless sky the trees and the broad fields of grayish cotton stalks, looking almost lavender in places, gave a kind of faded-tapestry effect.

After we crossed the Tennessee River at Savannah, the country changed. And it was as if the new kind of country we had got into depressed the two men. But it may have been only the weather, because the weather changed, too, after we crossed the river. The sky became overcast, and everything seemed rather closed in. Soon there was intermittent rain of a light, misty sort. I kept switching my windshield wiper on and off, until presently my uncle asked me in a querulous tone why I didn't just let the thing run. For thirty or forty miles, the two men had little to say to each other. Finally, as we were passing through a place called Waynesboro—a hard-looking hill town with a cement-block jailhouse dominating the public square—my uncle said that this town was where General Winfield Scott had made one of his halts on the notorious Trail of Tears, when he was rounding up the Cherokees to move them west, in 1838. The two men spoke of what a cruel thing that had been, but they agreed that one must not judge the persons responsible too harshly, that one must judge them by the light of their times and remember what the early settlers had suffered at the hands of the Indians.

Not very long after we had left Waynesboro, Mr. Lowder remarked that we were approaching the old Natchez Trace section and that the original settlers there had been a mighty rough lot of people. My uncle added that from the very earliest days the whole area had been infested with outlaws and robbers and that even now it was said to be a pretty tough section. They sounded as though they were off to a good start; I thought the subject might last them at least until lunchtime. But just as this thought occurred to me, they were interrupted.

We came over the brow of one of the low-lying hills in that country of scrub oaks and pinewoods, and there before us—in a clearing down in the hollow ahead—was a house with smoke issuing from one window toward the rear and with little gray geysers rising at a half-dozen points on the black-shingled roof. It was an unpainted, one-story house set close to the ground and with two big stone end chimneys. All across the front was a kind of lean-to porch. There was an old log barn beyond the house. Despite my uncle's criticism, I had switched off the windshield wiper a mile or so up the road, and then I had had to switch it on again just as we came over the hill. Even with the wiper going, visibility was not very good, and my first thought was that only the misty rain in the air was keeping the roof of that house from blazing up. Mr. Lowder and my uncle were so engrossed in their talk that I think it was my switching the wiper on again that first attracted their attention. But instantly upon seeing the smoke, my uncle said, "Turn in down there!"

"But be careful how you slow down," Mr. Lowder warned. "This blacktop's slick." Already he and my uncle were perched on the edge of the back seat, and one of them had put a hand on my shoulder as if to steady me.

The little house was in such a clearing as must have been familiar to travelers in pioneer days. There were stumps everywhere, even in the barn lot and among the cabbages in the garden. I suppose I particularly noticed the stumps because a good number were themselves smoldering and sending up occasional wisps of smoke. Apparently, the farmer had been trying to rid himself of the stumps in the old-fashioned way. There was no connection between these fires and the one at the house, but the infernal effect of the whole scene was inescapable. One felt that the entire area within the dark ring of pinewoods might at any moment burst into flame.

I turned the car off the macadam pavement, and we bumped along some two hundred feet, following wagon ruts that led more toward the barn than toward the house. The wide barn door stood open, and I could see the figure of a man inside herding a couple of animals through a door at the other end, where the barn lot was. Then I heard Mr. Lowder and my uncle open the back doors of the car. While the car was still moving, they leaped out onto the ground. They both were big men, more than six feet tall and with sizable stomachs that began just below the breastbone, but they sprinted off in the direction of the house like two boys. As they ran, I saw them hurriedly putting on their black gloves. Next, they began stripping off their topcoats. By the time I had stopped the car and got out, they had pulled their coats over their heads, and I realized then that each had tossed his hat onto the back seat before leaping from the car. Looking like a couple of hooded night riders, they were now mounting the shallow porch steps. It was just as they gained the porch that I saw the woman appear from around the far side of the house. At the sight of the hooded and begloved men on her porch—the porch of her burning house—the woman threw one hand to her forehead and gave such an alarmed and alarming cry that I felt something turn over inside me. Even the two intruders halted for an instant on the porch and looked at her.

I thought at first glance that she was an old woman, she was so stooped. Then something told me—I think it was the plaintive sounds she was making—that she was more young than old. After her first outcry, she continued a kind of girlish wailing, which, it seemed to me, expressed a good deal more than mere emotional shock. The noises she made seemed to say that all this *couldn't* be happening to *her*. Not hooded bandits added to a house-burning! It wasn't right; life *couldn't* be so hard, *couldn't* be as evil as this; it was more than she should be asked to bear!

"Anybody inside, Miss?" my uncle called out to the girl. She began shaking her head frantically.

"Well, we'll fetch out whatever we can!" he called. Glancing back at me—I was trying to make a hood of my own topcoat and preparing to join them—my uncle shouted, "Don't you come inside! Stay with that girl! And calm her down!" With that, he followed Mr. Lowder through the doorway and into the house.

Presently, they were hurling bedclothes and homemade-looking stools and chairs through the side windows. Then one or the other of them would come dashing out across the porch and into the yard, deposit on the ground a big pitcher and washbasin or a blurry old mirror with a carved wooden frame, and then dash back inside again. Now and then when one of them brought something out, he would pause for just the briefest moment, not to rest but to examine the rescued object before he put it down. It was comical to see the interest they took in the old things they brought out of that burning house.

When I came up to where the woman was standing, she seemed to have recovered completely from her first fright. She looked at me a little shamefacedly, I thought. Her deep-socketed eyes were almost freakishly large. And I noticed at once that they were of two different colors. One was a mottled brown, the other a gray-green. When finally she spoke, she turned her eyes away and toward the house. "Who are you-all?" she asked.

"We were just passing by," I said.

She looked at me and then turned away again. I felt she was skeptical, that she suspected we had been sent by someone. Each time she directed her eyes at me, I read deceit or guilt or suspicion in them.

"Where you coming from?" she asked in an idle tone, craning her neck to see what some object was that had come flying out the window. She seemed abundantly calm now. Without answering her question, I yanked my coat over my head and ran off toward the house. My uncle met me on the porch steps. He handed me a dresser drawer he was carrying, not failing to give the contents a quick inventory. Then he gave me a rather heavy punch on the chest. "*You* stay out there and keep that girl calm," he said. "You hear what I say! She's apt to go to pieces any minute."

The woman was taking a livelier interest in matters now. I set the drawer on a stump, and when I looked up, she peered over me to see which drawer it was I had brought and what extra odds and ends my uncle might have swept into it. On top lay a rusty fire poker and a couple of small picture frames with the glass so smashed up you couldn't make out the pictures. Underneath, there was a jumble of old cloth scraps and paper dress patterns and packages of garden seeds. Seeing all this, the woman opened her mouth and smiled vacantly, perhaps a little contemptuously. She was so close to me that I became aware of the sweetness of her breath! I could not have imagined that her breath would be sweet. Though the skin on her forehead and on her high cheekbones was clear and very fair, there were ugly pimples on her chin and at the corners of her mouth. Her dark hair was wet from the drizzle of rain and was pushed behind her ears and hung in clumps over the collar of her soiled denim jacket. She was breathing heavily through her parted lips. Presently, when our eyes met, I thought I detected a certain momentary gleefulness in her expression. But her glance darted back toward the house at once.

The two men had pressed on beyond the front rooms and into the ell of the house. Now the woman took a couple of steps in order to look through one of the front windows and perhaps catch a glimpse of them back there.

"We were coming from Memphis," I said. "We're *from* Memphis." But she seemed no longer interested in that subject.

"It's no use what they're doing," she said. "Unless they like it."

"It's all right," I said, still hoping to distract her. "We're on our way to a place in Alabama."

"They your bosses?" she asked. She couldn't take her eyes off the window.

"No, it's my uncle and his lawyer."

"Well, they're right active," she commented. "But there ain't nothing in there worth their bustle and bother. Yet some folks like to take chances. It's just the worst lot of junk in there. We heired this place from my grandma when she passed on last spring; the junk was all hern."

Just then, Mr. Lowder and my uncle came running from the house. Each of them was carrying a coal-oil lamp, his right hand supporting the base of the lamp and his left clamped protectively on the fragile chimney. I almost burst out laughing.

"It's gotten too hot in there," Mr. Lowder said. "We'll have to stop."

When they had set down their lamps, they began examining each other's coats, making sure they weren't on fire. Next, they tossed their coats on the bare ground and set about pulling some of the rescued articles farther from the house. I went forward to help, and the woman followed. She didn't follow to help, however. Apparently, she was only curious to see which of her possessions these men deemed worth saving. She looked at everything she came to with almost a disappointed expression. Then Mr. Lowder picked up an enameled object, and I noticed that as he inspected it a deep frown appeared on his brow. He held the thing up for my uncle to see, and I imagined for a moment that he was trying to draw laughter from all of us. It was a child's chamber pot, not much larger than a beer mug. "Did you bring this out?" Mr. Lowder asked my uncle.

My uncle nodded, and, still bending over, he studied the pot for a second, showing that he had not really identified it before. Then he looked at the woman. "Where's your child, ma'am?" he asked in a quiet voice.

The woman gaped at him as though she didn't understand what he was talking about. She shifted her eyes to the tiny pot that Mr. Lowder was still holding aloft. Now her mouth dropped wide open, and at the same time her lips drew back in such a way that her bad teeth were exposed for the first time. It was impossible not to think of a death's-head. At that instant, the whole surface of the shingled roof on the side of the house where we were standing burst into flames.

A few minutes before this, the rain had ceased altogether, and now it was as though someone had suddenly doused the roof with kerosene. My back was to the house, but I heard a loud "swoosh" and I spun around in that direction. Then I heard the woman cry out and I spun back again. Mr. Lowder set the chamber pot on the ground and began moving rather cautiously toward her. My uncle stood motionless, watching her as though she were an animal that might bolt. As Mr. Lowder came toward her, she took a step backward, and then she wailed, "My baby! Oh, Lord, my baby! He's in thar!" Mr. Lowder seized her by the wrist and simultaneously gave us a quick glance over his shoulder.

My uncle snatched up a ragged homespun blanket from the ground and threw it over his head. I seized a patchwork quilt that had been underneath the blanket, and this time I followed him inside the house. Even in the two front rooms it was like a blast furnace, and I felt I might faint. The smoke was so dense that you couldn't see anything an arm's length away. But my uncle had been in those two front rooms and he knew there was no baby there. With me at his heels, he ran right on through and into the first room in the ell, where there wasn't so much smoke—only raw flames eating away at the wall toward the rear. The window lights had burst from the heat in there, and there was a hole in the ceiling, so that you could look right up through the flames to the sky. But my eyes were smarting so that I couldn't really see anything in the room, and I was coughing so hard that I couldn't stand up straight. My uncle was coughing, too, but he could still manage to look about. He made two complete turns around the room and then he headed us on into the kitchen. There wasn't anything recognizable to me in the kitchen except the black range. One of the two window frames fell in as we ran through. The next instant, after we had leaped across the burning floorboards and had jumped off the back stoop of the house, the rafters and the whole roof above the kitchen came down.

There must have been a tremendous crash, though I hardly heard it. Even before my uncle and I could shed our smoldering blankets, we saw the man coming toward us from the

barn. "You're afire!" he called out to us. But we had
already dropped the blankets before I understood what he
was saying. He was jogging along toward us. One of his legs
was shorter than the other, and he couldn't move very fast.
Under one arm he was carrying a little towheaded child of
not more than two years. He held it exactly as though it
might be a sack of corn meal he was bringing up from the
barn.

"Do you have another baby?" my uncle shouted at him.

"No, narry other," the man replied.

My uncle looked at me. He was coughing still, but at the
same time he was smiling and shaking his head. "You all
right?" he asked me. He gave my clothes a quick once-over,
and I did the same for him. We had somehow got through
the house without any damage, even to our shoes or our
trouser legs.

By the time the man came up to the house, my uncle had
dashed off to tell the woman her baby was safe. I tried to
explain to the man about the mistake his wife had made.
"Your wife thought your baby was in the house," I said.

He was a stocky, black-haired man, wearing overalls and
a long-sleeved undershirt. "She *whut?*" he said, looking at
me darkly. He glanced up briefly at the flames, which were
now leaping twenty or thirty feet above the framework of
the kitchen. Then he set out again, in the same jogging
pace, toward the front of the house. I caught a glimpse of
the baby's intense blue eyes gazing up at the smoke and
flames.

"She thought the baby was inside the house," I said,
following the man at a trot.

"Like hell she did!" he said under his breath but loud
enough for me to hear.

As we rounded the corner of the house, I heard my uncle
call out to the woman that her baby was safe. She was
seated on a stump with her face hidden in her hands. My
uncle and Mr. Lowder once again began pulling rescued
objects farther away from the house. As the man passed
him, Mr. Lowder looked up and said, "Did you get all the
stock out?"

"Yup," said the man.

"I guess you're lucky there's no wind," Mr. Lowder said.
And my uncle said, "It must have started in the kitchen

and spread through the attic. You didn't have any water drawn?"

The man stopped for a second and looked at my uncle. He shifted the baby from one hip to the other. "The pump's broke," he said. "It was about wore out, and *she* broke it for good this morning."

"Isn't that the way it goes," my uncle said sympathetically, shaking his head.

Then, still carrying the baby, the man shuffled on toward his wife. The woman kept her face hidden in her hands, but I think she heard him coming. Neither of them seemed to have any awareness that their house and most of their possessions were at that moment going up in flames. I was watching the man when he got to her. He still had the baby under his arm. I saw him draw back his free hand, and saw the hand come down in a resounding slap on the back of her head. It knocked her right off the stump. She hit the ground in a sitting position and still she didn't look up at her husband. "J'you aim to git them fellows burned alive?" he thundered.

Mr. Lowder and my uncle must have been watching, too, because we all three ran forward at the same moment. "Lay off that!" Mr. Lowder bellowed. "Just lay off, now!"

"She knowed this here young'un warn't in no house!" the man said, twisting the baby to his shoulder. "I reckoned she'd like as not lose her head. That's how come I carried him with me, and I told her plain as daylight I was a-goin' to."

"Now, you look here, mister," my uncle said, "the girl was just scared. She didn't know what she was saying."

"Probably she couldn't remember, in her fright," Mr. Lowder said.

The man stood staring down at his wife. "She's feared of her own shadow, and that's how come I carried him to the barn."

"Well, you're not going to beat her with us here," Mr. Lowder said firmly. "She was scared out of her wits, that's all."

"Who sent y'all out here?" the man asked my uncle, turning his back on Mr. Lowder. "Ain't they goan send no fire engine?"

It was as he spoke the word that we heard the fire truck coming. The whine of the siren must have first reached us from a point three or four miles distant, because at least five minutes elapsed before the fire truck and the two carloads of volunteers arrived. It turned out that somebody else had stopped by before we did and had hurried on to the next town to give the alarm. I thought it strange that the woman hadn't told us earlier that they were expecting help from town. But, of course, there was little about the woman's behavior that didn't seem passing strange to me.

As soon as we heard the siren, she began pushing herself up from the ground. Without a glance at any of the rest of us, she went directly to her husband and snatched the baby from him. The baby's little face was dirty, and there were wide streaks on it, where some while earlier there must have been a flow of tears. But his eyes were dry now and wore a glazed look. He seemed to stare up at the flaming house with total indifference. Almost as soon as he was in his mother's arms, he placed his chin on the shoulder of her denim jacket and quietly closed his eyes. He seemed to have fallen asleep at once. With her baby in her arms, the woman strode away into the adjoining field, among the smoking stumps and toward the edge of the pinewoods. There she stopped, at the edge of the woods, and there she remained standing, with her back turned toward the house and toward us and toward all the activity that ensued after the fire truck and the other cars arrived. She was still standing there, with the baby on her shoulder, when we left the scene.

We stayed on for only a few minutes after the local fire brigade arrived. Mr. Lowder and my uncle could see that their work here was done and they were mindful of the pressing business that they hoped to transact in Alabama that afternoon. We lingered just long enough to see most of the articles they had rescued from the flames thoroughly soaked with water. The sight must have been disheartening to them, but they didn't speak of it. The inexpert firemen couldn't control the pressure from their tank, and whenever there came a great spurt of water they lost their grip on the hose. They seemed bound to spray everything but the burning house. We withdrew a little way in the direction of our car and joined a small group of spectators who had now come on the scene.

I didn't tell my uncle or Mr. Lowder what I was thinking during the time that we stood there with the local people who had gathered. I could still see the woman down in the field, and I wondered if my uncle or Mr. Lowder were not going to tell some local person how suspicious her behavior had been—and her husband's, too, for that matter. Surely there was some mystery, I said to myself, some questions that ought to be answered or asked. But no question of any kind seemed to arise in the minds of my two companions. It was as if such a fire were an everyday occurrence in their lives and as if they lived always among such queer people as that afflicted poor-white farmer and his simple wife.

Once we had got back into the car and were on our way again, I was baffled by the quiet good humor—and even serenity—of those two men I was traveling with. The moment they had resettled themselves on the back seat of the car, after giving their overcoats a few final brushings and after placing their wide-brimmed fedoras firmly on their heads again, they began chatting together with the greatest ease and nonchalance. I could not see their faces; I had to keep my eyes on the road. But I listened and presently I heard my uncle launch upon a reminiscence. "I did the damndest thing once," he said. "It was when I was a boy of just eight or nine. The family have kidded me about it all my life. One morning after I had been up to mischief of some kind, Father took me into the kitchen and gave me a switching on my legs with a little shoot he had broken off the privet hedge. When I came outside again, I was still yowling, and the other children who were playing there in the house lot commenced guying me about it. All at once, I burst out at them: " 'You'd cry, too, if he beat *you* with the shovel handle!" I hadn't aimed to say it; I just said it. My brothers kid me about it to this day.' "

"Yes," said Mr. Lowder. "It's like that—the things a person will say." He liked my uncle's story immensely. He said it sounded so true. As he spoke, I could hear one of them striking a match. It wasn't long before I caught the first whiff of cigar smoke. Then another match was struck. They were both smoking now. Pretty soon their conversation moved on to other random topics.

Within the next half hour, we got out of that hill country along the Tennessee River and entered the rich and beautiful section to the east of it, near the fine old towns of Pulaski and Fayetteville. I could not help remarking on the change to my uncle. "Seems good to have finally got out of that godforsaken-looking stretch back there," I said over my shoulder.

"How do you mean 'godforsaken'?" my uncle replied. I recognized a testiness in his tone, and his reply had come so quickly that I felt he had been waiting for me to say exactly what I had said.

"It's just ugly, that's all," I mumbled, hoping that would be the end of it.

But Mr. Lowder joined in the attack, using my uncle's tone. "I wouldn't say one kind of country's any better-looking than another—not really."

And then my uncle again: "To someone *your* age, it just depends on what kind of country—if any—you happen to be used to."

"Maybe so," said I, not wanting to say more but unable to stop myself. "Maybe so, but I could live for a hundred years in that scrubby-looking country without ever getting used to it."

No doubt the rolling pasture land on both sides of the highway now—still green in November, and looking especially green after recent rain—caused me to put more feeling into my statement than I might otherwise have done. And it may also have had its effect on the two men in the back seat.

There was a brief pause, and then my uncle fired away again. "Every countryside has its own kind of beauty. It's up to you to learn to see it, that's all."

Then Mr. Lowder: "And if you don't see it, it's just your loss. Because it's *there*."

"Besides, a lot you know about that country," my uncle went on, in what seemed to me an even more captious spirit than before. "And how could you? How could you judge, flying along the highway at fifty miles an hour, flapping that damned wiper off and on?"

"More than that," said Mr. Lowder with renewed energy, "you would have to have seen that country thirty years ago to understand why it looks the way it does now. That was when they cut out the last of the old timber. I've heard it said that when the first white men came through that section it had the prettiest stand of timber on the continent!"

Suddenly I blurted out, "But what's that got to do with it?" I was so irritated that I could feel the blood rising in my cheeks and I knew that the back of my neck was already crimson. "It's how the country looks now I'm talking about. Anyway, I'm only here as your driver. I don't *have* to like the scenery, do I?"

Both men broke into laughter. It was a kind of laughter that expressed both apology and relief. My uncle bent forward, thumped me on the shoulder with his knuckle, and said, "Don't be so touchy, boy." Almost at once, they resumed their earlier dialogue. One of them lowered a window a little way to let out some of the smoke, but the aroma of their cigars continued to fill the car, and they spoke in the same slow cadences as before and in the same tranquil tone.

We reached the town in Alabama toward the middle of the afternoon and we spent the night in an old clapboard hotel on the courthouse square. After dinner that night, the two men sat in the lobby and talked to other men who were staying there in the hotel. I found myself a place near the stove and sat there with my feet on the fender, sometimes dozing off. But even when I was half asleep I was still listening to see whether, in their talk, either Mr. Lowder or my uncle would make any reference to our adventure that morning. Neither did. Instead, as the evening wore on and they got separated and were sitting with two different groups of men. I heard them both repeating the very stories they had told in the car before we crossed the Tennessee River— stories about bird hunting and field trials and about my uncle's three-hour breakfast in the old house with the neo-classic portico.

Flannery O'Conner (March 25, 1925–August 3, 1964) was born in Savannah, Georgia, but moved with her family to her mother's family home in Milledgeville, Georgia when her father was diagnosed with disseminated lupus. She attended high school there and went on to college at the local Georgia State College for Women. Upon graduation she received a fellowship to the Writer's Workshop at the University of Iowa where she received an M.F.A. in 1947. A year later she went to Yaddo and began work on her first novel, *Wise Blood*. While visiting in New York she met Sally and Robert Fitzgerald and moved with them to Ridgefield, Connecticut, in 1949. In 1950 her own lupus was diagnosed and she returned to Andalusia, her mother's farm a few miles outside of Milledgeville. O'Connor loved peacocks and kept a menagerie of exotic birds. She continued to write in Milledgeville until her death in 1964.

Her publications include two novels—*Wise Blood* (1952) and *The Violent Bear It Away* (1960)—and two collections of short stories—*A Good Man Is Hard to Find* (1955) and *Everything That Rises Must Converge* (1965). Other books published posthumously include *Mystery and Manners* (1969), *The Complete Stories* (1971), and *The Habit of Being: Letters of Flannery O'Connor* (1979) edited by Sally Fitzgerald.

"Southern writers are stuck with the South and it's a good thing to be stuck with," said O'Connor. She wrote: "The best American writing has always been regional, but to be regional in the best sense you have to see beyond the region. The smallest history can be read in a universal light."

REVELATION

by Flannery O'Connor

The doctor's waiting room, which was very small, was almost full when the Turpins entered and Mrs. Turpin, who was very large, made it look even smaller by her presence. She stood looming at the head of the magazine table set in the center of it, a living demonstration that the room was inadequate and ridiculous. Her little bright black eyes took in all the patients as she sized up the seating situation. There was one vacant chair and a place on the sofa occupied by a blond child in a dirty blue romper who should have been told to move over and make room for the lady. He was five or six, but Mrs. Turpin saw at once that no one was going to tell him to move over. He was slumped down in the seat, his arms idle at his sides and his eyes idle in his head; his nose ran unchecked.

Mrs. Turpin put a firm hand on Claud's shoulder and said in a voice that included anyone who wanted to listen, "Claud, you sit in that chair there," and gave him a push down into the vacant one. Claud was florid and bald and sturdy, somewhat shorter than Mrs. Turpin, but he sat down as if he were accustomed to doing what she told him to.

Mrs. Turpin remained standing. The only man in the room besides Claud was a lean stringy old fellow with a rusty hand spread out on each knee, whose eyes were closed as if he were asleep or dead or pretending to be so as not to get up and offer her his seat. Her gaze settled agreeably on a well-dressed gray-haired lady whose eyes met hers and whose expression said: if that child belonged to me, he would have some manners and move over—there's plenty of room there for you and him too.

Claud looked up with a sigh and made as if to rise.

"Sit down," Mrs. Turpin said. "You know you're not supposed to stand on that leg. He has an ulcer on his leg," she explained.

Claud lifted his foot onto the magazine table and rolled his trouser leg up to reveal a purple swelling on a plump marble-white calf.

"My!" the pleasant lady said. "How did you do that?"

"A cow kicked him," Mrs. Turpin said.

"Goodness!" said the lady.

Claud rolled his trouser leg down.

"Maybe the little boy would move over," the lady suggested, but the child did not stir.

"Somebody will be leaving in a minute," Mrs. Turpin said. She could not understand why a doctor—with as much money as they made charging five dollars a day to just stick their head in the hospital door and look at you—couldn't afford a decent-sized waiting room. This one was hardly bigger than a garage. The table was cluttered with limp-looking magazines and at one end of it there was a big green glass ash tray full of cigarette butts and cotton wads with little blood spots on them. If she had had anything to do with the running of the place, that would have been emptied every so often. There were no chairs against the wall at the head of the room. It had a rectangular-shaped panel in it that permitted a view of the office where the nurse came and went and the secretary listened to the radio. A plastic fern in a gold pot sat in the opening and trailed its fronds down almost to the floor. The radio was softly playing gospel music.

Just then the inner door opened and a nurse with the highest stack of yellow hair Mrs. Turpin had ever seen put her face in the crack and called for the next patient. The woman sitting beside Claud grasped the two arms of her chair and hoisted herself up; she pulled her dress free from her legs and lumbered through the door where the nurse had disappeared.

Mrs. Turpin eased into the vacant chair, which held her tight as a corset. "I wish I could reduce," she said, and rolled her eyes and gave a comic sigh.

"Oh, *you* aren't fat," the stylish lady said.

"Ooooo I am too," Mrs. Turpin said. "Claud he eats all he wants to and never weighs over one hundred and seventy-five pounds, but me I just look at something good to eat and

I gain some weight," and her stomach and shoulders shook with laughter. "You can eat all you want to, can't you, Claud?" she asked, turning to him.

Claud only grinned.

"Well, as long as you have such a good disposition," the stylish lady said, "I don't think it makes a bit of difference what size you are. You just can't beat a good disposition."

Next to her was a fat girl of eighteen or nineteen, scowling into a thick blue book which Mrs. Turpin saw was entitled *Human Development*. The girl raised her head and directed her scowl at Mrs. Turpin as if she did not like her looks. She appeared annoyed that anyone should speak while she tried to read. The poor girl's face was blue with acne and Mrs. Turpin thought how pitiful it was to have a face like that at that age. She gave the girl a friendly smile but the girl only scowled the harder. Mrs. Turpin herself was fat but she had always had good skin, and, though she was forty-seven years old, there was not a wrinkle in her face except around her eyes from laughing too much.

Next to the ugly girl was the child, still in exactly the same position, and next to him was a thin leathery old woman in a cotton print dress. She and Claud had three sacks of chicken feed in their pump house that was in the same print. She had seen from the first that the child belonged with the old woman. She could tell by the way they sat—kind of vacant and white-trashy, as if they would sit there until Doomsday if nobody called and told them to get up. And at right angles but next to the well-dressed pleasant lady was a lank-faced woman who was certainly the child's mother. She had on a yellow sweat shirt and wine-colored slacks, both gritty-looking, and the rims of her lips were stained with snuff. Her dirty yellow hair was tied behind with a little piece of red paper ribbon. Worse than niggers any day, Mrs. Turpin thought.

The gospel hymn playing was, "When I looked up and He looked down," and Mrs. Turpin, who knew it, supplied the last line mentally, "And wona these days I know I'll we-eara crown."

Without appearing to, Mrs. Turpin always noticed people's feet. The well-dressed lady had red and gray suede shoes to match her dress. Mrs. Turpin had on her good black patent leather pumps. The ugly girl had on Girl Scout shoes and heavy socks. The old woman had on tennis shoes and the white-trashy mother had on what appeared to be bedroom slippers, black straw with gold braid threaded through them—exactly what you would have expected her to have on.

Sometimes at night when she couldn't go to sleep, Mrs. Turpin would occupy herself with the question of who she would have chosen to be if she couldn't have been herself. If Jesus had said to her before he made her, "There's only two places available for you. You can either be a nigger or white-trash," what would she have said? "Please, Jesus, please," she would have said, "just let me wait until there's another place available," and he would have said, "No, you have to go right now and I have only those two places so make up your mind." She would have wiggled and squirmed and begged and pleaded but it would have been no use and finally she would have said, "All right, make me a nigger then—but that don't mean a trashy one." And he would have made her a neat clean respectable Negro woman, herself but black.

Next to the child's mother was a red-headed youngish woman, reading one of the magazines and working a piece of chewing gum, hell for leather, as Claud would say. Mrs. Turpin could not see the woman's feet. She was not white-trash, just common. Sometimes Mrs. Turpin occupied herself at night naming the classes of people. On the bottom of the heap were most colored people, not the kind she would have been if she had been one, but most of them; then next to them—not above, just away from—were the white-trash; then above them were the home-owners, and above them the home-and-land owners, to which she and Claud belonged. Above she and Claud were people with a lot of money and much bigger houses and much more land. But here the complexity of it would begin to bear in on her, for some of the people with a lot of money were common and ought to be below she and Claud and some of the people who had good blood had lost their money and had to rent and then there were colored people who owned their homes and land as well. There was a colored dentist in town who had two red Lincolns and a swimming pool and a farm with registered white-face cattle on it. Usually by the time she had fallen asleep all the classes of people were moiling and roiling around in her head, and she would dream they were all crammed in together in a box car, being ridden off to be put in a gas oven.

"That's a beautiful clock," she said and nodded to her right. It was a big wall clock, the face encased in a brass sunburst.

"Yes, it's very pretty," the stylish lady said agreeably. "And right on the dot too," she added, glancing at her watch.

The ugly girl beside her cast an eye upward at the clock, smirked, then looked directly at Mrs. Turpin and smirked again. Then she returned her eyes to her book. She was obviously the lady's daughter because, although they didn't look anything alike as to disposition, they both had the same shape of face and the same blue eyes. On the lady they sparkled pleasantly but in the girl's seared face they appeared alternately to smolder and to blaze.

What if Jesus had said, "All right, you can be white-trash or a nigger or ugly"!

Mrs. Turpin felt an awful pity for the girl, though she thought it was one thing to be ugly and another to act ugly.

The woman with the snuff-stained lips turned around in her chair and looked up at the clock. Then she turned back and appeared to look a little to the side of Mrs. Turpin. There was a cast in one of her eyes. "You want to know wher you can get you one of themther clocks?" she asked in a loud voice.

"No, I already have a nice clock," Mrs. Turpin said. Once somebody like her got a leg in the conversation, she would be all over it.

"You can get you one with green stamps," the woman said. "That's most likely wher he got hisn. Save you up enough, you can get you most anythang. I got me some joo'ry."

Ought to have got you a wash rag and some soap, Mrs. Turpin thought.

"I get contour sheets with mine," the pleasant lady said.

The daughter slammed her book shut. She looked straight in front of her, directly through Mrs. Turpin and on through the yellow curtain and the plate glass window which made the wall behind her. The girl's eyes seemed lit all of a sudden with a peculiar light, an unnatural light like night road signs give. Mrs. Turpin turned her head to see if there was anything going on outside that she should see, but she could not see anything. Figures passing cast only a pale shadow through the curtain. There was no reason the girl should single her out for her ugly looks.

"Miss Finley," the nurse said, cracking the door. The gumchewing woman got up and passed in front of her and Claud and went into the office. She had on red high-heeled shoes.

Directly across the table, the ugly girl's eyes were fixed on Mrs. Turpin as if she had some very special reason for disliking her.

"This is wonderful weather, isn't it?" the girl's mother said.

"It's good weather for cotton if you can get the niggers to pick it," Mrs. Turpin said, "but niggers don't want to pick cotton any more. You can't get the white folks to pick it and now you can't get the niggers—because they got to be right up there with the white folks."

"They gonna *try* anyways," the white-trash woman said, leaning forward.

"Do you have one of the cotton-picking machines?" the pleasant lady asked.

"No," Mrs. Turpin said, "they leave half the cotton in the field. We don't have much cotton anyway. If you want to make it farming now, you have to have a little of everything. We got a couple of acres of cotton and a few hogs and chickens and just enough white-face that Claud can look after them himself."

"One thang I don't want," the white-trash woman said, wiping her mouth with the back of her hand. "Hogs. Nasty stinking things, a-gruntin and a-rootin all over the place."

Mrs. Turpin gave her the merest edge of her attention. "Our hogs are not dirty and they don't stink," she said. "They're cleaner than some children I've seen. Their feet never touch the ground. We have a pig-parlor—that's where you raise them on concrete," she explained to the pleasant lady, "and Claud scoots them down with the hose every afternoon and washes off the floor." Cleaner by far than that child right there, she thought. Poor nasty little thing. He had not moved except to put the thumb of his dirty hand into his mouth.

The woman turned her face away from Mrs. Turpin. "I know I wouldn't scoot down no hog with no hose," she said to the wall.

You wouldn't have no hog to scoot down, Mrs. Turpin said to herself.

"A-gruntin and a-rootin and a-groanin," the woman muttered.

"We got a little of everything," Mrs. Turpin said to the pleasant lady. "It's no use in having more than you can handle yourself with help like it is. We found enough niggers to pick our cotton this year but Claud he has to go after them and take them home again in the evening. They can't walk that half a mile. No they can't. I tell you," she said and laughed merrily, "I sure am tired of buttering up niggers, but you got to love em if you want em to work for you. When they come in the morning, I run out and I say, 'Hi yawl this morning?' and when Claud drives them off to the field I just wave to beat the band and they just wave back." And she waved her hand rapidly to illustrate.

"Like you read out of the same book," the lady said, showing she understood perfectly.

"Child, yes," Mrs. Turpin said. "And when they come in from the field, I run out with a bucket of icewater. That's the way it's going to be from now on," she said. "You may as well face it."

"One thang I know," the white-trash woman said. "Two thangs I ain't going to do: love no niggers or scoot down no hog with no hose." And she let out a bark of contempt.

The look that Mrs. Turpin and the pleasant lady exchanged indicated they both understood that you had to *have* certain things before you could *know* certain things. But every time Mrs. Turpin exchanged a look with the lady, she was aware that the ugly girl's peculiar eyes were still on her, and she had trouble bringing her attention back to the conversation.

"When you got something," she said, "you got to look after it." And when you ain't got a thing but breath and britches, she added to herself, you can afford to come to town every morning and just sit on the Court House coping and spit.

A grotesque revolving shadow passed across the curtain behind her and was thrown palely on the opposite wall. Then a bicycle clattered down against the outside of the building. The door opened and a colored boy glided in with a tray from the drugstore. It had two large red and white paper cups on it with tops on them. He was a tall, very black boy in discolored white pants and a green nylon shirt. He was chewing gum slowly, as if to music. He set the tray down in the office opening next to the fern and stuck his head through to look for the secretary. She was not in there. He rested his arms on the ledge and waited, his narrow bottom stuck out, swaying to the left and right. He raised a hand over his head and scratched the base of his skull.

"You see that button there, boy?" Mrs. Turpin said. "You can punch that and she'll come. She's probably in the back somewhere."

"Is thas right?" the boy said agreeably, as if he had never seen the button before. He leaned to the right and put his finger on it. "She sometime out," he said and twisted around to face his audience, his elbows behind him on the counter. The nurse appeared and he twisted back again. She handed him a dollar and he rooted in his pocket and made the change and counted it out to her. She gave him fifteen cents for a tip and he went out with the empty tray. The heavy door swung to slowly and closed at length with the sound of suction. For a moment no one spoke.

"They ought to send all them niggers back to Africa," the white-trash woman said. "That's wher they come from in the first place."

"Oh, I couldn't do without my good colored friends," the pleasant lady said.

"There's a heap of things worse than a nigger," Mrs. Turpin agreed. "It's all kinds of them just like it's all kinds of us."

"Yes, and it takes all kinds to make the world go round," the lady said in her musical voice.

As she said it, the raw-complexioned girl snapped her teeth together. Her lower lip turned downwards and inside out, revealing the pale pink inside of her mouth. After a second it rolled back up. It was the ugliest face Mrs. Turpin had ever seen anyone make and for a moment she was certain that the girl had made it at her. She was looking at her as if she had known and disliked her all her life—all of Mrs. Turpin's life, it seemed too, not just all the girl's life. Why, girl, I don't even know you, Mrs. Turpin said silently.

She forced her attention back to the discussion. "It wouldn't be practical to send them back to Africa," she said. "They wouldn't want to go. They got it too good here."

"Wouldn't be what they wanted—if I had anythang to do with it," the woman said.

"It wouldn't be a way in the world you could get all the niggers back over there," Mrs. Turpin said. "They'd be hiding out and lying down and turning sick on you and wailing and hollering and raring and pitching. It wouldn't be a way in the world to get them over there."

"They got over here," the trashy woman said. "Get back like they got over."

"It wasn't so many of them then," Mrs. Turpin explained.

The woman looked at Mrs. Turpin as if here was an idiot indeed but Mrs. Turpin was not bothered by the look, considering where it came from.

"Nooo," she said, "they're going to stay here where they can go to New York and marry white folks and improve their color. That's what they all want to do, every one of them, improve their color."

"You know what comes of that, don't you?" Claud asked.

"No, Claud, what?" Mrs. Turpin said.

Claud's eyes twinkled. "White-faced niggers," he said with never a smile.

Everybody in the office laughed except the white-trash and the ugly girl. The girl gripped the book in her lap with white fingers. The trashy woman looked around her from face to face as if she thought they were all idiots. The old woman in the feed sack dress continued to gaze expressionless across the floor at the high-top shoes of the man opposite her, the one who had been pretending to be asleep when the Turpins came in. He was laughing heartily, his hands still spread out on his knees. The child had fallen to the side and was lying now almost face down in the old woman's lap.

While they recovered from their laughter, the nasal chorus on the radio kept the room from silence.

> "You go to blank blank
> And I'll go to mine
> But we'll all blank along
> To-geth-ther,
> And all along the blank
> We'll hep eachother out
> Smile-ling in any kind of
> Weath-ther!"

Mrs. Turpin didn't catch every word but she caught enough to agree with the spirit of the song and it turned her thoughts sober. To help anybody out that needed it was her philosophy of life. She never spared herself when she found somebody in need, whether they were white or black, trash or decent. And of all she had to be thankful for, she was most thankful that this was so. If Jesus had said, "You can be high society and have all the money you want and be thin and svelte-like, but you can't be a good woman with it," she would have had to say, "Well don't make me that then. Make me a good woman and it don't matter what else, how fat or how ugly or how poor!" Her heart rose. He had not made her a nigger or white-trash or ugly! He had made her herself and given her a little of everything. Jesus, thank you! she said. Thank you thank you thank you! Whenever she counted her blessings she felt as buoyant as if she weighed one hundred and twenty-five pounds instead of one hundred and eighty.

"What's wrong with your little boy?" the pleasant lady asked the white-trashy woman.

"He has a ulcer," the woman said proudly. "He ain't give me a minute's peace since he was born. Him and her are just alike," she said, nodding at the old woman, who was running her leathery fingers through the child's pale hair. "Look like I can't get nothing down them two but Co' Cola and candy."

That's all you try to get down em, Mrs. Turpin said to herself. Too lazy to light the fire. There was nothing you could tell her about people like them that she didn't know already. And it was not just that they didn't have anything. Because if you gave them everything, in two weeks it would all be broken or filthy or they would have chopped it up for lightwood. She knew all this from her own experience. Help them you must, but help them you couldn't.

All at once the ugly girl turned her lips inside out again. Her eyes fixed like two drills on Mrs. Turpin. This time there was no mistaking that there was something urgent behind them.

Girl, Mrs. Turpin exclaimed silently, I haven't done a thing to you! The girl might be confusing her with somebody else. There was no need to sit by and let herself be intimidated. "You must be in college," she said boldly, looking directly at the girl. "I see you reading a book there."

The girl continued to stare and pointedly did not answer.

Her mother blushed at this rudeness. "The lady asked you a question, Mary Grace," she said under her breath.

"I have ears," Mary Grace said.

The poor mother blushed again. "Mary Grace goes to Wellesley College," she explained. She twisted one of the buttons on her dress. "In Massachusetts," she added with a grimace. "And in the summer she just keeps right on studying. Just reads all the time, a real book worm. She's done real well at Wellesley; she's taking English and Math and History and Psychology and Social Studies," she rattled on, "and I think it's too much. I think she ought to get out and have fun."

The girl looked as if she would like to hurl them all through the plate glass window.

"Way up north," Mrs. Turpin murmured and thought, well, it hasn't done much for her manners.

"I'd almost rather to have him sick," the white-trash woman said, wrenching the attention back to herself. "He's so mean when he ain't. Look like some children just take natural to meanness. It's some gets bad when they get sick but he was the opposite. Took sick and turned good. He don't give me no trouble now. It's me waitin to see the doctor," she said.

If I was going to send anybody back to Africa, Mrs. Turpin thought, it would be your kind, woman. "Yes, indeed," she said aloud, but looking up at the ceiling, "it's a heap of things worse than a nigger." And dirtier than a hog, she added to herself.

"I think people with bad dispositions are more to be pitied than anyone on earth," the pleasant lady said in a voice that was decidedly thin.

"I thank the Lord he has blessed me with a good one," Mrs. Turpin said. "The day has never dawned that I couldn't find something to laugh at."

"Not since she married me anyways," Claud said with a comical straight face.

Everybody laughed except the girl and the white-trash.

Mrs. Turpin's stomach shook. "He's such a caution," she said, "that I can't help but laugh at him."

The girl made a loud ugly noise through her teeth.

Her mother's mouth grew thin and tight. "I think the worst thing in the world," she said, "is an ungrateful person. To have everything and not appreciate it. I know a girl," she said, "who has parents who would give her anything, a little brother who loves her dearly, who is getting a good education, who wears the best clothes, but who can never say a kind word to anyone, who never smiles, who just criticizes and complains all day long."

"Is she too old to paddle?" Claud asked.

The girl's face was almost purple.

"Yes," the lady said, "I'm afraid there's nothing to do but leave her to her folly. Some day she'll wake up and it'll be too late."

"It never hurt anyone to smile," Mrs. Turpin said. "It just makes you feel better all over."

"Of course," the lady said sadly, "but there are just some people you can't tell anything to. They can't take criticism."

"If it's one thing I am," Mrs. Turpin said with feeling, "it's grateful. When I think who all I could have been besides myself and what all I got, a little of everything, and a good disposition besides, I just feel like shouting, 'Thank you, Jesus, for making everything the way it is!' It could have been different!" For one thing, somebody else could have got Claud. At the thought of this, she was flooded with gratitude and a terrible pang of joy ran through her. "Oh thank you, Jesus, Jesus, thank you!" she cried aloud.

The book struck her directly over her left eye. It struck almost at the same instant that she realized the girl was about to hurl it. Before she could utter a sound, the raw face came crashing across the table toward her, howling. The girl's fingers sank like clamps into the soft flesh of her neck. She heard the mother cry out and Claud shout, "Whoa!" There was an instant when she was certain that she was about to be in an earthquake.

All at once her vision narrowed and she saw everything as if it were happening in a small room far away, or as if she were looking at it through the wrong end of a telescope. Claud's face crumpled and fell out of sight. The nurse ran in, then out, then in again. Then the gangling figure of the doctor rushed out of the inner door. Magazines flew this way and that as the table turned over. The girl fell with a thud and Mrs. Turpin's vision suddenly reversed itself and she saw everything large instead of small. The eyes of the white-trashy woman were staring hugely at the floor. There the girl, held down on one side by the nurse and on the other by her mother, was wrenching and turning in their grasp. The doctor was kneeling astride her, trying to hold her arm down. He managed after a second to sink a long needle into it.

Mrs. Turpin felt entirely hollow except for her heart which swung from side to side as if it were agitated in a great empty drum of flesh.

"Somebody that's not busy call for the ambulance," the doctor said in the off-hand voice young doctors adopt for terrible occasions.

Mrs. Turpin could not have moved a finger. The old man who had been sitting next to her skipped nimbly into the office and made the call, for the secretary still seemed to be gone.

"Claud!" Mrs. Turpin called.

He was not in his chair. She knew she must jump up and find him but she felt like some one trying to catch a train in a dream, when everything moves in slow motion and the faster you try to run the slower you go.

"Here I am," a suffocated voice, very unlike Claud's, said.

He was doubled up in the corner on the floor, pale as paper, holding his leg. She wanted to get up and go to him but she could not move. Instead, her gaze was drawn slowly downward to the churning face on the floor, which she could see over the doctor's shoulder.

The girl's eyes stopped rolling and focused on her. They seemed a much lighter blue than before, as if a door that had been tightly closed behind them was now open to admit light and air.

Mrs. Turpin's head cleared and her power of motion returned. She leaned forward until she was looking directly into the fierce brilliant eyes. There was no doubt in her mind that the girl did know her, knew her in some intense and personal way, beyond time and place and condition. "What you got to say to me?" she asked hoarsely and held her breath, waiting, as for a revelation.

The girl raised her head. Her gaze locked with Mrs. Turpin's. "Go back to hell where you came from, you old wart hog," she whispered. Her voice was low but clear. Her eyes burned for a moment as if she saw with pleasure that her message had struck its target.

Mrs. Turpin sank back in her chair.

After a moment the girl's eyes closed and she turned her head wearily to the side.

The doctor rose and handed the nurse the empty syringe. He leaned over and put both hands for a moment on the mother's shoulders, which were shaking. She was sitting on the floor, her lips pressed together, holding Mary Grace's hand in her lap. The girl's fingers were gripped like a baby's around her thumb. "Go on to the hospital," he said. "I'll call and make the arrangements."

"Now let's see that neck," he said in a jovial voice to Mrs. Turpin. He began to inspect her neck with his first two fingers. Two little moon-shaped lines like pink fish bones were indented over her windpipe. There was the beginning of an angry red swelling above her eye. His fingers passed over this also.

"Lea' me be," she said thickly and shook him off. "See about Claud. She kicked him."

"I'll see about him in a minute," he said and felt her pulse. He was a thin gray-haired man, given to pleasantries. "Go home and have yourself a vacation the rest of the day," he said and patted her on the shoulder.

Quit your pattin me, Mrs. Turpin growled to herself.

"And put an ice pack over that eye," he said. Then he went and squatted down beside Claud and looked at his leg. After a moment he pulled him up and Claud limped after him into the office.

Until the ambulance came, the only sounds in the room were the tremulous moans of the girl's mother, who continued to sit on the floor. The white-trash woman did not take her eyes off the girl. Mrs. Turpin looked straight ahead at nothing. Presently the ambulance drew up, a long dark shadow, behind the curtain. The attendants came in and set the stretcher down beside the girl and lifted her expertly onto it and carried her out. The nurse helped the mother gather up her things. The shadow of the ambulance moved silently away and the nurse came back in the office.

"That ther girl is going to be a lunatic, ain't she?" the white-trash woman asked the nurse, but the nurse kept on to the back and never answered her.

"Yes, she's going to be a lunatic," the white-trash woman said to the rest of them.

"Po' critter," the old woman murmured. The child's face was still in her lap. His eyes looked idly out over her knees.

He had not moved during the disturbance except to draw one leg up under him.

"I thank Gawd," the white-trash woman said fervently, "I ain't a lunatic."

Claud came limping out and the Turpins went home.

As their pick-up truck turned into their own dirt road and made the crest of the hill, Mrs. Turpin gripped the window ledge and looked out suspiciously. The land sloped gracefully down through a field dotted with lavender weeds and at the start of the rise their small yellow frame house, with its little flower beds spread out around it like a fancy apron, sat primly in its accustomed place between two giant hickory trees. She would not have been startled to see a burnt wound between two blackened chimneys.

Neither of them felt like eating so they put on their house clothes and lowered the shade in the bedroom and lay down, Claud with his leg on a pillow and herself with a damp washcloth over her eye. The instant she was flat on her back, the image of a razor-backed hog with warts on its face and horns coming out behind its ears snorted into her head. She moaned, a low quiet moan.

"I am not," she said tearfully, "a wart hog. From hell." But the denial had no force. The girl's eyes and her words, even the tone of her voice, low but clear, directed only to her, brooked no repudiation. She had been singled out for the message, though there was trash in the room to whom it might justly have been applied. The full force of this fact struck her only now. There was a woman there who was neglecting her own child but she had been overlooked. The message had been given to Ruby Turpin, a respectable, hard-working, church-going woman. The tears dried. Her eyes began to burn instead with wrath.

She rose on her elbow and the washcloth fell into her hand. Claud was lying on his back, snoring. She wanted to tell him what the girl had said. At the same time, she did not wish to put the image of herself as a wart hog from hell into his mind.

"Hey, Claud," she muttered and pushed his shoulder.

Claud opened one pale baby blue eye.

She looked into it warily. He did not think about anything. He just went his way.

"Wha, whasit?" he said and closed the eye again.

"Nothing," she said. "Does your leg pain you?"

"Hurts like hell," Claud said.

"It'll quit terreckly," she said and lay back down. In a moment Claud was snoring again. For the rest of the afternoon they lay there. Claud slept. She scowled at the ceiling. Occasionally she raised her fist and made a small stabbing motion over her chest as if she was defending her innocence to invisible guests who were like the comforters of Job, reasonable-seeming but wrong.

About five-thirty Claud stirred. "Got to go after those niggers," he sighed, not moving.

She was looking straight up as if there were unintelligible handwriting on the ceiling. The protuberance over her eye had turned a greenish-blue. "Listen here," she said.

"What?"

"Kiss me."

Claud leaned over and kissed her loudly on the mouth. He pinched her side and their hands interlocked. Her expression of ferocious concentration did not change. Claud got up, groaning and growling, and limped off. She continued to study the ceiling.

She did not get up until she heard the pick-up truck coming back with the Negroes. Then she rose and thrust her feet in her brown oxfords, which she did not bother to lace, and stumped out onto the back porch and got her red plastic bucket. She emptied a tray of ice cubes into it and filled it half full of water and went out into the back yard. Every afternoon after Claud brought the hands in, one of the boys helped him put out hay and the rest waited in the back of the truck until he was ready to take them home. The truck was parked in the shade under one of the hickory trees.

"Hi yawl this evening?" Mrs. Turpin asked grimly, appearing with the bucket and the dipper. There were three women and a boy in the truck.

"Us doin nicely," the oldest woman said. "Hi you doin?" and her gaze stuck immediately on the dark lump on Mrs. Turpin's forehead. "You done fell down, ain't you?" she asked in a solicitous voice. The old woman was dark and almost toothless. She had on an old felt hat of Claud's set back on her head. The other two women were younger and lighter and they both had new bright green sunhats. One of them had hers on her head; the other had taken hers off and the boy was grinning beneath it.

Mrs. Turpin set the bucket down on the floor of the

truck. "Yawl hep yourselves," she said. She looked around to make sure Claud had gone. "No, I didn't fall down," she said, folding her arms. "It was something worse than that."

"Ain't nothing bad happen to you!" the old woman said. She said it as if they all knew that Mrs. Turpin was protected in some special way by Divine Providence. "You just had you a little fall."

"We were in town at the doctor's office for where the cow kicked Mr. Turpin," Mrs. Turpin said in a flat tone that indicated they could leave off their foolishness. "And there was this girl there. A big fat girl with her face all broke out. I could look at that girl and tell she was peculiar but I couldn't tell how. And me and her mama was just talking and going along and all of a sudden WHAM! She throws this big book she was reading at me and . . ."

"Naw!" the old woman cried out.

"And then she jumps over the table and commences to choke me."

"Naw!" they all exclaimed, "naw!"

"Hi come she do that?" the old woman asked. "What ail her?"

Mrs. Turpin only glared in front of her.

"Somethin ail her," the old woman said.

"They carried her off in an ambulance," Mrs. Turpin continued, "but before she went she was rolling on the floor and they were trying to hold her down to give her a shot and she said something to me." She paused. "You know what she said to me?"

"What she say?" they asked.

"She said," Mrs. Turpin began, and stopped, her face very dark and heavy. The sun was getting whiter and whiter, blanching the sky overhead so that the leaves of the hickory tree were black in the face of it. She could not bring forth the words. "Something real ugly," she muttered.

"She sho shouldn't said nothin ugly to you," the old woman said. "You so sweet. You the sweetest lady I know."

"She pretty too," the one with the hat on said.

"And stout," the other one said. "I never knowed no sweeter white lady."

"That's the truth befo' Jesus," the old woman said. "Amen! You des as sweet and pretty as you can be."

Mrs. Turpin knew exactly how much Negro flattery was worth and it added to her rage. "She said," she began again and finished this time with a fierce rush of breath, "that I was an old wart hog from hell."

There was an astounded silence.

"Where she at?" the youngest woman cried in a piercing voice.

"Lemme see her. I'll kill her!"

"I'll kill her with you!" the other one cried.

"She b'long in the sylum," the old woman said emphatically. "You the sweetest white lady I know."

"She pretty too," the other two said. "Stout as she can be and sweet. Jesus satisfied with her!"

"Deed he is," the old woman declared.

Idiots! Mrs. Turpin growled to herself. You could never say anything intelligent to a nigger. You could talk at them but not with them. "Yawl ain't drunk your water," she said shortly. "Leave the bucket in the truck when you're finished with it. I got more to do than just stand around and pass the time of day," and she moved off and into the house.

She stood for a moment in the middle of the kitchen. The dark protuberance over her eye looked like a miniature tornado cloud which might any moment sweep across the horizon of her brow. Her lower lip protruded dangerously. She squared her massive shoulders. Then she marched into the front of the house and out the side door and started down the road to the pig parlor. She had the look of a woman going single-handed, weaponless, into battle.

The sun was a deep yellow now like a harvest moon and was riding westward very fast over the far tree line as if it meant to reach the hogs before she did. The road was rutted and she kicked several good-sized stones out of her path as she strode along. The pig parlor was on a little knoll at the end of a lane that ran off from the side of the barn. It was a square of concrete as large as a small room, with a board fence about four feet high around it. The concrete floor sloped slightly so that the hog wash could drain off into a trench where it was carried to the field for fertilizer. Claud was standing on the outside, on the edge of the concrete, hanging onto the top board, hosing down the floor inside. The hose was connected to the faucet of a water trough nearby.

Mrs. Turpin climbed up beside him and glowered down at the hogs inside. There were seven long-snouted bristly shoats in it—tan with liver-colored spots—and an old sow a few weeks off from farrowing. She was lying on her side grunting. The shoats were running about shaking themselves like idiot children, their little slit pig eyes searching the floor for anything left. She had read that pigs were the most intelligent animal. She doubted it. They were supposed to be smarter than dogs. There had even been a pig astronaut. He had performed his assignment perfectly but died of a heart attack afterwards because they left him in his electric suit, sitting upright throughout his examination when naturally a hog should be on all fours.

A-gruntin and a-rootin and a-groanin.

"Gimme that hose," she said, yanking it away from Claud. "Go on and carry them niggers home and then get off that leg."

"You look like you might have swallowed a mad dog," Claud observed, but he got down and limped off. He paid no attention to her humors.

Until he was out of earshot, Mrs. Turpin stood on the side of the pen, holding the hose and pointing the stream of water at the hind quarters of any shoat that looked as if it might try to lie down. When he had had time to get over the hill, she turned her head slightly and her wrathful eyes scanned the path. He was nowhere in sight. She turned back again and seemed to gather herself up. Her shoulders rose and she drew in her breath.

"What do you send me a message like that for?" she said in a low fierce voice, barely above a whisper but with the force of a shout in its concentrated fury. "How am I a hog and me both? How am I saved and from hell too?" Her free fist was knotted and with the other she gripped the hose, blindly pointing the stream of water in and out of the eye of the old sow whose outraged squeal she did not hear.

The pig parlor commanded a view of the back pasture where their twenty beef cows were gathered around the hay-bales Claud and the boy had put out. The freshly cut pasture sloped down to the highway. Across it was their cotton field and beyond that a dark green dusty wood which they owned as well. The sun was behind the wood, very red, looking over the paling of trees like a farmer inspecting his own hogs.

"Why me?" she rumbled. "It's no trash around here, black or white, that I haven't given to. And break my back to the bone every day working. And do for the church."

She appeared to be the right size woman to command the arena before her. "How am I a hog?" she demanded. "Exactly how am I like them?" and she jabbed the stream of water at the shoats. "There was plenty of trash there. It didn't have to be me."

"If you like trash better, go get yourself some trash then," she railed. "You could have made me trash. Or a nigger. If trash is what you wanted why didn't you make me trash?" She shook her fist with the hose in it and a watery snake appeared momentarily in the air. "I could quit working and take it easy and be filthy," she growled. "Lounge about the sidewalks all day drinking root beer. Dip snuff and spit in every puddle and have it all over my face. I could be nasty."

"Or you could have made me a nigger. It's too late for me to be a nigger," she said with deep sarcasm, "but I could act like one. Lay down in the middle of the road and stop traffic. Roll on the ground."

In the deepening light everything was taking on a mysterious hue. The pasture was growing a peculiar glassy green and the streak of highway had turned lavender. She braced herself for a final assault and this time her voice rolled out over the pasture. "Go on," she yelled, "call me a hog! Call me a hog again. From hell. Call me a wart hog from hell. Put that bottom rail on top. There'll still be a top and bottom!"

A garbled echo returned to her.

A final surge of fury shook her and she roared, "Who do you think you are?"

The color of everything, field and crimson sky, burned for a moment with a transparent intensity. The question carried over the pasture and across the highway and the cotton field and returned to her clearly like an answer from beyond the wood.

She opened her mouth but no sound came out of it.

A tiny truck, Claud's, appeared on the highway, heading rapidly out of sight. Its gears scraped thinly. It looked like a child's toy. At any moment a bigger truck might smash into it and scatter Claud's and the niggers' brains all over the road.

Mrs. Turpin stood there, her gaze fixed on the highway, all her muscles rigid, until in five or six minutes the truck reappeared, returning. She waited until it had had time to turn into their own road. Then like a monumental statue coming to life, she bent her head slowly and gazed, as if through the very heart of mystery, down into the pig parlor at the hogs. They had settled all in one corner around the old sow who was grunting softly. A red glow suffused them. They appeared to pant with a secret life.

Until the sun slipped finally behind the tree line, Mrs. Turpin remained there with her gaze bent to them as if she were absorbing some abysmal life-giving knowledge. At last she lifted her head. There was only a purple streak in the sky, cutting through a field of crimson and leading, like an extension of the highway, into the descending dusk. She raised her hands from the side of the pen in a gesture hieratic and profound. A visionary light settled in her eyes. She saw the streak as a vast swinging bridge extending upward from the earth through a field of living fire. Upon it a vast horde of souls were rumbling toward heaven. There were whole companies of white-trash, clean for the first time in their lives, and bands of black niggers in white robes, and battalions of freaks and lunatics shouting and clapping and leaping like frogs. And bringing up the end of the procession was a tribe of people whom she recognized at once as those who, like herself and Claud, had always had a little of everything and the God-given wit to use it right. She leaned forward to observe them closer. They were marching behind the others with great dignity, accountable as they had always been for good order and common sense and respectable behavior. They alone were on key. Yet she could see by their shocked and altered faces that even their virtues were being burned away. She lowered her hands and gripped the rail of the hog pen, her eyes small but fixed unblinkingly on what lay ahead. In a moment the vision faded but she remained where she was, immobile.

At length she got down and turned off the faucet and made her slow way on the darkening path to the house. In the woods around her the invisible cricket choruses had struck up, but what she heard were the voices of the souls climbing upward into the starry field and shouting hallelujah.

Diane Oliver (July 28, 1943–May 21, 1966) was born in Charlotte, North Carolina. Her mother, Blanche Oliver, says, "As a child Diane read everything that was in the library. Once, when she had no new books to read, she remarked that when she grew up she would write stories for children so that they would have plenty to read."

Oliver graduated from West Charlotte High School in 1960 where she received the coveted Civitan Award for scholastic excellence and good citizenship. She entered Woman's College (now University of North Carolina-Greensboro) in 1960 at the beginning of a decade of transformation for civil rights in the South. Oliver was one of the first ten African-American students at UNC-Greensboro. Oliver studied writing with poet Randall Jarrell and served as feature editor, and later managing editor, of *Carolinian*, a student literary magazine. After receiving a B.A. degree in 1964 Oliver was among twenty young women selected from across the nation to be guest editors at *Mademoiselle* magazine for the month of June. Of the twenty selected Oliver was the only African-American. During the latter part of the summer of 1964 she spent eight weeks in Switzerland with "Experiment in International Living." From the fall of 1964 until her death in May 1966 she was a graduate student at the University of Iowa Writers' Workshop. In Iowa she was active in many campus activities, including civil rights and Vietnam protest demonstrations. Shortly before graduation Oliver died after a car hit the motorcycle she was riding as a passenger. A Master of Fine Arts degree was awarded to her posthumously.

NEIGHBORS

Diane Oliver

The bus turning the corner of Patterson and Talford Avenue was dull this time of evening. Of the four passengers standing in the rear, she did not recognize any of her friends. Most of the people tucked neatly in the double seats were women, maids and cooks on their way from work or secretaries who had worked late and were riding from the office building at the mill. The cotton mill was out from town, near the house where she worked. She noticed that a few men were riding too. They were obviously just working men, except for one gentleman dressed very neatly in a dark grey suit and carrying what she imagined was a push-button umbrella.

He looked to her as though he usually drove a car to work. She immediately decided that the car probably wouldn't start this morning so he had to catch the bus to and from work. She was standing in the rear of the bus, peering at the passengers, her arms barely reaching the over-head railing, trying not to wobble with every lurch. But every corner the bus turned pushed her head toward a window. And her hair was coming down too, wisps of black curls swung between her eyes. She looked at the people around her. Some of them were white, but most of them were her color. Looking at the passengers at least kept her from thinking of tomorrow. But really she would be glad when it came, then everything would be over.

She took a firmer grip on the green leather seat and wished she had on her glasses. The man with the umbrella was two people ahead of her on the other side of the bus, so she could see him between other people very clearly. She watched as he unfolded the evening newspaper, craning her neck to see what was on the front page. She stood, impatiently trying to read the headlines, when she realized he was staring up at her rather curiously. Biting her lips she turned her head and stared out of the window until the downtown section was in sight.

She would have to wait until she was home to see if they were in the newspaper again. Sometimes she felt that if another person snapped a picture of them she would burst out screaming. Last Monday reporters were already inside the pre-school clinic when she took Tommy for his last polio shot. She didn't understand how anybody could be so heartless to a child. The flashbulb went off right when the needle went in and all the picture showed was Tommy's open mouth.

The bus pulling up to the curb jerked to a stop, startling her and confusing her thoughts. Clutching in her hand the paper bag that contained her uniform, she pushed her way toward the door. By standing in the back of the bus, she was one of the first people to step to the ground. Outside the bus, the evening air felt humid and uncomfortable and her dress kept sticking to her. She looked up and remembered that the weatherman had forecast rain. Just their luck—why, she wondered, would it have to rain on top of everything else?

As she walked along, the main street seemed unnaturally quiet but she decided her imagination was merely playing tricks. Besides, most of the stores had been closed since five o'clock.

She stopped to look at a reversible raincoat in Ivey's window, but although she had a full time job now, she couldn't keep her mind on clothes. She was about to continue walking when she heard a horn blowing. Looking around, half-scared but also curious, she saw a man beckoning to her in a grey car. He was nobody she knew but since a nicely dressed woman was with him in the front seat, she walked to the car.

"You're Jim Mitchell's girl, aren't you?" he questioned. "You Ellie or the other one?"

She nodded yes, wondering who he was and how much he had been drinking.

"Now honey," he said leaning over the woman, "you don't know me but your father does and you tell him that if anything happens to that boy of his tomorrow we're ready to set things straight." He looked her straight in the eye and she promised to take home the message.

Just as the man was about to step on the gas, the woman reached out and touched her arm. "You hurry up home, honey, it's about dark out here."

Before she could find out their names, the Chevrolet had disappeared around a corner. Ellie wished someone would magically appear and tell her everything that had happened since August. Then maybe she could figure out what was real and what she had been imagining for the past couple of days.

She walked past the main shopping district up to Tanner's where Saraline was standing in the window peeling oranges. Everything in the shop was painted orange and green and Ellie couldn't help thinking that poor Saraline looked out of place. She stopped to wave to her friend who pointed the knife to her watch and then to her boyfriend standing in the rear of the shop. Ellie nodded that she understood. She knew Sara wanted her to tell her grandfather that she had to work late again. Neither one of them could figure out why he didn't like Charlie. Saraline had finished high school three years ahead of her and it was time for her to be getting married. Ellie watched as her friend stopped peeling the orange long enough to cross her fingers. She nodded again but she was afraid all the crossed fingers in the world wouldn't stop the trouble tomorrow.

She stopped at the traffic light and spoke to a shrivelled woman hunched against the side of a building. Scuffing the bottom of her sneakers on the curb she waited for the woman to open her mouth and grin as she usually did. The kids used to bait her to talk, and since she didn't have but one tooth in her whole head they called her Doughnut Puncher. But the woman was still, the way everything else had been all week.

From where Ellie stood, across the street from the Sears and Roebuck parking lot, she could see their house, all of the houses on the single street white people called Welfare Row. Those newspaper men always made her angry. All of their articles showed how rough the people were on their street. And the reporters never said her family wasn't on welfare, the papers always said the family lived on that street. She paused to look across the street at a group of kids pouncing on one rubber ball. There were always white kids around their neighborhood mixed up in the games, but playing with them was almost an unwritten rule. When everybody started going to school nobody played together any more.

She crossed at the corner ignoring the cars at the stop light and the closer she got to her street the more she realized that the newspaper was right. The houses were ugly, there were not even any trees, just patches of scraggly bushes and grasses. As she cut across the sticky asphalt pavement covered with cars she was conscious of the parking lot floodlights casting a strange glow on her street. She stared from habit at the house on the end of the block and except for the way the paint was peeling they all looked alike to her. Now at twilight the flaking grey paint had a luminous glow and as she walked down the dirt sidewalk she noticed Mr. Paul's pipe smoke added to the hazy atmosphere. Mr. Paul would be sitting in that same spot waiting until Saraline came home. Ellie slowed her pace to speak to the elderly man sitting on the porch.

"Evening, Mr. Paul," she said. Her voice sounded clear and out of place on the vacant street.

"Eh, who's that?" Mr. Paul leaned over the rail,. "What you say, girl?"

"How are you?" she hollered louder. "Sara said she'd be late tonight, she has to work." She waited for the words to sink in.

His head had dropped and his eyes were facing his lap. She could see that he was disappointed. "Couldn't help it," he said finally. "Reckon they needed her again." Then as if he suddenly remembered he turned toward her.

"You people be ready down there? Still gonna let him go tomorrow?"

She looked at Mr. Paul between the missing rails on his porch, seeing how his rolled up trousers seemed to fit exactly in the vacant banister space.

"Last I heard this morning we're still letting him go," she said.

Mr. Paul had shifted his weight back to the chair. "Don't reckon they'll hurt him," he mumbled, scratching the side of his face. "Hope he don't mind being spit on though. Spitting ain't like cutting. They can spit on him and nobody'll ever know who did it," he said, ending his words with a quiet chuckle.

Ellie stood on the sidewalk grinding her heel in the dirt waiting for the old man to finish talking. She was glad somebody found something funny to laugh at. Finally he shut up.

"Goodbye, Mr. Paul," she waved. Her voice sounded loud to her own ears. But she knew the way her head ached intensified noises. She walked home faster, hoping they had some aspirin in the house and that those men would leave earlier tonight.

From the front of her house she could tell that the men were still there. The living room light shone behind the yellow shades, coming through brighter in the patched places. She thought about moving the geranium pot from the porch to catch the rain but changed her mind. She kicked a beer can under a car parked in the street and stopped to look at her reflection on the car door. The tiny flowers of her printed dress made her look as if she had a strange tropical disease. She spotted another can and kicked it out of the way of the car, thinking that one of these days some kid was going to fall and hurt himself. What she wanted to do she knew was kick the car out of the way. Both the station wagon and the Ford had been parked in front of her house all week, waiting. Everybody was just sitting around waiting.

Suddenly she laughed aloud. Reverend Davis' car was big and black and shiny just like, but no, the smile disappeared from her face, her mother didn't like for them to say things about other people's color. She looked around to see who else came, and saw Mr. Moore's old beat up blue car. Somebody had torn away half of his NAACP sign. Sometimes she really felt sorry for the man. No matter how hard he glued on his stickers somebody always yanked them off again.

Ellie didn't recognize the third car but it had an Alabama license plate. She turned around and looked up and down the street, hating to go inside. There were no lights on their street, but in the distance she could see the bright lights of the parking lot. Slowly she did an about face and climbed the steps.

She wondered when her mama was going to remember to get a yellow bulb for the porch. Although the lights hadn't been turned on, usually June bugs and mosquitoes swarmed all around the porch. By the time she was inside the house she always felt like they were crawling in her hair. She pulled on the screen and saw that Mama finally had made Hezekiah patch up the holes. The globs of white adhesive tape scattered over the screen door looked just like misshapen butterflies.

She listened to her father's voice and could tell by the tone that the men were discussing something important again. She rattled the door once more but nobody came.

"Will somebody please let me in?" Her voice carried through the screen to the knot of men sitting in the corner.

"The door's open," her father yelled. "Come on in."

"The door is not open," she said evenly. "You know we stopped leaving it open." She was feeling tired again and her voice had fallen an octave lower.

"Yeah, I forgot, I forgot," he mumbled walking to the door.

She watched her father almost stumble across a chair to let her in. He was shorter than the light bulb and the light seemed to beam down on him, emphasizing the wrinkles around his eyes. She could tell from the way he pushed open the screen that he hadn't had much sleep either. She'd overheard him telling Mama that the people down at the shop seemed to be piling on the work harder just because of this thing. And he couldn't do anything or say anything to his boss because they probably wanted to fire him.

"Where's Mama?" she whispered. He nodded toward the back.

"Good evening, everybody," she said looking at the three men who had not looked up since she entered the room. One of the men half stood, but his attention was geared back to something another man was saying. They were sitting on the sofa in their shirt sleeves and there was a pitcher of ice water on the window sill.

"Your mother probably needs some help," her father said. She looked past him trying to figure out who the white man was sitting on the end. His face looked familiar and she tried to remember where she had seen him before. The men were paying no attention to her. She bent to see what they were studying and saw a large sheet of white drawing paper. She could see blocks and lines and the man sitting in the middle was marking a trail with the eraser edge of the pencil.

The quiet stillness of the room was making her head ache

more. She pushed her way through the red embroidered curtains that led to the kitchen.

"I'm home, Mama," she said, standing in front of the back door facing the big yellow sun Hezekiah and Tommy had painted on the wall above the iron stove. Immediately she felt a warmth permeating her skin. "Where is everybody?" she asked, sitting at the table where her mother was peeling potatoes.

"Mrs. McAllister is keeping Helen and Teenie," her mother said. "Your brother is staying over with Harry tonight." With each name she uttered, a slice of potato peeling tumbled to the newspaper on the table. "Tommy's in the bedroom reading that Uncle Wiggily book."

Ellie looked up at her mother but her eyes were straight ahead. She knew that Tommy only read the Uncle Wiggily book by himself when he was unhappy. She got up and walked to the kitchen cabinet.

"The other knives dirty?" she asked.

"No," her mother said, "look in the next drawer."

Ellie pulled open the drawer, flicking scraps of white paint with her fingernail. She reached for the knife and at the same time a pile of envelopes caught her eye.

"Any more come today?" she asked, pulling out the knife and slipping the envelopes under the dish towels.

"Yes, seven more came today," her mother accentuated each word carefully. "Your father has them with him in the other room."

"Same thing?" she asked picking up a potato and wishing she could think of some way to change the subject.

The white people had been threatening them for the past three weeks. Some of the letters were aimed at the family, but most of them were directed to Tommy himself. About once a week in the same handwriting somebody wrote that he'd better not eat lunch at school because they were going to poison him.

They had been getting those letters ever since the school board made Tommy's name public. She sliced the potato and dropped the pieces in the pan of cold water. Out of all those people he had been the only one the board had accepted for transfer to the elementary school. The other children, the members said, didn't live in the district. As she cut the eyes out of another potato she thought about the first letter they had received and how her father just set fire to it in the ashtray. But then Mr. Bell said they'd better save the rest, in case anything happened, they might need the evidence for court.

She peeped up again at her mother, "Who's that white man in there with Daddy?"

"One of Lawyer Belk's friends," she answered. "He's pastor of the church that's always on television Sunday morning. Mr. Belk seems to think that having him around will do some good." Ellie saw that her voice was shaking just like her hand as she reached for the last potato. Both of them could hear Tommy in the next room mumbling to himself. She was afraid to look at her mother.

Suddenly Ellie was aware that her mother's hands were trembling violently. "He's so little," she whispered and suddenly the knife slipped out of her hands and she was crying and breathing at the same time.

Ellie didn't know what to do but after a few seconds she cleared away the peelings and put the knives in the sink. "Why don't you lie down?" she suggested. "I'll clean up and get Tommy in bed." Without saying anything her mother rose and walked to her bedroom.

Ellie wiped off the table and draped the dishcloth over the sink. She stood back and looked at the rusting pipes powdered with a whitish film. One of these days they would have to paint the place. She tiptoed past her mother who looked as if she had fallen asleep from exhaustion.

"Tommy," she called softly, "come on and get ready for bed."

Tommy sitting in the middle of the floor did not answer. He was sitting the way she imagined he would be, crosslegged, pulling his ear lobe as he turned the ragged pages of *Uncle Wiggily at the Zoo*.

"What you doing, Tommy?" she said squatting on the floor beside him. He smiled and pointed at the picture of the ducks.

"School starts tomorrow," she said, turning a page with him. "Don't you think it's time to go to bed?"

"Oh Ellie, do I have to go now?" She looked down at the serious brown eyes and the closely cropped hair. For a minute she wondered if he questioned having to go to bed now or to school tomorrow.

"Well," she said, "aren't you about through with the

book?" He shook his head. "Come on," she pulled him up, "you're a sleepy head." Still he shook his head.

"When Helen and Teenie coming home?"

"Tomorrow after you come home from school they'll be here."

She lifted him from the floor thinking how small he looked to be facing all those people tomorrow.

"Look," he said breaking away from her hand and pointing to a blue shirt and pair of cotton twill pants, "Mama got them for me to wear tomorrow."

While she ran water in the tub, she heard him crawl on top of the bed. He was quiet and she knew he was untying his sneakers.

"Put your shoes out," she called through the door, "and maybe Daddy will polish them."

"Is Daddy still in there with those men? Mama made me be quiet so I wouldn't bother them."

He padded into the bathroom with bare feet and crawled into the water. As she scrubbed him they played Ask Me A Question, their own version of Twenty Questions. She had just dried him and was about to have him step into his pajamas when he asked: "Are they gonna get me tomorrow?"

"Who's going to get you?" She looked into his eyes and began rubbing him furiously with the towel.

"I don't know," he answered. "Somebody I guess."

"Nobody's going to get you," she said, "who wants a little boy who gets bubblegum in his hair anyway—but us?" He grinned but as she hugged him she thought how much he looked like his father. They walked to the bed to say his prayers and while they were kneeling she heard the first drops of rain. By the time she covered him up and tucked the spread off the floor the rain had changed to a steady downpour.

When Tommy had gone to bed her mother got up again and began ironing clothes in the kitchen. Something, she said, to keep her thoughts busy. While her mother folded and sorted the clothes Ellie drew up a chair from the kitchen table. They sat in the kitchen for a while listening to the voices of the men in the next room. Her mother's quiet speech broke the stillness in the room.

"I'd rather," she said making sweeping motions with the iron, "that you stayed home from work tomorrow and went with your father to take Tommy. I don't think I'll be up to those people."

Ellie nodded, "I don't mind," she said, tracing circles on the oil cloth covered table.

"Your father's going," her mother continued. "Belk and Reverend Davis are too. I think that white man in there will probably go."

"They may not need me," Ellie answered.

"Tommy will," her mother said, folding the last dish towel and storing it in the cabinet.

"Mama, I think he's scared," the girl turned toward the woman. "He was so quiet while I was washing him."

"I know," she answered sitting down heavily. "He's been that way all day." Her brown wavy hair glowed in the dim lighting of the kitchen. "I told him he wasn't going to school with Jakie and Bob any more but I said he was going to meet some other children just as nice."

Ellie saw that her mother was twisting her wedding band around and around on her finger.

"I've already told Mrs. Ingraham that I wouldn't be able to come out tomorrow." Ellie paused, "She didn't say very much. She didn't even say anything about his pictures in the newspaper. Mr. Ingraham said we were getting right crazy but even he didn't say anything else."

She stopped to look at the clock sitting near the sink. "It's almost time for the cruise cars to begin," she said. Her mother followed Ellie's eyes to the sink. The policemen circling their block every twenty minutes was supposed to make them feel safe, but hearing the cars come so regularly and that light flashing through the shade above her bed only made her nervous.

She stopped talking to push a wrinkle out of the shiny red cloth, dragging her finger along the table edges. "How long before those men going to leave?" she asked her mother. Just as she spoke she heard one of the men say something about getting some sleep. "I didn't mean to run them away," she said smiling. Her mother half-smiled too. They listened for the sound of motors and tires and waited for her father to shut the front door.

In a few seconds her father's head pushed through the curtain. "Want me to turn down your bed now, Ellie?" She felt uncomfortable staring up at him, the whole family looked drained of all energy.

"That's all right," she answered. "I'll sleep in Helen and Teenie's bed tonight."

"How's Tommy?" he asked looking toward the bedroom. He came in and sat down at the table with them.

They were silent before he spoke. "I keep wondering if we should send him." He lit a match and watched the flame disappear into the ashtray, then he looked into his wife's eyes. "There's no telling what these fool white folks will do."

Her mother reached over and patted his hand. "We're doing what we have to do, I guess," she said. "Sometimes though I wish the others weren't so much older than him."

"But it seems so unfair," Ellie broke in, "sending him there all by himself like that. Everybody keeps asking me why the MacAdams didn't apply for their children."

"Eloise." Her father's voice sounded curt. "We aren't answering for the MacAdams, we're trying to do what's right for your brother. He's not old enough to have his own say so. You and the others could decide for yourselves, but we're the ones that have to do for him."

She didn't say anything but watched him pull a handful of envelopes out of his pocket and tuck them in the cabinet drawer. She knew that if anyone had told him in August that Tommy would be the only one going to Jefferson Davis they would not have let him go.

"Those the new ones?" she asked. "What they say?"

"Let's not talk about the letters," her father said. "Let's go to bed."

Outside they heard the rain become heavier. Since early evening she had become accustomed to the sound. Now it blended in with the rest of the noises that had accumulated in the back of her mind since the whole thing began.

As her mother folded the ironing board they heard the quiet wheels of the police car. Ellie noticed that the clock said twelve-ten and she wondered why they were early. Her mother pulled the iron cord from the switch and they stood silently waiting for the police car to turn around and pass the house again, as if the car's passing were a final blessing for the night.

Suddenly she was aware of a noise that sounded as if everything had broken loose in her head at once, a loudness that almost shook the foundation of the house. At the same time the lights went out and instinctively her father knocked them to the floor. They could hear the tinkling of glass near the front of the house and Tommy began screaming.

"Tommy, get down," her father yelled.

She hoped he would remember to roll under the bed the way they had practiced. She was aware of objects falling and breaking as she lay perfectly still. Her breath was coming in jerks and then there was a second noise, a smaller explosion but still drowning out Tommy's cries.

"Stay still," her father commanded. "I'm going to check on Tommy. They may throw another one."

She watched him crawl across the floor, pushing a broken flower vase and an iron skillet out of his way. All of the sounds, Tommy's crying, the breaking glass, everything was echoing in her ears. She felt as if they had been crouching on the floor for hours but when she heard the police car door slam, the luminous hands of the clock said only twelve-fifteen.

She heard other cars drive up and pairs of heavy feet trample on the porch. "You folks all right in there?"

She could visualize the hands pulling open the door, because she knew the voice. Sergeant Kearns had been responsible for patrolling the house during the past three weeks. She heard him click the light switch in the living room but the darkness remained intense.

Her father deposited Tommy in his wife's lap and went to what was left of the door. In the next fifteen minutes policemen were everywhere. While she rummaged around underneath the cabinet for a candle, her mother tried to hush up Tommy. His cheek was cut where he had scratched himself on the springs of the bed. Her mother motioned for her to dampen a cloth and put some petroleum jelly on it to keep him quiet. She tried to put him to bed again but he would not go, even when she promised to stay with him for the rest of the night. And so she sat in the kitchen rocking the little boy back and forth on her lap.

Ellie wandered around the kitchen but the light from the single candle put an eerie glow on the walls making her nervous. She began picking up pans, stepping over pieces of broken crockery and glassware. She did not want to go into the living room yet, but if she listened closely, snatches of the policemen's conversation came through the curtain.

She heard one man say that the bomb landed near the edge of the yard, that was why it had only gotten the front porch. She knew from their talk that the living room window was shattered completely. Suddenly Ellie sat down. The picture of the living room window kept flashing in her mind and a wave of feeling invaded her body making her shake as if she had lost all muscular control. She slept on the couch, right under that window.

She looked at her mother to see if she too had realized, but her mother was looking down at Tommy and trying to get him to close his eyes. Ellie stood up and crept toward the living room crying to prepare herself for what she would see. Even that minute of determination could not make her control the horror that she felt. There were jagged holes all along the front of the house and the sofa was covered with glass and paint. She started to pick up the picture that had toppled from the book shelf, then she just stepped over the broken frame.

Outside her father was talking and, curious to see who else was with him, she walked across the splinters to the yard. She could see pieces of the geranium pot and the red blossoms turned face down. There were no lights in the other houses on the street. Across from their house she could see forms standing in the door and shadows being pushed back and forth. "I guess the MacAdams are glad they just didn't get involved." No one heard her speak, and no one came over to see if they could help; she knew why and did not really blame them. They were afraid their house could be next.

Most of the policemen had gone now and only one car was left to flash the revolving red light in the rain. She heard the tall skinny man tell her father they would be parked outside for the rest of the night. As she watched the reflection of the police cars returning to the station, feeling sick on her stomach, she wondered now why they bothered.

Ellie went back inside the house and closed the curtain behind her. There was nothing anyone could do now, not even to the house. Everything was scattered all over the floor and poor Tommy still would not go to sleep. She wondered what would happen when the news spread through their section of town, and at once remembered the man in the grey Chevrolet. It would serve them right if her father's friends got one of them.

Ellie pulled up an overturned chair and sat down across from her mother who was crooning to Tommy. What Mr.

Paul said was right, white people just couldn't be trusted. Her family had expected anything but even though they had practiced ducking, they didn't really expect anybody to try tearing down the house. But the funny thing was the house belonged to one of them. Maybe it was a good thing her family were just renters.

Exhausted, Ellie put her head down on the table. She didn't know what they were going to do about tomorrow, in the day time they didn't need electricity. She was too tired to think any more about Tommy, yet she could not go to sleep. So, she sat at the table trying to sit still, but every few minutes she would involuntarily twitch. She tried to steady her hands, all the time listening to her mother's sing-songy voice and waiting for her father to come back inside the house.

She didn't know how long she lay hunched against the kitchen table, but when she looked up, her wrists bore the imprints of her hair. She unfolded her arms gingerly, feeling the blood rush to her fingertips. Her father sat in the chair opposite her, staring at the vacant space between them. She heard her mother creep away from the table, taking Tommy to his room.

Ellie looked out the window. The darkness was turning to grey and the hurt feeling was disappearing. As she sat there she could begin to look at the kitchen matter-of-factly. Although the hands of the clock were just a little past five-thirty, she knew somebody was going to have to start clearing up and cook breakfast.

She stood and tipped across the kitchen to her parents' bedroom. "Mama," she whispered, standing near the door of Tommy's room. At the sound of her voice, Tommy made a funny throaty noise in his sleep. Her mother motioned for her to go out and be quiet. Ellie knew then that Tommy had just fallen asleep. She crept back to the kitchen and began picking up the dishes that could be salvaged, being careful not to go into the living room.

She walked around her father, leaving the broken glass underneath the kitchen table. "You want some coffee?" she asked.

He nodded silently, in strange contrast she thought to the water faucet that turned with a loud gurgling noise. While she let the water run to get hot she measured out the instant coffee in one of the plastic cups. Next door she could hear people moving around in the Williams' kitchen, but they too seemed much quieter than usual.

"You reckon everybody knows by now?" she asked, stirring the coffee and putting the saucer in front of him.

"Everybody will know by the time the city paper comes out," he said. "Somebody was here last night from the *Observer*. Guess it'll make front page."

She leaned against the cabinet for support watching him trace endless circles in the brown liquid with the spoon. "Sergeant Kearns says they'll have almost the whole force out there tomorrow," he said.

"Today," she whispered.

Her father looked at the clock and then turned his head.

"When's your mother coming back in here?" he asked, finally picking up the cup and drinking the coffee.

"Tommy's just off to sleep," she answered. "I guess she'll be in here when he's asleep for good."

She looked out the window of the back door at the row of tall hedges that had separated their neighborhood from the white people for as long as she remembered. While she stood there she heard her mother walk into the room. To her ears the steps seemed much slower than usual. She heard her mother stop in front of her father's chair.

"Jim," she said, sounding very timid, "what we going to do?" Yet as Ellie turned toward her she noticed her mother's face was strangely calm as she looked down on her husband.

Ellie continued standing by the door listening to them talk. Nobody asked the question to which they all wanted an answer.

"I keep thinking," her father said finally, "that the policemen will be with him all day. They couldn't hurt him inside the school building without getting some of their own kind."

"But he'll be in there all by himself," her mother said softly. "A hundred policemen can't be a little boy's only friends."

She watched her father wrap his calloused hands, still splotched with machine oil, around the salt shaker on the table.

"I keep trying," he said to her, "to tell myself that somebody's got to be the first one and then I just think how quiet he's been all week."

Ellie listened to the quiet voices that seemed to be a room

apart from her. In the back of her mind she could hear phrases of a hymn her grandmother used to sing, something about trouble, her being born for trouble.

"Jim, I cannot let my baby go." Her mother's words, although quiet, were carefully pronounced.

"Maybe," her father answered, "it's not in our hands. Reverend Davis and I were talking the day before yesterday how God tested the Israelites, maybe he's just trying us."

"God expects you to take care of your own," his wife interrupted. Ellie sensed a trace of bitterness in her mother's voice.

"Tommy's not going to understand why he can't go to school," her father replied. "He's going to wonder why, and how are we going to tell him we're afraid of them?" Her father's hand clutched the coffee cup. "He's going to be fighting them the rest of his life. He's got to start sometime."

"But he's not on their level. Tommy's too little to go around hating people. One of the others, they're bigger, they understand about things."

Ellie still leaning against the door saw that the sun covered part of the sky behind the hedges and the light slipping through the kitchen window seemed to reflect the shiny red of the table cloth.

"He's our child," she heard her mother say. "Whatever we do, we're going to be the cause." Her father had pushed the cup away from him and sat with his hands covering part of his face. Outside Ellie could hear a horn blowing.

"God knows we tried but I guess there's just no use." Her father's voice forced her attention back to the two people sitting in front of her. "Maybe when things come back to normal, we'll try again."

He covered his wife's chunky fingers with the palm of his hand and her mother seemed to be enveloped in silence. The three of them remained quiet, each involved in his own thoughts, but related, Ellie knew, to the same thing. She was the first to break the silence.

"Mama," she called after a long pause, "do you want me to start setting the table for breakfast?"

Her mother nodded.

Ellie turned the clock so she could see it from the sink while she washed the dishes that had been scattered over the floor.

"You going to wake up Tommy or you want me to?"

"No," her mother said, still holding her father's hand, "let him sleep. When you wash your face, you go up the street and call Hezekiah. Tell him to keep up with the children after school, I want to do something to this house before they come home."

She stopped talking and looked around the kitchen, finally turning to her husband. "He's probably kicked the spread off by now," she said. Ellie watched her father, who without saying anything walked toward the bedroom.

She watched her mother lift herself from the chair and automatically push in the stuffing underneath the cracked plastic cover. Her face looked set, as it always did when she was trying hard to keep her composure.

"He'll need something hot when he wakes up. Hand me the oatmeal," she commanded, reaching on top of the ice-box for matches to light the kitchen stove.

Arna Bontemps (October 13, 1902–June 4, 1973) was born in Alexandria, Louisiana, but grew up in Los Angeles, after his family left the South to escape racial oppression.

After graduating from Pacific Union College in 1923, he moved to New York and became one of the many writers associated with the Harlem Renaissance. In the 1920s and 1930s he worked as a teacher in New York City, Chicago, and Alabama. He won *Opportunity* magazine's Alexander Pushkin Poetry Prize in 1926 and again in 1927. His first novel, *God Sends Sunday* (1931), was later adapted as *St. Louis Woman*, the musical in which Pearl Bailey made her Broadway acting debut. *Black Thunder*, his most acclaimed novel, was published in 1936. From 1943 until 1965 he worked at Fisk University in Nashville, Tennessee, as university librarian and director of University Relations. In 1966 he resumed his teaching career, first at the Chicago Circle campus of the University of Illinois and in 1969 at Yale University where he also served as curator of the James Weldon Johnson Memorial Collection. He returned to Fisk University as writer-in-residence in 1971 and lived there until his death.

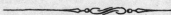

TALK TO THE MUSIC

by Arna Bontemps

You tells it to the music and
the music tells it to you.
                    —Sidney Bechet

My father used to say that when you heard one blues song, you've heard them all. He did not mean that all are the same, of course, or that one is enough to satisfy whatever it is in you that craves blues, but after you have listened to one blues, you can always recognize another. In the same way, when you've met one blues singer, you know the species. Ma Rainey, Mayme Smith, Bessie Smith—I could be talking about any one of them and you wouldn't be able to tell by the story which one I had in mind. But right now I'm thinking about the other Mayme— Mayme Dupree.

She never made records, and she never got to Broadway, and nobody ever called her Empress of the Blues, or Lady Day, or anything equivalent, but don't let that fool you. Mayme Dupree had what the others had and then some more. She could play the piano as well as sing and she made up her own songs. You've heard the Jelly-Roll Morton recording of the Mayme Dupree Blues. Well, that's what I'm talking about.

Chances are all this was before your time. What you know about women blues singers probably does not go back any further than Ethel Waters or Pearl Bailey or Billie Holiday, but ask Ethel or Pearl. They'll tell you about Mayme Dupree. Ask Kid Ory or Sidney Bechet. Mayme was singing blues before some of these were born.

There were still other things Mayme had that couldn't be matched by the three more celebrated women who brought the blues out of the South. She was a New Orleans woman with just enough Creole hauteur to make her interesting, and she was good looking. I'm still a bug about old New Orleans—though my own hometown was up the river a piece—and I can't remember a time when I had any objection to good looking women. Naturally I wanted to see and hear this Mayme Dupree people talked about.

But that wasn't easy. Mayme worked as an entertainer, but she worked in Storyville, and that was the legendary red-light district of the fabulous old city at the mouth of the Mississippi. I may have looked young, but age wasn't the obstacle. While there was a good bit of democracy in Storyville, believe me, there was not enough to open the doors of the place where Mayme sang to a black boy who was obviously not one of the employees.

As you know, Jelly-Roll Morton got around this by rushing the can; he made himself available for certain errands. He stood by to run around the corner with the beer can and get it refilled whenever this service was demanded. The wage was negligible, but the job gave the long-legged kid an excuse for being on the premises and provided excellent opportunities for him to hear the aching, heartsick songs of Mayme Dupree.

I, on the other hand, was never any good at masquerades of any kind. They still annoy me. The difference may have been that old Jelly was bent on learning Mayme's songs and nothing else, while I was curious about the singer herself and couldn't stop wondering what it was that troubled her and made her sing the way she did. In any case, I found out where she lived, and the time came when I went there to see her.

I put on my Sunday clothes, which was the only change I had at the time anyhow, fastened my two-toned shoes with a button hook, adjusted the stickpin in my tie, and gave an extra touch to my curly and rather flamboyantly parted hair. I was pleased with the raven sideburns, but my feathers fell when I looked at the mustache. Well, the devil with that, I sighed, but I remained confused as to the kind of impression I wanted to make. As an afterthought, when I had put on my hat and started for the door, I picked up my mandolin case and the leather-covered roll of sheet music beside it.

It was pointless to carry these things everywhere I went,

but I had formed the habit, and in almost any new situation I felt more comfortable with them than without. This was especially true in the late afternoon or early evening, and that was the time of day I had chosen to look up Mayme. I felt fine as I strolled on the wooden banquette that still served as a sidewalk in that part of town, but presently my feelings changed to dismay.

Neither the appearance nor the smell of the neighborhood was improving, and the quarters in which I asked for Mayme were over a pool hall. The steps were on the outside and the entrance was dirty; the hall beyond, dark. Here and there a shadow stirred. Something ponderous twisted and turned on a chair and finally spoke.

"You looking for somebody, ha'?"

It was the voice of an old woman, and the odd inflection with which she ended her question was pronounced as if she had started to say *hant* and cut it off in the middle.

"Mayme Dupree," I said.

"Mayme's apt to be sleep. She works at night."

"It's nearly dark now."

"Did you ever try to talk to Mayme when she's just waking up?"

"I don't know her yet, I just want to meet her," I explained.

"Well, you sure picked yourself a time." The old woman got out of the chair with more twisting and straining and started down the hall. "Mayme!" she blasted suddenly. "Mayme, somebody's asking for you here." She pounded the door in passing but continued on, finally disappearing down the hall.

Mayme came out soon afterwards, her lower lip hanging, her eyes almost closed, her hair in a tangle, a dingy garment thrown around her. "Do I know you?" she asked vaguely.

"I expect I've done wrong," I said, stuttering. "You don't know me; I'm from Rapides Parish. I just wanted to talk to you. I aimed to catch you when you were sitting around doing nothing."

"You never catch me sitting around doing nothing," Mayme muttered. "What's your name?"

"Norman Taylor."

Actually she didn't care what my name was. Before I could get the words out, she added, "If I was sitting around, I'd be drinking, I wouldn't be doing nothing."

"I mean I want to hear the blues," I ventured. "I want to hear the blues like you sing them."

Her mind seemed to wander but presently she blurted, "What in the name of God you doing with that thing?"

"Would you like to hear me play something on my mandolin?" I asked.

She shook her head. "Not this early in the evening. I got to get myself together now. I'm not too much on mandolin playing when I'm wide awake."

"I didn't mean to break in on you," I apologized again. "I'll move on now, but can't you tell me when I could hear the blues?"

She yawned, scratching her head with all ten of her fingers. "Come back," she nodded. "Come back again sometime."

I did—about an hour later. She had left her room, but I found her down the block sitting alone in the "family" section of a saloon. There was a bottle of gin on the table, beside it a tiny glass and nothing else. I waited at the door till she noticed me. She gave me a shrug which I took to mean 'suit yourself,' so I took the seat across the table, and she didn't seem to mind. In fact, she scarcely noticed me again after I sat down.

"Don't you ever talk to anybody?" I asked eventually.

She ignored the question. "I got a hack that picks me up here every evening. It takes me to—to where I go. I'm waiting for it now."

Suddenly Mayme emptied her glass and put the bottle in her handbag, and I looked up and saw the hack driver standing in the door. He was wearing a frayed Prince Albert and a battered top hat. His shoes were rough, his pants and shirt grimy.

"Well, good-bye," I called.

She turned and smiled rather pleasantly, but she kept on walking, and she didn't actually answer.

A saloon was not a place in which I could feel at ease in those days, but somehow I hesitated to leave. After a few moments I went to the bar in the adjoining section and asked for a glass of beer. I stood there a long time nibbling on the "free lunch" as I drank, and gradually became aware of the activity around me.

The telephone rang frequently. Each time it was answered by the bartender whose name, it seemed, was Benny, and each time the message had to do with someone's need for a musician or a singer or a group to entertain at a party, a dance, a boatride, or some other merry occasion. The men at the bar and those lolling about the premises would prick their ears as soon as Benny took the receiver off the hook, and as quickly as he indicated what kind of performer was sought, one who could fill the bill would step forward. Sometimes the request was for a specific individual or combination, and sometimes those requested were unavailable due to previous engagement. Some were in the pool hall around the corner and had left instructions as to how they might be fetched. A few were independent enough to ask a few questions about the hours, the distance, the pay, and other details before accepting a gig, as they called the engagements, but in the end no job went unfilled, and I was almost tempted to indicate to Benny my own availability.

But I had not come to New Orleans to seek employment as a musician, so I promptly dismissed the idea from my mind. Even though I had already let myself be drawn into several activities which I did not plan to write home about, the temptation to capitalize on my modest musical skills was not strong enough to lure me into another. I had left my parents with the understanding that I would enroll at New Orleans University, and I had every intention of doing so— eventually. My determination to hear the blues first was an irregularity which I considered amply justified. It was not based on mere whim or a casual desire. I had heard strains of the music, and I was haunted. With me the blues had become a strange necessity. I knew that before I could undertake anything else in New Orleans, I had to hear Mayme Dupree sing.

Before leaving that evening, I gained a general impression of the business end of the music game as the boys around New Orleans knew it. While Benny's saloon and Buddy's barber shop, which was mentioned several times during the half hour I stood at the bar, were not employment agencies, they did serve as clearing houses of a sort. There was no competition between the places, and neither expected cuts or payoffs of any kind from the musicians or the employers. Benny was satisfied to have the fellows hang around his place and do their drinking there, and apparently Buddy Bolden's shop was content to shave the musicians and cut their hair. Buddy, of course, was a powerful cornet player and bandman himself, and this made things a little different in his case.

Other women came in after Mayme Dupree left. Some were accompanied by escorts. Others were joined in the "family" section by men who spotted them as they arrived. I did not get the impression that any of these women had come into Benny's to pick up musical gigs. On the contrary, I concluded that most of them were there to be picked up themselves. Like the musicians, they appeared to have slept all day. Getting their eye-openers at Benny's, they looked fresh and sassy, and their perfume filled the saloon. When I turned around and discovered a particularly giddy-looking one trying to trap me with her eyes, I decided it was time for me to look at my watch and go through the motions of hurrying to an appointment.

What Mayme said about the hack picking her up at Benny's every evening was true. She never missed, and the hackman was always on time. I could have set my watch by him. But I did no more than speak and pass the time of day the next few times with her. Mayme did not encourage conversation. Absorbed in her own thoughts, she would come into Benny's saloon just as twilight was falling and go to the most isolated table in the family room. Benny would give her the usual pleasantry as he filled her tiny glass and left the flask of gin beside it, but Mayme's eyes were shadowed by her bird of Paradise hat, and I could see nothing on her face to indicate she even heard him. But I did not give up hope, and the time came when she invited me to come over and have some sit-down.

"You come here pretty regular," she chided.

"You told me to come back sometime," I reminded her.

Mayme smiled. "You're too young a boy to hurrah a woman old as me."

"I couldn't smart-aleck anybody if I wanted to, Mayme," I confessed. "Besides, I've got too much on my mind."

"You still hankering for the blues?"

"I'd give my eye teeth to hear them."

"You look like a boy that's had good raising. You keeps your shoes shined and your hair combed. You ain't got no cause to be hanging around saloons, much less trying to hear boogie house music. If you're a stranger in New Orleans, why don't you try to meet some nice quadroon girls? There's lots of parties going on all the time. Go rowing on

Lake Ponchartrain and play your mandolin. That's something you could write home and tell your people about."

"I aim to do all that sometime maybe," I admitted. "But I don't feel like it now. I had a girl at home, pretty as you please, but she couldn't wait. She said I was too slow. I don't want to think about courting or sweet music again for a long, long time. I'd like to hear something lowdown, Mayme."

"I don't sing the blues just to be singing them," she said. "Not any more, I don't. If you want to hear my blues, you got to go where I go, Norman, and I don't rightly think they'd let you in."

"Where's that?"

She put the cork in her bottle. "Storyville," she answered. "Do I have to say more?"

"The red-light district?"

"That's where I work. That's where this hack is waiting to take me."

The driver was standing in the doorway. She emptied her glass.

"You don't look like a fancy woman, Mayme, and you don't sound much like one."

"Along about nine or ten o'clock I sit down at the piano, and I sets my bottle of gin where I can reach it. I don't stop playing and singing till that bottle's empty. Then I get up and put on my hat. They pay me my money and I go home." She had started toward the door, but since she continued to talk, I followed her out to the hack. Seeing me standing there after she had climbed in, a sudden impulse seemed to strike her. "Get in if you want to," she said. "The hackman will bring you back this way. I don't keep him waiting around down there. He comes back for me in the morning."

Riding beside her in the rented carriage gave me a funny feeling. I had never considered myself a man of the world, but all at once I felt like one. "You ride in style," I told her.

"It takes a big cut out of what I make to pay for it, but it's the only way I can be sure of getting there." She fished in her handbag for cigarets, lit one in the darkness, and settled back for the slow drive. After a long pause she said, half-mischievously, I thought, "If you was out riding with a sure 'nough fancy gal, Norman, it wouldn't be like courting somebody you aimed to marry. You wouldn't study about age or color—things like that—so long as she smelled sweet and was soft to touch."

"If you're not careful, you'll be giving me ideas in a minute," I laughed.

She laughed too, but she added quickly, "Don't pay me no mind, boy. It ain't like me to carry on a lot of foolishness. I don't know what's come over me tonight."

"You're not as unfriendly as you try to make out," I encouraged.

Her answer was something between a sigh and a grunt. "Don't count on it," she added after a pause. "I'm a blue-gummed woman, and I know it. I'm poison, too."

"Aw, hush, Mayme."

"Don't hush me. I know what I'm saying. I bit a man once. It was just a love bite, but his arm swelled up like he'd been bit by a black widow spider or a copperhead snake."

"I don't pay any attention to the foolishness I hear people talk about blue-gummed women, women with crooked eyes, right black women. I'd go out with a girl that was black as a new buggy if I liked her, and I think blue gums are kind of interesting."

"Just go on thinking that," she scoffed, "and one of these days you'll find yourself all swoll up like a man with the dropsy."

The lights were coming on in Storyville as we reached the district, and there was a good bit of going and coming in the streets. Saloons were hitting it up, and in some the tinkle of glasses dissolved into a background of ragtime piano thumping. But the over-all mood, as I sensed it, was grim, and furtive shadows moved along the street. Can desire be anything but sad? I wondered as the carriage pulled up beside an ornate hitching post. I jumped out and waited for Mayme to put her foot on a large square-cut steppingstone.

"Is this as far as I can go?" I asked, looking up at the elegant doorway at the top of the steps.

"Here is where you turn back," she said.

"If there's any way you can fix it for me to hear you sing sometime," I reminded her, "I'll sure appreciate it, Mayme."

She didn't promise, but her voice still sounded indulgent as she let the hackman go, instructing him to drop me at a convenient point in the vicinity of Benny's.

I had enough mother wit to realize that Mayme was not the kind of woman you could persuade to do anything before she was good and ready. Having made it clear to her what I wanted, I settled back to another long wait, taking pains to let her see me occasionally and making sure she got a good chance to say anything that happened to be on her mind. Meanwhile, Benny's saloon hummed nightly. The telephone rang. Musicians were in and out, whistling for hacks, catching quick drinks before hurrying off to their gigs. Fancy women as bright as flamingos fluttered in and settled down languidly at the family tables. And the giddy-looking one who had taken a shine to me kept making eyes.

Mayme's hack driver had appeared in the saloon and she had followed him out one evening when the place was more crowded than usual, but a few moments later he returned and tapped me on the shoulder.

"She wants to speak to you," he said.

I didn't wait to finish my sweeten' water (gin and rock candy), and when I reached the carriage, Mayme was leaning out with something to tell me. "They need a boy tonight—out at the place. Did you ever work in a white coat?"

"Does it matter?" I asked, climbing in beside her. "I'll wear one tonight and like it."

"Well, just mind your p's and q's. Keep a duster or a broom or a towel in your hand all the time and don't sit down. Somebody might ask you to do something every now and then, but if you don't pay them no mind, they won't pay you none. Anybody looks at you right hard, just kind of ease around and go to dusting the woodwork or picking up empty glasses."

That was as much as I needed, and when Mayme presented me to the Madame as a boy who could take the place of some vague Leroy whom they did not expect to show up, we both nodded without speaking. She was a large woman, heavily jewelled, with glossy black hair piled on her head in great rolls. Her accent was French, but I couldn't be sure whether she was a Louisiana quadroon or a woman from southern Europe. It didn't matter. She led me out to the back and pointed to Leroy's closet. The equipment was in line with Mayme's description of the job: freshly starched white coat, a hanger for the one I was wearing, towels, lamp rags, dust cloths, mops, brushes, and the rest.

I put on the white coat and crept obsequiously into the big living room. When Mayme began playing the piano, I retreated into a corner where there were several pieces of erotic sculpture which I suddenly decided needed dusting. I think I succeeded in fading into the furniture and the fixtures, because neither the men who came through the front door nor the girls who glided down the stairs gave me a second glance. Presently Mayme took their minds completely away.

> *Good morning, blues,*
> *Heard you when you opened my door.*
> *I said, good morning, blues.*
> *I heard you when you opened my door.*

The sadness of the blues stabbed me with her first line, and immediately I wanted to ask Mayme Dupree who had hurt her and how and what made her take it so hard. Remembering how long she had kept me waiting to hear this first song and the price I'd had to pay—putting off my enrollment in college, hanging around Benny's, and now coming to this place with a dust cloth in my hand—I doubted that I could ever expect to learn what it was that made her sing as she did.

Men were calling for drinks and gals before she finished "Good-morning, Blues." The heavy beat of Mayme's song started things moving. When it was over, she reached for her bottle with one hand while the other hand kept up the rhythm. Then for a long spell the piano carried it alone, but more than once I was sure I saw Mayme press her lips together tightly as she played, like somebody deeply troubled in mind. Eventually she blurted another song as if she could hold it back no longer.

> *If I could holler like the mountain jack,*
> *If I could holler like the mountain jack,*
> *I'd go up on the mountain and call my lover back.*

This was heady stuff, even for the hard-bitten habitués of Storyville, and the way Mayme sang it promptly went to the heads of some. One of the men responded with a sort of hog-calling yell that was not intended as a joke and did not provoke laughter. A girl closed her eyes and fluttered her hands high in the air. A few couples stood together as if to dance but did not move. I began wondering when Mayme would sing the song for which she was becoming known and which I had heard about all the way up in Rapides Parish.

Finally she got around to it—the blues that she had made up herself and that had started a sort of craze among the few people who had been fortunate enough to hear her sing it.

> *Two-nineteen done took my baby away*
> *Two-nineteen done took my baby away*
> *Two-seventeen bring him back someday.*

Everyone seemed to expect her to repeat it several times, adding new verses as she sang, and she kept on until she could somehow get the folks to take their eyes off her and think about themselves again. But all I could think as I listened to Mayme Dupree sing her blues that night was that the blues are sad, terribly sad, and desire is sad too. The bottle of gin on the piano, the erotic sculpture, the motionless dancers, the girls with the flutters, the hog-calling man—all seemed to go very well with Mayme's blues. But I wondered if she thought so.

When I asked her, after I had been back several times, she did not show much interest. The blues she sang were just blues to her. There was nothing special about them. They were neither good nor bad. She could understand how some people might like them but not how anyone would want to talk about them. But I thought I would be ungrateful if I didn't make some effort to tell her how I felt about her songs.

I was convinced that there was power of some kind in the blues, their rhythms, and their themes. Fallen angels could never have wailed like this, no matter how they grieved over paradise. Adam and Eve might have perhaps, crying over their lost innocence, but somehow song was not given to them.

She pondered this conceit as the hack jogged homeward in the early dawn, and I thought it was making a good impression until she suddenly said, "You're crazy."

Doris Betts (June 4, 1932) was born Doris Waugh in Statesville, North Carolina, where she received her education before attending Women's College of the University of North Carolina at Greensboro (1950–1953), now UNC-Greensboro, and the University of North Carolina at Chapel Hill (1954). Betts says she seems to have always known she would be a writer. Before she learned to write, she began composing poems which her mother would write down for her. Born into a family of devout churchgoers, the Associate Reformed Presbyterian Church was an important influence in her life.

Her career began with the Statesville *Daily Record*. Over the next decade and a half Betts worked for several other North Carolina newspapers—Chapel Hill *Weekly*, Sanford *Daily Herald*, and Sanford *News Leader*. In 1958 she received a Guggenheim Fellowship in creative writing. Betts joined the English faculty of the University of North Carolina at Chapel Hill as a part-time teacher in 1966. She served as director of freshman composition (1972–1978) and as assistant dean of the honors program (1978–1981). Since 1980 she has been Alumni Distinguished Professor of English. In 1982 Betts became the first woman to chair the UNC English faculty. North Carolina honored her in 1975 with its Medal for Literature.

Betts's works include: *The Gentle Insurrection and Other Stories* (1954), *Tall Houses in Winter* (1957), *The Scarlet Thread* (1964) and *Beasts of the Southern Wild and Other Stories* (1973), "The Ugliest Pilgrim," reprinted from *Beasts*, has been adapted for film as part of the American Short Story series. The film entitled "Violet" won an Academy Award in 1982. Betts other books include *The Astronomer and Other Stories* (1966), *The River to Pickle Beach* (1972), and *Heading West* (1981).

Betts and her husband live on an 80-acre farm called Araby in Pittsboro, North Carolina, some twenty miles from Chapel Hill.

THE UGLIEST PILGRIM

by Doris Betts

I sit in the bus station, nipping chocolate peel off a Mounds candy bar with my teeth, then pasting the coconut filling to the roof of my mouth. The lump will dissolve there slowly and seep into me the way dew seeps into flowers.

I like to separate flavors that way. Always I lick the salt off cracker tops before taking my first bite.

Somebody sees me with my suitcase, paper sack, and a ticket in my lap. "You going someplace, Violet?"

Stupid. People in Spruce Pine are dumb and, since I look dumb, say dumb things to me. I turn up my face as if to count those dead flies piled under the light bulb. He walks away—a fat man, could be anybody. I stick out my tongue at his back; the candy oozes down. If I could stop swallowing, it would drip into my lung and I could breathe vanilla.

Whoever it was, he won't glance back. People in Spruce Pine don't like to look at me, full face.

A Greyhound bus pulls in, blows air; the driver stands by the door. He's black-headed, maybe part Cherokee, with heavy shoulders but a weak chest. He thinks well of himself—I can tell that. I open my notebook and copy his name off the metal plate so I can call him by it when he drives me home again. And next week, won't Mr. Wallace Weatherman be surprised to see how well I'm looking!

I choose the front seat behind Mr. Weatherman, settle my bag with the hat in it, then open the lined composition book again. Maybe it's half full of writing. Even the empty pages toward the back have one repeated entry, high, printed off Mama's torn catechism: GLORIFY GOD AND ENJOY HIM FOREVER.

I finish Mr. Weatherman off in my book while he's running his motor and getting us onto the highway. His nose is too broad, his dark eyes too skimpy—nothing in his face I want—but the hair is nice. I write that down, "Black hair?" I'd want it to curl, though, and be soft as a baby's.

Two others are on the bus, a nigger soldier and an old woman whose jaw sticks out like a shelf. There grow, on the backs of her hands, more veins than skin. One fat blue vessel, curling from wrist to knuckle, would be good; so on one page I draw a sample hand and let blood wind across it like a river. I write at the bottom: "Praise God, it is started. May 29, 1969," and turn to a new sheet. The paper's lumpy and I flip back to the thick envelope stuck there with adhesive tape. I can't lose that.

We're driving now at the best speed Mr. Weatherman can make on these winding roads. On my side there is nothing out the bus window but granite rock, jagged and wet in patches. The old lady and the nigger can see red rhododendron on the slope of Roan Mountain. I'd like to own a tight dress that flower color, and breasts to go under it. I write in my notebook, very small, the word "breasts," and turn quickly to another page. AND ENJOY HIM FOREVER.

The soldier bends as if to tie his shoes, but instead zips open a canvas bag and sticks both hands inside. When finally he sits back, one hand is clenched around something hard. He catches me watching. He yawns and scratches his ribs, but the right fist sets very lightly on his knee, and when I turn he drinks something out of its cup and throws his head quickly back like a bird or a chicken. You'd think I could smell it, big as my nose is.

Across the aisle the old lady says, "You going far?" She shows me a set of tan, artificial teeth.

"Oklahoma."

"I never been there. I hear the trees give out." She pauses so I can ask politely where she's headed. "I'm going to Nashville," she finally says. "The country-music capital of the world. My son lives there and works in the cellophane plant."

I draw in my notebook a box and two arrows. I crisscross the box.

"He's got three children not old enough to be in school yet."

I sit very still, adding new boxes, drawing baseballs in some, looking busy for fear she might bring out their pictures from her big straw pocketbook. The funny thing is she's looking past my head, though there's nothing out that window but rock wall sliding by. I mumble, "It's hot in here."

Angrily she says, "I had eight children myself."

My pencil flies to get the boxes stacked, eight-deep, in a pyramid. "Hope you have a nice visit."

"It's not a visit. I maybe will move." She is hypnotized by the stone and the furry moss in its cracks. Her eyes used to be green. Maybe, when young, she was red-haired and Irish. If she'll stop talking, I want to think about trying green eyes with that Cherokee hair. Her lids droop; she looks drowsy. "I am right tired of children," she says and lays her head back on the white rag they button on these seats.

Now that her eyes are covered, I can study that face—china white, and worn thin as tissue so light comes between her bones and shines through her whole head. I picture the light going around and around her skull, like water spinning in a jar. If I could wait to be eighty, even my face might grind down and look softer. But I'm ready, in case the Preacher mentions that. Did Elisha make Naaman bear into old age his leprosy? Didn't Jesus heal the withered hand, even on Sunday, without waiting for the work week to start? And put back the ear of Malchus with a touch? As soon as Job had learned enough, did his boils fall away?

Lord, I have learned enough.

The old lady sleeps while we roll downhill and up again; then we turn so my side of the bus looks over the valley and its thickety woods where, as a girl, I pulled armloads of galax, fern, laurel, and hemlock to have some spending money. I spent it for magazines full of women with permanent waves. Behind us, the nigger shuffles a deck of cards and deals to himself by fives. Draw poker—I could beat him. My papa showed me, long winter days and nights snowed in on the mountain. He said poker would teach me arithmetic. It taught me there are four ways to make a royal flush and, with two players, it's an even chance one of them holds a pair on the deal. And when you try to draw from a pair to four of a kind, discard the kicker; it helps your odds.

The soldier deals smoothly, using his left hand only with his thumb on top. Papa was good at that. He looks up and sees my whole face with its scar, but he keeps his eyes level as if he has seen worse things; and his left hand drops cards evenly and in rhythm. Like a turtle, laying eggs.

I close my eyes and the riffle of his deck rests me to the next main stop where I write in my notebook: Praise God for Johnson City, Tennessee, and all the state to come. I am on my way."

At Kingsport, Mr. Weatherman calls rest stop and I go straight through the terminal to the ladies' toilet and look hard at my face in the mirror. I must remember to start the Preacher on the scar first of all—the only thing about me that's even on both sides.

Lord! I am so ugly!

Maybe the Preacher will claim he can't heal ugliness. And I'm going to spread my palms by my ears and show him— this is a crippled face! An infirmity! Would he do for a kidney or liver what he withholds from a face? The Preacher once stuttered, I read someplace, and God bothered with that. Why not me? When the Preacher labors to heal the sick in his Tulsa auditorium, he asks us at home to lay our fingers on the television screen and pray for God's healing. He puts forth his own ten fingers and we match them, pad to pad, on that glass. I have tried that, Lord, and the Power was too filtered and thinned down for me.

I touch my hand now to this cold mirror glass, and cover all but my pimpled chin, or wide nose, or a single red-brown eye. And nothing's too bad by itself. But when they're put together?

I've seen the Preacher wrap his hot, blessed hands on a club foot and cry out "HEAL!" in his funny way that sounds like the word "Hell" broken into two pieces. Will he not cry out, too, when he sees this poor, clubbed face? I will be to him as Goliath was to David, a need so giant it will drive God to action.

I comb out my pine-needle hair. I think I would like blond curls and Irish eyes, and I want my mouth so large it will never be done with kissing.

The old lady comes in to the toilet and catches me pinching my bent face. She jerks back once, looks sad, then pets me with her twiggy hand. "Listen, honey," she says, "I had looks once. It don't amount to much."

I push right past. Good people have nearly turned me

against you, Lord. They open their mouths for the milk of human kindness and boiling oil spews out.

So I'm half running through the terminal and into the café, and I take the first stool and call down the counter, "Tuna-fish sandwich," quick. Living in the mountains, I eat fish every chance I get and wonder what the sea is like. Then I see I've sat down by the nigger soldier. I do not want to meet his gaze, since he's a wonder to me, too. We don't have many black men in the mountains. Mostly they live east in Carolina, on the flatland, and pick cotton and tobacco instead of apples. They seem to me like foreigners. He's absently shuffling cards the way some men twiddle thumbs. On the stool beyond him is a paratrooper, white, and they're talking about what a bitch the army is. Being sent to the same camp has made them friends already.

I roll a dill-pickle slice through my mouth—a wheel, a bitter wheel. Then I start on the sandwich and it's chicken by mistake when I've got chickens all over my back yard.

"Don't bother with the beer," says the black one. "I've got better on the bus." They come to some agreement and deal out cards on the counter.

It's just too much for me. I lean over behind the nigger's back and say to the paratrooper, "I wouldn't play with him." Neither one moves. "He's a mechanic." They look at each other, not at me. "It's a way to cheat on the deal."

The paratrooper sways backward on his stool and stares around out of eyes so blue that I want them, right away, and maybe his pale blond hair. I swallow a crusty half-chewed bite. "One-handed grip; the mechanic's grip. It's the middle finger. He can second-deal and bottom-deal. He can buckle the top card with his thumb and peep."

"I be damn," says the paratrooper.

The nigger spins around and bares his teeth at me, but it's half a grin. "Lady, you want to play?"

I slide my dishes back. "I get mad if I'm cheated."

"And mean when you're mad." He laughs a laugh so deep it makes me retaste that bittersweet chocolate off the candy bar. He offers the deck to cut, so I pull out the center and restack it three ways. A little air blows through his upper teeth. "I'm Grady Fliggins and they call me Flick."

The paratrooper reaches a hand over the counter to shake mine. "Monty Harrill. From near to Raleigh."

"And I'm Violet Karl. Spruce Pine. I'd rather play five-card stud."

By the time the bus rolls on, we've moved to its wider back seat playing serious cards with a fifty-cent ante. My money's sparse, but I'm good and the deck is clean. The old lady settles into my front seat, stiffer than plaster. Sometimes she throws back a hurt look.

Monty, the paratrooper, plays soft. But Flick's so good he doesn't even need to cheat, though I watch him close. He drops out quick when his cards are bad; he makes me bid high to see what he's got; and the few times he bluffs, I'm fooled. He's no talker. Monty, on the other hand, says often, "Whose play is it?" till I know that's his clue phrase for a pair. He lifts his cards close to his nose and gets quiet when planning to bluff. And he'd rather use wild cards but we won't. Ah, but he's pretty, though!

After we've swapped a little money, mostly the paratrooper's, Flick pours us a drink in some cups he stole in Kingsport and asks, "Where'd you learn to play?"

I tell him about growing up on a mountain, high, with Mama dead, and shuffling cards by a kerosene lamp with my papa. When I passed fifteen, we'd drink together, too. Applejack or a beer he made from potato peel.

"And where you headed now?" Monty's windburned in a funny pattern, with pale goggle circles that start high on his cheeks. Maybe it's something paratroopers wear.

"It's a pilgrimage." They lean back with their drinks. "I'm going to see this preacher in Tulsa, the one that heals, and I'm coming home pretty. Isn't that healing?" Their still faces make me nervous. "I'll even trade if he says . . . I'll take somebody else's weak eyes or deaf ears. I could stand limping a little."

The nigger shakes his black head, snickering.

"I tried to get to Charlotte when he was down there with his eight-pole canvas cathedral tent that seats nearly fifteen thousand people, but I didn't have money then. Now what's so funny?" I think for a minute I am going to have to take out my notebook, and unglue the envelope and read them all the Scripture I have looked up on why I should be healed. Monty looks sad for me, though, and that's worse. "Let the Lord twist loose my foot or give me a cough, so long as I'm healed of my looks while I'm still young enough—" I stop and tip up my plastic cup. Young enough for you, blue-eyed boy, and your brothers.

"Listen," says Flick in a high voice. "Let me go with you and be there for that swapping." He winks one speckled eye.

"I'll not take black skin, no offense." He's offended, though, and lurches across the moving bus and falls into a far seat. "Well, you as much as said you'd swap it off!" I call. "What's wrong if I don't want it any more than you?"

Monty slides closer. "You're not much to look at," he grants, sweeping me up and down till I nearly glow blue from his eyes. Shaking his head, "And what now? Thirty?"

"Twenty-eight. His drink and his cards, and I hurt Flick's feelings. I didn't mean that." I'm scared, too. Maybe, unlike Job, I haven't learned enough. Who ought to be expert in hurt feelings? Me, that's who.

"And you live by yourself?"

I start to say, "No, there's men falling all over each other going in and out my door." He sees my face, don't he? It makes me call, "Flick? I'm sorry." Not one movement. "Yes. By myself." Five years now, since Papa had heart failure and fell off the high back porch and rolled downhill in the gravel till the hobblebushes stopped him. I found him past sunset, cut from the rocks but not much blood showing. And what there was, dark, and already jellied.

Monty looks at me carefully before making up his mind to say, "That preacher's a fake. You ever see a doctor agree to what he's done?"

"Might be." I'm smiling. I tongue out the last liquor in my cup. I've thought of all that, but it may be what I believe is stronger than him faking. That he'll be electrified by my trust, the way a magnet can get charged against its will. He might be a lunatic or a dope fiend, and it still not matter.

Monty says, "Flick, you plan to give us another drink?"

"No." He acts like he's going to sleep.

"I just wouldn't count on that preacher too much." Monty cleans his nails with a matchbook corner and sometimes gives me an uneasy look. "Things are mean and ugly in this world—I mean *act* ugly, do ugly, be ugly."

He's wrong. When I leave my house, I can walk for miles and everything's beautiful. Even the rattlesnakes have grace. I don't mind his worried looks, since I'm writing in my notebook how we met and my winnings—a good sign, to earn money on a trip. I like the way the army barbers trim his hair. I wish I could touch it.

"Took one furlough in your mountains. Pretty country. Maybe hard to live in? Makes you feel little." He looks toward Flick and says softer, "Makes you feel like the night sky does. So many stars."

"Some of them big as daisies." It's easy to live in, though. Some mornings a deer and I scare up each other in the brush, and his heart stops, and mine stops. Everything stops till he plunges away. The next pulsebeat nearly knocks you down. "Monty, doesn't your hair get lighter in the summers? That might be a good color to ask for in Tulsa. Then I could turn colors like the leaves. Spell your last name for me."

He does, and says I sure am funny. Then he spells Grady Fliggins and I write that, too. He's curious about my book, so I flip through and offer to read him parts. Even with his eyes shut, Flick is listening. I read them about my papa's face, a chunky block face, not much different from the Preacher's square one. After Papa died, I wrote that to slow down how fast I was forgetting him. I tell Monty parts of my lists: that you can get yellow dye out of gopherwood and Noah built his ark from that, and maybe it stained the water. That a cow eating snakeroot might give poison milk. I pass him a pressed maypop flower I'm carrying to Tulsa, because the crown of thorns and the crucifixion nails grow in its center, and each piece of the bloom stands for one of the apostles.

"It's a mollypop vine," says Flick out of one corner of his mouth. "And it makes a green ball that pops when you step on it." He stretches. "Deal you some blackjack?"

For no reason, Monty says, "We oughtn't to let her go."

We play blackjack till supper stop and I write in my book, "Praise God for Knoxville and two new friends." I've not had many friends. At school in the valley, I sat in the back rows, reading, a hand spread on my face. I was smart, too; but if you let that show, you had to stand for the class and present different things.

When the driver cuts out the lights, the soldiers give me a whole seat, and a duffelbag for a pillow. I hear them whispering, first about women, then about me; but after a while I don't hear that anymore.

By the time we hit Nashville, the old lady makes the bus

wait while she begs me to stop with her. "Harvey won't mind. He's a good boy." She will not even look at Monty and Flick. "You can wash and change clothes and catch a new bus tomorrow."

"I'm in a hurry. Thank you." I have picked a lot of galax to pay for this trip.

"A girl alone. A girl that maybe feels she's got to prove something?" The skin on her neck shivers. "Some people might take advantage."

Maybe when I ride home under my new face, that will be some risk. I shake my head, and as she gets off she whispers something to Mr. Weatherman about looking after me. It's wasted, though, because a new driver takes his place and he looks nearly as bad as I do—oily-faced, and toad-shaped, with eyeballs a dingy color and streaked with blood. He's the flatlands driver, I guess, because he leans back and drops one warty hand on the wheel and we go so fast and steady you can hardly tell it.

Since Flick is the tops in cards and we're tired of that, it's Monty's turn to brag on his motorcycle. He talks all across Tennessee till I think I could ride one by hearsay alone, that my wrist knows by itself how far to roll the throttle in. It's a Norton and he rides it in Scrambles and Enduro events, in his leathers, with spare parts and tools glued all over him with black electrician's tape.

"So this bastard tells me, 'Zip up your jacket because when I run over you I want some traction.' "

Flick is playing solitaire. "You couldn't get me on one of them killing things."

"One day I'm coming through Spruce Pine, flat out, throw Violet up behind me! We're going to lean all the way through them mountains. Sliding the right foot and then sliding the left." Monty lays his head back on the seat beside me, rolls it, watches. "How you like that? Take you through creeks and ditches like you was on a skateboard. You can just holler and hang on."

Lots of women have, I bet.

"The Norton's got the best front forks of anybody. It'll nearly roll up a tree trunk and ride down the other side." He demonstrates on the seat back. I keep writing. These are new things, two-stroke and four-stroke, picking your line on a curve, Milwaukee iron. It will all come back to me in the winters, when I reread these pages.

Flick says he rode on a Harley once. "Turned over and got drug. No more."

They argue about what he should have done instead of turning over. Finally Monty drifts off to sleep, his head leaning at me slowly, so I look down on his crisp, light hair. I pat it as easy as a cat would, and it tickles my palm. I'd almost ask them in Tulsa to make me a man if I could have hair like his, and a beard, and feel so different in so many places.

He slides closer in his sleep. One eyebrow wrinkles against my shoulder. Looking our way, Flick smokes a cigarette, then reads some magazine he keeps rolled in his belt. Monty makes a deep noise against my arm as if, while he slept, his throat had cleared itself. I shift and his whole head is on my shoulder now. Its weight makes me breathe shallow.

I rest my eyes. If I should turn, his hair would barely touch my cheek, the scarred one, like a shoebrush. I do turn and it does. For miles he sleeps that way and I almost sleep. Once, when we take a long curve, he rolls against me, and one of his hands drifts up and then drops in my lap. Just there, where the creases are.

I would not want God's Power to turn me, after all, into a man. His breath is so warm. Everywhere, my skin is singing. Praise God for that.

When I get my first look at the Mississippi River, the pencil goes straight into my pocketbook. How much praise would that take?

"Is the sea like this?"

"Not except they're both water," Flick says. He's not mad anymore. "Tell you what, Vi-oh-LETTE. When Monty picks you up on his cycle" ("sickle," he calls it), "you ride down to the beaches—Cherry Grove, O.D., around there. Where they work the big nets in the fall and drag them up on the sand with trucks at each end, and men to their necks in the surf."

"You do that?"

"I know people that do. And afterward they strip and dress by this big fire on the beach."

And they make chowder while this cold wind is blowing! I know that much, without asking. In a big black pot that sits on that whipping fire. I think they might let me sit with them and stir the pot. It's funny how much, right now, I feel like praising all the good things I've never seen, in places I haven't been.

Everybody has to get off the bus and change in Memphis, and most of them wait a long time. I've taken the long way, coming here; but some of Mama's cousins live in Memphis and might rest me overnight. Monty says they plan to stay the night, too, and break the long trip.

"They know you're coming Violet?" It's Flick says my name that way, in pieces, carefully: Vi-oh-LETTE. Monty is lazier: Viii-lut. They make me feel like more than one.

"I've never even met these cousins. But soon as I call up and tell them who I am and that I'm here . . ."

"We'll stay some hotel tonight and then ride on. Why don't you come with us?" Monty is carrying my scuffed bag. Flick swings the paper sack. "You know us better than them."

"Kin people," grunts Flick, "can be a bad surprise."

Monty is nodding his head. "Only cousin I had got drunk and drove this tractor over his baby brother. Did it on purpose, too." I see by his face that Monty made this up, for my sake.

"Your cousins might not even live here anymore. I bet it's been years since you heard from a one."

"We're picking a cheap hotel, in case that's a worry."

I never thought they might have moved. "How cheap?"

When Flick says "Under five," I nod; and my things go right up on their shoulders as I follow them into a Memphis cab. The driver takes for granted I'm Monty's afflicted sister and names a hotel right off. He treats me with pity and good manners.

And the hotel he chooses is cheap, all right, where ratty salesmen with bad territories spend half the night drinking in their rooms. Plastic palm bushes and a worn rug the color of wet cigars. I get Room 210 and they're down the hall in the teens. They stand in my doorway and watch me drop both shoes and walk the bed in bare feet. When Monty opens my window, we can hear some kitchen underneath—a fan, clattering noise, a man's crackly voice singing about the California earthquake.

It scares me, suddenly, to know I can't remember how home sounds. Not one bird call, nor the water over rocks. There's so much you can't save by writing down.

"Smell that grease," says Flick, and shakes his head till

his lips flutter. "I'm finding an ice machine. You, Vi-oh-LETTE, come on down in a while."

Monty's got a grin I'll remember if I never write a word. He waves. "Flick and me going to get drunker than my old cousin and put wild things in your book. Going to draw dirty pictures. You come on down and get drunk enough to laugh."

But after a shower, damp in my clean slip, even this bed like a roll of fence wire feels good, and I fall asleep wondering if that rushing noise is a river wind, and how long I can keep it in my mind.

Monty and Flick edge into my dream. Just their voices first, from way downhill. Somewhere in a Shonny Haw thicket. "Just different," Monty is saying. "That's all. Different. Don't make some big thing out of it." He doesn't sound happy. "Nobody else," he says.

Is that Flick singing? No, because the song goes on while his voice says, "Just so . . ." and then some words I don't catch. "It don't hurt"? Or maybe, "You don't hurt"? I hear them climbing my tangled hill, breaking sticks and knocking the little stones loose. I'm trying to call to them which way the path is, but I can't make noise because the Preacher took my voice and put it in a black bag and carried it to a sick little boy in Iowa.

They find the path, anyway. And now they can see my house and me standing little by the steps. I know how it looks from where they are: the wood rained on till the siding's almost silver; and behind the house a wet-weather waterfall that's cut a stream bed downhill and grown pin cherry and bee balm on both sides. The high rock walls by the waterfall are mossy and slick, but I've scraped one place and hammered a mean-looking gray head that leans out of the hillside and stares down the path at whoever comes. I've been here so long by myself that I talk to it sometimes. Right now I'd say, "Look yonder. We've got company at last!" if my voice wasn't gone.

"You can't go by looks," Flick is saying as they climb. He ought to know. Ahead of them, warblers separate and fly out on two sides. Everything moves out of their path if I could just see it—tree frogs and mosquitoes. Maybe the worms drop deeper just before a footstep falls.

"Without the clothes, it's not a hell of a lot improved," says Monty, and I know suddenly they are inside the house with me, inside my very room, and my room today's in Memphis. "There's one thing, though," Monty says, standing over my bed. "Good looks in a woman is almost like a wall. She can use it to shut you outside. You never know what she's like, that's all." He's wearing a T-shirt and his dog tags jingle. "Most of the time I don't even miss knowing that."

And Flick says, disgusted, "I knew that much in grammar school. You sure are slow. It's not the face you screw." If I opened my eyes, I could see him now, behind Monty. He says, "After a while, you don't even notice faces. I always thought, in a crowd, my mother might not pick Daddy out."

"*My* mother could," says Monty. "He was always the one *started* the fight."

I stretch and open my eyes. It's a plain slip, cotton, that I sewed myself and makes me look too white and skinny as a sapling.

"She's waking up."

When I point, Monty hands me the blouse off the doorknob. Flick says they've carried me a soda pop, plus something to spruce it up. They sit stiffly on two hard chairs till I've buttoned on my skirt. I sip the drink, cold but peppery, and prop on the bed pillows. "I dreamed you both came where my house is, on the mountain, and it had rained so the waterfall was working. I felt real proud of that."

After two drinks we go down to the noisy restaurant with that smelly grease. And after that, to a picture show. Monty grins widely when the star comes on the screen. The spit on his teeth shines, even in the dark. Seeing what kind of woman he really likes, black-haired as a gypsy and with a juicy mouth, I change all my plans. My eyes, too, must turn up on the ends and when I bend down my breasts must fall forward and push at each other. When the star does that in the picture, the cowboy rubs his mustache low in the front of her neck.

In the darkness, Monty takes my hand and holds it in his swelling lap. To me it seems funny that my hand, brown and crusty from hoeing and chopping, is harder than his. I guess you don't get calluses rolling a motorcycle throttle. He rubs his thumb up and down my middle finger. Oh, I would like to ride fast behind him, spraddle-legged, with my arms wrapped on his belt, and I would lay my face between his sharp shoulder blades.

That night, when I've slept awhile, I hear something brushing the rug in the hall. I slip to my door. It's very dark. I press myself, face first, to the wood. There's breathing on the other side. I feel I get fatter, standing there, that even my own small breasts might now be made to touch. I round both shoulders to see. The movement jars the door and it trembles slightly in its frame.

From the far side, by the hinges, somebody whispers, "Vi-oh-LETTE?"

Now I stand very still. The wood feels cooler on my skin, or else I have grown very warm. Oh, I could love anybody! There is so much of me now, they could line up strangers in the hall and let me hold each one better than he had ever been held before!

Slowly I turn the knob, but Flick's breathing is gone. The corridor's empty. I leave the latch off.

Late in the night, when the noise from the kitchen is over, he comes into my room. I wake when he bumps on a chair, swears, then scrabbles at the footboard.

"Viii-lut?"

I slide up in bed. I'm not ready, not now, but he's here. I spread both arms wide. In the dark he can't tell.

He feels his way onto the bed and he touches my knee and it changes. Stops being just my old knee, under his fingers. I feel the joint heat up and bubble. I push the sheet down.

He comes onto me, whispering something. I reach up to claim him.

One time he stops. He's surprised, I guess, finding he isn't the first. How can I tell him how bad that was? How long ago? The night when the twelfth grade was over and one of them climbed with me all the way home? And he asked. And I thought, *I'm entitled*. Won him a five-dollar bet. Didn't do nothing for me.

But this time I sing out and Monty says, "Shh," in my ear. And he starts over, slow, and makes me whimper one other time. Then he turns sideways to sleep and I try my face there, laid in the nest on his damp back. I reach out my tongue. He is salty and good.

Now there are two things too big for my notebook but praise God! And for the Mississippi, too!

*   *   *

There is no good reason for me to ride with them all the way to Fort Smith, but since Tulsa is not expecting me, we change my ticket. Monty pays the extra. We ride through the fertile plains. The last of May becomes June and the Arkansas sun is blazing. I am stunned by this heat. At home, night means blankets and even on hot afternoons it may rain and start the waterfall. I lie against my seat for miles without a word.

"What's wrong?" Monty keeps asking; but, under the heat, I am happy. Sleepy with happiness, a lizard on a rock. At every stop Monty's off the bus, bringing me more than I can eat or drink, buying me magazines and gum. I tell him and Flick to play two-handed cards, but mostly Flick lectures him in a low voice about something.

I try to stop thinking of Memphis and think back to Tulsa. I went to the Spruce Pine library to look up Tulsa in their encyclopedia. I thought sure it would tell about the Preacher, and on what street he'd built his Hope and Glory Building for his soul crusades. Tulsa was listed in the *Americana*, Volume 27, Trance to Venial Sin. I got so tickled with that I forgot to write down the rest.

Now, in the hot sun, clogged up with trances and venial sins, I dream under the drone of their voices. For some reason I remember that old lady back in Nashville, moved in with Harvey and his wife and their three children. I hope she's happy. I picture her on Harvey's back porch, baked in the sun like me, in a rocker. Snapping beans.

I've left my pencil in the hotel and must borrow one from Flick to write in my book. I put in, slowly, "This is the day which the Lord hath made." But, before Monty, what kind of days was He sending me? I cross out the line. I have this wish to praise, instead of Him, the littlest things. Honeybees, and the wet slugs under their rocks. A gnat in some farmer's eye.

I give up and hand Flick his pencil. He slides toward the aisle and whispers, "You wish you'd stayed in your mountains?"

I shake my head and a piece of my no-color hair falls into the sunlight. Maybe it even shines.

He spits on the pencil point and prints something inside a gum wrapper. "Here's my address. You keep it. Never can tell."

So I tear the paper in half and give him back mine. He

reads it a long time before tucking it away, but he won't send a letter till I do—I can tell that. Through all this, Monty stares out the window. Arkansas rolls out ahead of us like a rug.

Monty has not asked for my address, nor how far uphill I live from Spruce Pine, though he could ride his motorcycle up to me, strong as its engine is. For a long time he has been sitting quietly, lighting one cigarette off another. This winter, I've got to learn smoking. How to lift my hand up so every eye will follow it to my smooth cheek.

I put Flick's paper in my pocketbook and there, inside, on a round mirror, my face is waiting in ambush for me. I see the curved scar, neat as ever, swoop from the edge of one nostril in rainbow shape across my cheek, then down toward the ear. For the first time in years, pain boils across my face as it did that day. I close my eyes under that red drowning, and see again Papa's ax head rise off its locust handle and come floating through the air, sideways, like a gliding crow. And it drops down into my face almost daintily, the edge turned just enough to slash loose a flap of skin the way you might slice straight down on the curve of a melon. My papa is yelling, but I am under a red rain and it bears me down. I am lifted and run with through the woodyard and into the barn. Now I am slumped on his chest and the whipped horse is throwing us down the mountainside, and my head is wrapped in something big as a wet quilt. The doctor groans when he winds it off and I faint while he lifts up my flesh like the flap of a pulpy envelope, and sews the white bone out of sight.

Dizzy from the movement of the bus, I snap shut my pocketbook.

Whenever I cry, the first drop quivers there, in the curving scar, and then runs crooked on that track to the ear. I cry straight down on the other side.

I am glad this bus has a toilet. I go there to cool my eyes with wet paper, and spit up Monty's chocolate and cola.

When I come out, he's standing at the door with his fist up. "You all right, Viii-lut? You worried or something?"

I see he pities me. In my seat again, I plan the speech I will make at Fort Smith and the laugh I will give. "Honey, you're good," I'll say, laughing, "but the others were better." That ought to do it. I am quieter now than Monty is, practicing it in my mind.

It's dark when we hit Fort Smith. Everybody's face looks shadowed and different. Mine better. Monty's strange. We're saying goodbyes very fast. I start my speech twice and he misses it twice.

Then he bends over me and offers his own practiced line that I see he's worked up all across Arkansas, "I plan to be right here, Violet, in this bus station. On Monday. All day. You get off your bus when it comes through. Hear me, Viii-lut? I'll watch for you?"

No. He won't watch. Nor I come. "My schedule won't take me this road going back. Bye, Flick. Lots of good luck to both of you."

"Promise me. Like I'm promising."

"Good luck to you, Vi-oh-LETTE." Flick lets his hand fall on my head and it feels as good as anybody's hand.

Monty shoves money at me and I shove it back. "Promise," he says, his voice furious. He tries to kiss me in the hair and I jerk so hard my nose cracks his chin. We stare, blurry-eyed and hurting. He follows Flick down the aisle, calls back, "I'm coming here Monday. See you then, hear? And you get off this bus!"

"No! I won't!"

He yells it twice more. People are staring. He's out of the bus pounding the steel wall by my seat. I'm not going to look. The seats fill up with strangers and we ride away, nobody talking to anyone else. My nose where I hit it is going to swell—the Preacher will have to throw that in for free. I look back, but he's gone.

The lights in the bus go out again. Outside they bloom thick by the streets, then thinner, then mostly gone as we pass into the countryside. Even in the dark, I can see Oklahoma's mountains are uglier than mine. Knobs and hills, mostly. The bus drives into rain which covers up everything. At home I like that washing sound. We go deeper into the downpour. Perhaps we are under the Arkansas River, after all. It seems I can feel its great weight move over me.

Before daylight, the rain tapers off and here the ground looks dry, even barren. Cattle graze across long fields. In the wind, wheat fields shiver. I can't eat anything all the way to Tulsa. It makes me homesick to see the land grow brighter and flatter and balder. That old lady was right— the trees do give out—and oil towers grow in their place.

The glare's in my eyes. I write in my notebook, "Praise God for Tulsa; I am nearly there," but it takes a long time to get the words down.

One day my papa told me how time got slow for him when Mama died. How one week he waded through the creek and it was water, and the next week cold molasses. How he'd lay awake a year between sundown and sunup, and in the morning I'd be a day older and he'd be three hundred and sixty-five.

It works the other way, too. In no time at all, we're into Tulsa without me knowing what we've passed. So many tall buildings. Everybody's running. They rush into taxis before I can get one to wait for me long enough to ask the driver questions. But still I'm speeded to a hotel, and the elevator yanks me to a room quicker than Elijah rode to Heaven. The room's not bad. A Gideon Bible. Inside are lots of dirty words somebody wrote. He must have been feeling bad.

I bathe and dress, trembling from my own speed, and pin on the hat which has traveled all the way from Spruce Pine for this. I feel tired. I go out into the loud streets full of fast cars. Hot metal everywhere. A taxi roars me across town to the Preacher's church.

It looks like a big insurance office, though I can tell where the chapel is by colored glass in the pointed windows. Carved in an arch over the door are the words. "HOPE OF GLORY BUILDING." Right away, something in me sinks. All this time I've been hearing it on TV as the Hope *and* Glory Building. You wouldn't think one word could make that much difference.

Inside the door, there's a list of offices and room numbers. I don't see the Preacher's name. Clerks send me down long, tiled halls, past empty air-conditioned offices. One tells me to go up two flights and ask the fat woman, and the fat woman sends me down again. I'm carrying my notebook in a dry hand, feeling as brittle as the maypop flower.

At last I wait an hour to see some assistant—very close to the Preacher, I'm told. His waiting room is chilly, the leatherette chairs worn down to the mesh. I try to remember how much TB and cancer have passed through this very room and been jerked out of people the way Jesus tore out a demon and flung him into a herd of swine. I wonder what he felt like to the swine.

After a long time, the young man calls me into his plain

office—wood desk, wood chairs, shelves of booklets and colored folders. On one wall, a colored picture of Jesus with that fairy ring of light around His head. Across from that, one of His praying hands—rougher than Monty's, smoother than mine.

The young man wears glasses with no rims. In this glare, I am reflected on each lens, Vi-oh-LETTE and Viii-lut. On his desk is a box of postcards of the Hope and Glory Building. *Of* Glory. *Of* Glory.

I am afraid.

I feel behind me for the chair.

The man explains that he is presently in charge. The Preacher's speaking in Tallahassee, his show taped weeks ahead. I never thought of it as a show before. He waits.

I reach inside my notebook where, taped shut, is the thick envelope with everything written down. I knew I could never explain things right. When have I ever been able to tell what I really felt? But it's all in there—my name, my need. The words from the Bible which must argue for me. I did not sit there nights since Papa died, counting my money and studying God's Book, for nothing. Playing solitaire, then going back to search the next page and the next. Stepping outside to rest my eyes on His limitless sky, then back to the Book and the paper, building my case.

He starts to read, turns up his glitter-glass to me once to check how I look, then reads again. His chair must be hard, for he squirms in it, crosses his legs. When he has read every page, he lays the stack down, slowly takes off his glasses, folds them shining into a case. He leaves it open on his desk. Mica shines like that, in the rocks.

Then he looks at me, fully. Oh. He is plain. Almost homely. I nearly expected it. Maybe Samuel was born ugly, so who else would take him but God?

"My child," the man begins, though I'm older than he is, "I understand how you feel. And we will most certainly pray for your spirit . . ."

I shut my eyes against those two flashing faces on his spectacles. "Never mind my spirit." I see he doesn't really understand. I see he will live a long life, and not marry.

"Our Heavenly Father has purpose in all things."

Stubbornly, "Ask Him to set it aside."

"We must all trust His will."

After all these years, isn't it God's turn to trust mine?

Could He not risk a little beauty on me? Just when I'm ready to ask, the sober assistant recites, " 'Favor is deceitful and beauty is vain.' That's in Proverbs."

And I cry, " 'The crooked shall be made straight!' Isaiah said that!" He draws back, as if I had brought the Gideon Bible and struck him with its most disfigured pages. "Jesus healed an impediment in speech. See my impediment! Mud on a blind man's eyes was all He needed! Don't you remember?" But he's read all that. Everything I know on my side lies, written out, under his sweaty hand. Lord, don't let me whine. But I whine, "He healed the ten lepers and only one thanked. Well, I'll thank. I promise. All my life."

He clears his long knotty throat and drones like a bee, " 'By the sadness of the countenance the heart is made better.' Ecclesiastes. Seven. Three."

Oh, that's not fair! I skipped those parts, looking for verses that suited me! And it's wrong, besides.

I get up to leave and he asks will I kneel with him? "Let us pray together for that inner beauty."

No, I will not. I go down that hollow hall and past the echoing rooms. Without his help I find the great auditorium, lit through colored glass, with its cross of white plastic and a pinker Jesus molded onto it. I go straight to the pulpit where the Preacher stands. There is nobody else to plead. I ask Jesus not to listen to everything He hears, but to me only.

Then I tell Him how it feels to be ugly, with nothing to look back at you but a deer or an owl. I read Him my paper, out loud, full of His own words.

"I have been praising you, Lord, but it gets harder every year." Maybe that sounds too strong. I try to ease up my tone before the Amens. Then the chapel is very quiet. For one minute I hear the whir of many wings, but it's only a fan inside an air vent.

I go into the streets of Tulsa, where even the shade from a building is hot. And as I walk to the hotel I'm repeating, over and over, "Praise God for Tulsa in spite of everything."

Maybe I say this aloud, since people are staring. But maybe that's only because they've never seen a girl cry crooked in their streets before.

Monday morning. I have not looked at my face since the pulpit prayer. Who can predict how He might act—with a lightning bolt? Or a melting so slow and tender it could not even be felt?

Now, on the bus, I can touch in my pocketbook the cold mirror glass. Though I cover its surface with prints, I never look down. We ride through the dust and I'm nervous. My pencil is flying: "Be ye therefore perfect as your Heavenly Father is perfect. Praise God for Oklahoma. For Wagoner and Sapulpa and Broken Arrow and every other name on these signs by the road."

Was that the wrong thing to tell Him? My threat that even praise can be withheld? Maybe He's angry. "Praise God for oil towers whether I like them or not." When we pass churches, I copy their names. Praise them all. I want to write, "Bless," but that's *His* job.

We cross the cool Arkansas River. As its damp rises into the bus and touches my face, something wavers there, in the very bottom of each pore; and I clap my rough hands to each cheek. Maybe He's started? How much can He do between here and Fort Smith? If He will?

For I know what will happen. Monty won't come. And I won't stop. That's an end to it.

No, Monty is there. Waiting right now. And I'll go into the bus station on tiptoe and stand behind him. He'll turn with his blue eyes like lamps. *And he won't know me!* If I'm changed. So I will explain myself to him: how this gypsy hair and this juicy mouth is still Violet Karl. He'll say, "Won't old Flick be surprised?" He'll say, "Where is that place you live? Can I come there?"

But if, while I wait and he turns, he should know me by my old face . . . If he should say my name or show by recognition that my name's rising up now in his eyes like something through water . . . I'll be running by then. To the bus. Straight out that door to the Tennessee bus, saying, "Driver, don't let that man on!" It's a very short stop. We'll be pulling out quick. I don't think he'll follow, anyhow.

I don't even think he will come. ·

One hundred and thirty-one miles to Fort Smith. I wish I could eat.

I try to think up things to look forward to at home. Maybe the sourwoods are blooming early, and the bees have been laying-by my honey. If it's rained enough, my corn might be in tassel. Wouldn't it be something if God took His own sweet time, and I lived on that slope for years and years, getting prettier all the time? And nobody to know?

It takes nearly years and years to get to Fort Smith. My papa knew things about time. I comb out my hair, not looking once to see what color sheddings are caught in the teeth. There's no need feeling my cheek, since my finger expects that scar. I can feel it on me almost anywhere, by memory. I straighten my skirt and lick my lips till the spit runs out.

And they're waiting. Monty at one door of the terminal and Flick at another.

"Ten minutes," the driver says when the bus is parked, but I wait in my seat till Flick gets restless and walks to the cigarette machine. Then I slip through his entrance door and inside the station. Mirrors shine everywhere. On the vending machines and the weight machines and a full-length one by the phone booth. It's all I can do not to look. I pass the ticket window and there's Monty's back at the other door. My face remembers the shape of it. Seeing him there, how he's made, and the parts of him fitted, makes me forget how I look. And before I can stop, I call out his name.

Right away, turning, he yells to me "*Viii*-lut!"

So I know. I can look, then, in the wide mirror over a jukebox. Tired as I am and unfed, I look worse than I did when I started from home.

He's laughing and talking. "I been waiting here since daylight scared you wouldn't . . ." but by then I've run past the ugly girl in the glass and I race for the bus, for the road, for the mountain.

Behind me, he calls loudly, "Flick!"

I see that one step in my path like a floating dark blade, but I'm faster this time. I twist by him, into the flaming sun and the parking lot. How my breath hurts!

Monty's between me and my bus, but there's time. I circle the cabstand, running hard over the asphalt field, with a pain ticking in my side. He calls me. I plunge through the crowd like a deer through fetterbush. But he's running as hard as he can and he's faster than me. And, oh!

Praise God!

He's catching me!

Alice Walker (February 9, 1944) was born in Eatonton, Georgia, the youngest of eight children of sharecropping parents. Her childhood years in the South were filled with stories of lynchings and other forms of racial violence prevalent in the deep South against black people. When she was eight years old Walker was blinded in one eye in an accident when her brother shot her with a BB gun. Her eye was covered with a scar until she was fourteen when an operation corrected the disfigurement. In this period in her life Walker says she began writing down her feelings and began observing the complex relationships of people to each other and to nature. "Books," she says, "became my world because the world I was in was very hard."

After graduating valedictorian of her senior class and receiving a "rehabilitation scholarship" from the state of Georgia, Walker attended Spelman College in Atlanta (1961–1963). In 1965 she graduated from the Sarah Lawrence College in Bronxville, New York. Walker's first book, *Once: Poems* (1968), was published after Muriel Rukeyser, writer in residence at Sarah Lawrence, sent the collection to her own editor. Between 1967 and 1974 Walker and her husband Melvyn Leventhal, an attorney who worked on school desegregation cases, lived in Mississippi and Georgia and worked in the civil rights movement.

Walker has published three other books of poetry— *Revolutionary Petunias & Other Poems* (1973), *Goodnight, Willie Lee, I'll See You in the Morning* (1979), and *Horses Make a Landscape Look More Beautiful* (1986)—four novels —*The Third Life of Grange Copeland* (1970), *Meridian* (1976), *The Color Purple* (1982), and *The Temple of My Familiar* (1989)—two collections of short stories—*In Love & Trouble: Stories of Black Women* (1973) and *You Can't Keep a Good Woman Down: Stories* (1982)—and two collections of essays—*In Search of Our Mothers' Gardens: Womanist Prose* (1983) and *Living by the Word.* Her novel *The Color Purple* won the American Book Award and the Pulitzer Prize in 1983 and was the basis of a major motion picture in 1985. In addition, she edited *I Love Myself When I Am Laughing: A Zora Neale Hurston Reader* (1979) and her short story "To Hell with Dying" was published as an illustrated children's book.

◦◦◦◦◦

EVERYDAY USE
for your
grandmama

by Alice Walker

I will wait for her in the yard that Maggie and I made so clean and wavy yesterday afternoon. A yard like this is more comfortable than most people know. It is not just a yard. It is like an extended living room. When the hard clay is swept clean as a floor and the fine sand around the edges lined with tiny, irregular grooves, anyone can come and sit and look up into the elm tree and wait for the breezes that never come inside the house.

Maggie will be nervous until after her sister goes: she will stand hopelessly in corners, homely and ashamed of the burn scars down her arms and legs, eying her sister with a mixture of envy and awe. She thinks her sister has held life always in the palm of one hand, that "no" is a word the world never learned to say to her.

You've no doubt seen those TV shows where the child who has "made it" is confronted, as a surprise, by her own mother and father, tottering in weakly from backstage. (A pleasant surprise, of course: What would they do if parent and child came on the show only to curse out and insult each other?) On TV mother and child embrace and smile into each other's faces. Sometimes the mother and father weep, the child wraps them in her arms and leans across the table to tell how she would not have made it without their help. I have seen these programs.

Sometimes I dream a dream in which Dee and I are suddenly brought together on a TV program of this sort. Out of a dark and soft-seated limousine I am ushered into a bright room filled with many people. There I meet a smiling, gray, sporty man like Johnny Carson who shakes my hand and tells me what a fine girl I have. Then we are on the stage and Dee is embracing me with tears in her eyes. She pins on my dress a large orchid, even though she has told me once that she thinks orchids are tacky flowers.

In real life I am a large, big-boned woman with rough, man-working hands. In the winter I wear flannel nightgowns to bed and overalls during the day. I can kill and clean a hog as mercilessly as a man. My fat keeps me hot in zero weather. I can work outside all day, breaking ice to get water for washing; I can eat pork liver cooked over the open fire minutes after it comes steaming from the hog. One winter I knocked a bull calf straight in the brain between the eyes with a sledge hammer and had the meat hung up to chill before nightfall. But of course all this does not show on television. I am the way my daughter would want me to be: a hundred pounds lighter, my skin like an uncooked barley pancake. My hair glistens in the hot bright lights. Johnny Carson has much to do to keep up with my quick and witty tongue.

But that is a mistake. I know even before I wake up. Who ever knew a Johnson with a quick tongue? Who can even imagine me looking a strange white man in the eye? It seems to me I have talked to them always with one foot raised in flight, with my head turned in whichever way is farthest from them. Dee, though. She would always look anyone in the eye. Hesitation was no part of her nature.

"How do I look, Mama?" Maggie says, showing just enough of her thin body enveloped in pink skirt and red blouse for me to know she's there, almost hidden by the door.

"Come out into the yard," I say.

Have you ever seen a lame animal, perhaps a dog run over by some careless person rich enough to own a car, sidle up to someone who is ignorant enough to be kind to him? That is the way my Maggie walks. She has been like this, chin on chest, eyes on ground, feet in shuffle, ever since the fire that burned the other house to the ground.

Dee is lighter than Maggie, with nicer hair and a fuller figure. She's a woman now, though sometimes I forget. How long ago was it that the other house burned? Ten, twelve years? Sometimes I can still hear the flames and feel Maggie's arms sticking to me, her hair smoking and her dress falling off her in little black papery flakes. Her eyes seemed stretched open, blazed open by the flames reflected in them. And Dee. I see her standing off under the sweet gum tree she used to dig gum out of; a look of concentration on her face as she watched the last dingy gray board of the house fall in toward the red-hot brick chimney. Why don't you do a dance around the ashes? I'd wanted to ask her. She had hated the house that much.

I used to think she hated Maggie, too. But that was before we raised the money, the church and me, to send her to Augusta to school. She used to read to us without pity; forcing words, lies, other folks' habits, whole lives upon us two, sitting trapped and ignorant underneath her voice. She washed us in a river of make-believe, burned us with a lot of knowledge we didn't necessarily need to know. Pressed us to her with the serious way she read, to shove us away at just the moment, like dimwits, we seemed about to understand.

Dee wanted nice things. A yellow organdy dress to wear to her graduation from high school; black pumps to match a green suit she'd made from an old suit somebody gave me. She was determined to stare down any disaster in her efforts. Her eyelids would not flicker for minutes at a time. Often I fought the temptation to shake her. At sixteen she had a style of her own: and knew what style was.

I never had an education myself. After second grade the school was closed down. Don't ask me why: in 1927 colored asked fewer questions than they do now. Sometimes Maggie reads to me. She stumbles along good-naturedly but can't see well. She knows she is not bright. Like good looks and money, quickness passed her by. She will marry John Thomas (who has mossy teeth in an earnest face) and then I'll be free to sit here and I guess just sing church songs to myself. Although I never was a good singer. Never could carry a tune. I was always better at a man's job. I used to love to milk till I was hooked in the side in '49. Cows are soothing and slow and don't bother you, unless you try to milk them the wrong way.

I have deliberately turned my back on the house. It is three rooms, just like the one that burned, except the roof is tin; they don't make shingle roofs any more. There are no real windows, just some holes cut in the sides, like the portholes in a ship, but not round and not square, with rawhide holding the shutters up on the outside. This house is in a pasture, too, like the other one. No doubt when Dee sees it she will want to tear it down. She wrote me once that no matter where we "choose" to live, she will manage to come see us. But she will never bring her friends. Maggie and I thought about this and Maggie asked me, "Mama, when did Dee ever *have* any friends?"

She had a few. Furtive boys in pink shirts hanging about on washday after school. Nervous girls who never laughed. Impressed with her they worshiped the well-turned phrase, the cute shape, the scalding humor that erupted like bubbles in lye. She read to them.

When she was courting Jimmy T she didn't have much time to pay to us, but turned all her faultfinding power on him. He *flew* to marry a cheap city girl from a family of ignorant flashy people. She hardly had time to recompose herself.

When she comes I will meet—but there they are!

Maggie attempts to make a dash for the house, in her shuffling way, but I stay her with my hand. "Come back here," I say. And she stops and tries to dig a well in the sand with her toe.

It is hard to see them clearly through the strong sun. But even the first glimpse of leg out of the car tells me it is Dee. Her feet were always neat-looking, as if God himself had shaped them with a certain style. From the other side of the car comes a short, stocky man. Hair is all over his head a foot long and hanging from his chin like a kinky mule tail. I hear Maggie suck in her breath. "Uhnnnh," is what it sounds like. Like when you see the wriggling end of a snake just in front of your foot on the road. "Uhnnnh."

Dee next. A dress down to the ground, in this hot weather. A dress so loud it hurts my eyes. There are yellows and oranges enough to throw back the light of the sun. I feel my whole face warming from the heat waves it throws out.

Earrings gold, too, and hanging down to her shoulders. Bracelets dangling and making noises when she moves her arm up to shake the folds of the dress out of her armpits. The dress is loose and flows, and as she walks closer, I like it. I hear Maggie go "Uhnnnh" again. It is her sister's hair. It stands straight up like the wool on a sheep. It is black as night and around the edges are two long pigtails that rope about like small lizards disappearing behind her ears.

"Wa-su-zo-Tean-o!" she says, coming on in that gliding way the dress makes her move. The short stocky fellow with the hair to his naval is all grinning and he follows up with "Asalamalakim, my mother and sister!" He moves to hug Maggie but she falls back, right up against the back of my chair. I feel her trembling there and when I look up I see the perspiration falling off her chin.

"Don't get up," says Dee. Since I am stout it takes something of a push. You can see me trying to move a second or two before I make it. She turns, showing white heels through her sandals, and goes back to the car. Out she peeks next with a Polaroid. She stoops down quickly and lines up picture after picture of me sitting there in front of the house with Maggie cowering behind me. She never takes a shot without making sure the house is included. When a cow comes nibbling around the edge of the yard she snaps it and me and Maggie *and* the house. Then she puts the Polaroid in the back seat of the car, and comes up and kisses me on the forehead.

Meanwhile Asalamalakim is going through motions with Maggie's hand. Maggie's hand is as limp as a fish, and probably as cold, despite the sweat, and she keeps trying to pull it back. It looks like Asalamalakim wants to shake hands but wants to do it fancy. Or maybe he don't know how people shake hands. Anyhow, he soon gives up on Maggie.

"Well," I say. "Dee."

"No, Mama," she says. "Not 'Dee,' Wangero Leewanika Kemanjo!"

"What happened to 'Dee'?" I wanted to know.

"She's dead," Wangero said. "I couldn't bear it any longer, being named after the people who oppress me."

"You know as well as me you was named after your aunt Dicie," I said. Dicie is my sister. She named Dee. We called her "Big Dee" after Dee was born.

"But who was *she* named after?" asked Wangero.

"I guess after Grandma Dee," I said.

"And who was she named after?" asked Wangero.

"Her mother," I said, and saw Wangero was getting tired. "That's about as far back as I can trace it," I said. Though, in fact, I probably could have carried it back beyond the Civil War through the branches.

"Well," said Asalamalakim, "there you are."

"Uhnnnh," I heard Maggie say.

"There I was not," I said, "before 'Dicie' cropped up in our family, so why should I try to trace it that far back?"

He just stood there grinning, looking down on me like somebody inspecting a Model A car. Every once in a while he and Wangero sent eye signals over my head.

"How do you pronounce this name?" I asked.

"You don't have to call me by it if you don't want to," said Wangero.

"Why shouldn't I?" I asked. "If that's what you want us to call you, we'll call you."

"I know it might sound awkward at first," said Wangero.

"I'll get used to it," I said. "Ream it out again."

Well, soon we got the name out of the way. Asalamalakim had a name twice as long and three times as hard. After I tripped over it two or three times he told me to just call him Hakim-a-barber. I wanted to ask him was he a barber, but I didn't really think he was, so I didn't ask.

"You must belong to those beef-cattle peoples down the road," I said. They said "Asalamalakim" when they met you, too, but they didn't shake hands. Always too busy: feeding the cattle, fixing the fences, putting up salt-lick shelters, throwing down hay. When the white folks poisoned some of the herd the men stayed up all night with rifles in their hands. I walked a mile and a half just to see the sight.

Hakim-a-barber said, "I accept some of their doctrines, but farming and raising cattle is not my style." (They didn't tell me, and I didn't ask, whether Wangero (Dee) had really gone and married him.)

We sat down to eat and right away he said he didn't eat collards and pork was unclean. Wangero, though, went on through the chitlins and corn bread, the greens and everything else. She talked a blue streak over the sweet potatoes. Everything delighted her. Even the fact that we still used the benches her daddy made for the table when we couldn't afford to buy chairs.

"Oh, Mama!" she cried. Then turned to Hakim-a-barber. "I never knew how lovely these benches are. You can feel the rump prints," she said, running her hands underneath her and along the bench. Then she gave a sigh and her hand closed over Grandma Dee's butter dish. "That's it!" she said. "I knew there was something I wanted to ask you if I could have." She jumped up from the table and went over in the corner where the churn stood, the milk in it clabber by now. She looked at the churn and looked at it.

"This churn top is what I need," she said. "Didn't Uncle Buddy whittle it out of a tree you all used to have?"

"Yes," I said.

"Uh-huh," she said happily. "And I want the dasher, too."

"Uncle Buddy whittle that, too?" asked the barber.

Dee (Wangero) looked up at me.

"Aunt Dee's first husband whittled the dash," said Maggie so low you almost couldn't hear her. "His name was Henry, but they called him Stash."

"Maggie's brain is like an elephant's," Wangero said, laughing. "I can use the churn top as a centerpiece for the alcove table," she said, sliding a plate over the churn, "and I'll think of something artistic to do with the dasher."

When she finished wrapping the dasher the handle stuck out. I took it for a moment in my hands. You didn't even have to look close to see where hands pushing the dasher up and down to make butter had left a kind of sink in the wood. In fact, there were a lot of small sinks; you could see where thumbs and fingers had sunk into the wood. It was beautiful light yellow wood, from a tree that grew in the yard where Big Dee and Stash had lived.

After dinner Dee (Wangero) went to the trunk at the foot of my bed and started rifling through it. Maggie hung back in the kitchen over the dishpan. Out came Wangero with two quilts. They had been pieced by Grandma Dee and then Big Dee and me had hung them on the quilt frames on the front porch and quilted them. One was in the Lone Star pattern. The other was Walk Around the Mountain. In both of them were scraps of dresses Grandma Dee had worn fifty and more years ago. Bits and pieces of Grandpa Jarrell's Paisley shirts. And one teeny faded blue piece, about the size of a penny matchbox, that was from Great Grandpa Ezra's uniform that he wore in the Civil War.

"Mama," Wangero said sweet as a bird. "Can I have these old quilts?"

I heard something fall in the kitchen, and a minute later the kitchen door slammed.

"Why don't you take one or two of the others?" I asked. "These old things was just done by me and Big Dee from some tops your grandma pieced before she died."

"No," said Wangero. "I don't want those. They are stitched around the borders by machine."

"That'll make them last better," I said.

"That's not the point," said Wangero. "These are all pieces of dresses Grandma used to wear. She did all this stitching by hand. Imagine!" She held the quilts securely in her arms, stroking them.

"Some of the pieces, like those lavender ones, come from old clothes her mother handed down to her," I said, moving up to touch the quilts. Dee (Wangero) moved back just enough so that I couldn't reach the quilts. They already belonged to her.

"Imagine!" she breathed again, clutching them closely to her bosom.

"The truth is," I said, "I promised to give them quilts to Maggie, for when she marries John Thomas."

She gasped like a bee had stung her.

"Maggie can't appreciate these quilts!" she said. "She'd probably be backward enough to put them to everyday use."

"I reckon she would," I said. "God knows I been saving 'em for long enough with nobody using 'em. I hope she will!" I didn't want to bring up how I had offered Dee (Wangero) a quilt when she went away to college. Then she had told me they were old-fashioned, out of style.

"But they're *priceless*!" she was saying now, furiously; for she has a temper. "Maggie would put them on the bed and in five years they'd be in rags. Less than that!"

"She can always make some more," I said. "Maggie knows how to quilt."

Dee (Wangero) looked at me with hatred. "You just will not understand. The point is these quilts, *these* quilts!"

"Well," I said, stumped. "What would *you* do with them?"

"Hang them," she said. As if that was the only thing you *could* do with quilts.

Maggie by now was standing in the door. I could almost hear the sound her feet made as they scraped over each other.

"She can have them, Mama," she said, like somebody used to never winning anything, or having anything reserved for her. "I can 'member Grandma Dee without the quilts."

I looked at her hard. She had filled her bottom lip with checkerberry snuff and it gave her face a kind of dopey, hangdog look. It was Grandma Dee and Big Dee who taught her how to quilt herself. She stood there with her scarred hands hidden in the folds of her skirt. She looked at her sister with something like fear but she wasn't mad at her. This was Maggie's portion. This was the way she knew God to work.

When I looked at her like that something hit me in the top of my head and ran down to the soles of my feet. Just like when I'm in church and the spirit of God touches me and I get happy and shout. I did something I never had done before: hugged Maggie to me, then dragged her on into the room, snatched the quilts out of Miss Wangero's hands and dumped them into Maggie's lap. Maggie just sat there on my bed with her mouth open.

"Take one or two of the others," I said to Dee.

But she turned without a word and went out to Hakim-a-barber.

"You just don't understand," she said, as Maggie and I came out to the car.

"What don't I understand?" I wanted to know.

"Your heritage," she said. And then she turned to Maggie, kissed her, and said, "You ought to try to make something of yourself, too, Maggie. It's really a new day for us. But from the way you and Mama still live you'd never know it."

She put on some sunglasses that hid everything above the tip of her nose and her chin.

Maggie smiled; maybe at the sunglasses. But a real smile, not scared. After we watched the car dust settle I asked Maggie to bring me a dip of snuff. And then the two of us sat there just enjoying, until it was time to go in the house and go to bed.